# HIGHLANDER IN HER DREAMS

RAVENSCRAIG LEGACY SERIES
BOOK 2

SUE-ELLEN WELFONDER

OLIVERHEBERBOOKS

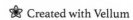 Created with Vellum

# PRAISE FOR HIGHLANDER IN HER DREAMS

*Aidan is a Romantic Times K.I.S.S Award Hero!*

"Highlander in Her Dreams is a fun, sexy story. HOT." ~ Romantic Times Magazine

*Highlander in Her Dreams is a RRAH Top Pick!*

"A magical tale ... exciting action and passionate romance." ~ Romance Reader at Heart

"When you pick up this book, you will feel Scotland surround you. Love, love, love Mackay's writing!" ~ Bookworm2bookworm

"Brims with Scottish charm, humor, and hot romance." ~ Night Owl Romance

"A charming and innovative paranormal romance." ~ Publishers Weekly

"An enchanting time travel. Super-hot!" ~ ParaNormalRomance

"Pleasing blend of wit, passion, and the paranormal ... a steamy romance that packs an emotional punch." ~ Romance Reviews Today

# PRAISE FOR SUE-ELLEN WELFONDER

"Welfonder pens stories that sparkle." ~ Angela Knight, USA
Today bestselling author

"Welfonder writes delightful paranormal romance." ~ Romantic
Times

"Artfully blending past and present, Welfonder pens well-written,
entertaining reads."
~ Fresh Fiction

"Welfonder knows what a Scottish romance novel needs and
socks it to you!"
~ A Romance Review

"I would follow Welfonder's hot Scots anywhere!" ~ Vicki Lewis
Thompson, New York Times bestselling author

"Welfonder brings Scotland to life for her readers." ~ Romance
Junkies

*In loving memory of my mother-in-law, Annegrete. Kind and soft-spoken, she was the heart and soul of her home, beloved by all who knew her. She was the mother-in-law I would wish for every bride and I feel blessed that she was mine.*

# ACKNOWLEDGMENTS

This book was originally published by Penguin NAL. Thanks so much to my then-editor, Anne Bohner. We had a grand ride together and I will always be grateful for her insight and enthusiasm, and above all, her kind heart. Likewise, thanks to the readers and reviewers who loved this book when it first released. I hope you'll enjoy the story anew.

# A PERSONAL NOTE TO READERS

Please note this is a work of fiction and not meant to reflect cold, hard reality. The following pages contain elements of fantasy such as Celtic myth and legend, the gift of far-seeing (being able to look into the past), time travel, ghosts, Highland magic, etc. A suspension of belief is therefore required. Likewise, this story was originally penned in a time without things I sometimes view as modern inconveniences. So you'll come across reminders of those days such as alarm clocks, answering machines, paper boarding passes, the UK's famous red telephone booths known across the Pond as phone boxes, old-fashioned maps rather than GPS automotive navigation systems, no smart phones, etc. Sure, I could have added the modern bits, but I chose to leave the story in the slower-paced world it was born in. As this is a romance novel, there is lovemaking. Such scenes are steamy and graphic. As a romance novel written by me, the story does not contain the F-word or other profanity. It does include hot Highlanders, the glory of Scotland's famed Isle of Skye, swordfights, all my love for Scotland, and locations there that are of deep meaning to me. Some place names have been changed, though even these are real. Above all, this story is about seizing your dreams and a love powerful enough to reach across the ages. The real world won't be found in this book's pages, only a reflection of how I wish the world could be. I hope you'll enjoy spending time there.

Wishing you Highland magic,
*Sue-Ellen Welfonder*

"Time is of little importance in the Highlands, a magical place of picturesque beauty, languorous and seductive, where you can easily believe the distant past was only yesterday. The faraway and long ago not lost at all, but waiting to be discovered by those with eyes to see."

— *WEE HUGHIE MACSPORRAN, HISTORIAN, STORYTELLER, AND KEEPER OF TRADITION.*

# FIRST PROLOGUE
## CASTLE WRATH, THE ISLE OF SKYE, 1315

"May the devil boil and blister him."

Aidan MacDonald, proud Highland chieftain, paced the battlements of his cliff-top stronghold, fury pounding through him, disbelief and outrage firing his blood.

Fierce blood, easily heated, for he claimed descent from a long line of fearless Norsemen as well as the ancient chiefs of the great Clan Donald, a race of men famed and respected throughout the Hebrides and beyond. A powerful man who believed that Highlanders were the equal of all men and better than most, he cut an imposing figure against the glittering waters stretching out below him.

Topping six foot four and favoring rough Highland garb, he was a giant among men, turning heads and inspiring awe wherever he went. Just now, with his dark, wind-tossed hair gleaming as bright as the great sword strapped at his side and his eyes blazing, the very air seemed to catch flame and part before him. Certainly, on a fair day, few were the men bold enough to challenge him. On a day such as this, only a fool would dare.

Aidan of Wrath had a reputation for turning savage. Especially when those he loved were threatened.

And this morn, he wanted blood.

More specifically, his cousin, Conan Dearg's blood.

"A pox on the craven!" He whipped around to glare at his *good* cousin, Tavish."I'll see the bastard's tender parts fed to the wolves. As for you"—he flashed a glance at the tight-lipped, bushy-bearded courier standing a few feet away, against the parapet wall —"if you won't tell us your name, then I'd hear if you knew what is writ on this parchment?"

Aidan took a step toward him, his fingers clenching around the damning missive.

"Well?"

The courier thrust out his jaw, his eyes cold and shuttered.

"Perhaps a reminder is in order?"Aidan's voice came as icy as the man's expression. "See you, this missive is scrawled with words that would have meant my death. My own, and every man, woman, and child in my clan."

Had the scroll been delivered to its intended recipient and not, by mistake, to him.

Anger scoring his breath, he let his gaze sweep across the choppy seas to the steep cliffs of nearby Wrath Isle, its glistening black buttresses spray-washed with plume. He fisted his hands, his eyes narrowed on the long, white-crested combers breaking on the rocks.

He would not be broken so easily.

This time Conan Dearg had gone too far.

He swung back to courier. "How many of my cousin's men knew of this plot?"

"Does it matter?" The man spoke at last, arrogance rolling off him. "Hearing their names changes naught. All in these isles know you've sworn ne'er to spill a kinsman's blood."

"He speaks true." Tavish gripped his arm, speaking low. "Conan Dearg is your cousin, as am I. He—"

"Conan Dearg severed all ties with this house when he sought to arrange our murder." Aidan scrunched the parchment in his hand, its rolled surface seeming almost alive. Evil. "To think he planned to slit our throats as we sat at his table, guests at a feast held in our honor!"

He stood firm, legs apart and shoulders back, the edge of his plaid snapping in the wind. "I cannae let it bide, Tavish. No' this time."

"We can put him out on Wrath Isle. His man, too, if he refuses to speak." Tavish glanced at the nearby islet's jagged cliff-face. "With the tide rips and reefs surrounding the isle, they'd ne'er escape. It'd be the closest place to hell a soul could find in these parts."

Aidan shook his head. He knew Wrath Isle, a sea-lashed hell-hole as wicked-looking this fair morn as on a cold afternoon of dense gray mist. But the isle's brooding appearance deceived. With cunning, a man could survive there.

It wasn't the place for Conan Dearg.

He drew a long breath, hot bile rising in his throat.

"He'd not find much foraging on the isle." Tavish spit over the parapet wall, the gesture more than eloquent. "No women either."

Aidan shot him a look, his frown deepening.

Conan the Red's handsome face flashed before him, his dazzling smile as false as the day was long. Not lacking in stature, charm, or arrogance, he was a man to turn female heads and win hearts.

Men, too, fell easy prey to his swagger and jaunty airs.

Foolish men.

As he, too, had been. But no more.

Fury tightening his chest, he turned back to the courier. "I ask you again – how many of my cousin's men knew of this perfidy?"

The man rubbed the back of his neck, his face belligerent.

He said nothing.

Aidan crackled his knuckles. "Perhaps some time in my water pit will loosen your tongue? 'Tis an old, disused well, its shaft open to the tides. Greater men than you have spilled their secrets after a night in its briny depths."

"I'll see you in hell first." Steel flashing, the man whipped a dirk from the cowled neck of his cloak and lunged. "Give my regards to the dev—"

"Greet him yourself!" Aidan seized the man's wrist, hurling him over the parapet wall before the dirk even fell from his fingers.

Snatching it up, Aidan tossed it after him, not bothering to look where man or knife landed. In the sea or on the rocks, the result was the same.

Beside him, Tavish coughed. "And Conan Dearg?"

Aidan dusted his hands on his plaid. "Have a party of warriors set out at once. Send them to his castle. To the ends of the earth if need be. I want him found and brought here alive."

"Alive?" Tavish's eyes widened.

"So I have said," Aidan confirmed. "Out of deference to our kinship – and my oath – I'll no' end his life. That he can decide on his own, whene'er he tires of the comforts of my dungeon and a diet of salt beef and soured water."

"Salt beef and soured water?" Tavish echoed again, comprehension spreading across his features. "No man can live long on suchlike. If he doesn't die of hunger, his thirst will drive him mad."

"Aye, that will be the way of it." Aidan nodded, feeling not a shimmer of remorse.

"And"—he took Tavish's arm, leading him from the battlements —"we'll have a feast to mark the craven's capture, the thwarting of his plan. See you that Cook makes preparations."

Tavish gave a quick nod as they stepped into the shadows of the stair tower. "It will be done."

"Indeed, it shall," Aidan agreed.

The moment he slid the bolt on Conan Dearg's cell, he'd treat his clan to the most raucous celebration Castle Wrath had ever seen. A lavish feast sparing no delicacies or merrymaking revels. With free-flowing ale and women equally generous with their charms, he'd make it a night to remember.

Always.

# PROLOGUE

## THE ISLE OF SKYE, MANY CENTURIES LATER...

O nly a few months after her eighteenth birthday and in the unlikely environs of a crowded tour bus, Kira Bedwell fell in love.

With Scotland.

Passionately, irrevocably, never-look-back in love.

Not as one might expect with a strapping, kilt-wearing hunky, all dimpled smiles and twinkling eyes. A powerfully built Celtic giant able to melt a woman at twenty paces just by reciting the alphabet in his rich, buttery-smooth burr.

O-o-oh no. That would have made things too simple.

Kira Always-Take-the-Hard-Way Bedwell had fallen in love with the land.

Well, the land and a few choice secret fantasies. Delicious fantasies that set her heart to pounding and made her toes curl. The kind of things that would have made her parents regret every dime they'd doled out for her graduation trip to Scotland.

*Land of her dreams.*

A place to stir and kindle female desires if ever there was one. Hers had been simmering for as long as she could remember – the tartan-clad fantasies sparked by the colorful tales spun by one-time Scottish neighbors. The MacIvers had moved else-where, but the magic of their stories stayed with Kira, as did her dreams of misty hills, heathery moors, and bold, sword-swinging men.

Frowning, she crossed her legs and stared out the window, the image of a braw, wild-maned Highlander striking out across that untamed, heather-covered land a bit too vivid for comfort.

She pressed a hand to her heart, determined to ignore the flutters in her belly. Prickly little flickers of giddiness that whipped through her each time she imagined such a man looming up out of the mist to ravish her. Her pulse quickened and she needed a few slow deep breaths to compose herself. Amazing, what the thought of a hot-eyed, handsome man in full Highland regalia could do to a girl.

Especially if such a man is bent on making a woman his.

What red-blooded woman could resist a Highlander with a wolfish smile and a tongue so honeyed his every word slid through her like a dream?

She wouldn't mind such a fate at all.

Indeed, she'd welcome it.

But the only kilties she'd encountered so far on her holiday coach tour through the Scottish Highlands were men over sixty. Each one ancient even if he did speak with deep, bone-melting burr. She recrossed her legs, her frustration minimal but defi-nitely there. Not a one of the over-sixty gallants had had cute knees.

Forget sexy calves.

As for filling out their kilts...

Pathetic.

She frowned again and shifted on her seat. A fine window seat, and one she wasn't about to relinquish. Not after she'd refused to leave the bus at the last three photo stops just to keep someone from snatching it from her.

After all, this was *Eilean a' Cheó*, the Isle of the Mist. Better known as Skye, and one of the highlights of the tour. A rapidly vanishing highlight, as today was the tour's only full day on the misty isle and she didn't want to miss a single moment.

Not a heartbeat.

Not one precious glimpse out her hard-won window.

A strange sense of nostalgia and romance welling inside her again, she twisted away from the potato-chip-munching woman beside her and pressed her forehead against the window glass. Who needed paprika chips and diet soda when you could devour the wonder-filled expanse of *Eilean a' Cheò*?

Just now, they were driving north along the cliff-hugging, single-track road through the heart of Trotternish, a landscape of rock, sea and brilliant blue sky almost too glorious to behold.

Indeed, wolfing junk food in the face of such wild, natural beauty should be illegal.

She knew better.

She appreciated the view.

The glistening bays of rocks and tide pools, the black-faced sheep grazing the greenest pastures she'd ever seen. Shining seas of deepest blue and dark, rugged coastline. Cliffs, caves, and ruined croft houses, the fire-blackened stones squeezing her heart.

Kira blinked. Unexpected emotion pricked at her eyes, threatening to water them. She touched her fingers to the glass, wishing she could feel the chill spring air, escape the coach tour and run through the bracken and faded heather, not stopping until she collapsed on the grass beside a sparkling, tumbling burn.

The woman next to her touched her elbow then, offering potato chips. Kira gave her a noncommittal head shake, a polite smile. She'd eat later, when they stopped at Kilt Rock for a picnic lunch.

For now, she only wanted to drink in the views. She was branding the vistas onto her memory, securing them there so they could be recalled at will when the tour ended and she returned to Pennsylvania, leaving her new love behind.

The MacIvers had been right. They'd sworn that no one could set foot in their homeland without losing their heart to Scotland's mist and castles. The wild skirl of pipes and vibrant flashes of plaid. She'd certainly fallen hard. Crazy in love as her sisters would say.

Crazy in love with Scotland.

And crazily annoyed by the constant drone of the tour guide's voice.

A deep and pleasing Highland voice that she would surely have found appealing if the speaker hadn't been such a bore. She glanced at him, then quickly away. That he seemed to be the only kilted Scotsman close to her age only made it worse.

Rosy cheeked, red-haired, and pudgy, he had a rather strong resemblance to a giant tartan-draped teddy bear.

Leaning back against the seat, she blew out a frustrated breath. If she'd harbored any illusions about romance on this tour, Wee Hughie MacSporran wasn't her man.

"...ancient seat of the MacDonalds of Skye, Castle Wrath stands empty, its once formidable walls crumbled and silent." The guide's voice rolled on, at last saying something that caught her attention.

She sat up, perking her ears.

Castle Wrath sounded interesting.

She could go for crumbled walls. Especially if they were silent, she decided, trying not to notice that her seatmate was opening a second bag of potato chips.

"Some say Castle Wrath is haunted," Wee Hughie went on, seemingly oblivious to crackling potato chip bags. In fact, his chest swelled a bit as he looked round to see the effect of his tale. "To be sure, its walls are bloodstained, each stone a reminder of the past. The turbulent history of the ancient warrior-chiefs who once dwelt there."

Pausing, he pointed out the ruin on its cliff, clearly pleased by the tour-goers' indrawn breaths. Their appreciative ooohs and ahhhs.

Kira ooohed too.

She couldn't help herself. Etched starkly against sea and sky, Castle Wrath, or what was left of it, looked just as dark and brooding as Wee Hughie described it.

Shivering suddenly, she rubbed her arms and nestled deeper into her jacket. She'd seen a lot of castle ruins since arriving in Scotland, but this one had her catching her breath.

It was different.

Romantic.

In a spookily delicious sort of way.

She shivered again, a whole rash of chills spilling down her spine. The solitary ruin exerted a pull on her that defied explanation.

Tearing her gaze away, she turned back to the guide, for once not wanting to miss a word he had to say.

"Castle Wrath was originally a Pictish fort," he told the group. "A *dun*. This first stronghold was seized by invading Norsemen until they, in turn, were dislodged by the Lords of the Isles." He looked around again, pitching his voice for impact. "These early MacDonalds were fierce and powerful. Their sway along Scotland's western coast was absolute."

He paused, his hands clenching the green vinyl satchel that Kira knew held his scribblings on Scottish history and lore.

Looking ready to impart that knowledge, he cleared his throat. "Deep grooves in the rock of the castle's landing beach attest to the MacDonalds' prowess at sea, for the grooves are believed to have been caused by the keels of countless MacDonald galleys being drawn onto the shore. These fearless men were the ones who raised the new castle, and it is their ghosts whose footfalls, knocks, and curses can be heard—"

"Have you seen our guide's beanstalk?"

Kira blinked. *"Beanstalk?"*

She looked at her seatmate, certain she'd misunderstood.

But the woman nodded, her gaze on Wee Hughie. "It's quite impressive."

Kira could feel her jaw drop. True, she hadn't seen that many naked men, but she'd seen enough to know that Wee Hughie's beanstalk was the only part of his anatomy that lived up to his name. She'd caught a glimpse of his *Highland pride* when some of the tour-goers photographed him at Bannockburn. Striking a pose beside the famous statue of King Robert the Bruce, he'd looked regal enough until an inopportune gust of wind revealed what a true Scotsman wears—or doesn't wear—beneath his kilt.

A wind blast that proved Wee Hughie MacSporran to be anything but impressive.

Wincing at the memory, she shot a glance at him. "I didn't think he was all that—"

"He's descended from the MacDonalds, Lords of the Isles," Kira's seatmate enthused, poking her arm for emphasis. "From the great Somerled himself. I know genealogists back home who'd sell the farm for such illustrious forebears." She paused to press a hand to her breast and sigh. "He carries a diagram of his lineage in that green satchel. It goes back two thousand years."

"Oh." Kira hoped the other woman hadn't guessed her mistake. She'd forgotten the guide's ancestral pedigree. His supposed claim to noble roots.

Kira didn't believe a word he said.

Any descendant of Robert Bruce and other historical greats would surely be dashing and bold, with dark flashing eyes full of heat and passion. Beautiful in a wild, savage way. Sinfully sexy. Well-muscled rather than well-fleshed—and definitely well-hung.

She squirmed on the seat, certain that her cheeks were brightening.

Sure, too, that she wouldn't be picnicking at Kilt Rock with full-of-himself MacSporran and the tour group. As if drawn by a force impossible to resist, she stared through the bus window at the ruin perched so precariously on the cliff-top. Bold men, mighty and strong, had called the romantic pile of stones their own, and if their echoes still lingered there she was of a mind to find them.

Or at least enjoy her packed lunch surrounded by the solitude.

Away from potato chip munchers and preening peacocks.

The bus could return for her later. If she could persuade the driver to indulge her.

Determination urging her on, she approached him a short while later during the obligatory roadside photo stop. A pleasant enough man about her father's age, he turned when he sensed her hovering, his smile fading at the lunch packet clutched in her hand.

"My regrets, lass, but there won't be time for you to eat that here." He shook his head. "Not if we're to make the craft and art shops on our way to Kilt Rock."

"I'm not interested in arts and crafts." Kira plunged forward before she lost her courage. "I'd rather picnic here than at Kilt Rock."

"Here?" The bus driver's brows shot upward. He eyed the clumpy grass at the roadside, the peaty little burn not far from where they stood. "Do you have any idea how many sheep pats are scattered hereabouts? Och, nae, here's no place for a lunch stop."

Looking sure of it, he glanced at the other tour-goers, some already filing back into the bus. "I cannae see anyone in this group wanting to picnic here."

"I didn't mean the others." Kira seized her chance. "I was thinking just me. And not here, along the roadway," she added, casting a wistful look toward Castle Wrath. "I'd like to spend an hour or two out at the ruins. Eat my lunch there and do a bit of exploring."

She looked back at the bus driver, giving him her most hopeful smile. "It would be the highlight of my trip. Something special that I'd cherish forever."

The driver stared at her for a few moments, then began rubbing his chin with the back of his hand. He said nothing, but the look he was giving her wasn't encouraging.

"You could pick me up on the way back to Portree." Kira rushed the words before he could say no. "Two hours is all I ask. More if you'd need the time to come for me. I wouldn't mind the wait."

"That ruin really is haunted," he warned her. "Wee Hughie wasn't lying. Strange things have been known to happen there. The place is right dangerous, too. It's no' one of those fancy historical sites run by the National Trust."

He turned piercing blue eyes on her. "Everything at Wrath stands as it was, untouched by man all down the centuries. Och, nae, you cannae go there. The cliff is riddled with underground tunnels, stairwells and rooms, much of it already crumbled into the sea."

"Oh, please," Kira pleaded, feeling as if the ancient stones were actually calling to her. "I'll be careful. I promise."

The bus driver set his jaw and Kira's heart plummeted when he glanced at his watch. "Come, lass. Think with your head, no' your heart. We'll tour Dunvegan Castle in the morning, before we leave for Inverness. You'll like Dunvegan much better. It's furnished and has a gift shop—"

"Which is why Castle Wrath is so special." Kira's throat began to thicken with her need to reach the ruins. "It's not overrun with tourists. It hasn't been spoiled." She paused to draw a breath. "My parents worked overtime for a year to give me this trip and I can't imagine ever getting back. Visiting Scotland again doesn't figure in my budget."

The driver grunted. Then he nudged at a cluster of heather roots, his hesitation giving her hope.

"I've ne'er had anything happen to anyone on my tours." He looked at her, a troubled frown knitting his brow. "One false step out there and you'd find yourself in some underground chamber, maybe even standing at the very wall of the cliff, the earth opening away at your feet and falling straight down to the sea."

"Nothing will happen to me." Kira lifted her chin, tightening her grip on the lunch packet. "There were abandoned coal mines near my grandparents' house. I know to be careful around such dangers," she said, omitting that her grandparents would have skinned her alive had she ventured near any of the mines.

"Besides," she spoke with confidence, "anyone used to walking around downtown Philly can poke around Scottish castle ruins."

"Ach, well." The driver gave a resigned sigh. "I still dinnae like it. No' at all."

Kira smiled. "I won't give you cause to be sorry. Nor Wee Hughie."

"We'd have to double back to fetch you," he said, rubbing his chin again. "It's a straight shot from Kilt Rock south to Portree. The others might not like—"

"I'll make it up to them," Kira exclaimed, her heart soaring. "I'll never be late getting back to the bus again, and I promise not to ask for extra time in the bookshops."

"Just have a care." He looked at her, his brow still furrowed. "Wrath is an odd place, true as I'm here. I'd ne'er forgive myself if harm came to you."

Then he was gone, striding away and herding his charges into the bus as if he needed a speedy departure to keep him from changing his mind.

A distinct possibility, she was sure.

So she didn't release her breath until the big blue and white

Highland Coach Tours bus rumbled away, disappearing at last around a bend in the road.

Alone at last, she allowed herself one doubtful glance at the nearest sheep pats, certain they'd suddenly increased in size and number. But she steeled herself as quickly, putting back her shoulders and lifting her chin. Making ready for the long march across the grassy field to get to the ruins.

The truth of it was, close as she was to Castle Wrath, nothing was going to keep her away.

Certainly not sheep pats.

She had eyes and would just watch where she stepped.

Besides, the many ewes and lambs gamboling everywhere were cute. Some even turned to stare at her as she started forward, their bleated greetings so different from the street noises of Aldan, Pennsylvania.

So perfect in this unhurried world of hills, clouds, and mist.

*Mist?*

She blinked. She'd heard how quickly Highland weather could change, but this was ridiculous.

She blinked again, but the mist remained.

The day had definitely darkened, turning just a shade uninviting.

She peered over her shoulder, scanning the road behind her, but the sky in that direction stretched as clear and bright blue as before. Cozy-looking threads of peat smoke still rose from the chimney of a croft house not far from where the bus had parked, and if the sea glittered any more brilliantly, she'd need sunglasses.

Only Castle Wrath had fallen into shadow, its eerie silhouette silent against waters now the color of cold, dark slate. Low gray clouds swept in from the sea, their swift approach heralded by the crashing of breakers on the rocks beneath the cliffs.

She took a deep breath and kept her chin lifted. Already, sea mist was dampening her cheeks, and the chill wetness in the air made the day smell peaty and old.

No, not old.

*Ancient.*

She started forward, refusing to be unsettled. She liked ancient, and this was just the kind of atmosphere she'd come to Scotland to see.

So why were her palms getting clammy? Her nerves starting to go all jittery and her mouth bone-dry?

Bedwells weren't known for being faint-hearts.

But *bone* hadn't been a wise word choice.

It summoned Wee Hughie's tales about wailing, foot-stomping ghosts, but she pushed his words from her mind, choosing instead to dwell on the other images he'd conjured. Namely those of the great and powerful MacDonald chieftains, preferring to think of them as they'd been in their glory days rather than as they might be now, skulking about in the ruined shell of their one-time stronghold, bemoaning the passing centuries, their ancient battle cries lost on the wind.

Thinking that she could use a battle cry of her own, she marched on, looking out for sheep pats and huddling deeper into her jacket.

Scudding mists blew across her vision, and the pounding of the waves grew louder with each forward step. She could still see Castle Wrath looming on the far side of the high, three-sided promontory, but the rocky spit of land leading out to it was proving more narrow and steep than she'd judged.

Not that she didn't have a good head for heights.

She did.

She just hadn't expected to make the trek hunched near double against gale-force winds. She'd wanted to picnic at Castle Wrath, not be blown from its cliffs. So she plunged on. There was no point in going back. The Highland Coach Tours bus wouldn't return for at least two hours. Besides, she was almost there.

The nearest wall of the ruin was already rising up out of the mist, its age-darkened stones seeming to beckon.

Kira's heart began to pound. She quickened her pace, her excitement cresting when she caught her first glimpse of Wrath Bay and the deep grooves scoring the smooth, flat rocks of its surf-beaten shore.

Just as Wee Hughie MacSporran had said.

Then she was there, the ruins opening up before her. Her breath caught, all thought of the medieval landing beach and its ancient keel marks vanishing from her mind.

Even the nippy air and howling wind no longer mattered.

Castle Wrath was perfect.

A labyrinth of tall rough-hewn walls, uneven ground, and tumbled stone, the ruins stopped her heart. The remains of the curtain walls clung to the cliff edges, windswept and dangerous, but what really drew her eye was the top half of an imposing medieval gateway.

Still bearing traces of a beautifully incised Celtic design, the gateway raged up out of the rubble, its grass-grown arch framing the sea and the jagged black rocks of the nearby island she knew to be Wrath Isle.

Without doubt, she'd never seen a wilder, more romantic place. A onetime Norse fortalice. Vikings once walked and caroused here.

Real live *Vikings*.

Big, brawny men shouting praise to Thor and Odin as they raised brimming drinking horns and gnawed on huge ribs of fire-roasted beef.

She drew a deep breath, trying hard not to pinch herself.

Especially when she thought about the Norsemen's successors. Wee Hughie MacSporran's Celtic warrior chieftains, the kind of larger-than-life heroes she loved to dream about.

Bold and virile men who could only belong to a place like this.

A place of myth and legend.

Looking around, she was sure of it.

Shifting curtains of mist swirled everywhere, drifting low across the overgrown grass and fallen masonry, softening the edges and making it seem as if she were seeing the world through a translucent silken veil.

And what a world it was.

The constant roar of the sea and the loud *whooshing* of the wind were fitting, too, giving the place an otherworldly feel she would never have experienced on a clear, sun-bright day.

She set down her lunch packet and stepped into the sheltering lee of a wall, not quite ready to spoil the moment.

Nor was she reckless.

Rough bent grass and fallen stones weren't the only things littering the ground that must've once been the castle's inner bailey. Winking at her from a wild tangle of nettles and bramble bushes, deep crevices opened darkly into the earth. Silent abysses of blackness that could only be the underground passages, stairwells, and vaults she'd been warned about.

Mysterious openings into nothingness.

Gaping black voids that were proving the greatest temptation she'd ever struggled to resist. Almost tasting her need to explore those abysses, she took a deep breath, drinking in chill air ripe with the tang of the sea and damp stone. She felt an irresistible shimmer of excitement she couldn't quite put her finger on.

The fanciful notion that Castle Wrath's once-pulsating heart still beat beneath the surface of its pitted, age-darkened stones.

She pressed her hands against a wall, splaying her fingers across the cold and gritty surface of the stones, not at all surprised to sense a faint vibration humming somewhere deep inside them.

Indeed, she felt a distant thrumming real enough to send a chill through her and even lead her to imagine bursts of loud masculine laughter and song. The sharp blasts of a trumpeter's fanfare. Barking dogs and a series of thin, high-pitched squeals.

Excited *feminine* squeals.

Kira frowned and took her hands off the wall.

The sounds stopped at once.

Or, she admitted, she recognized them for what they'd been: the rushing of the wind and nothing else. Even if the tingles spilling all through her said otherwise.

An odd prickling sensation she knew wouldn't stop until she'd peered into one of the earth-and-rubble clogged gaps in Castle Wrath's bailey.

Her lunch forgotten, she considered her options. She wasn't about to march across the nettle-filled courtyard and risk plunging into some bottomless medieval pit, meeting an early grave. Or, at the very least, twisting an ankle and ruining the remainder of her trip. But the shell of one of Castle Wrath's great drum-towers stood slightly tilted to her left, a scant fifty feet away.

Best of all, in the shadow of the tower's hulk she could make out the remains of a stairwell. A dark, downward spiraling turnpike stair that filled her with such a sense of wonder she didn't realize she'd moved until she found herself hovering on its weathered threshold. An impenetrable blackness stared back at her, so deep its dank, earthy-smelling chill lifted the fine hairs on her nape.

Something was down there.

Something more than nerves and imagination.

The sudden tightness in her chest and the cold hard knot forming in her belly assured her of it. As did the increasing dryness of her mouth and the racing of her pulse, the faint flickering torchlight filling the stairwell.

*Flickering torchlight?*

Kira's eyes flew wide, her jaw dropping. She grabbed the edges of the crumbling stairwell's doorway, holding tight, but there could be no mistake. The light was flaring brighter now, shining hotly and illuminating the cold stone walls and the impossibly medieval-looking Highland chieftain staring up at her from the bottom of the stairs, the vaulted hallows of his crowded, well-lit great hall looming behind him.

That it was *his* hall couldn't be questioned.

She'd bet her plane ticket back to Newark that a more lairdly man had never walked the earth. Nor a sexier one. A towering raven-haired giant, he was clad in rough-looking tartan-and calf-skin, and hung about with gleaming mail and bold Celtic jewelry. Power and sheer male animal magnetism rolled off him, stealing her breath and weakening her knees.

Making her question her sanity.

Perhaps someone on the bus tour had slipped something into her tepid breakfast tea.

Something that would make her hallucinate.

Imagine the hunky Highlander who couldn't really be there.

Just as she couldn't really be hearing the sounds of medieval merrymaking.

Feasting noises, she was sure. The same raucous male laughter and bursts of trumpet fanfares and song she'd heard earlier, the collective din of a celebrating throng—not that she cared.

A marching brass band could stomp past and blast her right off the cliff-top. As long as *he* stood glaring up at her, the world as Kira Bedwell had known and loved it ceased to exist.

And he *was* glaring.

Every gorgeous muscle-ripped inch of him.

He locked gazes with her, glowering at her as only a fierce, hot-eyed, sword-packing Highlander could do. A truth she hadn't known until this very moment, but one she'd take with her to her grave.

If she lived that long.

The too-dishy-to-be-real Highlander might have a patent on

sex appeal, but he was also armed to the teeth. A huge two-handed sword hung from a wide leather shoulder belt slung across his chest, and a glittering array of other equally wicked-looking medieval weapons peeked at her from beneath his voluminous tartan plaid. Not that he needed such a display of steel. O-o-oh, no. Such a man probably uprooted trees with one hand for exercise.

Big trees.

And at the moment, she felt incredibly treelike.

She swallowed hard, pressing her fingers more firmly against the stone edges of the door arch. Any further movement wasn't an option. Her legs had gone all rubbery and even if she could have taken a step backward, away from the opening, she just knew he'd charge up the stairs if she did.

Stairs that no longer looked worn and crumbling but new and unlittered, wholly free of fallen rubble and earth or the thick weeds that had clogged the top of the stairwell mere moments before.

She squeezed her eyes shut and opened them again. "This can't be happening," she gasped, jerking her hands off the now-smooth edges of the door arch.

"Nae, it cannae be," the Highlander agreed, his voice a deep velvety burr as he angled his head at her, his gaze narrowing. "Though I would know why it is!"

The words held a bold challenge, the suspicion in his eyes changing swiftly to something else.

Something darkly seductive and dangerous.

"Och, aye, I would hear the why of it." He tossed back his hair, the look he was giving her almost a physical touch. "Nor am I one to no' welcome a comely lass into my hall—howe'er strange her raiments."

"Raiments?" Kira blinked.

"Your hose, sweetness." His gaze dropped to her legs,

lingering there just long enough to make her squirm. "I've ne'er seen the like on a woman. No' that I'm complaining."

Kira swallowed. "Y-you can't be ... anything. You're not even there."

"Ho! So you say?" He looked down at his plaid, flicking its edge. "If my plaid's real, then I vow I am, too. Nae, lass, 'tis you who cannae be here."

"You're a ghost."

He laughed. "Since I haven't died yet, that's no' possible."

"I was told anything is possible in Scotland and now I believe it." Kira stared at him. "Whatever you are."

He flashed a roguish grin and started forward, mounting the tight, winding steps with long, easy strides. "'Tis laird of this keep I am." His deep voice filled the stairwell, rich, sonorous, and real as the chill bumps on her arms. "I'm also a man—as I can prove if you wish!"

Reaching her, he seized her shoulders, his grip strong and firm, warm even through the thickness of her jacket. He stepped close, so near that the hilt of his sword pressed into her hip. "Now, lass," he said, his gaze scorching her, "tell me. Do I feel like a ghost?"

Kira sucked in a breath. "No, but—"

"Aye, right." His mouth curved with a triumphant smile. "'Tis you who is out of place, no' me. Though I vow you dinnae feel like a ghost either."

Then his smile went wicked, his eyes darkening as he pulled her tighter against him, lowering his head as if to give her a hard, bruising kiss. Instead, his lips only brushed hers lightly, just barely touching her before he disappeared into darkness.

Kira screamed, but only the wind and the crashing sea answered her.

That, and the stairwell's emptiness. The same total blackness, icy cold and dank-smelling, that she'd been staring into all along.

Her imagination had run away with her. There could be no

other explanation. She'd wished for a Highlander with a wolfish smile and a honeyed tongue, and so she'd conjured him.

Simple as that.

She would just lean against the ruined wall of the drum-tower and wait until her knees stopped knocking before she gathered her untouched lunch packet and returned to the road to wait for the tour bus. It wasn't until she was halfway there that she realized she'd picked up more than her picnic goods.

Her heart still beating wildly, she looked at her left hand, slowly uncurling her fingers to reveal the squarish clump of granite she must've grabbed when she'd held so tight to the crumbling edges of the stairwell's door arch.

She frowned.

The stone seemed to stare at her in mute reproach, but rather than taking it back, she hurried on, clutching the stone like a precious treasure.

And to her it was.

A memento of her Highlander.

With a sigh, she paused a few feet from the road, looking back over her shoulder at the ruins. The sun had burst through the clouds, burning off the mist and gilding the tumbled walls with the bright blue and gold of the late-spring afternoon. Even the wind was lessening and the dark, jagged cliffs of Wrath Isle no longer looked quite so menacing.

The ruined castle no longer a home to ghosts.

An empty shell was all it was, she made herself believe, choosing as well to ignore the thickness in her throat and the stinging heat jabbing the backs of her eyes.

Whoever or whatever he'd been, her hunky Highlander couldn't have been real.

Never in all her dreams.

# 1

ALDAN, PENNSYLVANIA, A PLEASANT AND
RESPECTABLE DELAWARE COUNTY BOROUGH,
TWELVE YEARS LATER...

K ira Bedwell had a dirty little secret.
A towering plaid-hung secret, masterful and passionate, impossibly addictive.

Maddening, too, for he came to her only in her dreams.

Deliciously heated dreams that called to her now, teasing the
edges of her sleep and flooding her with tingling, languorous
warmth until she began to stretch and roll beneath the bedcovers.
She reached for an extra pillow, hugging it close as the walls of
her apartment's tiny bedroom shimmered and shimmied, taking
on a silvery translucence. As always, her pulse leapt at the trans-
formation, the rippling luminescence giving her a view of the
cliffs and the sea, a sheep-grazed hill and tumbled, mist-clad
ruins.

Ancient ruins, well loved and remembered.

Kira sighed, her heart catching. She bit her lip and splayed
her fingers across the cool linen of her bedsheets. She could
imagine him so well, her darkly seductive Highlander. If she
concentrated, she could almost see him in the shadows, waiting.
Mist swirled around his tall, strapping form, a strong wind
tearing at his plaid and whipping his raven hair. His hot gaze

would make her burn, the raw sensuality streaming off him flowing over her like pure, molten lust, rousing her.

He'd step closer then, a slow smile curving his lips, the sheer eroticism of him and his own insatiable need almost letting her forget she'd fallen asleep in her clothes.

Again.

The third night in a week, if she wished to keep note, which she didn't. Once was more than enough and three times bordered on seriously bothersome.

If she weren't mistaken, this time she'd even kept on her shoes.

Annoyed, she flipped onto her side. Yearning still swept her, but she cracked an eye, her dreamspun ardor vanishing as she peered into the darkness.

Her silent bedroom stared back at her, cramped, cluttered, and shabby chic. Pathetically empty of hot-eyed Scotsmen. But the pale glimmer of a new moon fell across the little polished brass carriage clock on her bedside table, the piece's stark black hands showing the hour as three a.m. Give or take ten minutes.

She blew out a frustrated breath. Like so many of her carefully accumulated treasures, the antique clock wasn't perfect, keeping time to its own rhythm. Sometimes accurate, sometimes ahead or behind, and every so often not at all.

Like her dreams.

They, too, couldn't be forced.

Aidan MacDonald, medieval clan chieftain extraordinaire, only slipped into her fantasies when it suited him.

Or so Kira thought.

Just as she assumed her bold dream lover could only be the MacDonalds' legendary leader. After her one trip to Scotland years ago, she'd spent months researching Clan Donald and Castle Wrath, finally determining Aidan as her Highlander.

The tantalizingly gorgeous Celtic he-god she'd glimpsed so briefly.

And never forgotten.

A man of any less mythic status couldn't possibly invade her sleep and ravish her with such wild, heart-pounding sex. Just the imagined scent of him made her dizzy with longing. Remembering the cool silk of his glossy, shoulder-length hair, or the hardness of his muscles, was enough to make her breath quicken. Thinking about his kisses, the skillful glide of his hands on her body, did things to her she never would have believed possible.

Watching him stride toward her, his sword hung low on his hip and a predatory gleam in his eye, positively melted her.

He was the essence of her deepest, darkest fantasies.

Her secret lover, he'd ruined her for all others.

Kira sighed, her fingers curling into the bed covers. Warmth pulsed through her just thinking about him. More than just a fantasy lover, he'd influenced her life in ways she'd never have believed possible. He'd initiated her into her special gift of far-seeing, the ability to catch a visual or mental image of the distant past. An inherited talent kept secret in her family and one she hadn't been aware of at all until the day she'd hoped to picnic at Castle Wrath and had peered down a ruined stairwell, looking straight into Aidan's torchlit hall and his dark, smoldering stare.

She shivered. She wanted that stare on her now.

Ached to see him.

Instead, nothing stirred except a chill wind whistling around her old brick apartment house. The faint *tap-tap* of tree branches against her window. All was still and quiet. Through a chink in the curtains she could see that the sky was low with clouds, the night cold and damp.

She stared out the window and sighed. Any other time she would have smiled. She liked cold and damp. Throw in a handful of mist and a bit of soft thin rain and her imagination could transport her to Scotland.

That other world where she longed to be, not here listening to the night wind sighing around Aldan, Pennsylvania's seen-better-days Castle Apartments, but hearing Hebridean gales blowing in from the sea. Long Atlantic breakers crashing on jagged black rocks.

Rugged cliffs and slate-colored seas, the tingle of salt mist damping her cheeks.

That was what she wanted.

*Needed.*

Unfortunately, on her budget, the closest she could hope to get to Scotland was dusting the framed tea towel of Edinburgh's Royal Mile that hung above her sagging sofa. Frustration welling, she twisted onto her side and pulled a pillow over her head. Truth was, she cherished that tea towel. Like the small tartan-covered armchair beside her bed, she'd found the tea towel at a garage sale. Along with the worthless wooden frame she'd used to mount it.

A thin purse sparked creativity.

And penning supposedly true tales of the strange and inexplicable for *Destiny Magazine*, a popular monthly focused on all things supernatural, didn't generate enough income for luxuries.

Even if some of her stories were fact.

Like her most recent. The reason she'd barricaded herself inside her postage-stamp-sized apartment and wasn't answering her phone or e-mail.

Kira groaned and knocked the pillow aside. Impossible, how a mere week could turn someone's life upside down. One excited phone call to *Destiny* from a group of wannabe archeologists, and there she was, using her far-seeing ability to help them locate the remains of a Viking longboat resting proudly at the bottom of a river-bisected Cape Cod lake, her discovery proving beyond a doubt that Norsemen were the first to land on the New World's shores. Overnight, she'd become everyone's most celebrated darling.

Or their worst nightmare.

Depending on whether one favored silver-helmed, ax-bearing

sea marauders or the tried and true. Either way, even if *Destiny* raised her salary to match her sudden and unwanted notoriety, the proponents of a certain Mediterranean mariner weren't too keen to see their hero's glory dinted.

A shudder rippled down Kira's spine and she clutched the covers tighter. She'd lost track of how many historical societies wanted her head, each one raking her over the coals for her blasphemy.

Christopher Columbus may have died centuries ago, but his spirit was alive and well in America.

His fans active.

Out there, and sharpening their claws.

She frowned. No, a raise wasn't going to help her. The means to purchase an air ticket meant diddly-squat if she ended up tarred and feathered before she could ever reach the airport.

Not to mention a Glasgow-bound plane.

Judging by the hate mail she'd been receiving, such a mob might even seize and burn her passport. Already, she'd found two nails thrust into her car tires, and some exceptionally witty soul who clearly lived in her apartment building had smeared some kind of unidentifiable goo on her doorknob. Icky, foul-smelling goo. Kira swiped an annoying strand of hair off her forehead. At least fretting about such nonsense took her mind off him.

The gorgeous, incredible-in-bed medieval Highlander she shouldn't be fantasizing about when she was in a pickle.

She sighed and shut her eyes, doing her best to forget him. The alpha Gael who not only could melt her with one heated, sensuous glance but who knew better than any real man how to ignite her passion.

A fool's passion, imagined and *un*real, regardless of how exquisite.

She pressed a hand to her forehead and massaged her temples. The broadcast reporters and television cameras camped in the Castle Apartments parking lot *were* real and she'd had enough of them. As the daughter of a ceramic tile salesman and a high school art teacher, she wasn't used to the limelight.

Nor did she like it.

Especially when they all seemed determined to make sport of her.

"Sleep." She breathed the word like a mantra, repeating it in her mind as she rubbed two fingers between her brows. A good eight hours of oblivion was what she needed.

Maybe then she'd wake refreshed, the snarl of television crews and other suchlike long-noses gone from outside her apartment's ground floor windows, the world a new and bright place, free of problems and cares.

Yes, she decided, settling an arm over her head, sleep was just what she needed.

*Lass ... your raiments.*

Deep and rich, the mellifluous words seduced the darkness, pure Highland and buttery-smooth. Familiar in ways that slid right through her sleep to curl low in her belly, warming and melting her. Making her tingle and sizzle in all the right places.

Aidan MacDonald's sinfully sexy burr could do that.

That, and many other things.

All delicious.

Her eyes snapped open. He stood in the dim moonlight near her window, his hands on his hips and his head angled as he looked at her. All male dominance and breathtakingly handsome, he caught and held her gaze, the heat of his own already stroking her, making her burn.

"The raiments," he said again, stepping closer. "Have done with them."

Kira's breath caught. Her heart leapt. Somewhere in the distance a siren wailed. Not that she cared. Her body refused to move. She could only stare, desire and need streaking through her, embarrassment flaming the back of her neck, scalding her cheeks.

He wanted her naked, as was his wont.

But unless she was mistaken, getting that way might dampen his ardor.

She was wearing her comfy, granny-style panties. High-waisted, white-cotton, and boring. Equally bad, she had on her favorite oversized training suit. The baggy one with the little tear in the knee.

She swallowed. "I wasn't expecting you tonight. It's been a while."

He shrugged. "I've had matters to see to," he said, flicking a speck of lint off his plaid. "That doesn't mean I haven't hungered for you. I have, and my need is great."

"I missed you, too," she stalled, trying to calculate how quickly she could rid herself of her less-than-flattering clothes and assume a seductive pose.

In dreams, anything should be possible, but her limbs remained stubbornly frozen, her fumbling fingers impossibly clumsy.

He started toward her, his own hands already unbuckling his sword belt. His eyes narrowing, he paused just long enough to set aside his great brand and whip off his plaid. Then, as was the way with sexual fantasies, he flashed a smile and was naked, without even having to stoop to yank off his rough-leathered brogues.

"Ahhh..." Her palms began to dampen. "Maybe tonight isn't a good time."

Towering over the bed now, he cocked a brow. "Sweetness, I've told you," he began, his gaze flicking the length of her, "any time we have is good." For an instant, his face clouded. "It isn't always easy to find you." He folded his arms, looking serious. "I dinnae ken what powers let us come together. Only that we must seize the moments we have."

She swallowed, her heart pounding. "But?"

"But you know I have ne'er cared for your way of dress." His eyes narrowed on her sweatshirt. "'Tis passing strange."

She burrowed deeper into the covers. Wait till he saw her granny panties.

"Clothes shouldn't matter in dreams." She met his gaze, her heart still hammering. "Besides, they're all I have—"

"You have an abundance, beautifully so." He reached for the covers and whipped them off the bed, some Highland slight of hand or dream-inspired magic leaving her unclothed.

Just as naked as he was.

She blinked. So much for cotton underwear and baggy sweatpants.

He looked at her, the covers dangling from his hand, her clothes nowhere in sight, and an expression of intense satisfaction on his handsome face.

"That's better," he said, letting the blanket fall.

*No, it's better than better,* Kira wanted to say, but the words lodged in her throat. She moistened her lips, her gaze flicking over his magnificence. Her heart swelled, her chest tightening even as her tender places went soft and achy. Just looking at him excited her. Need flamed through her, tingling and urgent as his dark eyes heated, flaring with passion as they swept her own nakedness.

"Sweet lass, were you not a *bruadar*, I'd keep you in my bed for a sennight." He reached to smooth strong fingers along the curve of her hip. "Nae, seven days wouldn't sate me. I'd double that, ravishing you again and again for a fortnight."

Kira sighed, her limbs going liquid.

But one thing he'd said troubled her. A word she didn't know.

"A broo-e-tar?" She could hardly speak, his touch and his buttery-rich voice, working the usual magic on her. "You've never called me that before."

"Perhaps I do not speak the word for I wish it were not so. *Bruadar* is the Gaelic for a dream. I would have you as a full-blooded woman, hot and alive in my arms." His eyes darkened. "Mine, alone."

"I am yours, and real." Kira's heart pounded, the truth of those three words slashing across her soul. The impossibility of them damned her. "You are the dream." She met his gaze, her own challenging him to deny it. "You're here in my bedroom. I'm not in yours."

"Say you?" One raven brow arced in a look of sheer male authority. "Yon walls look like mine to me," he said, flashing a glance at the windows.

Windows no longer there.

Kira gulped, unable to deny that her windows were gone. Likewise her carefully sewn tartan window dressings and even the entire wall. In their place, proud whitewashed stones gleamed with the soft glow of candles, and the tasseled edges of a richly colored tapestry fluttered in the draught of an unshuttered window.

A tall arch-topped window.

Very medieval-y.

Definitely not hers.

Her eyes widened. She could even feel the chill night breeze here in her bed. Catch the brisk tang of the sea; the pounding of waves onto a fearsome, rock-strewn shore. Then the illusion faded, leaving only the fragile luminescence of her dream, her plaid-patterned curtains faintly visible again, staring mutely from behind the shimmering silver. And instead of the roar of Hebridean waves, she heard only the tic-ticking of her clock.

The familiar tree branch scratching at the glass of her apartment windows.

Irrefutable evidence of just where she was and that despite the intensity of her his stare, she was indeed only dreaming.

"Nae worries, lass. It doesnae matter. No' where we are." He looked at her, his gaze going deep. "All that matters is that I want you. And"—he paused, desire blazing in his eyes—"that you want me. You do, don't you?"

"O-o-oh, yes." She reached for him and he obliged her, gathering her close for a hungry, lip-bruising kiss. Tightening his arms around her, he plundered her mouth, the mastery of his tongue blotting everything but sensation.

The wild thundering of her heart and the slight creaking of her secondhand bed when he stretched out beside her, the full hot and hard length of him pressed skin-to-skin against her own welcoming softness.

The creak made her frown, its intrusion reminding her this was all fantasy. A dream that could be so easily shattered, and often was.

Determined to hold onto him as long as possible, she slid her hands up his powerful back, gripping his shoulders as he rolled on top of her. At once, that very special hot, hard and glorious part of him probed her, seeking their bliss.

Still kissing her, he slipped a hand between them to explore her breasts. His fingers splayed over her fullness, tantalizing her. "You are mine," he growled, his breath warm against her lips. "I will ne'er let you go. No' if I must search to the ends of the earth to find you."

Something inside her broke on his words and she clung to him, returning his kiss with all the passion she had, refusing to accept the futility of his vow.

Aidan the Magnificent, as she sometimes thought of him, could search for her through all time, even turn the world on end, and never would he find her.

Not really.

Too many centuries stretched between them.

That truth scalding the backs of her eyes, she opened her mouth wider beneath his, welcoming the mad thrust of his tongue, needing the intimacy of his soul-searing kisses.

Wanting all of him.

Understanding that need as only he could, he deepened the kiss, swirling his tongue over and around hers as he eased himself inside her, the silky-smooth glide of each rock-hard inch deeper into her eager, clutching heat sent waves of pleasure spilling through her.

She matched his thrusts, losing herself to the elemental fury of their joining, reveling in the sexy Gaelic love words he breathed against her lips. Dark, lusty-sounding words, full of an untamed, earthy wildness that thrilled her, his every passionate utterance driving her closer to an explosive, shattering release.

Her own cries loud in her head, she writhed and arched her hips, her need breaking even as her cries turned shrill. Sharp, jangling cries so annoying and harsh they could never be coming from her throat.

Not now, on the verge of her climax.

The noise kept on, growing insistent, seeming louder with each passion-zapping shrill until she came awake with a start and recognized the sound for what it was.

Her telephone.

She groaned.

Aidan was nowhere to be seen.

If he'd been there at all—a peek beneath the covers proved she was still wearing her comfy training suit. The whole grungy works, complete with tennies. Worse, if her heavy-eyed grogginess and the bands of light sneaking in past her drawn curtains meant anything, she'd slept way too late.

Almost afraid to look, she groped for her little bedside clock, glanced at it, and then groaned again. Ten thirty a.m. A new record, even for her, notorious *un*-morning person that she was.

And still the phone rang.

Wishing she'd slept with earplugs, she scrambled to a sitting position and grabbed the phone. Squinting at the caller ID display, she almost put down the receiver.

Much as she loved her, her mother wasn't someone she cared to talk to before at least two cups of coffee.

Strong black coffee, the kind you could stand a spoon in.

Bracing herself, she drew a deep breath, determined to sound awake. "Hello?"

"Carter Williams called, dear," her mother gushed. "He wants to speak with you." She paused for a breath and Kira could hear her excitement bubbling through the phone. "I told him we could have coffee at three. Here at the house. He—"

"Wait a minute." Kira sat up, warning bells ringing in her head. "Who is Carter Williams?"

"*Kira.*" Her mother gave an exasperated sigh. "Would I invite him over if he weren't important?"

No, she wouldn't, but Kira wasn't about to point that out to her.

"Who is he?" she repeated instead.

Blanche Bedwell hesitated.

A pause that made Kira's stomach clench.

The only men wishing to speak to her lately were icky-pot media hounds. Worse, her mother not only worried about status, she was also a notorious matchmaker who believed every female under thirty should be married and having babies.

Like Kira's sisters.

"Well? Who is Carter Williams?" Kira was sure she didn't want to know.

"He's with the *Aldan Bee.* A nice young man who's going places. I play bridge with his mother. He only wants to ask you a few questions about your Viking ship."

"It isn't my Viking ship. It's what's left of a foundered Norse longship and a few ancient mooring holes and other artifacts that prove—"

"Whatever." Kira could almost see her mother waving an airy hand. "Carter Williams might give you an in at the *Bee* if you—"

"An in at the *Bee?*" The tops of Kira's ears started getting warm. "I don't want to work for the *Bee.*"

"It would be a real job, dear."

"I have a job." Kira glanced at the papers and books piled on her tiny desk across the room.

Research for her next assignment: *My Three Month Marriage To A Yeti.*

Suppressing a groan, she threw back the covers and stood. "*Destiny Magazine* pays well enough for me to cover my monthly bills. And"—she shoved a hand through her mussed hair—"writing for them lets me stretch my imagination. The readers who buy the magazine are entertained and I can pay my rent."

"Making up tales of alien abductions."

"If need be, yes." Kira shot another glance at her stack of Yeti books. She wasn't about to admit that she, too, was growing weary of penning such drivel.

Even so, she wouldn't barter her soul by working with the kind of wolf pack presently prowling the Castle Apartments parking lot. They were still there, the snarkies, as a glance out her window revealed. If she weren't mistaken, they might have increased in number overnight.

Like the plague of the giant toadstools she'd written about a few years ago.

Cringing at the memory, she turned away from the window and dropped onto the edge of her bed, not knowing whether to laugh or cry.

"Kira, child, Carter Williams is—"

"Not all my stories are about aliens," Kira cut in, thoughts of aliens and mutant toadstools making her testy. "The Norse long-ship is an important discovery. The excavation has drawn some of the nation's top archeologists. *Destiny* understands my special gift. No other magazine or paper would let me—"

"Carter Williams is single."

That did it.

Kira shot to her feet. "So am I. Happily so."

Her gaze slid to the glittery clump of granite sitting in a place of honor beside her computer's keyboard. At once, Aidan's face flashed before her and she could almost hear his deep burr again.

*You are mine.*

*I will ne'er let you go. No' if I must search to the ends of the earth to find you.*

Crossing the room, she picked up the stone. "Carter Williams will just have to do without me," she said, closing her fingers around the piece of granite. "You know I've gone off men for a while. I told you that the last time you tried to set me up with someone."

Her mother made an impatient sound. "There was nothing wrong with Lonnie Ward. Your father says he's certain Lonnie will be the next manager at the Tile Bonanza. You could have done worse."

Kira glanced at the ceiling. "Lonnie Ward doesn't like dogs." She tightened her fingers around the granite. "You should have seen him brushing at his pants after a dog ran up to him and sniffed him in the park. You know I could never be happy with a dog-hater."

"You don't have a dog, dear."

"I will someday."

As soon as she didn't live in an apartment the size of a fishbowl.

Her mother drew a breath. "I believe Carter Williams has a dog. I've seen him about town with a spaniel. And his mother has two—"

"It won't work, Mom." Kira puffed her bangs off her forehead. "I'm not biting."

"You're still mooning over that Highland chieftain," her mother said, and Kira almost dropped the phone. She'd never told anyone about her dreams. Not even her sisters. And especially not her mother. "It isn't healthy to obsess over someone who lived centuries ago, poring through history books and decorating your apartment like the set of *Brigadoon*."

"Lots of people love Scotland," Kira returned, relief sweeping her that her mother hadn't somehow guessed the truth about Aidan. "Even Kerry and Lindsay devour romance novels set there."

Blanche Bedwell sighed. "Your sisters are also well-balanced young women who have other interests."

Kira rolled her eyes. Her younger sister, Kerry's, only goal in life seemed to be squeezing into clothes too tight for her under-five-foot Rubenesque figure, eating sweets, and producing babies. Her older sister, Lindsay, was a hypochondriac tree hugger and such a clinging vine, Kira wondered how she managed to spend enough time away from their parents to run her own household, much less raise her two children.

"You should follow in your sisters' footsteps," her mother added. "Marry and raise a family."

Kira set down her stone and glanced at the drawn curtains. She couldn't see them, but she could feel the Carter Williamses of the world out there, clogging the parking lot, waiting for her to show herself.

She shuddered, her stomach knotting at the thought of facing them. But then she put her shoulders back and stood straighter. Silly or not, she knew Aidan wouldn't approve of a spineless woman.

Not in his century and not in her dreams.

As soon as she'd showered and had her coffee, she'd go outside and tell the long-noses to buzz off. Find someone else to make the centerpiece of their snarkfest.

She wouldn't cooperate. Nor would she be intimidated.

"Perhaps you're right—in part," she admitted. "Maybe I do need other interests. But don't forget, it was your own great-aunt Minnie's *inheritance* that got me into all this." She left out that her life might've taken an easier course if her mother hadn't kept silent about some females in the family having far-seeing talents.

A trait that had lain dormant for generations and that Blanche Bedwell had hoped would never surface again.

Unfortunately—or not—it had, and its startling arrival that day at the Wrath ruins had changed Kira's life.

"Great-aunt Minnie lived in a different time," her mother sniffed. "People were more impressionable then. You have the means to channel your talents in a more sensible direction."

Kira bristled. "Maybe I like the direction I've taken. I'm interested in the paranormal, though I wouldn't mind a better paying job where I wouldn't have to spend half my time making up nonsense about angels amongst us and Bigfoot sightings. It's the true supernatural that fascinates me. Ghosts, reincarnation, that sort of thing."

Her mother sighed.

Ignoring her, Kira began pacing. "I'd like to work quietly and behind the scenes, without being plunged into the limelight."

"Limelight isn't necessarily bad," her mother countered. "Such attention could draw the notice of—"

"Just the kind of man I'd not be interested in," Kira finished for her. "Not if flash and brass topped his list of the important things in life."

Her mother tsk-tsked. "You've set your sights too high, my dear. Phemie's stepdaughter is the only soul I've ever heard of who married a Scottish laird and went off to live happily ever after in a castle. Such things don't happen every day."

No, they didn't. Kira knew that.

The quick flash of green-tinged heat jabbing needles in her heart proved it.

A Scottish laird and living in the Highlands. In a real castle. She shot a glance at her desk, the silver-framed photo of the ruins of Castle Wrath claiming pride of place right next to her piece of granite. Her heart squeezed and the green-tinted heat began spreading through her chest, making each breath difficult.

"Phemie and the girl's father went over to see the couple last year," her mother was saying. "Though Phemie couldn't stomach sleeping in the castle, saying it was too damp and musty and full of ghosts. She—"

"Phemie as in Euphemia Ross?" Disbelief washed over Kira. "The sharp-tongued little wisp of a woman in your bridge club? The one everyone calls the Cairn Avenue shrew?"

"Now, Kira." Blanche Bedwell used her most placating tone. "She's Euphemia McDougall these days, and, yes, her stepdaughter, Mara, married a real live Highland chieftain. Sir Alexander Douglas, I believe Phemie called him. Their castle is near a place called Uban or something."

"Oban," Kira corrected her. "The gateway to the Hebrides. It's on Scotland's west coast. My tour years ago stopped there. We had a whole hour's look at Dunstaffnage Castle."

"Well, dear, if ever you go back, I'm sure Phemie would give you Mara's phone number and address. She'd surely be pleased to see you. Just—"

She broke off as the doorbell trilled in the background. "That will be Lindsay. She made a batch of organic brownies for your father. Call if you need me."

"I will," Kira said as her mother rang off.

Not that her mother—or anyone—could help her with what she needed.

Knowing she couldn't even help herself in that regard, she put down the phone and began peeling off her rumpled clothes, heading for the bathroom. Naked, she yanked back her thistle-covered shower curtain and made to step beneath the steaming, pounding spray.

Until her phone rang again. She listened as her answering machine clicked on and *Destiny Magazine's* executive editor's voice rose above the sound of running water, the man's tone giving her pause.

Dan Hillard sounded excited.

*Kira, girl.* His booming voice filled the bathroom. *I know you're in hiding and may even want to quit, but I've got a new assignment for you.*

"O-o-oh, no, you don't." Kira grabbed a towel and slung it around her as she hastened back into her bedroom to click off the machine. "Not for a while anyway."

*This is one you won't want to miss,* Dan's voice cajoled, almost as if he'd heard her. *It'll get you away from this media circus.*

Kira hesitated, her fingers hovering over the answering machine. Something in his voice was getting to her, making her heart skitter.

*Faraway, Kira. All expenses paid.*

She closed her eyes, breathed deeply, ready to reject—

Another voice broke in, interrupting Dan. *Come, lass, I'm waiting for you.*

Kira whirled around, the towel dropping to the floor. But only her empty bedroom stared back at her. Even if the echo of Aidan's voice still rang her in ears. Dark, rich, and sexy, and so full of longing her knees weakened.

He'd called to her.

She was certain of it.

Trembling, she stooped to pick up her towel, waiting for Dan to say something else. But he, too, was gone. Nothing remained of her boss or his cryptic message but the insistent little red light blinking on the answering machine.

Not that she needed to hear the words.

Her heart already knew.

She was going to Scotland.

## 2

"*Come, lass, I'm waiting for you. Burning for you.*"

Aidan MacDonald stood at the tall arch-topped window of his bedchamber, one hand clenched around his sword belt, the other clutching the tasseled edges of a richly embroidered tapestry proudly adorning his wall.

A brilliantly colored display of bold knights and fair, half-naked ladies romping in a wood, their erotic playfulness so explicitly depicted he could scarce bear looking at it.

Truth be told, if his temper didn't soon improve, he might just yank the thing from the wall and send it sailing out his window.

Letting go of it, he shoved a hand through his hair and scowled. For well over a sennight, he'd been unable to reach his *bruadar*. The comely, well-made vixen of his dreams he'd glimpsed but once and ne'er been able to put from his mind.

Or his heart.

Not to mention what she did to his body.

"Hell and damnation." He blew out a breath, the scent and feel of her haunting him. A bittersweet torment so real and vibrant he hurt inside. Ached with a deep, lancing pain that knew no healing.

Not without her. Her soft, lush lips parting beneath his, her bountiful curves, warm, silken, and smooth, crushed tight against him as he held her in his arms. Made her his again and again.

This time never letting her go.

His scowl deepening, he curled his hands to fists. "I burn for you, lass," he growled, staring out at the cold, wind-whipped waters tossing so indifferently beneath his tower chamber's window. The jagged cliffs of nearby Wrath Isle, each frowning, black-glistening fissure suiting his mood, firing his frustration.

His fury at such a foul turn of fate.

Setting his jaw, he braced his hands on the edges of the window arch, leaning out so the night wind could cool him. Take the heat out of his face if not his blood.

"Sakes, lass, I need you." The tightness in his chest let him know how much. "For the love of all the Ancient Ones, where are you?"

"She is long gone, that's what," a deep voice reproached from behind him. "God's eyes, man, what did you do to her?"

Aidan spun around. "What did I do to who?"

Tavish MacDonald merely cocked a brow. Aidan's most trusted friend and cousin—though some whispered half brother due to their strong resemblance—reached to pinch out the wicks of a hanging cresset lamp.

Aidan fixed him with a withering glare, trying for the life of him to recall if he'd ever fallen so deep in his cups as to regale his friend with tales of his dream lass.

"You ought know better than to have a lamp burning so near to the window on such a windy night." Tavish waved a hand through the dissipating smoke. "As for who I meant"—he slid a narrow glance at Aidan—"'twas the MacLeod widow. She herself and all her men."

Aidan relaxed. But only for a moment.

Turning again to the window, he clasped his hands behind his back and drew a deep breath, his gaze on the moon as it came and went through the clouds. He might not have spilled his heart to Tavish in a long ale-filled night in his great hall, but the departure of the MacLeod woman presented an entirely different kind of problem.

He'd counted on her men to help him scour the hills and surrounding islands for Conan Dearg.

Trouble was, the price of Fenella MacLeod's men and galleys was one he hadn't wished to pay.

"She left in a huff," Tavish informed him. "Away with the tide and a scowl darker than some of your own."

Aidan turned from the window and made for a polished oak table across the room, well laden with cold breast of chicken, oatcakes and cheese, and a freshly filled ewer of ale. The offerings were meant to be his evening repast, but circumstance had stolen his appetite.

Truth was, if his days didn't soon take a better turn, he might never regain it.

"Lady Fenella was quick to offer aid." Tavish hovered behind him again. "Few in these isles have a larger flotilla of longships. Or better-kept ones. Her men are fierce and strong-armed. She would have served you well."

Aidan almost spewed the ale he'd just poured for himself. Frowning in earnest now, he tossed back the rest in one great swig, slamming down the cup before he wheeled around.

"By the gods, Tavish! The lady wished to serve me, true enough." He glowered at his friend, felt heat surging up his neck. "She came here dressed in her bed-robe and nothing else, her hair unbound and hanging to her hips."

Aidan clamped his mouth shut, decency keeping him from revealing how she'd swept into his bedchamber, shutting and bolting the door behind her, then flinging open her robe to display her full, large-nippled breasts and the vee of jet-black curls topping her thighs.

"She made no mistake in letting me know why she came

knocking on my door so late of an e'en." Aidan's brows knit together at the memory. "The woman was brazen, I say you. Overbold."

To his annoyance, rather than answer him, Tavish moved to the table, taking his time to help himself to a towering portion of sliced chicken and a brimming cup of ale.

Worse, he then lowered himself into a chair beside the fire, setting his victuals on a nearby stool before he stretched his long legs toward the warmth of the softly glowing peats. Looking irritatingly comfortable, he pinned Aidan with an all-too-suspicious stare.

"Fenella MacLeod is an ardent woman. Generously made and vigorous, her eyes knowing." Tavish leaned back in the chair, his own gaze too wise for Aidan's liking. "Seldom have I seen a larger-breasted female. She has fine legs as well. I caught a glimpse of them once when she hitched up her skirts to board one of her late husband's galleys." He paused, lifting a hand to study his knuckles. "Indeed, many are the men in your hall who would bed her gladly."

Aidan quirked a brow. "Yourself included?"

"Nae, I, too, would have turned her from my door."

"I am glad to hear it. I would have doubted your honor otherwise." Aidan nodded, well pleased that his friend, too, drew the line at lying with the widow of a onetime ally. "Though I would not begrudge the men of my garrison such a dalliance. No' if the lady desired it."

"She comes and goes here at will, as you know," Tavish reminded him. "She isn't shy about displaying herself, dropping hints she'd welcome certain attentions. There are surely men amongst us eager enough to enjoy her charms. But the specter of her late husband is not the only reason you refused her."

Aidan lowered the cup he was about to refill. "What are you saying?"

Tavish looked up, his knuckles forgotten. "We were born and

bred together," he said, holding Aidan's stare. "I know you as few men can claim. I know the depth of your honor, the privilege of your trust, and the pleasure of your friendship. I've seen the rage of your battle-fury, felt secure knowing you were at my back. And"—he paused, leaning forward in the chair—"I know you are a well-lusted man."

Aidan folded his arms. "So? I wouldnae call myself a man were I not."

"To be sure, and neither would I," Tavish agreed, studying his knuckles again. "Nor," he added, looking up quickly, "did I abstain from the plump bed warmer that robber baron on Pabay thoughtfully provided for me when we sailed there to look for Conan Dearg."

Aidan frowned.

His friend's gaze grew more penetrating. "Despite the roughness of the men, the wenches on that isle of marauders were more than pleasing. Frang the Fearless offered you the comeliest of them all, yet"—he paused, lifting his ale cup to take a sip without his gaze leaving Aidan's face—"if memory serves, you slept alone."

"Leave be," Aidan warned him, unpleasantly aware of the muscle beginning to twitch in his jaw. "I am thinking you could no' have enjoyed your night on Pabay overmuch if you were so occupied observing mine."

Seemingly calm as a spring morn, Tavish crossed his ankles. "Lady Fenella is no' the first female to leave here looking soured in recent times," he drawled, brushing oatcake crumbs from his legs. "Nor have you tumbled Sinead, the Irish laundress, in longer than I can recall."

Aidan felt his face coloring. "Who I bed and when is my own business and no one else's," he snapped, especially furious to be reminded of the flame-haired Irish girl. There was only one fiery-tressed lass he hungered for and it wasn't Castle Wrath's light-skirted laundress.

Tavish lifted his hands in surrender.

Mock surrender, Aidan was sure.

"I'm only concerned for you," the lout declared, proving he wasn't about to let the matter lie. "You've been missed in the hall. Everyone knows you're up here brooding, locking yourself in your privy quarters or prowling the battlements at all hours, snarling like a chained beast."

*I'm feeling like a chained beast!* Aidan almost roared at him.

A deprived beast, trapped, ravenous, and filled with fury.

And about to do bodily harm to the one soul he loved above all men. If the great buffoon who looked so like him and knew his heart so well didn't soon have done with his badgering.

Turning away, lest his friend eye him any deeper than he already had, Aidan stalked back to the window and glared out at the expanse of dark water stretching between his own cliffs and the inky-black bulk of Wrath Isle. A strong swell was running, the swift current reminding him of the other matter weighing so heavily on his mind.

A problem he suddenly knew the answer to.

He almost smiled.

Under other circumstances, he would have.

As it was, it sufficed that he now had a clear enough head to squelch Tavish's concerns. Drawing a deep breath just in case he needed it, he returned to the fire, deliberately striking his most formidable pose and not for the first time silently thanking the gods for the one-inch advantage of height that he boasted over his friend.

"I haven't been brooding," he lied, blurting the untruth before the other had a chance to speak. "I've been thinking."

That, at least, was the truth.

Tavish looked at him, unblinking. "I daresay you have."

"No' about wenching." Another lie.

Knowing Tavish would see through a third, he put his shoulders back and shot another glance at the window, remembering well the treacherous journey the two of them had made to Wrath Isle a few days before.

A dangerous crossing that had led to naught, their hours spent searching the isle's caves and tumbled ruins turning up little more than angry seabirds and moldering sheep bones. Of Conan Dearg, there'd been nary a sign.

It'd been an undertaking he'd meant to make alone, not wishing to endanger anyone else's life but his own. Tavish, great and beloved meddler that he was, had declared himself of another mind, vowing he'd swim after Aidan's boat if he didn't let him board.

And Tavish MacDonald, may the gods e'er bless him, always kept his word.

Reason enough to welcome his company, however grudgingly.

Looking at him now, Aidan heaved a great sigh and spoke the only part of his heart he was able to share. "It grieves me to have caused the MacLeod widow distress, but it troubles me more that we haven't yet found Conan Dearg," he said, his hand going almost absently to his sword hilt. "We've upturned every stone on this isle and others, even sailing to that notorious robbers' den, Pabay, then scouring every tainted, treacherous inch of Wrath Isle as well.

"So-o-o," he concluded, reaching down to scratch his favorite dog, Ferlie, behind the ears when the great beast lumbered up to him, pressing his shaggy bulk against his legs, "while I regret losing the support of Fenella MacLeod and her birlinns, I doubt we will have needed them to find Conan Dearg."

Tavish tossed Ferlie a bit of roasted chicken. "Indeed?"

Aidan nodded. "Since we've looked everywhere the double-dyed bastard could have hid, there's only one place he can be," he said, growing more certain by the moment. "Ardcraig."

"His own holding?" Tavish blinked, seeming doubtful. "We've

already gone there, even searching his keep from the undercroft to the parapets."

"Aye, and seeing what we expected to see." Aidan touched his sword hilt, rolled his thumb over the jeweled pommel stone. "Next time we shall seek the unexpected. Then we shall find him. 'Tis a feeling in my bones."

"Then let us drink to your feelings." Tavish pushed to his feet, a smile tugging at his lips. "I've ne'er known them to be wrong."

"Neither have I,"Aidan agreed, watching his friend pour them both a generous portion of ale.

He only hoped his feelings about his *bruadar* were as accurate. That the shapely, hot-blooded woman he'd been thinking of as a dream vision wasn't that at all, but a *tamhasg*. Nightly visitations of the woman meant to be his future bride.

As soon as Conan Dearg was found and locked in his dungeon, his people safe from treachery, he meant to find out.

No matter what it cost him.

Nothing was surer.

❧

WORLDS AND AN OCEAN AWAY, Kira stood in the middle of the Newark Liberty International Airport check-in area, almost oblivious to everything but the precious Newark-Glasgow boarding pass clutched in her hot little hand. Gate C-127, seat number 24A. A window behind the wing, left side so that she could see the sun rise over Ireland and then the endless sweep of the Hebrides as the plane descended into Scotland.

She remembered it well. The views that had stilled her heart and stolen her breath as she'd stared out at the isle-dotted coast, feasting her gaze on soaring cliffs, deep inlets, and sparkling, crystal-clear bays. Long Atlantic rollers crashing over jagged, black-teethed reefs and tiny crescent-shaped strands of gleaming white sand, inaccessible bits of paradise, pristine and almost too beautiful to bear looking down upon.

Then at last the Highlands stretching away to the horizon, each ever-higher rising hill bathed in the soft, rosy-gold glow of a new morning.

The new day she'd yearned for so long.

A place of mist-hung peace and splendor so different from the hectic lifestyle she loathed that just thinking of being there soon nearly set her to swooning.

Ignoring the airport chaos, she traced a fingertip across the fresh black print on her boarding card. She kept her finger on the word *Glasgow*, certain each letter held magic. Truth was, she could feel it. The boarding card vibrated in her hand, its pulsating warmth making her fingers tingle.

Until she realized it wasn't the boarding card causing the sensation but the trembling of her own fingers, her hands as they shook with giddy excitement. Whether in the flesh or not, Aidan was there waiting for her. She'd felt him call to her, could feel him calling her now.

Chances were, once there, she'd catch another true glimpse of him. A daylight glimpse without the smoke-and-mirror effects of their dreams. If it'd happened once, it could again. That belief, combined with the thrill of finally getting back to Scotland, was pushing her over the edge.

Making her light-headed.

She took a deep breath, shoved her boarding card deep into a side pocket of her purse. Then she wiped her damp palms on her one great splurge: a fine and stylish, many-pocketed, weather-proof jacket complete with hood.

"Kira, you've gone pale. Are you okay?" Dan Hillard gripped her elbow, his blue eyes filling with concern. "We can still get your luggage back. You don't have to go if you don't want to."

"Are you kidding?" Kira blinked at him, all the whir, noise, and haste of the airport filtering back into her consciousness, pulling her into the crowded, bustling reality.

"*Of course*, I want to go. More than I can say." She placed her hand over his, squeezing his fingers. "I'm fine. It's just too warm for me in here. I don't think they ever run air conditioners in this airport."

"You're sure?"

"I'm positive."

A tall, middle-aged man with an open, ruddy face and an unfortunate haircut that made him look more like an Army general than executive editor for a magazine that specialized in paranormal oddities, Dan slung an arm around her shoulders, drawing her near in a fatherly hug.

"What about driving on the left?" He stood back to look at her, the simple question making her stomach flip-flop. "The last time you were there, you were on an escorted coach tour. This time there's a rental car waiting for you at the Glasgow airport. Will you be able to manage?"

Kira straightened her back against her belly flutters and hitched up the shoulder strap of her carry-on. "Of course, I'll manage," she said, willing it so.

*To get to Castle Wrath, I'd drive on water if need be.*

Left, right, or upside down.

Leaving those sentiments unsaid, she forced her brightest smile. "Americans drive in Scotland all the time," she added, the words meant for herself as well as to reassure Dan. "I've also studied maps and"—she paused, stepping aside to make way for a young woman tugging two wailing children behind her—"if I recall correctly, about the only traffic hazard to worry about over there is sheep jams."

"As long as you're sure." He still sounded doubtful.

"I am."

"Sure enough to make it all the way to those three fairy mounds I want you to investigate?"

"The Na Tri Shean?" Kira smiled, her exhilaration returning, banishing the little niggles of doubt about driving. Dan's three conical-shaped fairy hills were thought to open into the Otherworld, providing access into the Land of the Fae. Not that she cared where the hills might lead or what mythical entities might dwell there.

More interesting to her was that Dan claimed the Na Tri Shean were also rumored to be time portals.

A possibility he wanted her to explore.

And an opportunity she couldn't refuse. Not with the three supposed time-portalling-fairy-mounds located not far from the Isle of Skye.

More specifically, Castle Wrath.

The image of the cliff-top ruins blazed across her mind, and her heart skipped. She could see her Aidan standing there, so fierce and tall, his plaid slung proudly over one shoulder, his gleaming raven hair whipped by the stiff sea winds. He was looking west, searching for her, she was certain.

Catching her sigh before it could escape, she flashed Dan a confident smile. "I'll make it to your fairy mounds," she assured him. "I'd crawl on my knees to get there. Driving will be a breeze."

Seemingly mollified, he harrumphed, his gaze flickering to her carry-on. "You have all the information I gave you? Eyewitness local and tourist accounts of the strange goings-on around those three hills? Copies of the ancient Celtic legends that mention them?"

Kira nodded. "I have everything," she said, patting her bulging satchel bag.

Including a dog-eared copy of *The Hebridean Clans,* a slim but fascinating volume, its pages dominated by Clan Donald, Lords of the Isles and undisputed rulers of Scotland's medieval western seaboard.

She'd found Aidan in that book and she wasn't about to leave it behind.

"You've read the stories?" Dan was watching her. "The stress of the last days hasn't kept you from going over them? I don't want you running into anything unprepared. There's always a kernel of truth in old legends. Who knows what—"

"I'll be fine." Kira leaned up to kiss his whiskered cheek. "And don't worry, you'll get your story. One way or the other. If the Na Tri Shean don't speak to me, I have a few other ideas for sure-winning tales."

Dan's smile returned. "What? You visit Culloden and run into a handsome six foot four Highlander and discover you're soul mates? Reincarnations of long-dead star-crossed lovers? Maybe that infamous Wolf of Badenoch and his great lady-love, Mariota?"

A hot little rush shot through Kira. She wasn't planning on going anywhere near Culloden, but she had hung her heart on a six foot four Highlander.

At least she was pretty sure her sexy medieval warrior chieftain was about that height.

"I'm surprised you've even heard of the Wolf and his Mariota," she said, hoping Dan couldn't hear the thundering of her heart.

He shrugged. "I dated a girl from Inverness in college. A bit of a history buff, always going on about those two. She was obsessed by Scotland's most legendary love pairs." He paused to rub his chin. "So if not the notorious Wolf come back to life at Culloden, what other ideas do you have?"

Kira felt a jab of self-consciousness but brushed it aside. Dan and *Destiny* had been good to her. "O-o-oh," she said, shifting her carry-on again, "something along the lines of *I Was Seduced by a Selkie* or *I Found the Big Grey Man of Ben MacDui Sleeping in My Holiday Cottage.*"

"Ben Mac-*Who*-ee? Dan shook his head.

"A *ben* is a mountain. The Big Grey Man is like Bigfoot." Kira smiled. "He's the Yeti of the Scottish Cairngorms."

Dan laughed. "I'll be happy with any story you bring back. You just take care of yourself." His eyes took on that worried look again. "I have a feeling those fairy mounds might be the real thing. Like that lake in Cape Cod."

"If they are, just don't forget your promise."

"A time portal would be a bigger story than a sunken Viking boat, Kira." He hesitated. "You'd be world-famous."

"Not if you keep your word and leave my name off the story." Kira lifted her chin, not willing to budge. "I've had enough fame in recent days to last a lifetime. Give the honors to one of the horn-tooters who'll love the glory."

Dan looked uncomfortable. "You're sure?"

"Absolutely."

"Then off with you and be quick about it." He clutched her to him for a quick hug. "I hate long good-byes."

So did Kira, but before she could say her own, he was gone. Vanished into the teeming maze of hastening passengers and harried-looking airport personnel.

Shifting her carry-on yet again, she remembered what else she hated. Namely carting around unnecessary take-alongs pressed on her by her well-meaning family. No wonder her bag was digging a groove into her shoulder.

Determined to lighten her load—and avoid excess calories she really couldn't afford—she made for the nearest waste bin, then unzipped her carry-on, plucking out the bulky plastic bag stuffed with Lindsay's crushed and crumbling organic chocolate chip cookies.

A fat wedge of some kind of soybean imitation cheddar cheese and a mysterious home-baked energy bar her sister had sworn would keep her from suffering jet lag. Half a poorly wrapped hoagie her father must've secretly slipped into the bag after seeing Lindsay give her so much unappetizing health food.

Pitching it all, Kira dusted her hands and re-zipped her now much lighter bag. But not before her gaze fell upon her book, *The Hebridean Clans*.

Her heart thumped. Excited, she retrieved her boarding card and headed for the long line at the security checkpoint, thoughts of catching a glimpse of her own Hebridean chieftain in real live waking hours quickening her steps.

With a bit of luck and if her special gift of far-seeing didn't let her down, it just might happen.

She couldn't think of anything sweeter.

# 3

Many hours and even more transatlantic miles later, Kira pulled her fine-running hire car into a so-called lay-by, and rested her head against the steering wheel. She'd made it past Loch Lomond and even Crianlarich, carefully following the A-82, the most scenic route into the Highlands. But she wasn't sure she could go much farther. The many twists and turns were getting to her, each new one bringing her closer to defeat.

She'd lied to herself about left-handed driving.

It wasn't a breeze.

It was horrible.

Worse, she'd been sorely disillusioned to think that sheep jams were the only hazards of Scottish roads. Truth be told, to borrow the language of her medieval Highlander, the only sheep she'd spied so far were pleasant-looking woolly creatures seemingly content to keep to the verdant pastures rising from the impossibly narrow road.

She sighed. Leave it to her to make such a journey at a time when tiredness fogged her brain and heightened her fright factor.

Trying hard not to tremble and absolutely refusing to cry, she rolled down the window, hoping a good blast of clean and brisk air would bolster her confidence. Instead, the opened window only brought the approaching roar and passing *whoosh* of yet another speeding sports car.

A locally licensed car, flying past the lay-by at breakneck speed and disappearing into the wilds of Rannoch Moor before she could even blink, much less wonder why she ever thought she could tackle such a drive without a good night's sleep to recover from jet lag.

And if she wished to ponder her plight, the equally speedy *whooshes* of two coach tour buses and an over-wide recreational vehicle dashed her hopes of wallowing in self-pity.

"Holy guacamole," she breathed, clutching the steering wheel.

Maybe she would have to crawl on her knees to reach Castle Wrath. Pulling over to tremble and calm herself each time some impatient driver zoomed up behind her wasn't getting her anywhere. But maybe her handy-dandy map of the Highlands would. That, and her mother's carefully written instructions to the Cairn Avenue shrew's stepdaughter's castle near Oban.

Ravenscraig, the place was called if she remembered rightly. Supposedly, it even boasted a re-created Highland period settle-ment—One Cairn Village—with craft shops, a tearoom, and tourist lodgings.

Loosening her grip on the steering wheel, she twisted left, reaching for her purse, then digging inside its voluminous side pockets, searching for the folded piece of paper with her mother's notes. A quick scan of them and a glance at her map brought her an instant boost. She need only drive a bit farther north, then veer west onto the A-85, straight through Glen Lochy and the Pass of Brander before continuing along Loch Etive until she reached Ravenscraig Castle. According to her mother, she couldn't miss it, as the castle and its One Cairn Village were clearly signposted.

Kira smiled. Signposted was good.

Better yet, the A-85 would also take her along a short bit of

Loch Awe, allowing her a nice view of that loch's picturesque Kilchurn Castle. Her smile widened. Might as well enjoy the touristy stuff along the way.

And Ravenscraig was a good deal closer than the Isle of Skye, where she'd booked a room at a small family-run inn. With her eyes feeling like sandpaper, sleep riding her hard, and her jaw beginning to ache from repeating the words *stay left*, a hot shower and a soft, clean bed sounded like heaven.

Just how much like heaven astounded her when, a long but scenic stretch of Highland roads behind her, she stood in the heart of Ravenscraig's One Cairn Village and felt herself transported to Brigadoon.

This was Celtic whimsy at its finest.

Fine enough to blunt the worst of her jet lag.

"Oh-my-gosh." She stopped beside a large memorial cairn topped with a Celtic cross, the clutch of thick-walled, blue-doored Highland-y cottages surrounding it taking her breath and delighting her. A profusion of late-blooming flowers and heather rioted everywhere, spilling from rustic-looking halved wine barrels and crowding moss-grown paths. Curling wisps of fragrant peat smoke rose from several of the thatched cottages' squat chimney stacks, and although the afternoon light was failing, there was enough to cast a golden autumnal glow across the whole old-timey-looking village.

She glanced about, letting the place's magic close around her. It was like stepping into one of her books on Highland life, as if she'd blinked and suddenly found herself inside the sepia photographs of days long past and forgotten. The kind of photograph she was always mooning over.

"Oh-my-gosh," she said again, her eyes misting.

The strapping young Highlander beside her chuckled. Setting down her bags, Malcolm, as he'd introduced himself, flashed her a dimpled grin. "That's exactly what Mistress Mara said the first time she saw the castle," he told her, his soft Highland voice almost as exciting as the *Brigadoon*-like village. "Looks like you have a greater heart for the simple things?"

*A greater heart.* Kira sighed. Just the phrase, so old-fashioned and Scottish-sounding, thickened her throat. She blinked, tried to wipe the damp from her eyes as unobtrusively as possible.

Seeing it anyway, the red-haired Malcolm reached to dry her cheeks with a strong, callused thumb. "Dinnae shame your emotion, lass. I've seen grown men shed tears hereabouts. Scotland does that to people."

Kira nodded, his words making her eyes water all the more.

"I've always loved Scotland." She blinked, unable to keep the hitch out of her voice. "The mournful hills and deep glens, heather-clad moors and hidden lochs. And, yes, it's the simple things that stir me. A drift of peat smoke on chill autumn air or the laughter and song at ceilidhs. Real ceilidhs in crofts and cottages, not the kitschy Scottish song-and-dance evenings you see in big touristy hotels."

She paused, swiping at her eyes again. "I sometimes think I belong to another age. The time of clan battles and Celtic legends, back when a skirl of pipes and a war cry roused men to whip out their swords and—"

She broke off, heat flaming her cheeks. "I'm sorry, I get carried away—"

"You feel the pull o' the hills is what it is." Malcolm-of-the-red-hair picked up her bags again. "And I'm a-thinking if you don't have Scottish blood, then you did ... at one time," he added, the notion warming her like the sun breaking through clouds.

Before she could say anything, he nodded toward one of the cottages, its blue-shuttered windows glowing with the flickering light of what looked to be candles. "That's the Heatherbrae. Yours for the night, and, nae, those aren't real candles in the windows," he said, as if he'd read her mind. "They're electric. The cottages may look of another century, but they have all the comforts of our own.

"And that up yonder"—he indicated a well-lit cottage at the end of the path, one slightly larger than the rest—"is Innes' soap-and-candle craft and workshop. If you pop up there, you'll find she keeps a platter of shortbread and fresh-brewed tea ready for visitors."

Kira cast a longing glance at the Heatherbrae. "But—"

"I need a few minutes to ready your cottage." The young man offered an apologetic smile. "We didn't know for sure if you were coming, see you. Mistress Mara and her Alex insist on a true Highland welcome for their guests: a warming fire on the hearth grate and a waiting dram at your bedside."

"That sounds wonderful and so does Innes' tea and short-bread. Still"—Kira glanced at the large memorial cairn, according to its bronze plaque, dedicated to some long-dead MacDougalls —"I don't want to trouble the woman," she finished, her gaze also lighting on a nearby signpost marking the beginning of a wood-land path.

An evening walk would surely give her a second wind.

Following her gaze, Malcolm's rosy-cheeked complexion turned a slightly deeper red. "Sorry, lass, but Innes will be expecting you. She ... *er* ... watches out her shop windows, having nothing much else to do the day. Just smile and nod if she mentions Lord Basil."

"Lord Basil?" The words no sooner left her lips than the image of an elegantly-dressed, hawk-nosed man loomed up before her, his aristocratic stare haughty and cold.

Kira blinked and he vanished, leaving her with a rash of goose bumps, alone on the path.

Malcolm-the-red had left her, too. The cracked door of the Heatherbrae and the wedge of warm yellow light spilling out into the cottage's little garden left no doubt as to where he'd gone.

She also had no doubts that they'd been observed, for unless jet lag was playing tricks on her or her far-seeing gift was showing her yet another resident of Ravenscraig's past, there was a white-haired woman peering at her from behind one of the soap-and-candle craft and workshop windows.

A tiny white-haired woman, she discovered upon stepping inside the shop a few minutes later. A frilly-aproned, birdlike woman who beamed at her with a cheery, welcoming smile and a telltale faraway look in her bright blue eyes.

"Come away in!" she enthused, scurrying from the window to a plaid-draped table set with a tea service and an array of what looked to be home-baked shortbread. "I'm Innes, maker of fine soaps and candles. And you'll be herself, the young American Lord Basil told us we might be seeing," she added, pouring the tea with a shaky, age-spotted hand. "Lord Basil likes Yanks." She paused, her voice dropping to a conspiratorial whisper. "He even married one."

Kira looked at her, guessing she must mistake Mara McDougall's Highland chieftain husband for someone named Lord Basil. No doubt the stuffy-looking aristocrat she'd glimpsed on the path. She was pretty sure her mother had said Euphemia Ross' stepdaughter's husband's name was Alex.

Sir Alexander Douglas.

"You are a Yank, aren't you?" Innes came closer, holding out a rattling teacup and saucer.

"I'm Kira Bedwell. And, yes, I'm American. From Aldan, Pennsylvania near Philly." Kira accepted the tea and took a sip. "Philadelphia," she added, in case the old woman had never heard the term *Philly*.

"Lord Basil comes from London," Innes stated as if she hadn't spoken.

Determined to be polite, Kira opened her mouth to reply, but the words lodged in her throat, all thought of Innes and her apparent delusions forgotten as she blinked at a small display of books on local history and fauna.

A familiar face stared back at her.

Wee Hughie MacSporran. The puffed-up peacock of a tour

guide who'd accompanied her long-ago coach tour and repeat-edly regaled the company with his claims to lofty ancestry.

And there he was again, preening with self-importance on the cover of a book titled *Rivers of Stone: A Highlander's Ancestral Journey.*

Kira blinked again, half certain that this time jet lag really was getting to her. But when she looked a second time, there could be no mistaking.

It was the tour guide.

Even if he looked a bit more portly than she remembered. His name was on the book, too: Wee Hughie MacSporran, historian, storyteller, and keeper of tradition.

Kira almost dropped her teacup. How like the swellhead to tack on so many distinctions to his name.

Curious, she set down her tea and reached for the book. Her fingers were just closing on it when a richly timbred voice spoke behind her.

A deep Highland voice that sounded so much like Aidan that her heart leapt to her throat.

"A fine book," the voice said in endorsement, "written by a local man well versed in our legends and lore. You can have a copy if you like. A wee welcome-to-Scotland gift."

Kira spun around, the book clasped to her breast. "Thank you. I know the author. He guided a tour I was on years ago. And you must be—"

"No' Lord Basil," the Highlander returned, stepping aside to make way for an aging collie when the dog shuffled in, then plopped down at his feet. "He was the late Lady of Ravenscraig's English husband. And this is Ben." He cast an affectionate glance at the collie. "He's the true master at Ravenscraig."

The dog thumped his tail and looked up, his approving brown eyes saying he knew it.

"Myself, I'm Alex. Mara's husband." He took one of the short-breads off the table and gave it to Ben. "You have to be Miss

Bedwell? My regrets that we were unable to greet you, but"—he glanced at his kilt and shrugged—"we were having a folk after-noon for a gathering of school children at the Victorian Lodge."

He looked over his shoulder at the semidarkness framed by the shop's half-open door. "You may have seen the turrets of the lodge on your way here. It's a rambling old pile just the other side of the woodland path."

Kira gaped at him, well aware he was talking, but hardly regis-tering a word he said. Indeed, she was quite sure her jaw was hanging open, but found herself unable to do anything about it.

Sir Alexander Douglas had that kind of presence.

Tall, well built, and handsome, he had rich chestnut brown hair just skimming his shoulders and the kind of deep, sea green eyes she would've sworn existed only in the pages of historical romance novels.

She blinked again, surprised by his kilted perfection.

And he wasn't just wearing a kilt. Not like the kilt-clad Ameri-cans she'd seen at stateside Highland Games. O-o-oh, no. This man really *wore* his tartan. He was the genuine article, decked out in full Highland regalia, every magnificent inch of him making her weak in the knees.

Not because of himself, but because he reminded her of *him*.

Her Aidan.

Alex Douglas had that same medieval-y air about him. The only thing missing was the sword.

But then that, too, was there. A great, wicked-looking broadsword flashing silver at his hip as his plaid seemed to stir in some unseen wind, its eerie passage even riffling his hair.

Kira swallowed and the image slowly faded. The wind vanished quicker, but the sword lingered to the last. Then it, too, was no more, and the only flashing silver left on him was the large Celtic brooch holding his plaid at his shoulder and the cantle on his fancy dress sporran.

A MacDougall clan sporran of finest leather and fur with

tasseled diamond-cut chains—just like the assortment of various clan sporrans hanging on the wall behind the shop's till.

Kira's heart thumped. Imagining Aidan wearing such a grand sporran nearly made her swoon. If ever a man's best part deserved such an accolade it was his.

She swallowed again, feeling heat blaze onto her cheeks. "I'm sorry, I—"

"It's okay. Women always react to him that way." A pretty auburn-haired woman with a Philly accent stepped forward, extending her hand. "Especially mad-for-plaid American women," she added, her warm smile taking any sting out of the words. "I'm Mara—pleased to meet you. My father called and told us you might be stopping by. I'm glad you did."

Kira took her hand. "I am, too," she said, her blush deepening because she hadn't even noticed the woman standing there. "This place is like *Brigadoon*. Amazing."

Mara McDougall Douglas looked pleased. "That was our intent."

She threw a smile at her husband, then slipped behind the till to straighten a large framed print of three sword-brandishing Highlanders captured in the midst of what appeared to be a medieval battle fray.

The print hung beside the display of clan sporrans, and on closer inspection, Kira saw that the sword-wielding Highlander in the middle was none other than Mara's Alex.

"That's you!" She swung around to look at him, but he only smiled and shrugged again.

"Yes, that's him," his wife confirmed, clearly proud. "Alex, and two of his best friends, Hardwic— I mean, Sir Hardwin de Studley of Seagrave—and the big, burly fierce-looking fellow, that's Bran of Barra."

Kira's brows lifted. "Hardwin *de Studley*?"

Her hosts exchanged glances.

Alex cleared his throat. "An old family name. Goes back centuries."

He glanced at the print. "I've known him for ages. Bran as well. They were among the most fearsome fighters of their day, their sword skills second only to a certain Sassunach I also had the privilege to call my friend."

"Were?" Kira looked at the men on the print again. "You mean they're dead?"

"No." Mara came out from behind the till. "He means they're expert swordsmen. Alex and his friends are reenactors. They stage medieval battles for our visitors. Mostly in summer when we're full up here."

"Oh." Kira tightened her hold on Wee Hughie's book, certain she'd caught Mara flashing her husband a warning glance.

"I'm surprised Euphemia didn't mention the reenactments to your mother." Mara hooked her hand through her husband's arm. "Alex and his company put on quite a show when she and my father visited last year."

Innes tittered. "Ach, that biddie was too fashed about bogles to pay much heed to aught else," she said, pinning her gaze on Kira. "Be you afeart o' bogles?"

Kira blinked. "Bogles?"

"Ghosts," Alex explained, a smile quirking his lips. "Innes is asking if they frighten you."

"Maybe a better question would be if she believes in ghosts." Mara glanced from her husband to Kira. "In America, people aren't as receptive to such things as over here, where every house, pub, and castle is simply accepted as having ghosts."

"Indeed?" Alex looked amused. "So, Kira Bedwell, what do you think of them?"

"Ghosts? I rather like them. Or rather, the notion of them." Kira smiled, leaving it at that. She wasn't about to mention her talent and especially not having already glimpsed the previous Ravenscraig lord.

If he'd indeed been a spirit.

She could usually see through ghosts, so she suspected she'd only caught a brief glimpse of the past again, an image imprinted on a path the man often frequented.

Sure that was the way of it, she turned to Mara. "Do you have ghosts at Ravenscraig?"

"None that would bother you," Alex answered again, this time clicking his fingers at Ben, then holding open the door so the dog could amble outside. "You'll sleep well enough at the Heatherbrae. It should be ready now if you'd like us to see you there."

Opening her mouth to say she would, Kira was horrified when a ferocious yawn snatched the words. Blessedly, her hosts had already stepped out the door, and Innes appeared too busy humming to herself to notice.

Not wanting to intrude on the old woman's obvious happy place, she did allow herself a quick glance at Wee Hughie's book before she started after Alex and Mara. Skipping what looked to be long passages of flowery prose about his illustrious ancestors, she flipped to the illustrations and photographs in the book's middle, nearly dropping the book when the words *Na Tri Shean* leapt out at her.

Captured in a glossy black-and-white photo, the three fairy mounds sent an immediate shiver down her spine.

She'd either been there before or would be at some point in the future.

And in a way that had nothing to do with her assignment for Dan Hillard and *Destiny Magazine.*

Giving herself a shake lest her hosts look at her and think she'd seen a ghost, she shut the book and left the shop, walking straight into the next surprise.

Scotland's world-renowned gloaming.

In the short time she'd been inside the soap-and-candle craft and workshop, the evening had turned a deep bluish violet and soft, billowing mists were descending, sliding silently down the hillsides. The whole *Brigadoon*ish scene was now bathed in a gentle, never-to-be-forgotten luminosity she knew Highlanders thought of as the time between the two lights.

A special and magical time full of mystical promise.

Her heart jolting at the notion, she made her way down the path after Alex and Mara, hoping that the proximity to Castle Wrath and One Cairn Village's own magic might let Aidan come to her in her dreams that night.

He hadn't visited her in weeks and she needed him badly.

Almost feeling his hot and hungry gaze on her, she hastened her steps. Heatherbrae Cottage and her bed loomed just ahead. Soon she might feel his heated touch, lose herself in the mastery of his kisses, and glory in the deliciousness of the Gaelic love words he whispered against her naked skin.

Kira sighed.

O-o-oh, yes, she needed him.

Even if having him make love to her on Scottish soil might prove a greater sensual pleasure than she could bear.

She just hoped she'd have the chance to find out.

ONLY A FEW HOURS to the north by car, but many centuries distant in time, Aidan MacDonald prowled the lofty battlements of Castle Wrath, his features set in a fierce scowl. He was feeling every bit the harsh and embittered soul his good friend Tavish had accused him of being. A dark-tempered, coldhearted beast, some of his younger squires had called him when they hadn't known he'd heard. Remembering the incident now, he raked a hand through his hair and stifled a scornful laugh. Soon the wee kitchen lads would be claiming his eyes glowed red and he hid a tail beneath his plaid.

Even his guardsmen had fled from him, the whole lot of the quivery-livered night patrol taking themselves off to the far side of the parapets as soon as he threw open the stair tower door and strode out into the mist-hung evening.

Not that he blamed them.

In recent days, even his favorite hound, Ferlie, had begun to eye him as if he'd run mad.

And perhaps he had, he was willing to admit, stopping his pacing to stand before one of the open square-notched crenellations in the parapet wall.

Full mad and unable to do aught about it.

Lusting after a *dream.*

"Blood of all the gods," he growled, his folly cutting into him as sharply as the razor-edged steel of his sword. Thoughts of her bestirred him even now, filling his mind with the warm smoothness of her skin and the fine, plump weight of her breasts, the rosy crests beautifully puckered and begging his caress. The silky-soft heat between her thighs and her sweet sighs of pleasure when he touched her there.

Her fiery passion. For him, his land, and everything he stood for.

He saw it in the way she would reverently touch his plaid or run a finger over the intricate Celtic designs on his sword belt. How her breath would hitch, her eyes filling with wonder when his world intruded on their dreams and he knew she'd caught glimpses of his tapestried bedchamber, the glowing peat fire across from his bed or the black cliffs of Wrath Isle, visible through the room's tall, arch-topped windows.

*Marvels,* she called such things, shaking her head as if she'd never seen the like.

As if she loved them as much as he did.

That passion blazed inside her, too, and knowing it made him appreciate her in ways that had nothing to do with how good she felt in his arms. How just looking at her made him burn.

His loins heavy and aching with wanting her, needing her *now*, he jammed his fists on his hips and glared into the thick swirls of mist gliding past the battlements. Chill, cloying, and impenetrable, the mist seemed to mock him, its gray-white swaths blotting everything but the cold, damp stone of the crenellated wall right before him.

Just as his dreams had begun throwing up an unbreachable barrier, keeping him from reaching her and letting him see only the great void that loomed without her.

Until tonight.

Casting one last scowl at the mist, he started pacing again, as keenly aware of her as he'd been earlier, sitting at the high table in his hall, holding council with Tavish and several of his most trusted men, planning their surprise raid on Conan Dearg's Ardcraig, when a jolt had ripped through him and he'd sensed her.

Felt her presence, so vibrant and alive he would've sworn she'd somehow stolen into Castle Wrath and was suddenly standing right behind his chair.

Her sweet feminine scent, so fresh and clean, had swirled around him, filling his senses and making his heart slam against his ribs. A scent with him still, even here in the cold dark of the parapets.

To be sure, it wasn't his.

And with certainty not his guardsmen's, the fools still busying themselves on the other side of the battlements. Each one of the impressionable buffoons doing their best to pretend he wasn't there.

Nae, it wasn't coming from them. Their scent leaned toward armpit and old leather. Wool and linen that hadn't been washed in the gods knew how long, the whole charming effect enhanced by a slight whiff of stale ale, horse, and dog.

"Och, aye, 'tis you, my sweet," he breathed, certain of it.

His dream vision, *tamhasg*, or whate'er she was, was near.

So near he could almost taste her.

See her eyes light when she caught that first glimpse of him, feel her arms slide around him, drawing him closer, urging him to make her his.

"*Lass.*" The endearment came choked, burning his throat as he clenched his hands, willing her to appear.

When she didn't, he bit back a roar of frustration and whirled around, turning away from the empty night and striding toward the stair tower. The curving, torchlit steps that would take him back to his bedchamber.

The massive oak-framed bed and the sleep awaiting him there.

The dreams.

His last hope of finding her this night.

Several hours later, he believed he had, stirring in his sleep when soft kisses bathed his cheek, warm and wet, and hot breath hushed sweetly across his ear, waking him.

But instead of his *tamhasg's* shining eyes greeting him, the eyes meeting his were brown and soulful. Perhaps even a touch worried.

*Canine eyes.*

"Ach, Ferlie." He sat up and rubbed a hand over his face, his love for the great beast keeping him from letting his disappointment show. "She was here—or somewhere close."

But her scent was gone now. His bed most definitely empty, save himself and his huge, shaggy dog.

Only his surety remained.

Something in his world had shifted. A current in the air, a ne'er-before-there ripple in the wind. He knew not, but whate'er it was, he'd wager his best sword it had to do with *her.*

If the gods were kind, he would learn the answer soon.

# 4

S he was really here again.

Kira Never-Give-Up Bedwell, finally returned to the Trotternish Peninsula on the Isle of Skye.

Castle Wrath was no longer her dearest longing, distant and intangible, but a reality. Better yet, she was already halfway across the high three-sided promontory that held the ancient stronghold's ruins. A trek she was finding much easier than years before, since this afternoon was calm and bright, without the fierce wind gusts that had made her last visit so treacherous.

The sheep pats were still everywhere, though. A distinct quiver of *ick* slid through her, but she ignored it. She'd just watch her step and pretend the piles of black goop weren't quite so prevalent.

Not that she really cared.

She blew out a breath that fluffed her bangs as she shot a sideways glance at the nearest such obstacle. Fact was, she'd march right through the stuff if need be.

If doing so meant catching another true glimpse of her Highlander.

Savoring the possibility, she inched as close to the edge of the cliff as she dared and peered down at Wrath Bay. Its waters glistened blue in the autumn sunshine, the deep scorings in the smooth flat rocks of the small, crescent-shaped strand staring back at her just as she remembered.

Furrows that, according to Wee Hughie, tour-guide-cum-author, were caused by the keels of countless Clan Donald galleys being drawn onto the shore.

*War galleys.* She was sure.

Greyhounds of the Sea. Their heyday marked by grooves that must've taken centuries to form. Deep indentations in stone that might not even have been visible in her Aidan's time.

But they were there now—telltale remnants of long-ago days.

Kira's pulse quickened. Much as the past beguiled her, there was only one part of it she ached to seize.

If only she could.

Her heart pounding, she edged even closer to the precipice, a sheer and dizzying drop to the stony beach below. She squinted to see better, her gaze focused on the tide as it surged up and over the rocks and kelp. Brilliant sunlight glinted off the incoming swells, making the water glitter like jewels. But it was the ancient keel marks that continued to hold her attention. Each centuries-old groove was a not-to-be-denied reminder that *he* once walked there.

He'd been a part of this place where she now stood, and knowing that made her want to pull the clip from her hair, throw off her jacket, and run the rest of the way.

Fly across the grass until she reached Castle Wrath's tumbled walls and moss-grown arches, then collapse before the remains of *his* stairwell. The dark, downward-winding stair that led, she was sure, straight into Aidan's great hall.

There, where for a brief, torchlit moment she'd seen him.

Heard him speaking to her as he ascended the tight, corkscrew steps. She shivered, remembering how he'd reached for her, pulling her against him and lowering his head to kiss her, only to vanish before her eyes.

A feat he could not impossibly do again, she saw, reaching the place where she'd looked into his stairwell.

The steps were gone.

The inky darkness that had stared back at her only to suddenly blaze with torchlight was no more. Even the gap had vanished, leaving only a narrow crevice in its place. No longer yawning, it taunted her. A mere slit in the grassy, nettle-covered earth, the whole of it barely a foot wide and hardly adequate to peer into.

She gaped all the same, shaking her head at the pathetic little opening.

She put a hand over her mouth, disbelief slamming into her, freezing her heart. She'd been so certain, so sure nothing would have changed. Not after the stairs must've stood undisturbed for hundreds of years.

Only the briskness of the cold, clean Highland air remained the same. The incredible age of Castle Wrath's broken stones and the roar of the surf crashing into its jagged, impervious cliff foot.

"Oh, no." She dropped to her knees, sagging against what should have been the threshold to Aidan's world.

Instead, fallen debris and rubble filled the darkness, the lichen-and-weed-grown rocks blocking the ancient steps, each cold, silent stone and layer of rich, peaty earth creating an impassable barrier.

The way to Aidan's great hall—*to him*—was sealed.

Closed off for all eternity.

Unless she possessed enough spirit to brave the cliff's maze of underground tunnels, stairwells, and rooms, much of which were said to be crumbling into the sea.

Dangerous places where one false step could send her hurtling to certain death.

She blew out a breath, frustration warring with her refusal to give up.

She *did* have spirit.

And she thrived on challenges. Each broadsiding kick in the shins only made her roll her sleeves higher, more determined than ever to besiege whom-or whatever would hold her down. As if to prove it, she swiped a hand through her hair and kissed her palms for luck. Then, reaching deep into the crevice, she grabbed hold of the first chunk of weedy, nettle-stinging rock she could get a grip on.

Unfortunately, when she pulled, the rock didn't budge.

A second and third effort cost her two fingernails. Not that she cared. What mattered was not the attractiveness of her hands, but getting into Aidan's great hall. If the stairwell of their previous encounter was to remain off-limits, she would just have to find another way to reach him.

Beyond the wisps of a mere ghostly encounter, she'd felt him here so strongly on her last visit, as if he truly were flesh and bone and raw masculinity. As if he'd been waiting for her, just as she hoped he was now.

If only her gift, the magic of the place, or *whatever*, would kick in again and let him know she was near.

But first she needed to rest.

Shake off a bit more jet lag and gather her strength for the assault it would mean, creeping down into damp, dank-smelling passages. Icky places where she would be able to see no more than a few feet ahead of her flashlight.

And she was glad she had one. Bright blue, plastic and beautiful, it rested in her trusty backpack, along with two sets of extra batteries.

Thanks to Alex and Mara Douglas.

She also had the perfect place to rest. The great grass-grown arch of what she was sure had once been the entry into Castle Wrath's bailey. It, at least, was still there as she remembered, the top half of its imposing bulk rising up out of the cliff-top to wink at her in all its Celtic rune-incised glory. A medieval wonder, undisturbed by time, the arch looked as inviting now as it had twelve years ago.

Strangely beckoning.

Kira frowned. Regrettably, the tangle of brambles and nettles surrounding the arch didn't beckon at all. Unlike the caved-in entrance to Aidan's stairwell, the crevices and holes scattered throughout the castle's empty courtyard appeared anything but filled in.

Just the opposite—they looked deep, dark, and dangerous. She wasn't about to search for one with an intact stairwell until her eyes no longer felt like sandpaper and she'd fortified herself with a tuna sandwich and a thermos of tea.

Tea solved everything, the Brits always claimed.

Hoping it was so, she started forward, carefully avoiding the worst of the brambles and nettles, but especially watching where she stepped. She had no desire to get better acquainted with one of those black-staring holes-in-the-ground until she was good and ready.

Sadly, when she reached the arch and managed to scramble on top of it, Castle Wrath's pièce de résistance proved to have a few cracks of its own. Some looked rather crumbly around the edges, while others had a fern or two thrusting up from their depths. Thankfully, none looked wide enough for her to fall through.

Almost tired enough not to care if she did, she quickly claimed the most solid-looking spot the arch top offered, pleased because her chosen picnic site also seemed to have the thickest, most cushiony grass.

Soft, cushiony grass was good.

A crackless resting place even better.

Proud that she'd made it to the arch without mishap, she shrugged off her backpack and pulled it onto her lap, eager to dig out her treasures. A tightly rolled tartan picnic rug, waterproof on one side and just one of several souvenirs picked up at One Cairn Village. Her tea thermos and packed lunch. Her father's borrowed mini-binoculars and her two special books.

*The Hebridean Clans* and Wee Hughie MacSporran's *Rivers of Stone: A Highlander's Ancestral Journey.*

Thinking of the tour guide—no, *author*, she corrected herself—reminded her of the other treasure in her backpack. The most special one of all. A fine MacDonald dress sporran she'd plucked off the wall display in Innes' soap-and-candle craft and workshop.

Now hers to cherish, she meant to have it altered into a handbag when she returned to Aldan.

Not wanting to think about her return journey, she unrolled her tartan picnic rug and spread out her goodies, determined to enjoy her afternoon despite her disappointment over the collapsed stairwell.

Filling her stomach and taking time for a soul-soothing glance through her books would do her good. Then she'd be ready to search for access into Castle Wrath's heart.

Or rather she'd be ready if the words on the page stopped blurring before her eyes. The book, Wee Hughie's little tome, also felt heavier than it should. In fact, it slipped right from her fingers, bouncing off her knee to disappear into the nearest crack in the arch top.

"Oh, no!" Too late, she lunged for it, a sudden wave of dizziness making her clumsy.

The book was gone, and it was her fault for being such a butterfingers.

Frowning, she sat back and rubbed a hand over her face.

What she needed was some of that tea.

Cure-all of the British Isles.

Yes, good old Earl Grey would give her a boost.

If only she could remember where she'd placed her thermos

and packed lunch. But her mind felt fuzzy and the picnic goods were nowhere to be seen, the smooth stone surface of the arch top pitifully bare.

Worse, the afternoon had darkened and a chill wind now whistled past her ears, its keening making it hard to think. Not that she'd be able to concentrate even if the day had remained as clear and still as it'd been. Not with all the shouting and dog barking going on around her.

*Loud shouting and dog barking.*

Even if she couldn't see anyone or their frenzied canines, the noise was deafening enough for her to jam her fingers in her ears and wriggle them. Something she did with great gusto—until she noticed that Wee Hughie's tome and her trusty tea thermos weren't the only things missing.

Her world was missing.

Beginning with her tartan picnic rug and ending with her father's much-prized mini-binoculars. Most alarming of all, the thick carpet of grass covering the arch top had vanished, replaced by smooth, polished stone. The whole sweeping lot of it not showing a single weedy crack. And, surprise-surprise, the arch now raged much higher than before.

She stared down at the cobbles. Yep, her perch was definitely up there.

She swallowed, little chills beginning to streak up and down her spine.

If the well-swept paving stones were an illusion, the arch's height wasn't.

Never in a million years could she have climbed such a towering monstrosity.

Leaping down was unthinkable.

If she could even tear her gaze away from Castle Wrath's bailey and curtain walls long enough to consider the risk. Castle Wrath's teeming, bustling bailey and its mighty, notably *un*tumbled walls.

Thick, crenellated walls of medieval mastery. Massive, white-washed, and impregnable-looking, they soared proudly into the moody Highland sky, every magnificent foot of them daring her to challenge their existence.

Kira blinked, not about to do the like.

After all, she decided, clutching her jacket closer against the wind, there wasn't a need. Her wits had finally returned, and with them, her heart slowed a pace. She really was seeing Castle Wrath as it had once been. She looked about the bailey, noting its splendor, how blazing torches made the walls glow as if hewn of gold. Awe swept her and she pressed a hand to her breast, ready to appreciate the moment for what it was: another fleeting time slip.

A tantalizing glimpse into the past, visible for the space of a blink and then forever gone.

Just as she'd seen flashes of Norsemen landing in America. Or, more recently, at One Cairn Village, when she'd caught a look at Ravenscraig's onetime English lord.

She recognized the moment for what it was because her gift always let her see time slip images as real and solid. Only true ghosts and spirits appeared somewhat translucent.

But this time the image was lasting longer.

*Much longer.*

She shifted, the fine hairs on the back of her neck beginning to rise.

Never had she enjoyed such a lengthy viewing of the long ago. A medieval curtain-walled bailey no longer teeming with mere chickens, goats, and scurrying washerwomen, but now also filled with out-for-blood ferocious-looking dogs. Leaping, barking beasts larger than some ponies she'd seen at state fairs back home. Equally oversized and nearly as shaggy were the wild-eyed, gesticulating clansmen who appeared in the same moment as the dogs, the whole unruly lot of them looming up out of nowhere.

One instant there'd been only barking and shouts. The next, the barkers and shouters were there, bold as life, and wanting her.

At least that was the impression they gave her.

Her heart began to race again. Something was seriously not right. She blinked several times, but the men and the dogs remained.

Garrulous, frowning, and garbed in rough tartan clothing, the clansmen poured out of the wooden buildings lining the curtain walls or stormed from the keep, a flood of plaid-hung outrage bursting from a door she recognized as the one leading into Aidan's hall.

Her breath caught when she recognized it, but she had no time to digest the meaning of the stairwell's intact appearance. On and on the men came, hollering as they ran at her across the bailey, some wielding swords, others shaking fists, a few carrying torches, brandishing them like weapons.

All stared.

Looking furious, they crowded beneath the arch, gaping up at her as if she were some two-headed monster.

"A fairy!" one cried, pointing with his dirk.

"Nae, a witch!" another corrected, glowering at the other. "I'd ken the like anywhere."

Kira stared back at them, too startled to move. Never had one of her past-glimpses felt so real.

Or so threatening.

She could hear the crackling of their hand-held torches. The flames leapt, casting red stains across the cobbles and curtain walls. Smoke blew on the wind, smelling hot, acrid, and real, threatening.

She shuddered.

This wasn't how she'd envisioned her return to Aidan's world. She'd hoped to sneak into the shell of his ruined great hall and catch a glimpse of him sitting there. See him lairding it at his high table, all sexy and magnificent. Perhaps even catching his eye and exchanging glances before the image faded.

Maybe even share one brief *real-time* kiss.

Facing a pack of raving, wild-looking Highlanders who thought she was a witch wasn't her idea of bliss.

Especially when a great, bearlike man with a mane of thick black hair and an even bushier black beard shouldered his way through the throng. He stopped at the base of the arch, where he stretched his arms above his head, loudly cracking his knuckles.

"Come!" he roared at his kinsmen. "If she's a witch, the laird will be wanting us to seize her. I'll hoist any souls brave enough onto the arch to get her."

"O-o-oh, no, you won't," Kira disagreed, scooting away from the arch's edge. She pushed quickly to her feet, knowing from experience that the sudden movement would break the spell, plunging Castle Wrath into splendid ruin and sending its long-ago occupants back into their own day.

To her surprise, nothing happened.

The image, and the angry men, remained. Behind them, above the curtain walls, she saw the clouds part briefly to reveal the rising moon. It'd been daylight when she reached the ruin, now it was clearly gloaming.

And the men below the arch were as flesh-and-blood as her.

"You aren't really there," she said anyway, looking down at them. She shook her head against the cold knot forming in her belly. "Any moment you'll be gone—and so will I!"

But the icy wind kept whipping past her, the bailey dogs continued to bark, smoke from the torches burned her eyes, and the bear was readying himself to hurl the first sword-swinging Highlander onto the arch.

"No swords, you lackwit!" He snatched the other man's blade and sent it scuttling across the cobbles, instantly endearing himself to Kira.

Until he swung the other man high into the air, informing

him, "If there's any head-lopping to be done, I'll do it myself. Seeing as I'm the laird's own ax-man."

"*The laird won't want a hair on the maid's head harmed—whoe'er or whate'er she is.*"

Kira froze, looking on as *he* cut a path through the crowd.

It was Aidan. Every inch of him just as bold and glorious as she knew him. Even if his eyes currently blazed with anger, not passion. Fury directed at his men, not her.

And o-o-oh was he beautiful in a rage.

Her heart flip-flopping, Kira released the breath she'd been holding and looked on, watching as he scorched the gathered men with a glare, then upbraided them.

"Your chief will have the tender parts cut off any man who'd dare lift a hand against a woman—any woman," he warned, throwing back his plaid to reveal the wicked-looking long sword beneath. "As would I."

*His chief*? Kira's jaw slipped. She would've sworn Aidan was laird. The history books said so, too.

"Ach, Tavish," the bear argued, solving the riddle.

Looking disgusted, he set down the man he'd been about to hurl onto the arch. "Where'er your eyes? That be no woman on the arch—she's a witch, plain as day. Have a good look at her."

And he did. This Tavish who looked so like her Aidan that her heart was still galloping madly in her chest. He let his plaid fall back into place and tilted his head, staring up at her with Aidan's own dark eyes.

Intelligent, measuring eyes, she noted with relief.

"I can see she is dressed oddly." His gaze swept her from head to toe and back again. "She's also passing fair and nothing like any witch I've e'er had the discomfort to meet."

"Bah!" Her would-be captor snatched up his fallen sword, resheathing it with a scowl. "The laird's gone off women—as well you know. He won't care how fair the wench is. Witch, or no'."

"He'll care that no woman is mistreated on MacDonald soil."

The man called Tavish planted his hands on his hips and glared round again, raking the others with a cold stare until, one by one, they backed away.

"Be warned, my friends," he added, "if you value your bollocks."

Then, in a whirring blur of plaid and steel, he vaulted onto the arch, landing on his feet in front of Kira before she could even cry out.

"Have no fear," he said, narrowing his eyes at her all the same. "I mean only to see you to my liege. He'll decide your fate, though it willnae be beneath an ax-man's blade. That I can promise you —whoe'er you are."

"I'm Kira." She blinked at him, his resemblance to Aidan unsettling her, making her knees tremble. "Kira Bedwell of Aldan, Pennsylvania."

His brow furrowed. "Pen-*where?*"

"It's a long way from here." She tried to smile, but the way he was studying her made it impossible. "A distant place. You won't know it."

"It matters not, *Kee-rah*." He reached to finger one of the buttons on her jacket. "Though it wouldn't be wise to let the others see you as closely as I have," he added, whipping off his plaid and swirling it over her shoulders. "This will shield you from the worst of their stares. I shall tell them you were shivering with cold."

"They've already seen me."

His lips quirked. "What men think they see can be corrected," he said, patting his sword hilt. "Pay no heed to those blunder-heads below."

"And your chieftain?" Kira wrapped the plaid around her. It smelled of man and woodsmoke. "I can't imagine he'd be easily persuaded."

"Aidan is a fair and reasonable man." He looked toward the keep, then back at her. "Crazed as it sounds, I suspect he might even be expecting you."

*Aidan.*

The breath froze in Kira's throat.

She said nothing, her tongue too thick for words.

Her champion shrugged, his gaze dipping to her feet and the hill-walking boots she'd bought before leaving on her trip. "Och, aye," he drawled, "I'd wager my soul you won't be a surprise."

Kira took a deep breath. "Why not?"

"Would that I could explain it. 'Tis a feeling I have here." Looking slightly sheepish, he pressed a hand to his heart.

Kira bit her lip, her own heart pounding so wildly, she wondered he didn't hear it.

Showing no signs of doing so, he stepped closer, his expression unreadable.

"Come now, let me get you down from here before you do catch a chill." He reached for her, sweeping her into his arms. "Aidan's in the great hall, holding council, though I doubt he'll mind the disruption," he added, hefting her over his shoulder as he made to jump from the arch.

But not before Kira caught a quick glimpse of Wrath Bay.

Wrath Bay, the incoming tide, and the little crescent-shaped strand.

A picturesque, moonlit cove now crowded with moored, medieval-looking galleys.

Nary a keel mark to be seen.

AIDAN SLAMMED down his ale cup, well pleased with the decisions of his war council. "'Tis settled, then." He lifted his voice so it was heard not just at the high table and on the dais but throughout Castle Wrath's hall. "Conan Dearg's time has come to pass. We ride for Ardcraig on the morrow. At first light and not a heartbeat later."

"Aye, let the bastard's days of bluster and swagger be ended!" someone yelled from the shadows.

"To his capture!" Another grabbed an ale jug, waving it in the air before taking a great swig. "May Wrath's dungeon give him a foretaste of hell!"

Cheers rose to the rafters, the hall resounding with agreement as men stamped their feet and rattled swords. Aidan looked on, scarce hearing them. Only his own voice echoing in his ears. Unable to rid himself of it, he pinned a furious stare on the platter of spiced salmon set before him and did his best to fight back a grimace.

A groan, too, were he honest.

*Not a heartbeat later.*

Odin's knees, but he'd made a poor word choice. A thoughtless mistake that only reminded him that his heart still thundered with thoughts of *her.* Certainty that she was near pounded through him, not letting go despite the impossibility of such a fool notion. He felt her all the same. Even now, when he could so easily swipe an arm across the table, sending feasting goods and ale hurtling to the floor.

At least the dogs would thank him.

And still she'd haunt him.

He scowled, his temples beginning to throb. "Thor's blood," he growled, snatching his ale cup and downing the frothy brew before such mooning got the better of him.

Now was not the time to dwell on her.

Now was—

The time for his world to upend. Spin around him, stealing his breath. The ale cup slid from his hand, landing on the table with a loud *clack* and spill of gold-tinged foam. Eyes wide, he shot to his feet. Uproar filled the hall, a ruckus unfolding near the shadowed entry. Scores of kinsmen shoved through the door, loud and boisterous. Murder on their faces. His best friend, cousin, what-have-you, led the fray, his *dream woman* clutched in the lout's arms.

"By the gods," Aidan bellowed, staring. "What goes on here?"

"A witch!" Mundy, his Irish-born ax-man, raised his voice above the din. "We caught her dancing nekkid on the gatehouse arch, a horde o' winged demons flying round her head."

Hoots and guffaws accompanied Mundy's outburst, one man slapping him hard on the back before leaping onto a trestle bench.

The trestle leaper's mirth vanishing, he peered round, his eyes glinting in the torchlight. "That flame-haired vixen wasn't nekkid and if Mundy saw flying demons, I saw none." He raised an arm to point at the lass. "She *is* garbed like no maid I've e'er seen, and Tavish is the only soul I ken able to vault to such heights. Seeing as she doesn't have wings, there's only one thing she can be—just what Mundy says. A witch!"

"She is none the like." Tavish's face darkened as he mounted the dais steps, Aidan's beauty still cradled protectively in his arms. "Ne'er have I carried a more womanly female," he vowed, setting her on her feet in front of the high table.

"I daresay you'll agree," he added, his gaze seeking Aidan's.

"Without doubt!" Still staring, Aidan tamped down the urge to challenge his friend to a round in the lists for daring to touch his woman.

A thought that brought an immediate jab of guilt when he caught a closer look at his kinsmen's faces. Murder wasn't the only emotion painted on the fierce and bearded countenances he loved so well. Ranging from suspicion, to fear, to bloodlust, their expressions made it clear he owed Tavish much for coming to his *tamhasg's* rescue.

"Where did you find her?" He glared at Tavish all the same, the blood roaring in his ears making it hard to think. "How did she get here?"

"I don't know how I got here." His *tamhasg* answered,

brushing at the plaid slung loosely about her shoulders. "Not exactly. I—"

"She spelled herself here!" someone yelled.

Others chimed in, those standing near making the sign against evil as they edged away from her.

"Cease!"Aidan slammed his fist on the table, jarring cutlery and tipping over wine goblets."I'll no' have you babbling like women!" he roared, his fury squelching the foul-tempered rumbles.

For good measure, he put back his shoulders and looked round, letting his stare act as a further warning. Fear was something he couldn't condone within his walls. A MacDonald feared nothing. Even if his men seemed to have momentarily forgotten. He folded his arms, watching them. It also appeared to have slipped their minds that he didn't tolerate injustice. Another trait he expected all MacDonalds to adhere to.

Most especially in regard to females.

He drew a deep breath, schooling his features. He knew better than anyone else present that the woman was no witch.

Not that he meant to share how he knew it.

She *was* something he couldn't fathom. Not that he cared. All that mattered was that she stood before him. Scarce able to believe it, he came around the high table and put a hand on her arm, that one touch—her physical nearness—shooting jolts of white-hot flame all through him.

Fighting the urge to clutch her to him, he drew himself to his fullest height, feigning a look of fierceness lest his superstitious kinsmen doubt his ability to deal with a woman they held for a witch.

There would be time enough to win them over to her—if she wasn't an illusion.

Hoping she wasn't, he raised her arm and raked the hall with all the lairdly sternness he had in him. "I can feel this woman's warmth through her clothes. Even"—he jerked a glance at Tavish

—"the thickness of Tavish's plaid. All ken witches have blood of ice. If she's of the Fae, or merely a troubled woman here to find succor, it will be to me to decide. No one else shall touch her or even glance askance at her. I forbid it."

Displeased grumbles answered him. A sea of shifting, nervous manhood, all with doubting, belligerent faces. Only a few looked down, swatting at sleeves and hitching sword belts.

"Come, Aidan." A gap-toothed man stepped forward, clearly speaking for them all. "You ken the damage a witch can wreak. Only last year, Widow MacRae's best cow started giving soured milk after the old woman granted a night's shelter to a witch. The same creature caused the widow's daughter to lose her bairn. And—"

"Nonsense!"Aidan cut him off, silencing the rest with another cold stare. "I'll have no such foolery spoken in my hall. The lass is no witch, and it will go poorly for the man who dares say so again. Mark it and be wary."

Beside him, his *tamhasg* drew in a breath. "Of course, I'm not a witch. Or a fairy," Aidan thought he heard her say, though he couldn't be sure because the scent of her was clouding his wits. The closeness and heat of her sweet, lush body making him crazy.

"Your name." He looked at her, hoping that only he heard the thickness of his voice. "I would know it at last," he added, the words so low he wasn't even sure he'd said them.

Her eyes widened, the slight tremble of her lips telling him he had. "I'm Kira," she said, saying her name for the second time that evening. "Kira Bedwell."

"Kee-*rah* Bedwell," he repeated, pronouncing the name as her champion had, only with an even richer, sexier burr. "'Tis an apt name."

Kira blinked, not certain she'd heard a slight emphasis on the last words.

His scowl told her she'd imagined it.

Not that it mattered.

With a voice like that he could set a woman into ecstasy just reading the back of a cereal box. He'd sounded sexy in her dreams. In person, he undid her. Six foot four inches of pure, wild, and savage Highland masculinity was almost more than she could take. Especially when those inches were put together so well. His tall, muscle-ripped frame made all the more irresistible by the thick, silky black hair just brushing his shoulders and his dark, smoldering gaze.

"Lass." He looked at her, his eyes narrowing ever so slightly. "I'll ask you again—how did you get here?"

"It was a time slip." She lowered her voice, not wanting his men to hear. "One that expanded. Or ... oh, let's just say I've come a long way," she blurted, too awestruck to manage anything better. "From Aldan, Pennsylvania."

*And I think I am going to faint.*

Her heart had surely stopped. And with it, her ability to breathe. She stared up at him, everything in her world slamming to a halt. Nothing existed except the man before her. His gaze held hers, commanding and possessive. He towered over her, all medieval male and gorgeous, the look in his eyes melting her.

She blinked, swallowing against the fluttering in her stomach. The bite of so much smoke-filled air. An acrid haze that stung her eyes, while the reek of peat, over-spiced food, dogs, and ale made her nose twitch. She stood frozen, taking it all in, her ears ringing with the grumbles of angry, tartan-draped men. Harried servants rushed past, their faces averted, the general, noisy chaos like nothing she could have imagined. It all whirled around her in a great, dizzying cacophony. The wild, torchlit, colorful place she'd dreamt of so long.

Diminished to nothing when compared with the wonder of his hand on her arm.

"See that no one disturbs us." He spoke again, his voice smooth, deep, and flowing right through her.

Even if his words were directed at the man called Tavish rather than her. "Settle the hall—even if you must draw blood."

Tavish nodded.

Aidan frowned and turned away, pulling her along beside him. Kinsmen and dogs made room as they passed, heading for the shadowed arch of a nearby stair tower.

"I'd have words with you in my privy quarters," he told her, not breaking stride as he swept her off her feet, scooping her into his arms. "Words long overdue."

Then he was carrying her up the winding, torchlit stair, mounting the steps two at a time. Kira slid her arms around his neck, holding fast and biting her lip. The truth of her situation becoming more clear the higher they climbed up the tight, circular stair.

A very *new*-looking stair, lit by stinking, sputtering rush lights and whatever pale moonlight fell through the narrow, deep-set arrow slits.

This was for real.

She was no longer dreaming about the ancient past—she was in it.

And judging by Aidan's frown, he was anything but pleased to see her there.

---

## 5

Aidan was no longer scowling by the time he climbed the last few rounds of the stair tower and stopped outside his bedchamber door. Far from frowning, his countenance must now be thunderous. Indeed, he was certain he could feel the flames of anger licking the back of his neck and scalding his cheeks.

For two pins, he'd tear back down to the hall, whip out his blade, and lop the heads off the first loose-tongued kinsmen who dared utter the word *witch* again.

Instead, he blew out a hot breath and kicked open his oak-planked door. Striding inside, his *tamhasg* still in his arms, he took some small satisfaction in slamming the door behind them.

"So-o-o, lass." He released her at once. "Tell me, what magic brought you here?"

"I already told you I don't know." She stared back at him, her face as flushed as he suspected his must be. "Or rather, I'm not sure. I think I'm trapped in a time slip, though that's never happened before. All I know is that I was on the top of your arch and—"

"I know that." Aidan frowned, not about to admit he hadn't understood half of what she'd said. Not just the words, but how she'd pronounced them. A problem he'd never had in their dreams. "It's how you got there, that interests me."

*If you know me.*

Not that he was going to ask. Not yet anyway.

First he needed to know what the blazes was going on.

Doing his best to look as if he did, he folded his arms."Well?"

"If I knew I'd tell you." She shot a glance at the window arch, her eyes rounding at the dark outline of Wrath Isle. Recognition flashed across her face, her eyes widening even more when she saw the colorful tapestry hanging so close to the window, his huge four-poster bed placed not far away.

"Holy moly." She pressed a hand to her breast, looking round.

Aidan's frown deepened. He understood *holy,* but *moly* was new to him. Not that the word was of any great import. Her astonishment spoke worlds.

She knew his room.

And that could only mean one thing.

She'd lived their dreams as vividly as he had.

The possibility enflamed him and he reached for her, seizing her shoulders. "You've been here." He tightened his grip on her, willing her to admit it. "I can see it all o'er you."

She twisted free, turning back to the window. Stepping closer, she touched the shutter hinges. She examined them, flattening her hands on the stone of the embrasure before trailing her fingers down the tasseled edge of his tapestry.

"I can't believe how real all this is." She glanced at him. "How real *you* are. For this long, anyway."

Aidan harrumphed. "I'm as real now as I was when I woke this morn. 'Tis you I'm concerned about." He looked at her, the whole situation making his head pound. "You're no' making a word of sense."

The admission slipped out before he could stop it, but rather than laugh at him as he'd almost expected, she shook her head, looking as dumbfounded as he felt.

"It doesn't make sense to me either," she said, proving it. Her gaze flitted to his bed and then back to him. "If this had happened at the Na Tri Shean, I might not be so surprised, but—"

"The Na tri Shean?" A chill sped down his back. "'Tis a bad place, that. Good folk would ne'er set foot there."

"I'm not a witch." She drew Tavish's plaid more tightly about her. "I had business at the fairy mounds. That doesn't make me one of them."

"I ken what you are." Aidan closed his eyes, wishing he did.

He also tried not to breathe in her scent.

He wouldn't have believed it, but it was even more wondrous than in their dreams. So enticing, it befuddled his wits. If he succumbed to it, he'd have her naked and beneath him in a flash and such a breach of honor would haunt him all his days.

MacDonalds wooed their women. Winning them with sensual prowess and charm. With the exception of a few aberrations like Conan Dearg, ne'er would a man of Aidan's race take an unwilling female.

And Kira Bedwell wasn't just any female. She was special beyond words. No matter how many fairy mounds she knew about. Everyone knew of such places. What mattered was that he wanted and needed her to desire him as much now as she did in her dream state.

Only then would he touch her. And only after a suitable wooing period. She deserved as much and, as laird, his dignity required it of him.

Much as the waiting pained him.

He looked at her, his heart thundering. "You're been here," he said again, the truth of it pounding through him. "Tell me, Kira, tell me you know."

She swiped a hand through her hair, the movement sending Tavish's plaid fluttering to the floor. "Of course I know." Color bloomed on her cheeks. "I've been here in my dreams. *Our* dreams."

Aidan nodded. "Aye, lass. How much do you remember of them?"

Her throat worked. "I remember everything."

"Even this?" He slid his arms around her, forcing himself to hold her gently. "You must tell me, Kira. If this, too, is familiar?" He smoothed one hand across her back and with the other caressed the curve of her hip, drawing her just a bit closer. "Or this?" He lowered his head to lightly brush her lips with his. "Speak true, sweetness. I would hear the words. Exactly what you recall."

Kira's face flamed. "I think you know."

"That's no' an answer." He watched her coolly, every inch the proud, self-assured laird.

And so flesh-and-blood, staring-at-her real, she was sure she must be one big goose bump.

She shivered. His huge stone hearth and peat fire ranked all kinds of prizes in the romance department, but those little orange-glowing bricks of turf couldn't compete with central heating.

With the exception of her face, she was suddenly freezing.

He blazed like a furnace.

Somehow her hand had become trapped between them, her splayed fingers pressed against the rough weave of his plaid. He tightened his arms around her, pulling her closer against him. Blessed heat poured off him, warming her even through the heavy wool. She could also feel the steady thumping of his heart and, a bit lower, the hard buckle of his sword belt digging into her belly. A discomfort as tangible and eye-opening as the cold and one that underscored that he wasn't just a real living and breathing man, he was a *medieval* man.

If she discounted Halloween and Ren Faires, there weren't too many times a man in her world walked around with a giant broadsword slapping his thigh.

Aidan MacDonald looked like he was born wearing his.

She swallowed, just a bit daunted by so much muscle and steel.

"I'm waiting, Kee-*rah*."

"Ahhh..." The words lodged in her throat.

No way was she going to recite the explicit details of their nightly encounters.

She slid another glance at the tapestry near the window. The one she knew from her dreams. Moon glow slanted across it, the silvery light gilding each bright-gleaming thread and breathing life into the nude and half-clad figures artfully blended into an idyllic forest scene.

Figures entwined in intimate embraces that couldn't hold a candle to the kind of wild, uninhibited lovemaking they'd enjoyed in their dreams.

Unfortunately, at the moment she did feel a bit less daring.

And who wouldn't?

Hot, earthy sex with a dream man was one thing, but getting all touchy-feely within minutes of a first real meeting, was a whole 'nuther kettle of fish, as her mother would say. Her mother also loved reminding her that no man bothered to buy a cow if the milk was free; whether Aidan had *dream-sampled* her offerings or not, wasn't the question.

She'd never been a first-date-bedding kind of girl and she didn't want to start now, no matter how strong and wonderful his arms felt around her.

No matter how kissable his lips.

How good he smelled. An intoxicating blend clung to him, a mix of peat smoke, clean wool, cold air, and man. The scent teased her senses, tempting her to lean in and nuzzle her cheek against his plaid-draped shoulder, just for the heady pleasure of breathing him in.

She really did want him.

So she lifted her chin and met his stare, hoping she didn't have take-me-I'm-yours flashing on her forehead.

To her dismay, his arched brow and the heated look he pinned on her indicated she just might.

"So, will you say the words? Tell me true what you remember of our dreams?" He smoothed her hair back from her face, his touch sending a cascade of pleasure through her.

Pleasure so sweet, each shivery wave put a major dent in her jitters.

She clamped her lips together, not quite ready to admit it.

He angled his head. "Come, sweet, I already know you to be a bold-hearted lass."

Kira glanced aside. If she looked at him, she'd be a goner. He was that intoxicating.

"Well?" He lifted a handful of her hair, letting the strands glide over his fingers.

She pulled back a bit, needing to catch her breath. "There are no *wells* about it. No wondering, either. You know what I remember. Every bit, I'm sure."

To her annoyance, he smiled.

Another of those conquering alpha-male hero smiles.

"O-o-oh, I believe I know well enough," he admitted, his smooth, whisky-rich burr making it all the more difficult not to throw her arms around his neck and cling to him.

He was, after all, a very *clingable* man.

So curl-her-toes-clingable that she slipped out of his arms before she made a spectacle of herself. Much better to give herself a little space and do some pacing.

Besides, it wasn't every day she could walk on medieval floor rushes. Not knowing how long she would remain in his time, she dug one toe into the thick layer of fragrant meadowsweet or whatever such herb-strewn rushes were called, then took care to step beyond his reach.

"You cannae deny it, lass." He folded his arms, watching her. His voice poured over and into her, the beauty of it making the impossible so incredibly real. "Wearing a track in my floor willnae change anything."

"I know that," she said, pacing anyway. "But moving around helps."

And she definitely needed help. Never would she have believed such a thing could happen.

A single fleeting glimpse, yes.

But never this.

She slid another glance at him, half expecting him to be gone, but he hadn't budged. He was still there. Bold as day and looking more fiercely handsome than the hottest hero she'd ever seen on the cover of a historical romance novel. Above all, he seemed so amazingly real, and she just couldn't wrap her mind around that.

Her Aidan. His Castle Wrath no longer a confused tumble of stones and broken walls, but a thriving, *living* place where he reigned supreme and had just tossed her over his shoulder and carried her up winding castle steps and into his bedchamber. An act that made the centuries between them as meaningless as a dust mote.

Her throat began to thicken and she swallowed. Never had she felt so overwhelmed.

She stopped her pacing to look at him. "You were angry in the hall. As if you weren't pleased that I—"

"Angry?" His dark brows arced upward. "Precious lass, I was furious, but no' at you. I was wroth with my men and their foolery. What might have happened had Tavish not crossed the bailey when he did."

He stepped close to caress her face. "Ach, sweetness, you thought wrong." He smoothed his thumb over her lips, his tone softening. "Seeing you appear was like having the sun and the stars burst into my hall. I've burned for you, searching nightly. Waiting, always waiting, and ne'er giving up hope."

Kira's breath caught, something inside her stirring as never before.

Making her bold.

"Hoping what? That I would step out of a dream, materialize before you?" She held his gaze, his touch melting her. Heating her. Even the room's chill seemed less biting. In fact, it was almost beginning to feel stuffy. Sure of it, she slipped out of her heavy waxed jacket and let it drop onto the discarded plaid.

He looked at the jacket, then at her. "O-o-oh, lass." His eyes darkened. "You shouldn't ask what I hoped for—not if hearing the answer will frighten you."

"I'm not frightened." She flipped back her hair and assumed her most unfrightened expression. "I only need time to adjust."

He shook his head slowly, clearly not buying her denial.

He was touching her hair now, his fingers skimming along her nape. "Would a kiss put you at ease?"

Kira blinked, not sure she'd heard the softly spoken words.

"A kiss?" She spoke quickly before her courage fizzled.

He nodded.

"I don't think a kiss is a good idea just now."

In fact, she knew it wasn't. Just his thumb sliding back and forth across her lips had set her on fire. Each word he spoke in his deep, smooth-as-sin burr took her breath and made her fear she might even drown in its richness. A *kiss* would be the end of her.

"No kisses," she emphasized, shaking her head.

"Ach, lass, dinnae think it willnae cost me, too. If I kissed you but once, I'd burn to kiss you for hours. Even days. But know this"—he paused to glide his knuckles down the side of her face—"I mean to court you properly, as is fitting. For the now, I'll only kiss you. Naught else until you're ready."

Kira almost choked.

She glanced aside, not wanting him to see how very ready she was.

He captured her chin, tilting her face upward. "I also mean to chase the worry from your eyes. You ought to know I would ne'er let anyone harm you."

Kira's heart skittered. "It isn't a person I'm worried about."

"Then what?"

"Something far more impossible than our dreams."

He frowned. "It cannae be as impossible as you being here."

"It has everything to do with me being here."

She looked down, searching for words, and ending up plucking at her clothes. The fine weave of her top and the stretch wool of her pants at such odds with his rough Highland garb. Her wristwatch, a gleaming incongruity in his world of rush-strewn floors and smoking torchlights, his massive timber-framed bed and the colorful tapestries covering his walls.

Centuries old adornments she'd only ever seen on her one long-ago visit to Scotland. Or, more often, in the glossy colored pages of coffee-table books on castles.

Ancient castles that belonged to a world as distant from hers as the moon.

She nudged the floor rushes again, remembering with a pang the times he'd loved her so fiercely that the power of their passion ripped away her apartment walls, letting her see through her dreams and into the time and place he called his own.

*This place*, where she'd never thought to stand.

She bit her lip, her eyes burning. Any moment she could be whisked away, swept right out of his arms and back to her time. The place she did belong, but that would feel so empty now—now that she had finally felt his arms around her for real.

However briefly.

She swallowed and broke away from him, not wanting him to see her concern. But he must have, because he moved with lightning speed, his strong fingers clamping around her arm and yanking her back against him.

"You needn't be so troubled, Kee-*rah*." His embrace almost

crushed her. "Whate'er it is that fashes you has yet to face a MacDonald."

She shook her head, about to tell him that all of Clan Donald's medieval might couldn't conquer the hands of time, but before she could, he gripped her face and his mouth crashed down over hers in a searing, demanding kiss.

A deep, soul-slaking kiss full of hot breath, sighs, and tangling tongues. A beautiful melding to cross time and space and ignite a man and woman in a pleasure so exquisite that she would have melted into a puddle on his rushy floor if he hadn't been squeezing her to him in such a fearsome hold.

Clutching him just as fiercely, she opened her mouth wider, welcoming the deep thrustings of his tongue. The hot glide of his hands roving up and down her back, exploring all her curves and hollows, the way his skilled fingers sought and held her hips.

"Och, lass. I knew you were near." He breathed the words against her lips. "I've felt you close for days, looked for you."

"Yesss..." She curled a hand around his neck, tangling her fingers in his hair. "I'd hoped that was so, dreaming it, and aching for this to happen."

"Kee-*rah*." He kissed her again, claiming her lips with open-mouthed hunger.

Time stopped, no longer of importance. He tightened his arms around her, his kiss making her forget everything except their passion. The raging need to be one with him and have him touch and taste her, to forget all caution and just lose herself in the madness of his raw, sensual heat.

Heat she knew so well and wanted again.

This time for real.

She sighed, the heavy silk of his hair spilling through her fingers as he kept kissing her, each delicious swirl of his tongue against hers making her burn.

Sweet, hot tingles raced across the softness between her thighs, igniting a fire that made her wild. She leaned into him, the feel of his thick, rigid arousal electrifying her. The sexy Gaelic love words he whispered against her throat driving her beyond reason.

Until one of his roaming hands slid across her wristwatch, his seeking fingers hooking around the elastic metal watchband. Breaking the kiss, he stepped back and lifted her arm to the light of a softly hissing oil lamp. His brow pleated as he peered at the timepiece.

"It's a watch," Kira told him, his frown making her stomach clench.

Clench, and growl.

*Loudly.*

After all, she hadn't eaten since leaving Ravenscraig's One Cairn Village. Substantial as her full Scottish breakfast had been, she was now so ravenous, she'd gladly devour every crumb of Lindsay's crushed and crumbling organic chocolate chip cookies.

Instead, more pressing matters plagued her.

Namely, Aidan's furrowed brow as he eyed her bargain basement imitation of a Swiss masterpiece.

"Where did you get this?" He fingered the smooth glass of the watch face. "You didn't wear it in our dreams."

"It's my watch." Kira glanced at it. "I take it off before I sleep. That's why you've never seen it. It tells the time."

He scoffed. "I'm no fool, lass," he countered, his sexy burr still making her burn, no matter how fiercely he glowered at her watch. "I know it's a timepiece. My grandfather had one no' unlike yours. A second century bronze Roman sundial, small enough to fit in the scrip he wore from his belt."

"*Scrip?*" This time Kira blinked.

"Aye." He slanted his mouth over hers in another swift, bruising kiss, then jerked his head toward an iron-studded strongbox at the foot of his bed. "Yon is my scrip."

Kira followed his gaze, noting a rough-leathered sporran

resting atop the chest's domed cover, the sight of it only reminding her how far back in time she'd spiraled.

And of the fine MacDonald sporran she'd hoped to make into a purse.

A treasure that would have made a fine gift for Aidan, had it not gone missing when she'd been swept back in time.

She stared at the scrip for a long moment, then looked again at her watch, not wanting to think about the centuries dividing them.

Apparently feeling the same, he unlatched the watch with surprising ease and tossed it onto her jacket. "It willnae do if my men see you wearing suchlike." His voice came low and husky, a deliciously deep burr that made a little thing like an imitation Swiss watch seem ever so insignificant. "While I might no' have trouble accepting the Fae can fashion such a timepiece, my men might disagree. To be sure, they'd see it as proof you're a witch."

Kira swallowed, the significance of her watch returning like a fist to the gut.

"I told you," she said, amazed by the steadiness of her voice, "I am neither a fairy nor a witch. I'm Kira Bedwell of Aldan, Pennsylvania. I'm a far-seer. A paranormal investigator. And I come from the future. The early twenty-first century to be exact."

"Indeed? So many years ahead?" He arched one raven black brow, clearly not believing her. "Sweetness, I already ken you aren't of these parts and I'll personally take down the first man who calls you a witch. But there's no wrong in being of the Fae. I doubt there's a Highlander walking who'd deny them, and many are they who've even wed with them. We all ken the tales."

He pressed two fingers to her lips when she tried to protest. "Be that as it may, I'd warn you no' to say aught about them to anyone but me. Above all, dinnae mention any tall tales about para-*whate'er* or the future. If my men heard you speak the like, even I might have difficulty controlling them."

"But it's the truth." She puffed her bangs off her forehead, the last of her Scottish-accent-inspired tingles flying out the window. "If you believe in witches and fairies, why can't you accept someone who can step into a time slip? Look into the past as I do? Or see ghosts, for that matter."

"I've no' problem with bogles." He waved a dismissive hand. "These hills are full of haints. 'Tis this far-seeing and Penn-*seal* business I'm concerned about."

"I know it sounds crazy." Kira sighed, a hot, tight knot forming at the base of her neck, just between her shoulder blades. "Far-seeing is a gift I have—as do many others. It runs in my family, on my mother's side, though I'm the first to have it in generations. I only learned I'd inherited it when I saw you years ago, that very first time. Now, I use it to look into haunted sites and legends. Supernatural phenomena. *Destiny Magazine* employs me and I—"

"You're wearing those wretched raiments again." He stepped back and folded his arms, the medieval laird in him blocking his ears to everything she'd said. "All I care about is how it is I saw you at the top of my stair all those years ago only to have you vanish out of my arms. Then"—his gaze held hers, dark with smoldering passion—"you appear in my dreams, night after night, making me burn for you and no other. And now you're here."

Kira felt her pulse quicken, certain her entire body would start humming with anticipation if he kept that heated gaze on her.

"I've been trying to tell you. My gift let us see each other on the stair." She tried not to squirm. "How can I explain it to you? I'm able to see things, to look beyond what's actually there and into the distant past. I don't know how the dreams worked. Or why I'm here now. I never really believed in time travel until—"

"*Time travel?*"

She nodded.

His lips curved into a slow, sensual smile. No, an indulgent smile. The kind that would have been insulting were he not, well, medieval.

"I think you should sleep," he declared, clearly tired of their conversation. "Aye, a good long rest will serve you well."

Definitely meaning it, he scooped her into his arms and carried her across the room, lowering her onto the soft fur coverings of his bed. "A good sleep without those raiments. Ne'er have I cared for the like, and you cannae wear them here."

"I don't think I'll be around long enough for them to bother anyone."

He cocked a brow. "Och, lass, you'll no' be going anywhere," he said, looking sure of it. "I'll no' allow it."

Kira frowned at him. "I don't think that would matter much. Not against Father Time."

"As for your raiments," he said as if she hadn't spoken, "they bother *me* enough to twist my head in knots. I'll no' have my men going gog-eyed o'er them."

He reached to finger the button above her zipper, his brows snapping together when it popped off and arced through the air.

"By the gods!" He jerked his hand back, staring first at the suicidal button, resting so innocently on the floor rushes, then at the metal teeth of her zipper.

Kira winced. She could well imagine what it must look like to him.

"It's just a zipper," she said, the strange word making his head throb even more.

She clasped her hand over it and scooted away from him across the bed. Almost as if she feared he'd harm the thing. Aidan almost snorted, and would have, had the wee disk flying off her hose not rattled him to the core. Ne'er had he seen the like. He frowned and rammed a hand through his hair. Och, nae, by a thousand red-tailed devils, he wasn't about to touch the zip-*her*.

Nor would it do to let her see how much her outlandish garb unsettled him.

He was, after all, a man with a reputation to uphold. A brave-hearted chieftain who'd faced death on the battlefield more times than he could count. And he'd defy the flames of Hades and all its winged demons to keep this woman safe, flying disks and zip-*hers* or nae. So he attempted his most worldly pose, standing as tall as only a MacDonald could, his hands clasped loosely behind his back.

"Have done with these garments and sleep," he ordered, the commanding tone a wee nod to his fierce Highland pride. "I'll keep my back turned the while, then take my own rest in yon chair." He indicated his resting chair, a great oaken monstrosity beside the hearth fire.

Not that he meant to sleep this night.

O-o-oh, no.

This night, at least, he'd keep a sharp eye on her. Anything else struck him as extremely unwise. Perhaps he'd even shove his strongbox in front of the door later. Every female he knew could unbolt a drawbar without difficulty, but he knew nary a one who would be able to budge his heavy, iron-banded coffer.

Feeling better already, he stretched his hands to the fire, warming them. Behind him, he could hear her scrambling out of her clothes, then settling beneath his covers. He ached to join her there—but such pleasures would come soon enough.

Perhaps even sooner than was wise if the twitchings in his tender parts were any indication.

Determined to ignore them, he stood unmoving, waiting until he was sure she slept before he went to his chair. A chair that suddenly struck him as uncomfortable as the stirring at his loins. Why he'd e'er deemed it his *resting chair* he didn't know.

How he expected to sleep in it was well beyond him.

Scowling once more, he leaned his head back against the hard, cold wood and threw a spare plaid over his knees. Only then, safely hidden from possibly prying glances, did he ease one hand beneath the plaid and squeeze a certain part of himself until his eyes watered and all desire left him.

A drastic measure he suspected he might have to employ more than once before the night was over.

Sleep was certainly out of the question.

Especially since the fool night wind was picking up, its wretched blasts rattling the window shutters. A persistent, ongoing racket, the likes of which would've kept a deaf man from a good night's slumber.

He cursed beneath his breath and shifted on the chair.

Unfortunately, his best efforts at ignoring the noise only caused the din to increase. Even yanking the spare plaid over his head proved futile. The wind's howling rose to a teeth-grinding pitch, and the banging shutters became so loud he considered ripping them from their hinges the instant he felt awake enough to see to the task.

Awake enough?

He blinked, the thought jarring him so thoroughly that he sat bolt upright.

He *had* fallen asleep.

And though a fuzzy-headed glance at the bed showed that his lady yet slumbered deeply, the new day broke in a wild cacophony around him.

"By the gods," he grumbled, rubbing his hands over his face. Chaos rang in his ears, loud and penetrating. Poor Ferlie's howls, which he'd mistaken for the wind, and the sharp rapping at his door that wasn't rattled shutters at all.

"Sir!" came the voice of one of his squires, followed by another burst of knocking.

Ferlie gave a piercing bark and charged the door.

Aidan swore and leapt from his chair. Still half asleep, he grabbed his clothes and his sword, then bounded across the room, the name Conan Dearg pounding through his mind in rhythm to his squire's door hammering.

This was the morn they rode to Ardcraig.

The day he was sure they'd finally capture his dastardly cousin.

Aidan scowled, his pleasure in the deed dampened by the thought of such a fiend beneath the same roof as Kira—even with the craven secure in Castle Wrath's dungeon. Pushing the notion from his mind, he reached for the drawbar, only to stub his toe on his strongbox.

"Odin's balls!" he roared, pain shooting up his leg.

Furious, he unbolted the door. Flinging it wide, he realized too late that he'd latched his sword belt around his naked hips.

His plaid lay bunched around his feet, where he must've dropped it when he opened the door.

Not that his slack-jawed squire paid his appearance any heed.

Far from it. The youth's stare shot past him, homing in on a naked form far more pleasing than his own. And thanks to the carelessness of sleep, a ripe, well-made nakedness that left little to the lad's red-faced imagination.

Or Aidan's.

His gaze, too, flew straight to Kira's bared and creamy breasts, the triangle of flaming curls visible between her slightly parted thighs.

"You've seen nothing." He whipped back around, fixing the squire with his sternest laird's look. "No' if you wish to properly enjoy such sweetness yourself when you're old enough."

Not giving the lad a chance to see it was an empty threat, for he'd ne'er harm a youth—certainly not for ogling a fetching, bare-bottomed female—Aidan stepped into the doorway, making sure his shoulders blocked the view.

"Tell Tavish to see our men mounted at once," he ordered, trying to maintain as much dignity as he could, garbed as he was in naught but his great sword. "I'll join them anon."

As soon as his big toe quit throbbing and he was more suitably dressed. He also had to see to a few other urgent matters. Things that bit deeply into his conscience but he deemed necessary.

Indeed, vital.

Things that would ensure that his *tamhasg* would find it difficult to leave him.

**6**

---

K ira awoke to absolute stillness.
She also had a raging headache, a twitching nose,
and, she'd bet on it, horribly swollen eyes.

Frog eyes. Red, bulging, and achy.

Even without the luxury of a peek in her bathroom mirror,
she knew she must look like death warmed over served on icy-
cold toast.

She felt that bad.

Not an unusual occurrence in recent times, considering her
irritation with the media hounds who'd persisted in dogging her
every step since she'd owned up to the discovery of the Viking
longship and its New England moorings. Since then, every new
morning had seen her reaching for the aspirin and glass of water
she kept handy on her night table. Just as sleepless nights spent
tossing and turning resulted in aching, puffy eyes.

Annoyances she'd grown accustomed to.

But the thick and furry covers tickling her nose *were* beyond
the norm, as was the undeniable scent of dog. Much more than a
hint of dander on the cold, peat-tinged air, the smell was over-
powering and definitely there.

A big, smelly dog odor as real as the massive, richly carved medieval bed in which she found herself.

Even if the beast himself wasn't anywhere to be seen. He'd been there. That stood without question. Just as the bed was certainly real, its heavily embroidered curtaining parted enough to give her a view of tall arch-topped windows and the burgeoning morn. A new day that was *not* breaking over the crowded parking lot of Aldan, Pennsylvania's low-budget Castle Apartments.

Nor the small and cozy car park of the tiny Skye inn she hadn't even spent a night in.

Indeed, she couldn't be in a more different place if she'd stowed away on a rocket to Mars.

Kira's heart began to pound and her mouth went dry. Her headache worsened, and although she would have preferred not to admit it, rarely had she felt so miserable. If she didn't soon feel better, she'd suspect she was allergic to time travel.

Or medieval Scotland.

Much as the notion displeased her.

There could be no doubt that she'd landed there. Even if she weren't peering through the bed curtains at the proof, the lack of noise was a giveaway. There *was* a stiff wind. It blew and moaned, and from somewhere above her came the snapping of what might have been a banner flying from the parapets. She also heard the muffled barking of dogs and the repetitive wash of waves on the rocks below.

What she didn't hear was the twenty-first century.

The maddening blare of leaf blowers and you-ride-'em-cowboy lawn mowers or old Mr. Wilson's television droning through her apartment's bedroom wall. No rattling of garbage trucks or distant sirens. Not even the low hum of her computer or the weird pops and shudders her ancient refrigerator was always making.

She heard simply nothing.

She listened hard, the silence almost hurting her ears. Half certain that her admittedly wild imagination was conjuring the stillness, she squeezed her eyes shut and opened them again, but the quiet remained. As did the whole medieval-y room, the doggy smell, and the great, dark bulk of Wrath Isle so visible through the tall, arched windows.

Her stomach gave a funny little dip. Last she'd looked, Aldan, Pennsylvania, couldn't claim such a view.

Nor could Castle Wrath—leastways not in the ruinous state she knew it.

Her heart still thumping, she held the furry covers to her breasts as she peered through the gap in the bed curtains. In addition to the window alcoves and view, she was greeted by whitewashed walls and the erotically decadent tapestries that had so startled her the night before.

Her first true indication that she stood in the medieval bedchamber she recognized from her dreams.

Now, some hours later, she swallowed hard. The room's not-so-savory-looking floor rushes and the torchlights in their heavy iron wall brackets took away any last doubt that she was still in Aidan's world.

Trapped there and … naked.

Unless time traveling had not just given her a shattering headache but affected her memory as well. She dug her fingers into the pillow, considering the possibility. To be sure, she remembered undressing beneath the covers, but a quick scan of the floor refused to reveal where she'd dropped her clothes.

Or, better said, where she'd flung them.

In particular, her panties and her bra.

Neither bit of crucially important underwear was anywhere to be seen. And for the life of her, unless she was horribly mistaken, the rest of her clothes had gone missing as well. Everything was gone. Including her beloved hill-walking boots, and even her bargain basement Swiss watch.

Nothing remained to remind her of her own left-behind world.

Even more alarming, Aidan had vanished, too.

Heaven help her if she'd only imagined him.

Conjured his hot-eyed stares and his heart-stopping kisses, the old-fashioned, take-charge sense of chivalry she found so endearing.

*Woo her*, indeed.

He'd made only one mistake. Hiding her clothes wasn't the way to her heart. Nor was leaving her behind in a strange, doggy-smelling bedchamber, even if she did know the room from their dreams. Too many big, hairy people here seemed to want a piece of her, and not the way she knew their laird did.

Those against her also carried swords.

And being medievals, they'd know how to use them.

Medieval Highlanders were especially bloodthirsty. Everyone knew it.

She bit her lip, her pulse beating rapidly. It was one thing to be stuck in medieval Skye with Aidan at her side during the day and guarding her come nightfall, and something else entirely to be stranded here alone.

Nearly as distressing, she was hungrier than she could recall being in her entire life and—gasp! horrors!—she felt an urgent need to visit what she knew medieval people called the jakes. If the fates were kind, she would find one of the miniscule water closets tucked away in a discreet corner of Aidan's oh-so-lairdly bedchamber.

If not, she'd simply have to find something to wrap around her nakedness and go looking for one. But first she took a deep breath and peered around the room one more time, just to make sure the dog wasn't lurking in some dark and musty corner, waiting for her.

Not that she didn't like dogs.

She loved them.

But the ones she'd seen barking at her in the bailey weren't the garden-variety, toddle-down-the-sidewalk-looking-happy kind of dogs she was so crazy about. The shaggy, fang-toothed beasts that had gathered beneath the gatehouse arch had looked anything but friendly.

Shuddering at the memory, she slipped from the bed, certain she didn't want anything to do with such monsters. She could still feel their agitated stares.

Or someone's.

A disturbing sensation that came at her from two places—the other side of the closed oak-paneled door and, oddly, from outside the tall arched windows.

The back of her neck prickled, and she grabbed a pillow, holding it in front of her just in case the room was outfitted with one of those peekaboo *squint holes* she knew could be found in medieval castles. Half afraid that might be the case, she crept around the corner of the huge curtained bed, relief washing over her when she spied the mound of clothes piled on top of Aidan's massive iron-banded strongbox.

Not her clothes, unfortunately, but clearly meant for her.

If she could figure out how to wear them.

Not sure that was possible, she picked up what could only be an *arisaid*. "A *yarusatch,*" she breathed, pronouncing it as she knew was correct for the female version of the ancient belted plaid.

But whether she could say the name properly or not, it still looked like an overlong bedsheet, finely made of a white-based plaid shot through with thin stripes of black, blue, and red. There wasn't any way she could manage to drape it on without ending up looking like a ghost.

Despite the heavily carved silver brooch someone had thoughtfully tucked into its folds.

"No-o-o, I think I'll pass." She shook her head, then carefully refolded the cloth and placed it on the bed. Celtic shoulder brooch and all. Exiting the room dressed like Casper-in-drag would only have Aidan's scowling-faced clansmen growling at her again.

Sure of it, she examined the other garments, pleased to see that they appeared easier to slip into. A basic-looking woolen gown in a rich shade of dark blue and an emerald green over-dress that could only be made of silk. It spilled across her fingers, cool and luxuriant to the touch. The third gown, clearly a light-weight cotton undershift, proved equally delicate.

Regrettably, it also appeared to be the only underwear in the pile.

She frowned. Hoping it wasn't so, she searched through the garments again, only to have her dread confirmed. Underwear as she knew and appreciated it apparently didn't exist in Aidan's world, even if he could afford fine silks and silver brooches.

At least there were shoes.

She stared at them, not surprised she'd overlooked them, for in the shadow cast by the bed, the deer hide *cuarans* were difficult to see against the floor rushes. Little more than longish, oval-shaped slippers laced all around with a thin leather cord, they would have reminded her of moccasins if they didn't look so ridiculously big.

Big or not, she had to *go,* so she pulled on the silk undergown and the remaining clothes as quickly as she could, pointedly ignoring the *arisaid* and its brooch. She also tried not to notice how awkward the soft-soled, giant *cuarans* felt on her feet.

She wasn't even going to think about her lack of underwear.

Instead, she steeled herself and took a few trial steps in the clumsy shoes. Nothing like her comfortable hill-walking boots, they flipped and flopped with every step, making it next to impos-sible to walk, as did the long, loose skirts swishing around her legs. Frowning again, she hitched them above her knees so she could march to the door and sail through it on her quest to find a latrine.

She had a pretty good idea where one might be located, but when she pulled open the door, sweeping through it proved impossible.

A tartan-hung boy stood there, a huge platter of food clutched in his hands. He gasped, his face beet-red and his eyes darting any which way but in her direction.

"Oops!" Kira dropped her skirts at once, the near collision only causing the boy to flush all the deeper. Delicious smells wafted up from his food tray, making her mouth water, but *other urges* took precedence.

Even over politeness.

"Sorry." She forced a smile as she tried to squeeze past him. "If that's breakfast, I thank you. Just put it anywhere and I'll dig into it when I get back."

"There'll be no need to be a-getting back as you willnae be going anywhere." A burly, great-bearded Highlander stepped from the shadows, the steel glinting all over him underscoring the authority of his deep, don't-argue-with-me voice. "The laird gave orders you are no' to leave his chamber."

A second man snorted. Every bit as well built and ferocious-looking as the other, he snatched the food tray from the boy's hands and narrowed his eyes at her, suspicion rolling off him. "If you even eat the like, you can break your fast alone. We'll keep watch that no one disturbs you."

Kira bristled. "You are disturbing me," she said, planting her hands on her hips. "I have to go to the ladies' room. The *loo* if that makes more sense to you."

Apparently it didn't—the two men merely stared at her, blank-faced and clearly not willing to budge.

Realizing retreat wasn't an option, she held her ground. "Your laird wouldn't wish me to be so discomforted," she said, trying for a more medieval tone. "He'd—"

"Lord Aidan isn't here." The man with the food tray stepped closer, seeming to swell in size as he towered over her. "He's charged us to see to your comfort, and we have—by bringing you sustenance."

"We can take it away as easily," the other informed her. "If the offerings don't please you."

Kira pressed her lips together, trying hard not to shift from foot to foot. "It isn't that," she began, wondering if she could make a run for it. "I have to—"

"I think she has to use the jakes," the boy chimed in, his embarrassed gaze flicking from one angry-looking Highlander to the other. "The laird said she might have to—"

"The laird isn't himself of late." The first man grabbed her arm and dragged her back inside the room. "If she has suchlike needs, the pot beneath the bed will suffice."

"Not with you looking!" Kira jerked free of his grasp and glared at him. "With *no one* looking," she added, rubbing her arm as the dog shuffled into the chamber and plopped down beside the fire, his milky gaze watching her every move.

"No one," she repeated, folding her arms.

The second man plunked down her breakfast tray on a table near the window embrasure. "Watch your tongue, lassie. The laird loses interest in wenches sooner than an autumn wind blows leaves from the trees."

Kira sniffed. Not about to show any weakness, she put back her shoulders and strode over to the hearth, where she ruffed the dog's head, taking courage from her firm belief that such an ancient creature, however fearsome-looking, was well past the days of biting.

Proving her right, the beast licked her hand.

Kira smiled, as did the red-faced youth still hovering on the threshold.

The two burly Highlanders frowned at her. "We'll be outside yon door," the first one said, jerking his head in that direction. "You willnae be winning o'er the rest o' us as easily as old Ferlie."

As if on cue, the dog bared his teeth and growled at the man, his protectiveness earning a scowl. "The laird ought be returned by nightfall," the second man announced, already moving toward the door. "See you dinnae cause us any trouble, lest you wish to meet his dark side."

And then the two men were gone, closing the door behind them and leaving her with a full-laden breakfast tray, a moony-eyed geriatric dog, and a pee-pot she couldn't wait to get her hands on.

Fortunately, once she knew where the thing was, it didn't prove difficult to find. Or use. Not that she could imagine ever growing overly fond of such quaintness. All things considered, there were worse annoyances in her own world.

Leaf blowers came to mind.

Or the persistent shrill of the telephone whenever she sat down to concentrate on one of her stories for *Destiny Magazine*. By comparison, a medieval chamber pot was definitely the lesser evil.

Even the dog, a creature that looked like a cross between an Irish wolfhound and a donkey, no longer seemed quite so daunting. She'd reserve judgment on his buddies down in the bailey.

"You're not quite a Jack Russell, but I like you," she said, watching him watch her.

Still feeling someone else's gaze on her, she shivered as she washed her hands with cold water from an ewer and basin. She hadn't noticed such amenities earlier, but enough gray morning light was now seeping in through the windows for her to quickly spot what she'd missed. Not just the ewer and basin, but also a small earthen jar of lavender-scented soap and even a comb. A short, folded length of linen she assumed was a medieval drying cloth.

Whether it was or not, she made good use of it.

Just as she would do justice to her breakfast, even if she wasn't quite sure what everything was. Determining to find out, she sat at the table, pleased to recognize oatcakes and cheese, while a green-glazed pottery bowl appeared to be filled with mutton stew. Another dish of the same type held what she suspected might be spiced and pickled eels, a delicacy she doubted she'd try. A small crock of honey and a jug of heather-scented ale rounded out the offerings.

Not too shabby, and certainly more edible-looking than some of the health food her sister Lindsay tried to palm off on her at times, even though just looking at the eels made her feel like gagging.

Her new four-legged friend suffered no such aversion. His scraggly ears perking, and wearing the most hopeful look she'd ever seen on a dog's face, he pushed to his feet and crossed the room to circle the table, eyeing everything on her breakfast tray as a potential tidbit.

"Okay, Ferlie." She handed him an oatcake. "You win this battle, but the war's not over."

Pasting on a smile for his benefit, she helped herself to one as well, smearing her own with the soft cheese and honey. Unfortunately, despite her best efforts at trying to stay upbeat, waves of ill ease kept sluicing through her, and the odd prickling at the back of her neck increased tenfold just since she'd sat at the table.

Someone really was staring at her.

And she could no longer deny where the sensation was coming from. Not now, sitting so close to the source. Chills running up and down her spine, she stood, her gaze on the tall arched windows.

Whoever—or whatever—was staring at her was out there, beyond the opened shutters.

*"Aieeeeeeeeeeeeee!"* The piercing scream, a woman's, proved it.

Heart pounding, Kira ran into the window alcove, horror slamming into her when she leaned out the first arched opening to see a woman bobbing in the rough waters beneath Wrath Isle's deadly, perpendicular cliffs.

"Dear God!" She clapped a hand to her throat, disbelief and shock stopping her breath.

The woman thrashed frantically and appeared to have a rope tied around her waist—a rope with dead seabirds dangling from its entire length.

Not trusting her eyes, she leaned farther out the window, but there was no mistake. Even through the scudding mists, she could see that the poor woman was encircled by dozens of seabirds-on-a-rope, their buoyant white bodies keeping her afloat as the swift current swept her out to sea.

"*Eachann!*" the woman wailed, her voice full of despair. "I cannae reach the rocks!"

"Get help! Anyone! *Please!*" a second voice cut through the morning, louder and deeper. A man's cry, his terror sounding even greater than the woman's.

"Hold, lass, I willnae let you drown!" he yelled, and Kira saw him then, dashing back and forth along Wrath Isle's cliff-tops.

Waving his arms and staring her way, he clearly hoped someone at the castle would see or hear and send help. A boat and men to rescue the woman Kira knew instinctively was his wife.

No, she was the man's life.

His everything, and his anguish seared Kira to the bone.

Waving her own arms, she called to them. "Hang on! Help is on the way!" she shouted, even as she whirled and raced for the door.

She reached to yank it wide, but needn't have bothered for it flew open in her face. Her two guardsmen stood there, hands fisted on their hips and glaring at her.

"Have you lost your wits?" The bigger of the two stared at her as if she'd sprouted horns. Making a din and ranting like a mad woman. The laird—"

"The laird will have your hide if you allow a poor woman to drown!" Kira gave him an adrenalin-powered shove and streaked down the corridor, shouting as she ran. "Help! Someone get a boat! There's a woman in the water!"

"Ho! Come back here, you!" The men bounded after her, their pounding footsteps spurring her on. Hitching her skirts, she careened around a bend in dimly lit passage, the flapping, over-sized *cuarans* making her clumsy.

"Damn!" she swore when one of them went sailing off her foot. Snatching it, she raced on, but the guardsmen caught up with her, the bigger one grabbing her arm.

"Foolish wench! That was ill done." He glowered at her. "Think you we'd no' aid a drowning woman?"

"If she saw one." The other man stood panting, fury all over him. "I dinnae believe her."

"Of course, I saw the woman," Kira insisted, trying to jerk free. "She'll soon be dead if you don't stop arguing and go save her!"

The bigger man shot the other a glance. "I'll no' stand by and have a woman drown. I say we make haste to look for her." Hefting Kira off her feet, he tossed her over his shoulder and hurried for the stair tower. "Someone in the hall can keep an eye on this one until we return."

"She'll have slipped away by then," the other scoffed, huffing after them. "She's lying. No woman within these walls is fool enough to fall off the cliffs."

"Bah!" the first man disagreed. "She could've slipped on the rocks down at the landing beach. Perhaps one of the laundresses or—"

"No." Kira twisted in the man's arms. "She fell from the cliffs of Wrath Isle."

The man carrying her stopped short. "That cannae be," he said, dropping her to her feet. "No one lives on Wrath Isle. 'Tis a scourged place."

Kira lifted her chin. "I didn't see her fall from there, but I know she did. I saw her husband running along the cliff-top. She called him Eachann."

The big man's eyes rounded. "*Eachann,* was it?"

Kira nodded.

The two men exchanged glances. "Would there have been anything else you noted about the woman?" the big one wanted to know. "Something ...odd-looking?"

Kira swallowed. She didn't like the way they were watching her. "The woman had a rope tied to her," she said anyway. "A rope with dead seabirds attached to it."

"By the gods!" The big man jumped back and made the sign against evil.

The other turned white as a ghost. "I told you there was something no' right about her!"

"No, please." Kira looked from one to the other. "You must help the woman. She'll drown if you don't."

"That's no' possible." The big man shook his head. "Eachann MacQueen's wife already drowned. Her life-rope broke when he lowered her down the cliffs to gather seabirds. Happened nigh onto a hundred years ago. The bards still tell the tale."

Kira's blood froze. She should've realized she was far-seeing the tragedy. But the woman's cries had sounded so real, and she'd tasted the man's terror, alive and coiling around her, squeezing the breath from her.

Somehow, having already gone so far back in the past, she hadn't expected to catch any glimpses of an even more distant time.

But apparently she'd guessed wrong, and although her two tormentors hadn't yet said the *w*-word, their opinion of her was plain to see.

"I am not a witch." She put up her hands, palms outward. "Please don't be afraid. I can explain everything."

The big man shook his head and took another step or two backward.

The other snorted. "Aye, and you will, but no' to the likes of us. 'Tis the laird who'll want to know how it is you saw something that happened before any of us were even born. Lest you're indeed a fairy or one of those other creatures we've been forbidden to call you."

"I'm neither," Kira protested, her eyes flying wide when the man pulled a dirk from beneath his belt and began prodding her down the corridor, away from Aidan's bedchamber.

"Where are you taking me?" she demanded, scooting along ahead of his jib-jabbing dirk all the same.

Bravado only went so far and hers stopped at a knife edge.

Apparently the two guardsmen's willingness to speak to her had also ceased. A glance over her shoulder showed them stony-faced and tight-lipped. Not that she needed any clues as to her destination. They were herding her into a narrow side corridor, a sloping, dank-smelling passage with a small, unpleasant-looking door at its end.

Kira's heart began to thunder and her mouth went dry.

She'd seen such passageways on her long-ago tour to Scotland and she knew exactly where they always led.

"O-o-oh, please!" Pride forgotten, she dug in her heels and braced her hands against the cold, slime-coated walls. A sharp prick of the dirk to her back got her moving again. "Please don't take me down there," she pleaded. "I won't bother any of you, I promise. Just let me go back to your laird's room. Please. You won't even know I'm around."

One of the men snorted.

The other opened the door and dragged her across its threshold. Mercifully darkness hid the things she knew she didn't want to see, but the *squish-squish* beneath her feet was bad enough. Especially since one of them was still bare. As for the scurrying sounds of what could only be rats, she'd just do her best to pretend she hadn't heard them. Or the *drip-drip* of what she was sure would be fouled and rancid water.

The smell was blinding.

She shuddered, thinking that now would be a very good time to be zapped out of medieval Scotland.

Instead, she found herself shoved into a pitch-black cell, the heavy-sounding door slamming shut behind her before she could even blink.

"Wait!" She spun around to pound on the door as one of the men slid home the drawbar. "Please listen to me!"

"Och, you'll be heard soon enough," one of the men assured her. "As soon as the laird returns from warring."

"*Warring?*" The ground dipped beneath Kira's feet. Medieval warfare could take ages. Heaven help her if he didn't return. "Where did he go? I thought you said he'd be back by evening?"

No answer came.

Panic gripping her, she strained to see through the small hole in the door, but it was impossible. The men were already gone, leaving her alone in Castle Wrath's dungeon.

So she did what Bedwells were famous for when faced with adversity.

She blew out a breath and began pacing, doing her best to not to cry.

## 7

About the same time, Aidan stood in the middle of Ardcraig's smoke-hazed great hall and struggled to ignore the softly crying women huddled together by the hearthside. Pale-faced and hand-wringing, they posed a trial to his already thin patience. He shot another glance their way, then scowled, dignity alone keeping him from thrusting his fingers in his ears. Truth was, he couldn't bear to hear any women cry, especially when he bore the brunt of causing their grief.

A weakness Conan Dearg's womenfolk were using to their fullest advantage.

Sure of it, he paced the length of his cousin's hall, cursing under his breath. Something was sorely amiss, and if his foe's teary-eyed females would cease their sniffling and sobbing long enough for him to think clearly, he'd surely figure out what the devil it was.

In any event, it had little to do with despairing women and even less with the sad state of Ardcraig's dingy, foul-smelling hall. O-o-oh, nae, it was the same niggling sense of *not-rightness* that had ridden him the last time he and his men had come here, the whole lot of them scouring Conan Dearg's keep from dungeon to parapets, searching pointlessly and making fools of themselves in the process. An embarrassment he wasn't going to endure again.

Especially if it meant having to admit failure to Kira.

Flashing a glance at the blackened ceiling rafters, he clenched his fists in frustration. Truth be told, he was also growing mightily weary of the sideways looks his men had been giving him ever since he'd left his chamber to join them that morn. Their silence rode his last nerve, but he'd deal with such annoyances later. After he'd routed his nefarious cousin and tossed him into Castle Wrath's dungeon.

The blackguard was here somewhere.

Aidan could smell him.

Furious that he hadn't yet found him, he strode over to the dais end of the hall, where Tavish and a few others guarded those of Conan Dearg's garrison who'd had the misfortune of sleeping too soundly when Aidan and his men burst into the hall, swords at the ready and flashing.

Surprisingly, though naked and weaponless, not a one amongst them seemed concerned. They certainly didn't appear sleep-befuddled. If anything, they looked smug. And that was what gave him such an uneasy feeling. Almost as if they'd let themselves be caught unclothed and defenseless, knowing any Highland chieftain with a smidgen of pride would refrain from wielding steel on an unarmed man.

Aidan blew out a breath and slid a glance at them, their bare-bottomed, muscle-bound bulk limned by torchlight and the reddish glow of Conan Dearg's hall fire.

Nary a one of them could meet his eye, each one glancing aside whenever he wheeled to fix him with a penetrating stare.

He shivered, drawing his plaid against a cold that had little to do with his cousin's crowded, untidy hall.

The bastard's men were hiding something.

And he was certain that *something* would prove to be Conan Dearg. The chill creeping up and down his spine left no room for doubt, even if they had searched everywhere. Half expecting to see the craven come crashing out of some hidden corner, swinging a battle-ax, he scanned the shadows, but saw only emptiness.

Even so, his every nerve ending hummed, his warrior instincts screaming with each indrawn breath. He tightened his grip on his sullied blade, his heart heavy with the need to stain his steel with the blood of kin.

Tavish stepped closer and put a hand on his shoulder. "Kin or no, the deaths couldn't be helped," he said, as always seeming to read Aidan's mind.

"The bastard is here," Aidan seethed, anger shielding him from the morning's horrors. "He's sacrificed his men, hiding behind them as he would a woman's skirts."

Tavish shrugged. "They should not have refused us entry." His gaze flicked to Aidan's sword, then to his own. Its blade, too, dripped red. Looking back at Aidan, his lip curled. "Better they died nobly than lying silent and feigning sleep."

Aidan arced a brow. "So you agree something is amiss?"

"To be sure." Tavish lifted his sword, eyeing its bloodied edge. "I just cannae grasp where Conan Dearg is hiding. We've upturned every stone and peered into each corner."

Aidan rubbed the back of his neck, thinking. "We're missing something, but it will come to me soon."

Frowning, he glanced again at the captured garrison men. Others were joining them, men brought in by the patrol he and Tavish had sent around Ardcraig's perimeter. Men now stripped of arms and clothes, just as their brethren from the hall. Their leader was nowhere to be seen. To a man, they stood sullen and defiant, some shifted restlessly, others exchanging edgy glances. All refused to talk, a stubbornness Aidan secretly admired, not that he cared to admit it.

Instead, he shoved his reddened sword into its scabbard and folded his arms. Sooner or later, one of them would let his guard slip, revealing the truth through a gesture or a glance, a word spoken too quickly. Moving to the high table, he settled himself in his cousin's chair, deigning to wait.

"You will grow cold, standing there naked," he observed, speaking to the men but pretending to study his knuckles. "Yet stand you shall, for I will have the bollocks cut from the first man who dares sit."

He leaned back in the chair, watching them. "I am a patient man. It willnae cost me to while here for days if need be. Indeed, I intend to stay put until one of you tells me where my cousin is keeping himself."

None of the men said anything, though several tightened their jaws and glared at him.

One spat into the floor rushes.

Another slid a nervous glance at the screens passage and the arched entry to the kitchens.

*The kitchens.*

At once, the hall tilted and dipped, spinning around Aidan as the answer hit him like a fist in the gut.

"Thor's thunder!" He leapt to his feet, his own words echoing in his head: *He's sacrificed his men, hiding behind them as he would a woman's skirts.*

He wheeled to face Tavish, triumph surging through him, hot and sweet. "I know where he is!" he cried, and slapped his mailed thigh. "The bastard is in his kitchens—disguised as a scullery wench!"

Tavish's jaw dropped. "By the gods! The unfortunate creature we saw sitting in a corner, querning grain. The big-boned woman with a head veil and her face turned away from us!"

Aidan nodded. "That'll be him. I'd bet my life on—"

"Your life is over!" One of Conan Dearg's men lunged forward, snatching the sword of Aidan's youngest guardsman. "'Tis you who shall die!"

"I think not." Aidan whirled with eye-blurring speed, his own sword already drawn as the man rushed him, swinging his blade in a stroke that would have been deadly against any other foe. As it was, steel met steel, the clang of clashing metal and angry snarls filling the air as Aidan parried the man's every slashing blow, then closed in, his arcing blade cutting a mortal wound in the other's side. The man folded in a pool of his own blood, his roar of pain echoing in Aidan's ears.

Jerking his sword free, he swept Conan Dearg's men with a heated stare.

"Should any others amongst you feel honor-bound to defend my cousin, come forward now or hold your peace," he challenged them, bile rising in his throat that he'd been forced to cut down yet another kinsman. "I'll see that you're given a blade and even a shield to counter my blows, but I'd have it a fair fight. No' the likes of what just transpired."

A sea of hostile gazes met his own cold stare, but no one made a move to accept his dare.

"You have no right to speak of fairness when you'd have us ride to Castle Wrath only to be slaughtered by your allies on the journey!" An older man pushed past the others, glancing hotly at the fallen guardsman before turning his glare on Aidan. "Your treachery is the reason we—"

"*My treachery?*" Aidan stared at him, a chill dread icing his blood. Suspicions too blasphemous to consider. He strode forward, clutching the man by the arms. "What is this you'd accuse me of? If we have our differences, every man within these walls is of my blood. Ne'er would I harm a kinsman without due reason."

He paused to shove the hair from his brow, taking heart in the doubt beginning to flicker in the man's eyes. "I see you know it," he said, releasing him. "I would think every man in these isles knows it as well."

"Your words spoke otherwise." The man rubbed his arms, his face darkening again. "One of Conan's riders intercepted the courier you sent to the MacKenzies of Kintail. Your missive fell into Conan's hands. He told us of your perfidy. How you planned to invite us to feast with you and how the MacKenzies would lay in wait, falling upon us when we passed through the narrow gorge not far from your holding." The man put back his shoulders, fury blazing in his eyes. "Your orders were to give no quarter, that not a one of us should be left alive."

Heat swept Aidan, scalding the back of his neck. He felt his face flush, well aware that his jaw was working, but no words were coming out.

"By the blood of all the gods," Tavish swore beside him, "ne'er have I heard a greater pack of lies."

Aidan's accuser set his mouth in a grim line, his gaze angry and unflinching. Behind him, others surged forward, their own faces red with outrage. "He speaks the truth," one of them called. "The MacKenzies were to ambush us—"

"Who amongst you saw these orders?" Aidan thundered, his temper fraying. "Speak up and prove your lies. Here and now, that I might dispel them."

"I will speak." A young man barely sporting a beard elbowed his way to where Aidan stood. Ignoring the disapproving glances of his fellow guardsmen, he straightened his shoulders and drew a great breath. "We did not see the missive," he said, his tone respectful. "We but believed what our lord told us he'd seen. He claimed his fury was so great upon learning of your plans, that he tossed the parchment into the hearth fire. All know of the strife between the two of you, so why should we have doubted his word?"

He paused to clear his throat, his cheeks reddening a bit. "I ask you, sir, would you not expect the same trust from your own men?"

"Indeed, I would." Aidan folded his arms and did his best not to scorch the louts with a listen-and-learn-from-this-lad glare. "I would know your name." He eyed the boy, judging him to be not more than fifteen summers. "Your name and if you are skilled with horses."

"I am Kendrew. I was orphaned and left at Ardcraig's gates, or so I was told." The boy flushed anew, his gaze darting to Conan Dearg's silent, set-faced men, then back to Aidan. "And I am good with beasts, aye. Especially horses," he added, shifting legs already longer than most of the men crowded near him. "I also know my letters and am handy with both a blade and a battle-ax."

Aidan nodded. "So-o-o, Kendrew"—this time he did flash a narrow-eyed glance at his men—"are you afraid of witches?"

The boy blinked, then shook his head. "I do not fear them, no. From my experience, the older ones are naught but healers and the young ones are often women who've fallen out of favor with powerful men. There are some who say my mother was such a woman, but I cannae believe she was bad. Were that so, I think I'd feel it here"—he paused to clap a hand over his heart— "though I'm sure there are many things in these hills we'll ne'er understand."

Under other circumstances, Aidan would have smiled. As it was, he made a swift decision. Turning to the man at his left, he ordered, "Mundy, see Kendrew's clothes returned to him and give him a blade." Before the oversized Irishman could protest, he took the boy's arm and drew him forward. "You, lad, shall hie yourself outside and help my men tend their horses. Then you'll return with us to Castle Wrath, where I have other duties in mind for you."

The lad's flush deepened, turning as bright a red as his hair. "But, sir, I cannae leave Ardcraig." He pulled back, clearly torn. "I am Conan Dearg's man. I—"

"Go, and dinnae make me regret my rashness." Aidan turned from him to Mundy. "See him into the bailey, then set others to gathering my cousin's horses and weapons. We'll be leaving anon. With Conan Dearg."

"No-o-o, please!" One of the sobbing women ran at him, clutching his sleeve. "You cannae take the laird from us! See you, I carry his child." She ran her hands down the front of her skirts, displaying the bulge at her middle. "Several of us are heavy with his seed," she added, gesturing to the clutch of females. "We need him—"

"My regrets." Aidan shook his head, wishing his cousin's manhood was long enough to be tied into a knot. Unfortunately, he knew from earlier years that it wasn't.

Frowning, he disentangled himself from the woman's grasp. A comely wench with fiery red hair and a lush, creamy bosom fair spilling from her low-cut bodice, she smelled fresh and sweet, her scent reminding him of Kira and what would happen to her should she land in his cousin's hands. He shuddered at the thought, thanking the gods he knew her to be safe and guarded in his own bedchamber.

"Please, sir," the woman pleaded again.

Aidan schooled his features, not wanting to frighten her.

"You shall have all you need and more, my lady," he promised, hoping she'd believe him. "My own patrols will guard your walls, and I will make certain your stores and fuel remain plentiful."

He didn't add that he would also attempt to find more suit-able *fathers* for her and the other maids' bairns.

"No one here will suffer—lest you repeat my cousin's mistakes," he added, turning back to the captive men. "I give you my word."

"Your word!" A swarthy man spat at his feet. "A snake's honor," he sneered. "We'll no' have your leavings."

Great shouts of agreement rose from his fellow men and the older man stepped forward again, anger rolling off him in waves. "Hear me, Aidan of Wrath, I am Walter of Ardcraig and have dwelt here since before your birth. I, too, share your MacDonald pride. You may well slay us here where we stand if you mean to leave us unable to defend ourselves. We do not want or need your men riding our lands." He glared at Aidan with withering scorn. "In your place, Conan Dearg would ne'er—"

"Let us speak plainly, Sir Walter." Aidan lifted his voice now that the woman had scurried back to her friends and young Kendrew was out of earshot. "My cousin would and has done many things—including deceiving you." Reaching beneath his plaid, he withdrew the rolled parchment, penned by Conan Dearg's own hand.

The blackguard's seal, cracked and broken, still dangled from the missive, attached to the end of a crumpled bit of red ribbon.

Red as blood and just as damning, as were the words inked inside.

"Read this and then tell me I've no right to put an end to my cousin's villainy once and for all time." Aidan thrust the scroll into the man's hands, then stepped back to wait. "Read it aloud if you will."

Walter of Ardcraig glanced at the scroll, looking up as quickly. His face was ashen. "My lord—this is beyond reason."

"Reason was ne'er one of my cousin's better points," Aidan agreed. "Nevertheless, I'd have his words known. Read on, and loudly enough so all may hear."

Looking miserable, Walter complied. A great silence descended when he finished. Again, Conan Dearg's men avoided Aidan's eye, but this time shame stained the faces of most. Regrettably, not all, so he took back the parchment and tucked it carefully into his plaid.

Then he cleared his throat. "Since my cousin intended to slay me and any of my clan who cared to accompany me to his feast, there will be some amongst you who knew of his plans," he said, his voice ringing. "Be glad I am not him. I willnae damn innocent men for the dark deeds of others, but I will keep your horses and your weapons until I've decided I have no further reason to distrust you. Or until those brave enough to throw yourself on my mercy step forward and admit your guilt."

"I cannae think of a man present who'd be party to the like," Walter spoke up again. "Not a one."

"Then so be it." Aidan gave him a curt nod. "I charge you to ensure I have no cause to return here in anger. If I must, not a stone will remain uncharred."

Before the other could reply, Aidan turned on his heel and strode for the screens passage and the arched kitchen entry, quickening his pace as he neared the torchlit steps spiraling down into Ardcraig's heart.

He took them two at a time, Tavish and a few others fast on his heels. At the bottom, his heart bounded as he found a cluster of his best guardsmen, standing at ease as they watched over the seemingly innocent kitchen scene. Young boys stirred the cook pots, and a straight-backed graybeard kneaded bread at a table laden with butter, milk, cheese, and other goods obviously meant for the evening meal. Conan Dearg still sat quietly in the corner, his back angled to door as he ground his grain, clearly unaware his hours were measured.

The old man looked up, his expression as tight as his posture. "Can we not be left in peace to tend our work?" he demanded, his voice thrumming with indignation. "Your guardsmen frighten the wee fire laddies and I'm too old for the likes o' such scrutiny!"

"Indeed," Aidan agreed, stepping deeper into the kitchen, the zinging *hiss* of his sword leaving its scabbard announcing his purpose. "We are not here to plague you or yon laddies, though you'd be wise to stand clear lest you get injured in the fray."

"There'll be no fray! Only your death!" Conan Dearg whipped his sword from beneath a pile of grain sacks and leapt to his feet. He lunged forward, overturning a bench as he swung wildly, his movements hampered by his skirts. "You'll no' leave here alive," he snarled, crashing into the table before he regained his balance and attacked again.

Aidan's mouth twitched. "But you shall—leave here alive," he shot back, easily sidestepping the other's charge. "You'll meet your end in my dungeon, where you'll need neither grain nor a woman's skirts."

Conan Dearg lunged again, his blade meeting Aidan's with an earsplitting *clang*. "You're mad," he bellowed, jumping back when his sword went flying. His face red with fury, he dived for the table, grabbing a kitchen knife, but Aidan was on him in a heartbeat, knocking the knife from his hand before he could even blink.

"Och, I'm no' mad." Aidan tossed aside his own sword, then slammed his fist into his cousin's nose. "I'm reminding you that no one threatens my people and lives to tell the tale." Another blow sent Conan Dearg to his knees, where he pressed a hand against his nose and gaped up at Aidan for a split second before sprawling facedown on the floor.

Satisfied, Aidan glanced at the grim-faced old man and the three wee boys. They cowered in a corner, their distress only deepening his anger. Wiping his hands on his plaid, he turned to Tavish.

"See that someone looks after them." He started toward the kitchen door arch, snatching up his sword on the way. "As for Conan Dearg, we are cousins no more. Have someone get him out of those skirts and properly clad. I'll no' have him shaming us on the journey back to Wrath."

He just hoped he didn't shame himself by yanking Kira into his arms and having his way with her the instant he returned.

After the ordeal he'd just put to an end, his need for her was that great.

❧

UNFORTUNATELY, when Aidan and his party approached Castle Wrath a few hours later, all such urges were swiftly replaced by an odd sense of ill ease. Nothing he could put his finger on, but something out of place all the same. A muscle began to twitch in his jaw, and a hard, tight knot started pulsing somewhere deep inside him.

Willing the twitching to cease, he adjusted his plaid to better shield him from the sudden cold he suspected only he'd noticed.

Were he a superstitious man, he might fear someone had hexed him, feeling such an uncanny chill twice in one day. As it was, and just for the sake of good Highland prudence, he shot a glance at Conan Dearg, half thinking he might be attempting to blast him with the evil eye, but the double-dyed blackguard sat straight in his saddle, his expression stony and his gaze fixed stubbornly on the back of the man leading his horse.

Tavish, his other men, and even young Kendrew appeared oblivious. Some of Aidan's younger kinsmen whooped and jested with each other before kicking their beasts into flat-out gallops in their eagerness to reach Castle Wrath's looming walls and the warm welcome of its great hall. The promise of a seat beside the fire, free-flowing ale, and a trencher piled high with fine roasted meat.

Perhaps, too, the celebratory feasting he'd sworn would mark Conan Dearg's capture.

Aidan frowned. He'd hoped to enjoy a bit of celebratory wooing, perhaps steal a few sweet kisses or more from his dream woman. A quiet evening spent in bliss that would help him banish the distastefulness of the morn.

Instead, he grew more wary the farther he rode along the steep and twisting track leading out to his cliff-girt home. And for no apparent reason, as the day had turned fair, with a fine deep blue sky and a bracing autumn wind. Not far ahead, Castle Wrath with its square keep and high curtain walls stood tall and proud as ever on its pinnacle of rock, Aidan's own banner raised and snapping in the wind. Everything looked as it should, and from what he could see of the landing beach and the little harbor below his stronghold, nothing was amiss there, either.

He turned in his saddle, craning his neck to make certain.

The seas were running steep, but his flotilla of longships and galleys appeared safely moored in the choppy, sun-dazzled water. Several of the galleys had been drawn up onto the shore for repairs and the fires of the beachside smokehouses looked well tended, with the usual number of men going about their business drying fish and mending nets.

Even so, something wasn't right.

Sure of it, he placed a hand over the worn leather scrip hanging from his sword belt, hoping the clutch of freshly picked heather tucked within would banish his dark thoughts and put him back in fine fettle.

But as so much of his luck seemed to be going of late, Tavish caught sight of the movement and cocked a knowing brow. "Think you a handful of crushed heather will win a lady's heart?" He edged his horse nearer, his implied superior knowledge of wooing only worsening Aidan's mood.

Leaning close, he lowered his voice, "You'd be better served to seat her next to you in the hall, pouring her wine and hand-feeding her fine morsels. Whispering sweet nothings in her ear and letting your men see—"

"It would seem my men see all too much!" Aidan shot back, glaring at him. "Since when can a man no' pause to tend nature's call without some long-nosed kinsman who claims to be his friend spying on him while he's at the deed?"

Tavish chuckled. "Mayhap since it was the first time I've known you that I've seen you call for such a halt on such a short journey?"

Aidan harrumphed. "Mayhap I drank too much watered-down ale before we left Ardcraig. The morn's doings left a bad taste in my mouth and I but sought to wash it away."

"Then why not tend such matters standing beside your horse as you usually do? Why sneak off behind a great outcrop where a particularly bonnie patch of heather is known to bloom?"

Aidan bit back a curse.

"I'm no' the only one who saw you," Tavish continued, making it worse. "Perhaps it's a good thing for the men to know you're so smitten. They've been worried about you."

"Grinding on my patience is what they've been doing." Aidan flashed him a dark look. "You most of all!"

"You wound me, my friend."

"Be warned! I'll do more than that if you dinnae soon leave me be," Aidan groused. He clamped his lips together, refusing to be goaded any further.

"Ho!" Tavish called, leaning over to thwack him on the shoulder not a breath later. "We've been seen. The drawbridge is down. But isn't that Geordie and Ross with the gatehouse guards? I thought you'd ordered them to guard your lady?"

"I did." Aidan's stomach dropped.

He stared ahead, squinting against the afternoon sun. Disbelief washed over him, but there could be no doubt. The drawbridge had been dutifully lowered and the gatehouse's heavy iron portcullis was rattling upward even as they approached, his best guardsmen hastening to swing open the second, inner gates.

As was expected of them.

Them, and *not* Geordie and Ross, two of his most trusted men.

The apparent lackwits who'd sworn they'd watch over Kira with their very lives.

A score of dire possibilities making his head reel, Aidan spurred his horse across the last stretch of rough, cattle-dotted grass. But when he thundered over the drawbridge's hollow-sounding planks and through the arched gatehouse pend, the only men crowding the guardroom doorways were the ones he'd assigned duty there.

His relief great, he swung down onto the cobbles, tossing his reins to a running stable lad. "The sun must've blinded us," he said, striding over to Tavish the instant his friend dismounted. "I should have known Geordie and Ross could be trusted not to leave their post."

"The sun?" Tavish snorted. "My vision has yet to fail me, though I'll agree I see nary a sign of them now." He jammed fisted hands on his hips and glanced round, wearing a frown as dark as some of Aidan's own. "What I *do* see isn't pleasing. Too many of your men are avoiding your eye."

"They will think more kindly of me when they see my cousin hauled into the dungeon."

Looking doubtful, Tavish glanced to where a handful of Aidan's stoutest guards were already escorting Conan Dearg across the bailey.

"Then let us make certain he's put in a cell he cannae escape," he said, starting after them.

Hesitating, Aidan threw a last look at the gatehouse, pleased to see his younger men crowding around Kendrew, Conan Dearg's man or no. He had no wish for the lad to witness his former liege laird being hustled away.

"Come you." Tavish signaled, waiting for him. "I want surety. We've both seen the bastard wriggle himself out of the worst scrapes and come back to jeer at us."

"He'll no' have the strength this time." Aidan kept pace with him. "No' living on salt beef and soured water."

"'Tis you who'll wither away on such rot—and in your own foul pit." Conan Dearg twisted round to sneer at him. Arrogant and contemptuous as always, he spat on the ground, showing no fear as Aidan's men tightened their grip, bundling him through the low-ceilinged door that led to the steep stone steps winding down into the dungeon.

"The sun will ne'er rise on the day you get the better of me," he boasted, squaring his shoulders to walk proud along the cold and dank passage.

"Some might say that day came this morn." Aidan fell in step beside him. "Salt beef and soured water ne'er sustained any man for long and I've yet to meet one who can live on bluster alone."

Conan Dearg snorted. "I am a hard man. Rancid victuals and darkness will not break me. Soon I shall prove it to you."

Aidan glanced over his shoulder, not surprised to see the dirk raised in Tavish's hand.

"That isn't the way," he warned, hoping his way wasn't a mistake. "Each hour he spends in his cell will repay one of the lives he's taken. We both know how great the number is. A swift death is a mercy he won't find here."

"I dinnae trust him." Tavish frowned, but thrust his knife back beneath his sword belt all the same. "He'll charm the water rats into bringing him cheese and wine."

Despite himself, Aidan chuckled, his spirits lifting for the first time that day. His cousin *was* a charmer. And even with a blackened eye and swollen nose, his looks were still dazzling enough to blind any woman who caught a glimpse of him.

That his flashing smiles and swagger would be lost on all but scuttling vermin and whate'er nameless creatures slithered in the matted rushes scattered across the dungeon floor, was a meet end for a man of Conan Dearg's vanity and stature.

Aidan opened his mouth to say as much, but shut it the instant they rounded a corner, entering the oldest and dankest part of the dungeon. A familiar smell hit him square in the face and he stopped short, blinking into the musty, dimly lit passage even as a pitiful, canine wail filled the darkness.

"Odin's balls!" Aidan hurried forward, almost slamming into his guardsmen and Conan Dearg, who'd stopped a few paces ahead, their passage blocked by the howling beast's great bulk. Aidan stared at his dog, his jaw slipping. "'Tis Ferlie!"

An absolute impossibility, for the dog feared the dark and especially avoided the dungeon.

Yet there he was, sitting on his shaggy haunches beside one of the blackened, iron-hinged doors, and clearly intent on staying there.

"Heigh-ho! So you've arranged a mourner for me." Conan Dearg laughed. "A pity you couldn't have chosen a less offensive creature. The beast stinks."

"He is worth a thousand of you." Reaching past him, Aidan snatched one of the rush lights out of its wall bracket and stepped forward, his surprise complete when the sputtering torch illuminated not just his afraid-of-the-dark dog, but two sets of masculine legs standing in the shadows behind Ferlie.

Legs, as a lifting of the torch revealed, that belonged to none other than Geordie and Ross.

"What mummery is this?" Aidan thrust the torch at them, his blood icing. "You swore to guard my lady, vowing to see to her safety even if the Valkyries themselves came calling for you."

"Ah. See you, we ... m'mmm ..." Geordie, the larger of the two twisted his hands, looking uncomfortable. "Your lady, sir, is—"

*His lady?* Conan Dearg looked on with interest. "I'd heard he'd gone off women."

"You'll hold your tongue or lose it," Tavish growled, his own face dark with anger as he rammed an elbow into Conan Dearg's ribs, then pressed the tip of his dirk beneath the lout's chin. "Be silent if you know what's good for you."

Scarce hearing them, Aidan felt his knees water, sure as the day that for whatever reason he'd found his two guardsmen and his dog in the deepest bowels of his dungeon, it had something to do with Kira.

Something he was not going to like.

"What has happened?" he demanded, laying on his sternest tone to mask the sick feeling spreading through his gut. "Where is she? And why aren't you guarding her?"

The two men exchanged glances, their misery palpable.

"Um," Geordie tried again, sweat beginning to bead on his brow.

Ross drew a deep breath. "We're guarding you, sir. Not the lass. She doesn't—"

"Guarding me?" Aidan's eyes flew wide.

"Aye, sir." Ross bobbed his head. "She did something that proved our suspicions about her. We brought her down here for the good of the clan," he added, speaking quickly now. "Her powers—"

"Have you lost your wits?" Aidan roared, blood thundering so loudly in his ears that he scarce heard himself shouting. "She's here? In the dungeon?"

The two guardsmen nodded.

Or so Aidan thought, whirling away before he could be sure. He'd already wasted too much time, should have guessed the truth the instant he'd spotted Ferlie and seen the fear in his guards' faces.

Fear for his dream woman squeezing his heart, he shoved past Tavish and leapt over Ferlie, fumbling at the heavy drawbar of the nearest cell door with fingers that had gone impossibly cold and clumsy.

"Kira!" He yanked at the drawbar. "Sweet lass, can you hear me?"

"The entire keep can hear you." Tavish grabbed the bar and helped him slide it aside. "Go fetch your lady," he said, shoving Aidan into the cell. "I'll see to Conan Dearg and the others."

But his lady wasn't anywhere to be fetched.

The cell was empty.

Then, peering into the darkness, he saw her standing in a corner, her shoulders straight and her hands clasped tightly before her, her eyes squeezed shut.

"Kee-*rah*!"

Her eyes snapped open. "Aidan!" She ran at him, her arms outstretched. "Thank God! I didn't think you'd ever get back!"

"I'm here now." He crossed the cell in two quick strides,

catching her when she launched herself at him. "Shush, lass, I have you."

He pressed her head against his shoulder, absorbed her shiver, then kissed her hair, not caring that Tavish and the others gawked through the door.

Ferlie barked and pushed past them, hurling himself at their legs, his tail wagging.

"He followed when they brought me here." Kira reached down to pet the shaggy, tail-thumping beast. "He's been outside the door the entire time."

Aidan glanced at the aged dog, rubbed his ears. Only his pride and the knowledge that his cousin looked on kept him from acknowledging that his dog had guarded Kira better than his men.

There'd be time enough later to reward Ferlie and have words with Geordie and Ross.

Time, too, to discover the reason they'd put her into the dungeon. What terrible thing she'd done to give two burly Highlanders such a dreadful fright.

Heaven help them both if he didn't like the answer.

———————

## 8

"*I want to go home.*"

Not sure if she'd spoken aloud or just thought the words, Kira took a deep, calming breath. She needed calm. The backs of her eyes stung, her misery reaching new heights as she stood near the hearth of Aidan's bedchamber and watched a parade of young, flush-faced boys carry pails of steaming water into the room. Carefully avoiding looking at her, each one tipped his burden into a wooden bathing tub that looked exactly like a sawed-in-half wine barrel.

A linen-lined wine barrel, praise God for small mercies.

The last thing she needed was a medieval splinter in her behind.

Her ordeal in Castle Wrath's dungeon had been torture enough. Almost as bad was having Aidan toss her over his shoulder and charge out of the cell, pounding up the stairs with her and then flying through his great hall, knocking over benches and sending people jumping out of their way, poor Ferlie loping after them and barking furiously at anyone who didn't leap aside quickly enough.

She cringed just remembering. It'd been a humiliation she

wasn't sure she could swallow.

Not because he'd rescued her.

And not even because he'd gone so caveman wild.

Far from it—she'd rather liked that part. All wind-torn and travel-stained, with his sword clanking and eyes ablaze, he could have burst from the pages of a book about ancient clan warfare. But when he'd raced through the hall, cursing and shouting for a bath to be readied for her, his rubber-necked kinsmen had gaped at her, bug-eyed and slack-jawed, every last one of them looking on as if he'd run mad and she was a two-headed alien.

Maybe even a three-headed alien.

And now she was supposed to take a bath.

Kira frowned and folded her arms. She didn't want a bath. She wanted to go home. Back to the twenty-first century where she belonged and where she could moon all over books about medieval Scotland and framed secondhand Edinburgh castle tea towels, living in a fantasy that suited her so-o-o much better than the real thing.

Across the room, the best *real thing* in this nightmare threw off his plaid and unlatched his sword belt, then sent the last of the pink-cheeked water boys on their way, closing and bolting the door behind them. Turning, he strode over to her, no longer looking so fiercely angry, but not smiling either.

"This could be your home, Kee-*rah*," he said, his words letting her know she had spoken aloud. "I know well that you love this place. That it means as much to you as to those of us who have called it our own since before time. When you walk here, you see more than rock and heather and mist. Your heart recognizes the true spirit of these hills." He paused, studying her so intently that she caught her breath. "I know this from our shared dreams."

Kira swallowed, not wanting to think about their dreams just now. Or her great passion for Scotland. Last she'd heard being a card-carrying Scotophile didn't include half the things she'd endured since landing here.

Looking down, she fussed at the folds of her skirts, still finding them as cumbersome and awkward as she had the moment she'd first slipped into them. Even worse, the bottom six inches or so were soiled with goop from the dungeon. As were her feet, since somewhere during the awful journey down there, she'd lost the blasted *cuarans*.

"Come, lass, you cannae deny you belong here." He sounded sure of it. "I've seen you go misty-eyed just watching cloud shadows drift across the heather."

Kira dug her toes into the floor rushes. "I did love it here," she admitted, glancing up at him. "In my time and, yes, in our dreams. But the reality is wa-a-ay different and it scares me."

"Ach, lass." He smoothed the hair back from her face. "Surely you have seen that I willnae let aught happen to you?"

She blinked, hating the way her throat was thickening. "Did you know," she began, "that they brought me food when I was in the dungeon?"

When he only looked at her, his expression unreadable, she went on. "A bowl of slaked oats, I think you call it. Porridge. It didn't look too bad, but I couldn't eat, so I set it in a corner. Within minutes, three mice crawled up out of the floor rushes and ate it." She paused to moisten her lips. "Or rather, they would have, if the biggest rat I've ever seen in my life hadn't appeared to claim the porridge for himself."

He took her hand, twining their fingers. "The like will ne'er happen again. I promise you."

She bit her lip. "How can you? It's impossible for you to be at my side every minute, and your men don't like me. They're afraid of me and think I'm a—"

"Then we shall change their minds." He drew her close, tightening his arms around her. "You already have a strong champion in Tavish, and I've a promising young lad in mind to give duty as your personal guard."

"If only it were that simple."

"I will make it so."

Kira tried to smile, but her smile muscles wouldn't cooperate.

Instead, she sighed and rested her head against his shoulder. "You are a medieval warrior chieftain," she began, trying to ignore how good his arms felt around her. "You live in a world of clan feuding, sword fights, and cattle raids, a time when a mere bad tooth or ingrown toenail could kill someone, not to mention battle wounds and childbirth. You have enough to deal with without worrying about—"

"Do you not trust me to care for you?" He pulled back to look at her, his dark eyes narrowing. "I've dealt with the things you name since I drew my first breath, as has any other Highland chieftain worthy of the style. What I need"—he paused, holding her gaze—"is for you to relax and then tell me what happened with Geordie and Ross. Only when I understand what frightened them enough to take you to the dungeon can I dash the fear from their hearts. Your bath will—"

"I don't want a bath."

"It will soothe you," he countered, the richness of his burr almost letting her believe him.

Smooth, husky, and deep, his voice slid through her, its soft Highland beauty seducing her, making her forget where and *when* she was, lulling her into doing whatever he asked.

Almost.

Biting her lip again, her gaze snapped to the *wine barrel*, its steaming water scented and waiting. Truth was, she did want a bath. Desperately. But taking one meant getting undressed, and she was suddenly more aware than ever that she wasn't wearing any underwear.

She didn't need her sixth sense to know that even if Aidan turned his back, he'd peek before she could clamber into his wooden bathing tub.

He had that look about him tonight.

The wild, hot-eyed-predator look that could mean only one

thing, no matter how hard he was clearly trying to play the chivalry card.

As if to prove it, he put his hands on her shoulders, easing her down onto a stool next to the bathing tub before she could even splutter a protest. The determined gleam in his eyes holding her in place, he knelt before her, reaching for a basin and a still-filled pail of heated water.

"Give me your foot." He glanced at her as he filled the basin. "It willnae do for you to get into the bathing tub until your feet are clean."

Kira tensed. "I can wash them myself. You needn't help me."

In answer, he cocked a brow and flipped her skirts up over her knees. Making it worse, he flashed an arrogant smile, then clamped a strong hand around her left ankle, lifting her foot and placing it in the basin.

Frowning, she tried to jerk from his grasp, but he only slanted her a look of lairdly admonishment, his fingers tightening on her like an iron-cast ankle bracelet.

"You can see to yourself once we have you settled in your bath."

She lifted her chin. "There will be no *we* about it. If I use the bathing tub, you can leave the room."

"Och, you will bathe," he said, dipping a soap-smeared cloth into the water and then plunging it between her toes, scrubbing vigorously. "I shall keep my back turned."

"I don't trust you."

"Then you shall have to learn. As I, too, am trying to do." He looked up, fixing her with a long, level stare as he carefully washed the arch of her foot. "Do not think it is easy for me to accept a place called All-den, Pen-seal-*where'er*, tiny flying disks, and zip-*hers*."

Kira almost smiled, remembering his expression when her button went sailing through the air. "Okay. You've made your point, but no peeking."

"I do not need to peek," he observed, soaping her other foot. "I already know every inch of you. Including a certain bit of sweetness I can see just now."

Kira's eyes flew wide. "What do you mean *a bit of sweetness*?"

He only smiled.

Her own face flaming, she looked down, embarrassment crashing through her when she saw that her gown had slid much higher up her thighs than she'd realized. Even worse, she'd been sitting with her knees open.

"O-o-oh!" She jumped off the stool. "I don't want to talk about our dream-times and what you think you know about me." Shaking out her skirts, she frowned. "You can't compare something from a dream with the reality—"

"Nae, you cannot," he agreed, standing. "The real you fires my blood a thousand times more than any dream vision." He captured her chin and kissed her. Hard, rough, and fast. "Dinnae you e'er forget that, even when we must speak of unpleasant things."

Kira angled her head, regarding him in the flickering glow of the hearth fire. "I think I've had enough unpleasantness for one day."

"Even so," he said, his expression serious, "there are matters we must discuss."

"Does it have to be now?"

He nodded, and then lowered his head to kiss her again, this time gently.

When he straightened, she pulled away, her heart thundering. There was something both unsettling and electrifyingly delicious about being kissed when she wasn't wearing any panties, and now wasn't the time to go all hot and tingly. A sensation that vanished when he began pacing between the *wine barrel* and the window embrasure.

Without breaking stride, he slanted her a dark look, all fierce warrior chieftain. "Remove your soiled clothes now, before the water cools," he said, seven hundred years of authority shimmering all over him. "While you bathe, I would hear about your morning. You must tell me what frightened my men."

"What I must do is find a pair of glittery red shoes," Kira snapped, her fingers busy at her gown's lacings.

He stopped to look at her. "Glittery red shoes?"

"Never mind."

"Ah, lass, but I do." He stood watching her, another frown settling on his brow. "You must've said something the like to Geordie and Ross. Perhaps mentioned this future of yours, or the Na Tri Shean?"

"It was neither, but close."

He arched a brow. "That willnae do, sweetness. No' when your *whate'er-it-was* made my men gibber with fright."

"I didn't mean to scare them," she returned. "I just wanted them to save what I thought was—oh, no!" She gasped when the bodice lacings ripped and both her gown and overdress fell open to her waist.

Aidan's eyes darkened with *that look* again, his men's fright clearly forgotten as his gaze snapped to her breasts. Planting her hands on her hips, she glared at him, not needing to look down to know that her thin excuse for a medieval undershift hid absolutely nothing. The thing was practically transparent. Just as bad, the room's chill was tightening her nipples. She could feel them thrusting against the delicate linen, just as she could feel the heat of his stare.

An intense, heavy-lidded perusal that only made them pucker all the more.

She bristled, irritated by his effect on her. "You said you'd turn your back."

"And so I shall." He reached to glide his knuckles down the curve of her cheek. "Now hie yourself into yon bathing tub, lest I forget my vow to woo you properly."

The words spoken, he wheeled around, clasping his hands as

casually as possible behind his back and fixing his stare on the
night coming down outside his bedchamber's tall, arch-topped
windows. He also tried to close his ears to the furious rustling of
cloth and the sloshing of water as she rid herself of her garments
and climbed into the bath.

"So-o-o," he began, turning only when he was certain it was
safe to do so, "what was it that you wished Geordie and Ross to
save?"

She looked at him, clouds of steam from the bathwater rising
around her like tendrils of fairy mist. "A drowning woman," she
said, jutting her jaw as if she suspected he wouldn't believe her. "I
saw a woman's death—apparently one that took place nearly a
hundred years ago. She had seabirds tied to a rope about her
waist and—"

"Her name was Annie," Aidan finished for her, his innards
twisting. "Her tale is a sad one and well known in these parts. She
was married to Eachann MacQueen, a farmer who scratched a
living off Wrath Isle's barren slopes, sustaining his family by
lowering his wife down the cliffs to gather seabirds and their eggs
whene'er hunger drove them to such privations."

"Whoever she was, I saw her." She peered at him, her naked,
soapy breasts jiggling as she gripped the edge of the bathing tub
and leaned forward. "I didn't see her as a ghost or because of
witchcraft, but as a glimpse of the past. The *once-was*, as my gift of
far-seeing reveals to me."

Aidan frowned and began pacing again, too aware of the
rivulets of water streaming over her full, well-rounded breasts to
wrap his mind around something that happened so long ago, and
what it had to do with her and his gog-eyed, clack-tongued
kinsmen.

"So you are a seeress." He paused by one of the windows and
stared across the dark water at the black, serrated cliffs of Wrath
Isle. "The sight is common hereabouts and shouldn't have fashed
my men," he said, keeping his back to her. "I'll wager they fear

you because of the way you appeared atop the gatehouse arch. We must find a way to explain that. Then they will accept you."

Behind him, Kira sighed. "I don't have second sight," she argued. "At least not if you mean divination and prophecy. I told you, I'm a far-seer. Sometimes I'm able to look back in time, that's all. Now I have gone back in time and that's the only explanation I can give you. That, and that your gatehouse arch is a portal to the past."

Aidan snorted before he could help himself.

"Scoff all you will," she tossed at him. "If you have a better theory, I'm all ears. Fact is, in my time, that arch of yours was half buried in the grass, its top covered with moss and ferns. I was sitting on it, having a picnic, when suddenly my world vanished and I saw your men running across the bailey at me."

Aidan considered telling her he wasn't dim-witted enough to believe the like, but decided against it. The matter of their dream encounters and her zip-*her* made it difficult for him to doubt her.

Not to mention the wee *flying disk*.

He shuddered, his head beginning to throb with the immensity of it all. "Ach, what a tangle," he muttered, turning from the window and going to his table, where he poured a generous cup of his strongest ale—a fine, rich brew flavored with just a hint of heather. He took a long swallow, then wiped his mouth on his sleeve.

"I will not lie to you, Kee-*rah*." He swirled the ale in his cup, looking down into its frothy, honey-colored depths. "What you claim is no' easy to accept. Even when my heart tells me you speak true."

"Then you believe me?"

Aidan let out his breath slowly. "Let us say I can think of no other explanation," he said, setting down the ale cup. He wasn't about to admit how much the zip-*her* and the little disk she called a button bothered him. Instead, he folded his arms and tried to look worldly.

She put her shoulders back. "There's not another explanation because I've told the truth."

"Be that as it may, my men will have to be told a different tale."

Her brow furrowed at that, but before she could protest, he raised a silencing hand. "We will put it about that one of my allies brought you here, spiriting you onto the gatehouse arch as a jest. Many of my friends are bold enough to have attempted such foolery," he said, thinking in particular of the Barra MacNeils.

Hebridean devils to a man, and great ravishers of women as well, any one of his friends from the Isle of Barra could have done the deed. Best of all, if ever his tall tale reached the MacNeils, they'd be quicker to throw back their heads and roar with laughter than draw their swords and demand he redeem their honor.

O-o-oh, aye, the MacNeils were the answer.

His aching head beginning to feel better already, he smiled.

Kira Bedwell frowned.

She'd wrapped her arms around her knees and sat staring at him from the bathing tub, clearly not agreeing with a thing he'd suggested. "It means a lot to me that you don't think I'm a witch," she said, her tone proving it, "but whether you believe me or not, I am still out of place here. I—"

"Thor's thundery knuckles!" Aidan crossed the room in a flash. "Your place is with me and has been since that long ago day we first glimpsed each other. If there be any truth between us, it is that." He frowned down at her, seeing not her nakedness but the stubborn set of her jaw. "Come, lass, you know it as well as—"

"*If there be any truth between us* are words that prove there can be nothing between us," she returned, staring right back at him. "Just like 'Thor's thundery knuckles.' People don't talk like that where I come from, and they sure don't talk like me here." She looked down then, plucking at the tub's linen lining. "Don't you see? Much as I would have wished it otherwise, my being here is a mistake. A weird quirk of fate—a slip in time—that should only have been a fleeting glance. I'd hoped to catch a glimpse of you in your hall, but in my heart I wanted more."

She looked up again, her eyes shining. "I think my longing was so strong that it caused a *bump* in our destinies, sort of like when the needle of an old-fashioned record player skipped to the wrong groove."

Aidan dropped on one knee beside the bathing tub. He didn't understand all the words she'd used, but he knew well enough what she meant. "The fates do not err," he told her. "Leastways no' Gaelic ones. If they saw fit to send you here, you can be sure that was their intention."

To his annoyance, she didn't look convinced.

Just the opposite, she snatched back her hand when he reached for it, hoping to gentle her with a soft kiss to her palm.

"I'm not so sure ancient Gaelic gods have much control over Americans," she said, tucking her hands beneath her bent knees. "We're always told we make our own beds, and this one"—she glanced around his sumptuous, candlelit room—"is a bed I'm not supposed to be sleeping in. Especially when my being here is causing you so much grief. I can't allow—"

"*Grief?*"Aidan shot to his feet, pulling her up with him. Scowling, he lifted her from the tub, then swirled a linen drying cloth around her shoulders as he stood glowering at her. "Misery was the long years without you. The empty nights when I wondered if you were indeed naught but a dream. I thought my heart would split when Tavish carried you into my hall and I recognized you."

She gave him a look that made his head start to pound again. "You looked furious when you saw me," she said, clutching the drying cloth to her breasts. "In medieval-speak, you'd probably say black-browed and ready to flay me to ribbons."

"No' you, lass. I was ready to punish my men—as I've told you," he reminded her. "I was wroth with them for their treatment of you."

"And that's the very reason I must leave." She moved to stand before the hearth fire, turning her back to its warmth. "I can't stay on and see my presence cause such disruption in your hall. If I'm gone—"

"If you are gone, there will be no hall, for I should spend my days searching for you." He went to her, putting his hands on her shoulders. "My men would become rovers, broken men without direction—"

"You're trying to make me feel good, but it won't work." She ducked away and snatched up another linen towel, using this one to dry her hair. "If I stayed on, you'd be miserable. You'd end up spending every night like this one, stomping about and scowling, grilling me because one of your men misunderstood something I said or did."

*Stomping and scowling?*

Aidan shoved a hand through his hair. Was he truly guilty of the like? Half certain that he was, he snapped his brows together, his head now throbbing in earnest. Frowning as well, he turned on his heel and did his best not to stomp to the window. Once there, he drew a deep breath of the bracing sea air and scowled all he wished.

Truth was, it felt good.

But he didn't need Tavish Long-nose to tell him that black moods and storming through halls weren't ways to win a lady's heart. What he needed was a clear head and a plan. A new approach, guaranteed to impress.

Stepping closer to the window, he braced his hands on the cold stone ledge and took another deep breath. And another. The chill air would surely help him think. Hopefully, when the answer came, it would be one he could stomach.

Something that wouldn't make him look foolish.

Not that he'd allow such a trivial matter to keep him from gaining his heart's desire.

He sighed. It was amazing what love could do to a man.

# 9

Aidan stood at his bedchamber window, no longer looking out at the night's mist and murk but down at his own two hands. Still planted firmly on the broad stone ledge of the window arch, they were hands a man could be proud of. Strong, large, and capable, they'd swung swords, wielded axes, and were no strangers to hard, back-breaking work.

And, it finally occurred to him, neither were they the hands of a man incapable of claiming the woman he wanted.

The *only* woman he wanted.

Despite the small matters of All-den, Pen-seal-*where'er,* and his men making the sign against evil each time she walked past. The gods knew, he'd fought and besieged greater battles. With one last gulp of the cold night air, he straightened his back and turned, ready to take on this new challenge.

A formidable foe, she watched him from near the hearth. Across the length of his chamber, to be sure, but after the distance of dreams, so close he could taste her. Without doubt, he could smell her. The scent of clean, freshly washed woman filled the room, a fine, heathery scent laced with just enough *her* to befuddle his senses and torment him.

Truth was, she drove him beyond reason.

She met his gaze steadily, her sleek flame-bright hair gleaming in the torchlight, the drying cloth still clutched tight around her. The thin, damp cloth clung to her, molding her full, round breasts and tempting him with the sweetness of her shapely hips and thighs.

Even more distracting, she was tapping one foot, the rapid movement making her breasts jig, while the flush of irritation on her face only drew his attention to her soft, kissable lips.

Tiny droplets of water glistened on her shoulders and as he watched, one pearled and trickled down her breasts, disappearing beneath the knotted cloth.

When a second droplet did the same, his mouth went dry.

"A plague on it," he hissed, trying hard not to groan or frown. Clenching his hands, he struggled to ignore the sudden heavy pounding at his loins. He raked a hand through his hair, blotting all thought of her lush, warm curves, the fragrant, heated place hidden between her thighs.

A slick, succulent delight he couldn't wait to get his hands on.

His hands, and more.

Much more.

"Return my clothes, and I'll be on my way," she said then, her words dashing cold water on his ponderings. "If the gatehouse arch brought me here, it can surely take me back."

"Och, lass, I fear it is too late for that," he said, frowning after all. With long strides, he crossed to her. "There are clothes a-plenty for you here. Fine clothes. Raiments my sister left behind when she wed a Border chieftain. I'll also have new ones made for you. As for the gatehouse arch, I cannae let you near it. Leastways unescorted. No' that I think there's aught amiss with it, but—"

"What is this?" Her eyes flashed. "First you take my clothes and riddle me with questions, and now you'd deny me access to the one place—"

He grabbed her shoulders, silencing her with a fierce, bruising kiss. "Ach, lass," he panted, releasing her. "It was my hope to woo you this e'en. My questions were so I can understand what we're facing. I need to know so we can find a way to make things work, together."

"You have a strange way of wooing a woman," she said, hitching up the drying cloth where it'd dipped a bit.

"Perhaps because I dinnae do the like every day," Aidan shot back, his frown blacker than ever. "I have ne'er met a woman like you. One I so wished to please. A future woman."

She blinked, then sank onto a stool before the fire. "You wished to please me because I come from the future?"

"Nae!" Aidan almost roared. "Because you are *you*. And dinnae tell me it's no' possible to know you that well. Sweet lass, I have lived with you day and night for years now, though I cannae explain what brought us together."

He paused, looking at her deeply. "All that matters is that we *are*. No' how we came to be."

She blinked again and bit down on her lip, her eyes sparkling suspiciously. "You sound like you mean that, MacDonald."

"I do. More than anything," he owned, remembering the handful of heather tucked into his scrip.

Wondering why he hadn't thought of it before, he wheeled about and strode across the room, making for his discarded plaid and sword belt.

"Here!" he announced, seizing the ratty-looking leather pouch and waving it at her. "Now I shall prove to you how I meant us to spend this e'en."

Kira swallowed, not sure she wanted to know.

She'd already resigned herself to leaving him. If she even could. She took a deep breath, forcing herself not to think about how much she would miss him. She would even miss his world, wine barrel baths, stewed eels, and all. Shivering with a cold she suspected had little to do with the room's temperature, she scooted her stool closer to the fire and focused on keeping a neutral look on her face. What she needed to do was concentrate not on how crazy she was about him but on how much better off he'd be once she was gone.

A feat she was mastering beautifully until he plunged his hand into his ancient scrip and withdrew a fistful of crumpled purplish-brown heather, thrusting his prize beneath her nose with as much glowing pride as if he were offering her a dozen long-stemmed roses.

"O-o-oh, no," she cried, her heart squeezing.

She pushed slowly to her feet, her every refusal melting away as he pressed the crushed heather into her hands, closing her fingers around the dried, brittle stems.

Closing her fate, too, for the instant her fingers tightened on the heather, she knew herself lost. She opened her mouth to thank him, but shut it as quickly, the thickness in her throat making it impossible to speak.

She looked down at the heather, touching a finger to the tiny, bell-like blooms until they began to swim before her eyes. Blinking furiously, she pressed the gift to her breast, more delighted than if he'd showered her with diamonds and gold. Love, happiness, and wonder swept her, filling her with sweet, golden warmth that chased all else from her mind.

Certainly the Castle Apartments in distant Aldan, Pennsylvania, and even her love's grumbling, grim-faced men and their giant, porridge-eating rats. The three mice that surely lived with a gazillion twitchy-nosed pals beneath the dungeon's matted floor rushes. Even those great annoyances of her own time, every hapless landscape worker who ever wielded a leaf blower.

They were all banished. Gone, as if they'd never been.

Nothing mattered but the tall, fierce-looking Highlander standing so proudly before her. He took a step closer, his dark eyes watching her, waiting.

"You brought me heather." She looked at him, her voice cracking. "Th-thank you."

Aidan humphed, her pleasure affecting him more than was seemly. Tavish, that great gowk of a self-professed wooing expert, would no doubt place his hand o'er his heart and declare himself ready to lay all the heather in Scotland at his fair maid's feet.

He was so besotted, he'd throw in every Highland sunset and all the stars in the heavens if such were possible. As it was, he reached for her, gently brushing his lips back and forth over hers, letting his kisses and the fine heat crackling between them say the fancy words he couldn't.

As if she heard them, she slid her arms around his neck and twined her fingers in his hair. "I know the significance of heather," she said, her eyes shining. "You wouldn't have given me such a gift if you didn't care."

"*Care*?" He jerked, his entire body tight with longing, so ready and needful he could scarce breathe. "Have you no' been listening to me? Lass, I burn for you," he said, bracketing her face and kissing her. "I've waited for you so long."

"We've both waited, but we're together now." She touched his face. "Maybe we really were meant to be."

He lifted a brow. "No more talk about returning to that future place beyond our dreams?"

Kira shook her head.

He stood quiet for a moment, the night breeze coming in the windows riffling his dark, unbound hair, the look in his eyes letting her know there'd be no going back.

Her throat was burning now, her emotions almost overwhelming her, but she kept her back straight, her chin lifted. Not that it was easy. She wanted to lean into him, let him catch and hold her forever. She'd almost swear he made her soul tremble. She knew she could still feel his kisses, the shivery tingles each one sent spilling through her.

She just needed surety.

As if he knew, he shook his head slowly. Then he reached to touch her lips, her hair.

"I will ne'er let you go, Kee-*rah*." He glanced at the crumpled heather, then back at her. "You say you know the significance of heather," he said, watching her carefully. "Do you also know that if a woman accepts it from a man, she has as much as bound herself to him?"

"No, I didn't," Kira admitted, her heart pounding. "But it wouldn't have made any difference."

His eyes lit with triumph. "Ach, lass, you will ne'er regret it. I promise you."

She said nothing, sure she'd regret it indeed, but the heather felt so right in her hand. Almost like magic, something changed the instant she'd curled her fingers around the little clutch of blooms, the tiny purplish flowers not just making her heart soar, but giving her courage and hope.

The faith to believe in miracles.

*No, the impossible*, a voice inside her chided. Ignoring it, she took a deep breath, the warning spiraling away when he pulled her to him and slanted his mouth over hers, kissing her until the room spun.

When he released her, she gasped and touched a hand to her lips. No man had ever kissed her so hotly, dragging her hard against him as he'd plundered her, slaking his hunger for her as if he wanted to devour not just her lips but the very essence of her.

She drew a shaky breath. "O-o-oh, my."

He gave her a slow smile as he took the heather from her and placed it on the table. "That, sweetness, was only the beginning," he vowed, the roughness in his voice exciting her, the simmering heat in his eyes making her tingle with anticipation. "I have told you how much I want you. Now I will show you."

His burr turned her knees to jelly. Surely a sexier, more provocative man had never walked or breathed. And the trappings of his medieval bedchamber only heightened his appeal.

Fire glow bathed him in a sensual, gold-flickering light, while the impressive length of his broadsword and his massive curtained bed reminded her of other huge things he had. Everything about him excited her, and she burned to rub herself against him, forgetting her cares and just running her hands over every hard, muscle-ripped inch of him.

Especially his most magnificent inches, the most impressive such inches she'd ever seen.

She flicked a glance in that direction, a very different kind of heat scalding her cheeks. The old adage *tilt in a kilt* flashed through her mind and her face flamed hotter. *Tilt* didn't begin to describe it. If the real Aidan was anything like the dream one, she might climax just looking at him. He was that much of a man and she wanted him badly. Heaven help her when he touched her.

Really touched her.

"Have you studied me enough, Kee-*rah*?" His eyes darkened as he grasped his tunic and pulled it over his head, tossing it aside. "I hope so, for I would now look upon you."

Not taking his gaze off her, he rid himself of the rest of his clothes faster than she could blink. At ease in his nakedness, he flashed her a smile and stretched his arms above his head, cracking his knuckles.

"That's better," he said, tossing his hair over his shoulders. "Look your fill, lass, for I'm no' shy. But have done quickly for I cannae wait much longer."

"Look?" She stared at him, doing just that. "I can hardly breathe."

His smile turned wicked. "That's good, lass. Then I shall give you a few moments more," he said, clasping his hands behind his back, his steely self-control clearly not extending to a certain very masculine part of him.

Kira's eyes widened as her gaze settled there, a fierce need stirring deep inside her. She watched in amazement as he ran even harder beneath her stare. Her mouth went dry. Nothing she remembered from their dream lovings had prepared her for this.

She'd been right—*tilt* didn't begin to cover it.

He could be some mythic Celtic sex god and, heaven help her, the longer she gaped at his blatant male perfection, all she could think about was her overlarge breasts and the not-bad-but-definitely-there roll at the top of her belly.

"Oh, dear," she blurted, tightening the knot in the drying cloth as discreetly as she could. Her breasts still swelled over the top of the wrap, but at least her tummy and her hips were covered.

Turning away, she dipped her hand in the bathwater, twirling her fingers in it as cheerily as she could. "The water's still warm," she said, risking a glance at him. "If you don't mind sharing, it just occurred to me that maybe you'd like a bath, too?"

His smile faded. "I had a quick wash at a spring when I collected your heather. It was enough."

"You might enjoy a real bath more."

He seized her water-swirling hand and pressed a kiss to her fingers. "You know well what I'd enjoy. What I need."

She pulled back her hand and scooted around the tub. "Still, I think—"

"Odin's bones!" He was on her in a heartbeat, swooping her off her feet and carrying her across the room. "Have done with such nonsense," he said, lowering her onto his bed. "You ought to know how much I desire you."

Kira pulled a pillow on top of her belly. "I do know..." She trailed off, remembering how he'd almost worshipped her curves in their dreams, calling her lush and claiming that her soft, warm body would fire his blood on even the coldest Highland nights. How he'd smoothed his hands all over her as he said the words, kissing her everywhere. Even so, this was now and no dream, and her belly was definitely a tad too soft.

Angry that she hadn't taken better care of herself, she dug her fingers into the pillow, holding it firmly in place.

"What is bothering you, Kee-*rah*?" He glanced at the table, then back at her. "Shall I bring you an armful of heather next time? I will if a few sprigs weren't enough to properly woo you."

Her heart dipped. "I loved your heather. One sprig would've melted me. It isn't that." She paused, struggling to find the right words. "It's that I've gained a bit of weight since the last time we dreamt together."

His brows shot upward. "By all the ancients! Think you I'd want a stick-woman in my bed?"

"No, but—"

"Ne'er have I desired another woman more than you." His gaze slid across her breasts and her pillow-padded belly, then swept down her thankfully good legs. "Alas," he added, rubbing his chin with the back of his hand, "it would seem I must prove it to you."

He stepped closer, pure male heat pouring off him.

Her pulse jumping, she watched as he pried her fingers from the pillow. He set it carefully aside, then stood back and folded his arms.

"Now the drying cloth." He waited, every fierce, muscled inch of him daring her to defy him.

No, every fierce, muscled, *scarred* inch, for standing this close and beneath the blaze of a well-burning wall torch, she could see a scoring of faint, silvery scars winking from his hips and thighs. A rather fresh one slashed the side of his left arm. Sword marks, Kira knew. Battle tokens that she'd not noticed in their dreams. Not surprising, he wore them well, each one only making him more irresistible.

Dark, dangerous, and bearing marks of medieval warfare.

Kira swallowed, the notion making her pulse quicken. She looked up at him, her tummy roll forgotten. "Your scars—"

"My battle scars are no' near as interesting as the sweetness beneath that drying cloth," he said, his burr thicker than ever before. "Have done with it—I would see you naked."

With trembling fingers, Kira obliged. She untied the knot and yanked the linen from beneath her, letting it fall to the floor. Cold air swept her, bringing gooseflesh and chilling her, but she resisted the urge to reach for the covers. She couldn't have moved if her life depended on it. Not with him looking at her as if he wanted to devour her whole.

He was not looking at her as if tummy rolls mattered to him.

His expression said he wanted to eat her alive.

"You take my breath," he said, proving it. "Every luscious curve of you. Your breasts"—he paused, his gaze latching onto them—"are magnificent." He reached for them, lightly caressing, then splaying his fingers across her fullness, palming and squeezing. "I will ne'er get enough of you," he vowed, the words sending delicious shivers spilling all through her.

Especially there where he hadn't yet looked.

Tingling flames of pleasure danced and pulsed between her legs, the fiery ache making her burn for more. She shifted on the bed, rocking her hips and biting back a plea to take her. She didn't want to rush the moment, the sweet savoring of this first real joining. Then a single whimper escaped her and something flared in his eyes. Something primal and untamed, and so arousing she nearly choked on her need.

"That's my Kee-*rah*," he praised, gliding one hand over her belly, then tracing a finger right down the center of her, the intimacy of his touch electrifying her, shattering her control.

"I *am* yours," she cried, bending her legs and opening her knees, all reservations fleeing.

"You minx!" He looked down at her, his gaze burning as he swept his hands beneath her hips, his grip firm and demanding. "You, lass, ought e'er be clothed in naught but your skin and moon glow," he vowed, his fingers digging into her smooth, plump flesh.

"And you—I've ached for you since the first moment I saw you," she confessed, her throat getting thick again. "I dreamt of you even before our dreams began."

"Och, sweetness, if you only knew how I longed for you, too. How I searched for you." He leaned down to kiss her. A ravenous openmouthed kiss so incredible it was all she could do not to drag him down on top of her, wrapping her legs around his hips and then plunging her hand between them, closing her fingers around him and guiding him home.

There, where she needed him so badly.

Instead, he pulled back to rain kisses down the side of her neck. He nuzzled his face against her breasts, rubbing back and forth, losing himself in her scent and warmth, the smooth, satiny feel of her. "Lass," he breathed, teasing at her nipples with light, barely there touches before he shoved his hair out of the way and drew one peak deep into his mouth, tasting and savoring her. Losing his soul. Each sweet drawing pull enflamed him more, the blaze of his need rivaling anything he'd ever felt in their dream-passions.

Dream-lust.

Nae, *love,* a bold voice shouted in his head.

He drew harder on her nipple, grazing it with his teeth, the immensity of his need for her almost stopping his heart. Whate'er it was, love, lust, or both, it filled him now. A great roaring hunger inside him, all-consuming and out of control, its fury blinding him to all else. Only the woman on his bed mattered. His need to make her his, scorching him to the bone.

"This is how I need you." He looked up, locking gazes with her. "Just so," he vowed, smoothing a hand down her hip, then tracing light circles across her abdomen, his fingers just brushing the flame-red curls of her sex. "Naught but skin and pleasure between us."

She gasped, her body quivering beneath him. "Yes, just skin to skin," she agreed, lifting her hips until his fingers were on her sleek, female heat, the silky-soft feel of her breaking his restraint.

"Och, lass, you shouldnae have done that," he warned, his mouth curving in just the kind of smile he knew would make her burn. "See you, now that I'm touching you with my fingers"—he slid his middle one right inside her—"I've a powerful need to feel you with all o' me."

"I want all of you." She writhed on the bed, her breath hitching. "Love me for real this time. I told you, I've ached for that since the first time I saw you."

He looked at her for a long moment, not missing the flush of arousal staining her breasts or the brilliance of her eyes. Her kiss-swollen lips and the way she kept rocking her hips, pressing against his hand.

"You truly want this?" He had to ask. "There will be no regrets?"

"Yes! And no!" she cried, sliding a hand around his nape, pulling his mouth to hers for a kiss. "No regrets ever."

Something inside him wound tight on her words, a hot-spinning fire that set him hard as granite. "Then so be it," he breathed, stretching his fingers across her, cupping her intimately. He rubbed with just enough pressure, circling his thumb over her most sensitive spot.

"O-o-oh!" She arched her back, nearly shooting off the bed.

Exultation flashed through him, making him even hotter and harder than before. "Now, sweetness, you will see just how real I am," he promised, straddling her. "A more real man ne'er walked and breathed. Nor one who desires you more."

He smoothed her hair back, wanting to see her face as he touched her. "You are mine." He made the words an oath, his voice roughened by passion. "Now, and for all days to come. I will ne'er let you go."

"I don't want to go anywhere." She peered up at him, her gaze slipping right inside him. "Not ever."

"The only place we're going is where we've already been in our dreams." He wound his fingers in her hair and claimed her lips in a deep, slaking kiss.

She pulled away, her face troubled. "But our dreams are over," she protested. "What if—"

"A MacDonald doesn't allow what ifs." He looked at her, willing her to believe him. "We've already walked a long path together. Now, this night, we join at the meeting of our destiny."

Certain of it, he lowered his head to her breasts again, swirling his tongue over first one crest, then the other. He needed the taste, feel, and scent of her, couldn't live without drinking her in.

She was his destiny.

His life.

His heart fell wide with the knowledge. Everything about her felt so familiar. He couldn't remember having ever felt this way about a woman before. They shared an intimacy deeper than their dreams, almost as if he'd spent lifetimes holding her. And this was one he wasn't going to let pass without her.

No matter what keeping her might cost him.

Need and longing filling him, he rained soft kisses across the swell of her breasts, her shoulders, and neck. He wanted to savor her so fully that he would forever carry her scent, wouldn't be able to breathe without the essence of her flooding his senses.

A husky moan rumbled low in his chest. A strangled sound some might call capitulation. Maybe even surrender. It mattered not. Only that he never again blink or waken and find her gone, his bed cold and his arms empty.

"Dinnae e'er say what if again." He breathed the words against her skin. "Our joining is writ across our souls. Ignoring such a truth would be like trying to stem the tide with one's bare hands."

"Oh, I believe." She locked her arms around him, holding him close. "I think I always have."

"Then let me love you, lass. Now." He reached down between them, nudging her thighs wider as he covered her body with his. "*Mine*," he vowed, his throat too thick for anything else, his vitals so tight he half feared he'd burst before he could thrust into her.

But then she arched her hips and did some reaching of her own, curling her fingers around him and angling him closer. So near that he could wait no longer.

He plunged into her, his soul splitting when she cried his name. Again and again, he kissed her, matching the strokes of his tongue to their mating, riding her harder and deeper and faster until she gripped him tighter, her nails scoring his shoulders. A woman on fire, she clung to him, her every gasp of pleasure a deeper satisfaction than his own spilling seed.

The room tilted and whirled, the little flames of the oil lamps and the glow from the hearth fire blending into a crazed blur of fast-wheeling stars until his heart slowed and his breath came easier.

Even then, his body still shuddered and her tight, female heat kept convulsing around him, the mingled scent of their pleasure a heady, intoxicating proof of the realness of their loving.

As was her soft, quiet breathing as she nestled close, her warmth and the soft, sated feel of her as reassuring as the solidness of his bedchamber's walls. The sturdy thick-timbered frame of his great curtained bed and the familiar night darkness filling the tall arched windows. All was as it should have been.

He hadn't even realized he'd fallen asleep until he felt a persistent tapping on his shoulder.

He rolled off the bed and leapt to his feet, groping for his sword until he spied the still-bolted door. Relief flooding him, he wheeled around—and knew instantly why he'd been having such sweet dreams.

Kira sat peering at him from the middle of the bed, beautifully naked and tempting, her hair sleep-tousled and her every curve limned by moonlight and shadow. The shadows prevailed, but there was enough silvery light to catch tantalizing glimpses. Now fully awake, he swept his gaze over her lush breasts, dipping briefly to her fine legs, curled sweetly beneath her, before settling on the red curls between her thighs.

He drew a sharp breath, instantly hard.

She shifted on the bed, that one move giving him a quick flash of *all* of her.

Aidan's blood ran burning hot. He stepped closer, his mouth curving in a devilish smile. "I would ne'er have believed you'd be more eager than in our dreams," he said, tossing a glance at the window, where the stars hadn't even begun to pale. "'Tis nowhere near daylight and already you want—"

"I couldn't sleep." She glanced aside, something in her tone freezing his smile.

"What is it?" He sat on the edge of the bed, looking at her. "Dinnae tell me you're sorry we mated?"

"Oh, no, it isn't that," she said, her eyes troubled all the same.

He reached over and touched her face, then sifted his fingers through her hair. "I dinnae like seeing you fashed, sweetness. Tell me what's worrying you."

She hesitated only a moment before she seized his hand, gripping hard. "I remembered your men saying you'd gone warring. You didn't mention it, so I worried."

Aidan's smile returned. "Ach," he said, lifting her hand for a kiss, "I wasn't warring, only chasing vermin."

She blinked. "You mean rats?"

He laughed. "So you could say, aye. But he's caught now and whiling in my dungeon, so you needn't concern yourself o'er him."

"Oh," she said in a relieved voice, "you mean rats of the two-legged variety?"

"Indeed," Aidan confirmed, kissing her fingertips. "My own cousin, Conan Dearg. A blight to our clan and the worst scourge to e'er walk the heather."

She gasped.

Aidan's smile faded.

*"Conan Dearg?"* She stared at him, wide-eyed. "Did I hear you correctly? He's the man in your dungeon?"

"Unless the weasel's transformed himself into another, aye, that'll be him. Conan Dearg, my cousin. Only remaining son of my father's baseborn half brother." He looked at her, not liking the way her face was paling. "'Tis rumored he had done with his sire, then his own brothers, one by one, hoping to lay claim to Ardcraig Castle. With that ambition long accomplished, he's set his sights higher in recent times, casting his eye on Wrath as well."

"Dear God," Kira gasped, even whiter than before. "I can't believe I forgot him. I should have warned you straightaway. But everything happened so fast and I—"

"Whoa, lass." Aidan pushed to his feet. "How can you know Conan Dearg?"

"I don't know him," she said, scrambling off the bed after him. "I know *of* him. From books."

Aidan frowned, one of his best. "You've read of him in books? In this future time of yours?"

She nodded, looking miserable. "According to Scottish history, he's the man who killed you."

Aidan stared at her, feeling the floor give way and the room spin wildly.

This time not in bliss.

# 10

Several hours later, Kira sat in a heavy oaken chair in Aidan's privy solar, once again properly dressed in fitting, period-suitable clothing, up to and including a fresh and floppy pair of oversized *cuarans* and not a stitch of underwear. Most importantly, she was more convinced than ever that she now knew the reason she'd been sent back in time. She also had a pretty good idea of what she was supposed to do about it, even if a certain fierce and stubborn warrior chieftain felt otherwise.

*She knew.*

And all his pacing and bluster wouldn't change a thing.

Pointedly ignoring the tempting platter of bannocks, butter, and honey winking at her from the table beside her chair, she folded her hands in her lap and waited calmly for his next barrage of questions.

When they didn't come, she took a deep breath. "It must be as clear to you as it is to me." She lifted her voice just in case Aidan couldn't hear her where he stood across the solar, glaring out a window. The day had turned cold and dark, with a sleety wind blowing off the sea. Not that she'd let howling gales and glowers stop her from saying what needed to be said. "There can be no question," she contended. "I was sent here to save you and—"

He huffed. "I dinnae need a lass to save me."

Kira pressed her lips together and stared at his back, willing him to be reasonable. "I believe the gatehouse arch will work in reverse. My purpose is to return us to my world."

He spun around. "Us? Why would I be wanting that?" he asked, his hands curling around his sword belt. "I like my world fine and dinnae want to leave it. Nor, I thought, did you." He narrowed his eyes at her, his look challenging. "Or did my ears fool me when you said you wished to stay?"

"That was before you reminded me about Conan Dearg." Kira sighed. "Now things are different. Besides, I meant I wished to stay with you. It doesn't matter to me in what time that is."

"It matters to me." He strode to the hearth and took an iron poker to jab at the glowing peats. "I cannae just disappear through some *time portal*, as you call it. I have duties here," he said, straightening. "A Highland chieftain's life is no' just filled with cattle raiding and leading men into battle. Teaching the young lads to swing a sword and stand unafraid no matter what comes at them. We must also speak true at all times, keep our promises, and honor the clan elders. We care for the weak and ill, and give shelter to our widows and orphans."

Setting aside the poker, he clasped his hands behind his back and began pacing. "We hold councils and are allies, e'er ready to support our friends when they need us, just as we punish those men who behave badly."

Kira frowned and reached down to stroke old Ferlie's head. Newly washed and pleasant-smelling, thanks to her insistence, her used bath water, and two somewhat reluctant kitchen lads, the great beast lay curled on the floor rushes beside her chair, snoring contentedly. Unfortunately, sweet-smelling or no, his shaggy, medieval-looking bulk, as well as the smoking, hissing flames of a nearby wall torch, only underscored the harshness of Aidan's world. As did the solar's thick, whitewashed walls and the eye-stinging peat haze tingeing the air.

The discreet but there-all-the-same door to the one-holed chute garderobe tucked into a hidden corner of the room. A tiny, foul-reeking chamber that had never seen the likes of petal-soft toilet paper or spring-scented air freshener. Yet the soft golden glow from the many beeswax candles and the jeweled colors of the richly embroidered tapestries lent an irresistible air of the distant and faraway.

It truly was a world so like the romantic whimsy of her dreams, yet so different, too.

A world that belonged to Aidan, not her.

Just as her world was a place where Conan Dearg couldn't reach him.

"Clan Donald's name has e'er been a testament of greatness." He glanced at her, his gaze heated. "I will no' pass from history as the first to break such a noble line."

"I know you have duties, and pride." She looked up, not caring for the tight set of his jaw.

"They are more than duties and go deeper than pride." He dropped to one knee before her, taking her hand with both of his. "I have responsibilities that my honor will not allow me to turn my back on."

She blew out a breath. "Your responsibilities won't matter if you are dead."

To her annoyance, he squeezed her fingers and flashed one of his smug, alpha-male smiles. "Then tell me again, Kee-*rah*, how the books say I died."

"Exactly as I've already told you." Kira shoved a lock of hair away from her face and tucked it behind her ear. "Every book I have says you died at the hands of your cousin, Conan Dearg. One, a self-published book by a man called Wee Hughie MacSporran, goes into greater detail, claiming Conan Dearg locked you in your own dungeon, leaving you to starve on a diet of salt beef and fouled water."

The alpha-male smile turned triumphant, spreading across his face. "Och, lass, dinnae you see? You are fashing yourself for naught." He sprang to his feet, pulling her up with him. "Your books erred, though the self-published one, whate'er that means, is closer to the truth than the others. Conan Dearg did not lock me in my dungeon. 'Tis the blackguard himself who whiles there, wasting away on salt beef and soured water. Wee Hughie MacSporran, whoe'er he claims to be, mistook us, switching my fate with my cousin's."

Kira smoothed back her hair again, fighting the desperation beginning to spin inside her.

Looking bolder and more confident than ever, he folded his arms. "I am no' concerned about this Hughie man."

He made a dismissive gesture. "It matters not. His book is wrong."

She hesitated. The image of Wee Hughie's book flashed across her mind, his name and the words *historian, storyteller, and keeper of tradition* almost larger than the slim volume's title. She suppressed a shudder, memories of the self-inflated tour guide-cum-author's preening on her long-ago coach tour flooding back to her.

Never would she forget his grand camera poses in front of the Robert Bruce statue at Bannockburn and how he'd gone on and on about being directly descended from the well-loved hero king, as well as every other great name in Scottish history.

Including Clan Donald!

She winced, hearing the swellhead's boasts as clearly as if she'd last seen him yesterday.

Too bad for her, she also remembered Mara McDougall-Douglas' husband, Alex, claiming that *Rivers of Stone: A Highlander's Ancestral Journey* was a "fine book" and that Wee Hughie

MacSporran was exceptionally well versed in Highland legends and lore.

A notion that made her stomach twist into a cold, tight knot.

Alex Douglas hadn't struck her as man who'd give praise where it wasn't due.

Wishing she felt otherwise, she turned to the table and poured herself a cup of the odd-tasting medieval wine, just another difference she hadn't yet adjusted to. But wet was wet, and she needed to do something about her dry mouth before she could speak.

Draining the cup, she set it down with a *clack*, then turned back to face Aidan, not at all surprised to see him still wearing his smug look.

"I hate to say it," she began, bracing herself, "but I think the book is right and you're wrong."

He lifted one brow. "Why would you be thinking that?"

"Because I've met the author." She lifted her chin, ignoring how the cold knot inside her was drawing tighter, even starting to pulse. "He was a tour guide on my first trip to Scotland, the one I saw you on. He's even related to you, if he wasn't lying. Either way, I didn't like him. He struck me as being quite full of himself, but he did seem to know a lot about Scottish history."

Aidan humphed. "I'll wager he was full of naught but too much Highland wind."

"He was, as far as boasting about his illustrious ancestors," she agreed. "A shame, because he was also filled with fascinating anecdotes about the places we visited. He's the one who told us about Castle Wrath as our tour bus approached your cliff. If his tales hadn't been so stirring, I might not have felt such an urge to trek out here and have a look. Had I not, we might never have met."

She paused. "Even so, the real reason I believe his book is right is because someone I trust praised his knowledge. I stopped near Oban on my way here, at Ravenscraig Castle, and—"

"*Ravenscraig*?" He looked at her, his brows almost on the ceiling. "That place is a den of cross-grained MacDougall devils. They can't be trusted farther than the length of a sword."

"They were nice to me." Kira bristled. No one bad-talked her friends, no matter how hunky or good in bed. Or even medieval. "Mara McDougall is American like me. She's a friend of my family and just happened to marry a Highlander. His name is Alex, *Sir* Alex Douglas, and they own Ravenscraig in my time. He's the one who gave me a copy of Wee Hughie's book. It was in their gift shop."

"Ah, well, that's good to hear—a Douglas lairding it at Ravenscraig," he announced, not looking a bit remorseful. "Theirs is a fine name, one of the strongest in the land. After MacDonald, of course."

"You'd like Alex. He reminded me of you. He has this air about him, almost as if he could stride right into your time and be instantly at home." She glanced aside, surprised by a sudden rush of emotion. Images of Ravencraig's One Cairn Village whirled across her mind, her throat thickening as she remembered the warm welcome she'd received there. "If you met Alex, you'd understand why I trust his word on Wee Hughie's book."

Aidan humphed again, his admiration for the great Clan Douglas clearly not going that far.

Kira sighed. "I wish I could have showed you the book, but I lost it when I time traveled. It slipped from my fingers and fell into a crack in the top of the gatehouse arch."

"I would hear of Ameri-*cains* and tour buses," he declared as if she hadn't spoken. He helped himself to a cup of wine, then eyed her over its rim as he sipped, clearly no longer interested in discussing Wee Hughie and his book. "Are these tour buses only used by Ameri-*cains* and are they anything like the flying machines you told me of earlier?"

She frowned.

This conversation wasn't running in the right direction.

Wishing she'd never let him maneuver her from modern-day books on Clan Donald to airplanes, she put back her shoulders and lifted her chin. "Tour buses are like the flying machines, but on wheels and without wings. They're smaller and never leave the ground. And, yes, lots of American tourists use them. In the Scotland of my time, they're called *coaches*."

Aidan nodded, sagely.

"I thought as much," he said, clearly attempting to appear knowledgeable.

"*A-hem*," Tavish's deep voice cut in, surprising them both. "Pardon the intrusion," he said, stepping out of the shadows by the door, "but Cook is in a dither o'er the preparations for the feast to celebrate Conan Dearg's capture. He wants your permission to dip into the better spices and—"

"If you didn't mean to disturb, you could have knocked." Aidan flashed a frown at the gaping door, then at his long-nosed friend. "Yon door was closed, if I recall. No' that the like has e'er bother you."

The lout feigned a look of innocence. "Had I known you weren't alone, I would have called out before I entered."

"And had I not seen you standing in a niche in the stair tower, kissing one of the laundresses as my lady and I made our way down the steps, I might be inclined to believe you. As is"—Aidan looked down to flick at his plaid—"I caught your quick, sideways glance as we passed."

Tavish gave a half shrug. "That was hours ago."

Aidan glared at him, his frown deepening when Tavish lifted his hands in mock surrender, then crossed the room to kiss Kira's hand with an unnecessary flourish.

An exaggerated flair that almost made Aidan forget how much he loved the man. Displeased all the same, he eyed him. "I think you have better to do than skulk about plastering your ears to doors and hiding in shadows."

"Be that as it may," Tavish said, straightening, "Cook is driving everyone in the kitchens half mad with his rantings. I thought you ought know."

Not believing a word, Aidan slung an arm around his friend's shoulders and led him toward the table. Pouring a brimming cup of wine, he thrust it into the other's hands. "Cook has ne'er cared to consult me on kitchen matters so long as he's wielded his stew ladle. We both know he'll be fussing about something on the day we lower him into God's good earth."

"That may well be," Tavish agreed.

Folding his arms, Aidan watched him take an all-too-leisurely sip of wine. "Out with it, my friend. How long were you standing there, straining your ears?"

"He only just walked in. I saw him out of the corner of my eye." Kira defended him, lying just as surely as Tavish.

"See?" Tavish smiled and set down his wine cup. "You insulted me for naught."

Aidan grunted. "'Tis impossible to insult you. Your hide is thicker than an ox's. Further, even if Cook wished my consent to plunder our stores of spices, he would have sent a kitchen lad. So tell me why you're here."

Tavish's jaunty smile vanished. "Would you believe to save your hide? Leastways, to inform you of certain stirrings in the hall."

Aidan sighed, believing his friend indeed.

Not that he was wont to admit it.

Instead, he folded his arms and cocked a brow, waiting.

To his credit, Tavish didn't squirm. He did cast an uncomfortable glance at Ferlie. "Your men are no' pleased about having been ordered to bathe the castle dogs," he said, a frown marring his handsome face. "I suspect they fear they'll be next."

"Oh, dear," Kira said. "That's my fault—"

Aidan held up a hand to silence her. "Nae," he said, snatching a choice bannock and tossing it to Ferlie. "The time is long past that Wrath's dogs stop fouling the air with their stink. My men, too, now that I think of it."

"As you wish." Tavish didn't bat an eye. "Shall I see that they cease their bickering?"

In answer, Aidan took him by the elbow and ushered him toward the door. "Just tell them that any that are no' bathed and clean-smelling within two days will find themselves scouring the cesspit and then scrubbing each other until their buttocks shine like a bairn's. Now off with you, and dinnae return unless we're attacked."

Tavish nodded, but jerked free just before Aidan could shove him out the door. Twisting round, he looked across the room to Kira. "The parchments and scribing goods you wished have been left in Aidan's bedchamber," he said, making her a slight bow. "If you need more, let me know."

Then he was gone.

Disappearing into his infernal shadows before Aidan could have the pleasure of closing the door on him.

He shut it, regardless. Even sliding home the drawbar, though there really wasn't any need. What he needed was to get to the bottom of the goings-on in his castle. Things he wouldn't mind at all had a certain flame-haired, big-bosomed vixen taken the time to mention them to him.

"When did you ask Tavish for scribing goods?" he demanded, turning to fix her with his best I-am-laird-and-you'd-better-answer-me-now stare.

She jutted her chin, not looking a bit impressed. "This morning," she admitted, her gaze bold. "But I didn't ask Tavish directly. I asked the woman who brought me new clothes when you stepped out of the room to leave me to my ablutions."

Aidan nodded. "One of the laundresses, then."

Kira shrugged. "Whatever. I wanted the parchment and ink to keep record of my thoughts."

She blew out a breath of relief when he nodded again, apparently believing her.

Not that she wished to deceive him, but at the moment she didn't want to discuss her need to put together a story for Dan Hillard. *Her story*, though she'd add a caveat at the end never to reveal her identity.

Whether she ever made it back home or not, she didn't want to be plunged into the limelight. Heaven forbid, to be made an object for dissection on the internet. The Viking affair had been bad enough. If ever her account of her experiences came into Dan's hands, he need only have the parchment carbon-dated to prove the validity of her tale.

Such a story would thrust *Destiny Magazine* into the big league and bring Dan a fortune.

A good turn he deserved, even if it meant being a bit secretive.

Aidan, too, had his duties and loyalties, as he'd said himself.

So she took a deep breath and squared her shoulders, preparing to use her mother's best strategy for avoiding sticky wickets.

*Diversion*.

"Are you really going to hold a feast to celebrate your cousin's capture?" she asked the instant he rejoined her beside the solar's hearth fire.

Aidan slid his arms around her, pulling her close. "Aye, I must," he said, resting his chin on her head. "My people expect and deserve it. Locking him in the dungeon is no' enough. They need the *forgetting* of a feast. With luck, a fine and rollicking one can be arranged within a fortnight."

"Your cousin is that bad?" Kira couldn't believe it.

"He is worse," Aidan owned, his gut clenching at the thought of all the souls on Conan Dearg's conscience. "He has but one redeeming quality, though I am at a loss to explain it."

"What?" Kira angled her head, peering at him. "Is he a horse whisperer or something?"

Aidan frowned, not sure what a *horse whisperer* was, but

knowing full well that wasn't what he'd meant. "Och, nae," he said, shaking his head. "Conan Dearg is none the like. What he is, is a charmer. There hasn't been a maid yet born who can resist him."

"I don't think he'd impress me." She flicked an invisible speck off her skirts. "From what I'm hearing about him, I'm surprised women even glance at him."

"Och, they look." Aidan refilled his wine cup, drinking deeply. "They look and go all moony-eyed, flocking to him like bees to a hive. He's a great fiery-haired devil, bold and handsome, and strong as a wild Highland bull."

"It sounds like he needs to be de-bulled."

Aidan threw back his head and laughed, then caught himself, stunned to realize he hadn't laughed in longer than he could remember. "Aye, lopping off his bits should've been done long ago," he agreed, serious again. "But he's suffering a meet end now. No' that his passing will bring back the victims of his viciousness."

Dismay flickered in Kira's eyes. "There were many?"

"More than a soul can rightly count." Aidan leaned a hip against the table, considering how much he should share with her. "He used to send large stones sailing down from the battlements of Ardcraig's keep onto the heads of any unwelcome visitors who'd somehow slipped past his gatehouse. The gods only know how many hapless wayfarers seeking no more than a night's lodging were brained in such a manner. He'd designed a special stone-throwing device and tied ropes around the stones, using his contraption to haul them up to be dropped again if the first aim failed to flatten a man."

Pausing, he sighed deeply and looked away. The gusting wind was lessening now and great swaths of mist rolled past the solar windows, turning the night into a shifting mass of chill, damp gray.

"Dinnae worry—the career of his stone-throwing device was

short-lived," he said, rubbing the back of his neck. "Those days ended when he accidentally dropped a stone on his favorite mistress, killing her. She was the wife of one of his best allies and had taken it upon herself to pay him a surprise visit. Sad for the lady, she disguised herself as a man, and although she gave her identity to the guards, passing unhindered through the gatehouse, in the dark of night Conan Dearg mistook her for a stranger. Someone he didn't care to be pestered by."

He turned back to Kira, not surprised to find her staring at him with rounded eyes.

"Good heavens." She pressed a hand to her breast. "Too bad the husband didn't kill him."

"Och, he tried, well enough," Aidan told her, stretching his arms over his head and cracking his knuckles. "He rode hotfoot to Ardcraig to challenge him as soon as he heard. Their clash lasted all of a heartbeat, with Conan Dreag cleaving the man in two before he'd scarce whipped his blade from its scabbard." He lowered his arms, looking at her. "My cousin is an expert swordsman."

Kira shuddered. "I think he's also crafty," she said, now more determined than ever to persuade Aidan to return to her time with her.

"Aye, that he is," he agreed, glancing at the windows again, his expression hardening. "Cunning and devious as the wiliest fox."

"I've always liked foxes." Kira smoothed the soft, red-gold wool of her skirts, thinking how much the rich color resembled a fox pelt. "I once read a book where a really cute one with magical eyes was a meddling wise woman's familiar. She was called Devorgilla and I think his name was Somerled."

"*Somerled?*" Aidan shot a sharp glance at her. "I dinnae think my like-named forebear, who styled himself *King of the Isles*, would've cared for that. And you, sweetness, wouldn't care for my cousin's kind of foxing," he said, reaching to pull her against him. "With surety, not."

"No doubt." Her heart began to thunder as he took her in his arms, drawing her close.

"Indeed." He slid a hand beneath her hair, gently massaging the back of her head. "Conan Dearg's craftiness would put Satan's most devious minions to shame. Once, many years ago, he took a dislike to one of his younger garrison men. The lad was a bit of a rogue and bonnie enough to catch the eye of one of my cousin's ladyloves. Much to Conan Dearg's annoyance, because of the lad's sunny disposition and ready laughter, he was also popular with the other men."

She shivered, guessing the outcome. "Don't tell me he ended up in two pieces?"

Aidan shook his head. "Nae, praise the gods, he was one of the few to escape my cousin's grasp. But only by the grace of a passing MacKenzie galley and the good eyes and ears of those who happened to be on board."

Her jaw slipped. "Did your cousin set him adrift in a leaky boat or something?"

"Or something, aye," Aidan told her in a voice like steel. "Because of the lad's popularity, he bided his time, not wanting to rouse suspicion. Opportunity finally arose when a ewe tumbled off a cliff, landing unharmed on a narrow rock ledge halfway between the cliff-top and the sea."

Releasing her, he pushed away from the table to pace again, distaste making it impossible to stand still. Even with his sweet *tamhasg* pliant and warm against him.

"Agility was another of the lad's many talents, and so my cousin approached him, saying he'd chosen him to fetch the poor ewe," he continued, a chill passing through him as he remembered the deed. "Together with two other men, they went out to the cliffs, a remote place far from prying eyes and where a call for help wouldn't be heard. Eager to please, and just as keen to rescue the ewe, the lad let himself be lowered on a rope down the cliff to the small foothold of a ledge."

"Ropes and cliffs again?" Kira looked at him with a frown. She didn't shudder, but her opinion of his world's harsher aspects rippled all over her.

His mouth twisted. "Ach, lass," he said, wincing inside, "such is our way of life. The cliffs hold a rich harvest for us. Seabirds, with their eggs and oil, the latter being a fuel we use to light our lamps. When a beast loses its footing and slips o'er an edge, if it survives the fall, we fetch it. Men here learn to brave the cliffs soon after their first steps. Some women as well, as you know from Annie MacQueen's fate."

"So what was the young man's fate? Did he, too, plunge into the sea?"

"Nae..." He hesitated, wishing he'd ne'er mentioned the lad. "He reached the ledge with ease, but before he could secure the end of the rope around the ewe, the rope went slack in his hands. Looking up, he saw its other end sailing down toward him, and the two other men, apparently sacrificed to guarantee their silence."

Kira gasped. "That's horrible."

"To be sure." He came back to her, crossing the room with purposeful strides. "Had it not been for the MacKenzies hearing his cries when they sailed past, a shade too close to the cliffs, he'd surely have died there," he said, putting his hands on her shoulders. "As it was, the MacKenzies anchored in the next cove, sending men to climb the cliffs and then toss down a fresh rope, rescuing both the lad and the ewe."

"Thank goodness." Kira exhaled. "But how did you find out? Did he come here after his rescue?"

"Ach, nae, he had more sense than that and sailed on to Kintail with the MacKenzies, settling and eventually marrying there. The tale did not reach us here at a Wrath until some years later when a wandering bard mentioned having met him at a feast at Eilean Creag Castle, the MacKenzie stronghold."

He paused to stroke her cheek. "You needn't look so worried, sweetness," he said, lighting a finger across her lips. "The bard told us the MacKenzie chieftain, a man styled as the Black Stag of Kintail, took a great liking to the lad and saw that he received every comfort and a warm welcome into that clan."

"But—" Kira broke off, frowning. "Didn't anyone wonder what happened to the three missing men?"

Aidan arched a brow. "You mean before the bard's arrival?"

She nodded.

He gave a half smile. "I told you my cousin is cunning," he reminded her. "He crafted an explanation no one would question, claiming the men set sail for the Isle of Barra, hoping to enjoy a bit of carouse and wenching with our allies, the MacNeils. They are generous, openhanded hosts and notorious wenchers. Many of the younger clansmen hereabouts like paying calls there. Some of the older ones, too."

"And you?"

"Me?" Amusement sparked in his eyes. "I will no' lie to you, lass. To be sure, I've enjoyed visiting the Barra MacNeils. And, aye, I've savored the lustier revels they offer their guests, but"— he took her hand and pressed a quick kiss to her palm, another to the back of her wrist—"the MacNeils have no' seen me in recent times."

She blinked. "Why not?"

"Ahhh, sweetness, I think you know," he said, his half smile broadening into a grin.

"Maybe I'd like to hear the words."

"Then you shall have them." His gaze dipped to her breasts as he carefully undid her gown's laces, then eased open her bodice, allowing him to caress her naked skin. "My world isn't all harshness and cruelty," he said, his touch causing an immediate melting between her thighs. "Many are the pleasures, including those that men find on the Isle of Barra. You are my pleasure and have been since that first day I saw you. Since then, my only reason for e'er sailing to Barra has been to quench my need for you."

"With other women—oh!" Her breath caught when his fingers brushed a nipple.

Squeezing gently, he looked down, watching as it tightened beneath his lazy strokings. "With. Other. Women. Aye." He spoke the words slowly, his gaze riveted on her breasts. "Poor substitutes for the one woman I burned to have for my own."

"Oh, Aidan." She bit her lip, her heart melting this time.

He looked up at her, the blaze in his eyes scorching her soul. "'Tis you I want, Kee-*rah*. You and no other for the rest of my days."

She nodded, her throat once more too thick for words.

"I cannae recall the names of those other women, nor even their faces, save that I sought out ones that reminded me of you," he said, cupping her breasts with both hands now, kneading and plumping them. "All I can remember is the emptiness I felt inside each time I left their beds. That, and my gnawing need for the woman in my dreams."

*Aidan!* Her voice sounded strange in her ears, urgent and roughened, blurred by the roar of her pulse, the wild thundering of her heart. "I couldn't bear to lose you," she tried again, wrapping her arms around his neck, willing to plead. "Please come back to my time with me. You can't stay here. I know your cousin will kill you. He—"

"Will no' have me running away with my tail between my legs like a frightened dog," he finished for her. "MacDonalds do not flee from their foes. They fight them and win the day. Conan Dearg's days are past."

Kira glanced away. "He doesn't sound like someone easy to defeat," she said, worry squeezing her chest. "You said he's an expert swordsman."

He snorted. "You doubt that I am as good?" He arched a brow, all arrogant chieftain again. "Sweet lass, I am better."

"Even so—"

"He is in my dungeon and powerless." His mouth crashed down over hers, claiming her lips in a deep, searing kiss. Hot, hard and demanding. "All this talk of him has left a bad taste on the back of my tongue," he vowed, breaking away to look at her. "I've a powerful need to banish it with something sweet!"

In a blink, he was on his knees, her skirts shoved up to her hips and his face but a breath away from that-part-of-her-that-should-be-wearing-panties.

Kira froze, unable to move. Not wanting to. She looked down, the way he was staring at her there, exciting her.

"Oh, no," she gasped.

"O-o-oh, aye," he purred, his sexy Scottish voice deep with passion. "*This* is the sweetness I crave. You, all hot and slippery."

He glanced up, the heat in his gaze sizzling her as he jerked her skirts up even higher, then leaned close, nipping and kissing his way up the inside of her thighs before he buried his face between her legs and licked her.

Crying out, she fisted her hands and threw back her head, arching into him and almost climaxing the first time he flicked his tongue over her most sensitive place.

"Don't stop," she breathed, her knees nearly giving out on her when he replaced his tongue with a circling finger and then licked along the center of her, plunging his tongue right into her. Deep, deep inside her. "O-o-oh, Aidan—"

*Aidan!*

The rough and urgent voice again, not hers at all, and this time followed by a loud pounding on the door.

They both froze, passion doused.

Tavish shouted, "Come, man! Open the door!"

Aidan shot to his feet, his face a mask of fury. "I'll kill the bastard," he snarled, storming across the room and yanking open the door. "Did I no' tell you—"

"'Tis the young lad, Kendrew," Tavish panted, bursting into

the room. "He's been hurt, out by the gatehouse. Men just carried him in the hall."

Aidan swore. "The gatehouse? What happened? Was there trouble with the other lads?"

"He had a skirmish, aye. But not with any lad."

"Then who?"

Tavish looked uncomfortable. "If he's to be believed," he said, slanting a look at Kira, "it was your cousin."

"*Conan Dearg*?" Aidan stared at him. "That's no' possible."

Tavish shrugged. "Aye, it cannae be. Conan Dearg is still in the dungeon. I checked myself."

"What exactly happened?" Kira put in, joining them. "Kendrew was in a scuffle at the gatehouse? Could he have mistaken one of the guards for Aidan's cousin?"

"My guards wouldn't fall upon the lad." Aidan shot her a frown.

Tavish snorted. "That, my friend, is what Kendrew claims happened."

Aidan's eyes widened. "What? That Conan Dearg *fell* on him?"

"Nae." Tavish shook his head. "He said the blackguard *leapt* onto him. From the top of the gatehouse arch. Kendrew babbled that he saw Conan Dearg up there, creeping about on his hands and knees. When he called to him, he says the lout jumped down on top of him, knocking him into the mounting block before running away across the bailey."

Aidan rubbed his jaw. "That doesn't make sense."

Kira looked at him, Kendrew's tale making perfect sense to her.

Aidan's cousin had an accomplice at Wrath. Someone willing to let him in and out of the dungeon. Even scarier, he'd learned about the gatehouse arch.

And he was trying to find out how to use it.

## 11

---

Kira noticed two things the moment she followed Aidan and Tavish into the smoke-hazed, torchlit great hall. How quickly two plaid-wrapped, sword-toting Highlanders could plow their way through a teeming, jam-packed crowd of men, and the sharp, metallic smell of blood.

Trying to close her nose against the latter, she hurried after them, not missing the way half the men in the hall hastily glanced aside as she dashed past them. Not surprisingly, the other half gaped at her openly, their bearded faces filled with suspicion.

Or hostility.

Only one soul ignored her.

A portly, ruddy-faced giant of a man who needed only a furred, sleeveless jerkin and a silvered helmet to look like one of the Vikings who'd once ruled Wrath. Tall, broad-shouldered, and with a wild mane of reddish-blond hair, he would've looked genial dressed in anything but his somber, dark robes. Maybe even like a merry, red-cheeked Norse Santa, were he not so focused on the strapping youth sprawled on his back across the rough planks of a trestle table pushed close to the hearth fire.

Clearly a healer, the man stood at the head of the table, gently probing an egg-sized lump on Kendrew's forehead. He glanced up at Aidan's approach. "He's not by his wits," he said, the words loud in the quiet of the hall. "The blow to his head is making him spout foolery. He'll fare better once he's rested."

Aidan humphed. "I'd hear what happened. From the lad, or whoe'er. And someone—anyone—send men to comb the castle and grounds." Stepping up to the table, he frowned when Kendrew moaned. "The lad didn't end up like this from tangling with a mist wraith."

The healer shrugged. "The sharp edge of the mounting block could've cut his shoulder. The knot on his head might be from the block's stone as well," he suggested, pulling on his beard. "Depends on how he fell."

"Pah!" quipped an older woman hovering close. "He didn't fall. Conan Dearg attacked him. The lad swore it."

A second, equally grizzled woman clucked in agreement. She held a laver while the other dipped a rag into the bloodied water, then swabbed at the gash in Kendrew's shoulder. "Aye," she gabbled, turning bright eyes on Aidan, "the laddie said your cousin waved something strange at him, laughing that he'd now 'beat every foe, because he'd see them coming before the battle began.'" Straightening thin shoulders, the crone flashed a gap-toothed smile and lowered her voice to a conspiratorial whisper. "Conan Dearg then leapt down from the arch, knocking the poor laddie into the mounting block and dashing him on the head with the object."

"The object?" Aidan folded his arms.

"The thing he claimed would let him see any foe's approach," the other old woman chirped, once more dipping her rag into the laver.

Kira stared at the two women in horror, scarce hearing their babbling. She saw only the youth's shoulder gash and the filthy rag clutched in the woman's gnarled and age-spotted hand.

Medieval healing at its finest.

Hygiene at its worst.

Shuddering, she clutched Aidan's arm, pulling him back from the table.

"Make them stop," she urged him, her voice rising when the rag-dipping old woman tossed the dripping cloth onto the floor rushes, then produced another, promptly blowing her nose into its ratty-looking folds before plunging the thing deep into Kendrew's wound. "He'll get an infection! Maybe even die. Those filthy rags are full of germs."

"Hush, Kee-*rah*."Aidan patted her hand. "Nils and the birthing sisters know what they're about."

"Oh, no, they don't," she shot back, her whole body trembling. "They'll only make it worse."

"Leave be, lass," Aidan warned again, but three startled faces were already looking her way.

The tiniest, most wizened woman peered sharply at her, her lips tightening to a thin, disapproving line. The rag-dipper appeared confused, her knotty hand still pressing the offending cloth against Kendrew's shoulder until Nils swelled his broad chest and plucked the rag from her hand, tossing it not onto the rushes, but into a pail at his feet.

"Lass!" he boomed, fixing Kira with a twinkling blue-eyed stare. "I dinnae understand half of what you said, but what I did grasp is just what I've been trying to get through the thick heads of these she-biddies for years!"

Planting beefy hands on his hips, he cast a frown on the two old women. "To think they call themselves midwives," he scolded, his tone good-natured all the same. "Me, having seen the work of the great healers of the East, and some here still choose not to heed me when I tell them to use clean lengths of linen and fresh water on wounds."

"Fresh, *boiled* water," Kira allowed, sensing an ally in Nils the healer.

Even if the so-called clean bits of linen he was now pulling from some hidden cache in his robes looked anything but snowy white.

They'd surely never been bleached or disinfected.

But they were a vast improvement over the ghastly rags the birthing sisters seemed so fond of.

A chill running through her, she opened her mouth to say more, but glanced at Aidan first, relief sweeping her when he jerked a quick nod, giving her his approval.

At his elbow, Tavish grinned. "Nils learned the healing arts in Jaffa," he said, edging close so only she could hear him. "He went there as a lad, tagging along on an uncle's pilgrimage to the Holy Sepulchre, but the poor man succumbed to the journey. Nils was stranded there for years, learning much before he could return. Naught you might say will shock him."

*No' even talk of flying machines and tour buses filled with Americains?* Kira was sure she heard Aidan mutter beneath his breath.

She wasn't about to comment, not here in his hall.

She did hesitate, her gaze flicking from the healer, to Tavish, to Aidan.

Then she glanced at Kendrew, his pale face and glittering eyes, deciding her.

She had to help him.

"These, too, should be boiled." She indicated two impossibly large-looking bone needles lying on a nearby stool, a suspicious coil of horse-tail thread revealing their purpose. "Kendrew could catch an infec—... I mean, it could go bad for him if these things aren't properly cleaned before they're put to use."

The two old women sniffed in unison.

The same men who'd narrowed eyes at her when she entered the hall crowded round, looking on expectantly. Those who'd averted their gazes shook their heads and grumbled, but pressed forward just the same, curiosity winning out over stubbornness.

Nils the Viking hooted and grabbed her arm, pulling her

closer to the table, thrusting one of his almost-clean cloths into her hands.

"She'll bespell him!" someone objected from the throng.

"Be wary, Nils!" another agreed. "You might find those healing cloths turned into snakes next time you reach for one!"

Ignoring them, Nils handed her a bowl of unsavory-looking paste. "'Tis woundwort," he told her. "My own special betony healing salve. If you aren't faint of heart, you can apply it to Kendrew's shoulder. It'll help draw out the evil."

"Of course," Kira agreed, steeling herself. "I should wash my hands first." She forced a smile, not wanting to offend. "You should, too. Anyone who touches—"

"Ho, Nils! You speak of evil. I say *she* be evil." A female voice cut her off, rising clear and angry from somewhere near. "Telling a healer and his helpers how to care for the lad!"

Spinning about, Kira almost collided with the speaker, a beautiful woman with the creamiest skin and brightest hair she'd ever seen. Flame-bright hair that glistened in the torchlight, her braid swinging as she plunked down a basket of fresh linens at Nils' feet, then whipped around to disappear into the crowd without a further word.

Kira opened her mouth to protest, but the rag-dipper scuttled forward then, snatching the cloth and bowl. "Sinead and the others speak true." She shunted Kira aside with a bony elbow. "With so many strange goings-on these days, it willnae do to have *you* poking and prodding at the laddie."

Bristling, Kira rubbed her ribs. "I only wanted to help," she said, amazed the tiny old woman could pack such an elbow jab. "I know you mean well, but—"

"And what do you know?" A big, great-bearded clansman stepped up to them, eyeing her critically. "You dinnae look like a healer to me!"

"My father was a healer." Kira lifted her chin, hoping the lie wasn't flashing on her forehead. But better a fib than tell them she knew what she did from life in a future century. "He worked for a king," she added, borrowing the name of her dad's boss, Elliot King, at the Tile Bonanza.

An uproar rose from the hall. Men pushed closer, scores of bushy brows snapping together as they glared at her, skepticism in every eye.

Aidan was frowning, too. He stood watching her, his arms still folded and his dark expression saying exactly what his tightly clamped lips didn't.

He'd warned her to keep out of it and she hadn't.

"My father *did* work for a king." She put her hands on her hips and glanced round, letting her own dark look dare any of them to challenge her. "I helped him sometimes."

She left off that her helping consisted of long-ago summer jobs at the tile shop's checkout.

"Then prove it." One of the men edged closer, clearly unimpressed. He pointed at Kendrew, sleeping soundly now. "Do something for the lad."

Kira swallowed.

Heat was beginning to bloom inside her. Any minute now it would sweep up her throat and burst onto her cheeks, revealing her for the impostor she was.

"It isn't that easy." She straightened her back, aware of every stare. "My knowledge isn't very fresh. It's been years since I assisted my father," she added, almost choking on the words.

It was more than years.

Considering where she was, her father hadn't even yet been born.

And even if he were here, he was a ceramic tile salesman, not a healer of kings.

She bit back a groan. She'd really flubbed it this time. Aidan had every right to be frowning at her.

"Good lass." He stepped forward then, slinging an arm around her shoulders. "I will have water boiled for the cloths and stitching needles," he said, nodding to Nils and the two birthing sisters. "Now tell us what else you know. Perhaps something that will ease young Kendrew's pain?"

Kira sighed and shoved a hand through her hair.

*What Kendrew needed was morphine and penicillin.* A clean, freshly laundered bed in a sterile-smelling hospital, with cute and smiling nurses cooing over him, rather than being cared for by a dark-robed giant who looked like a Viking and two tiny, bird-like women who smelled like they hadn't bathed in a hundred years.

If ever.

She slid a glance at them, hoping Aidan's threat to make his men bathe applied to them as well. Not that their stares would be any less hostile if their bodies were sweet-smelling.

"See?" The rag-dipper pointed at her. "She cannae answer you, my lord," she gloated, beaming at Aidan.

"Well, lass?" He squeezed her shoulders, the gesture giving her courage. "Prove to Ella and Etta that you know what you're about."

Kira took a deep breath and closed her eyes, concentrating.

Silence filled the hall as everyone waited. A great, ominous silence, unbroken until a long-ago memory flashed through her mind, filling her ears with her dad's grumbles and groans. His endless fussing the day he'd been brought home from work with a huge lump on his head after a box of tile had tumbled off a shelf, grazing him.

Kira almost smiled, remembering, too, how her mother had immediately slapped a cloth-wrapped bag of frozen peas onto his head and given him two aspirins.

Her eyes snapped open and she did smile, certain she had the answer.

"I know how to care for that lump on Kendrew's forehead," she announced, pitching her voice to sound like a healer's daughter. "I'll need something cold. Really cold." She slipped out from under Aidan's arm and faced the crowd, hands on her hips. "What can you bring me that is cold as winter ice?"

A sea of blank faces stared back at her.

"The siege well in the kitchen has cold water," Tavish spoke up. "Would that do?"

Before she could answer, Mundy the Irishman pushed forward. "There's a wee spring out near the byres with water much colder than the kitchen well. One sip is enough to make a man think his teeth will crack."

"That's it!" Kira clapped her hands. "Go, and bring me buckets of it. And"—she glanced at Aidan—"send someone to the kitchens for several small sacks of dried peas."

He looked at her, his brows starting to pull together again. "Dried peas?"

"Yes." She nodded. "Just make sure the sacks are as clean as possible," she added, hoping ice packs made of dried medieval peas soaked in spring water would decrease the swelling as quickly as her mother's bags of frozen veggies.

A muscle jerked in Aidan's jaw. "Right. Peas," he said, not looking entirely convinced.

"Don't worry. I know what I'm doing." Kira reached to touch his plaid, willing him to trust her. "We'll soak the sacks of peas in the icy water," she explained. "When they're cold enough, we'll place a cloth-wrapped sack on Kendrew's forehead, leaving it there until the sack isn't cold anymore. We'll then apply a new one, so someone will have to keep bringing chilled water from the spring."

"Tavish! Mundy!" Aidan swung around to the other men. "See that her orders are followed," he said, nodding in satisfaction when they took off at a run.

He glanced back at her. "Aught else?"

"Only that we need to get the icy sacks onto Kendrew's fore-head as quickly as possible."

"It will be done." He looked at her and something flared in his eyes.

Something heated that went straight to her toes.

"Aye, it will be done," he repeated. "Whate'er you want."

She blinked, her heart pounding. What she wanted was to continue what they'd started in the solar.

But now was clearly not the time.

So she touched a grateful hand to Nils the Viking's sleeve and gave Ella and Etta her best smile, hoping they'd accept a truce if poor Kendrew's goose egg went down as quickly as she hoped.

Aidan looked hopeful, too, and that pleased her more than she would have believed.

Folding his arms again, he raked his men with a triumphant stare. "Soon, Kendrew will be well," he announced, his voice ringing.

Almost as if *he'd* suggested the chilled pea sacks.

Not that she minded.

O-o-oh, no, she didn't care at all. Not as long as he made it up to her the instant they were alone again. Then she'd tell him exactly what she wanted.

Judging by the way he'd just looked at her, he was more than ready to indulge her desire.

She smiled, already melting.

For a night that had soured so quickly, things were definitely looking up now.

᠁

SEVERAL HOURS LATER, Kira sat alone at a heavy oaken table in Aidan's room, frowning at a stack of parchment sheets. Moonlight slanting through a nearby window arch and two heavy wax candles illuminated the unwieldy scrolls. Her efforts to record her time traveling experiences for Dan. Everything that had happened to her since arriving in Scotland, up to and including

Kendrew's mysterious scuffle and how she'd subsequently introduced ice packs to the good folk of Castle Wrath.

Unfortunately, she couldn't yet write about whether they'd worked or not, having gladly let Aidan usher her from the hall when Nils the Viking placed a smooth bit of wood between Kendrew's teeth just before the birthing sisters set to work with their bone needles and horse-tail thread.

She shuddered, certain she'd been wise to leave.

At least, thanks to Aidan's nod and the healer's open-mindedness, the sisters had used sterilized needles.

Not sure that they would make much difference, all things considered, she helped herself to a small sip of the wine someone had thoughtfully left sitting beside her parchments. Still not fond of the rather piquant taste of medieval spirits, she wrinkled her nose, restricting herself to a very small sip.

A cloud passed over the moon, dimming her vision. She blinked and edged the two candles closer, needing better light to see. Ink splotches blotted some of her words, the sight of them making her head pound with annoyance. Rubbing her temples, she peered down at the squiggled lines, not sure if she should credit the messiness of her scribbles to the awkwardness of using an inkwell and quill or if working on a keyboard had just ruined her handwriting.

Either way, she could only hope that if ever the parchments reached Dan, he'd be better at deciphering her script than she was.

She also hoped Aidan would return soon.

The moonlight was making her ache for him, its pale glow spilling not just across the table and her blasted parchments, but across the luscious coverings of his great timbered bed on the other side of the room as well. Every time she glanced that way, a delicious curl of anticipation warmed the deepest part of her, making her tingle with excitement. He'd promised to hurry back, the swift, heated kiss he'd given her at the door, suggesting even more.

Shivering, she took a deep breath, her scribblings forgotten as his words from earlier circled through her like heady, honeyed wine.

*Whate'er you want.*

Chills sweeping her, she smiled. The words sent heat coiling through her even as her body trembled. Her breath quickened, and her heart began to thump with a slow, erratic beat. She could almost feel him striding into the room, claiming it and her as his own as he crossed over to her. Possession in mind, he would raise her skirts and settle himself beneath them, telling her that he knew what she wanted so badly and that his need was even greater.

Hot and cold in turns now, she bit her lip, not wanting to get too worked up before his return. She also needed to write more. Now, with everything so fresh in her mind. But it was hard to concentrate, and the squiggly lines were beginning to look even squigglier, some of them seeming to dance and swim before her eyes.

"Was your father truly a healer of kings?" Aidan spoke from right beside her.

"Oh!" She jumped, her heart skittering. She looked up, the quill slipping from her fingers, its ink splashing across the parchment.

Pushing to her feet, she swayed, nerves or the lateness of the hour making her clumsy. "Sheesh!" She frowned and grabbed the chair, grateful for its support.

She swallowed hard, pulling up all her strength to stand tall and look normal.

Unfazed by tiredness and immune to moon glow. Wholly unaffected by her Highlander's dark, penetrating gaze, or whatever it was that had her mouth so dry and her legs feeling like rubber bands. The way he changed the very air just by being there.

She blinked, her fingers still clutching the chair. "Is Kendrew okay?"

To her relief, he smiled.

"The lad sleeps." He looked pleased. Equally good, holding her gaze as he did, he didn't seem to notice her death grip on the chair. "Nils gave him a strong sleeping draught after Ella and Etta did their stitching. I doubt he'll wake till the morrow's noon."

"What about the lump on his forehead?" She was almost afraid to ask. "Did it go down?"

Bemusement lit his eyes. "Och, aye. With remarkable speed, much to everyone's astonishment."

Kira released a ragged breath. "Thank goodness."

"So tell me, lass." He stepped back and folded his arms, once more assuming his most lairdly tone. "Was your father truly a healer? And of kings?"

"Ahhh..." She trailed off. She'd meant to tell him the truth, but her tongue wouldn't form the words, even felt too big in her mouth.

She swallowed and tried again. "No, he isn't a healer. It just seemed like the most diplomatic thing to say. He's a ceramic tile salesman."

One raven brow lifted. "No royal connections?"

Kira shook her head. "Only through a name. He works for a man named King."

His smile returned. "Hah!" He gave a short laugh. "I thought as much."

"You aren't mad? Not even a bit disappointed?"

She'd thought he would be.

At least until she explained herself.

Instead, he stood looking at her, his smile slowly broadening into a grin. The warmth in his gaze slid right into her, wrapping around her heart and making her rubbery knees even more unsteady.

"You, lass, could ne'er disappoint me." He spoke softly, his voice almost a caress. "And, nae, I'm no' mad."

"You didn't want me to interfere. I saw it on your face in the hall." She swallowed again, still finding it hard to form words. "Then—then I lied, making my father something he's not."

He touched a finger to her mouth, tracing the curve of her lips. "You delighted me this e'en and have won o'er my men with naught but a few sacks of dried peas and icy water from a spring."

"What?" She blinked. "They're no longer calling for my head?"

"They think you most wise. Even Ella and Etta paid you grudging respect."

"The birthing sisters?" She could hardly believe it. "What about the redheaded woman? The one with the milk-white skin?"

He frowned, looking puzzled. "Ach," he said after a moment, "you must mean Sinead, the laundress?"

Kira nodded, even now feeling the stab of the woman's resentful stare. "She doesn't like me at all."

"She isn't fond of any women." He gave a half shrug, dismissing her. "Especially beautiful ones who are far more desirable than herself."

His words made her heart soar. "I think you are a flatterer."

"I speak but the truth," he said, leaning close to lightly kiss her brow. "Sinead is of no consequence. You needn't fret about her."

"Then why is she here?"

He sighed. "She is a laundress, and—more. In a castle with so many unmarried men, such women are a necessity. She means naught to me."

"Oh." She should have known.

Wishing she'd never mentioned the woman, much less seen her, she took a deep breath. As deep as she could with her chest feeling so tight and achy. She pressed a hand to her breast, trying to ease the pressure.

"Forget the woman. There are one or two others like her here. You needn't pay heed to any of them." He kissed her again, on the cheek this time. "Every man in Wrath's hall drinks to your health this night. Even Ross and Geordie."

"They were that pleased to see Kendrew's swelling go down?"

"To be sure, though I'd wager their pleasure is more self-serving." He drew her to him, sliding his arms around her back. "You wouldn't believe what they're doing just now. Nor would I, had I no' seen it myself."

He pulled back to look her, a smile hovering on his lips. "If you were to slip down there, you'd find at least half of them lying about with chilled sacks of dried peas pressed to whate'er body parts they claim ails them. The others are glaring at them, impatiently waiting their turn because there aren't enough pea sacks to go around."

Kira let go of the chair to wrap her arms around his neck. His smile was getting to her, the dark gleam in his eyes making her breath hitch.

"You look surprised."

His voice was deep, low and soft with a richness that strummed her soul. Holding fast to his shoulders, she leaned into him, certain she'd melt at his feet if she didn't. Her legs *did* feel seriously like rubber.

She frowned. "I think there's something wrong—"

"Naught for you to fash yourself about." He caught one of her hands, bringing it to his lips. "My men are no' bad, Kee-*rah*. I knew they would warm to you in time." Releasing her hand, he smoothed the hair back from her face. "Any who still bear doubts will lose them soon. I promise you."

Not so sure, she looked at him, trying to focus. She wished the clouds would stop blotting the moonlight. Or the candles on the table would burn brighter. At times, his face seemed to blur, lost in the darkening shadows.

She blinked, then squinted, relieved when the dimness receded. "Maybe I should tell your men about hot water bottles?" she offered, her voice sounding far away.

Almost *tinny*, as if she were speaking in a drum.

"Hot water bottles?" He looked amused. "Are they another future healing method?"

She nodded, regretting it instantly for the swift movement nearly split her head. "They are like the heated stones you put in beds to warm them, but better. You need only fill a small leather pouch with boiling water to have soothing heat wherever you need it."

His smile turned wicked. "I can think of a different kind of soothing heat." He took her hand again, this time pressing a kiss into her palm. "A slick, slippery heat I've been hungering for all e'en."

"Oh." Kira caught her lip between her teeth, the *heat* he meant pulsing in hot response. "I—"

"I need you naked," he finished for her. "Need us both naked. I've an urge to devour every inch of you."

"Oh, please, yes!" She leaned into him, her excitement so intense the room began to spin. Mercy, she tingled everywhere. Even her mouth and lips, her fingers.

*This was what she wanted, needed.*

His smile positively wolfish now, he reached for the large Celtic brooch at his shoulder, unclasping it faster than her eyes could follow. He whipped off his plaid with equal speed, his sword belt, tunic, and everything else vanishing in a blur until he stood naked before her.

Naked, proud, and leaving her no doubt about how much he wanted her.

He raised his arms over his head, cracking his knuckles, then tossed his hair over his shoulders, the look in his eyes making her pulse quicken. "I am ravenous for you," he growled, reaching for her and stripping her so quickly, she was naked in his arms before she could even blink.

Crossing the room with swift, easy strides, he lowered her onto the bed. He joined her, kissing her long and deep, one hand kneading her breasts while he slid the other between her thighs, rubbing and probing the sleek, womanly softness there. His gaze locked on hers, he cupped her firmly, her hot readiness and the musky scent of her arousal making him run hard as granite. She went soft and pliant against him, her sweet sighs and the way she opened her mouth beneath his firing his blood, making him burn for her.

"I must taste you," he vowed, covering her body with his and turning his attention to her breasts, smoothing his face against their fullness. He licked and laved them, flicking their crests with his tongue, then drawing one deep into his mouth as he continued to rub her silken heat, taking special care to keep a circling finger on her most sensitive spot.

She whimpered, rocking her hips and pressing herself against his hand, then went limp again, a great shudder rippling through her. "Don't stop," she begged, her voice a mere whisper, her legs opening, giving him greater access.

"Och, lass, I may no' stop for days." He pushed up on his elbows to look at her, the sight of her parted, kiss-swollen lips and passion-heavy eyes making him even harder.

His heart pounding as fiercely as the hot throbbing in his loins, he returned to her breasts, once more savoring her satiny-smooth flesh before moving lower, trailing hot, openmouthed kisses down her stomach, stopping only when he reached her triangle of soft, female curls, the wonder of her almost splitting his soul.

"By the gods!" He reached down and gripped himself, squeezing hard until the sharp edge receded, not wanting to spill before he'd had enough of her.

"Aidan ..." Her voice came even softer, a faint shiver in the air, a barely-there gasp in the wild thunder drumming in his ears.

But she opened her legs wider, giving him what he needed, her slick woman's flesh, ready, glistening, and beautiful in the candlelight, his for the taking.

Needing her badly, he stared down at her, drinking in her beauty as he slid his hands up and down her inner thighs. He stroked her again and again, urging her knees even wider apart with each possessive pass of his hands. Far from resisting such intimacy, she only moaned softly, allowing him to open her fully.

Then, just when he was sure he'd burst no matter how fiercely he might squeeze himself, he plunged his face between her legs and nuzzled her roughly, pulling in great, rousing breaths of her hot, womanly scent. Consumed, he opened his mouth over all of her, drawing hard, needing the taste of her, craving and burning for her with a madness he'd never felt for any other woman.

"I will ne'er get enough of you," he vowed, breathing the words against her glistening flesh. "Ne'er in a thousand lifetimes. You are mine—forever."

She said nothing, but another little quiver sped through her. And, he'd swear, the scent of her arousal deepened, leaving no doubt as to her eagerness.

"Ach, but you are sweet!" He rubbed his head back and forth against her, tasting, licking, and nipping.

Most especially licking.

Long, leisurely broad-tongued strokes, each greedy sweep of his tongue thorough and claiming. The fierceness of his desire enflamed him, his need so powerful he thrust his hands beneath her, digging his fingers into her buttocks as he lifted her hips, needing her even closer to his questing, licking tongue.

The same tongue that would have had her writhing in ecstasy were he ravishing her in their dreams.

Only this time, she wasn't writhing at all.

Truth was, she wasn't even moving.

The wild pounding of Aidan's heart slowed a beat, the furious thunder of his blood in his ears quieting just enough for him to note that her sweet cries and whimpers had stopped too.

Frowning, he slowed his licking, his tongue coming to rest in the sleekness of her feminine heat. Something was wrong.

Horribly so.

His passion ebbing, he sat up, his pride stinging to see that she'd fallen asleep. Her lips were still parted, but her eyes had fallen shut. Eyes, he now suspected, that hadn't looked at him with lust-heavy need, but had been weighted with imminent sleep.

"Thor's bluidy hammer!" He pulled a hand down over his face, then blew out a breath. Frustration warring with his wounded pride and a certain still-aching *problem*, he considered helping himself to ease but cast aside the notion at once.

Kira slept too deeply.

His curse alone should have wakened her.

Yet she slept on, her sweet body still as stone, her face pale in the moonlight.

"Kee-*rah!*" He leapt from the bed and reached for her, shaking her by the shoulders, but she remained limp, her eyes closed and her head lolling to the side.

"Sakes, lass, speak to me!" He shook her again, his blood once more roaring in his ears and his heart galloping, each fearing beat slamming against his ribs. "What ails you?"

But only silence answered him.

"Damnation!" He eased her back against the pillows, relief flooding him when he pressed his ear to her breast and heard the beat of her heart.

Faint, but steady.

Her skin felt cold, her soft breath tinged with something he hadn't noticed before. Trying to place it, he rammed a hand through his hair, dismissing the first thought that came to mind.

Ne'er would he have been so crazed with lust not to have noticed such a piquant scent.

He frowned again.

He'd been wild with wanting her.

Wild enough that the hot scent of her musky womanliness must've swept his senses, blotting all else.

Dread piercing him, he sniffed her breath, then ran across the room, grabbing the ewer sitting so innocently beside her parchments. The half-filled cup of wine she'd clearly been sipping from.

Both the wine in the ewer and the cup smelled strongly of monkshood. The same herb in the potion Nils had given to Kendrew.

A fine painkiller and sleep-bringer, but a deadly poison if dosed by the wrong hands.

Cold terror racing up his spine, he threw the ewer and the cup into the hearth, then snatched up his plaid. Grabbing his sword as well, he pounded from the room, two things on his mind. Saving Kira and murdering whoe'er had tried to poison her.

But most of all, keeping Kira alive.

Anything else was unthinkable.

## 12

"*Nils! Tavish!*"

Aidan burst into the shadowed hall, thundering names and frowning darker than ever. With the castle already settled for the night, scarcely a torch remained lit, but he strode over to one of the few and grabbed it from its wall bracket, raising it high. Even so, he could barely see beyond the flame's wavering, smoky glare.

A fury on him like ne'er before, he stormed past sleeping, snoring men, not stopping until he reached the middle of the hall. If he stomped on someone, woe be to them for being in his way. But all was silent save his men's assorted night noises and a few muffled but telltale rustlings and moans floating out from the darkened window alcoves.

"Hellfire everlasting!" he roared when no one stirred.

The fools carousing in the window embrasures had surely heard him.

Blessedly, the castle dogs did. Their sudden barking and his own shouts soon had men jumping from their pallets, pea sacks and ale cups flying everywhere as they scrambled to their feet, grabbing swords and blinking through the shadows, their sleep-bogged eyes searching for the source of such clamor.

Satisfied, he thrust the flaring torch into the startled hands of a spluttering, half-naked kinsman, then leapt up onto a trestle bench, scanning the darkness for the two men he needed most.

"Tavish! Nils!" He jammed fisted hands on his hips as he looked round, trying to penetrate the shadows. "You!" He wheeled toward the torch-holder. "See that every torch is relit. Each candle. I need to see faces!"

The guilt that would show him whose head needed lopping.

But as the man hastened to do his bidding, the only souls to peer back at him were gaping and confused. Men startled from deep, innocent sleep. Nary a one looked blameworthy. They all merely gawped at him as if he'd sprouted horns and a tail.

And lost his wits in the bargain.

"Where is Tavish?" He glared back at them, not caring what they thought. "Nils?"

"I am here." Tavish emerged from one of the window alcoves, his voice raised above the dogs' frantic barking. "Where I e'er sleep," he added, starting forward.

Aidan scowled at him, not missing the lout's disheveled state, or Sinead's bright head gleaming in the depths of the alcove, her naked breasts and a length of bare leg revealed by the newly blazing torches.

"If you were sleeping, I am a mewling bairn!" Aidan jumped down from the trestle bench at his friend's approach. "Where is Nils?" He grabbed Tavish's arm, gripping tight. "Kira's been poisoned—with monkshood!"

Tavish's swagger vanished immediately. "Good gods!" He stared at Aidan, eyes wide. "Monkshood? You're sure?"

Aidan snorted. "She lies abed still as the grave and with the damnable herb on her breath." Letting go of Tavish's arm, he glanced round. "Where is Nils?" he repeated, seeing the healer nowhere. "He'll know a cure."

"But who would—"

"Devil if I know! Only that someone served her tainted wine." Aidan swept his gawking men with another glare. "I must find Nils before I—"

"If the culprit were here, your bellowing would've put him to flight already." Tavish tugged at his tunic, smoothed his rumpled plaid. "I heard your hollering before you reached the hall. Sinead—"

"How long has she been with you?" A dark suspicion whipped through Aidan's mind. "Did she carry wine abovestairs?"

Tavish's eyes rounded. "Come, man, you cannae think she had aught to do with it?"

Aidan dragged a hand through his hair. "I dinnae know what to think. But I *will* hear where she was. From you or the wench herself—if need be!"

"If you think to put a scare in her, you won't be—dressed as you are," Tavish declared, his gaze flicking the length of him.

The nearly bare length of him, not that he cared.

A hastily donned plaid and well-honed steel were more than enough. His bare hands would do the job—once he knew who bore the guilt.

Male or female.

Putting his hands on his hips, he gave Tavish a look that said so. "Where was she?"

"With me," Tavish owned, his gaze unwavering. "As were Maili and Evanna."

"All at once?" Aidan's brows flew upward.

Tavish shrugged. "Until a short while ago, aye. Only Sinead remained with me after—"

"Enough." Aidan raised a stilling hand. "Where did the other two go?"

"Who knows?" Tavish rubbed his beard, considering. "They are lustful wenches. I saw Maili and Evanna with Mundy earlier, but I think they went to the kitchens to see to laundering Kendrew's bloodied linens. Nils should be there, too. He was after fetching a bite to eat, having watched over Kendrew all night. He—"

"Now you tell me!" Aidan spun on his heel, racing for the screens passage to the kitchens before his friend could finish. "Find the birthing sisters and send them abovestairs!" he called over his shoulder as he ran. "Tell them what happened."

He'd assume they had no hand in poisoning Kira's wine.

Unfortunately, when he barreled into the kitchens, skidding to a halt on the slick, stone-laid floor, he once again encountered a scene of innocence. Panting, he dragged a hand across his brow, immediately dismissing the two wee spit laddies sleeping on pallets before the double-arched hearth. Cook stood beside them, calmly stirring a fine-smelling mutton stew in his great iron cook pot, while a tired-looking graybeard scrubbed the wooden surface of the bread table, quietly conversing with a second equally ancient man who sat nearby, plucking feathers from a plump hen.

None of them looked like evildoers.

"Where is Nils?" he boomed, regardless.

Cook wheeled around, his stew ladle flying from his fingers. "You'll curdle my stew with your yelling," he scolded, casting him an indignant glare as he stooped to swipe the spoon off the floor.

Stalking forward, Aidan snatched the spoon from him and tossed it aside, letting the thing fall where it may. "'Tis more than stew that will go bad if I do not soon find Nils or learn who sent tainted wine to my bedchamber!"

"Tainted wine?" Cook hitched up his belt, his considerable girth jigging even as his eyes widened. "Ne'er would I send fouled spirits to you. To anyone."

Aidan glowered back at him. "It would seem no one has, yet my lady lies abed near death! I'll have the heads of any bungling fools who—"

"Heigh-ho, lad! What are you shouting about?" Nils strode out of the murk of a hidden corner, Maili the laundress trailing after him, her tumbled flaxen curls and loose bodice leaving no doubt as to what had been going on in the deep shadows of Wrath's kitchens.

"He'd accuse us of serving bad wine." Cook snatched up his stew ladle a second time.

"No' bad wine, *tainted* wine." Aidan ignored him, whirling to Nils. "Someone laced the wine with monkshood and my lady drank it."

The healer's bluster evaporated. "That's not possible. Only I have access to my herb stores," he said, jangling a ring of keys at his belt. "I mixed Kendrew's sleeping draught myself. Here in the kitchens I did, as aye. Then I locked away my medicines in yon strongbox."

"No one but Nils has touched those herbs," Cook put in, pointing his spoon in the strongbox's direction.

Aidan glanced at the large, dome-topped coffer. Not one but two heavy locks held it secure.

As long as Nils' keys remained in his possession.

The healer *was* fond of women. By his own accounts, he'd been fleeced more than once by light-fingered lassies, taking advantage of his need for a snooze after pleasure.

Aidan looked at Maili, not surprised that she hadn't bothered to re-lace her gown. Of Wrath's three laundresses, she loved her craft best, baring her flesh often and freely. Using her charms to win favors and trinkets from the most jaded, hardened men.

Nils was anything but hardened. Beneath his Nordic bluster, the healer was a lamb.

As for Maili...

Aidan narrowed his eyes at her, thinking. He wasn't overly fond of the lass, but he was sure she craved her comforts too much to risk losing her position at Wrath.

Cook stepped forward, his bearded chin jutting. "I say the

lady simply guzzled too much wine. Aye, I doubt the wine was bad at all."

Aidan frowned. "I smelled the monkshood on Kira's breath, even stronger in the wine."

"How much did she drink?" Nils' brow crinkled, his face as dark as Aidan's own.

"I cannae say. There was a half-full cup on the table."

Nils drew a sharp breath. "A sip would be enough."

"Enough for what?" Aidan didn't really want to know.

"If she's had more than a pinch…" Nils shook his head, not needing to say more.

Aidan grabbed his arm, propelling him out the door. "Come!" He was running now. "Her heartbeat is steady and she yet breathes. Make haste so you can help her!"

"Would that I could!" Nils threw him a grim look as they dashed for the stairs. "There isn't a cure for monkshood."

WORDS FILTERED through the blackness enveloping Kira. Unlikely words like *monks* and *hoods*. Then Ameri-*cains* and tour buses. Grumblings about lairdly duty and love. Gaelic mumblings that sounded like low, softly muttered prayers, then sharp, furious bursts of anger. Heated words she couldn't decipher, only the outrage behind them. Clucking tongues, hurrying footsteps, the banging of doors. Sometimes, she was certain, the soothing patter of rain. It was a strange mishmash that made no sense, sounds flaring briefly in the darkness only to blur and dim as quickly.

Images came and went, too.

Frightful things, mostly. A gnarled hand plucking what looked to be fat garden slugs from an earthen jar, then dangling the icky beasties above her, only to have a larger, stronger hand sweep into view, knocking the slugs from curled, ancient fingers.

Two sets of bright, beady eyes peering at her through the mist, a glimpse of grizzled gray hair, or the weaving flame of a candle held too close to her face.

A bold swirl of plaid and a glint of raven black hair, proud, wide-set shoulders, and the silvery flash of a flourished sword, the bright red jewel in its pommel shining like a sunburst.

And then there was the cold.

Never had she felt so frozen. Buried under an icy avalanche of snow. A heavy, weighty drift of the white stuff that seemed to come and go, chilling her to the bone, then easing slightly, only to freeze her anew before she could gather strength to crack her leaden eyelids to see where all the snow had come from.

Or if she'd been thrust forward in time again and had accidentally landed inside a giant hotel ice machine. The kind that always seemed to be right outside her hotel room door and that made weird popping and *grrr'ing* noises all night. Not to mention the clatter and commotion when someone just had to fetch a bucket of ice in the wee hours.

Thinking about it now, though, made her laugh.

Or rather, she'd have laughed if she could.

Too bad for her, her mouth felt drier than a dustbin and her tongue had turned to sandpaper.

Just as bad, she still couldn't seem to open her eyes.

"Sir!" cackled a high-pitched voice just above her ear. "I do believe she's trying to speak."

"No, you fool," chimed a second voice. "'Tis laughing she is!"

"Gods be praised!" A third voice filled the room, this one deep, rich, and very Scottish. The joy in it made her want to weep. "Kee-*rah*! Sweet lass, speak to me."

She couldn't do that, so she blinked—or tried to. Especially when her eyes began to water and burn, hot tears damping her lashes and trickling down her cheeks.

Bedwells didn't cry, dammit.

But apparently she was, because not one, but two pairs of

knotty old hands were suddenly dabbing cloths at her cheeks. Gentle old hands, so caring, she swallowed against the emotion welling in her throat. Unfortunately, dry as her mouth was, her swallow caused an odd rasping sound, ghastly even to her own ears.

So awful it was almost a croak.

No, it was worse.

Kira grimaced. That, she could do.

"You she-biddies are hurting her!"A second male voice boomed, some distant corner of her mind recognizing it as belonging to Nils the Viking. "I told you she didn't need bleeding."

"Pah!" One of the old women sniffed. "You said she might survive the monkshood if she didn't catch a fever. Her own chilled pea sacks prevented that, but who's to say our leeches didn't draw off whate'er other evils might've been in her?"

"The only evil in her was the poison she drank!" a third manly voice declared.

Mundy, the great black-bearded Irishman, if Kira wasn't mistaken.

But poison? She started to ask about that, but her tongue stuck to the roof of her mouth.

As if sensing her discomfort, one of the knotty hands returned, this time to dab a cool wet cloth at her lips.

"Aye, 'tis the leeching that saved her," the owner of the knotty hand insisted. "That, and the powder of newt we sprinkled on the hearth fire. Everyone knows powdered newt fumes cleanse the air o' bad vapors."

"Hah!" Nils the Viking snorted. "Newt fumes do naught but make good men sneeze."

Knotty Hand teetered. "Be that why *you* haven't done?"

"Cease! All of you." Aidan's voice came again, sweet as a dream. "Away with you, the lot of you. I'll watch o'er her alone now. 'Tis clear she'll soon be waking." Then, in a sterner, don't-argue-with-me tone, "I'll no' have her frightened if she opens her eyes to see so many ugly faces peering at her. And—Tavish! Take Ferlie with you. I willnae have her upset by his whining."

"And your bellowing? Ferlie's whimpers and groans are nowise as loud. She's fond of the old beast and might be pleased to know he's pined for her," another deep male voice countered.

Tavish's own. Her champion the day she'd found herself perched atop Aidan's gateway arch.

She smiled, remembering, but the smile made her lips crack. Even worse, she suspected they were bleeding. "Owww," she moaned before she could stop herself.

"See?" Aidan roared, bellowing indeed. "You're upsetting her. Now begone—all of you!"

A great ruckus followed. The departure, Kira assumed, of those souls at Wrath who'd cared to look in on her. From the number of trudging feet and muttered complaints as Aidan ushered them from the room, it must've been a goodly number indeed.

But only one mattered so much to her that she wanted to throw her arms around him and tell him how glad she was that he was there. How her heart had nearly burst when she'd heard his voice.

His beautiful, melt-her-at-ten-paces Scottish burr.

Listening to him now, she judged he was close.

Possibly on his knees by her bedside. Hoping it, she tried to lift her arm and reach for him, feeling a great need to touch him. But her arm refused to move. Her fingers still tingled a bit. In fact, she'd done a lot of tingling, if she remembered rightly.

Just not the good kind.

Far from it. Every inch of her throbbed and ached with mind-numbing intensity. A nightmarish stiffness worse than the time she'd tried to cram a year's worth of gym workouts into two days and ended up nearly creeping around her apartment on all fours, finding it too painful to stand and even worse to move.

She felt that bad now.

Having enough of it, she struggled to open her eyes, then tried even harder to raise herself on an elbow. Instead, all she managed was heaving a great, trembling sigh.

Aidan leaned close and kissed her cheek. "Hush, sweet, and lie still," he said, smoothing the hair from her brow. "You'll feel better once we get some broth into you."

Broth?

She tried to smile again. She knew he didn't mean chicken noodle soup, but as long as it was hot broth, she'd feel better indeed. Even lukewarm would do. Her feet felt like a block of ice and even the tips of her fingers were tingling-numb with cold.

"I-I'm f-freezing," she rasped, her teeth chattering.

"You won't be for long." He put a hand to her forehead and she could see his relief through her lashes. "There isn't a fever, and if you're awake now, there's no longer a need to keep you mounded with these chilled pea sacks."

Her lips twitched. So that was why she'd felt buried under an avalanche. It was funny, really. But what she needed was water, not frozen peas.

"I'm thirsty, please." Her voice was thick again, hoarse and unintelligible.

She tried to will him to understand, but the concentration only made her head throb harder.

"Sakes, but you gave me a fright!" He shoved a hand through his hair, looking almost as haggard as she felt.

Then, leaping to his feet, he threw back the covers and began removing the ice bags, pitching them into a large wooden tub nearby, another cut-in-half wine barrel-y bathing contraption, this one apparently empty.

But what really caught her eye was the flashy sword propped against a chair near the wine barrel. Much longer and definitely more magnificent than his usual one, its blade reflected the flames of the hearth fire, the whole length of it shining and sparkling like a well-polished mirror. An elaborately scrolled inscription was inlaid along the blade's fuller, the blood-channel running down from the hilt, but she couldn't make out the letters. The inscription just made the sword look special.

Magical or enchanted.

Much like what she imagined King Arthur and his knights would've carried.

She squinted, trying to see it better. The cross-guard looked rather straight and plain, and the hilt was leather-wrapped and worn. As if it had been used often, and hard. Her breath caught when she focused on the sword's pommel. That was the real attention-getter.

Hers anyway.

A circular, wheel pommel, its centerpiece was an enormous bloodred gemstone. Polished smooth and brilliant, dazzling rays of bright, ruby-colored light streamed in every direction from its jeweled surface, the radiant bands dancing crazily on the room's whitewashed walls and the ceiling.

It was definitely the sunburst blade.

The one she'd seen whipping through the blackness as she'd slept.

She moistened her lips, her heart pounding. Her eyes fluttered completely open.

"I saw that sword." She peered at it now, looking from the blade to Aidan. "You swung it—I saw you in my dreams."

"I raised it, aye." He spoke after a hesitation. "Once."

She blinked, remembering the blade's great sweeping arc through the quiet and darkness. A flashing, lightning-quick arc, the memory of it brought a horrible thought.

"You weren't trying to put me out of my misery, were you?"

Aidan felt his jaw slip. "I was trying to save you." He stared down at her, the neck opening of his tunic suddenly so tight he could scarce breathe. "That sword has been in my family for centuries. Some claim it brings us good fortune. I thought its presence might—"

"Help me?" She pushed up on her elbows, her gaze flitting to the sword again. "Like a good luck talisman or something?"

Aidan nodded. "Many clans have the like," he admitted, hoping that would suffice.

He wasn't about to tell her how he'd dropped to his knees and raised the sword to the Old Ones, vowing on the bloodred pommel stone that he'd grant Kira any wish if only they'd intervene and spare her life.

He knew well what her greatest wish might be and even if the Ancients smote him for it, now that she was clearly back amongst the living, he'd prefer not to tempt fate any further.

It was one thing to hear about Ameri-*cains* and their flying machines and tour buses, and something else entirely to be surrounded by such impossibilities.

Pushing them from his mind, he poured her a small bit of water. "Drink this," he said, slipping his hand behind her head, steadying her as he held the cup to her lips.

She took a few sips and fell back against the pillows. "I must've been in pretty bad shape if you thought only a magic sword could cure me."

"It isn't a magic sword, but a *family* sword. In these hills, we see strength in blood ties. The continuity of our clans." Aidan tossed aside the last of the pea sacks. "I wanted to share that strength with you, that was all."

She still looked skeptical. "There isn't any mumbo jumbo running down the sword's blade?" she asked, slanting another glance at it. "Those cryptic letters aren't a charm or a hex or anything?"

Aidan laughed despite himself. "The inscription reads 'Invincible,'" he told her, speaking true. "'Tis the blade's name. Family tradition says it came to us from one of the great Somerled's sons, though we cannot say which. The red of the gemstone is supposed to be his blood, frozen forever inside the pommel stone. That, however, is questionable."

"Who knows..." She trailed off, her attention on the sword.

"It doesn't matter." He reached for her hand, not liking the shadows beneath her eyes. "Only that you are well now."

Her gaze returned to his. "How long did I sleep? One night? Two?"

"Four." Letting go of her hand, he took a large plaid from the end of the bed and swirled it over her, taking care to smooth it into place. "Tonight would have been the fifth." He touched her cheek, not wanting to frighten her. "You will be fine, Kee-*rah*. Dinnae you worry."

But she did.

Especially since learning he'd tried some quirky medieval voodoo to save her. No matter what he cared to call it, that's what it had been.

Frozen ancestral blood indeed.

Not that such a notion was any wackier than time travel. Or ghosts. She certainly knew both existed. She also knew someone must've tried to poison her.

Or him.

She glanced at the water cup, grateful when he picked it up immediately, once more helping her to drink. Before he could take it away, she lifted a shaky hand and grasped his wrist. "The wine I drank," she began, then needed another sip to finish. "It was laced with something, wasn't it?"

He nodded. "It was a careless mistake, Kee-*rah*," he lied, the twitch in his jaw giving him away before he even finished the sentence. "Nils mixed a sleeping draught for Kendrew and someone mistook it for simple wine."

"You aren't fooling me." She struggled to a sitting position, every inch of her screaming protest, but determination made her strong. "Someone here tried to kill me. Or you."

"It willnae happen again." He folded his arms, no longer denying it. "I'll no' have you worrying."

She blew out a breath, puffing her bangs off her forehead. "I've been worrying ever since I remembered reading about your cousin locking you in your own dungeon to die."

Aidan frowned.

Her worries couldn't compare to the concerns splitting him. No matter how he turned it, he'd failed her. Conan Dearg wallowed in Wrath's deepest, darkest pit. Every man within Aidan's own walls feared, respected, and, he hoped, loved him. Yet someone he knew, someone close to him, had tried to take Kira's life.

And he'd been unable to prevent it.

Indeed, while she'd sipped the tainted wine, he'd stood laughing in his hall, looking on as his men gallivanted about, making merry with her pea sacks.

Thinking all was well with his world.

It was inexcusable. A mistake he couldn't allow to happen again.

He drew a deep breath, hoping to convince her it wouldn't. "I've ordered my cousin placed in a different part of the dungeon. He's in a larger, more comfortable cell, but there's an oubliette running through its middle. He—"

"A what?"

Aidan sighed and began to pace. "An oubliette is a bottle dungeon," he told her. "A narrow crack in the floor just wide enough for a man to fall through. When he does, the chutelike opening widens into a small round space only large enough to crouch in. There's no escape unless someone is hauled out by a rope."

"That doesn't change the history books."

Aidan glanced at her, annoyed that she kept repeating the same argument, but pleased to hear her voice sounding stronger.

He paused at the table to pour himself a measure of ale, downing it in one quick swallow.

"What it changes is that my cousin may well be tempted to use the oubliette to end his misery. He's a vain man, fond of his appearance and comforts. He'll weary of confinement. The lack of baths and a comb for his hair. If he managed to sweet-talk his way out of the dungeon to climb up onto the gateway arch the night Kendrew claims to have seen him, or if he persuaded someone to taint your wine, he'll have no further chances to do so. He—"

"How do you know?"

Aidan closed his eyes. "Because I will do all in my power to keep you safe."

But as soon as the words left his tongue, his stomach clenched and he fisted his hands.

Truth was, he didn't know.

Not when someone at Wrath conspired with his cousin.

He could only hope.

He started pacing again, well aware that Conan Dearg had been known to wriggle through crevices too tight for a mouse. The bastard had more charm than a whore had favors. But no matter what Kira's history books might say, Aidan wouldn't allow her to become one of Conan Dearg's victims.

Even if keeping her safe meant putting certain plans into action.

Things he'd discussed earlier with Tavish and hoped would ne'er be necessary.

He closed his eyes again and ran a hand down over his face, forcing himself not to worry about that road until it loomed up before him, leaving him no choice.

After a moment, he drew another deep, lung-filling breath and put back his shoulders, schooling his face into his best expression of lairdly confidence before he strode back across the room, ready to ply his lady with sweet words and kisses until

Cook finally sent up a kitchen laddie with her long-overdue broth.

But when he reached the bed, he saw that she'd fallen asleep again.

A restful sleep this time, praise the gods.

Sweet color tinged her cheeks, and for the first time in days her breathing sounded soft and easy. No longer labored and harsh.

Leaning down, he smoothed his knuckles along the side of her face. His heart catching, he kissed her brow. He burned to stretch out beside her, gathering her close and holding her against him all the night through. But she needed her rest and he needed a distraction.

Something to take his mind off that road he did not want to journey down.

It'd been bad enough discussing such eventualities with Tavish.

Frowning at the memory, he made certain Kira was comfortable, then went straight to the table, meaning to help himself to another generous cup of ale and then settle in his chair for the night.

He'd spent the last four nights in its cold embrace. One more wouldn't make that much difference.

But when he reached for the ale jug, he noticed something amiss. There was a new parchment sheet resting atop Kira's stack of scribbled notes.

A parchment he was sure hadn't been there before.

Nor were the boldly inked words slashed across it anything like Kira's.

They were hateful, fate-changing words.

As he looked at them, his eyes narrowed. He snatched up the parchment and held it closer to the flame of a candle, just to be certain. Unfortunately, he'd not been mistaken. The words didn't change and the threat remained the same. *Next time it will not be monkshood in Kira's wine but cold steel in her back.*

"Nae, it will be neither." Aidan stared at the words until his blood iced.

A surprising calm settling on him, he walked across the room and dropped the parchment into the hearth fire. He looked on as the thing curled and blackened, disappearing as surely as its meaningless threat. Whoe'er had penned and delivered it wouldn't be able to reach Kira where he meant to take her.

Perhaps she'd been right all along and they were meant to be together in her time, not his.

How he fared there mattered not.

Only her safekeeping.

Quickly, before any niggling doubts could assail him, he dusted his hands and settled himself in his chair. There'd be much to do on the morrow and a good night's sleep would serve him well. With Tavish's help, the upcoming feast night would likely be their best opportunity to slip away unnoticed.

His mind set, he curled his fingers around the hilt of his family's precious sword, wondering if fate had caused him to prop the well-loved sword against his chair. Or if he'd brought them to this pass by vowing on its ancient, bloodred pommel stone.

Either way, he wouldn't fail.

Not with Kira Bedwell as the prize.

## 13

A full sennight later, seven days and nights unlike any Aidan had ever known, he stood in the shadows of his great hall's entry arch, oddly detached from the chaotic preparations for the evening's celebratory feast. Everywhere, men bustled about, laughing and jesting, their arms laden with long, streaming garlands of autumn leaves and bright red rowanberries, which they took great pleasure in hanging on the walls and draping wherever they could. Harried servants ignored them, too busy themselves, spreading white linen over row upon row of trestle tables while red-cheeked kitchen laddies dashed after them, looking excited and self-important as they laid out trenchers, ale and wine cups, and knives. Delicately carved spoons of bone that had been his mother's pride. Extra torches already blazed, too, as did a well-doing log fire in the hall's massive hearth.

Tempting aromas drifted from the kitchens, enhancing the hall's smoke-hazed air with mouthwatering hints of what was to come: a bountiful parade of roasted meats, simmering stews, and freshly baked breads. Not to be overlooked, at least two silver candelabrums gleamed on every table, each one boasting fine wax candles waiting to be lit the instant Aidan gave his nod. Even the floor rushes had been replaced, the fresh new layer fragrant with sweet-smelling herbs and dried lavender, much to the frustration of the castle dogs, used to scrounging for scraps of food buried in the matted older rushes.

Not that the new rushes kept them from looking. They did, capering and getting underfoot, barking wildly each time someone paused in their work to shoo them away. Excited, the dogs wagged tails, ran in circles, and made general mayhem. As did Aidan's men, their zeal for the day breaking his heart.

Steeling himself, he drew a deep breath and released it slowly. Whether it pained him or nae, he remained where he stood. The gods knew this might be the last time he gazed on such a scene. It was wise and good to brand the memories into his soul. With all respect to Kira's world, he doubted it could be as colorful and joyous as his.

Despite the dark bits that were driving him away.

As if to prove it, a great burst of ringing laughter rose from the far side of the hall and he glanced that way, not surprised to see Nils and Mundy holding court with Sinead, Evanna, and Maili. The maids wore rowanberry sprigs in their hair and were dancing gaily around the two laughing men as they balanced on trestle benches, trying in vain to festoon the ceiling rafters with bold swaths of tartan.

Nearby, at the high table, young Kendrew did his part as well. Sitting quietly, he busied himself folding the linen hand towels that would be offered to each celebrant, along with a bowl of fresh, scented washing water.

Watching him, Aidan frowned. He'd grown fond of the lad and had plans for him. A muscle twitched in his jaw and his throat thickened. An annoying condition that worsened when the two birthing sisters hobbled past, sprays of ribbon-wrapped heather clutched to their breasts. Adornments he knew they'd made with great care, intending to place them before Kira's seat at the high table.

In her honor, too, they'd bathed. More than one soul had commented on such a wonder. He'd noticed it now himself, catching a hint of rose-scented soap and fresh, clean linen wafting after them.

Putting back his shoulders, Aidan swallowed hard and blinked. He was a warrior chieftain, after all. He had no business going soft around the edges just because a young lad he scarce knew sat folding hand towels at his table and two bent old women chose this day to bathe for the first time since he'd known them.

The stinging heat piercing the backs of his eyes had nothing to do with the like.

Nothing at all.

And it *especially* had nothing to do with how difficult it was to see his people so ready and eager to finally welcome Kira into their hearts. Now, when the time had come for them to leave.

A cold nose nudged his hand then, and the fool lump in his throat almost burst. "Damnation!" He started, reaching to stroke Ferlie's head when the old dog pressed against him, whimpering. "Ach, Ferlie. Dinnae you go making me feel worse."

"You needn't go anywhere, you know."

Aidan jumped at the sound of the deep, well-loved voice behind him. Whirling round, he glared at the only soul besides Kira who knew his plans.

Tavish, good and trusted friend, cousin, possible half brother, and soon to be new laird of Wrath, stood lounging against the wall, his arms folded and his dark eyes glittering challenge.

"You, of all people, know why I must leave. Why it must be tonight." Aidan met his gaze, trying not to see the hurt behind his friend's piercing stare. "No one will miss us if we slip away when the revelries are at their highest, everyone deep in their cups. And"—he glanced out an arrow-slit window—"it will be full dark tonight, no moon."

"Ach! How could I forget?" Tavish slapped his forehead with

the ball of his hand. "The night's blackness and the mist will shield you from curious eyes when you clamber up onto the gate-house arch, looking for your time portal."

"Sakes, Tavish." Aidan grabbed his friend's arm, gripping hard. "Dinnae you start on me too," he said, keenly aware of Ferlie's sad, unblinking stare. "We cannae stay. I'll no' have Kira's life threatened."

Tavish arched a brow. "Since when has a MacDonald e'er run from a foe?" He flipped back his plaid, patting the hilt of his sword. "Together we can protect your lady. Here. Where you belong. Both of you."

Aidan shook his head. "I am no' running away. I'm seeing Kee-*rah* back where she belongs and where I know she'll be safe." Whipping back his own plaid, he displayed the Invincible's proud hilt, having asked Tavish earlier to give his old sword to Kendrew once he was gone.

Curling his fingers around the sword's ruby red pommel stone, he willed his friend to understand. "Have you ne'er loved a woman, Tavish?" He spoke as plain as he could. "Loved her so much that you know you'd no' be able to breathe without her? Enough no' to care about your pride? So much that you'd do anything to keep her safe? Even if the doing might rip your soul?"

Tavish just looked at him.

"That is how I love Kee-*rah*." He let his plaid fall back into place, covering the ancient sword. "Too much to trust even a blade as worthy as the Invincible. No' when my foe is invisible and dwelling within my own castle walls."

Tavish shrugged. "Kill Conan Dearg. Let me kill him. There has to be a connection. Once he is no more, whoe'er it is will surely slink into the shadows."

Aidan sighed. "You know I cannae do that."

The weight of the Invincible seeming to increase at his hip, Aidan held his friend's stare, amazed that Tavish could forget how, many years ago when they'd been boys, his father had accidentally slain his own brother, not recognizing him in the fury and bloodlust of a fierce battle melee.

The tragedy had marked Aidan's father for life, and he'd made both boys kneel with their hands on the Invincible's jeweled pommel, swearing on its sacredness ne'er to take up a sword against a kinsman.

No matter the reason.

It was an oath Aidan had broken a time or two, much to his sorrow. But he'd ne'er acted in cold blood, and he simply couldn't. Not when he remembered how haunted his father's eyes had been all his living days.

And now he'd made yet another vow on his family's holiest relic, this time calling on the Ancient Ones to save Kira from death by poisoning.

A plea they'd answered.

He couldn't risk their anger by breaking not one but two such pacts.

As if he guessed, Tavish glanced into the festive hall, then back at him. "You truly mean to leave us? Nothing will change your mind?"

"My mind was set the instant I found that parchment." He still felt how his blood had chilled, the shock hitting him like a kick to the gut. "It was no empty threat, but penned with true venom."

"Then I shall go with you." Tavish clapped a hand on his shoulder, looking quite taken by the notion. "I wouldn't mind seeing those flying machines and tour buses."

"Nae, you must stay here to laird in my place." Aidan reached up to press his friend's hand. "The clan will follow you well. Our friends and allies respect you. Equally important, our foes know not to cross you."

"There are others. Good and worthy men—"

"It will ease my mind to know Wrath is in your hands. Yours and no one else's." Aidan paused, needing to swallow. His damnable throat was closing again. "I'll have your word, Tavish. Only so can I go in peace."

Tavish scowled at him and turned away, only to swing back around and grab Aidan by the arms, dragging him into a swift, crushing embrace. "Sakes, but I shall miss you!"

"Ach, chances are we'll be rejoining you in the hall—back before the sweet courses are served." Aidan almost wished that would be the way of it. "We cannae be sure anything will happen. It is a chance, naught more."

"Nae, it is more. You will be sent forward to Kira's time." Tavish pressed a hand to his heart. "I feel it here."

"We shall see," Aidan said, trying to make light of the possibility.

Truth was, he felt it too.

Almost as if the air around him was already shifting and the cold afternoon mist beginning to drift across the bailey was lying in wait, silent and watching. Anticipating just the right moment to thicken, swirl, and speed him away.

A chill tripping down his spine, he grabbed his friend's shoulders, pulling him close one last time. "I must see to Kira," he said, releasing him. "I've returned her old clothes and she may need help hiding them beneath proper raiments for the feast."

Tavish nodded. "How long will you remain with us? Before you go?"

"Not long." Aidan glanced back into the hall. It was more crowded now, and louder, some of his men already carousing. "Perhaps you can help by making sure the ale flows a bit faster than usual?"

Again Tavish nodded. "As you will."

"So be it, my friend." Aidan turned away, suddenly needing to be gone. "Live well."

But before he'd gone three paces, Tavish halted him with a hand to his arm.

"There might be one unexpected difficulty," he said, looking pained.

Aidan waited. Something told him he wasn't going to like whatever his friend had to say.

"Well?" He looked at him. "What is it?"

"Not it, her."

"Kee-*rah*?"

"Nae." Tavish shook his head. "The MacLeod widow. She—"

*"Fenella MacLeod?"* Aidan's brows lifted. He hadn't heard word of the she-devil since he'd spurned her attentions some long while ago. "What of her?"

"She is here and will surely expect a welcome at the feast."

"How can she be here?" Aidan rubbed the back of his neck, the thought of the predatory widow making his flesh crawl. "The MacLeod holding is on the other side of Skye. I didn't send her word about tonight's celebrations."

"Be that as it may, she is here." Tavish looked miserable. "Down on the landing beach with one of her galleys. She sent word a short while ago, claiming her vessel has sprung a leak. I was coming to tell you when I saw you standing here, looking into the hall."

Aidan snorted. "MacLeod galleys ne'er spring leaks. Their fleet is almost as well kept as our own."

"My thoughts exactly," Tavish agreed. "The woman is curious. She's heard of Kira and wants to see her."

"Ah, well." Aidan considered. "There we have your first duty as Wrath's new laird."

Tavish blinked. "My first duty?"

Aidan nodded.

"You must keep the MacLeod woman occupied tonight. By fair means or foul."

❦

HOURS LATER, Kira sat beside Aidan at the high table in Wrath's crowded great hall, worrying about what might or might not happen when they finally managed to sneak away from the feast and out into the bailey. Beyond that, only a few other things really concerned her.

How wonderful it was to finally have good-fitting, comfortable shoes on her feet again.

That the panties she'd missed so much now felt constricting. That wearing her medieval garb over her regular clothes made her look fat.

And that if the big-breasted, raven-haired siren sitting with Tavish at the other end of the table didn't stop sending slow, knowing smiles Aidan's way, she and Aidan would be on *their* way well before he intended.

A departure she would truly regret, because if everything went as planned, she'd likely never again have the chance to experience this kind of medieval pageantry.

Not for real, anyway.

And she knew without having ever attended one, that a twenty-first-century medieval banquet place couldn't hold a candle to Aidan's feast. No matter how flashy and fancy, how expensive, or how many supposedly hunky male models they engaged to play at being knights.

"*Aidan.*" The siren's low, husky voice slid around the name like a caress. "You didn't tell us your good news," she purred, leaning forward just enough to display the generous swell of her breasts. "How proud you must be—an heir for Wrath at last."

Kira's face flamed.

Aidan, man that he was, fell for the ploy.

He blinked, his gaze flitting to Kira, then back at the woman. "Heir?"

The woman's gaze dipped pointedly to the bulge at Kira's middle. She said nothing, her red, berry-stained lips simply curving in another slow, intimate smile.

A nasty, catty smile that lasted only until Maili materialized beside her, a huge tray of stewed oysters and cooked herring balanced on one hand—a hand that flicked just enough to the side to send the tray's wet, steaming delicacies spilling into the beauty's lap.

"Ohhh!" The woman leapt to her feet, her eyes snapping with fury. "You careless chit!" she cried, swiping at her ruined skirts, her scoldings and jigging drawing all eyes.

Then, before Kira knew what was happening, two strong hands were lifting her to her feet, releasing her almost as quickly to thwack Aidan roughly on the back, then give him a great shove toward the deep shadows at the rear of the dais.

*Tavish*, she saw, barely catching her breath before he yanked back a tapestry and swept open a door she'd not known existed. "Fair means or foul," he said, practically pushing them through it, into the cold, sleety dark of the bailey.

True to the end, he'd created a diversion for their escape.

Then the door slammed behind them and they were alone, running hand in hand across the deserted courtyard, the swirling night mist so thick around them that Castle Wrath and its sturdy walls already seemed little more than a long-ago dream.

Somewhere, muffled and distant, a dog whined and howled, but otherwise the night was eerily quiet. Great rolling curtains of mist damped all sound, even the pounding of their feet on the bailey's dark, rain-slick cobbles. Then, as they reached the gatehouse, for once emptied and silent, its heavy oaken doors closed and barred, the impassable iron portcullis lowered to keep out any unexpected intruders, even the dogs' howls faded away, dwindling until not even a faint echo remained.

What did remain was a ladder, tucked into the deepest shadows in the concealing lee of the curtain wall and giving access to the top of the gatehouse arch.

Looking at it, so real and *waiting*, Kira felt her mouth go dry and she began to tremble.

"Aidan..." She pulled him back when he grabbed hold of the ladder, his foot already on the first rung. "I know you ordered men to take turns on the battlements," she said, scanning the wall-walk but seeing only swirling mist and thin curtains of fine, slanting rain. "What if one of them sees us?"

"They won't." He kept his hands on the ladder, already ascending. "They know to keep their eyes trained on the cliffs and the sea. No' on the empty bailey and the gatehouse arch behind them."

Even so, Kira cast a last glance at the top of the curtained walling, so difficult now to see in all the thick, whirling mist. And even if she could make out the battlements, somehow she doubted she'd see any men there.

Not now.

The queasy feeling in her stomach and the prickles at the back of her neck told her it was already too late.

Aidan's men were gone.

Blessedly, *he* was still there. On top of the arch now, and reaching down for her, encouraging her. "Come, Kee-*rah*, give me your hand and I will pull you up."

Kira blinked. She hadn't even realized she'd already scrambled nearly all the way up the ladder. Her heart pounding, she felt his hand grasp hers even as the ladder rung seemed to vanish from beneath her feet.

"Gah!" Her breath caught as she hovered just a split second in thin, empty air. But Aidan's arm swept around her like a band of steel, his strong hand heaving her up onto the arch top with him. "I think it's happening already," she gasped, clutching at him. "The ladder disappeared beneath me."

"Aye, lass, I know." He kept his arms locked around her, holding her so tight against him she could hardly breathe. "I cannae see much through all this mist, but I think more has disappeared than the ladder."

Kira wrapped her own arms around him, clinging to him just

as fiercely. She pressed her head against his chest and closed her eyes, not really wanting to see whatever it was he'd meant had disappeared.

It couldn't be helped that they'd find Wrath in ruin if indeed they returned to her time, but she'd come to love the real Wrath and didn't want to watch it dissolve before her eyes. It would be difficult enough to see Aidan's face when he saw what had become of his proud home.

She winced.

That was something she should have thought about before. Something she might not have to worry about now because nothing was happening.

Nothing at all.

Even the light patter of the fine, misty rain was no more. Total silence swelled around them, almost like the proverbial quiet before the storm, a thought that made her shudder, then cry out when her foot slipped on the slick stone surface of the arch top.

"Hold, lass!" Aidan's arms tightened around her, righting her before she lost her balance. "Try no' to move, Kee-*rah*. Just hold on to me."

"I will—Iieeeee ..." Her foot slipped again, this time plunging knee-deep into a mossy, fern-lined crack in the arch's stonework.

Crumbling, ancient stonework, grass-grown and riddled with cracks—just as she remembered.

Equally amazing, her tartan picnic rug and her backpack were wedged in a clump of ferns near her ankle.

"Aidan!" She pulled her foot from the crack, her heart thundering. "We're here! My things, too!"

Her entire body shaking, she reached into the crevice, her fingers closing around a strap on her backpack just when all hell broke loose. An earsplitting *boom* shattered the quiet, knocking the breath from her as wave after wave of brilliant white light flashed across the arch top, ripping away the mist and darkness until every tiny age line and lichen pattern stood out in bold relief on the ruined stone.

Then the world went black.

Total darkness.

Even the cold was gone. The fine, sleety rain. She felt and heard nothing.

Until a great blaring blast pierced her ears and she slammed down onto the stone again, this time landing on her buttocks with a hard, bone-jarring *thunk*.

"Bluidy hell, woman! Have you gone daft?"

Kira jerked, a man's angry voice ringing in her ears.

An angry Scottish voice, burred and all, but so unpleasantly startling it took her a moment and a few mad eye-blinks to realize that the owner of the voice was standing beside the open driver door of a bright red car.

"Damned tourists, anyway!" He glared at her, tapping his temple with a forefinger. "I could've hit you! Flying across the car park like there was no tomorrow!" he huffed, jumping back in his car and roaring off.

*Car park?*

Kira blinked again, only now fully grasping that she *was* in a car park and not on Wrath's gatehouse arch. Far from it, she was sitting right smack in the middle of a large paved and graveled car park crammed full with cars, square-shaped recreational vehicles, and tightly packed rows of coach tour buses.

Her stomach beginning to do funny things, she recognized the place as the Spean Bridge Mill, a popular tourist trap on the scenic A-82, just north of Fort William and not far from the turnoff to Skye.

This was definitely her time, but something had gone wrong.

They weren't supposed to return here.

Nor was it autumn anymore, but late spring or early summer. She'd lost six or seven months. Her palms starting to dampen, she hoped she hadn't lost more.

Aidan was gone.

Trying not to panic, she pushed to her feet and looked around, searching for him. Her backpack was still clutched tight in her hands and her tartan picnic rug lay a few feet away, unharmed. But her medieval clothes were gone, as was he.

"Aidan!"

A family of four turned to give her weird looks. She scowled at them, not caring what they thought. "Aidan!"she called again, her mouth fully dry now, blood starting to pound in her ears.

There was no sign of him anywhere.

Only other people.

Lots and lots of other people. Mostly American and English tourists, from the looks of them. They streamed in and out of the mill-and-tea shop, weaving through the parked cars, and crowding the pretty arbored walkways. An especially noisy bunch blocked the entrance to the mill's busy public restrooms.

Separated from the main gift shop by a flower-lined walkway and a series of dark-wooded pergolas, they were the cleanest and finest public restrooms along the entire A-82. An insider tip for those in the know, complete with a lovely view of the Spean River's rushing, tumbling rapids.

They were also where she needed to go. *Now.*

Not for the usual reason, but because panic and dread were making her ill. Gorge was rising in her throat, hot, bitter, and scary. Worse, she was finding it increasingly difficult to breathe.

She needed to splash cold water on her face and calm down.

She needed to *think.*

Plan a way to find Aidan, wherever he'd landed. Or get back to him if he was still standing on his gateway arch top, possibly just as panicked and looking for her.

Moving fast now, Kira headed straight for the restrooms. If need be, she'd use her elbows, or even swing her backpack, to plow a way through the tight knot of tourists blocking the entrance.

She needed a clear head more than they needed to *go*.

But when she neared them, she saw they weren't waiting to get into the fancy restrooms at all. They were taking pictures. Snapping away like mad, oooh'ing and ahhh'ing over something she couldn't see.

Then two of them moved and she did see.

They were photographing Aidan!

He stood ramrod straight between two wooden barrels of spring flowers, the Invincible raised threateningly, and such a fierce glower on his face he would have scared her if she hadn't known him. Unmoving and unblinking, he could have been a life-sized statue. The tourists apparently mistook him for a reen-actor, posing for their benefit.

A little old lady on the edge of the crowd gave Kira a gentle tap on the arm. "He's been standing there like that for at least ten minutes," she gushed, aiming her diggy camera at him. "My granddaughters back in Ohio will swoon when they see his picture. He's just the kind of wild Highlander they're always dreaming about."

*Don't I know it*, Kira almost said.

Instead, she gave the woman a tight smile and pushed her way forward. "Aidan! There you are. Come, we're late." She laid on her most businesslike tone. "Your appearance at the Loch Ness Medieval Festival is in an hour." She grabbed his arm, his muscles hard and tense and ready for battle. She flashed an apologetic glance at the crowd as she pulled him away. "We'll just make it if we hurry."

"Wait!" A family father with three little kids hurried after her. "There's a medieval festival at Loch Ness today?"

Kira nodded. "All day," she improvised, praying Aidan wouldn't contradict her.

Not that he looked keen on saying much of anything.

His mouth was still set in a firm, hard line, and he'd clamped his jaw so tight she wouldn't be surprised if he never got it open again.

He also refused to let her pull him farther than a few yards from where he'd been standing. His scowl darkening, he sheathed the Invincible with such force, the English family father and the rest of the crowd scattered at once, leaving them alone on the walkway.

Others, those just now exiting the gift shop, made a wide circle around them.

"Wise souls." Aidan spoke at last, eyeing them as they scuttled past.

Planting his legs apart and folding his arms, he assumed his most regal mien. A posture that lasted until one of the monstrous *things* he assumed was a coach tour bus rumbled past them, only to come to a shuddering, smoke-belching halt, then disgorge a small throng of chattering, oddly garbed people who looked very much like the ones who'd cornered him the moment he'd landed in this horrid, dreadful place.

One turned to gape at him—a female, and not unattractive, all things considered—but when she paused and aimed one of those little silvery objects at him, he smiled wickedly and whipped the Invincible a foot or two out of its sheath.

It was enough.

The woman ran away faster than he would have believed.

"Aidan, please. That was just a camera. She liked you and wanted to take your picture." Kira put a hand on his arm. "You can't do things like that here. Times are different. You're scaring people."

He closed his eyes and drew a deep breath, trying to ignore the way the foul-smelling smoke from the tour bus tainted the pure Highland air.

"I am sorry, Kee-*rah*," he said, the words costing him much. "I—"

"You aren't sorry you're here with me, are you?" She looked at him, the worry in her eyes lancing him. "Or ... or mad at me?"

"Ach, lass." He rammed the sword back into its sheath and grabbed her, crushing her to him and slanting his mouth over hers in a ferocious, demanding kiss that would surely set the gawkers' tongues wagging.

Not that he cared.

Setting her from him at last, he straightened his plaid and tossed back his hair. "Sweet Kee-*rah*, where'er you are, is where I need to be. I am no' sorry, nor mad. Just ..."

*Terrified.*

He couldn't say the word, but he could see in her face that she knew. Her eyes filling with the tears she was e'er swearing she ne'er shed, her whole expression softened, and she slid her arms around him, pressing close.

"It will be okay," she said, her voice thick, husky. "You'll see. But we can't stay here and I don't think it's a good idea to go to Wrath. Not yet, anyway."

Aidan nodded, his own throat tightening.

Hearing the name of his home spoken aloud in this strange place that his beloved Scotland had become pinched his heart more than was good for a man.

But he *was* a man. A fine, braw one, he hoped. So he drew another deep breath of the odd-smelling air, then braced his hands on his hips and looked round, once more assuming his lairdly airs.

"So-o-o, Kee-*rah*!" he boomed. "Where shall we go?"

She considered a moment, then beamed. "I think ... I think south to Ravenscraig."

"That MacDougall nest?" His brows snapped together—until he remembered she'd told him a Douglas now lairded it there. "To your friends?" he amended, silently thinking a journey to people she knew would be wise indeed.

"Yes. To Mara McDougall Douglas and her husband, Alex."

Still smiling, she looked down and opened her travel pouch with one of those infernal zip-*hers,* then plunged her hand inside it and rummaged about until she withdrew a tiny gold piece of parchment.

A thin, bright, and shiny thing that she waved at him.

"My credit card," she said, clutching it as if it were made of gold indeed. "It will get us a rental car ... I think there's a small local agency somewhere here in Spean Bridge. Maybe Roy Bridge. If not, I'll find one in Fort William and ask them to deliver the car."

Aidan nodded again, trying his best to look sage.

Truth was, he hadn't understood a word she'd said.

He did, though, have a very unpleasant suspicion that getting to Ravenscraig—near distant Oban, by all the gods!—would entail a journey in one of the smaller tour-bus-looking things crowded so thickly across the Spean Bridge Mill's busy courtyard.

He certainly didn't see any stables about.

Indeed, horses didn't seem to exist in her world. Which left his original notion.

The one that he didn't care for at all.

Needing to know, he put back his shoulders again and cleared his throat. "Ahhh, Kee-*rah*, lass," he began, pleased by the strength of his voice, "this *rental car* you mention? Would it be anything like these small tour buses sitting about here?"

To his dismay, she nodded. "Yes. Those are cars." Then, starting forward, she added, "There's a phone box just down the way. I'll call Mara McDougall and let her know we're coming. Then I'll find us a car. Don't worry—we'll be on our way before you know you know it."

Aidan nodded again, beginning to feel like a head-bobbing fool.

But he dutifully followed her down the road, away from the frightful Spean Bridge Mill and its horrors.

Hoping worse ones weren't awaiting him.

If the speed of the rental cars whizzing past them on the road gave any indication, the journey to Oban would be a nightmare.

Something he became absolutely certain of when, a short while later, she stopped beside a tall, bright red metal and glass container and opened its door. Popping inside, she punched at tiny numbers on a metal plate, then spoke rapidly into a strange silver thing she pressed to the side of her head.

Just watching her made *his* head throb and ache.

When two earth-shaking, earsplitting *flying machines* zoomed past just overhead, he knew for sure this modern Scotland was not for him.

"They were RAF military jets," Kira told him, stepping out of the red-and-glass box at last. "They fly over like that all the time. Even in the most remote parts of Scotland." She smiled. "Just ignore them."

Aidan gave the most casual shrug he could. "I scarce noticed them," he lied, glad his knees hadn't buckled when they'd sped across the sky.

"Anyway, we're all set." Looking pleased, she stretched up on her toes to kiss him. "Mara and Alex are delighted we're coming and they can't wait to meet you."

He grunted. "And the *rental car*?"

"It's called a 'hire car' here, and we'll have to go back to the Spean Bridge Mill to wait for one," she said, hooking her arm through his for the walk back to that awful place. "Someone will bring it up from Fort William shortly."

Aidan harrumphed this time, having never heard of Fort William either.

"There's just one thing you should know." She stopped just before they reached the large courtyard with all the tour buses and rental-hire cars. "I'm not very good at driving on the left."

"It doesn't matter, Kee-*rah*," he lied again.

Something told him *driving on the left* might be very important in this place.

Not that he was in a position to do much about it.

Instead, he did what he could.

He walked proud and curled his hand around his sword's ruby red pommel, taking comfort in the blade's name.

Sooner or later, he would surely be able to convince himself that he was just as unshakable.

A surprisingly short while later, considering how long such
journeys took in his day, Aidan decided he liked Fort
William even less than the Spean Bridge Mill. Unfortunately, he
was also quite sure he'd prefer walking the town's crowded,
strange-looking streets to spending much more time trapped
inside Kira's rental-hire car.

She hadn't been exaggerating when she'd claimed she wasn't
very good at driving left. Indeed, he strongly suspected she might
even have similar difficulties driving right if such a thing existed.

He had no idea and didn't care to know.

For himself, once they were settled where'er that might prove
to be, he would secure himself a fine and capable steed. Perhaps
even a whole stable of them. Cars, tour buses, and the rolling
nightmares Kira called recreational vehicles were not for him.

And from what he'd seen of her *RAF military jets*, he knew
without doubt that flying machines would disagree with him
even more.

But for now, he had other worries. Another huge, square-
shaped recreational vehicle was heading straight at them and he

didn't need to sneak a glance at Kira to know she'd spotted it, too, and was fearful.

Each time one of the monstrosities approached, she gritted her teeth and tightened her hands on the thing she called a *steering wheel*. Even more alarming, he was certain she also shut her eyes at the critical moment when the horrors thundered past them. Considering the narrowness of the road, he understood her distress.

Sadly, her ill ease only worsened his own.

Frowning, he wished the Invincible had fit inside the car rather than having to be stashed in the storage area she called the trunk-boot. He felt naked and vulnerable without the great brand at his hip. Aye, to his mind, there weren't many advantages to this driving.

No matter how quickly the rental-hire car might get them to Oban.

If they even arrived alive.

Something he wasn't all too sure would be the case.

Casting a cautious glance at his lady, he wriggled his jaw as unobtrusively as possible. He'd been clenching it since they'd left the Spean Bridge Mill and his teeth were beginning to ache. His head ached even worse. Truth was, even though Kira had taken great pains to explain her world and tried so valiantly to ready him for her life before he'd landed in her time, none of those details and descriptions could have prepared him for what he was facing now.

He doubted even Tavish would have been pleased by Kira's Scotland.

Much as the lout declared his eagerness to see it.

Thinking of his friend made his heart hurt, so he fixed his attention on the road ahead, regretting it immediately when he spotted another recreational vehicle in the distance, heading determinedly their way. Dreading Kira's reaction as much as the coming encounter, he looked down at the wee bit of tartan cloth clasped so tightly in his hands.

An *eye mask,* Kira had called it.

She'd plucked it from her travel pouch and offered it to him when he'd balked at being strapped into the rental-hire car. Naturally, he'd refused to use it, preferring to see death coming than hide behind such a fool thing.

Even so, if they didn't soon reach their destination, he might reconsider.

"Why don't you put that in your new sporran?" Kira glanced at him, and he immediately ceased fiddling with it.

Driving left was danger fraught enough without him distracting her. But apparently it was too late to worry about it, because her gaze dipped briefly to the eye mask.

"If you haven't used it by now, there'll be less need soon," she said, blessedly returning her attention to the road. "We're almost to Ballachulish now. After the bridge, we'll leave the A-82 for the A-828, the coast road that'll take us right down to Ravenscraig Castle. That road won't be as busy."

Aidan harrumphed.

He wasn't at all sure driving left on a less-traveled coast road would prove any less harrowing than constant encounters with recreational vehicles on a busy one. Coast roads presented other hazards as even he knew.

Things like cliffs and sharp, hair-raising turns.

He frowned. If either one caused Kira to shut her eyes as she did each time a recreational vehicle or tour bus whizzed past them, he would insist she halt immediately. He would then wisely proceed to Ravenscraig on foot, whether she laughed at him or nae.

"I thought you liked the sporran." She reached over to flick one of the scrip's tassels, clearly misinterpreting his scowl.

"I like it fine." He hoped the quick answer would get her hand back on the steering wheel.

Relieved when it did, he looked down, admiring her gift. He did like it. Indeed, he was more than pleased. Ne'er had he seen such a fancily fashioned scrip, all fine leather and fur and decorated with flashy silver-beaded chains and tassels. It even boasted the MacDonald crest. Had he possessed such a treasure in his time, he'd have been the envy of every other laird in the Highlands.

A notion that pleased him.

"So you do like it?"

His frown returned. "To know I smiled means you took your eyes off the road again, Kee-*rah*." It was high time to warn her about such things. "'Tis a mighty fine gift and I am proud to wear it."

"I wish I'd been able to give it to you at Wrath."

He swallowed. He wished that too. But there wasn't any point in being sad about something they couldn't change. So he forced a smile, aiming for a wolfish one.

Just in case she was peeking at him again.

"If your friends at Ravenscraig give us private quarters, I shall show you exactly how much your gift pleased me, Kee-*rah*. How much *you* please me." He glanced at her, deliberating deepening his burr. He'd learned fast how much she loved what she called his sexy Scottish accent. "A man might think this time traveling business makes a body ravenous."

Kira's heart flipped to hear him sound himself again. Another, entirely different part of her tingled. She knew just the kind of hunger he meant and she couldn't wait.

"Don't make me think of such things while I'm driving," she said, only half meaning it. "I might just pull over and demand you take care of that hunger now. But we're almost there and Mara said they have a big surprise for us, so we'd best keep going."

"As you wish, my lady." He sat back, her tartan eye mask still clutched tight in his hands, his white-knuckled grip letting her know how much his bravura cost him.

Kira bit her lip and drove on, pretending not to notice.

With any luck, Mara McDougall's surprise would be something special enough to take his mind off all he'd left behind. Make him less sad and help him adjust better to her world. From Mara's excitement on the telephone, she could almost believe that might just happen.

Then, about an hour and a good stretch of lonely coast road later, Ravenscraig Castle's double-turreted gatehouse finally loomed ahead and she did believe it.

A large banner stretched across the gatehouse, welcoming them with the traditional Gaelic greeting *Ceud Mile Failte!*

A Hundred Thousand Welcomes!

Aidan snorted. "The MacDougalls have grown friendlier since my day."

Kira glanced at him. "I told you—they *are* friendly. To everyone."

But the greeting made her smile. Even if she suspected that the banner remained in place all summer, there to greet the scores of MacDougalls and others who visited Ravenscraig from all over the world, eager to enjoy One Cairn Village's *Brigadoon*-ish charm or to take advantage of Mara's state-of-the-art genealogical center.

The welcome banner wasn't the surprise.

A cluster of signposts lining the drive and the overlarge placard in front of the rhododendrons flanking the gatehouse had to be it. Bold and colorful, the signs announced the second annual Ravenscraig Highland Games.

Not that they wouldn't have discovered the day's significance the instant they drove beneath the gatehouse's raised portcullis and through its dark, tunnellike pend. The castle came into view as soon as they did, but only the tall, parapeted towers.

Everything else was blocked from view, the entire expanse of endless, emerald green lawn crowded with colorful tents and tartan-draped platforms. Rows of refreshment booths and trinket stalls lined the perimeter, as did a large U-shaped area of bleachers.

Chaos reigned, with competing pipe bands standing in tight circles everywhere, playing their hearts out, while solo pipers stood on the scattered platforms, giving skirling accompaniment to young girls performing the Highland fling.

On the far side of the lawn, the kilted heavies were already in full swing, throwing hammers and weights, and tossing the huge, telephone pole-like caber. Closer by, more kilties engaged in a fierce tug-o'-war, much to the delight of the female spectators. From their flushed faces and laughter, Kira suspected they were more keen on catching beneath-the-kilt flashes than watching to see which team of huffing, straining tuggers actually won.

Kira beamed as she drove past them, slowing to a snail's pace as she followed the parking instructions of a young, freckle-faced lad in a kilt. Beside her, Aidan was silent, but she caught a suspicious gleam in his eye when he clambered out of the car.

A gleam that was getting brighter by the moment. So she held her silence, not wanting to embarrass him by saying anything he'd have to comment on. Not until she was sure he'd caught himself.

Her throat was thick too.

Pipes always did that to her. She also knew that such games went back well over a thousand years. That medieval chieftains like Aidan used the competitions to select the clan's strongest and fastest men. Those with the most stamina and the greatest hearts. Men who became the chieftain's personal *tail*, or bodyguards. His most prized fighting men.

Trusted friends.

She shivered. The medieval games must've been full of pageantry and color. Things she was certain Aidan was remembering now. She could tell by the way his hands shook just a bit as he refastened his sword belt, then smoothed his plaid, his head held high.

Looking proud.

And so out of place against the backdrop of milling T-shirted, sneaker-footed American tourists that she could have sat down and wept.

"Aidan, my love." She reached for his hand, lacing their fingers. "We can leave now. No one yet knows we've arrived. We can go back—"

"You call me your love." He looked at her, his gaze going so deep she'd swear he'd brushed her soul. "Am I, lass? Do you love me as much as I love you?"

Kira's heart burst. He'd never yet mentioned love, but she'd guessed, hoped."Oh, Aidan, you know I do." She slid her arms around him, squeezing tight. "I love you more than there are sands on the shore. More than all the stars in the night sky. I have always loved you. I think since that very first day."

He nodded, taking her hands and kissing both palms. "Then all is good, Kee-*rah*. We shall stay here and visit your friends. After that ... I cannae say. But we are no' going back to Wrath. No' so long as Conan Dearg breathes and a faceless enemy threatens you in my own bedchamber."

Kira looked down, nudging at a pebble on the graveled path. She'd almost hoped he'd say they *would* go back to Wrath. Her world felt funny to her, too, now.

She never would have believed it, but she was actually homesick for the fourteenth century.

"Nae, lass." He shook his head, almost as if he'd read her thoughts. "We are here now and shall make the best of it."

"And if—" She broke off, her jaw dropping.

Just ahead a small book stand claimed pride of place in the middle of the Games' row of trinket stalls. Two large flags flew above it, the red and gold Lion Rampant, so often associated with Robert the Bruce, and the blue and white Scottish Saltire. Both snapped proudly in the afternoon wind, but it was the giant poster of RIVERS OF STONE: A HIGHLANDER'S ANCESTRAL JOURNEY and the many teetering stacks of the little book that drew attention.

As did the tall, kilted Highlander preening beside the book table, surrounded by a clutch of female Australian and American tourists. Loud and giggly, they wore their national flags on the backs of their sweatshirts. All except one, a brassy-looking older woman who appeared to be hanging on to every word the Highlander said.

In addition to the Australian flag, the back of her sweatshirt declared that she was ELIZABETH: WORLD CHAMPION KILT-TILTER.

Kira almost choked. "Oh, no! It's him." She grabbed Aidan's arm. "Wee Hughie MacSporran."

Aidan stopped. "The scribe who claims Conan Dearg locked me in my dungeon to starve to death?"

"The very one—I think. He's a bit heavier and has less hair than the last time I saw him. But"—she squinted, straining to catch a better look at him through the clustering women—"Yes, I'm sure now. It's him."

Aidan narrowed his eyes at the man, then smiled.

His wickedest smile. "Then, come." He started forward, his hand on the Invincible's hilt. "I shall give him a history lesson."

Reaching the little book stand, he whipped out the sword and plunged it into the earth a few inches from Wee Hughie's feet. "Greetings, kinsman!" he boomed, clapping the startled Highlander on the shoulder. "I'm told you're of good Clan Donald blood?"

The women giggled.

Wee Hughie's face colored, but he nodded, his Adam's apple bobbing. "I—"

"He's related to Robert the Bruce," the Kilt-Tilter trilled, eyeing Aidan with equal interest.

Kira frowned at her.

Aidan arched a brow. "Indeed?"

Wee Hughie stepped back a pace, brushing at his kilt. "The Bruce was my great-great-great-grandfather. Eighteen generations in a direct line."

Aidan closed the space between them. With a wink at Kira, he lowered his voice. "I cannae claim eighteen generations from the man, but I have fought and wenched at his side. Welcomed him at my table and hearth."

Wee Hughie lifted his chin, clearly annoyed. "Ancestral roots should not be mocked. I can document my lineage back through two thousand years of Scottish history."

Aidan didn't look impressed. "Lad, if you do have Clan Donald blood, I *am* your history."

"Come, let's move on." Kira put a hand on his arm, not surprised when he brushed it away.

"And"—he yanked the Invincible from the ground, resheathing it without taking his gaze off the author—"I am here to tell you that your book is wrong. Aidan MacDonald of Wrath didn't die in his own dungeon. That was his cousin, Conan Dearg."

Wee Hughie puffed his chest. "You, sir, are the one who has your history skewed. I never wrote that. Conan Dearg drowned."

Aidan frowned and picked up one of the books, tucking it inside his plaid. "I shall read this and see what other errors you've made," he said, once more clapping the author on the shoulder. "If I find more, kinsman, we shall meet again."

*"Spoken like a true Highlander of old."*

A tall, darkly handsome man fell into step beside them the minute Aidan turned and pulled Kira away from the book stand. Dressed like a prosperous knight of old, he made them a gallant bow, clearly taking pains not to dislodge the studded medieval shield he held in front of his groin.

A beautiful Highland targe, round and covered with smooth,

supple-looking leather, it was the finest example of a medieval shield Kira had ever seen outside a museum.

"You must be one of Sir Alex's reenactor friends," she said, certain of it. "I'm Kira. Of Aldan, Pennsylvania." She glanced at Aidan. "And this is Sir Aidan. The MacDonald of Wrath," she blurted, his true identity somehow spilling from her.

The dark knight's casual, easy grace could have pulled even more from her had she not been careful.

There was something about him.

"I know who you are, Lady Kira." He smiled, his gaze passing knowingly to Aidan before returning to her. "You have been expected. Both of you. We are here to help you."

"We?" Kira blinked.

"Many of us." He gave a slight nod, his mailed shirt gleaming in the afternoon sun. "I am Sir Hardwin, onetime companion-in-arms to Alex of Ravenscraig, and late of my own fair Seagrave in the north."

Kira's brow furrowed. "Late?"

He shrugged and flashed her a dazzling smile. "So to speak, my lady."

For one crazy mad moment, she was certain she could see Wee Hughie MacSporran and his fan club of tourist women right through the man and his medieval targe.

But then a cloud passed over the sun and the illusion faded, leaving him looking as solid as everyone else.

Including the giant bearlike man with a shock of shaggy red hair and an equally wild beard who suddenly appeared at his side.

"Dinnae fash yourself, Kira-lass. We are friends." The bushy-bearded newcomer slung an arm around the first man's shoulders, then winked at Aidan. "Friends of old."

Kira slid a glance at Aidan, not surprised to see him watching the two men with skeptical, narrowed eyes.

"You have the looks of the MacNeils about you," he said, his gaze fixed on bushy-beard.

"Aye, and I suppose I do!" The man rocked back on his heels, mirth rolling off him. "'Tis Bran of Barra I am," he added, looking quite pleased about it. "And you are a Skye MacDonald—a son of Somerled, as I live and breathe!"

And then he was gone.

As was the first man, both swallowed up by a new surge of holidaymakers pushing past them into the rows of trinket stalls and refreshment booths.

Nothing of the strange encounter remained ... until a bright flash of glitter struck Kira's eye and she stooped, examining the grass where the two men had stood.

Two gold rings lay there, glinting in the day's fading light. Celtic rings identically patterned with slender-stemmed trumpets, birds, and delicate swirls. A man and a woman's rings, both looking suspiciously medieval.

So beautifully medieval, her heart dipped the instant her fingers closed around them.

*We are here to help you.* The dark knight's words came back to her and she suddenly knew.

As she should have known right away, and would have, had the day's trials not taken such a toll.

She turned to Aidan, the rings clutched tight in her hand. "They were ghosts," she said, the wonder of it sending warmth all through her.

"I know that." He snatched the rings and frowned down at them, not about to admit he'd not known indeed.

He'd been about to draw the Invincible again and challenge the cheeky bastards.

As it was, he chose to bow to the greater wisdom of his lady regarding the spirits of her time. He also didn't want to overlook the possibility that the Ancient Ones of his own time might still be looking after them.

If that were the case, the rings had a definite purpose and had best be worn.

Sure of it, he grabbed her hand and shoved the smaller-looking ring onto the fourth finger of her left hand, then worked the other onto the same finger of his own left hand.

And with no time to spare, it would seem, because no sooner were the rings in place than a wild-eyed older couple came tearing across the grass toward them, calling his lady's name.

"Kira!" A tall, slender woman threw her arms around Kira, sobbing and laughing at the same time. "Dear heavens, girl, *where* have you been? We've been here for weeks, searching for you!"

The balding, potbellied man puffing after her wasn't looking at Kira at all, but at him. "So you're the man who's married my little girl?" he demanded, eyeing him as if he were one of the birthing sisters' newts. "Without so much as a by-your-leave!"

Quick on his heels, a running, panting couple about Aidan's own age burst through a hedge of rhododendron, then drew to a skidding, slip-sliding halt.

Keeping a few paces behind the older couple, they winked and gesticulated, the man's magnificent Highland regalia and the woman's simple flame-haired beauty letting him know they were his hosts.

Mara McDougall of Penseal-*where'er* and her Douglas husband, Alex.

That they'd informed Kira's parents that he and Kira had married was more than obvious. Not that he cared. Far from it, the notion pleased him.

He'd meant to wed her anyway, as soon as he'd managed to settle their future.

It scarce mattered if he claimed her as his wife already.

In his heart, she'd been his since time was.

Perhaps, he sometimes believed, many lifetimes before that as well.

They fit together that beautifully.

Secure in that knowledge, he put back his shoulders and smoothed his plaid, understanding now why the Ancient Ones had sent the ring-bearing bogles.

"Well?" Kira's father glared at him, both his chins quivering. "What have you to say for yourself?"

"The only thing of import, sir." Aidan cleared his throat, regretting the temporary deception. "I am the man who loves your daughter. And, aye, I've taken her to wife."

"Taken her to wife?" The man's face reddened. "That's an odd way to put it."

"He's a reenactor, George." Kira's mother spoke up. "Don't you see his costume? He's speaking in period. Like the guides at Pennsbury Manor back home. Or Colonial Williamsburg."

"Humph." George Bedwell glared at his wife. "I'd have him speak to me as my daughter's father, not some tourist!"

"Oh, George, calm down," the woman said. She threw Aidan an apologetic smile. Turning back to George, she gave him one as well. "Now, dear, you know how long we've waited to see Kira settled. I'll not have you scaring the boy off before the ink is dried on their marriage license."

"I hope to God he has one." George produced a small square of white linen and mopped his brow. "I'll have answers if he doesn't."

"We are properly wed." Aidan extended his hand, showing the man his ring.

George peered at it, looking only somewhat mollified.

Aidan nodded, then did his best to assume the most respectful mien he could manage.

The only consolation he was willing to give, considering his position.

"My sorrow, sir, that we were unable to inform you until now. It simply wasn't possible."

"Not possible?" George's face went red again. "In this day of high-speed internet and email? Good old-fashioned telephones?"

Aidan sighed and pulled a hand down over his face. "Where my home is, we do not have such amenities."

Kira pulled away from her mother to hasten over to him. "You don't understand, Daddy," she began, sliding an arm around Aidan. "Aidan is—"

"*Aidan?*" Her mother pressed a hand to her throat, her eyes rounding. "Dearie me, it's him!"

"What do you mean him?" Her husband shot another angry look at her. "Have you met this man already? Met him, and not told me?"

Blanche Bedwell shook her head. "No. I've never met him, but I've heard of him. For years. He—"

"Years?" Kira's father's gaze flew from her mother to her and then back to her mother again. "You've known of him that long and I wasn't informed?"

His wife pursed her lips. "You weren't informed because there was nothing to say. He was a dream. An obsession of Kira's since her graduation trip to Scotland. He's a legendary historical hero who lived over seven hundred years ago."

Kira's father laughed. "Are you telling me my daughter married a ghost?"

Blanche shrugged.

Alex Douglas chose that moment to stride forward, placing a hand on both their shoulders. "Aidan of Wrath is no ghost." He spoke in a level tone. "Trust me, I can sense spirits within a hundred paces. Your new son-in-law is a good man."

He paused, his gaze dropping to the Invincible's hilt, lingering there, before he fixed Aidan with a deep, knowing stare.

"He simply hails from a distant time."

"From seven centuries ago?" George frowned at him. "Look," he added, glancing first at Kira, then the others, "our family has had its share of oddballs. Far-seers, ghost-seers, and other assorted fruit-loops. But I've yet to hear of anyone marrying someone seven hundred years dead."

Mara McDougall Douglas coughed. Joining them, she put a hand on George Bedwell's arm. "I know it sounds impossible," she said, her voice so calm *anything* sounded possible, "but you have to remember this is Scotland. It's an ancient land, full of magic. I've had to learn that myself. Strange things can happen here that you'd never hear of elsewhere."

She exchanged a quick glance with her husband. "Strange and wonderful things."

George grunted. "I don't see anything wonderful about my daughter marrying a dead man."

"Oh, Daddy. He's not dead." Kira reached for Aidan's hand, grasping it hard. "You can't imagine what he's sacrificed for me."

"Seven-hundred-year-old men have to be dead." George insisted, bent on being belligerent.

"Nae, that is not so. I can prove it to you, if you desire." Aidan spoke with his laird's voice. "But I warn you, it is not wise to tamper with such things. The consequences can be dire and wreak more harm than your simple doubts can stir in a lifetime."

"And where—*how*—do you intend to live your lifetime?" Kira's father eyed them. "Even Elliot King at the Tile Bonanza wouldn't hire you on a résumé that says you're a seven-hundred-year-old legendary historical hero."

Aidan set his jaw, unable to answer him.

Worse, he understood the man's outrage.

Given the circumstances, he would have reacted in a similar fashion. Nae, he'd ne'er have tolerated such a discussion in the first place and would have silenced the upstart young man with a swift, swinging pass of the Invincible.

Kira, apparently, had other thoughts.

Shrugging off her backpack, she undid the zip-*her* and withdrew a bundle of rolled parchments. No longer fresh and supple as he knew they'd been at Wrath, the scrolls now appeared ancient. Thin and brittle, they crackled in her hands, the frayed red ribbon tying them looking ready to crumble to dust.

"Here." She thrust them into her father's hands. "This is a record of my time in medieval Scotland. I wrote it for Dan Hillard and would appreciate it if you'd see he gets it. He can have the paper and ink carbon-dated. That'll prove the year it was written, and you, Daddy, cannot deny that it's in my hand-writing."

Her father grunted again.

Some of the angry red color left his face as he peered down at the parchments. "That still doesn't tell me where you mean to live? And how?"

Kira glanced at Aidan. "We'll stay here in Scotland," she said, knowing that would please him. Turning back to her parents, she hugged them both. "You know it's always been my dreamland. Now it is also the home of the man I love."

She kissed them each on the cheek, willing them to under-stand. "Someday ... maybe ... we'll return to Aidan's time. If such a thing is even possible. But if we did, you will now have seen us together and will know how happy we are. If it came to that, I'd try to somehow let you know we made it back. That we were okay and thriving in Aidan's world."

"Humph." Her father pressed his lips together and scowled, reminding her so much of Aidan that she would have laughed had the circumstances allowed.

"You are well and truly married?" He grabbed her hand, examining the ring Aidan had slipped onto her finger only moments before.

"Yes," she said, knowing in her heart that they soon would be.

"And you love my daughter?" He shot another glance at Aidan. "Have the means to keep her fed and clothed? Happy?"

Aidan smiled, sensing the man's softening. "She is my life, sir. I'd be honored to have your blessing ... but I'm keeping her whether it pleases you or nae."

"Then take good care of her, by God." Her father marched over to him, thrusting out his hand.

"I will, sir," Aidan said, meaning it. He surprised himself by ignoring the older man's hand and, instead, grasping him by the shoulders for a quick, tight embrace. "Ne'er worry about her. She is more precious to me than all the world's coin, even my life. I would kill the man who'd even glance sideways at her."

*There are some men who deserve killing,* he thought he heard Alex Douglas speak low at his shoulder. But when he released Kira's father and looked at Alex, his host stood across the little clearing again, one arm slung casually around his wife.

"We've readied the Heatherbrae for you," he said.

Looking so like the men of Aidan's own day that his heart squeezed.

"It's the same cottage Kira had before." Mara McDougall Douglas slipped away from her husband. Coming forward, she handed Aidan a key. "I think you'll find it comfortable. It's a bit old-fashioned, but has everything you need."

Unfortunately, when he took himself there a short while later, hoping to give Kira some time alone with her family, he found himself unable to enjoy the luxuriously appointed cottage's amenities.

The *lights*, as a cheery young man named Malcolm had called the bright-glaring contraptions, hurt his eyes. And the chattering little moving people in the so-called *telly* unsettled him so much he was sure his head would soon burst just trying to comprehend such a wonder.

Almost as bad, when he'd tried to use the *shower* he'd scalded his back. Then, a short while later, he'd raised a blister on his finger when he'd touched one of the *lights*, trying to see how the fool thing worked.

But none of those horrors came anywhere near to the nightmare spread across the bed in the Heatherbrae's tidy bedchamber.

Going there now, he stared down at the books he'd examined earlier. Wee Hughie's *Rivers of Stone: A Highlander's Ancestral Journey.* Kira's other little volume, *The Hebridean Clans,* and several others.

Eight altogether. Kira's two, plus six he'd plucked from a shelf on the wall.

Each one said the same thing.

Conan Dearg drowned.

Not that he'd really care—were it not for the rest.

Sinking onto the edge of the bed, he picked up his kinsman's little tome, once more opening it to the damning passage. Tracing the words with a blister-tipped finger, he swallowed against the thickness in his throat and wondered how the fates could be so cruel as to let him save Kira only to cause Tavish's death.

Aidan closed his eyes and groaned. Never had he felt more helpless and miserable. Until Alex Douglas' cryptic words came back to him.

*There are some men who deserve killing.*

His eyes snapped open. When the first thing that leapt into view was the Invincible, its bloodred pommel jewel glittering like a dragon's eye, he knew what he had to do.

Leaping to his feet, he grabbed the sword, feeling better, *stronger,* the instant his fingers clenched around the leather-wrapped hilt.

Power—and rage—swept him, heating his blood until it was all he could do not to throw back his head and shout his clan's battle cry.

Instead, the words he'd said to Tavish the morning of the feast echoed in his ears: *Chances are we'll be rejoining you in the hall —back before the sweet courses are served.*

He closed his eyes again, his heart thundering. If they could manage that, all might not be lost.

It was a risk he had to take.

# 15

"You want to go back?"

Kira slowly closed the door of the Heatherbrae behind her, then set down the glossy monthly, *Scotland Today*, that she'd brought back from the Ravenscraig library. She stared at Aidan, her initial euphoria on hearing him declare he wanted to return to his time giving way to queasiness and dry mouth now that she looked at him more closely.

He no longer looked like Aidan-out-of-water, but rather the fierce laird of Wrath she knew so well from his own time.

His jaw was set in a formidable line and his eyes blazed. Most telling of all, he'd strapped on the Invincible.

Crossing the cottage's little sitting area, she slid her arms around him. "What's wrong? What's happened?" She looked up at him, not surprised when he disentangled himself and started pacing. "Why do you want to go back now? I know things aren't ideal, but we just got here."

"It's no' that I want to go back, though the gods know I do." He whirled to face her, his expression giving her chills. "We must. According to your history books, our leaving caused Tavish's death."

Kira's eyes widened. "What? How can that be?"

He disappeared into the bedroom, returning a moment later with an armful of books. Dumping them onto a tartan-upholstered armchair, he snatched up one and began flipping through its pages.

"Here! The lines in the middle of the page." He thrust the book at her, pointing to a brief paragraph on page 57. "Read it and you'll understand."

Kira looked down at the clear black print, her stomach dropping as she read the words. "Oh, God." She tossed down the book and pressed a hand to her chest. "Conan Dearg slew Tavish while escaping Wrath's dungeon? Then drowned? With that MacLeod woman?"

"So the books say." Aidan folded his arms. "All of them. Even that fool, Wee Hughie's. Some just say Conan Dearg killed *the laird of Wrath*, but the result is the same. After we left, Tavish took my place. Had we remained, he would still be alive."

"And you'd be dead." She didn't like that possibility either.

Aidan snorted. "Nae. Conan Dearg would be dead, and by my sword. No' from drowning."

Kira dropped onto a chair. "I don't get the drowning part. Or the connection with that awful woman."

"That's because you don't know my cousin. Or Fenella MacLeod." He gave her an alpha-male look, all medieval chieftain again. "I wouldn't be one of the most respected warrior lairds in the Highlands if the answer weren't clear to me."

Kira looked at him. It wasn't clear to her at all.

"'Tis simple, lass." He picked up Mara McDougall Douglas' welcome decanter of single malt and poured himself a hefty dram. He started to pour a second measure for her, but she shook her head to stop him. Tossing down his own whisky in one quick swig, he wiped his mouth with the back of his hand. "Lady Fenella devours men faster than I just swallowed that whisky.

Conan Dearg will have attracted her like a lodestone. Especially since she was grieved with me."

"She didn't like you?" Kira lifted a brow.

"She liked me too much. Some while before you came to Wrath, she visited, offering her men and her fleet of longships to help me to search for Conan Dearg." He paused to run a hand through his hair, a look of distaste passing over his face. "Not surprisingly, she offered other services as well. When I declined, she left in a fury."

"And you think she then hooked up with your cousin? To get back at you?"

He nodded. "I'd bet my sword that was the way of it. I should have thought of it before, but I was distracted."

Kira swallowed. She knew he meant her. "I still don't understand the drowning part. Especially if the MacLeod woman is supposed to have drowned with him."

"I can only guess, but I'd vow Lady Fenella helped him escape at some point during the feast and they tried to leave Wrath Bay in her galley." Coming over to her, he placed his hands on her shoulders. "Tavish and I suspected her of damaging her own craft as a ploy to pull up on my landing beach. If her flight with Conan Dearg caused as much confusion as I suspect it might have, and my men pursued them, in the rush to get away she may have set sail in her own galley rather than taking one of mine as I imagine she'd planned to do."

"You think her boat sank?" Kira blinked up at him. "As they tried to sail away?"

"I was told when she arrived that there was quite a hole gouged in her galley's hull. They wouldn't have made it past Wrath Isle if they sought to flee in such a vessel."

Kira shuddered. "If this is true, I'll bet she was behind my poisoning."

"I thought the same," he agreed. "Though if she'd been slipping into Wrath to visit Conan Dearg, or harm you, someone there must've been helping her."

"That has to be how your cousin got up onto the arch that night." Kira bit her lip, a hundred thoughts churning in her head. "I suspected he'd somehow learned about me. How I got there. Someone must've helped him sneak out of the dungeon so he could examine the top of the arch."

"Indeed. You're a wise lassie." A touch of admiration lit his eyes. "Poor Kendrew must've startled him—and suffered the consequences."

"But who would've helped your cousin?" Kira couldn't wrap her mind around it. "Your men can't stand him. And the women, those laundresses—" She broke off, suspicion making her breath catch. "Do you think one of them did it?"

He frowned. "Help my cousin?" He started pacing again, rubbing the back of his neck as he walked. "Could be. I've told you, Conan Dearg exerts a weird influence on women. But I can't see any of the laundresses doing Lady Fenella any favors."

Stopping by the table, he helped himself to another dram of whisky. "It doesn't matter, Kee-*rah*." Confidence rolled off him. If she didn't know better, she'd have sworn he'd grown several inches. That his powerful shoulders had gone even wider. "Now that I know what to be wary of, I'll get to the bottom of the matter when we go back. Hopefully we can get there the same night we left. If so, I'm sure I can save Tavish."

Kira's heart sank. "Oh, dear," she said, half certain the shadows in the room had just deepened, turning as dark as the blackness she felt bearing down on them. Her gaze slid to the little pine table by the door. The slick and colorful issue of *Scotland Today* lying on the tabletop. "I don't think we can get back."

She hadn't wanted to say so yet, but now, watching and listening to him talk about saving his friend, she couldn't keep quiet any longer. "The gatehouse arch—"

"Worked once and will serve us again." He set down the little crystal dram glass. "You just need to *left drive* us back to Wrath. We'll leave in the morning, as soon as you've said your farewells to your family and friends."

"You don't understand." Kira pressed her fingers to her temples. "It won't matter if we go back to Skye. Even if we did, we wouldn't be able to get to the arch top. Not even the outermost ruins of your castle."

He looked at her, uncomprehending.

"The site's under construction," she tried to explain, pushing to her feet. Going to the little table near the door, she grabbed the *Scotland Today* and waved it at him. "It's all in here. You can even see pictures. In the months I've been away, Wrath has gone to the National Trust for Scotland. That's a historical preservation society and they're currently developing the ruins into a tourist exhibition. They—"

"*A what*?" He stared at her, the blood draining from his face. "You mean a place overrun with Ameri-*cains* and tour buses?"

Kira nodded, her heart breaking that she had to tell him. "Mother said they tried to go there weeks ago when they first arrived, but it's all roped off and guarded. Even at night. No one can set foot on the property."

"I see." He looked at her, all the flash and gleam in his eyes, vanished. "Put that thing away, Kee-*rah*," he said, glancing at the magazine in her hands. "I dinnae want to see the images. No' now."

Turning away from her, he went to the cottage's front window. The one with the view of Mara McDougall Douglas' One Cairn Village memorial cairn. Its stones and great Celtic cross shimmered silvery blue in the pale luminosity of the late-summer night, the beauty of it twisting Kira's heart.

Aidan seemed to be staring at it, too, his shoulders sagging more the longer he stood there, stiff and silent, his hands clenched tightly at his sides.

Kira moved to join him, but stopped halfway there, her stare going past him to the big memorial cairn, a smile splitting her soul the instant she made the connection.

"Oh, wow!" she cried, starting to tremble. "I know what we can do!"

Aidan whipped around, the hope on his face making her heart soar. "You know of another *time portal*, Kee-*rah*? Another way we can return?"

"I might." She couldn't lie to him. "Let's say there's a chance. If"—she snatched Wee Hughie's book off the chair and thumbed through its pages until she found what she needed—"we go here! The Na Tri Shean."

His brows shot upward. "That accursed place?"

Kira nodded. "My boss, Dan Hillard, had reason to believe the cairns there aren't just fairy mounds, but a portal to the Other-world and all places beyond and between. A *time portal*." She thrust the book beneath his nose, forcing him to look at the black-and-white photograph of the three piles of stone on their hill. "If we go there, maybe, just maybe, we can get back to Wrath."

"Cnoc Freiceadain—the Na Tri Shean—is far from here, Kee-*rah*." He rubbed his forehead. "Getting there would mean crossing almost the whole of Scotland."

"Does it matter?" She tossed aside the book and wrapped her arms around him, squeezing tight. "It's our only chance."

He drew a deep breath, then hugged her back. "Then we shall seize it. I owe Tavish no less."

Kira grinned. "I can't wait to see the look on his face when he sees you."

That he might not was something she wouldn't consider.

After all, as Mara McDougall Douglas had said, Scotland was a place of miracles.

&

IT WAS past nightfall the next day by the time they passed through the tiny hamlet of Shebster in Scotland's far north and finally reached the great grass-grown hill that held the three long-chambered cairns known as the Na Tri Shean. A stout, rib-sticking full Scottish breakfast, a swift but emotional farewell from George and Blanche Bedwell and their hosts at Ravenscraig, along with hope, sheer will, and a seemingly endless ribbon of narrow, winding Highland roads had brought them here. And now, turning off the ignition at last, Kira had to struggle to hide her disappointment.

Dan's supposed time portal par excellence proved nondescript.

Little more than a huge, treeless hill stood before them, outlined against the eerily light late-summer night sky. The hill's summit showed the telltale fairy mounds, said to date back to the third millennium BC, but rather than the massive, well-defined cairns she'd expected, only a scattered jumble of boulders and stones showed that anything really significant had once stood there.

Getting out of the car, she pushed back her shoulders and glanced at Aidan. "Not very impressive, hmmm? I'm sorry. I thought—"

"You are thinking like a woman who no longer believes in magic, Kee-*rah*." Tossing back his plaid, he whipped out the Invincible and held its blade to the soft, silver-glowing sky. At once, the combined light of the bright crescent moon and the pale northern sun caught the sword's edge, making its cold, hard steel shine and glow like a living thing. "The power of a place like this remains through time and eternity. It matters little that the man-made cairns are tumbled. Besides"—he reached for her hand, then started forward, up the hill—"the stones only marked what was beneath. It is there, deep under the earth, that we must go."

"Under the earth?" Kira stopped, digging in her heels.

Suddenly the great grassy hill no longer looked so harmless. "What are you saying?"

He looked at her, his dark eyes glittering in the strange silvery-blue light. "I thought you knew what long-chambered cairns are."

Kira swallowed, not wanting to admit she hadn't given it that much thought. At least not as far as entering the cairns and going down into the cold, dark earth.

"I will be with you, Kee-*rah*. You needn't fear." He traced his knuckles down the curve of her cheek. "Now, come. Get out your flashlight, or whate'er you call it, and help me look for an entrance. There should be three. They'll be low in the ground, and perhaps hidden by rocks or underbrush. I doubt it matters which cairn we enter. The magic will be powerful in each."

Hoping that he was right, Kira fished the flashlight out of her backpack and let him pull her higher up the grassy slope. They found an entrance quickly, with surprising ease. The dark, low-linteled opening seemed to stare right at them, an impenetrable-looking black hole in the hillside, its contours softened by thick-growing underbrush.

It was also painfully small.

A rabbit hole she doubted either one of them could squeeze into.

Her stomach tightening, she flicked on the flashlight and aimed it into the darkness. A few moss-covered stone steps gleamed weakly in the thin band of light. Nothing else was discernible except the narrowness of the dank, low-ceilinged entry.

"I don't think anyone above four feet can get down those steps." She turned to Aidan, sure he'd agree. "Especially not you."

To her surprise, he simply shoved the Invincible back into its scabbard and stretched his arms, flexing his fingers. "Once we've mastered the steps and crept through the long passage, we'll come to the inner chamber, Kee-*rah*. We'll be able to stand upright then. You'll see. It willnae be so bad."

He pulled her close, tightening his arms around her before he released her and grabbed the flashlight. "Come, now," he said, ducking low and stepping into the darkness. "Follow close behind me and keep your head down. Dinnae straighten until I tell you."

And then he was gone, the blackness swallowing him as he descended deeper into the cairn.

"Oh, man." Kira threw one last glance at the parked rental car, then dipped her head to hurry after him.

Cold, damp, and silence slammed into her, the smell of earth and old stone.

Catching the back of Aidan's plaid, she hoped her feet wouldn't slip on the mossy steps. Then, before she knew it, they'd reached the bottom and were crouching along a tight, cobbled passage, its walls seeming to grow more constricting the farther they went.

"We're almost there, Kee-*rah*." Aidan's voice echoed in the darkness. "Dinnae be afraid."

Then he was straightening, pulling her up with him and wrapping a strong arm around her waist, holding her close. They were in a small, oval-shaped chamber with high, stone-slabbed walls and a corbeled ceiling. Kira thought she saw a few tipped-over urns and the remains of an ancient-looking fire, but before she could be certain, Aidan clicked off the flashlight.

"I dinnae think it's wise to use your light now, sweetness." He took her hand, easing her down onto the cold stone floor beside him. He gathered her against him, keeping their fingers tightly laced. "We'll just sit here and think of Wrath and hope the magic works."

In the silence, she heard the soft *hiss* of the Invincible leaving its sheath, then the rustle of his plaid as he settled the great sword across his knees. Its pommel stone glowed a faint red in the darkness, but all else was black. A deep, cloying blackness that suddenly zoomed in on them, then snapped back, exploding into a wild, spinning vortex of bright, eye-piercing color.

Icy wind rushed past them and the ground shook, tilting crazily as the tornado-like wind swirled faster. Kira's skirts flew up into her face, covering her head until she yanked them down.

"Aidan—my clothes!" She grabbed his arm, digging her fingers into him. "My medieval clothes are back!" She twisted around, straining to see him, but where he should have been, was only a flash of a black and wild glen, the kind that could have been inhabited by witches and demons. Lightning crackled and *zished* across the chamber's ceiling, booming thunder splitting her ears.

"Wha—" she cried out, but the image vanished instantly, replaced by a young girl in peasant's clothing, a willow-wand basket clutched to her hip.

The girl disappeared, too, swept away before Kira even really saw her. More images followed, each one whizzing past at light speed, whirling and whirling, the colors and roar of the wind making her dizzy.

"Kee-*rah!* Hold on, lass!" Aidan's voice rose above the chaos.

Kira felt his arm tighten around her, almost squeezing the breath from her as a yelling, helmeted Viking war band sped past them, followed immediately by quick glimpse into the splendor of a Victorian great hall, complete with dark-paneled walls hung with stag heads, weaponry, and gilt-framed portraits. A swirl of cloud and mist came next, then a broad, open stretch of empty moorland, thick with heather and broom.

A field of daffodils, giving way to the sudden skirl of bagpipes as an army of Highlanders crested a hill, their swords glinting in brilliant sunshine, their banners streaming in the wind.

Then the cloud and mist returned, the loud wail of the pipes melting into the darkness, leaving only cold and silence, the soft red glow of the Invincible's pommel stone, and the distant howls of a dog.

"By my soul! That's Ferlie." Aidan shot to his feet, pulling her up beside him. "Kee-*rah*, sweet, it's over. We've made it. We're on the arch."

Kira kept her death grip on his arm, her heart pounding. "Thank God!" She glanced at him. "But do you think it's real? Not like all those images that just whirled past?"

"Och, 'tis Wrath, aye." Aidan laughed. "Sure as I'm standing here. I can even see my men patrolling the far side of the parapet walk. And the ladder—it's still here, propped against the gatehouse, just as we left it."

Kira swallowed. Joy swept her when she saw the top of the ladder peeping up over the edge of the arch, the two burly guards on the opposite wall-walk. Ross and Geordie, if she wasn't mistaken. The Invincible rested on the smooth stone of the arch top, the red gleam of its pommel now matched by the flickering orange-red glow of the smokehouse fires down on the landing strand.

They were home.

"Come, lass, I've a score to settle." Aidan snatched up his sword, sheathing it, before he turned toward the ladder. "Let's hope we're no' too late."

Scrambling down, he held up his arms for her, helping her descend. He tossed a quick glance through the swirling mist toward his keep, relieved to see torchlight glimmering at the window slits. With luck, the feasting would still be in full swing, his cousin yet locked in his dungeon cell.

They pounded across the cobbles and burst into the hall. Aidan skidded to a halt, disbelief stopping his heart. Instead of being full of stir and mayhem, shouts and laughter, the hall was empty. No one sat at the rows of long tables. On the dais, his overturned laird's chair and a toppled bench indicated a hasty departure. As did the many filled trenchers and ale cups, the still-burning candles in the silver candelabrums.

Aidan's blood ran cold.

Now he knew why the hall door had stood wide and poor Ferlie howled somewhere, deep in the bowels of the castle.

The other castle dogs were gone, though by straining his ears, he heard them now. Barking in the distance, along with the muffled cries of men. A woman's sudden piercing wail, the sound making his gut clench.

"Guidsakes! It's happening!" He grabbed Kira's hand, pulling her with him from the hall, racing to the low arched door that led to the dungeon. "Tavish!" he roared, shouting as they ran. "Hold, man! We're coming!"

But when they rushed down the dark, narrow stair and reached Conan Dearg's cell, the heavy iron-bound door stood cracked, a fresh-looking pool of blood near the threshold leaving no doubt as to what transpired.

"Mercy!" Beside him, Kira clapped a hand to her throat, her face paling as she stared at the blood. "We're too late."

"Nae! Dinnae say it." Aidan whipped around, pressing his hand against her lips. "It could be my cousin's blood. It *must* be— I'll no' allow otherwise."

Kira looked at him, her stomach clenching. "Then they'll be down at the boat strand—the drowning part."

"That'll be the way of it," he agreed, already sprinting down the fetid passage. "Pray the gods we get there in time."

Streaking after him, Kira kept a hand pressed to her ribs, half afraid her heart would jump right through them if she didn't. Aidan almost scared her. Never had she seen him look so fierce.

So deadly.

He shot up the stairs and through the hall with explosive speed, gripping his sword hilt as he ran, not breaking stride until they'd crossed the bailey and neared the small postern door in the curtain walling. As at Conan Dearg's cell, they found the door ajar. Ferlie paced to and fro in front of the opening, howling and fretting, his lame back legs keeping him from bounding down the cliff steps to the landing beach below.

"He's no' dead, Ferlie," Aidan tossed at him, pausing just long enough at the top of the steps to reach again for Kira's hand. "I can see him! Tavish. And my cousin." He glanced at her, his eyes wild, blazing. "They're at the water's edge, fighting."

And they were. Kira saw them now as well. Aidan's men and a pack of crazed, barking dogs crowded the little strand, Tavish and Conan Dearg going at each other in the middle of a small cleared circle. She saw, too, that the reddish-orange glow she'd noticed from the arch wasn't caused by the strand's smokehouses, but came from the torches that many of Aidan's men held above their heads. The flames gave the scene a hellish taint, the men's shouts and the clashing shriek of steel meeting steel filling her with terror.

In Wrath Bay, a lone galley sped seaward, its hoisted sail declaring the MacLeod colors, the widow's face as she stood clutching the rail bathed as red as the torch flames. Her raven hair streamed in the night wind and her galley was already beginning to founder, lurching heavily to one side as it raced toward the rocks of Wrath Isle.

"Oh, no," Kira cried as they flew down the steep cliff-side steps. "It's just like you said it would be! That boat's going to hit those rocks any minute, and Tavish—"

"—is holding his own," Aidan panted as they tore down the last few steps and leapt onto the pebbly strand, "and I'm about to relieve him!"

Aidan wrenched the Invincible from its scabbard. Men leapt back, freeing a path as he ran across the beach, sword raised, fury in his eye. Ahead, Tavish and Conan Dearg circled each other, blades feinting and slashing, both men bloodstained and sweating.

His own sword already lashing, Aidan hurled himself at his

cousin, sweeping the Invincible in a great, eye-blinding figure-eight motion. "Conan Dearg!" he roared, "'tis time for a reckoning!"

"A mercy!" Tavish spun around, his eyes flying wide. "Aidan!" he cried, his relief evident. "You're here! I dinnae believe it!"

The distraction cost him. Quick as lightning, Conan Dearg dove, swinging his blade in a wide arc that would've lopped off Tavish's head if Aidan hadn't whirled round, kicking Tavish so hard he flew back against the wall of gathered men.

From the corner of his eye, he saw Mundy catch him, seizing Tavish's sword and tossing it aside as he snaked a quick arm around Tavish's waist, holding him so he couldn't rush back into the circle.

"So it comes down to the two of us!" Conan Dearg taunted, Tavish forgotten. "I've waited long for the day!"

"'Tis the day you die, Cousin." Aidan lunged, taking a first cut on Conan Dearg's arm. "Breathe your last while you can."

Conan Dearg laughed and came at him, his sword glinting red in the torchlight as it crashed against Aidan's with a loud, arm-jarring *clank*. With a ferocious burst of strength, Aidan knocked him back, grunting with satisfaction when Conan Dearg lost his footing on the slick shingle, his blade nearly flying from his hand.

Aidan smiled, advancing before Conan Dearg could right himself. "You're tired, clumsy. Come, let me help you find rest!"

"A pox on you!" Conan Dearg yelled, swaying on his feet. "You will rue—"

"That I didn't do this years ago!" Aidan finished, ramming the Invincible deep into his cousin's chest. Hoisting him in the air, he snarled, "May you find the Devil good company."

Conan Dearg stared at him, his eyes bulging, a trickle of blood bubbling from his lips. Glaring at him, Aidan withdrew his blade and resheathed it, grabbing his cousin before he could topple to the ground.

With a great heave, he pushed him into the surf, dusting his hands as Conan Dearg landed with a splash, a flicker of life still gleaming in his eyes as he stared up at Aidan.

"So you die by drowning," Aidan informed him, stepping closer to the water's edge. "As the history books decried."

"The *history books*?" Tavish spoke at his shoulder, looking on as Conan Dearg went limp, his eyes glazing as the tide claimed him.

Aidan drew a deep breath, then slung an arm around his friend, pulling him close. "I'll explain later," he panted, releasing Tavish to drag his sleeve over his forehead. "After I've seen to whoe'er poisoned Kee-*rah*." He glanced round at his men, raising his voice when they pressed closer, their cheers and shouts loud in his ears. "Or do you think it was Conan Dearg? Fenella?"

"It doesn't matter." Kira finally managed to push through the circle of men. She ran forward, flinging herself into Aidan's arms. "All that counts is that we're back here and Tavish is safe."

Tavish looked at her and laughed. "Safe? Me?" Grinning, he jammed his hands on his hips. "I could say the same to the two of you! Sakes, but I've worried about you."

"We were fine." Aidan stood taller. "A mere day's journeying. Naught more." He looked down at Kira, kissed her brow. "Aye, lass?"

"There were moments." She leaned into him, sighed. "I'm just so glad we made it back."

"So am I." Tavish thwacked Aidan on the arm. "I'd hear all about it, regardless."

But Aidan didn't answer him, his gaze sliding away to probe the crowd, searching faces and finding two missing. Nils, whose fierce Viking looks and great height should have had him standing head and shoulders over the fray. And Maili. She was notably absent from where the other two laundresses stood with a small group of kitchen laddies.

A dark suspicion made his jaw clench. "Love-of-thunder." He

looked over Kira's head to Tavish. "Dinnae tell me Nils or Maili had aught to do with all this?"

"Not Nils," Tavish said, no longer smiling. "It was Maili. She helped them, though you should know she's the one who warned me of their escape when Fenella disappeared from the hall not long after you left. Maili followed her and—"

"Maili?" Aidan's jaw dropped. "But she helped us get away when she dumped the oysters and herring into Fenella's lap." Glancing to the sea, he shuddered. The MacLeod galley was almost gone, its wreckage gleaming dully on the choppy waves. "I cannae believe Maili would—"

"She did it for love of a man." Tavish looked uncomfortable. "Apparently, she'd set her sights on one of Fenella's men and the widow promised she'd arrange a marriage between them—in exchange for Maili's help in slipping in and out of Wrath. And, aye, serving Kira poisoned wine."

Aidan shook his head. "But she helped you," he repeated, puzzled.

"To be sure," Tavish agreed. "She also confronted the widow a few days before the feast, demanding to know about the supposed marriage pact. Fenella laughed at her, claiming no MacLeod would lower himself by wedding a laundress."

"I see." Aidan nodded. "Where is she now?"

"In your solar with Nils. He's looking after her." Tavish shoved a hand through his hair, let out a breath. "Maili followed Fenella into the dungeon and they argued. Fenella dirked her in the ribs in front of Conan Dearg's cell. It was Maili's cry that alerted us to their escape. She then told us everything, before she lost consciousness."

Aidan frowned. "Will she live?"

Tavish shrugged. "Nils says there is a chance. But she'll need care. You may not want—"

"Give her the best care possible." Kira pulled out of Aidan's arms. She glanced up at the keep, high on the cliff. When she turned back to him, she stood straighter, squared her shoulders. "Nothing happened to me and she did help us get away."

Aidan looked at her. "You dinnae mind, Kee-*rah*? The monks-hood could have killed you."

Kira shook her head. "But it didn't." She smiled and blinked at him, her eyes starting to mist and her throat closing. "I doubt she'll do anything like that again. And, besides, I can understand a woman's desperation to win the man she loves." Swiping a hand across her cheek, she lifted her chin. "I might have done the same. If I thought it was the only way to win your heart."

"Och, lass." Aidan reached for her, wrapping his arms tight around her. "I lost my heart to you that day I saw you standing at the top of my stair tower. As I have told you."

"A-hem." Tavish tapped his arm, interrupting just as Aidan was about to kiss her. "There's one more thing."

Aidan glared at him. "By all the living gods! What is it?"

"This." His smile returning, Tavish reached beneath his plaid and withdrew a small black object. Two cylinderlike rolls, topped with double rounds of bright, clear-shining glass. "I found this buried in the floor rushes in Conan Dearg's cell. I dinnae know what it is, but—"

"My dad's field glasses!" Kira grabbed them, her heart pounding. "Oh, Aidan! Conan Dearg must've found them on the arch. That night Kendrew saw him crawling around up there. They must be—"

"The *strange object* he used to hit Kendrew on the head with." Aidan took them from her, peering at them curiously. He looked into the glass part, dropping them at once. "By thunder!" he cried, bending to pick them up again. He peered into them once more, but from the other end.

This time he smiled.

"Another mystery solved." He handed them to Tavish. "Now we know what Conan Dearg meant when he said he'd 'see his foes coming before any battle could begin.'"

Tavish nodded, looking equally pleased. "I thought the same when I found them." He clapped Aidan on the arm again. "Now *we* shall enjoy that advantage. Woe be to our enemies!"

"And woe be to my men if they don't soon clear the strand and return to the feast."Aidan reached for Kira's hand, linking their fingers. "I'd have a few quiet moments with my lady before we rejoin you."

"As you wish." Tavish nodded, his smile broadening to a grin when his gaze dipped to the gold rings on their fingers. "Dare I hope the remainder of the feast might be spent celebrating something other than Conan Dearg's demise?"

"You might." Aidan's voice was gruff, husky and thick. "Now get them all back up to the keep before I lose patience."

Tavish laughed, but did as he was bid.

Alone at last with Kira, Aidan took a deep breath. "So, lass," he began, putting his hands on her shoulders. "Shall we give my brave men something to celebrate?"

Kira blinked, her throat too thick for words.

"Well?" He looked at her."Dinnae tell me you're wishing a longer wooing period? No' now, after all we've been through together?"

She swallowed. "Aidan MacDonald, if you're asking me to marry you, you know I'd love nothing more, but—"

"But?" He frowned. "That's another thing you should know by now. I dinnae care for *buts*. Though"—he folded his arms, looking quite the fearsome laird again—"something tells me I ought to hear this one."

Kira looked down, nudging her toe into the pebbles. "It's just that ... well, you know I've always felt that I was sent back in time to save you?"

He nodded.

"Now that I have ... I mean, now that everything's been resolved, I'm wondering if I won't soon be zapped back to my own time."

His frown deepening, he lifted her chin. "That willnae happen, Kee-*rah*. Your place is here with me. I know it."

"How can you?"

He smiled. "Because you are my *tamhasg*, that's why."

Kira's brows lifted. "Your what?"

"Och, lass." He drew her into his arms again, kissing her. "I ne'er believed you were sent here to save me. That, too, I've told you. MacDonald men dinnae need lassies to rescue them. We're together because we were meant to be. That's what a *tamhasg* is."

This time Kira frowned. "I don't understand."

He laughed and kissed her again. "Then I'll speak plainly. A *tamhasg* is the sighting of a future bride or groom. I knew you were mine not long after seeing you that first time. I've always known it and it's why I know time isn't going to whisk you away from me."

"Oh, Aidan." She blinked, unable to say more.

Not that it mattered.

She could see in his eyes that he knew how happy he'd just made her.

Proving it, he grinned and offered her his arm. "Come, sweetness, shall we go share our good news with my men?"

Kira nodded, not about to say no.

# EPILOGUE

## CASTLE WRATH, HIGHLAND SCOTLAND, FIVE MODERN-DAY YEARS LATER

"I knew it was a waste of money to come here." George Bedwell stood in the middle of the National Trust for Scotland's Castle Wrath car park, his resentful stare fixed on the closed Visitor Centre. "We've spent half our trip here bugging those people, and no one has offered a clue as to what happened to Kira or that man of hers. If he even *was* 'Aidan of Wrath.'"

"You know he was." Blanche Bedwell looked on as the last coach tour bus of the day belched a plume of exhaust fumes before rumbling out of the fast-emptying parking lot. "Just because we haven't found out anything doesn't mean fate wasn't good to them."

Her husband snorted and hitched up his belt. "She promised she'd try and leave some kind of sign for us. With all the nutty far-seeing and time travel she was capable of, you'd think she'd have been able to manage something as simple as leaving us a clue."

"Now, George—"

"Och! A thousand pardons." A tall, dark-haired man bowed courteously. "I didn't mean to bump into you," he said, holding a deep blue National Trust for Scotland gift bag in front of his groin.

Flashing a smile, he straightened, keeping the shop bag carefully in place. "I trust this lass can help you. She has the answers you seek."

"What?" George Bedwell put back his shoulders and huffed. But when he adjusted his camera strap, ready to scald the nosy bugger with an angry, all-American stare, he could only splutter and gape.

The man was gone.

In his place, a young girl stared at them, her eyes wide. A badge declared her to be an employee of the National Trust and she held a clutch of business folders pressed to her breast.

"Oh! I'm sorry. I was daydreaming and didn't see you." She smoothed a hand through hair so like Kira's that George Bedwell's jaw dropped.

"It's all right, dear." Blanche touched her arm. "We were distracted, too. That man—"

George stomped on her toe.

The girl smiled, looking more like Kira by the moment. "I don't know who you mean, but maybe I can be of service? It's after hours, but if you have any questions about the site, just ask."

"Ahhh, errrr..." George hesitated, the back of his neck flaming.

He'd definitely ingested too much haggis at the hotel ceilidh the night before.

"Your ring." His wife peered at the girl's hand. "I've seen that design before."

George shot her a glare. "Pay her no heed," he said to the girl. Ignoring his wife, he brushed at his jacket, trying to look distinguished.

With luck, Blanche would follow his lead and not say something that would embarrass them.

"Our daughter once had a ring like that," she said anyway. "She—"

"Oh? That's amazing. I wouldn't have thought that possible." She glanced down at the heavy gold ring.

A Celtic-looking ring, engraved with slender-stemmed trumpets, birds, and delicate swirls.

"You see, it's an old family design," she explained. "The ring has been passed down through the centuries." She cast a glance at the closed Visitor Centre. "An uncle of mine believes it goes back to Aidan of Wrath and his wife, Katherine."

Blanche coughed.

George frowned. "Katherine?"

The name was the reason for his foul humor.

They'd been so close, everything falling into place until they'd stumbled across the archives claiming Aidan of Wrath had wed and lived his long life with a woman called Katherine, not Kira.

The girl nodded, once more looking so much like Kira that their hearts stopped.

"Ach," she cooed, her soft Highland voice drawing them in, letting them hope. "Katherine is only the name in the annals." Lifting her hand, she touched the gold ring, her smile going wistful. "There are actually two rings. A man's and a woman's, both with a simple 'A' and 'K' engraved on the inside. No one knows what Aidan of Wrath's wife's name really was. Unfortunately, history has lost her true name. Scholars replaced it with Katherine because of the 'K.'"

"We see." Blanche slid a glance at her husband.

He was frowning again, his gaze on the perimeter wall of the Castle Wrath grounds. "Did this *Katherine* have any children?" he asked, clasping his hands behind his back as he stared down at Wrath Bay.

"Oh, there were many." The girl beamed at him even if he wasn't looking. "Her firstborn was named George."

"Indeed?" George nodded, ready to believe at last.

And when they drove away a short while later, their eyes

damp and their hearts content, a shadow materialized in the middle of the car park. A shimmering, crackling *cloud* that took on more density the closer it drifted to the low stone wall at the edge of the castle grounds.

Then, just when it appeared as if all Ameri-*cains* and tour buses were finally gone, a tall, dark-haired man stepped out of the mist and dusted his hands. Then he winked at the burly, bushy-bearded man sitting on the wall.

"That was well done." Bushy-beard slapped his thigh, then stood. "Great fun to watch."

"It was the least I could do." The dark-haired man adjusted the shop bag at his groin. "Though, next time, I think you should do the honors."

"What?" Bushy-beard wriggled his eyebrows. "And spoil your fun?"

The dark-haired man looked past him to Wrath Isle, his lips curving in a slow smile. "My fun is about to begin."

Bushy-beard looked skeptical. "Down on that accursed isle?"

"Nae, you loon. I feel a need to go have a closer look at our ring."

His friend lifted a brow. "The ring or the girl wearing it?"

The dark-haired man laughed. "If you have to ask, you don't know me as well as you should."

With that, he clapped Bushy-beard on the arm, then turned and set off across the car park toward the Visitor Centre, his grin broadening with each step he took.

It was good to be *alive*.

# AUTHOR'S NOTE

ε●

Did you know?
Reviews are worth gold to authors – these days more than ever.
When readers share their thoughts on a book, other readers
listen. There's no better way to spread word about stories you
love. A win-win for readers and authors.
If you enjoyed Highlander in Her Dreams, I would be really
appreciative if you would review the book online – Amazon,
BookBub, and Goodreads are the best options. A review needn't
be long. Something as simple as 'I really loved this story' is great.
My heartfelt thanks.

ε●

Dear Readers,

As with so many of my books, this story was inspired by my
own adventures in Scotland. The settings are real although I
usually change the names. I love these places dearly and hope to
have painted them as beautifully as they truly are. My goal as a

writer is to *take you there*, transporting you into the magical world of Highland Scotland. I want readers to feel as if they are living the story right alongside my characters.

Read on to discover behind-the-ink tidbits and musings about Highlander in Her Dreams. I hope you'll find them interesting...

~ Insta-love: Adding this as Kira and Aidan know their hearts pretty much upon meeting. Well, it is said to *'write what you know'* and I do that in my books, especially this one. I met my German husband on an airline layover in Munich. Obviously that happened in my flying years. I was a young stewardess and out for dinner with the cabin and cockpit crew. We were in a Bavarian pub and having a great time when the door opened and my husband walked in. Our eyes met, the proverbial 'electricity' crackled between us, and I jabbed my elbow into the stew-friend beside me and said, "Here comes my dream man - I'm going to marry that man." And I did. We've now been happily married for more decades than I care to note, but I will say ... I disagree with the opinion that there's no such thing as insta-love.

~ Scotophile: To be correct, it should be noted that the word for someone who loves all things Scottish is actually Cale-donophile, taken from Caledonia, the Latin name for Scotland. Even so, I chose to use Scotophile as many of us who are wild about Scotland use this word, technically correct or not.

Scotophile's proper meaning is *'someone who loves and flour-ishes in darkness.'* I find that fitting, too, as for many months of the year, darkness falls quite early in Scotland and Scotland's famed gloaming also falls as the evening begins to draw in.

Also, although I am now a lark, rising before dawn to cycle out to enjoy the tropical sunrises here in southwest Florida, during the years I wrote most of books, I was a dedicated night owl, tapping away at the keyboard after midnight and through the small hours. I enjoyed the peace and stillness of the night's darkness to slip away into my stories. So either way, Scotophile works fine for me.

~ Brand: Old English and also old Norse (brandr) for sword. The word only appears a time or two in this story and should be understood in context, but any fascinated by word origins might enjoy delving into the history of sword/brand. Interesting stuff!

~ Diggy camera: If you caught this mention, it wasn't a typo. The usage was a nostalgic nod to the time when digital cameras first hit the scene. For whatever reason, I called my first one a 'diggy' camera.

~ Left driving: Sorry friends and readers across the Pond, but even after all these years and many Scotland trips behind the wheel *(driving really is the only way to get to the best places)* well, I would rather face hordes of swarming Florida noseeums—think midges—than drive over there. Jellies my knees every time. So all quips about the terrors of thread-thin Highland roads, racing locals, and dinosaur-size recreation vehicles are from my own experiences and remain my scariest nightmares. *(I still love the UK.)*

~ Castle Wrath: This ruin/castle actually exists. Its true name is Duntulm and the ruins there are very much as described in this story. Only the medieval arch is missing although it, too, can be found on Skye. I borrowed the arch, transplanting it to Castle Wrath from another Skye castle ruin, Dun Sgathaich.

Like Kira, I have enjoyed picnics atop the grass-grown arch at Dun Sgathaich. I've also spent time at Duntulm, my attention always drawn to a certain deep, dark opening in the earth. One that, I strongly suspect, leads down into Duntulm's haunted dungeon where Hugh, a one-time Duntulm laird's evil cousin was imprisoned. His cries and rantings are said to be heard to this day and I can vouch that Duntulm does indeed echo with the possibilities of such ghostly residents.

I must admit that I tweaked the truth by having the National Trust for Scotland turn the site into a major tourist attraction at the end of Highlander in Her Dreams. Thank goodness, that isn't so. It just suited my story to add such a twist. If you visit Skye, I hope you'll make the journey out to the ruins. They are deliciously atmospheric and you never know what you might find there. Perhaps an Aidan of your own, as the ruins are indeed haunted.

~ Spean Bridge Mill: Also real. And the name is the correct one. I was a bit hard on Spean Bridge Mill in the story, but that angle fit the telling of the tale as I hope you'll agree. I actually love the place and always nip in there when driving along Scotland's scenic A-82. I have used the classic red 'phone box' there many times. Often when I've done so, RAF fighter jets would roar by overhead, jolting me and disrupting my call. Those fond memories spurred me to have the same thing happen to Kira and Aidan.

~ Sassunach: There are several spellings for this Scottish word for the English. Sassenach is probably the most popular these days. The Irish use Sasanach. I prefer Sassunach with 'u' because it is the spelling I've come across most often in my nonfiction research books on medieval Scotland. After decades of feeling at home with this spelling, it would seem odd to me to use another version.

~ Ravenscraig Castle: This castle is pure fiction, but based on several castle hotels and country manor estates I know and love in Scotland. You can revisit this enchanting castle and those who live there in all Ravenscraig Legacy books and in my stand-alone book, The First Knight, which is largely set there.

~ The Ravenscraig Legacy: These stories have always been my favorites. All these books were originally published by Penguin and *Highlander in Her Dreams* was the second of the series. All of these books combine the glory of medieval Scotland with the fun of a contemporary paranormal romance with time travel, ghosts, and magic.

If you'd like to read the entire Ravenscraig Legacy series, here are the books, noted in the best reading order...

Highlander in Her Bed
Highlander in Her Dreams
Tall, Dark, and Kilted
Some Like It Kilted
Must Love Kilts
Haunted Warrior
(most are also available in audio)

Thank you for reading Highlander in Her Dreams. If you love Scotland as much as I do, I hope the hours spent with Kira and Aidan took you there.

Wishing you Highland Magic,

*Sue-Ellen Welfonder*

# DON'T MISS THE NEXT RAVENSCRAIG LEGACY STORY...

## TALL, DARK, AND KILTED

*A good man is hard to find.*

Cilla Swanner has been jilted by her lover, and she is struggling with a jewelry business that's far from sparkling. She needs a getaway someplace quiet and remote. Someplace like Dunroamin Castle in Scotland, where her aunt and uncle run a retirement home in the majestic Highlands. But what she finds there may be more than she can handle.

*Or is it the other way around?*

Centuries ago, the roguish Scots knight known as Hardwick was renowned for his swordmanship, both on and off the battlefield. But a traveling bard cursed him to wander the world forever, pleasing a different woman each night with no hope of fulfillment or true love. Then Hardwick meets Cilla, who may be his only chance for salvation.

"Outlandishly funny one minute and seductively sensual the next." ~ Wild on Books

## MINI-EXCERPT:

### A HERO'S WARNING

"Who are you?" Cilla regarded him warily. "Where did you come from?"

"From a place more distant than you'd believe." He ignored her first question. "I've good advice for you. If you're after a true taste of Scotland, hie yourself—"

"Hie myself?" She blinked.

"Take yourself," he clarified, scowling. "Quit this place and journey south. Inverness, the Isle of Skye, Stirling and Perth, perhaps even down to Edinburgh. Or Glasgow. Aye." He appeared to warm to the idea. "Glasgow is where you should be. Loch Lomond is there and—"

"I saw Loch Lomond on the drive up here." Cilla frowned back at him. "We stopped there for lunch and I've never seen so many tour buses. If that's Scotland"—she made a wide sweeping gesture with her arm, taking in the rain-dampened parapet—"I'd rather be here."

"Be warned then." He stepped closer, his dark gaze piercing her. "Sutherland is filled with lonely moors and dark bogs. Mountains so vast they'd eat a lass like you bones and all and no one would ever be the wiser."

"I like wild places." She tossed back her hair, defiant.

He snorted. "This is the end of the world."

Cilla smiled. "Exactly."

# ABOUT THE AUTHOR

"Sue-Ellen Welfonder brings legends and love to life."

— FRESH FICTION

USA Today bestselling author Sue-Ellen Welfonder won Romantic Times Best Historical Romance Award for her debut title, Devil in a Kilt. Many of her books have been RT Award nominees, and have received RT Top Picks and K.I.S.S. Hero Awards. She is thrilled to be a winner of InD'Tale's RONE Award. Her favorite reader compliment is that her stories transport them to medieval Scotland, the setting of most of her books. She is also known for her strong heroines, Alpha heroes, and weaving Highland magic and humor into her tales.

Sue-Ellen also writes as Allie Mackay, penning contemporary paranormals, mostly set in the Scottish Highlands.

Connect with Sue-Ellen Welfonder
*(aka Allie Mackay)*

Join the newsletter mailing list:
https://madmimi.com/signups/102456/join

Sue-Ellen's website:
www.welfonder.com
www.alliemackay.com

# ALSO BY SUE-ELLEN WELFONDER

**Ladies' Knight**

The First Knight

**Highland Warriors**

Sins of a Highland Devil

Temptation of a Highland Scoundrel

Seduction of a Highland Warrior

Once Upon a Highland Christmas

A Yuletide Promise

**Highland Knights**

Knight in Her Bed

Master of the Highlands

Wedding for a Knight

**Clan MacKenzie Series**

Devil in a Kilt

Bride of the Beast

Only for a Knight

**Return to Kintail Scottish Romances**

Winter Fire

The Taming of MairiMacKenzie

**Highlander Regency Romances**

The Kiss at Midnight

The Laird of Lyongate Hall

**Short Stories**

The Seventh Sister

Falling in Time

**Available Allie Mackay Titles**

**Ravenscraig Legacy**

Highlander in Her Bed

Highlander In Her Dreams

Tall, Dark and Kilted

Some Like it Kilted

Must Love Kilts

**Highland Ghostbusters**

Haunted Warrior

**Audio**

WEDDING FOR A KNIGHT

HIGHLANDER IN HER BED

HIGHLANDER IN HER DREAMS

TALL, DARK, and KILTED

SOME LIKE IT KILTED

HAUNTED WARRIOR

# Always Mine

## Book 3 of the Always Trilogy

# CHERYL
# HOLT

# Praise for *New York Times* Bestselling Author
# CHERYL HOLT

"Best storyteller of the year . . ."
*Romantic Times Magazine*

"A master writer . . ."
*Fallen Angel Reviews*

"The Queen of Erotic Romance . . ."
*Book Cover Reviews*

"Cheryl Holt is magnificent . . ."
*Reader to Reader Reviews*

"From cover to cover, I was spellbound. Truly outstanding . . ."
*Romance Junkies*

"A classic love story with hot, fiery passion dripping from every page. There's nothing better than curling up with a great book and this one totally qualifies."
*Fresh Fiction*

"This is a masterpiece of storytelling. A sensual delight scattered with rose petals that are divinely arousing. Oh my, yes indeedy!"
Reader to Reader Reviews

## *Praise for Cheryl Holt's "Lord Trent" trilogy*

"A true guilty pleasure!"
*Novels Alive TV*

"LOVE'S PROMISE can't take the number one spot as my favorite by Ms. Holt—that belongs to her book NICHOLAS—but it's currently running a close second."
*Manic Readers*

"The book was brilliant . . . can't wait for Book #2."
*Harlie's Book Reviews*

"I guarantee you won't want to put this one down. Holt's fast-paced dialogue, paired with the emotional turmoil, will keep you turning the pages all the way to the end."
*Susana's Parlour*

". . . A great love story populated with many flawed characters. Highly recommend it."
*Bookworm 2 Bookworm Reviews*

# BOOKS BY CHERYL HOLT

ISBN: 978-1-64606-927-9 (Print version)

Cover Design Angela Waters
Interior format, Dayna Linton, Day Agency

# Always Mine

# PROLOGUE

———✦✦✦———

"I want to go home."

"You are home, so be silent."

Rebecca glared at her Cousin Beatrice, but her firm look had no effect. She was only a little girl, and her cousin was a big, scary adult. Her voice was loud, her hands rough and quick to lash out.

In Rebecca's prior world, she'd never been pinched or slapped. She'd definitely never been scolded and sent to bed without supper, but even after so much time had passed, her circumstances were so confusing, and the grownups in her new world were cruel, angry, and impatient.

She didn't want to stay with them. She wanted to live where she'd previously lived. Her life there had been perfect, and she'd been treated like a princess. Why didn't Cousin Beatrice understand how precious Rebecca was?

"Where are Mother and Father?" Ever since Rebecca had been forcibly conveyed to Cousin Beatrice's house, she'd been posing the same question. "Nanny told me they're in Heaven. Could I fly up to Heaven too? I'd like to be with them again."

"Your nanny was lying. Your parents were sinners. They're not in Heaven. They're in Hell, and they'll be there forever."

Rebecca scowled. "Hell is a bad place. My parents weren't bad."

Cousin Beatrice was sitting at the dining room table, eating her breakfast. Rebecca wasn't supposed to bother her when she was eating, but she refused to accept all the rules that had been foisted on her.

She was Viscount Blake's daughter, so she was very special.

Her father had always told her so, her mother too. They'd been the best parents ever. At least she *thought* they'd been wonderful. She was five now, and she'd resided with Cousin Beatrice for ages, so her memories were fading. She was starting to forget her parents, was starting to forget what was true and what wasn't.

"Where is Sissy?" she asked. "I shouldn't be separated from her, and I have to find her."

"You don't have a sister. Stop pretending."

Rebecca's scowl deepened. She'd once been sure that she'd had a sister. They were exactly alike, and they'd spoken in a secret language others didn't comprehend, but *they* had comprehended it. They'd been like one person, with not a speck of difference between them. People hadn't been able to tell them apart.

"I had a sister," Rebecca said, but less adamantly. "I know I did."

"You have a vivid imagination, and I've warned you about making up stories. Will I have to whip it out of you?"

"She'll be hunting for me."

Cousin Beatrice leaned down from her chair, so she and Rebecca were nose to nose. "You're not allowed in the dining room. Go away."

"I don't like it here, and I don't like you," Rebecca bravely stated.

"Well, we don't like you either."

"I'd like to leave. I'd like to live with Sissy and Brother again, and Nanny must be worried over where I am."

Rebecca had asked about her old life so often and for so long that it had begun to be a habit. It wasn't so much that she missed it anymore, but she suffered from a profound sense that she should continue to inquire. If she tucked away her concerns, she was terrified her family would become invisible, and she would hate to have them be invisible.

Yet she was feeling less and less certain over what she recalled. Perhaps Sissy and Brother didn't really exist. Perhaps Mother and Father weren't in Heaven. Perhaps they hadn't liked her and had given her away as Cousin Beatrice repeatedly claimed.

"You were spoiled as a child," Cousin Beatrice said, "and your mother did you no favors by letting you sass and disobey. It's obvious you never learned your place. It's beyond me why I should have to tolerate your cheeky impertinence."

"My mother loved me," Rebecca insisted.

"No, she didn't. You were born wicked, and you constantly caused trouble. You were very expensive to raise too. Your parents were sick of you and that's why they dumped you in my lap. They didn't want you."

"I don't think that's right. When my brother comes for me, you'll be sorry."

"Don't get your hopes up." Cousin Beatrice grinned an evil grin. "Your brother detested you even more than your parents. He was glad to be shed of you, so he'll never search."

A maid entered, and Cousin Beatrice straightened and said to the woman, "I have no idea why this brat is pestering me. She's not permitted to, and you're aware of the rules. If she disturbs me again during my breakfast, I'll have you flogged."

The maid hurried over and grabbed Rebecca. "My apologies, Mrs. Carter. I didn't realize she'd snuck in."

The maid dragged Rebecca out and marched her up the stairs and down the deserted halls to her dark, cold bedchamber at the rear of the manor.

The woman pushed Rebecca inside as she scolded, "Why antagonize Mrs. Carter? It only lands you in hot water."

"I need to talk to my father."

"Your father is dead, and you're five already. Quit acting like such a baby. It's pointless to whine about the past. You can't change what occurred."

"Did I have a sister?" Rebecca asked.

"No, you didn't. You'll stay in your room today and ponder your behavior. Maybe, when I let you out, you'll have remembered to guard your tongue."

She yanked the door closed and spun the key in the lock. Her footsteps retreated down the hall, then it was very quiet. But Rebecca was used to the quiet, was used to being all alone—with just her odd memories to entertain her. She simply wished they weren't fading so quickly.

She walked to the window and stared out, content to listen to the birds chirping in the trees. It was a comforting noise, and she would watch them for hours—until the sun began to set and a footman brought her supper on a tray.

In her mind, she sent a message to her sister as she always had when she was tiny. Or was it her guardian angel? How could she know for sure?

*Are you there?*

The reply surged back immediately. *Yes, I'm here—and I always will be.*

# CHAPTER

1

*Twenty-two years later . . .*

REBECCA CARTER STROLLED BY the stables where a quartet of horses had arrived from a London auction house. For several minutes, she dawdled in the shadows, observing the beautiful animals as they stomped and snorted in the corral.

Her cousin, Clayton, was a connoisseur of fine horseflesh. He owned many more of them than he needed or could afford to feed, but he was very spoiled. Where money was involved, he thought it grew on trees. No one—not even his mother, her Cousin Beatrice—could convince him to rein in his expenses.

She scanned the area, eager to catch a glimpse of the two men who'd delivered them, but she didn't see them anywhere. A housemaid had mentioned they were a pair of handsome, dashing rogues and definitely worth a glance, so Rebecca had come outside.

It was always interesting to meet someone new or to chat with someone from town. Rebecca had never been to London—or any place else for that matter. The city sounded so exotic and was so far away, it might have been up on the moon.

In their small corner of the kingdom, that being her cousins' estate of Carter Crossing, they didn't have many visitors, mostly because they were located in such an isolated spot on the coast, with the English Channel at their backs. But also, her relatives weren't the easiest people to like.

Her cousin Millicent, who was twenty, could be cheery and pleasant when she tried, but her mother, Cousin Beatrice, had a knack for making enemies.

She viciously disciplined her servants, rudely fought with the neighbors, and constantly bickered with merchants in the nearby town of Frinton. Her foibles and quarrels were so renowned that she'd garnered an open reputation as a shrew and a harpy. Because of it, they rarely had callers.

The men who'd brought the horses would tarry for awhile to get them settled, so there would be chances to socialize, which was exciting.

Rebecca seldom crossed paths with any bachelors. The neighborhood was filled with families, but as with her cousin, Clayton, young men liked to revel in London, so they were hardly ever home. It was difficult to arrange a party or a dance when there were no fellows to partner with all the girls.

Clayton would slither in the next day to celebrate his thirtieth birthday. His appearance could be a blessing or a curse, depending on his mood. He was addicted to fast living and gambling, so if he'd had a run of bad luck at the card tables, he would be especially irritable.

Or if he'd drained the bank accounts again, he'd have epic battles with Cousin Beatrice over his being such a spendthrift.

Rebecca couldn't abide their spats. They disrupted the entire house. She was an optimist though and would hope for a successful sojourn. He'd invited a dozen friends to join him for the festivities, and he had many lofty acquaintances. When any of them accompanied him to the country, he was on his best behavior.

There was a rumor circulating too that—on this occasion—a member of Sir Sidney Sinclair's African expedition team would be included in the list of guests. Sir Sidney was a national hero who'd died on his latest excursion to Africa. The explorers who went with him were all famous too, and the staff was atwitter over the prospect of him showing up.

Rebecca couldn't believe Clayton rubbed elbows with such a grand person. It would be like having the King stay with them, and Clayton wasn't exactly a luminary. How could he have befriended such an icon?

As to herself, she'd love for the rumor to be true. She wanted to pepper the man with questions about his life and activities. What was it like to be out on the ocean, to ride a canoe in the jungle, or to mingle with native tribes? She couldn't imagine.

Men were so fortunate. They were allowed to travel and have adventures, while women had to sit at home and read about their trips in the newspaper.

With Carter Crossing being situated on the coast, there were plenty of cliffs and coves where she could loaf and ponder the bigger world. She frequently climbed the nearby headland to stare out at the water. Most days, a ship or two would pass by, the sails whisking it through the waves, and she'd experience such a surge of wanderlust that it left her sick with desire.

She'd give anything to leave Carter Crossing, to bluster off to a better future, but a female such as herself had scant opportunities to alter her fate.

When she realized how dreadfully she was moping, she yanked away from the barn and marched over to the trail that led up to the promontory. She had no reason to sulk, and it was futile to pine away. She was stuck where she was, with no money and just her Carter cousins to offer her shelter.

Why lament? She had so much more than most people. She had food to eat and clothes to wear, chores to attend and servants to manage. What more did a woman need?

She clambered up the path, stopping every so often to catch her breath, but to study the horizon too. The sight was so spectacular. The blue sky and blue ocean stretched to infinity.

It was a chilly September afternoon, autumn approaching with a vengeance, and the wind whipped at her hair and shawl. She pulled it more tightly around her body, scolding herself for failing to grab a cloak or even one of Clayton's wool coats. The temperature was cold and warranted more layers.

She reached the top, and the trail leveled out. It remained flat for a bit, then descended down the other side to the abandoned Oakley estate. Old Mr. Oakley had died without any heirs, and the property had been vacant for years.

When she had a free minute, she'd walk all the way across to Oakley. She liked to snoop around the deserted mansion, to peek in the windows and envision the place restored to its prior glory, with her living in the refurbished rooms.

At noting her flight of fancy, she chuckled and shook her head.

"What is wrong with me today?" she asked herself.

Usually, she ignored her circumstances and was content to muddle through. Perhaps it was her advanced age of twenty-seven, but recently, she was chafing more and more, yearning for her plight to change, but this was Carter Crossing where nothing ever changed.

On the uppermost point of the hill, there was an ancient stone bench that had been carved into the rocks. Once she'd been old enough to flit off by herself, she'd regularly snuck up to sit on it, vanishing for hours to enjoy the solitude and escape the pressures of the manor.

It was her secret spot and always empty, so when she saw a man hogging it, she was incredibly aggravated. Who was he? How had he stumbled on her private haven? And why would he feel it was all right to linger?

He was thirty or so, and he appeared sinister, being dressed all in black: black shirt and coat, black trousers, black boots. His hair was black too, and it was tied with a strip of leather and hanging far down his back, as if he'd fired his barber.

He hadn't shaved for a week or two either, and a beard shadowed his face. He was wearing a hat, and it shielded his eyes so she couldn't discern their color. She wondered if they'd be black to match his hair and clothes.

Because he was seated, she couldn't guess his height, but she suspected he'd be very tall, six feet at least or maybe even taller than that. He was broad-shouldered and lanky, and looked sturdy and tough, as if he'd been swamped by many disasters in his life and had skipped by with nary a scratch or a scar.

The brisk wind had concealed the sound of her footsteps, so he hadn't noticed her. Since he exuded the aura of a brigand or highwayman and had no business being where he was, she didn't suppose she ought to tarry.

She would have spun away and tiptoed off, but as she began to turn, he glanced over, and when he observed her, he blanched with astonishment.

"Miss Robertson?" he asked as if they were acquainted.

"No, sorry, I'm not Miss Robertson."

"Yes, you are," he absurdly said. "Don't jest."

"I'm not jesting, and I'm not Miss Robertson."

"Liar. Just because we loathe each other, you don't have to pretend. I won't bite you."

"That's good to hear."

"Why are you out on the coast? How did you travel here? You don't have a penny in your purse. What brought you?"

"I believe, sir, that you have me confused with someone else."

He pushed himself to his feet, and he was as tall as she'd predicted he would be. She was only five-foot-five in her slippers, and he towered over her—but not in a frightening way. She didn't perceive any menace. He was simply big and masculine in a manner she'd never previously encountered.

He was very handsome too, with an aristocratic face—high cheekbones, strong nose, perfect chin—but it was his eyes that were most riveting. They were a striking shade of blue, enhanced by the sapphire of the sky above and the water below.

A woman could get lost in those eyes.

He stomped over to her, and if she'd been smarter or quicker, she'd have run off, but she stood her ground, watching him warily and concerned about what he intended.

He continued until they were toe to toe, coming so close that her skirt tangled around his legs. He scrutinized her white-blond hair, her blue eyes. Though her lengthy locks were tied with a ribbon, the breeze was wreaking havoc. He grabbed a strand and wrapped it around his finger so he could draw her nearer.

The move was so brazen and so unexpected that she was astounded by it. It was rare that anyone touched her, that anyone really looked at her. He was such a severe, forceful fellow that she found the moment to be very thrilling.

"I'll be damned," he muttered as he released the strand and stepped back. "You were telling the truth. You're not Sarah Robertson. You must be her sister then. Her twin?"

At his voicing the word *twin,* a fierce wave of gladness swept through her.

For the briefest second, she suffered a vision from when she was tiny and still living with her father. She had so few recollections of that time, and she viewed it as a precious gift. There was a little girl with her, one who—in Rebecca's dreams—she assumed was her guardian angel. They were nose to nose, an unspoken conversation darting between them as they talked inside their heads.

Then Rebecca blinked and the vision vanished. The worst sense of loss gripped her, but she shook it away.

"I don't have any siblings," she said.

"That can't be right. Two women can't be so similar without their being twins."

"I'm serious. I'm an orphan and an only child."

It was a small lie. She had a half-brother with whom she had no contact, but she never mentioned him.

The stranger studied her again, then smirked. "You're lying. Why? You have a twin. Why deny your connection?"

"I have no sister. How can I convince you?"

"Let's hope you're not as bossy and obstinate as she is."

"I'm never bossy or obstinate."

"Praise be," he grumbled. "I'd take you to town and introduce you to her, but there's no point in meeting such a shrew."

"It seems she made quite an impression on you."

"And not in a positive way. I don't care for uppity women."

"Then you'll love me," she sarcastically said. "I'm the most biddable, sweet-tempered female in the kingdom."

"There's no such thing as a biddable female."

"You have a very low opinion of my gender."

"It's all deserved. Since you're not the odious Miss Robertson, what is your name? You have to be a Robertson too. How are you related to her?"

"I'm not related to any Robertsons. I'm a Carter."

At the revelation, he assessed her even more meticulously. "*You* are a Carter?"

"Yes. This headland is part of the Carter Crossing estate, so don't be surprised to find a family member walking by."

"You don't resemble Clayton in the slightest, so you can't be his sister, Millicent."

"No. I'm a cousin."

"Not with those eyes, you're not."

She scowled. "What's wrong with my eyes?"

He scoffed in a manner that might have meant anything, then he spun away to gaze out at the ocean.

"It's amazing up here," he said.

"Yes. It's always been my favorite spot."

"I'd forgotten it was so spectacular."

"Are you from the area?"

"No."

"Then how could you have forgotten it was spectacular?"

She waited for him to explain himself, but he didn't. They were at the top of the promontory. In one direction, the trail led down to the Carter manor house. In the other, it led down to the abandoned Oakley mansion. No one stumbled over the hill by accident.

"What sort of cousin are you?" he asked.

"The usual sort, I guess."

"Indicating what? You're an orphan, so you must have moved in as a little girl who had nowhere else to go, and you never left."

She nodded, irked by how swiftly he'd deduced her situation. She liked to think she was a tad mysterious, but evidently, she wasn't.

"You're very perceptive," she said.

He looked her up and down, his appraisal nearly impertinent. "Women are never hard to figure out."

"You're a bit rude too."

"I've heard that accusation occasionally."

"Were you raised in the forest by wolves?"

"Close enough." He noted her scuffed shoes, and he snorted. "You're the poor relative, aren't you?"

"You don't have to insult me."

"I wasn't insulting you. I was stating the facts."

He leaned a hip on the bench, his arms folded across his chest. He appeared as if he had all the time in the world to chat, but *she* didn't.

She worked like a dog for Beatrice, managing the servants, managing the house. She was like an indentured servant, but one who had no contract, so she could never buy it out and have her term of servitude end.

Beatrice didn't warrant any kindness, but Rebecca placated her anyway. It was an impulse she couldn't shake. Her stubborn attitude was deeply ingrained from listening to Beatrice's repeated complaints that Rebecca was lazy and foolish and would, no doubt, turn out just as awful as her immoral, sinful mother.

Rebecca had grown up chafing at Beatrice's derision, but she'd slowly developed a very thick skin and a very entrenched need to prove that Beatrice was mistaken. She constantly tried to please Beatrice, but there was no pleasing her.

Rebecca never snuck off for long, not wanting an incident to arise where Beatrice would blame her for some minor catastrophe. As Beatrice never ceased to remind her, she stayed at Carter Crossing because Beatrice let her stay. If Rebecca enraged her, or if Beatrice got tired of supporting her, she could be kicked out, and her predicament was no different than it had been when she'd first arrived. She still had nowhere to go.

When Rebecca had been small, Beatrice had frequently terrorized her with threats of eviction. She'd suffered for years, planning how she might be able to live on the beach or in the woods, but it had gradually dawned on her that Beatrice simply enjoyed being horrid and would never follow through.

Besides, the property was actually Clayton's, and his sister, Millicent, was cordial. If Beatrice ever became overly vile, she could prevail on Millicent to make her mother behave.

Then again, Rebecca wouldn't court trouble. She would never rock a boat or initiate a quarrel. In all circumstances, she was the happiest, most helpful person ever.

But it was difficult to maintain such an agreeable façade. On the inside, she was boiling with fury over the injustices she'd endured. Every so often, she started to feel as if she couldn't breathe in the manor, as if she was suffocating, and she'd dash off for a walk—like the one she was engaged in at that very moment.

She was anxious to sit on her bench and relish the solitude before she had to head down to supervise the preparations for supper. Why didn't he leave? How could she persuade him to depart so she could have a few minutes to herself?

She glowered to inform him that he was loafing where he shouldn't be, but he was an obtuse oaf, and he didn't budge.

"How old were you when you were brought to Carter Crossing?" he asked.

"Three, and I have to categorically state that you are very nosy."

"How did it happen that your Carter cousins took you in?"

"My parents died. How would you suppose?"

"Who were they? Were they Robertsons—like your twin, Sarah Robertson? Or were they Carters?"

"My mother was a Carter."

"Who was your father?"

Her father had been Matthew Blake, Viscount Blake, but Rebecca never mentioned it. He'd seduced her mother, Mary, when she'd been young and gullible and far from home. He'd been a widower with a baby son—Rebecca's half-brother, Nathan—and he'd hired Mary to work as Nathan's nanny.

According to Beatrice, Mary had been beautiful, but stupid and naïve too. She'd fallen for the Viscount's charms, and Rebecca had been the result. It was why she'd likely never marry. No man worth having would pick a bride with such sordid bloodlines.

She changed the subject. "You haven't told me who you are or why you're up here."

"No, I haven't," he maddeningly retorted.

"It's not exactly a popular trail. Should I be worried about you?"

"Yes."

She wasn't sure what she'd expected as an answer, but it hadn't been that. She sputtered with amusement. "Yes? Setting aside the fact that you look sinister as the Devil, why should I be concerned about you?"

"I'm tough and dangerous."

"I'm certain you are, but there is no menacing situation for you to encounter on this promontory. It's simply peaceful and serene, so it invites contemplation."

He tsked. "It's hardly peaceful. The wind could blow a cow off this cliff."

"I like it anyway. I like to watch the ships passing by."

"When you espy one, do you yearn to be on it?"

"Yes. I've never been on a ship before. How about you?"

"Yes. I've journeyed to the wildest places on the globe."

He casually tossed out the remark, as if he'd trekked great distances, but he was attired like a laborer who needed to locate his barber as quickly as possible. How could he have traveled? How could he have afforded it?

She was betting that London was the farthest venue in his itinerary.

"I can't decide if you're being truthful or not," she said.

"Why would I lie?"

"You're very enigmatic, so there are probably a dozen reasons."

"You think I'm enigmatic?"

"Well, you won't tell me your name or your purpose."

"Perhaps I'm merely rude and unsociable."

"Perhaps," she concurred.

"Is Beatrice Carter your aunt?" he asked.

"She was my mother's cousin, so she's mine too."

"Millicent and Clayton are your cousins as well?"

"Yes."

"You poor girl."

She clucked her tongue with offense. "I won't listen to you denigrating my relatives, especially when you and I haven't even been introduced. You're being positively surly."

"I'm a surly fellow."

"You definitely are. Do you always dress all in black?"

"Yes."

"It makes you appear quite ominous."

"That's the point."

"You like to frighten people?"

"Yes. Am I frightening you?"

"No, you're annoying me."

"I have that effect." He was almost bragging.

"I'm not surprised to hear it, so you should be on your way before it occurs to me that you're lurking where you shouldn't be."

"I don't feel like leaving."

"If you won't go away, *I* will have to depart."

"Why? You said I don't scare you."

"I have to get back. I have chores."

"I thought you were a cousin. Why would you have chores? Or are you treated like a servant?"

He was such an astute wastrel, and he'd nailed her position exactly. She couldn't mask a frown, and he crowed, "I was correct! I should have guessed."

"They don't force me to pitch in. I simply like being helpful."

"Sure you do. How hard are they making you work?"

"They don't *make* me work. I run the manor for Cousin Beatrice, and I enjoy having so much responsibility. I'm useful and valued for my contributions, and I'm lucky to have such an important post."

He pushed away from the bench, and he stepped in so they were toe to toe again. Stunning her, he clasped hold of her hand, and he lifted it so he could examine her palm. It was covered with calluses.

He stroked his thumb over the roughest spot, and his touch had her wishing she were a damsel in a fairytale so he'd think she was beautiful and spoiled. But from the condition of her skin, it was obvious there had never been any chance of that.

She peered up at him, and for a moment, she was drowning in his riveting gaze. His eyes were so blue, and he was so tall. She liked how he towered over her, how she felt small and insignificant next to him. He had wide shoulders, the kind a woman could lean on if she was weary or distressed.

What would it be like to have such a strong, strapping man by her side? What changes might it render? How comforting might it be? She couldn't imagine.

She drew her hand away and tucked it in the folds of her shawl so he couldn't grab it again.

"You're too pretty to be so abused," he said. "I hate that you are."

"I'm not abused. My life is fine, and I should go."

"Don't leave because of me. How about if we tarry for awhile and see how many ships we can count?"

"I've frittered away all the minutes I can for one afternoon."

"That's too bad."

She should have turned away then, but she didn't. She studied him, committing every detail to memory so she could reflect on them later. It seemed as if something was supposed to happen or as if she should offer a profound remark, but she couldn't fathom what it might be.

"Goodbye," she told him.

"I hope I'll bump into you again someday."

"And *I* hope you won't. You won't tell me who you are, so you shouldn't be sitting on my bench."

"Your bench?"

"It's as much mine as anyone's."

"I'll keep that in mind."

He smiled at her, and it was a wicked, sinful smile, filled with temptation. It was the type of smile that could drag a girl into all sorts of trouble. It was very likely the type of smile Rebecca's father had flashed at her mother all those years ago.

How did a woman deflect that look? Why would she want to?

She whipped away and started down the hill, figuring she should warn Beatrice about him, but it would mean having to admit she'd been woolgathering on the promontory. It would simply bring about a sound scolding for her being lazy and unreliable.

Perhaps she'd corner a stable boy and ask him to climb up and chase the man off. It was a better idea.

She wound down the trail, determined not to glance at him, but every fiber of her being was urging her to catch a final glimpse. At the last bend in the path, she stopped and peeked back.

She'd expected him to be watching her depart, maybe as bewitched by her as she'd been by him, but he'd already forgotten about her. He was over by the cliff, staring out at the ocean. His feet were braced, his fists on his hips, as he scrutinized the horizon. He was clearly in his element, as if he owned the whole world.

He was quite magnificent, and she could only pray he wouldn't cause any problems. If he did, Beatrice would find a reason to blame Rebecca, and she'd never hear the end of it.

She sighed and continued down the hill.

# CHAPTER

# 2

"Don't gamble with the stable hands."

"Why shouldn't I?"

"How about because you don't need the money and they do. Besides, you cheat, and they don't realize it. It's not fair to them."

Raven Shawcross glared at his younger brother, Lucas, trying to wear him down with a firm glower, but unfortunately, no one could coerce Lucas into behaving.

"Who said life is fair?" Lucas asked. "I've certainly never thought it was. If I steal a few pounds from them, they should consider it a lesson."

"What lesson would you be imparting?"

"They shouldn't gamble with a stranger from the city."

Raven rolled his eyes, saddened that he hadn't had a chance to act as a father figure to his brother over the years. Lucas had always required firm guidance, but circumstances had guaranteed he'd never received it. He was a shining example of how wicked propensities could fly free if they weren't drummed out at a young age.

They were both driven and determined, but Raven had scruples. He wouldn't deliberately lie or transgress, and he debated moral issues. His recent experience in London was typical.

He was a member of the famous group of explorers who'd traveled in Africa with Sir Sidney Sinclair. Sir Sidney had been murdered in a violent melee, caused by his fraternizing with a jealous tribal chief's wife. Upon their return to England, there had been an inquest by the trip's financial backers who'd felt compelled to dig to the bottom of what had occurred.

The team had worshipped Sir Sidney, and they would never have uttered a word to tarnish his legacy, so they'd concocted a false, but believable tale to explain his demise, and it hadn't included any mention of illicit fornication or jealous tribal chiefs.

Normally, Raven wouldn't have participated in that sort of subterfuge, but they'd fabricated for the greater good. They'd saved Sir Sidney's reputation as a national icon, but they'd also saved his widow and daughter from having to hear the lurid facts surrounding his death.

Wasn't that kind of sin allowed? Couldn't a man be forgiven if he prevaricated for a principled reason? Raven had persuaded himself that the answers to those two questions were *yes* and *yes*. Their deception had been for the best.

Lucas, on the other hand, wouldn't have suffered any qualms about lying. He wouldn't have dithered over right and wrong. He'd have simply proceeded with his usual reckless abandon, and he'd have looked like an innocent choirboy while doing it.

Raven deemed Lucas to be the more dangerous sibling. A fellow with no conscience didn't ever stop to mull the consequences.

"I met a Carter woman this afternoon," he told his brother.

"You crossed paths with Miss Millicent already?" Lucas asked.

"No, it wasn't Millicent. There's a cousin living here. Her name's Rebecca."

"Is she pretty?"

"Very pretty, but she's the poor relative. I was left with the distinct impression that she's lonely and unhappy."

"Aren't all poor relatives lonely and unhappy? You ought to be able to use her to pry out tons of information."

"It's what I assume."

"I thought you were setting your sights on Millicent."

"I'm a man of many talents," Raven said. "I can pursue both females at the same time."

He had many tasks to accomplish during his visit to Carter Crossing. One of them was to flirt with twenty-year-old Millicent Carter so her hopes would be terribly dashed when his attention vanished.

"You'll trifle with one and toy with the other?" Lucas asked. "That seems awfully devious. Where have you hidden honorable, decent Raven Shawcross?"

"You constantly accuse me of being honorable, but your tone indicates you view it as a dubious trait. I have never been particularly honorable, but I wish I was. Most people would describe integrity as a positive attribute."

"Not me or you. Where did honor or integrity ever take us?"

"Nowhere worth being," Raven said.

"Precisely."

They were in the barn at Carter Crossing, having been invited to bunk down in the hay loft. The hired hands lived there, and they'd emptied two cots to accommodate the Shawcross brothers.

Lucas was sitting on one of them and drinking a whiskey, but Raven was pacing. Now that the end of his scheme was so close, he was impatient to get moving. Typically, he was calm and composed. His prior adventures in Africa, where he'd been the expedition scout, had guaranteed he could focus intensely.

He supposed, after events at Carter Crossing were concluded, he'd regain his unruffled aplomb, but just then, he was eager and edgy.

They'd brought some horses to the estate for Clayton Carter and were pretending to be horse traders, utilizing the animals as an excuse to linger for a few days. They'd leave soon to head next door to the adjoining Oakley property Raven had recently purchased.

When they returned to Carter Crossing, it would be for Clayton's birthday party, and they'd arrive in grand style as befitted Raven's status as a member of the Sinclair team of explorers. At the moment though, Raven's true identity was concealed, so they were gleaning all sorts of gossip.

The servants always knew every secret, and they were delighted to reveal every scurrilous detail to a pair of friendly men from out of town.

Raven was obscenely rich, his travels in Africa furnishing partial owner-ship of several diamond mines, so he'd had the funds to garner every finan-cial crumb there was to learn about the Carters. He'd employed accountants, bankers, and investigators to dig into their records, but they'd supplied num-bers jotted down on paper.

He'd been anxious to accumulate more personal tidbits so that when he lashed out at Beatrice and Clayton, he could be certain he'd extract the most excruciating penalties available.

For two decades, it had been his single, riveting goal: He would revenge himself against the Carter family for the damage they had inflicted on Raven's own. It was a vow he'd made at age ten, and he'd never wavered from it.

He was thirty now, so he'd been fuming and plotting for twenty years, and it would be an enormous relief to have it over. Perhaps, once he was finished, he would finally find some peace and figure out how to be content.

His only regret was that Beatrice's husband, Charles, was deceased. Charles was the biggest culprit in their sad saga, his many felonies initiating the catastrophes that had ruined Raven's parents, but Beatrice had had a huge role too. Later, Clayton had piled on a colossal dose of shame and grief.

They would all pay. He'd sworn it on his father's and mother's graves, and he wouldn't rest until every Carter was destroyed.

He was a man who kept his promises.

"I'm going for a walk," he said.

"Good," Lucas replied. "I can't have you hanging over the card table and glowering at me. You'd give me away, and I'd rather not be caught."

"If you wind up getting shot someday, don't complain to me."

"I wouldn't dream of it." Lucas grinned his devil's grin. "But I won't ever suffer any punishment for my sins. I'm lucky, remember? I always emerge unscathed."

"Your unbridled confidence might eventually bring you down."

"It hasn't yet."

Lucas downed his whiskey and sauntered over to the ladder to climb down and locate the stable boys and footmen who had agreed to gamble with him. Raven sighed with exasperation.

Lucas was twenty-four, and though Raven had arranged a trust fund for him so he'd never have to work or worry about money, his brother couldn't help but engage in mischief. It was simply his nature to be wild and negligent.

Their father's disaster had meant they'd been separated when Raven was ten and Lucas was four. With their father imprisoned, and their mother dead from a broken heart—the tragedy due to Charles Carter's embezzlement—Raven and Lucas had been sent off to different orphanages, then different charity schools.

Raven had staggered through the debacle without too many problems, but Lucas had grown up to be a criminal and rogue.

He'd been locked away in juvenile reformatories and was fortunate he hadn't been transported to the penal colonies as a public nuisance. Raven had been in Africa by then and unable to intervene, so Lucas's unsavory attributes were totally ingrained, and there could be no saving him.

Raven had been serious when he said he hoped some angry card player didn't shoot his brother. Or he might cuckold the wrong husband, and Raven couldn't bear to think of Lucas meeting a bad end. He'd already lost his parents, and their only sister, Lydia, was gone too.

She'd been seduced by a scoundrel, then she and her baby had died in childbirth. Again, Raven had been far away in Africa, and he hadn't learned of it until fourteen months later. So he had a strong incentive to keep Lucas alive and out of trouble. If his brother perished in a stupid mishap, Raven would be all alone in the world.

He climbed down the ladder too, more slowly than Lucas had. He was just six years older than Lucas, but he felt a hundred years older. Lucas had wiled away his time in London, loafing in gaming halls and brothels. Raven had spent them hacking his way through thick jungle, ducking poisoned arrows, becoming sick with jungle sweats and rashes.

His bones and joints ached, his old wounds ached, and occasionally, he'd fall ill from recurring fevers that never completely went away. Lucas carried on like a carefree, violent puppy, but Raven trudged along like a decrepit codger whose every step was painful.

He left the barn and strolled to the park behind the manor. The moon was up, and he thought about scaling the promontory again, but he probably shouldn't be out on any cliffs in the dark. Instead, he meandered down the path that led to the beach.

The waves were crashing on the shore, and the sound stirred his wanderlust, making him question the wisdom of tarrying in England. It was nearly autumn, and winter would arrive shortly.

He ought to be on a sailing ship and racing south, but apparently, he'd given up his itinerant existence. He'd bought Oakley, and when he was finished with the Carters, he'd own Carter Crossing too. He'd own their shipping company of Carter Imports as well, together with anything else Beatrice had glommed onto in the past two decades.

He couldn't deduce how he felt about his decision to stay put. Starting at age eighteen, he'd traveled with Sir Sidney, but the man's death had destroyed Raven's prior life.

His best friends had been Sir Sidney's son, Sebastian, and another member of their team, Nathan Blake, who was Earl of Selby. They hated each other now, due to how events had unraveled after Sir Sidney's murder.

Raven had dawdled for months at Sebastian's home of Hero's Haven outside London, waiting for him to declare that he was heading back to Africa in his father's place, but Sebastian was too traumatized to go again.

Raven had finally accepted that the expeditions were over, and he'd moved on to deal with his family's ancient business. But he doubted he'd ever stop gazing at the horizon and wondering what was over the next hill.

He paused to stare at the manor off in the distance, and he let his ire sink in, let it sizzle and bubble up. Every little piece of the Carters' wealth had been stolen from his unsuspecting father, and it was galling to witness it up close.

He smiled a grim smile. It wouldn't be theirs much longer. He'd already implemented the plot that would yank it from their greedy, covetous hands, and he received enormous satisfaction from imagining how distressed they would be when they lost everything in the blink of an eye.

Having endured that very scenario when he was ten, he could definitely admit that it was a wrenching state of affairs.

As he turned to the beach, he noticed there was a woman sitting on a log not far from where he was standing. From how her white-blond hair shone in the moonlight, he recognized Rebecca Carter immediately, and the realization was more thrilling than it should have been.

He'd met her earlier in the afternoon, up on the promontory, and he'd been thinking about her ever since. Because she was so gorgeously beautiful, it was difficult to *not* think about her, but he was intrigued for other reasons too. She was trusting and sociable, so it would be easy to ingratiate himself, then wheedle out details he shouldn't ever discover.

She intrigued him for another reason too. She so exactly resembled the harpy, Sarah Robertson, that they had to be twins. He didn't care what Miss Carter claimed about it. The bloody woman had a twin sister.

He didn't want to startle her, so he neared, then waved to catch her attention.

"Hello again, Miss Carter," he said.

"I'd greet you too, but you're too vain to tell me who you are."

"I'm Raven Shawcross."

He froze, giving her a chance to react, but she didn't. The Carter servants were tittering over the news that one of Sir Sidney's men was coming for Clayton's birthday party, but his identity hadn't been announced. He'd been curious if the family members might have heard, but evidently, they hadn't.

"Is that your *real* name?" she asked. "Or did you make it up?"

"It's my real name."

Well, it was as real as could be managed under the circumstances. His actual surname had been Stone, his father Harrison Stone, but with him being a notorious felon who'd hanged himself in prison, Raven and his siblings had been persuaded to begin using their mother's maiden name of Shawcross.

No one was aware of his past, not even Sir Sidney and Sebastian Sinclair with whom he'd traveled for over a decade. It was a secret he would take to the grave.

"If we weren't outside in the dark," she said, "I'd study your eyes to see if you're lying or not."

"Why would I lie about it?"

"You probably have a thousand falsehoods buried in that devious mind of yours."

"I'm merely a horse trader," he fibbed. "I brought some animals from London for Clayton Carter."

"I was told that two men had arrived with the horses, but I wouldn't have pegged you to be one of them."

"Why not?"

"If forced to offer an opinion, I'd have declared you to be a bandit."

"A bandit! Why would such an absurd notion have occurred to you?"

"Perhaps it's your black clothes. Or it might be your furtive behavior this afternoon and your sly refusal to answer any of my questions."

"I wasn't furtive. I was just rude."

"Yes, you were. After I left you, I sent a footman to run you off, but you'd vanished."

"I went exploring in the other direction. There's an abandoned property on the other side of the hill."

She sighed with what sounded like regret. "Yes, it was owned by poor Mr. Oakley."

As he had already purchased Oakley, he'd gleaned every fact about the place, but he asked, "Was he poor? Was he bankrupt? Is that why it's in such a sorry condition?"

"I don't know if he was fiscally poor. I was referring to him personally. He didn't have any relatives, so there were no heirs to inherit."

"How long has the house been empty?"

"A few years. It's such a splendid mansion. If I had a fortune, I'd buy it and restore it to its former glory."

"Are you a dreamer, Miss Carter?"

"Absolutely."

She patted the spot next to her on the log, and he walked over and sat down. The wind was brisk, and she was bundled in a man's coat. Her magnificent hair was tied back with a ribbon, but could barely be restrained. Lengthy strands whipped about, and she kept tucking them behind her ears.

He couldn't stop gaping at her. She was so arresting; he couldn't deny it.

"This is the second time in a single day," he said, "that I've bumped into you when you'd snuck away from the manor."

"It's a terrible habit of mine. I like to gaze at the horizon and wonder what's beyond it."

He snorted with amusement. "I'm familiar with that feeling. It's called wanderlust."

"Is that what's plaguing me? Is it a case of wanderlust? Here I thought it was just my advanced age of twenty-seven. I've never been away from Carter Crossing, and I think I'm suffering from the lack."

"Wanderlust is a hideous malady. At least when a man catches it, he can appease it by taking a trip. I'm not sure what women do."

"We loaf on beaches and stare at the passing ships."

"I've always been glad I wasn't born a female."

"You should be glad. It can be positively exhausting."

He shifted to focus his attention on her. She had a classic face, her features arranged in the most striking way. She was slender but shapely, her figure rounded and alluring.

Her white-blond hair was striking too and different from any he'd ever previously observed—except for on her twin, Miss Robertson. It was long and curly and untamed. In the moonlight, it appeared silver, so she might have been a fairy sent to tempt him.

But it was her eyes that were most remarkable. They were big and blue, and they sparkled with delight. Out on the promontory, they'd seemed almost violet rather than blue. As with her hair, he'd never previously seen eyes like hers. They were the kind of eyes that could hold a man rapt, that could have him blustering over to introduce himself, then coming off like a fool because he was so tongue-tied.

He clasped a wayward strand and traced his thumb across it.

"Your hair is the most interesting color," he said.

She grabbed his wrist and yanked him away. "You are so impertinent, Mr. Shawcross. I can't imagine why you'd assume it's appropriate to touch my hair."

"I'm a cheeky rogue. I admit it. I've lived in wild circumstances, so any manners I once possessed have vanished."

"What were your wild circumstances?"

"You wouldn't believe me if I told you." She'd soon find out who he was, so there was no reason to explain. He gestured to her hair. "It's such a stunning shade."

"Was that a compliment? If you keep it up, my head will swell with pride."

"Who did you inherit it from? Your mother or father?"

"I have no idea. They died when I was three, and I don't remember them."

"Who were they?"

She peered at him as if it was the oddest query ever voiced. "They were just . . . people."

"I doubt that."

He nearly added, *you're too extraordinary to have sprung from anyone ordinary*, but he bit down the words.

There was an intriguing aura emanating from her. It seemed as if waves of goodness were wafting out. He deemed her to be a very sweet person, a very loyal person, a very nice person.

He rarely socialized with gently-bred women. His interactions with the fairer sex typically involved dalliances with doxies in port towns. His life was filled with tough, vigorous men, and there were no females in that world. It was refreshing to tarry with her, and he was enjoying himself very much.

He'd like to dawdle with her all night. It would be lovely to watch the moon set and the sun rise. He thought, if he spent those quiet hours with her, he'd feel much better at dawn. Maybe some of his anger and bile would be tamped down.

Or maybe not.

She was pretty and very charming, but she was a Carter. He couldn't forget it. He would use her to get what he wanted, that being revenge against Beatrice and Clayton, but the whole family would be ensnared in his scheme. She would be caught too, so he wouldn't grow attached because he refused to pity her in the end.

"You constantly flee the house," he said. "Why is that? I've already deduced that your cousins are awful to you. Are you wishing you could escape your fate?"

"You are a brash devil, aren't you? Even if I was chafing and miserable, which I'm not, I would never confess such a dreadful secret to a stranger."

"You don't have to think of me as a stranger. You're quite lonely, so I'm probably the closest thing you have to a friend."

"Not only are you brash, you're very vain too."

"Yes, I'm impossibly vain. It must be difficult for you to stagger through here."

"It's fine, Mr. Shawcross."

"How come you never married?"

"Honestly! What kind of question is that?"

"You seem very engaging to me."

"There you go with your compliments again."

"Why has no local fellow snatched you up?"

She stared at the water, her expression a tad haunted, then she smiled sadly. "I almost married once, but it . . . didn't work out."

"Why not?"

"He changed his mind."

"How old were you?"

"Seventeen."

"And you've been a spinster ever since?"

"I'm not a spinster! I'm unwed by choice, and if you plan to insult me, I'll stomp off in a huff. Please don't make me leave just yet."

"I wasn't insulting you," he said. "I was stating the facts."

"You tossed out the same excuse up on the promontory. You don't get to be rude to me, then rationalize your appalling manners by claiming you're simply being candid."

"You're twenty-seven, so I rest my case. You're a spinster."

She shrugged. "It's not so bad here. I run the house, and I manage the servants. I have an enormous amount of authority—much more than most females are allowed to have—and I have a young cousin I'm raising. All of it keeps me busy."

This was news Raven hadn't uncovered. "Who is the young cousin?"

"Alex? He's an orphan who's been with us since he was a toddler. It's as if

I have my own son, but without the bother of a husband."

"Without the *bother* of one? Every woman wants a husband."

"I suppose, but I've become convinced that most of them aren't worth having."

"Why would you utter such a ridiculous comment?"

"Well, men drink and gamble. They can be bossy, stubborn, and cruel. Many of them are violent."

"You must have crossed paths with some very terrible marital candidates."

"There aren't a lot of options in the country. Mostly, they're Clayton's friends."

"I hear they're all horrid—and Clayton is the worst of them."

He paused, expecting her to offer a denigrating remark, but she scoffed. "I'm not about to chime in with offensive gossip, so don't sit there grinning at me as if I might."

"I wouldn't dream of it," he lied.

"My mother's kin took me in when I was tiny, and they've given me a home and a purpose. I'll always be grateful to them."

"But if you could escape this life, if you had the money and the liberty to pick up and go wherever you wanted, where would it be?"

She didn't hesitate to reply. "I'd walk into Frinton and board a ship at the harbor. I'd order the captain to whisk me around the world and to not stop until I'd visited every corner of it."

It was a romantic's response, and it tugged at his heartstrings.

He'd met many poor relatives, and he'd been in much the same position after his father had died: a charity case, an unwanted burden. It was such a heavy weight to carry, yearning to belong, but never being accepted or even particularly liked.

His investigations had revealed all he needed to know about Beatrice and Clayton Carter. They were petty, greedy people, and he was surprised she hadn't been corrupted by them.

"How about your cousin, Millicent?" he said. "Will you gossip with me about her?"

"No, and you are much too nosy for your own good."

"The stable hands tell me she's a spoiled tart."

"Mr. Shawcross! Cease your disparagement of my cousins!"

"I like how it makes your eyes flash with temper."

"It's so dark out here that you can't possibly see my eyes, so don't pretend you've been gazing into them. You're simply trying to goad me into chatting about topics I have no interest in discussing, but I can't imagine why."

"I'm not very adept at casual conversation."

"You're right about that."

"While I'm in residence," he said, "I should spend some time with you so you can smooth over my rough edges."

It was the perfect moment to scoot a little nearer, to start the false flirtation he intended to pursue. Yet as he did, the strangest thing happened. Their sides were forged fast all the way down to their feet, and the most powerful surge of energy was flowing from his body to hers.

If he'd pointed a finger, sparks might have shot out the end. He'd never felt a commotion like it, and it was obvious she felt it too. She glanced up at him, and suddenly, his senses were aroused and inflamed. He was giddy with a curious sort of joy he'd never previously experienced.

"You're sitting much too close to me," she said.

"I'm not sorry."

"You should move over."

"I don't think I will."

She laid a palm on his chest to push him away. Her hand was directly over his heart, and it had begun to hammer quite fiercely.

What was wrong with him? He was overcome as a green boy with his first girl.

Before he could dissuade himself, he leaned down and kissed her. In the entire history of kisses, it wasn't all that intimate. He simply brushed his mouth to hers, then drew away.

He was aghast over his folly and assumed she would utter a remark that would humiliate him to his bones, but she smiled and told him, "I haven't been kissed in the moonlight in a very long time."

He smirked. "Is it a habit of yours to dawdle in the dark and allow men to kiss you?"

"I had that beau when I was seventeen. I won't claim I never let him."

"I want to do it again." The words practically burst out of him.

He dipped in and initiated a second embrace, and she permitted it for a minute or two, then she eased away.

A thousand comments swirled between them, and he was being pelted by the worst urge to confess his woes to her. He was positive she'd be a good listener, that she'd chew over every morsel and absolve him when he was through.

He was guilt-ridden over everything that had transpired in Africa. He was anxious to describe how Sir Sidney—his hero and mentor—had been murdered, how the incident had generated a vortex that had sucked away what he'd loved about his life.

Their adventurous journeys were over. His friend, Nathan Blake, hated them all and with valid reason. They'd left him for dead and had sailed home without him. He would never forgive them.

Raven had resigned his spot on the expedition team so he could finally chase down the revenge he was owed by the Carter family, but he'd reveled in the world Sir Sidney had provided, and with it destroyed, he was feeling lost and adrift.

His foundations had been yanked away. He loathed being on the coast, scheming on strangers and trying to achieve the result he'd sought forever. He was terribly afraid the conclusion might not bring him the satisfaction he craved.

What if it didn't? Where would he be then?

But he would never voice such needy observations to anyone.

She studied him, then stood and said, "I'd better return to the house."

"Must you?"

"You're a bit too much *man* for me, Mr. Shawcross."

"I'm a bit too much man for every woman."

"I'm certain that's true, but for me, it's particularly pertinent."

"Will you climb to the promontory tomorrow?" he asked. "If you'll tell me when, I'll join you."

"I can't sneak off to secluded locations with you."

"I beg to differ, Miss Carter. *I* might be just what you require to brighten your dreary existence."

"My existence is fine, and I doubt you could ever brighten anything, but I suppose you're allowed your little fantasies."

He couldn't bear to have her depart, which was incredibly odd. He was a solitary individual who was used to being alone and on his own. He liked it that way, but he reached out and linked their fingers as if they were adolescent sweethearts.

"If you won't climb to the promontory," he said, "how about if we meet out here tomorrow night?"

"No, and stop tempting me. You're like the Snake in the Garden, filling my head with ideas that are dangerous and wrong."

He grinned. "I've tempted you?"

"Yes, you rogue, and you know you have too. Aren't you leaving for London soon?"

"I'm in no hurry. I'd tarry if I could be convinced there was a good reason."

"I could never be the reason."

"Are you sure about that?"

"Very sure."

He was still holding her hand, and he pulled her to him and kissed her yet again. She participated with an amount of joy that was thrilling, but she was the one to end it.

"You are a menace, Mr. Shawcross." Her tone was scolding. "And I can't figure out why I loafed with you a single second."

"You're bored and lonely, and I think you could let yourself like me."

"I *think* you might be right, but I won't roll the dice to find out if you're correct."

She jerked away and dashed off, and he glanced over his shoulder and called, "It's late and very dark. Would you like me to walk you to the house?"

"I don't dare be seen with you."

"Would I get you in trouble?"

"In more trouble than you could ever imagine."

"I might be worth it."

She laughed. "No, you wouldn't."

Then she was gone. He watched the path, hoping he might catch a glimpse of her as she strolled across the park, but there were too many trees in the way. Finally, he sighed—with what sounded like melancholia—and he turned toward the water and stared at the breaking waves.

Off on the horizon, he observed the lamp on a passing ship, and he wondered where it was headed and why he wasn't on board.

# CHAPTER

## 3

"THE BIRTHDAY GUESTS WILL be arriving today and tomorrow."

"Yes, and we'll be living in a madhouse."

"My father will be here."

Rebecca nodded at Alex. He was a handsome boy of ten and her cousin Clayton's bastard son.

He'd been sired a decade earlier when Clayton had been a young man reveling in town with little guidance or supervision. He'd had an affair with a pretty girl, and she'd died shortly after Alex was born.

Clayton had met her in London during the Christmas holidays when he'd been at university. According to Beatrice, she'd been a doxy who'd enticed him in the hopes of glomming onto some of his fortune. Beatrice refused to provide more information than that, so Rebecca had no idea what sort of person Alex's mother had truly been.

But she was painfully aware of what his lazy, spoiled father was like. Alex had inherited only stellar traits, and they hadn't been supplied by Clayton, so

Rebecca suspected the tales about Alex's mother were false. His mother had likely been a beautiful, perfect saint.

No one at Carter Crossing had had any notion of Clayton's spurious conduct until a vicar had contacted Beatrice and demanded she assume custody of Alex. She'd been shamed into bringing him to Carter Crossing, but she'd always been aggravated that she'd relented.

She'd dumped him in Rebecca's lap when she was nineteen. She'd raised him ever since, and he was the sole aspect of her life at Carter Crossing that was palatable. He made her feel as if she was accomplishing a worthwhile goal, and they were kindred spirits, despised by their Carter kin, not really wanted, and viewed as a heavy burden.

Beatrice pretended to be very pious, liking how it shaped her reputation in the community. She disdained the lower classes, being especially contemptuous of the poor, whom she deemed to have created their own problems. She never donated to charities, insisting it simply encouraged the downtrodden.

She was particularly scornful of people with base antecedents, with Rebecca and Alex being the most prominent examples of immorality she could find.

She never ceased to complain about how their dubious ancestries were a stain on the family. When Rebecca was a child, Beatrice's insults about her parents had cut into her like a sharp knife, but she'd gradually learned to ignore the taunts.

She was teaching Alex to ignore them too, but he hadn't required much training. He was confident, cocky, and a master at exhibiting condescension in a quiet manner. Beatrice could never rattle him or deflate his massive ego. She was his grandmother, but she acted as if he didn't exist, which was probably just as well.

It meant he rarely had to suffer the brunt of her rage or derision, and her words bounced off him like dull arrows.

Rebecca had come to the estate at age three, and there had been no protector or champion to watch over her. She'd been frightened and lonely, and she hadn't comprehended what had happened to her. Alex had shown up as a rambunctious toddler, and he'd had Rebecca firmly planted by his side.

His relationship with his father was difficult, but then, Clayton was more pompous and vain than Beatrice. He behaved as if he had no illegitimate child, and he never glanced in Alex's direction.

Clayton's snubs didn't bother Alex. Though he didn't recall his mother, he possessed a great affinity for her, and he understood how badly she'd been treated by his father. He wasn't very forgiving.

"Yes, your father will be here," she said.

"I suppose I'll have to spend the next two weeks in hiding."

"I think that would be for the best."

Beatrice would expect Alex to be invisible while they had company, and he had a stoic attitude about the entire situation. He didn't want to fraternize with his father's friends anymore than Clayton wanted him too.

"I was wondering about something though," he said.

"What is it?"

"One of Sir Sidney's team members will be at the party."

"I heard that. It's exciting, isn't it?"

Sir Sidney had been murdered by a native tribe in Africa. The whole kingdom had staggered through months of funerals and memorial services as he'd been extensively eulogized. The men who'd trekked with him were famous too, and one of them was about to be in residence!

"I'd like to meet him," Alex said. "I'd like to listen to some of his stories."

"I might be able to introduce you, but we'd have to be careful."

"I've decided I'd like to be an explorer when I grow up. I'd like to journey to Africa and other wild places like the Sinclairs."

"Really?"

"Yes. Sebastian Sinclair and Lord Selby began traveling with Sir Sidney when they were ten. Why couldn't I do that? I don't know how to start though, and I thought I could ask him some questions that might help me figure it out."

Alex had never previously voiced such an exotic dream. In the past, he'd talk about being a soldier or a sailor—normal pursuits that a typical British male might relish. But an African explorer? Why would such a peculiar notion have occurred to him?

"What brought this on?" she inquired. "I had no idea you were pondering such a big path."

"I've been reading Sebastian Sinclair's travelogue about when he was a boy. He rode camels and camped in desert tents and sailed down jungle rivers in canoes. His book is very thrilling. Would I be a good explorer?"

"You'll be terrific at whatever profession you choose."

They were on the rear verandah, with Rebecca having stepped outside to relax for a minute. The maids were dusting the parlors, in a frenzy to have the house in pristine condition for when Clayton arrived.

While Beatrice was ostensibly in charge of the manor, Clayton owned the property. It was *his* home and *his* servants. He was hardly ever in the country though, preferring to wallow in his more extravagant activities in town. When he deigned to visit, they were all anxious that he be happy with how things were rolling along.

Suddenly, Beatrice called from a parlor window, "Rebecca! Come here at once! I must speak with you!"

"I'd better go," she murmured to Alex.

"Don't stand too close to her. Rumor has it that she bites."

Rebecca grinned. "Don't be impertinent. You'll only land yourself in trouble."

He grinned too. "I'm never impertinent. I'm simply stating the facts."

She chuckled, realizing it was exactly the sort of comment Mr. Shawcross would have made, and Alex was very much like him, both in looks and cocky temperament. He had Shawcross's same dark hair and blue eyes, their features so similar they could almost be related.

He whirled away and flitted down the stairs into the garden. He had chores in the stables and was supposed to work there, but he wasn't very conscientious. The Carter family blatantly pretended he wasn't one of them, and he felt little loyalty.

For a boy of ten, he was very mature, very shrewd in his assessment of people, and she wished she had half of his steely aplomb.

She watched him depart, pausing to adjust her attitude, then she spun and went inside. It was always difficult to confer with Beatrice. She'd grown more adept at it over the years, had learned sly methods for dealing with the persnickety woman, but it was never easy.

Beatrice was in the dining room, the windows facing the verandah, so she'd have had a clear view of Rebecca chatting with Alex, and she'd be irked to have been reminded of their fond connection.

What had she expected though? Rebecca had been given full authority over him since he'd first been delivered to Carter Crossing. Of course they were fond.

She breezed into the room, determined to skip through the conversation without letting Beatrice goad her. It was a lovely day, and she'd been kissed in the moonlight the night before. She was walking on air and wouldn't allow Beatrice to ruin her merry mood.

Beatrice was seated at the table, as usual nibbling on a plate of sweets. As a result, she was very fat. She was fifty, her gray hair pulled into a tight bun, her eyes a pale gray that were icy cold. She never smiled, and Rebecca wondered if she'd ever experienced an enjoyable moment in her life. Most likely not.

Millicent was seated with her mother. She was twenty, fetching and curvaceous, having managed to avoid her mother's passion for desserts, so she was still slender and shapely. She was blond and blue-eyed, a very classic British girl in her habits and tastes, and as with her brother Clayton, she was very spoiled.

She and Rebecca got on well enough, kind of like sisters who weren't particularly affectionate. Normally, they were cordial, but every once in awhile, Millicent would forget herself and treat Rebecca like a servant. When Rebecca had been younger, she'd tolerated Millicent's occasional disregard, but they'd come to an agreement about mutual respect, and Millicent was unfailingly polite.

"What did you need, Cousin Beatrice?" Rebecca asked, her tone soothing and helpful.

Millicent answered. "She's about to browbeat you over nothing. What would you imagine she needs?"

Beatrice frowned at her daughter. "Don't be smart, Millicent. You know I can't abide it."

Millicent scowled. "Does that mean you're not going to browbeat her?"

"Your presence isn't necessary for this discussion," Beatrice told her.

"Can you stand to be alone with her?" Millicent asked Rebecca. "Would you like me to stay?"

Rebecca never jumped in the middle of their petty spats. "You're being a nuisance, Millicent. Please don't upset your mother."

"Yes, Heaven forbid that we *upset* her."

Millicent leapt up and sauntered out, her attitude making it clear that she wasn't happy with her mother, and Rebecca would hear about it soon enough. Millicent deemed Rebecca to be a confidante and ally, when in reality, she just tried to keep her head down and remain on everyone's good side.

As Millicent's footsteps faded, Beatrice said, "Clayton will arrive shortly. Are we ready for him?"

"Yes, ma'am."

"And the guest bedchambers? You've checked those?"

"Of course. Don't worry. Everything will be fine."

"The man from the Sinclair expedition team isn't traveling with Clayton, so he'll be here tomorrow. He's to have the blue suite overlooking the park. It's the fanciest we have."

"I figured that's what you'd want, and I've informed the staff."

"Be sure there's an array of liquor in his sitting room. That sort of fellow probably likes to have a brandy before bed. Or he might prefer whiskey. Give him several choices, so he's not left questioning our hospitality."

"You must cease your fretting, Beatrice. It will be a splendid party."

Beatrice was an obnoxious person and an awful hostess, but the servants would make certain their company was cosseted and content.

"You have to talk to the boy," Beatrice said.

By *boy,* she was referring to Alex. She never called him by his name, and Rebecca couldn't deduce why—when Beatrice had such harsh feelings about him—she'd brought him to Carter Crossing. Rebecca frequently speculated the same about her own circumstance. Beatrice loathed them both, so why had she inflicted them on herself?

Beatrice liked to be viewed as doing her Christian duty—even though it annoyed her. A vicar had begged her to aid Alex after his mother was dead, and she likely hadn't been keen to appear uncharitable in his eyes.

When Rebecca's parents had died, and Beatrice had agreed to assume custody of her, the demand had come from Rebecca's lofty Blake relatives. Her grandfather had been an earl, and her father a viscount. A Blake aunt had insisted Beatrice take Rebecca to Carter Crossing, and Beatrice had complied without argument.

For all her posturing and pretention, she wasn't very tough when confronted by those she pictured as her betters.

"I presume you mean Alex," Rebecca said. "What is it you'd like me to tell him?"

"He should stay out of sight and not admit his identity to anyone. If he's asked about it, he should claim to be a stable hand. That's what he is anyway."

"I've spoken to him," Rebecca blithely said.

Beatrice's opinion about Alex was exhausting. Clayton wasn't the first man in history to sire a bastard, and Alex wasn't the only natural son living with his father's kin. There was shame attached to the situation, but not much.

Clayton was never home, and his friends were a bunch of rich, gambling-addicted wastrels. They'd probably all sired bastards and wouldn't blink at learning that Clayton had too.

"I ought not see him on the verandah again," Beatrice warned.

"You won't."

"And he should avoid Clayton."

"Believe me, Cousin, he knows what you expect."

Beatrice flapped her napkin at Rebecca. "You're excused."

"If you need anything else, just send a servant to find me."

Rebecca rushed out before Beatrice could think of another issue about which to complain. She went down the hall toward the foyer, but as she marched along, a burst of claustrophobia gripped her, and she couldn't breathe. She headed for the rear of the house instead, to the kitchen where she kept an old coat on a hook by the door.

She murmured to a footman that she was going for a walk, and he nodded as she continued outside.

The servants were kind to her. They labored under difficult conditions, and they understood that Rebecca bore the brunt of Beatrice's temper and spite. Rebecca was the bulwark that protected them from Beatrice's worst impulses. If she raged at Rebecca, she didn't have to rage at them.

Usually, Rebecca didn't mind her role as a human rampart, but every so often, like that very moment, she felt as if she was choking on her life.

She dashed into the fresh air, and she peered around quite frantically, anxious to vanish. There wasn't time to climb up to the promontory, so she hurried across the garden to the beach. The waves always soothed her, and she'd calm down fast. Shortly, she'd be good as new. She was sure of it.

As she reached the trees at the end of the park, she was practically running. It seemed as if hounds or demons were chasing her. Anymore, her reflections were so tormented, her discontentment so vast, that she wondered if she wasn't growing deranged.

Beatrice claimed that her mother had been mad. Had she been? Had Rebecca inherited her tendencies as a lunatic?

She lurched onto the rocky shore, eager to stagger over to her log and sit down for a few minutes, but to her consternation, Mr. Shawcross was seated there. He was gazing out at the ocean, looking very much as if he'd been waiting for her, as if he'd been positive she'd arrive.

The sight of him set a dozen odd emotions swirling. She was delighted to stumble on him. She was irked that he'd taken over her favorite spot. She was thrilled to have the chance to chat with him again. She was irritated that he'd been flirting with her. She wished he'd stop. She also wished he'd *never* stop.

Since he'd kissed her—three times!—she'd been in an absolute state. Every second after she'd flitted back to the manor, she'd been pondering him and why he'd done it. She recognized that it was fueling much of her current restlessness.

Her world was so small and quiet. He simply stoked the fires of the injustices that consumed her, making her covet and chafe over how little she'd been given. It required such effort to accept her place, to accept her lot. Her father's elevated blood—her Blake blood—coursed through her veins, constantly reminding her that she shouldn't be living as she had been since she was three.

She deserved so much more than she had, and she craved the life she should have led as a Blake daughter, which was insane.

When her wayward thoughts raced off on their tangents, it was so hard to tamp them down. She valiantly worked on her attitude, to keep it at a sustainable level. If she considered her predicament overly much, she would begin to seethe with dissatisfaction, and it was pointless to mope and lament.

The wind and waves should have covered the sound of her footsteps, but he'd heard her approaching. He glanced over his shoulder, standing when he saw her.

His nose and cheeks were red from the cold, his hair unbound and the long strands flowing free. His blue eyes were intense, the stunning color enhanced by the sky and water. He resembled a Greek god who might have been painted in a mural on a church ceiling.

She'd never met a man like him, one who was so dynamic and fascinating. She already suspected, when he departed for London, she'd be bereft for weeks.

"What's wrong?" he asked. "What happened?"

A thousand words flooded to her tongue. She never mentioned her problems. It was all bottled up inside, and for once, it was begging to spill out.

She yearned to confide how lonely she was, how she struggled to be liked and appreciated by her cousins. She wanted to tell him how horrid her childhood had been, how Beatrice had convinced her—and she'd grown up believing—that she'd been unwanted and despised by her parents.

She'd been twelve before an elderly servant had whispered that Beatrice's taunts weren't true. Rebecca's father had loved her mother very much, but he hadn't married her, and when they'd died in an accident, Rebecca had been orphaned.

Her grandfather had refused to let her come to live at the family's estate of Selby. He'd demanded her Carter relatives support her, and Beatrice had brought her home.

With that dubious history dragging behind, how was she supposed to muddle forward in a rational manner? She'd first have to admit that she was utterly damaged, but she would never confess any of that.

Instead, she blurted out, "I'm having the worst day."

"I see that."

"Sometimes, I can't abide my life. I wish I had wings like a bird. I'd fly away to a better place."

"It's why you stare out at the passing ships. You dream of where they might take you—if you could only escape where you are."

"Yes."

It was exhilarating to realize that he understood her. No one ever paid her much attention. No one ever asked how she was faring or what she was thinking. Alex was kind and sweet, but he was a child and could never fill the holes in her soul.

She felt empty and used up, and she desperately needed to save herself or she might become invisible.

He opened his arms, and she rushed over and fell into them. Then he was kissing her and kissing her. He held her as if she was precious and unique, as if she was his and he had a duty to protect her from the daily slings and arrows that repeatedly impaled her.

He sampled her mouth, as his curious hands roamed over her torso. He caressed her in a gentle way, in a soothing way, as if he sensed her distress and knew precisely how to dispel it.

She couldn't figure out what was driving her to participate, but she was anxious for someone to notice her, to fuss over her. He seemed to gaze at her and see what others had missed.

It was a refreshing insight, and she was so pathetically morose that she would glom onto whatever crumb of interest he deigned to bestow. But why shouldn't she?

She'd had a fleeting romance when she was seventeen and that was it.

A young carpenter from Frinton had been working at the manor, and they'd been sufficiently close that Rebecca had started to assume he'd propose, but Beatrice had scuttled her opportunity. She'd spoken about Rebecca to her beau's father, and he'd never come to the estate again.

She'd bumped into him at church, and she'd tried to talk to him, to find out what had occurred, but he'd been cool and detached, providing the distinct impression that he no longer cared for her. She had no idea what Beatrice had said about her or why she'd ruined Rebecca's sole chance to be a bride.

Rebecca would have predicted Beatrice would have been delighted to get rid of her, but it was entirely possible that Beatrice simply couldn't bear to let Rebecca have a happy ending.

Rebecca saw her prior flame occasionally. He'd wed a local girl, and they had six children already. His wife was chubby and surly, looking haggard and quite decrepit, being overwhelmed by parenting and motherhood.

Rebecca didn't exactly begrudge her former swain for his choice, but whenever she observed his wife, she suffered a sinful surge of pride that she was still thin, beautiful, and charming.

In light of her grueling experience with him, she'd never pushed herself forward again. It had been too humiliating to be tossed over, but she was an adult now and not a seventeen-year-old girl. Why shouldn't she pursue a brief amour?

Mr. Shawcross would only be at Carter Crossing for a quick visit. Why not grab for all the amusement and joy he could supply? Beatrice would never know, and hopefully—after he departed—some of her restless hunger would have abated.

She couldn't guess how long they kept at it, but for once, she wasn't concerned.

Eventually, he slowed and drew away. He nestled her in the circle of his arms, her body crushed to his all the way down. She was warm and safe in his embrace, and she didn't want him to ever release her.

He smiled down at her and asked, "Are you calmed down? Have I cheered you a bit?"

She smiled too. "I'm much better."

"What happened at the house? Why were you so upset?"

"It was nothing out of the ordinary. Often, it seems as if I'm trapped."

She was surprised that she'd admitted it, but he was from London. After he left, she'd never see him again. If she confided some personal secrets, who would he tell them to?

He smirked. "So when you previously insisted your life was all wine and roses, you might not have been completely truthful?"

"Maybe not. It's difficult to live with my cousins, but to never really be welcome."

"It's the curse of every poor relative."

"I'm aware of that, so I shouldn't feel sorry for myself."

"Was your mother a Carter? Isn't that what you told me?"

"Yes, she was."

"Do you know your father's family? Could you live with them? Is that an option for you?"

"No, I couldn't go to them."

He was polite enough not to press for information about them, which was a huge relief. She never liked to confess that she was a bastard daughter, that her mother had been young and gullible and had fallen for a nobleman's lies. It was the most dismal story ever, one that had ensnared unsuspecting females over and over throughout history. It was always tragic. It was always exasperating.

"I'll be here a few more days," he said. "We should sneak off and misbehave whenever we can."

"You would think that."

"I guarantee, by the time I return to London, I'll have totally vanquished your low mood."

"Yes, but if I constantly fraternize with you, I'll start to like you, then I'll be miserable after you leave. It's probably best for me to *not* start liking you."

"That's the gloomiest attitude I've ever encountered, and you can't mean it. Are you claiming you don't want to be happy now because you might be unhappy later? You're being silly."

"Since you put it like that, yes, it's silly."

"When can you get away from your chores?"

Excitement rattled her. She envisioned tiptoeing off, sharing furtive kisses, reveling in the danger of discovery. Initially, she'd considered it, but it was madness in the extreme. Beatrice wielded a large cudgel that she held over Rebecca's head. If she ever disgraced herself—as her mother had with Viscount Blake—Beatrice would kick her out the door.

So even though the notion of an illicit fling was thrilling to imagine, she couldn't proceed. She had too much to lose.

She sighed with regret. "I can't."

"Yes, you can." He studied her, then said, "You're afraid."

"Yes. If we were caught, I'd be in so much trouble. My Cousin Beatrice can be very cruel, and she wouldn't tolerate immoral conduct. Especially not from me."

"I'm not scared of her," he ridiculously stated.

"Well, you don't have to be, but I would never deliberately cause a quarrel with her."

He grinned. "I won't stop tempting you."

"I'd like it if you'd keep on, but please don't be aggravated if I can't oblige you."

"Who says you won't oblige me? I'm a master at seduction. I'll wear you down until you can't resist."

"Your comment makes me certain you're a scoundrel, so I have no business standing out in the open—where anyone could stumble on us—and allowing you to kiss me senseless."

"Have I kissed you senseless? I like the sound of that." His grin widened. "Tell me it was worth it."

She nodded. "It might have been."

"We're going to do it again. You realize that, don't you?"

"No, I don't realize it, and I have to get back. We have guests coming, and I'm sure everyone is searching for me."

"Let's meet tonight," he said. "After the men are playing cards and enjoying their liquor—and you decide you can head to bed—I want you to head out to the beach instead. I'll be here at eleven. You have to join me."

"I won't. I can't." Her pulse raced at the very idea. "You're deranged. I'm certain of it."

"I've heard that a time or two."

"Don't wait for me. It's cold in the evenings, and I can't bear to think you might take a chill because of me."

She yanked away and sprinted off, and she didn't slow down until she was halfway across the park and worried people inside the manor might glance out and see her running like a lunatic.

She calmed herself and smoothed her expression, and it dawned on her that she was feeling much improved, wasn't jittery and anxious. Apparently, he'd fixed what was wrong, and she wondered if she shouldn't sneak to the beach at eleven.

Why not? What could it hurt? It might help her in innumerable ways. Why shouldn't she?

As she recognized the path her wicked thoughts were traveling, she groaned with dismay and continued on to the house, determined—once she entered—that not a hint of gladness would show on her face.

# CHAPTER

## 4

"How was your trip from town?"

"Fine."

Beatrice stared across the dining table at her son, Clayton. He'd staggered in late the prior evening, and he'd just crawled out of bed. It was noon already, and he was in awful shape. His blue eyes were streaked red, his blond hair mussed as if he didn't own a comb. His breath could knock over a bull.

It was obvious he was hung over. He'd been drinking too much for ages, but she wasn't allowed to comment on his bad habits. Over the years, they'd had their share of fights about it, and she'd lost each and every one.

He was in full control of every facet of their lives. Her dead husband, Charles, had bequeathed everything to him: the house, the estate, the money, and the family company of Carter Imports. Charles's sole request was that Clayton *take care of* Beatrice and Millicent. Beatrice had no authority to tell him anything.

He ran with a fast crowd in London, all of whom had more income and assets than he did, but he was determined to belong to their dissipated, wealthy group. She couldn't dissuade him to cease his overindulgence.

He'd previously been slender and dapper, concerned about his wardrobe and his physique, but recently, he'd deteriorated. He had a definite paunch around his waist, and his shoulders drooped—as if he didn't have the energy to stand up straight.

Had he realized it? If not, she wasn't about to mention it. He would be so upset to be apprised of how swiftly he was falling apart. Although they were about to celebrate his thirtieth birthday, he looked closer to fifty, debauchery and intemperance wearing him down.

He appeared to have slept in his clothes, not bothering to change before coming down to demand breakfast. His laziness and sloth were galling.

He hadn't deigned to visit in months. In the city, he understood that *image* mattered. Why couldn't he figure out that the same standard should be applied at home? With his slovenly condition so evident, how could he hope to generate respect from the servants?

"The weather's been good," she said, anxious to fill the void. "It's supposed to rain, so I was worried about the roads. I wasn't sure you'd be able to get here."

"Mother!" he snapped. "My head is pounding! Will you blather on through my entire meal? Let me eat in peace."

She sniffed with offense. "I rarely see you, so we rarely confer. I deem this encounter to be a minor miracle. I'm not about to dawdle in silence."

He shoveled food into his mouth as if he was a starving pauper, and she couldn't hide her disdain. He was her only son, and she should have been proud and fond, but she wasn't. He'd been a difficult boy to like, and he'd become a surly, rude man. Nor was she the most maternal person. It was hard for them to maintain a firm bond.

Finally, his plate empty, he shoved it away. He'd had the butler bring in a bottle of brandy, and he splashed some into his tea and swallowed down a hefty gulp.

"Ah . . ." he groaned, "hair of the dog. Just what I needed." He drank a second swallow, then glared over at her. "What are you so eager to discuss? Make it quick, would you? I intend to nap for a few hours before my guests begin to arrive."

They were alone, the door shut, the servants shooed out, so it was the perfect moment to address thorny issues. Once his friends were in residence, he'd be busy and distracted and in no mood to talk about business. Then he'd leave for London again, and who could guess when he'd return?

Clayton was ostensibly in charge of Carter Imports, but he didn't think he should have to dirty his hands in the commerce that was their sole source of revenue. He attended no meetings, strategized with no employees, convened with no ship captains or suppliers.

He left it all to Beatrice, but she wasn't very adept at management. Men hated dealing with a woman. They wouldn't listen to her, heed her suggestions, or carry out her orders, and she didn't trust any of them.

As to Clayton, he simply spent like an aristocrat, believing money grew on trees and would never run out. He was such a fool, but she couldn't tell him he was. If she tried, he'd stomp out and their conversation would be over.

He'd never been informed of the shaky underpinnings by which she and Charles had bought the estate and started Carter Imports. It had been accomplished with what some people might have called *stolen* assets.

Not that Beatrice would call it that. Not that Charles would have admitted it. But they'd pilfered it from Charles's old boss, Harrison Stone.

After Charles's lengthy embezzlement had been exposed, after he'd shifted the blame to innocent, clueless, Harrison, Mrs. Stone had visited Beatrice. In what had definitely sounded like a curse, she'd warned, *Everything you plan will collapse. My husband's ghost will haunt you forever. None of your dreams will come true.*

Beatrice had never forgotten those words, and they still had the power to rattle her. With how Charles had dropped dead without notice, with how indolent and spoiled her children had turned out to be, with how Clayton was addicted to vice and drink, it certainly seemed as if Mrs. Stone's admonition had been an omen.

She tamped down a shudder and pushed the disturbing memory away.

"It's Carter Imports," she said. "The books are a mess, and our accountant insists we're on the verge of bankruptcy."

"Is that all?" He tsked with exasperation and waved away her comment. "You needn't fret."

"How can I not? We're not noblemen. We own a shipping company, and it's how we earn our income. If it folds, how—precisely—will we support ourselves?"

"I found a silent partner, so our problems are solved. Quit nagging."

"What sort of *silent* partner? What do you mean?"

"A lawyer approached me. He had a client who was interested in making some investments, particularly in imports and exports. He's willing to shore up our ledgers with a huge infusion of cash."

The scenario was too good to be true, and she scowled. "Why would a rich man assist us?"

"He has some sugar and rum plantations in the West Indies, and he thinks he can use our vessels to lower his shipping costs."

"Can he?"

Clayton scoffed. "Gad, no. If a wealthy idiot wants to hand me a fortune, it doesn't follow that I have to hand him a boon in exchange."

"I suppose we could consider an agreement. Why don't you provide me with the contracts, and I'll have our banker and accountant look into it."

"I've already agreed to bring him on, Mother."

"But you didn't seek my opinion."

"It's *my* company. Why would your permission be required?"

"You're not exactly skilled in business matters."

"Neither are you," he snidely retorted.

She was wary and alarmed. "What are you expecting to happen?"

"I'm *expecting* that my purse is about to be filled with the dolt's money."

"Do you even know who he is?" she asked.

"What part of *silent* investor don't you understand? No, I don't know, but it will be fine. Now, if you'll excuse me, I'm off to take that nap I mentioned."

"There is one more thing," she said before he could scoot out.

He sighed heavily, as if she was the greatest burden in the world. "What is it?"

"I've been pondering the boy."

They never spoke the little bastard's name. There was no need. Clayton was aware to whom she referred. According to him, he'd only sired one illegitimate child. If she ever discovered there were more, she couldn't predict how she'd react.

"What about him?" Clayton sneered.

"He's ten. We should make arrangements for him."

"What kind of arrangements?"

"He could start an apprenticeship. Or we could enlist him in the army."

"I'm not about to waste funds buying him an internship or a military spot."

"He could join as a private when he's twelve. That way, we wouldn't have to put up any money. If nothing else, we should send him away to boarding school."

"I just told you I won't waste the funds." He frowned. "Why this sudden urge to be shed of him?"

"He's growing up, and he can't stay here forever. He has to learn a trade or get an education, so he can eventually support himself."

"Why would I care if he can support himself or not? I can't fathom why he's living here now. It's still a mystery to me why you allowed him to come in the first place."

It was a mystery to Beatrice too, and she'd never had a viable explanation. A vicar had called on her and demanded she shelter the boy. He'd been such a stern, righteous fellow that she hadn't been able to decline.

It had been the same with Rebecca. Her lofty relatives had insisted Beatrice help her after her mother died, and Beatrice hadn't known how to refuse. She hadn't thought Godwin Blake, Rebecca's grandfather, would let her refuse.

At least she'd dumped off Rebecca's twin and had avoided that obligation. On the day Beatrice had been forced to take Rebecca home, her twin—a tiny runt named Sarah—had been sickly and coughing incessantly as if she'd contracted lung fever. Beatrice had managed to skate away with one girl rather than two. It was a small blessing, and Rebecca hadn't turned out that bad.

She worked like a dog, groveled like a slave, and was unceasingly biddable. It was like having a competent servant, but never having to pay her any wages.

"I won't have the boy flaunting himself to any of your friends," she said.

Clayton blanched, as if the notion hadn't occurred to him. "He better not."

"I warned Rebecca to keep him out of sight, and our conversation simply underscored the problem of having him on the premises. We should get rid of him."

"If you want to be rid of him, I have no opinion about it. Just don't request that I fork over any money or effort for it to transpire."

He stood to march out, and she felt slighted and weary. It didn't seem as if they'd discussed any of the important subjects facing them.

"When will the Sinclair team member arrive?" she asked. "I should tell the servants so they can make a special fuss."

"I have no idea, but he's attending the party tomorrow night. His brother will accompany him, so they'll require two rooms."

"How did you cross paths with such a famous man?"

"He was in London for the inquest about Sir Sidney's death. We played cards at my club, and we've become cordial."

"It will be interesting to meet him."

"He's a severe, ruthless person—sort of like you. You'll probably like him very much."

Then he was gone, and she eased back in her chair.

For the next two weeks, the house would be crammed with guests, so she'd be occupied with various tasks as hostess, but the minute she had an extra second, she'd visit their banker to talk about Clayton's new *partner*.

Clayton was an inept dunce, and he had no ability to judge a man's character. She only had to look at his friends who were all dandies and wastrels. Most of them lived in profligate circumstances, but couldn't afford their ostentatious existences.

There was no telling what type of associate had glommed onto him, and she was terrified over the debacle that might unfold because of it. She had to start an investigation and start it fast.

Her fiscal security was always in jeopardy because of Clayton's reckless ways, and she wasn't about to let some unknown idiot make things even worse.

---

"HELLO, MISS CARTER."

"Hello, Mr. Melville. What brings you by?"

"I'm coming to your brother's birthday party."

"So is the whole neighborhood," Millicent said more snottily than she'd intended.

His smile slipped, and he yanked it into place. "You're so popular. I thought I should ask you to dance the opening set with me—before anyone else has a chance."

"Yes, I can do that."

"And if you're not busy this afternoon, I was wondering if you'd like to go for a ride. I drove my gig in case I can coerce you into joining me."

They were in front of the manor. He frequently popped in, eager to catch her at her leisure, so she'd have no excuse to avoid him. She tamped down a sigh, not wanting to hurt his feelings, but she couldn't help it.

They'd been acquainted for over a year, and she supposed—technically—they had an understanding about the future. His grandfather had been the vicar, and after he'd passed away, the family had left the area for a few decades. Now Mr. Melville was back and hoping to be selected as the new vicar. The job included a small income and a modest residence for a parsonage.

The appointment never seemed to materialize though, and he couldn't get answers from church officials. Apparently, the Good Lord worked slowly and couldn't be rushed, which—in her opinion—was just as well.

If the post was finally offered to him, he'd likely propose immediately. Her mother was fine with the match, mostly because there weren't many bachelors in the neighborhood, and Beatrice wasn't keen to have her daughter marry someone from another town where she might end up moving far away.

Millicent had constantly begged to have a Season in town, where she could have been introduced to a more elevated group of candidates, but Beatrice had refused to pay for it. So Millicent was stuck at Carter Crossing, with Preston Melville as her only suitor.

Yet she viewed him as her backup plan. He was very nice and not bad looking: thirty, thin and dapper, with unremarkable brown hair and kindly brown eyes. But he was short, probably five-foot-nine or so, and with her being five-foot-five in her slippers, he wasn't much taller than she was. It was impossible for him to tower over her in a manly way.

He was steady, sympathetic, and reliable though. He'd be a marvelous husband and father, but he was so boring! She thought—if she was forced to spend decades as his wife—she'd go insane from how dull it would be.

Her whole life had been boring. Carter Crossing was boring. Her mother and brother were boring. Their rural world was boring. Clayton was a male, so he'd been allowed to gambol in town. He'd had an illicit amour and had even sired a bastard child. That's how exciting his existence had been.

She was a female, so she'd had to tarry in the country with her mother and be courted by a tedious oaf whose great goal was to be their next vicar. Her cousin, Rebecca, was the lone person who delivered any stimulation or gaiety to their humdrum home.

Millicent was already twenty, and she felt she deserved a much grander spouse than Preston Melville, but she was on the verge of being a spinster. She'd told herself that she'd dither until her birthday, and if she hadn't met a viable contender by the time she turned twenty-one, she'd swallow her pride and settle for ordinary, dependable Preston.

"I can't socialize this afternoon," she said. "My brother just arrived, and his friends are beginning to roll in from town. It's too hectic."

"I will admit to being horribly disappointed." He smiled a sweet smile. "I'll see you tomorrow night—if not before!"

"I'm looking forward to it."

He went over to his gig. It was painted bright yellow, with huge red wheels, and it was such a flashy vehicle for a man who was expecting to be a minister. When he bounced down their rustic lanes, he created quite a spectacle.

She suspected he'd purchased it to impress her, and she wouldn't deny that it was very fun to race down the road in it. But the gaudy carriage couldn't fix what was wrong between them.

He climbed up, having a bit of trouble maneuvering the high step, then he plopped onto the seat and grabbed the reins.

"Don't forget you promised me the first dance!" he cheerily said, and he called to the horse.

The animal took off like a shot and nearly threw him out into the dirt. He was clutching his hat, struggling to balance himself, and failing to make the dramatic exit she was sure he'd been yearning to make.

After he vanished, she wandered over to the stables. She'd heard the housemaids tittering over the horse traders who'd brought Clayton's horses to the estate for him. Supposedly, they were too handsome for words. Millicent was dying to catch a glimpse of them, and she'd come outside numerous times without managing to stumble on them.

She was terribly afraid they might leave before she had a chance to chat with either of them. It was rare when a bachelor visited. Of course several of them would attend her brother's party, but she'd met Clayton's friends. For the most part, they were lazy, rich, unlikable idiots.

As she approached the corral, a man was standing over by the water trough. She observed him, her interest extreme. He was a few years older than she was, twenty-four or so, and he was tall and lanky, with black hair and very blue eyes. He saw her and focused in on her with a grin she felt clear down to her toes.

With her blond hair and blue eyes, her curvaceous figure and expensive clothes, she knew she was gorgeous, and as she sauntered over to him, he didn't stop watching her for a single second. He stared at her as if she was a delicious morsel, and he might gobble her up. He was being very impertinent, and she was thrilled to the marrow of her bones.

"You must be Miss Millicent," he said, his hot gaze meandering down her torso.

She gave her fetching curls a firm shake. "I might be."

"I've been hoping we'd cross paths."

The comment was exhilarating. "You have? Why?"

"The stable hands were talking about you."

Her jaw dropped. "What were they saying?"

"They claim you're pretty as a picture, but spoiled rotten."

She couldn't decide whether to be offended or not. She liked to have people talk about her, but it didn't seem appropriate for it to be the male servants.

"I'm not spoiled," she said. "I'm fussy."

"Are you?"

He sidled over to her, and he had a smooth, casual stride, as if he glided through life without any barriers to obstruct him.

"I'm Lucas," he said.

"Lucas what?"

"Just . . . Lucas."

"Well, Mr. *Just* Lucas, I have to inform you that you're being incredibly forward."

"Girls always insist I am, but usually, they end up being glad. How about you? Do you think you'll end up being glad?"

"I have no idea. As I mentioned, I'm fussy."

"I'm betting you'll like me."

She tsked with exasperation. "You're so cocky. After I get to know you, I might not like you at all."

"I doubt that. There's never been a girl who didn't fall in love with me."

"You might be the vainest person I've ever encountered."

"You might be right." He stepped even closer, so close her cloak swirled around his legs. "Can you guess what else the stable hands say about you?"

"No, what? And if it's horrid, I'll have a few of them whipped. Then they won't be so quick to gossip about their betters."

"They told me you have a beau."

She shrugged. "I might have."

"According to them, he's boring and persnickety, and in my view, you're feisty and spirited. Why would you shackle yourself to a dreary dolt?"

"I'm not promised yet. We're just friends." She stuck her nose up in the air. "Don't denigrate him. He's actually very nice."

"Is that what you're looking for in a man? A fellow who's *nice?*"

"Maybe I am and maybe I'm not."

"Would you like to know a secret about me?" he asked.

"I suppose."

"I'm not ever nice."

He leaned down so they were nose to nose, and he slipped a hand inside her cloak and rested it on her waist. He was being so flirtatious that she wondered if he might kiss her. Was that what he intended? What an insolent devil!

She might have squirmed away, but she wasn't about to let him discover how he intimidated her. Nor did she want the moment to conclude. She was quite breathless, eager to learn what he planned.

"I hear your mother watches you like a hawk," he said.

"She does, but I can sneak away if I feel like it."

"I'm going out to the beach tonight. Probably around ten—after it's good and dark."

"Are you requesting I join you?"

"Yes, and I can guarantee you won't be sorry."

She couldn't imagine what her response might have been, but from over in the barn, a man snapped, "Lucas! Get over here."

"My brother," he whispered. "He's as bad as your mother about making sure I don't have any fun."

"Lucas!" the man called again.

He winked at Millicent and pulled away much too slowly, his hand taking forever to be removed from her waist. Then, with the grace of an athlete, he leapt over the corral fence and strolled over to his brother.

The brother was older, but resembled Lucas exactly: black hair, blue eyes, lanky, muscular physique. They disappeared into the building without glancing back.

She dawdled for an eternity, anxious for him to return, but he didn't. Ultimately, she stomped off, and she was vexed and annoyed and very, very excited.

Would he really go to the beach at ten o'clock? Had he been jesting or was he serious? Was it a genuine invitation? Should she accept? What might happen if she did? Dare she find out?

She had many hours to answer those questions, and she was afraid she might be about to behave recklessly—which was precisely what she'd always dreamed of doing.

---

REBECCA CLIMBED THE STAIRS to head for her bedchamber. It was late, and she was exhausted.

Clayton had arrived from town, but none of his friends had arrived with him. The staff had been waiting impatiently, to no avail. He claimed they were all coming the next day, that his mother had misconstrued the dates.

It didn't matter when they showed up. The house was ready, and the actual birthday party would be held the following night. The important neighbors would attend, along with the main merchants from town and the upper-level clerks from Carter Imports.

Clayton and Beatrice weren't particularly liked, but people would set aside their detestation for the evening and revel in grand style. It would be a marvelous gala, with plenty of food, liquor, and dancing.

She'd been feeling on edge, so she'd taken a lamp and had walked out to the beach, hoping Mr. Shawcross might be there, but he hadn't been. She'd heard a rumor that he was leaving in the morning, and the news had panicked her much more than it should have.

What if she never saw him again? The prospect was too dismal to contemplate.

Her bedchamber was located at the end of a deserted wing on the third floor. It was the room Beatrice had put her in when she'd been conveyed to Carter Crossing at age three. Alex's room was across from hers. They were far from the rest of the family, far from the servants' closets in the attic.

In the early years, when she'd been so little, the spot had been very scary. Now it fit her needs perfectly. She could escape for lengthy periods.

She reached the landing, when suddenly, Clayton emerged from the shadows. She was carrying her lamp, so she could clearly observe it was him. Still though, she hadn't expected to encounter anyone, and her heart raced a bit.

"Why are you wandering the halls?" she asked him. "You should be in bed. Tomorrow will be busy."

"Rebecca, Rebecca! Let down your hair!" He scowled. "No, no, that's not correct."

"I believe you're thinking of Rapunzel in the fairytale."

"Yes, that's who I meant. I'm certain her hair was just as blond as yours."

He was off balance, swaying, and she could smell alcohol on his breath. From the potent odor, it was obvious he'd over-imbibed. It was a ghastly habit that was getting worse.

He approached her in an aggressive manner, and while she'd never feared him in the past, his swagger left her uneasy. She glanced over her shoulder, wishing someone had accompanied her. A frisson of concern slid down her spine, and for a brief instant, she considered turning and dashing away. But she didn't.

This was *Clayton*. He could be rude and boorish, but he'd never physically harm her. There was no reason to be frightened.

"You're too pretty for your own good," he said like a complaint. "And you're so damned regal. You don't have any right to be so regal."

"Don't curse in front of me. You know I don't like it."

"Saint Rebecca, the beloved maiden of Carter Crossing."

His tone was surly, his bravado disturbing, and she decided to simply hurry on by, but as she did, he grabbed her arm and yanked her to a halt.

"Clayton!" she scolded. "You're being a nuisance! Stop it!"

"I let you live here. You understand that, don't you?"

"Of course I understand it."

"You've never had to pay me a penny. Perhaps it's time you start."

"You're drunk, and if you accost me again, I'll speak to your mother."

She flashed her fiercest glower, but it had no effect. She tried to jerk away, but he was gripping her so tightly she was positive she'd have bruises. She wasn't about to wrestle with him, but she was growing alarmed.

She couldn't predict what might have happened, but suddenly, Alex said, "Rebecca! There you are! It's late, and I've been searching for you."

At having Alex's voice emanate from the dark hall, Clayton frowned, appearing confused, as if worried a ghost was hovering. He whipped around as Alex stepped into the light. Clayton studied him, his confusion spiraling, as if he couldn't quite recollect who Alex was.

Alex ignored him and said, "Rebecca? You're aware that I never go to bed until you're there too, and I'm tired. Can you come now?"

If was a huge lie, but she sighed with relief. "Yes, I'm sorry I've kept you waiting."

She skittered by Clayton and rushed to Alex. He slipped his hand into hers, and he faced down his father. Even though he was only ten, he looked furious and violent, as if he wasn't scared of anything.

"Well, well," Clayton taunted, recognition finally dawning, "if it isn't my little bastard."

Rebecca couldn't imagine what other insults Clayton might have hurled. Nor could she imagine how Alex might have reacted to them, but she wasn't about to tarry and find out.

"You're in no condition to chat, Clayton," she said. "We'll talk in the morning."

She and Alex marched away, and after they'd turned the corner, they began to run, and they continued running all the way to their rooms. As they reached Rebecca's door, they were gasping for breath, and she was trembling.

"Did he hurt you?" Alex asked.

"He merely grabbed my arm. I'll survive."

"I'm glad I decided to hunt for you."

"Why did you?"

"I simply had a feeling that I should."

"My hero!" she teased, and she batted her lashes.

"I'm embarrassed that I have his blood in me."

"Just because you share his blood, it doesn't mean you have to ever be like him."

"I know, and I never will be."

"Good," she said.

"Would you like me to stay with you tonight? What if he stumbles in? I'm not afraid of him. I could sleep on the floor."

"He won't stumble in," she said with more confidence than she should have had.

She truly didn't believe Clayton had any idea where her bedchamber was located, and she suspected—the next day—he wouldn't remember molesting her.

"Are you sure?" Alex asked.

"I'm sure." She nodded to his room. "You go on. I'll be fine."

"All right, but lock your door for once."

"I will. You lock yours too."

She watched until he went inside, and she listened as he spun the key. Then she went into her own room. She spun her key too, and she stood in the middle of the floor, angry, shaking, and wondering if this was the beginning of some new horror she'd have to endure.

She really—*really!*—didn't think she could bear it.

She clasped hold of her dresser and dragged it in front of the door—adding an extra barrier of protection. Just in case.

# CHAPTER

# 5

Rebecca stood in the corner, observing the festivities. She hadn't been asked to dance, but she desperately hoped she would be.

She occupied an odd position in the household. She was a family member, but treated like a servant. She managed the staff, but Beatrice could counter any command or suggestion.

Due to Millicent being very spoiled, Rebecca had a wardrobe filled with pretty clothes. Her cousin never liked a garment for long, and she gave her cast-offs to Rebecca, so she was attired as a party guest ought to be attired: a lavender gown, with a high waist, capped sleeves, and a flowing skirt.

Her slippers and hair ribbon matched the gown, and the color enhanced the silver in her white-blond hair and the blue of her eyes so they appeared almost purple.

She wasn't being vain when she said she looked beautiful, wealthy, and glamorous. The neighbors weren't fooled into believing she'd suddenly stumbled on a fortune, but Clayton's friends were probably curious about her. She didn't care for any of them, but she'd like it if they thought she was someone's fetching sister.

Yet she had to be certain she wasn't enjoying herself too overtly. If Beatrice noticed, she'd nip Rebecca's jollity in the bud.

The first set had just ended, and Preston Melville had handed Millicent off to her next partner. As opposed to her mother and brother, she was popular in the neighborhood. She hadn't had as many chances to annoy people, so she was generally viewed as sweet and spirited. She wouldn't sit down all evening.

Mr. Melville wasn't very nimble and had no sense of rhythm, so he was an awful dancer, and Rebecca prayed he wouldn't approach her. She didn't think he would, and she had her fingers crossed that one of the bachelors from town would step forward instead. So far, she'd had no luck.

Like an idiot, she kept watching the door, wishing Mr. Shawcross would stroll in, even though he never would. He was simply a horse dealer from London, so he hadn't been invited, and she'd heard a footman claim he'd left early that morning. She hadn't exactly been devastated by the news, but she was definitely feeling glum.

In her pathetic, deluded mind, she'd convinced herself that they'd established a close bond, but obviously, she'd misconstrued the situation. She wondered if she'd ever see him again. Unless Clayton bought more horses from him, there would be no reason for him to return to the estate, and the notion was too sad to ponder.

"Are you having fun, Miss Rebecca?" Mr. Melville asked as he walked up.

"I'm having a marvelous time. How about you?"

"It's terrific. I wanted to be sure to tell you how much I appreciate your hard work. You must have been overwhelmed with getting everything ready."

"Thank you. I'm grateful for your compliment."

Being a genuinely kind man, he never failed to offer a courteous remark, but he was a bit of an inept bungler, the sort of clumsy character who'd have provided comedic relief in a theatrical play. She liked him very much, but worried about him too.

She suspected he was madly in love with Millicent, but when she'd discussed him with Millicent, her cousin had declared him to be *just fine*, which was tepid praise.

Apparently, she deemed Mr. Melville to be her second choice. If she never found a better spousal candidate, Rebecca supposed her cousin would break down and settle for Mr. Melville. If that happened, they'd both be miserable forever. Mr. Melville was doting and nice, and Millicent was spoiled and exhausting.

She'd crush him with her whims and quirks and, on a vicar's salary, he'd never be able to support her in the manner to which she was accustomed.

"How have you been?" he asked.

"I'm always all right."

She couldn't guess how much he'd gleaned about her sorry existence, but he was the sole person who ever inquired as to how she was faring. It was an endearing gesture, and she cherished his interest.

"Have you seen my gig?"

"Yes. You look quite dashing in it."

His cheeks reddened. "Considering that I hope to be the new vicar, it probably wasn't the best decision. But I couldn't resist purchasing it."

"A man is only young once," she said. "You deserve to have some excitement."

"The next time I take Miss Millicent for a ride, would you like to come too?"

"What a sweet question. I would love to."

"When the horse really gets trotting, it's a little fast, but you're the type of female who would buck up and enjoy it."

"I'm positive I would."

There was a kerfuffle by the door, and she glanced over to find out who had arrived. They didn't have a formal receiving line, but Beatrice and Clayton were there to welcome people. Millicent, when she wasn't dancing, went over too. They were all there now, with others milling, so Rebecca didn't have a clear view.

Suddenly, guests were whispering, pointing, gossip sweeping by like wildfire:

"It's that Africa explorer, the one who traveled with Sir Sidney!"

"He's here? Clayton claimed to know him, but I didn't believe it!"

"His name is Shawcross. Raven Shawcross."

The last remark had her whipping around.

*Raven Shawcross? What?*

There couldn't be two men in the kingdom with that same name.

She rose on tiptoe, trying to peer over everyone, as beside her, Mr. Melville muttered, "My, my, but aren't we lucky. A national *hero* at Carter Crossing!"

Rebecca peeked at him. Was that sarcasm in his tone? Why would he be irked to have a famous explorer show up? The whole team was so legendary it was like having an angel fly down from Heaven to mingle in their paltry company.

For a brief instant, the crowd parted and . . . ?

There he was—the cad who'd stolen her heart. At the same time, it couldn't possibly be him. The man who'd flirted with her had seemed to be a laborer, dressed in scruffy clothes, with hair that was too long and a beard that had needed shaving.

This fellow was another species entirely. He'd been barbered, his unkempt beard removed, his hair trimmed. It was still long, but much shorter than it had been, so it was neatly restrained with a ribbon. And of course, he was wearing all black.

Now though, rather than a working man's attire, his garments were sewn from the finest materials and obviously stitched by the best tailors. His coat was velvet, his trousers a smooth fabric she couldn't identify. His knee-high boots had been polished to a shine.

His shirt was black too, his cravat a stunning black lace. He should have looked sinister, but with his outfit so luxurious, he looked wealthy, gorgeous, and elegant.

The only specks of white on his person were the diamond rings that glittered on his fingers. It was an odd affectation for someone so masculine, then she remembered that the Sinclair expedition team had gotten obscenely rich from the discovery of African diamond mines. He was likely flaunting gemstones from his very own mines.

The prospect annoyed her immensely. They were having a country house party, with many of the guests being local merchants and landowners who were basically farmers. It was pompous and condescending to parade his good fortune in such an ostentatious way.

There was a second man hovering at his elbow. He was a few years younger, and he resembled Mr. Shawcross so strongly that they had to be brothers. He was dressed just as immaculately, but he'd donned a more typical blue velvet coat, tan trousers, and a white shirt with white lace cravat. His fingers displayed the same gaudy rings.

He had to have been the other horse trader, and she was hurt to realize Mr. Shawcross had never mentioned having a sibling or that he was in residence too.

For some reason, the notion that they hadn't been introduced was particularly galling. It was silly to feel slighted, but she couldn't help it. Her meeting him was the sole interesting thing that had happened in so long. She was crushed to learn that it had been a chimera.

He was chatting with Beatrice and Millicent, and Clayton was puffed up like a rooster, relishing how he'd impressed the group by having such a famous friend. Rebecca couldn't hear any of them. She was too far away, but he reached into his coat and extracted a small gift box, which he handed to Millicent with a grand flourish.

She preened with delight and ripped off the silver wrapping paper. When she lifted the lid, she—and those surrounding her—gasped with astonishment.

Excited utterances raced by:

"It's diamond earrings!"

"How bloody rich is the man?"

"He can afford to dole out jewels like candy!"

He glanced over Millicent's shoulder, and he noticed Rebecca lurking in the corner with Mr. Melville. Their eyes locked, and he winked at her, acting as if they shared a joke that no one else understood. Then the crowd closed in, and she lost sight of him.

She whirled away, refusing to gawk and not wanting to be caught staring at him in case the crowd parted again.

Mr. Melville frowned at her. "Were people saying his surname is Shaw-cross? Was that it?"

"Yes, why?"

"I think I went to school with him as a boy, and I'm sure his name is Raven Stone." Mr. Melville glared across the milling mob, searching for Mr. Shawcross, but he wasn't much taller than she was. Finally, he shrugged. "It was many years ago. I'm probably mistaken."

"Well, I've conversed with him recently, and when he originally came to Carter Crossing, he claimed to simply be delivering some horses Clayton had bought."

"If he's that African explorer, why would he pretend to be a horse dealer?"

"I have no idea."

"He must be playing some game with us. What could it be?"

"I can't imagine."

His frown deepened. "Did he . . . he . . . give Miss Millicent some dia-monds? I couldn't see what was in the box. Could you?"

Rebecca shook her head. "No, I couldn't see."

The musicians struck up another tune, and as she and Mr. Melville con-tinued to watch, Mr. Shawcross escorted Millicent into the line of dancers and joined in the fun. He was graceful and regal, and Millicent appeared charmed and thrilled to have been singled out.

Rebecca felt sick to her stomach. Poor Mr. Melville looked ill too. He observed Millicent for a bit as she twirled and strutted, then he sighed with what sounded like resignation.

"Would you excuse me, Miss Rebecca?" he ultimately said. "I'm not feel-ing all that well. I believe I'll sneak out while everyone is busy."

"Must you go?"

He smiled a tight smile. "I'm afraid I must."

"Millicent is a dedicated flirt, Mr. Melville," Rebecca pointed out, "and she's very young. Don't read anything into this situation that isn't there."

He stared at Millicent forever, his expression incredibly glum. "I'm not reading anything into it. I'm just tired. Thank you for the lovely party. Please give my regards to Mrs. Carter."

"I will."

He slinked away, and she was left alone, standing with the other wallflowers, gaping at the man of her dreams as he danced with her cousin. She'd like to leave too, but Beatrice would expect her to stay until the bitter end, so she *would* stay—even if it killed her.

———

REBECCA STOOD ON THE verandah. It was too cold to tarry outside, but she was overheated and hoping the chilly evening air might cool her down. She'd retrieved a wool shawl before stepping out of the manor, and it provided some protection from the frigid breeze, but not much.

Through the windows, she could see into the parlors where the festivities were winding down. The musicians had packed up their instruments, and the dancing was over. Millicent had gone to bed, Beatrice too. The neighbors had departed, so it was mostly Clayton's London guests who remained.

They had removed their coats, rolled up their sleeves, and were preparing to play cards and, Rebecca was certain, engage in some vigorous gambling.

Beatrice would have been aghast if she knew, but it was Clayton's house. If he wanted to wager with his friends, who was there to tell him he couldn't?

She remembered how drunk he'd been the prior night, how he'd accosted her in the hall. If Alex hadn't come to check on her, there was no predicting what might have happened.

She'd avoided Clayton all day, so she had no idea if he recalled the incident or not. She'd yearned to confront him, but it would have been futile. If she'd scolded him, he'd have pretended he didn't recollect the event, then he'd have found a way to retaliate later on.

She hadn't told anyone about the encounter, but she had five very distinct fingertip bruises on her arm from when he'd grabbed her. With her gown having shortened sleeves, they'd been visible during the soiree, but no one paid enough attention to her to notice them, so she hadn't had to explain their origin.

She smelled smoke from a cheroot, and she glanced down the balustrade to discover Mr. Shawcross's brother, Lucas, was there. She'd been introduced to him inside, but they hadn't had a chance to chat, and she hadn't minded.

He and his brother had seized control of the party, dancing with the ladies and conversing with the men. People had been fascinated by their good looks, charisma, and stories. They were so handsome and dashing, so obviously wealthy and well-connected, that it seemed as if a pair of kings had dropped by.

Both of them had spent an inordinate amount of time with Millicent, and her cousin had been bowled over by their interest. Rebecca was glad Mr. Melville had fled so he hadn't had to witness the depressing scene. She'd have been ecstatic to not have witnessed it either.

Through it all, Raven Shawcross hadn't approached her, and she couldn't decide why he'd ignored her. Had she been so insignificant to him that he didn't feel the need to say hello? Was he worried she might reveal his fake identity? Was he afraid she might divulge facts he didn't care to have exposed?

He needn't have fretted. The last thing she would ever do was quarrel in public.

It was evident he had mischief brewing, and she was concerned over what it was. Mr. Melville didn't even think his real surname was Shawcross. What was Rebecca to make of it?

The whole day, she'd been despondent over how she assumed he'd crept off without a goodbye. Now she simply wished he'd never arrived in the first place. There was some type of peril swirling over all of them that she couldn't quite discern.

What would it be? What route would it take? When it was over, what would become of them?

She wondered if Lucas Shawcross had seen her, and she considered sneaking away without greeting him, but the opportunity vanished when he said, "Miss Carter? Is that you lurking in the shadows?"

"Yes, hello, Mr. Shawcross," she replied.

He sauntered over and rested a hip on the balustrade. "You shouldn't be outside in such cold weather, and you're definitely not dressed for it. You'll probably catch an influenza."

"I'll try not to." She sounded snippy, which she never was, so she added, "It's so hot and stuffy in the house. I thought I'd cool down before I call it a night. How about you? Will you gamble with the men or are you as weary as I am? Are you about to head off to your bed?"

"I gamble plenty in town," he said, "so I've arranged an amorous assignation instead."

It was a brash comment, and she couldn't guess if he was telling the truth or not. Candles glowed in the parlor windows, and they provided enough illumination for her to study his eyes. They were twinkling with merriment.

"You're having an assignation?" Her tone was skeptical.

"Yes. It should be much more entertaining than winning money from a bunch of London idiots. I spend nearly all my time with dolts like them. I'd much rather flirt with a pretty girl."

She tsked with annoyance. "I don't know you, so I can't judge if you're being candid or if you're teasing me."

He grinned a scoundrel's grin, and she suspected he had a habit of breaking hearts.

"I might be pulling your leg." His grin widened. "Or I might not be."

Her mood was incredibly dour, and she might have pleaded fatigue and hurried off, but she was so intrigued by him and his despicable sibling. If she asked him some questions, would he supply any believable answers?

"I have to confess, Mr. Shawcross," she tentatively started, "that I'm terribly curious about you and your brother."

"Well, we're curious fellows."

"You brought Clayton's horses, didn't you? The ones he purchased in town? You slept in the hay loft and pretended to be horse traders."

"Yes. That would be us."

"Why would you do that?"

He assessed her, pondering his response, his behavior making her suppose he was a deceptive wastrel—perhaps even dangerous too.

"We wanted to arrive quietly," he said. "When my brother's status is disclosed, there's too much of a fuss."

"Why would you need to arrive quietly? He was invited, and we were expecting him. Why not show up like a normal person?"

"What fun would that have been? Besides, we were eager to learn as many details as we could about all of you. We knew if we loafed in the stables for a bit, the servants would gossip incessantly."

"What was it you hoped to find out from them?"

He smirked. "I'll let it be a surprise."

"Should I be humored or alarmed by your remark?"

"You should be . . . ready for anything, I guess."

"Whatever can you mean?"

"You seem very nice. Just watch out in the coming days and weeks."

"Watch out for what?"

"I'll let that be a surprise too."

A shiver slid down her spine. "You appear to like my cousin, Millicent."

"I'm always tantalized by a fetching female. I can't help myself, and it drives my brother mad with frustration."

"She has a beau."

"Not much of a one, from what I'm told. She's not promised, is she? The footmen claim there's no betrothal—and there probably won't ever be. She's too spoiled and picky for the poor oaf."

"The footmen said that to you? I'll have to have a stern talk with them. You're a stranger to us, and they were being entirely too indiscreet."

"You'd be amazed by what we've discovered."

"No, I wouldn't. You're too cheeky by half."

"I am," he agreed.

"I only mentioned Millicent's beau because—when your brother initially strolled into the party—he thought they might have gone to school together as boys."

He shrugged. "It's possible."

"He swore your brother's name is Raven Stone."

He paused forever, then grinned again. "Isn't that interesting?"

"Is your surname Stone? There's something dodgy about the two of you, which is why I'm inquiring."

"Dodgy?" He considered the word. "I wouldn't think the term should apply to me. With me, what you see is what you get, but you definitely ought to be wary of my brother. He can be an absolute terror when he's riled."

"Why would he be riled with any of us?"

He leaned nearer and whispered, "It's a secret."

"I've never liked secrets."

"Don't worry. You'll learn what it is very soon."

"You haven't reassured me in the least."

"Keep your head down. That's my advice to you."

His insolent attitude was infuriating, and she'd like to order him to mind his manners, but she had no right to boss him.

Her temper was flaring though. Clearly, the devious pair had a scheme in the works that would be hideous and shocking when it was revealed. She imagined—with their having involved themselves with Clayton—it might be any sordid business.

First thing in the morning, she had to sit Beatrice down and have a blunt discussion. The woman had to be warned about problems developing, but Rebecca couldn't clarify what they might turn out to be.

"Your brother is a famous explorer." Her snippy tone was back. "What are you?" It was a rude query, but she posed it anyway.

"I'm a nuisance and a troublemaker. Can't you tell?"

"Oh, yes, I can tell."

Movement out in the garden caught his eye, and he raised a brow. "My assignation is about to commence. It's been lovely chatting, but you'll have to excuse me."

"Who are you meeting?" she asked, as she rolled through the list of maids who might have been coerced into a scandalous tryst.

"You wouldn't believe me if I told you," he cockily retorted.

He winked at her—as his brother had during the party—then he whirled away and strutted down into the garden. She watched him until he was swallowed up by the shadows.

She yearned to chase after him, to march right up to the girl who was risking everything for him, and drag her back to the house. Or maybe she should storm inside, grab his brother, and demand he fetch her back.

Or maybe—just maybe—she should stay out of it. She'd had about all of the Shawcross siblings she could stand, and she hoped that the foolish ninny breathlessly waiting on the beach wouldn't be too heartbroken when handsome, rich Lucas Shawcross returned to London and never thought of her again.

Rebecca whipped away and hurried to the servant's door so she could sneak up the rear stairs to her dark, quiet room, and the depressing night would end once and for all.

• ──── ✦✦ ──── •

MILLICENT STOOD ON THE dark beach, wondering if she might have gone insane. What was she doing?

Her brother's party had been the greatest event of her life. He'd repeatedly boasted that one of Sir Sidney's explorers would attend, but he was a braggart and a liar, and she hadn't believed him. No one had.

But Raven Shawcross had actually arrived. He'd charmed their mother—who was impossible to charm. He'd befriended Clayton who wasn't worth befriending. And he'd given Millicent a pair of diamond earrings, with the gemstones being from his very own African diamond mine.

She had no idea why he'd present her with such a spectacular and inappropriate gift. Was he signaling that he'd like to marry her? What else was she to think?

She was rippling with anticipation, obsessing over what it would be like to be courted by him. What if they wed? What if he swept her away from boring, dull Carter Crossing and took her to London?

He was so rich! He could furnish her with the exact sort of luxurious existence she'd always thought she deserved to have.

She'd spent the night dancing. Mr. Shawcross had partnered with her several times, which everyone had noticed, but on the fringe of all that socializing, his brother had been lurking on the edge of her vision.

Toward the end of the evening as the guests were beginning to depart, he'd casually whispered in her ear that she should announce she was tired, pretend to head to her bedchamber, then meet him on the beach.

She'd told him she absolutely wouldn't, but despite her protestations, she was anxiously waiting for him. He'd invited her the prior day, and after sufficient mental scolding, she'd managed to keep herself from joining him, but his second invitation had been too enticing to resist.

She couldn't figure out what game the two brothers were playing. They'd waltzed in as horse traders, had slept in the barn and acted like laborers, then they'd promenaded in the front door, dressed like wealthy princes.

What was she to make of such furtive, peculiar behavior? Nothing exciting ever happened at Carter Crossing, but something was definitely happening now.

The weather was chilly and windy, and she'd just decided she shouldn't have come, when Lucas Shawcross emerged from the trees. The moon was up, clouds blowing by, so she had a perfect view of his handsome features, his expensive clothes, his lanky, masculine physique.

He was, by far and away, the most striking man she'd ever seen. Her pulse raced just from looking at him. What might he want? What might he do?

Oh, but she was mad to have obliged him!

"I doubted you'd show up," he said as he sauntered over. "I was convinced your courage would fail you—as it did last night."

"You were here?"

"Of course. Where were you?"

She'd never admit to being a coward, so she said, "I'm freezing, so I'm heading back to the house."

"Why would you leave?"

"I shouldn't be alone with you."

"That's what girls always say when they first sneak off with me, but I change their minds. Will I be able to change *your* mind?"

"You're so vain, which I hate."

"Well, you're spoiled and fussy, which I hate too."

"I don't have to stand here and be insulted by you."

"You're free to go whenever you like."

He stared blandly, as if he didn't care one way or the other, and his nonchalance was so annoying. He was daring her to stay, but certain she'd never be brave enough. Clearly, he didn't comprehend how lucky he was that she'd joined him.

She was the prettiest girl in the whole Frinton area, and her family was very rich. Probably not nearly as rich as his, but still!

If she was spoiled, it was for a reason: She'd been raised like a princess and considered herself to be one. She would never let him best her, would never let him assume he had the upper hand.

"I'm not leaving," she said, "but I'm awfully cold. I should have guessed you'd pick such an unpleasant spot for a clandestine rendezvous."

"I could have snuck to your room."

"My room!" It was a shocking comment, and her jaw dropped with astonishment.

"I didn't know where it was though," he said, "and I didn't think I should inquire of the footmen."

"You'd better not!"

He grinned. "Will you tell me where it is?"

"No!"

"We could go there now. We'd be much more comfortable."

"It's right across the hall from my mother!"

"Then we could go to mine. It's on the floor above hers. The other guests are lodged there though. We might be observed tiptoeing in, and if we were, you're not worth the trouble it would cause me."

She tsked with offense. "I can't decide it you're serious or not. Do you really bring females to your bedchamber? Do you really sneak into theirs?"

"How old are you?" he asked.

"Twenty."

"You truly are an innocent country mouse, aren't you?"

There was no remark he could have uttered that would have irked her more.

She detested that she was trapped at Carter Crossing. Her mother hadn't even let her attend boarding school, insisting there was no need. A governess had been hired instead, and of course, Millicent had begged for years for a Season in town.

She'd never understood why her mother had constantly refused, but she'd once heard two housemaids gossiping. They'd claimed there was no money for a Season, that Clayton had spent it all, so Millicent was left to scrape by on pennies. But with their being so wealthy, she couldn't believe they were correct.

"I'm not an innocent," she fumed, "and I'm not a mouse. If you just plan to tease me, I'm going inside."

"I told you it doesn't matter to me. You're terribly young anyway. I shouldn't trifle with you."

He pulled a flask from his coat and sipped what she assumed would be liquor. He held it out to her, offering her some, and she asked, "What's in it? Hard spirits?"

"Yes, whiskey."

"I can't."

"Why not?"

"I'm not allowed to imbibe of alcoholic beverages. My mother wouldn't like it."

The instant the words were out of her mouth, she wished she could retract them, and she was glad it was dark so he couldn't see her blushing.

"Your *mother* wouldn't like it?" he snidely said. "Do I look like I care what your mother thinks?"

"No."

"Then why should you? She seems like a shrew to me. You must realize that. Is she deserving of your fawning obedience? Have you ever asked yourself that question? If you have, perhaps you should answer it for once."

Millicent should have risen to her mother's defense, but his criticism was spot on. "My mother can be overwhelming."

He smirked. "You don't have to be polite with me. When we're together like this, you can say whatever you like."

He waved the flask at her, and she yanked it out of his grasp. She sniffed the contents, then took a cautious sip. It had an odd taste she couldn't quite describe—like smoky heat—and it slid down her throat in a soothing manner. She drank another swallow, liking it much more than the first.

She attempted to give it back, but he retrieved a second one from his coat. He tipped it toward her. "I have my own. You can have that one."

They tarried silently, enjoying their drinks, and much too soon, she'd finished all of hers. It had a potent, swift effect. Her limbs felt rubbery, her body hot all over—even though it was so cold. All in all, the sensation was extremely pleasant, and she wondered why she hadn't sampled any liquor before.

The sideboards in the manor were filled with decanters. From this point on, she'd steal some whenever no one was looking.

She handed him the flask, and he stuck it in his coat, then he emptied his and put it away too.

"Now that you've tried a man's libation," he said, "what is your opinion?"

"It was very good."

He nodded as if she'd provided the right response. "I intend to corrupt you, Miss Carter. I'm predicting it will be very easy."

"I doubt it. I'm not interested in developing bad habits."

"Yes, you are. I'm an expert at judging people, and the minute I met you, I perceived your true inclinations. Aren't you bored in the country? Doesn't all this sky and land drive you mad?"

"Yes."

"I can't wait to get back to London," he suddenly declared.

"When will you depart?"

"Not just yet," he said, which wasn't much of a reply.

"What are you and your brother really doing at Carter Crossing? Initially, you were pretending to be a horse trader, but you're not."

"My brother raises horses, so technically, *he* is a horse trader. I merely came along to help him."

"Help him with what?"

"You'll find out," he said.

"Why did he give me those earrings?"

"Why would you suppose? He's hoping to tantalize you. Has he?"

"Yes, but he must want something in exchange."

His torrid gaze wandered down her torso, and it lingered on her feminine areas, as if he was undressing her with his eyes. He scoffed and facetiously said, "Yes, Miss Carter, he wants something from you."

"What is it?"

"I'll let it be a surprise."

"Are the diamonds genuine?"

He chuckled. "If I were you, I wouldn't take them into a pawn shop. You'd simply embarrass yourself."

Were they fakes? Could it be? Ooh, he was so aggravating. How could she decide if he was telling the truth or not?

She didn't like him. He was smug and condescending, but then, she'd never met anyone like him, and she was absolutely fascinated. She ought to stomp off and never talk to him again, but she was mesmerized in a manner that was dangerous.

He stared out at the ocean, and a ship was passing by, a lone lamp swinging as it cut through rough water.

"My brother has sailed the ocean," he said, "but I've never been anywhere. How about you?"

"I've never gone anywhere either."

"You must be about to expire from all this tedium."

"Occasionally, it feels that way. I'd like to have the chance to travel someday."

"No, you wouldn't. You'd like to have some fun every so often. You'd be delighted to just head to London. That's about as far as your borders will ever extend."

When he put it like that, she sounded dull and immature, but she envisioned herself as being glamorous and sophisticated. She wasn't about to have him cataloguing her faults though, so she switched subjects.

"Your brother is a hero and a horse trader, but what are you?"

"I'm a gambler and a criminal."

"You are not." She frowned, then tentatively inquired, "Are you?"

"Yes, I was quite incorrigible when I was a boy, and I grew up causing trouble. It's just my nature, and I was never stopped from engaging in mischief.

I finally realized I enjoyed it immensely, and there was no point in behaving."

"Where were your parents? Didn't they try to mold you into a better person?"

"They died when I was four."

She actually suffered a bit of compassion for him. "How did they die?"

He shrugged. "The way everyone does, I imagine. They simply drew their last breaths, and it was over."

"Who raised you after they were deceased?"

"No one. That was my problem: a lack of supervision. But it was coupled with my complete absence of any concern about moral restraint."

"Where was your brother?"

"For awhile, he was at a different school. Then, once he was older and had cheated and lied to accumulate some funds, he bought a spot with Sir Sidney. I rarely saw him after that. If I had, he'd likely have kept me on the straight and narrow."

"And you chose a life of crime? Seriously?"

"Yes."

Her annoyance flared. "I think you've been pulling my leg from the start. I'll bet your parents are alive and well and living in a grand mansion in London. They're probably merrily spending all your brother's diamond money. You probably had a totally ordinary childhood."

He snickered, but didn't dispute her assessment. Instead, he asked, "What about you, Miss Carter? Have you ever done a bad deed? Have you ever had a wicked thought? Have you ever lied or cheated or tricked anyone?"

"Gad, no. I've been the perfect daughter, the perfect sister."

"Don't you ever get tired of being so uninteresting? Haven't you ever wondered how thrilling it might be to throw caution to the wind?"

He'd precisely described her feelings. She was so sick of Carter Crossing, sick of her mother and brother, sick of their rural estate and their quiet neighborhood. Her path currently led in one direction, that being marriage to stable, boring Preston Melville.

If she wound up having to wed him, she sincerely expected she'd jump off a cliff.

"You're correct about me," she said. "I'm choking on my life."

"I'm ecstatic to hear you admit it. You have to recognize a dilemma before you can begin to solve it."

He turned away from the water, and he stepped in very close. He slid his hand under her cloak and rested it on her waist as he had the prior afternoon at the corral. Then he dipped down and kissed her. He didn't ask if he could. He simply forged ahead with no warning whatsoever.

She was so astonished that she staggered away and gaped up at him like an idiot, but she couldn't help it. She'd never been kissed, and her greatest complaint about Mr. Melville was that he'd never tried to initiate an amorous embrace.

For a few years, she'd had a friend in Frinton, and the girl had liked to read romantic novels. She'd secretly shared them with Millicent. In them, the heroes were always grabbing the heroines and kissing them as if they were off to the gallows and would never again have the opportunity.

Millicent dreamed of having an experience like that, but Mr. Melville was exhaustingly polite. She suspected that he didn't even like the notion of passion. She might marry him only to discover that he never intended to proceed. Ever.

"I take it you've never been kissed before," he said as if in accusation.

"Oh, I have been," she fibbed. "Dozens of times. You just surprised me, that's all."

He wiggled a finger at her, indicating she should approach. "Let's do it again. You know you want to."

"Maybe."

"I invited you to engage in an assignation." His voice was soft and coaxing. "Will you go back to the house without a single illicit thing happening? Is that how you'd like this evening to end?"

The whiskey she'd drunk was coursing through her body. It was making her reckless, was making her feel braver than she actually was. He was right that—if she returned to the manor without participating in scandalous activity—she'd regret it forever.

And he'd gloat forever.

She squared her shoulders and marched over to him.

"I'm not afraid of you," she said.

"I never thought you were."

"I'm not a scared rabbit either."

"Are you ready to prove it?"

"We'll see, Mr. Shawcross. We'll see what you can convince me to do."

"You'll like it," he boasted, "and since it appears this tryst has just gotten much more intriguing, you should probably call me Lucas."

# CHAPTER

6

RAVEN HEARD REBECCA COMING from quite a long distance. Her bedchamber was located in a decrepit, deserted wing of the house, far from the family and the servants, and her footsteps echoed as she climbed the stairs.

He wondered if she'd picked it for herself or if it had been assigned to her by Beatrice Carter. If so, it would be typical that Mrs. Carter would treat her badly. From the reports he'd read, she was a shrew who enjoyed doling out punishment to people who were weaker than she was.

Evidently, she had abused poor Rebecca for years and was never happy with Rebecca's efforts on her behalf. Rebecca was a sort of whipping girl who was blamed for whatever went wrong.

It was easy for Mrs. Carter to inflict herself on a helpless female who couldn't defend herself, but they'd soon discover how she fared when she was forced to confront a really angry, really powerful man who wasn't afraid of anything. He didn't suppose she'd like the experience very much.

He was delighted to find himself in such an isolated spot. It meant he could sneak in and out undetected—*if* he felt like committing such a reckless act. Apparently, he did.

He'd assumed he was simply having a bit of fun with Rebecca, entertaining himself as he waited for Clayton to arrive. The idiotic cretin was finally in residence, so Raven should have been too busy to trifle with her, but he'd had to accept that he wasn't finished with her.

He had the energy and focus to accomplish two goals at once. He could ruin Clayton and Beatrice Carter, *and* he could amuse himself with pretty, lonely Rebecca.

Her room was small and modest, much like he envisioned a nun's cell would be in a convent. There was a dresser, chair, and narrow bed with a lumpy mattress that needed re-stuffing.

There was a wardrobe too, filled with stylish clothes, and he figured her cousin, Millicent, gave her cast-offs. While he wouldn't have pictured himself to be particularly sentimental, she was so beautiful that it seemed a crime against nature for her to have to attire herself in her cousin's discarded garments.

He was much more intrigued by her than he should have been, so he'd rummaged through her possessions. She didn't have any mementoes, and considering her poverty, he couldn't deduce if that was normal or not. Was she simply not the type to hoard tokens from her past? Or had there never been tokens to save?

As a fellow who'd had every item in his home taken from him when he was ten—even the silverware in the drawers—he traveled light too. He didn't amass keepsakes to remind him of better times because the *better* times had occurred so long ago that they were like a dream.

But also, his itinerant years on the Sinclair expedition team had guaranteed he was usually away from England. Why accumulate chattels? What was the point?

When she entered, she shrugged off her shawl and hung it on a hook by the door. She looked drained and weary, her expression glum. She probably believed he'd ignored her at the party, but in reality, she enticed him like a moth to a flame. He hadn't been able to stop himself from constantly peeking at her.

She was carrying a candle, and he let her set it on the dresser before he said, "Hello, Rebecca. Where have you been?"

She hadn't noticed him sitting in the chair by the window. She jumped a foot and whirled around, barely managing to tamp down a squeal of alarm. Not that it would have done her any good to cry out. Who was there to hear a call for help?

"Mr. Shawcross!" she wheezed when her pulse slowed enough that she could speak. "Oh, my lord, I thought you were . . . were . . ."

She didn't complete her sentence, but her fear was palpable. Clearly, someone was terrorizing her, and he was curious as to who it might be.

"Who did you think I was?" he asked.

"No one," she hastily said. "You just startled me."

"I see that."

"I have no idea why you're in my bedchamber. I can't imagine how you learned where it was—or *why* you'd wish to know—but you are leaving immediately."

She made a shooing motion with her fingers, urging him out as if he were a misbehaved hound. Of course he didn't obey.

"I'm fine right where I am." He smiled a cocky smile.

"You are not staying in my room!"

"I didn't have a chance to chat with you during the party."

"Whose fault is that?" she furiously inquired.

"I decided I should rectify the situation."

"I happen to disagree. I can't guess what game you're playing at Carter Crossing, but I won't play it with you. I won't scheme against my relatives, and I won't fraternize with you when you have dubious motives with regard to all of us."

"That's a mouthful. It sounds as if you assume I'm about to engage in spurious conduct."

"I'm sure you are, and I plan to warn Beatrice first thing in the morning."

It was much too late for Beatrice Carter to protect herself, and he chuckled. "What will you tell her?"

She didn't clarify what her remarks would be, but asked, "Do you recall a classmate from your school days named Preston Melville? His father and grandfather were vicars. He's hoping to be one too."

"No, I don't recall him."

"Well, *he* recalled you quite vividly. After he saw you tonight, he informed me that you are Raven Stone, *not* Raven Shawcross."

Stone had been his father's surname, the one that had been ruined throughout the kingdom when he'd been accused by Charles Carter of embezzling from Lord Coxwold and other wealthy men. A friend of their father's had encouraged Raven and his two siblings to conceal their connection to him, so they'd begun using their mother's maiden name of Shawcross instead.

Raven had always been ashamed that he'd betrayed his father in such a weak way. If he'd been older and tougher, he wouldn't have succumbed. But his father had been totally disgraced, and after he'd hanged himself in prison, he'd not only had his earthly reputation destroyed, but he'd destroyed his immortal soul too.

Because he'd committed suicide, he'd been denied a Christian funeral or burial in a church cemetery. His father, Harrison Stone, had been pious and devout, and his ending—suffered without the blessings of his faith—was galling.

What benefit could there have been to keep their reviled name? As his orphaned children, they'd had plenty of obstacles to conquer, and they hadn't needed to carry forward extra burdens.

"Raven *Stone?*" he mused. "Never heard of him."

She scoffed. "A likely story—that I will *not* debate with you. Go away!"

"No."

"My young cousin, Alex, is asleep across the hall, and I can't have him discover you loafing. How would I ever explain it?"

He shrugged. "So close the door."

She bristled with offense. "I'm not about to sequester myself with you. I can't deduce your intent, but I'm positive I wouldn't approve of it."

"You previously mentioned your young cousin to me. Is he being abused by Beatrice too?"

"Honestly!"

"She's hidden the two of you in this deserted wing of the manor. How long has she forced you into this paltry room?"

"She didn't force me. I'm certain it will come as a huge surprise to your grand self, but I *like* to be off on my own. After a busy day, I enjoy the solitude."

"Sure you do."

He stood and pushed the door shut, then he spun the key in the lock and stuck it in his pocket.

"Mr. Shawcross! You can't be in here with me."

"I already am, so your complaints are silly."

The tiny space provided no escape for her. He stepped over and trapped her against the dresser. Then he dipped down and kissed her. Their lips touched briefly, then she yanked away, so he placed soft kisses on her cheek and jaw, down her neck to her nape.

"I like the way you smell," he murmured, biting her tender skin.

She tsked with exasperation and tried to pull away, but he wasn't about to release her.

"You didn't talk to me all night," she said, "and now, you bluster in as if I should be happy to see you."

"You *should* be happy."

"You're deranged. You understand that, don't you?"

"If I'm acting crazy, you're the one who's driven me insane."

"There are so many absurd parts to that comment that I don't know where to start in addressing them. I've never driven a man insane in my life, and I would have no idea how."

"Maybe you're more of a vixen than you realize."

She squirmed away and lurched over to the end of the bed. She stared at him like an irritated nanny.

"What do you want, Mr. Shawcross?"

"Call me Raven."

"No. You show up at Carter Crossing with your brother. You pretend to be horse traders, and you begin a flirtation with me."

He raised a brow. "It's been very fun too."

"You depart the property—without a goodbye to me."

"Did I break your heart?"

She didn't answer his question. "Then you strut in to attend Clayton's birthday party. You proclaim yourself to be Raven Shawcross, famed African explorer. What am I to make of such an odd sequence of events?"

"I have some business dealings with Clayton," he said, which was putting it mildly. "I decided to conduct an investigation first, so I could learn more about the sort of man he is."

"You spied on us."

"Yes," he bluntly confessed.

"You lied—about your identity, about your purpose."

"Perhaps."

"Is your name really Shawcross? Are you really an African explorer? For all I know, you might be a confidence artist who's merely declared himself to be Mr. Shawcross."

"Sir Sidney's son is Sebastian Sinclair, and he's my friend. So is Nathan Blake. He's Lord Selby. Should I have them send you a letter to verify who I am?"

He was watching her closely, and at his mentioning Sebastian and Nathan, she blanched with surprise—or it might have been dismay. He wondered why. She was an orphan, living on an isolated, rural estate. Why would they mean anything to her?

"You deceived me," she said, and her cheeks flamed bright red, as if she was embarrassed.

Yes, he had, but she was in the dark as to which facts. She'd be apprised very soon though. "How have I deceived you? I told you who I am. I told you I'm a horse trader, and it's one of my many commercial ventures. I delivered the animals to Clayton as I promised I would. What part of that is a deception?"

"Don't twist my words," she scolded, looking very forlorn. "I thought you liked me. I thought you enjoyed my company, but your interest was fake. Every minute I spent with you—it was fake."

"It wasn't fake."

"What was it then? At the very least, I believed we were cordial, but this morning, I had to hear from a footman that you'd left. You couldn't even be bothered to inform me."

"I wasn't actually leaving," he said.

"How was I supposed to know that? You completely ignored me at Clayton's party. Why? Are you too marvelous to socialize with lowly old me? Are you so impressive that you couldn't have your snooty chums realize we were connected?"

"It wasn't that at all. I was busy with Clayton and his mother."

"And let's not forget Millicent. You were certainly *busy* with her."

He grinned. "Are you jealous?"

"I'd have to *like* you to be jealous, and I don't like you. I hate you."

"You do not."

"Have you even the slightest clue what my life is like?"

"I have a fairly good idea."

"No, you don't. You couldn't possibly imagine it."

She was wrong, but he wouldn't try to convince her.

After his father had been arrested, Raven's world had collapsed in an instant. The scandal had been splashed across the newspapers, with spurious charges leveled by Charles Carter. His father had been too stunned to figure out how to save himself. He'd killed himself in prison, and it had ignited a downhill spiral of tragedy.

His mother had died of shame, then he and his siblings had been separated. The sole ally who'd stood by his father through the debacle had found schools to admit them, but they'd been charity students, dressed in worn clothes from the church basket and no pennies to ease their way.

Raven had quickly learned how poverty and disgrace were like a stench a boy couldn't wash off.

The early period had been incredibly difficult. He'd felt such a burden to support himself so he could afford a home and bring his brother and sister to live with him, but he'd only been ten when it had started. It had taken him years of dubious scheming and rigged gambling to accumulate sufficient funds to purchase a spot with Sir Sidney when he was eighteen.

By the time he'd grown rich from his travels and could have rescued his siblings, Lydia had been seduced by a scoundrel and had passed away in child-birth, and Lucas had become a delinquent with a criminal history.

Raven had discovered what it meant to be scorned, to not belong anywhere. The difference between him and Rebecca Carter was that he'd had a grand life, a wealthy father, a doting mother, and a beautiful property in the country.

In the blink of an eye, it had all been yanked away. What was worse? To once have had so much and to lose it? Or to never have had anything in the first place?

"Let's not quarrel, Rebecca," he said. "I'm not about to fight with you."

"We're not fighting. I'm simply telling you that you're an ass, and I'm delighted that you've listened to my complaints. I'm finished voicing them though. And *don't* call me Rebecca. You don't have my permission."

"I don't care if you like it or not. I always behave precisely as I please, so I'll do it anyway."

"That doesn't surprise me. You are a bully and a fiend. Feel free to leave whenever you're ready."

He smiled at her as if she was being ridiculous. She stomped to the door and grabbed the knob, having forgotten it was locked and the key was in his pocket.

"Give me the key," she fumed.

"No."

"Are you intending to keep me as your prisoner?"

"Maybe."

"For how long? I insist you apprise me, so I have some idea of how long I'll be forced to tolerate your odious company."

"You think I'm odious?"

"It's the nicest term I can use to describe you. I'm much too polite to tell you my true opinion, for I would never utter the hideous words it would require."

She was bristling with indignation, and he was so intrigued to witness her fit of pique. Her hands were on her hips, her shoulders squared, and she was balanced on the balls of her feet, as if she were a pugilist in the boxing ring.

Her phantom twin, the loathsome Miss Robertson whom she denied knowing, stood the same way when she was angry. Her eyes flashed with the same heat.

When he'd initially met Rebecca, he'd thought she resembled Miss Robertson exactly, but now, he deemed them to be even more similar. The odd parallels made him want to throw her in a coach and convey her to London where he would push the two of them together. What reaction might it produce? If they were in such close proximity, might the whole world explode?

He reached out and clasped hold of her arm, and even though he barely touched her, she winced and jerked away.

"Ow!" she protested.

"What? I couldn't have hurt you."

"No, I just ... ah ... have a bad bruise."

He seized her arm and stretched it out, examining it to find several very clear bruises that definitely looked as if they'd been left by fingerprints. No doubt about it, someone had marked her in a livid, violent manner.

"Who was it?" he demanded.

"It doesn't matter."

She stared mulishly, and he said, "You might as well confide in me. I won't stop pestering you until you do."

She wrenched away, showing him her back.

"If you must know," she said, "it was Clayton. But it was ... nothing. He was drunk, and it was late."

Raven's blood ran cold. No, not cold. It ran red hot, pouring like lava through every limb and vein.

"You excuse him because he was inebriated?" he asked.

"Well, he *was* drunk. It *was* late."

"How did you get away?"

"My young cousin, Alex? He interrupted us, and Clayton is a coward. Alex and I walked off, and the incident was over."

"Are you scared of him?"

She pondered, then shook her head. "No. I'm sure it won't happen again. In fact, I bet if I scolded him about it, he wouldn't even remember what occurred."

Raven recalled how—when she'd entered the room—she'd suffered a terrible fright. Had she assumed he was Clayton? Had she any notion what a rogue like Clayton could do to a woman?

Since she was a spinster, probably not.

He snuggled himself to her, his front pressed to her back, and he bent down and kissed her on the shoulder.

"He'll never touch you again," he said. "I swear it."

"How could you prevent it? Besides, I don't need to worry. I'll simply stay out of the halls at night until he's departed for London."

Raven thought of her, afraid in her own home, afraid in her own bedchamber, and his rage spiraled to an alarming height. He had quite a bit of revenge to extract from Clayton Carter, and she'd just given him a reason to remove yet another pound of flesh.

Clayton was the type who would feel strong when he was inflicting himself on a defenseless female. As with his mother, Beatrice, Raven couldn't wait to see how brave he was when he was facing a really irate, really powerful man.

He'd spent enough time chatting with her, and he was weary from the lengthy day of plotting and socializing. He wrapped an arm around her waist, spun her, and tumbled them onto the bed. It was scant more than a cot, and he was surprised it could support their combined weight, that it hadn't crashed to the floor.

They were lying on their sides, nose to nose, and she glared at him as if he'd lost his mind. Perhaps he had.

"Mr. Shawcross! Let me up."

"No."

"I can't be on a bed with you!"

"You already are."

She attempted to scoot away, but he wasn't about to allow her to escape. He pinned her to the mattress, a hand on her tummy, a leg over her thigh, then he dipped in and kissed her.

"I'm exhausted tonight," he said. "Don't be angry with me."

"I am so far beyond angry that it's not possible to clarify what I'm feeling."

"I think you like me a little. Can't you try to recollect that you do?"

"First, you'd have to explain the scheme you're hatching."

"I can't. You have to find out with everyone else."

"Why?"

"Because you're a Carter, and I can't abide any of you."

"If you can't abide me, why—pray tell—are you in my room?"

"I have no earthly idea."

"Ooh, I'll likely get in so much trouble because of you."

"I'm tired of our bickering," he said, "and I'd like you to supply me with some hint of why I've bothered with you a single second."

"I can't guess why you've bothered with me."

"I'm going to kiss you, and you're going to kiss me back."

"You are so arrogant," she said, "and you were horrid to me all night! Why would I have any fond sentiment remaining?"

"Maybe you don't, but kissing is fun anyway."

He gazed at her, and suddenly, he was considering things he'd never considered with a female before. What would it be like to keep her by his side forever? With a girl like her, that sort of arrangement only transpired through matrimony, and he would never marry a Carter. So what was he planning?

He couldn't imagine. She just made him feel better, so he kissed her again, and for once, she ceased her complaints and simply participated.

He wasn't much of a talker. He didn't dither and debate. He let his actions speak for him. He let his vicious tendencies speak for him. He let his courage and daring-do speak for him. His life had been filled with vigorous, manly men, and he'd liked it very much, but it was refreshing to snuggle with her. It wasn't an activity he'd engaged in very often, and he was thrilled to have the opportunity.

As she relaxed into the embrace, he pulled her nearer so their bodies were forged fast all the way down. Her pert breasts were pressed to his chest, her tummy and thighs crushed to his own. Her secret womanly places were riveting him, his cock hard as stone.

He rolled her onto her back, and he shifted so he was on top of her, and he was quickly growing overwhelmed, which was incredibly peculiar.

With his looks, money, and status as a member of the Sir Sidney expedition team, women threw themselves at him, hoping for a connection. He was never interested though, so it had been ages since he'd waded into such deep waters. He was definitely in over his head.

He yanked his lips from hers and buried his face at her nape. He hovered there, being swamped by various qualms: that he shouldn't dally with her, that he shouldn't flirt with her, that he shouldn't notice her at all. But he thought she was extraordinary. When she was amazingly beautiful, when she was kind and amusing and loyal, how could he fail to be charmed?

He drew away so he could study her, and she appeared irked, but worried about him too. Had anyone ever worried about him? He supposed his mother must have when he was a boy, but he couldn't recall what it had been like.

"Why have we stopped?" she asked.

"You drive me wild," he told her.

"That can't be true."

"It is, so I should probably get out of here before I do something I'll regret."

"What might you regret?"

"Your question reminds me of how innocent you are."

"Of course I'm an innocent. I'm a maiden and a spinster. How am I to know what you might accomplish if I let you proceed?"

"You'd like it. I can promise you that."

"Vain beast."

He sat up, and she popped up on an elbow and caressed a palm over his chest, directly over his heart where it always ached with remorse.

"You look positively morose," she said. "Have I upset you?"

"You could never upset me, and I'm not morose."

"I can see in your eyes that you are."

Usually, he was adept at hiding his emotions, and he couldn't believe she'd sensed his melancholy mood. He was elated that she'd noted such a personal detail, and it left him terribly afraid he might start to babble about issues that were none of her business, so he changed the subject.

"You might observe me trifling with your cousin, Millicent, but I'm not serious."

"Then why do it?"

He shrugged. "Because I can."

"You're a scoundrel—I agree—but why make me witness your bad behavior?"

"It won't continue for long."

"I'll have to warn her about you."

He chuckled. "What will you say?"

"I'll say you're a cad, and she should avoid you like the plague."

He nodded. "You can tell her all of that—just so *you* don't avoid me later on. And don't be jealous."

He leaned down and kissed her a final time, wondering if he'd have many more chances. On how many more occasions would he be with her like this?

Fleetingly, he fretted about what would become of her after her relatives were evicted. Where would she end up?

*You could support her...*

The prospect slithered by, shocking him with how much he liked the sound of it. He'd never previously considered having a mistress. Might she be amenable?

If she wound up with nowhere to live, she might be. Poverty had a swift way of focusing a woman's attention, of forcing her to settle for options she wouldn't normally have pondered.

"I'll see you tomorrow," he said.

"Does your comment indicate you'll grace us with your magnificent presence for at least one more day?"

"Yes, for at least another day." He clasped her hand and linked their fingers. "Tell me you're glad about it."

"I'm not telling you that."

"Why not?"

"Because your ego is so massive, if I stroke it any further, you won't be able to walk out of here."

He laughed. "You know me so well."

He stood, straightened his clothes, then went to the door. He unlocked it, then tossed her the key.

"Lock up after me," he said.

"I will."

"I'm not joking. I don't want you to have any unexpected visitors."

"Clayton won't stumble in. I'm sure of it."

"Lock up for me anyway," he said more sternly, "and when I come down to breakfast, you better be in the dining room and eager to serve me."

"I never *serve* anyone. Go away, you insolent oaf."

He missed her already, and he nearly declared the ridiculous sentiment, but he managed to bite down the words.

As he would have exited into the hall, she asked, "Would you talk to your brother for me?"

"About what?"

"I last saw him down on the verandah, and he claimed to have an assignation out on the beach. He wouldn't admit who it was with, but I really wish he wouldn't ruin any of our housemaids."

Raven sighed, suspecting he could guess precisely who Lucas's target had been. "I'll speak to him, but it's probably pointless."

He stepped out and pulled the door closed. He waited to hear her jump up after him, but she didn't, and he murmured, "Rebecca! Lock the door."

"Oh!"

The bed creaked, then she scurried over, and the key was spun.

"Goodnight, Raven," she whispered.

"Goodnight, Rebecca. Sleep tight."

He laid his palm on the wood, and he held it there. He shut his eyes and imagined her doing the same.

Then he realized he was behaving like a smitten fool, and he whipped away and tiptoed off. He considered heading to his own bed, but first, he had to track down Lucas and order him to leave Millicent Carter alone.

When the swaggering boy turned on his charm, no girl was safe.

# CHAPTER

## 7

"CLEARLY, HE FANCIES HER."

"I suppose."

Rebecca's response was tepid and noncommittal.

She was sitting at the breakfast table, with Beatrice as her only companion. Clayton and his guests had reveled late into the night, so none of them would stagger down for hours. She and Beatrice had the room and the food to themselves.

"Why else would he give her those blasted earrings?" Beatrice asked. "I was awake until dawn, trying to figure it out. He must want to marry her."

"He's very rich. Maybe it's simply his nature to make grand gestures."

"Rich men are never generous. How do you imagine they become rich? It certainly isn't by throwing their money away on diamond earrings for a silly girl who's barely out of the schoolroom."

"Then he might have merely been showing off."

"What if I wound up with him as my son-in-law? My goodness! What a stroke of luck that would be!"

Rebecca couldn't bear the conversation another second, and she wasn't about to continue participating in it. Her own relationship was developing with Mr. Shawcross, and she was about to bust with the dangerous news that he'd snuck into her bedchamber.

How could she keep herself from being buried by all the secrets that were piling up?

She swallowed her last bite of food, then said, "I realize you've placed Mr. Shawcross up on a pedestal, but may I share an issue about him that's vexing me?"

"You may share whatever you like—so long as it's not derogatory."

Rebecca was conflicted and feeling horridly guilty. Beatrice was eagerly mulling the possibility that Mr. Shawcross might wed Millicent, but Rebecca was sure it would never happen. He was raising their expectations for no reason Rebecca could discern, *and* he'd told her he wasn't sincere about her cousin.

It was obvious he had a scheme proceeding, and Clayton was at the center of it, but Clayton was a buffoon who wouldn't notice a runaway carriage barreling down on him until it was too close to avoid being trampled.

It would never occur to him to wonder why he'd been befriended by such a wealthy, notorious fellow. Clayton believed he was interesting and remarkable, and he'd view the alliance as being precisely what he deserved.

There was so much chaos brewing that Rebecca simply thought she should brace herself and be ready to duck when they began to be pelted by the rubble of the mess Mr. Shawcross fomented.

"It's not exactly derogatory," she said, "but there are a few facts I think you should know."

Beatrice tossed down her fork. "Such as?"

"He and his brother have been here for several days. They delivered Clayton's horses, and they camped out in the barn and pretended to be ordinary working men."

"Why would they do that?"

"I have no idea, but perhaps—before you get too excited about his flirting with Millicent—you should find out."

"I don't need to find out. Clayton has vouched for him and that's all the information I require."

"There's one other piece of it."

"I'm absolutely on pins and needles waiting for you to apprise me."

"When Mr. Shawcross arrived at the party, Mr. Melville was still present. He watched Mr. Shawcross dance attendance on Millicent, and he was very hurt by it."

"Why would I care about that?"

"He plans to marry Millicent. You can't act as if you're unaware of his intentions."

"Well, he might be dreaming about having her as his bride, but he's never taken any steps to make it a reality. If Mr. Shawcross asks for her hand, I won't hesitate to accept. Mr. Melville is nice enough, but there's no comparison between them."

Rebecca inhaled a deep breath, then slowly let it out. "Mr. Melville recognized him. They were acquainted at school as boys."

"So? Mr. Melville went to school forever. He likely had many classmates."

"He claimed Mr. Shawcross's surname is Stone. That it's Raven *Stone.* He was quite adamant about it."

At Rebecca voicing the name *Stone,* Beatrice blanched with astonishment, but she quickly recovered her aplomb as she casually inquired, "*Stone,* is it? I've never heard of the family."

Beatrice might have denied any knowledge, but she glanced away, her furtiveness providing blatant evidence that she was lying.

"We should contact Sir Sidney's son, Sebastian Sinclair," Rebecca said.

Beatrice scowled. "Why would we?"

"I'm not positive Mr. Shawcross is who he says he is. He might be an imposter. Even as we speak, the *real* Mr. Shawcross might be sitting in London and not at Carter Crossing at all."

"Why would he impersonate the real Mr. Shawcross?"

"Who can guess? He has a plot hatching, and I predict—when he reveals what it is—we'll all be burned by it. I hope Clayton hasn't loaned him any money."

Beatrice huffed with aggravation. "Clayton's finances aren't any of your concern."

"No, they're not, but if Mr. Shawcross is a confidence artist, and he's duping Clayton, we'll all be sorry."

"Your comments are noted." Beatrice gestured to Rebecca's empty plate. "You're finished eating, so you're excused. With so many guests in residence, you have plenty of chores."

Rebecca sighed. What more could she do? She'd tried to warn Beatrice that dodgy events were occurring, but she wouldn't listen.

She pushed back her chair and stood. "If it all blows up later on, please don't blame me."

"You're *excused,* Rebecca," Beatrice stated more sharply. "If you stumble on Millicent, notify her I have to talk to her right away."

"About what?"

"If I thought it was any of your business, I'd tell you Mr. Shawcross is taking her on a carriage ride."

"After what I just told you, you'll encourage her to join him?"

"Why wouldn't I? Besides, you've always been jealous of her. You're merely sowing seeds of distrust in my mind, so I'll reject Mr. Shawcross if he proposes."

"*I* am jealous of Millicent? Are you joking?"

"No. It wouldn't surprise me in the slightest to learn you'd like to wreck this for her."

"That might be the worst thing you've ever said to me."

"I doubt that. I'm sure I've said many other things that were much more horrid, and I've had enough of you for one morning."

Beatrice began eating again, making it clear that Rebecca was dismissed. She spun away and stomped out.

"WHAT IS IT, MOTHER?" Millicent asked. "Rebecca demanded I attend you at once. I was hardly dressed."

"I have some news."

"About what?"

"About Mr. Shawcross."

Beatrice was still seated at the dining table, having continued to feast after Rebecca's departure. Millicent plopped into the chair across and inquired, "Which Mr. Shawcross?"

"The older one."

"What about him?"

"He's taking you for a carriage ride this afternoon."

"Oh." Millicent wrinkled up her nose. "Must I go?"

When Beatrice was a girl, she'd never been pretty or popular. She'd never had suitors lined up at her door, but if she'd ever had a dashing rake like Raven Shawcross stroll in her parlor, she'd have fainted dead away.

"Must you *go*?" She was aghast. "You act as if it would be a huge burden."

"He's so grouchy, and with all those black clothes, he seems quite sinister to me. He and I would have nothing in common."

"He's rich as Croesus," Beatrice pointed out, "and he's famous to boot. It doesn't matter if you *like* him or not. If he deigns to spend time with you, you'll agree with a smile on your face."

"I like his brother much better. He's much more charming."

"His brother? Don't be ridiculous."

"They're not aristocrats. If I set my cap for the other one, it's not as if I'll be losing out on a dukedom."

"A woman never picks the younger brother. It's ludicrous."

"Maybe so, but he's much more handsome and much less odious."

Beatrice shook her head with disgust. "Raven Shawcross owns diamond mines and possesses a fortune. *He* is a member of Sir Sidney's team of explorers. If Lucas Shawcross has a penny in his purse, it's because Raven Shawcross put it there."

Millicent rolled her eyes in a way that made Beatrice yearn to reach across the table and slap her.

"You fixate on the silliest issues," Millicent said, but Beatrice ignored her.

"He'll meet you in the driveway at two o'clock. Wear your most fetching gown."

"You're not listening to me!" Millicent protested. "I don't want to flirt with him, and I can't bear to get to know him. For some reason, he's noticed me, and I wish he hadn't!"

"You will obey me in this. I won't argue about it."

"There's something dodgy about them. I ought not to speak with either one."

"What do you mean?"

"I *mean* that I ran into Mr. Lucas Shawcross on the verandah last night, and he told me I shouldn't pawn those earrings his brother gave me because they're fake."

"They wouldn't be."

"And he and his brother actually arrived a few days ago to deliver Clayton's new horses. They were pretending to be horse dealers, and now, they're ensconced in the manor and strutting about like a pair of lazy kings. Who behaves like that?"

Beatrice was taken aback. Rebecca had voiced the same concerns, and she'd claimed Mr. Melville and Shawcross had been school classmates when they were boys—and that his true surname was Stone.

The name *Stone* always sent a shiver down her spine, and ever since Rebecca had mentioned the prospect, she'd been pondering Harrison Stone. She'd never met him. Her husband, Charles, had worked for him, and the Stones had lived in London and Beatrice and Charles in Frinton.

Charles had been a trusted clerk at Harrison's company of Stone Shipping. The offices had been located at the wharf in Frinton, where he'd overseen the loading and unloading of the ships.

Harrison had been married, and his wife was Blanche. They'd had some children, but for the life of her, Beatrice couldn't recollect how many or what their names had been.

Charles had bankrupted Harrison Stone and had nearly bankrupted Lord Coxwold who'd been their biggest customer. Then, when his embezzlement had begun to unravel, he'd blamed it all on Harrison, but Charles had had a felonious heart, and he'd been prepared for that eventuality.

He'd skillfully covered his tracks, and he'd scooted away unscathed, painted as a hero in the newspapers and the law courts. Harrison had been sentenced to prison, a broken man who'd had no money left to hire a lawyer to defend himself.

Early on, Beatrice had occasionally felt guilty over what Charles had done to Harrison. But as the years had passed, and she'd stepped into Harrison's affluent world, she'd gradually convinced herself that she deserved what Charles had stolen from the Stone family.

Could any of the Stone children have survived their ordeal?

She'd never considered the situation before, had never wondered about them. Surely, after their father had died in prison, their lives had been ruined too. There was no way one of them could have grown up to rub elbows with Sir Sidney or own African diamond mines. The notion was too preposterous to contemplate.

No, Raven Shawcross was not Raven Stone. Mr. Melville had to be mistaken.

"I have no idea why Mr. Shawcross initially stayed out in the barn," she said. "Perhaps he likes animals, and he was happy there. His motives don't matter to me."

"Well, they matter to me," Millicent snottily retorted. "I'd like to know what he's about. Wouldn't you?"

"I *know* what he's about. For reasons I can't fathom, he's developed an interest in you, and he's asked that you join him for a carriage ride at two. You *will* join him. If you refuse, I will drag you out to the driveway. Don't make me. I'm certain you would hate to have me reveal what a spoiled brat you are."

She could have eaten for another hour, but her insolent daughter had quashed her appetite. She tossed down her napkin, pushed back her chair, and stormed out.

PRESTON BOUNCED UP THE lane to Carter Crossing in his yellow gig. He wasn't a sporty fellow, so he shouldn't have purchased such a flashy conveyance. But he was anxious to show Millicent a more confident, fun-loving side to his character.

She was such a pretty, vivacious girl, and so far, he hadn't presented himself as the type of spouse she'd be eager to have. She was still young, and he had no doubt—when she fantasized about a husband—he wasn't anywhere near to being who she envisioned.

He'd be good for her though. He was kind, reliable, and very patient. He thought he'd be able to tolerate her quirks better than anyone else she might choose. Yet the possibility wouldn't have occurred to her, and he could hardly mention it.

He pulled up in front of the manor, and he tied the reins and jumped down. It was such a high leap to the ground, and he always wished he appeared jaunty when he descended, but he probably didn't. Two footmen came over to admire the vehicle, and he left them to it.

He planned every visit to Carter Crossing with enormous care, but he'd pretend he was stopping by on the spur of the moment. Whenever he attempted to arrange a specific activity with Millicent, she'd insist she was otherwise engaged, but if he arrived unannounced, he often caught her bored and at loose ends.

Hopefully, he'd catch her today too, and he'd coax her into taking a ride with him. If she couldn't be enticed, Miss Rebecca might like to go instead. She was a grand girl, and he liked her very much. She was the nicest person in the house really, and it was too bad he'd never become attached to her.

She'd have been a perfect wife, but the heart was an inexplicable organ. He'd set his sights on Millicent, and he couldn't be dissuaded from that goal.

As he marched up to the door, it opened, and Raven Shawcross exited. At Clayton's party, Preston had viewed Shawcross from across the room, so he hadn't gotten a close look at him. But he was getting a close look now.

"Mr. Shawcross?" he said. "Please forgive me for being presumptuous, but I believe we've met."

Shawcross studied him, his precise gaze roaming down Preston's torso in a rude manner. "I don't think so."

"I knew you at school—when we were nine. I'm Preston Melville. It's been a long time, and you won't remember me, but I definitely remember you."

Shawcross smirked. "You have me confused with someone else."

"I'm positive I don't, and I'm not confused." He forced a smile. "You were so popular, and you were smart and tough too. I always yearned to be just like you. I could have guessed you'd wind up as an African explorer. Your lofty career path is exactly what I would have expected from you."

"I'm delighted you approve."

Shawcross's tone was sarcastic. It was obvious he was irked by Preston's prattling, and with the exciting life Shawcross had led, Preston understood he would seem tedious, but he was terribly hurt by how Shawcross had been flirting with Millicent. If he was serious in his attentions, Preston wouldn't stand a chance.

"I'm curious about one detail though." Preston gulped, convinced he as about to ask a question that shouldn't be asked. "When we were boys, your name was Raven Stone. I'm certain of it. Why are you claiming a different identity?"

They were almost toe to toe, so Preston could clearly observe Shawcross's expression. He didn't flinch, didn't glanced away. He simply said, "I can't imagine what you're talking about. Now if you'll excuse me, I'm busy."

Footsteps sounded in the foyer, and Millicent burst outside, her maid following behind. She looked pretty as a picture, wearing a white dress with blue piping on the bodice and skirt. A blue ribbon encircled her waist, emphasizing how small it was. A straw bonnet framed her blond curls.

She didn't even see Preston and walked right by him.

"There you are!" She beamed at Shawcross. "I was so slow in getting ready, I was afraid you'd have departed without me."

Preston spoke up. "Hello, Miss Carter."

She peered at him and frowned. "Mr. Melville? What are you doing here?"

"I was . . . ah . . . in the neighborhood, and I thought you might like to go for a ride."

"I'm sorry, but I have plans this afternoon."

Shawcross offered his arm to her. She clasped hold, and they sauntered toward the stables. Preston watched them, and he was so forlorn it was pathetic.

A few minutes later, she and Shawcross promenaded by in a carriage, the two of them snuggled together on the front seat, her maid in the back as a chaperone. As they rounded the driveway, Miss Rebecca emerged from the manor and came over to him.

"Mr. Melville!" She appeared kind and happy as always. "This is a nice surprise. What brings you by?"

"I was hoping to socialize with Miss Carter, but it wasn't convenient."

Miss Rebecca stared at Millicent's carriage that was being swallowed by the trees. She sighed, comprehending his despondency.

"Yes, Millicent is occupied, but how about me? I'm eager for that ride you promised."

"Will you be dreadfully disappointed if I tell you I don't feel like it just now? Could we do it another time?"

"Of course," she gently agreed, and she laid a hand on his wrist. "I hate that you saw them leaving, but don't despair. He has no genuine interest in her."

"It seemed quite genuine to me."

"You're wrong. I talked to him about her, and he admitted that he's playing some sort of game with all of us. And she's so young; he'll soon tire of her."

"You're such an optimist, Miss Rebecca, but in this situation, it might be misplaced."

"You're exactly the fellow she needs, Mr. Melville. I refuse to let you give up."

"I pressed Mr. Shawcross about his surname. I accused him of being Raven Stone, but he insisted he's not."

"I mentioned that he's toying with us," she said. "I'm sure of it. He's toying with Millicent too, for reasons I can't begin to fathom."

"His father was Harrison Stone. I'd suggest you ask your Cousin Beatrice about his connection to her late husband, Charles, but you shouldn't."

"Why shouldn't I?"

"Because she'd likely kill the messenger." He couldn't bear to tarry, and he tipped his hat to her. "I'll bid you good day, Miss Rebecca. It was marvelous to see you."

"You too, Mr. Melville. Don't you dare go home and sulk."

"I won't," he lied.

"You must come back tomorrow and try again with Millicent. I'm positive she won't be busy."

He glared down the lane where Millicent had finally vanished with handsome, dashing Mr. Shawcross/Stone. "I don't know if I'll come tomorrow. I just don't know."

He trudged to his vehicle, climbed up, and left. He could have called to the horse and had it start to run, but he went as slow as possible, not keen to overtake Millicent. He wasn't certain what direction she'd traveled after she'd turned onto the main road, but he was too miserable to have to witness her smiling at Raven Shawcross ever again.

⁂

"ARE YOU MR. SHAWCROSS?"

Raven halted and spun around to find a boy of ten or so standing in the shadows by the barn. With his black hair and blue eyes, his slim physique and lanky frame, he reminded Raven of how Lucas had looked when they'd last spoken before he'd headed off to Africa. His brother had never been the same after that.

He'd just finished his tedious ride with Millicent Carter. Their fraternization had forced him to realize that he couldn't abide her, and it was stupid to drag her into his scheme. She was immature and exhausting, and he didn't have to trifle with her to accomplish his goals with regard to Beatrice and Clayton.

His actions toward Millicent had been for mere spite, and he had bigger fish to fry.

He could have handed her off to Lucas and let him break her heart, but that would have been a recipe for disaster. Raven had already warned him to stay away from her, and Lucas swore he would.

When Raven had confronted him about his sneaking off to the beach for a tryst, he'd claimed it had been with a housemaid, but Raven couldn't decide if he believed Lucas or not. Lucas was the best liar in the world, and if Raven learned his target had been Millicent after all, he'd have to beat his brother to a pulp. It was the only type of explanation that ever sank in.

"Yes, I'm Mr. Shawcross," he said. "May I help you?"

"I don't mean to bother you, but I'd like to ask you a question—if you might have a minute to answer it."

"Ask away. I'll answer if I can, but first, it's obvious you've learned my name, so I should probably know yours."

"It's Alex. Alex Carter."

So this was Rebecca's cousin, the one of whom she was so fond.

"You don't look like a Carter." They were all blond-haired and blue-eyed. From his black hair alone, he couldn't have much Carter blood in his veins. "How are you related to Clayton and Mrs. Carter?"

The boy hesitated, then said, "They're . . . ah . . . cousins."

"What's your question, Mr. Alex Carter?"

"I'm aware that Sir Sidney is deceased."

Raven should have guessed the topic would be Sir Sidney. Everyone inquired about him. He'd been a national icon, and people couldn't stop obsessing over him. Children included.

"Yes, he's passed on," Raven said.

"I was wondering if his son, Sebastian, might be planning another expedition to Africa."

"I doubt it, Alex. He was traumatized by his father's death."

"How about you? Might you schedule your own expedition?"

"I have no intention of returning either. I was traumatized too."

"Do you think any explorers will go again? Or do you imagine the British missions are finished?"

"There are other men there now," Raven said. "We'll never abandon the Dark Continent. There's too much to discover that's fascinating."

"Then this is what's vexing me: I'd like to join an expedition someday, and I've read Sebastian Sinclair's books about it, but he never mentions how much it costs."

"It's an enormous amount," Raven told him.

"How did you earn your initial stake? Did your father pay it for you? How did you manage?"

Raven had gambled and cheated at cards. He had a precise memory for numbers, and apparently deep down, he possessed much of Lucas's dubious character. He had a real knack for deception and fraud, and he'd figured out all sorts of ways to dupe acquaintances who shouldn't have been wagering with him in the first place.

He never gambled anymore. He didn't need the money, but also, he still regretted how he'd tricked all those ignoramuses. As penance, he never played cards.

He didn't suppose he ought to chat about nefarious activities with a child though. Nor should he talk about how he'd *cheated* to accumulate the necessary sum.

"I had a trust fund," he lied.

Alex nodded. "I was afraid it would be something like that."

"Is it hard for you to live here?"

"Yes. Occasionally, I feel as if—should I never escape Carter Crossing—I'll simply grow mad with longing. I spend all my time on the promontory, staring out at the ships sailing by. I always ponder where they're headed and wish I could be on one of them."

"You have a bad case of wanderlust, which I completely understand."

Alex sighed. "Sebastian Sinclair and his great friend, Lord Selby, started their treks to Africa when they were my age. Are there any other exploration teams that would take a boy like me? If I could find the money, that is."

He was so solemn in his query, and Raven smiled, trying to remember if he'd ever been that young, that innocent. He hoped Alex never suffered a dire moment in his life. He hoped it would be all sunshine and roses for him, but as a Carter, there was no chance for that optimistic ending.

"You're stuck with your Carter kin," Raven said, "so it must be difficult to envision a future."

"It is."

"In my opinion, a man can achieve whatever goal he sets his mind to, so

I'm sure you'll eventually devise a way to get to Africa."

"I'll tell myself you're correct."

Raven liked Alex very much and worried about what would become of him when the older Carters faced Raven's wrath. Fleetingly, he considered sending him away to school or maybe buying him a commission in the army in a few years.

A friend of Raven's father had helped him when his own world had fallen apart. Should Raven do the same? No! As with Rebecca, it didn't matter how much he liked Alex. The boy was a *Carter,* so Raven wouldn't let a flicker of sympathy flare.

He couldn't predict what might have happened, what he might have offered—or not—but Alex glanced out into the park. He frowned, so Raven glanced out too.

Rebecca was walking toward the beach for an afternoon stroll. Clayton was in the park too, with some of his male guests. They'd already been drinking and were being obnoxiously rowdy and rude. With Rebecca coming around the side of the house, she hadn't observed them yet.

"Would you excuse me, Mr. Shawcross?" Alex said. "I see my cousin, Rebecca, and I have to speak with her."

"Certainly, young Mr. Alex, and if any other questions occur to you, feel free to accost me again."

"I will, and thank you for bothering with me."

"It was no bother."

Alex hurried off, and Raven watched as, shortly, he caught up with Rebecca and deftly steered her away from Clayton. He continued to watch as Alex escorted her out to the beach. They appeared affectionately close, with Alex determined to protect her from Clayton.

Raven liked that type of behavior, and he was impressed that Alex would exhibit it. He was a bit jealous too that the boy was alone with Rebecca. Raven wanted to join them so desperately that he could practically taste it, but that was insane thinking.

He whipped away and went to the manor where he would lock himself in his fancy bedchamber and review his plans. It was time to make several moves that no one was going to like—except him.

# CHAPTER

## 8

REBECCA WAS ON THE promontory up above Carter Crossing and staring out at the water. She'd been particularly claustrophobic and had had to get out of the manor, so she'd climbed up the hill.

Ever since Mr. Shawcross had arrived, she'd been feeling trapped and unhappy. For reasons she couldn't clarify, he was making her question her circumstances. She was a viscount's daughter and an earl's sister, but throughout her life, she'd been denigrated and maligned.

Why had she put up with so much vilification? Why had she been content to settle for so little?

Her parents were a forbidden subject at Carter Crossing, but she found herself constantly pondering them. She always avoided the subject simply because Beatrice never uttered a positive comment about them.

When she'd been small, Beatrice had claimed they'd given her away because she'd been naughty and expensive to raise. As she'd grown older and had ceased to believe she'd been abandoned by them, Beatrice would harangue about how—when they'd died—Rebecca's lofty Blake relatives had been ready to send her to an orphanage, but Beatrice had saved her from that fate.

Rebecca didn't think any of Beatrice's stories about her parents were true. She had a few memories from her earliest years. Her mother had been beautiful and kind, her father handsome and dashing. Her brother, Nathan, had been brave and fearless, and she suspected she might have lived with him once.

Might he recall that he had a sister? If so, did he ever wonder what had happened to her? If she contacted him, how might he react?

Recently, she'd been desperately anxious to correspond with him, but he was Lord Selby now, and no man liked to be apprised that his father had been a libertine. If he didn't recall Rebecca being his half-sister, she didn't suppose he'd be pleased by the information.

Suddenly, an odd sensation swept into her mind. It was a peculiar thing that occurred occasionally. She had a guardian angel who watched over her and who appeared in her dreams. The angel spoke to Rebecca in her head too, and it seemed as if she was reaching in with her fingers and massaging Rebecca's thoughts.

*Are you there?* her angel asked.

*Yes, I'm here,* Rebecca answered.

*I'm searching for you. Where are you?*

*Come to me while I'm sleeping.*

The sweetest perception of safety washed over her, and it would persist for hours. It was such an interesting phenomenon, and whenever it transpired, she wished she could capture it in a bottle so the experience would last longer.

She pulled away from the water, but she couldn't bear to return to the manor just yet. She went over to the other side of the promontory to gaze at the Oakley mansion. It was such a pretty residence and too lovely to have fallen into disrepair.

As she glanced down, she was stunned to see the front doors were open. There were wagons in the driveway, and they were filled with lumber, tools, and other supplies, as if construction work was about to begin.

Had the property been sold? Was someone fixing it up with the intent to move in?

She'd be delighted to have the neglected place refurbished, but she was sad too. She'd always frivolously hoped it might be hers someday. The notion was a complete fantasy, but she clung to it anyway.

She walked down the trail to the house, not sure who she'd encounter, but she displayed her best smile. If the new owner was present, she'd be the first to welcome him.

The foyer was empty, and she called, "Hello? Is anyone home?"

When Raven Shawcross emerged from the shadows, she probably shouldn't have been surprised, but she was.

"Hello, Rebecca. I didn't expect you to stumble in."

She didn't bother to scold him for using her Christian name. He never listened, so what would be the point?

Since he'd taken his carriage ride with Millicent, she hadn't seen him, and she was relieved she hadn't. Even though he'd insisted he wasn't serious about Millicent, she couldn't help but be hurt by his behavior.

She was jealous of Millicent and brimming with envy. In a weird way, she'd started to view him as her own. She'd started to view herself as being special to him, but she should have realized how ridiculous the prospect was.

"The door was open," she told him, "and I assumed there might be a new neighbor I'd like to meet. I guess I was wrong."

She spun to leave, and he said, "I'm glad you're here."

"You are not. Don't tell lies. It's so annoying."

She kept on, and he snapped, "Rebecca!"

His tone was exasperated, as if no one ever ignored him and he couldn't deal with her disobedience.

*Don't stop!* she chided. *Don't turn around!*

She turned around. "What?"

"I just arrived myself. How about if you snoop through the rooms with me?"

"I'd rather not."

He sauntered over, approaching until they were toe to toe. He studied her expression and said, "Why are you so angry?"

"I'd have to care about you to be angry."

He chuckled. "You are so funny. You always entertain me, which is no small feat."

"How was your carriage ride with my cousin?"

She shouldn't have inquired. If she'd been a bigger person, she'd have pretended she wasn't peeved, but the words slipped out before she could swallow them down.

"You're jealous." He scoffed. "I told you not to be."

"I'm not jealous. I'm aggravated. It's clear you're courting my cousin, and with that as your ploy, you have no business flirting with me."

"I like flirting with you."

"Her erstwhile beau, Mr. Melville, was at Carter Crossing when you traipsed off with her. He was devastated."

"I'm finished with her, so he can have her back."

"How magnanimous you are!"

Her comment was very sarcastic, but she couldn't be more polite. Every paltry detail of her life—including him—was irritating her.

"She's too young for me," he said.

"You just noticed?"

"Well, I suspected it from the outset, but I didn't think the age difference would matter so much."

"And now?" she snidely asked.

"Now I'd throw myself off a cliff before I'd spend another afternoon with her."

She bristled. "I should be insulted on Millicent's behalf, but I'm actually relieved. I was certain there could be no benefit for her to have an association with you."

"What about you?" he asked. "Do you suppose there could be a benefit for *you* to have an association with me?"

"No. I believe I've previously indicated—if you get me in trouble—you'd never be worth it."

"I might surprise you."

"You haven't so far," she churlishly responded.

He laughed, and—as if they were adolescent sweethearts—he linked their fingers and started for the stairs.

"Where are we going?" she asked.

"I haven't been up to the bedchambers yet. Or to the servants' rooms in the attic. Look through them with me."

"Why are you in here? You appear to have a key. Have you bought it?"

"Yes, I bought it." He hesitated, then admitted, "It used to belong to my family. We'd visit occasionally when I was a boy."

She tripped, and he reached out to steady her. Mr. Melville's warning, about his being Raven Stone, rushed back.

"Your family owned this house?"

"Yes, my father."

"When we met that day up on the promontory, we talked about this property. You never mentioned your connection to it."

He shrugged. "I don't generally discuss my past."

"Why not?"

"I just don't." Then he said, "We had a shipping company on the coast."

"Did you grow up in the Frinton area?"

"No, London. My father was out here quite a bit though."

She tried to remember if she'd known his father, but if they'd crossed paths, she couldn't recall.

"Are your parents still alive?" she asked.

"They've been deceased for twenty years."

"How old are you now?"

"Thirty."

"They died when you were ten."

"Yes."

"After you were orphaned, what became of you?"

"I traveled an interesting road," was all he would say about it. "Quit pestering me with questions and come upstairs. Let's see what sort of mess I have to clean up."

"Are you planning to restore the place? Will you live in it?"

"Maybe. Or maybe not. It depends on how things shake out the next few weeks."

"What things?"

"Since my parents passed away, I've never really belonged anywhere. I can't decide if I'm ready to put down roots, and if I am, whether this should be the spot. I might simply tear down the house so nature can reclaim it."

Her jaw dropped. "Don't you dare tear down this house! If you don't want it, give it to me. I'll cherish it forever—as you apparently don't."

"Come," he said again, and she relented and accompanied him.

A grand staircase ascended to a landing with a balustrade that looked down on the foyer, and she enjoyed a quick vision of children peeking through the railing as fancy guests arrived. It was a happy image that galvanized her affection for the decrepit building, and she wouldn't permit him to raze it.

If she accomplished nothing else during their acquaintance, she would nag at him until he understood the value of renovating it.

Halls went in three directions, and they proceeded down the one that would take them toward the ocean. They walked to where it ended at an ostentatious suite.

"This was my father's bedchamber," he said. "My siblings and I were never allowed inside it."

"Siblings?" she asked. "You have others besides your brother?"

"We had a sister, but she's deceased too."

"You've suffered so many losses! If you keep telling me about them, I might begin to feel sorry for you. It certainly helps to explain why you're so difficult."

"I'm not difficult," he huffed. "Well, I might be a *little* difficult."

They entered the sitting room, the bedchamber behind it. There was furniture present, but it was covered with sheets. Paintings had been removed and were piled on the floor. The rugs had been rolled and stacked along the wall.

"I've noticed the furniture is still here," she said. "Is any of it from your family? Might you stumble on some heirlooms?"

"I doubt it. We lost everything—in a tragedy—so every item here must have been Mr. Oakley's. Our possessions were all sold, right down to the spoons in the drawers."

"My goodness! Stop sharing your sob stories. You're breaking my heart."

"I like the sound of that. Will you be nicer to me now?"

"I've been plenty *nice* to you, much nicer than you deserve."

He grinned. "Perhaps."

He led her over to a window, and he unlatched the shutters and shoved them open. They looked out on the weedy, overgrown park that stretched to the beach.

Once again, she pictured herself living in the house, waking up every morning and peering out at a beautiful garden that was lovingly tended. He was so ungrateful about the property. Why should he be lucky enough to own it?

They dawdled for an eternity, staring out at the stunning vista, and, to her great joy, he flung an arm over her shoulders and nestled her to his side. She shouldn't have snuggled with him so intimately, but when he was near, she simply couldn't behave as she ought.

"What was the tragedy that occurred in your past?" she eventually asked. "What happened to all of you?"

"I *might* tell you about it someday."

"Is it hard for you to talk about it?"

"It's not hard especially. It just makes me angry. On such a splendid afternoon, I'd rather not ponder it."

"Will you ever get to the point where it doesn't make you incredibly angry?"

"Probably not."

"If you'd like to confide in me, I'm a good listener."

"Yes, you are," he agreed, "but that doesn't mean I'll spill my secrets to you."

She smiled at him, and when she did, he dipped down and kissed her. She couldn't say she hadn't been hoping he would, and she knew she shouldn't participate, but she couldn't convince herself it was wrong.

He pulled her to him, so the front of her body was pressed to his all the way down. He towered over her, his chest so broad, his shoulders so wide. They were the kind of shoulders a woman could lean on when she was lonely or afraid.

She bet he wasn't afraid of anything, and she wondered what it would be like to have such a fierce, tough man in her life.

Thrilling ideas flitted through her mind. He seemed to like her very much, and while she constantly told herself she *didn't* like him, it was a lie. Could they have a future? What might he think about that?

There appeared to be some destiny at work in their meeting. She'd always adored Oakley, had always imagined the grand old mansion superbly restored and her residing in it. And here she was, kissing him in the master's suite.

Why couldn't they wind up together? Why couldn't she have him for her very own?

She never reached out and grabbed for what she craved because her dreams never came true. But why not reach for Raven Shawcross? Why not toss the dice for once?

"You make me feel better," he said as he drew away.

"I'm glad. Are you really finished with Millicent?"

"Yes."

"Good."

He smirked. "My jealous little Rebecca. I wouldn't have pegged you as a possessive type."

"I'm not usually. I simply can't bear to have you focused on anyone but me."

"I can tell. I'm a very vain fellow, so I will admit to being delighted that you're fixated on me."

He was smiling too, and she realized that she'd rarely seen him smile. Was it because of the disaster that had happened to his family when he was a boy? Or had his whole life been hard?

She'd like to quiz him about his travels with Sir Sidney Sinclair. How had an orphan managed to join in such a fantastic adventure? And she suspected it hadn't all been fun and games. He was back in England because Sir Sidney had been brutally murdered in Africa, so she supposed his itinerant existence hadn't been all that glamorous.

There was such poignant emotion in the air. It was the perfect time for speaking frankly. When he gazed at her so fondly, she was sure he was suffering from the same affectionate feelings that were plaguing her.

She was so eager for him to provide some hint of his intentions. She'd previously engaged in that one fleeting amour when she was seventeen, so she couldn't guess how a romance bubbled into a bigger connection. Unless he professed heightened sentiment, she never could.

He kissed her again and murmured, "Let's check out the bedroom."

It wasn't close to the comment she'd been dying to hear, and she could have kicked herself for being so foolish. She'd always been told that women and men were totally different animals, that they honed in on completely different issues as being important, and he'd just proved that adage.

She was pondering love, and he was pondering lust.

"Let's not," she said. "The blankets are probably dusty anyway."

"Does that mean—once I've had it cleaned—you'll be happy to loaf in there with me?"

"No, it doesn't mean that, and merely because you snuck into my bedchamber, you shouldn't automatically assume that I'm loose. I don't plan to lie down on a bed with you ever again."

"That sounds like a challenge. It makes me want to corrupt you."

"I am *not* corruptible."

He snorted. "We'll see about that."

He started in again, kissing her as if they were the last two people who would ever kiss. He was holding her so tightly, his palms roving over her back, arms, and hips. She felt as if her body had been electrified, as if he'd imbued it with an energy she'd never be able to tamp down.

Suddenly, from behind them, a man cheerily called, "Hello? Hello? Is anyone up here?"

They jumped apart as Preston Melville strolled in. He looked dapper as ever, in the tidy suit and bowler hat he wore when he was trotting through the countryside.

Rebecca couldn't decide which of them was more astonished, her or Mr. Melville. She was aghast to have been caught in such a shocking circumstance, and *he* was obviously shocked to have caught her in it. As to Mr. Shawcross, he never exhibited much excitement in any situation.

"Miss Rebecca?" Mr. Melville said, as he stumbled to a halt. "Ah . . . fancy meeting you here. And Mr. Stone! Or should I say Shawcross?"

Rebecca smoothed a nervous hand across her hair. "What did you need, Mr. Melville? May we help you?"

"I was driving up the lane to Oakley." His concerned gaze flicked from her to Mr. Shawcross, then back to her again. "I like the curve in the driveway; it's thrilling to race around it in my gig."

"I'm sure it is," she tepidly agreed.

"I saw the wagons of lumber and the open door, and with Oakley being vacant for so long, I figured someone must have finally purchased it. I wanted to greet our new neighbor."

"I purchased it," Mr. Shawcross said.

"Well . . . isn't that something?" Mr. Melville mused. "So . . . ah . . . I'm sorry to interrupt, and I'll just be going."

"May I walk you out?" she asked him.

"No, no, I can find the way." He spun away, then he stopped and whipped around. His look was beseeching. "Miss Rebecca, would you come with me? Please? I don't believe I ought to leave you alone with him."

She sensed Mr. Shawcross bristling—as if he might hurl an insult—and she hurriedly said, "I'm fine, Mr. Melville."

"Are you?" The question hung in the air, and his furious attention shifted to Mr. Shawcross and stayed there.

"You should be off, Melville," Mr. Shawcross told him. "There's naught occurring in this room that is any of your business."

Mr. Melville focused on Rebecca again. "I'm certain Mrs. Carter wouldn't like this, and I'd hate for you to get yourself into trouble with her."

"Don't fret, Mr. Melville. I'm about to depart myself."

"Come with me!" he earnestly repeated.

Mr. Shawcross stepped in front of her, blocking her from Mr. Melville's view, as if he was protecting her from the kindly man.

"Goodbye, Melville," he said. "You claimed to know the way out or would you like me to show you?"

"No, I can go on my own."

He hovered another second, giving Rebecca a chance to change her mind, but she couldn't force herself away. Her entire encounter with Mr. Shawcross had been divine, and she wasn't ready for it to conclude so abruptly.

Mr. Melville's shoulders slumped. "I guess I'll see you at Carter Crossing then. Be careful."

Then he marched out, and they listened as his strides faded down the hall.

Once it was silent again, she began to shake, and Mr. Shawcross pulled her into his arms. He held her until her trembling abated.

"Oh, my lord!" she muttered. "That was hideous."

"Will he tattle to Mrs. Carter?"

"I doubt it. He's very nice. He wouldn't deliberately harm me."

"If you're imperiled because of this, track me down immediately. Your cousins won't have many more opportunities to be awful to you."

"I won't ask what you mean by that."

"You'll find out very soon." Tears flooded her eyes, and he frowned and inquired, "Are you about to cry on me?"

"No, I'm simply so embarrassed. I want others to think the best of me, and I try hard to guarantee that they do. I never like to diminish myself in anyone's esteem."

"He's a tedious dolt. His opinion of you is irrelevant."

"No, it's not. He lives nearby, and he's an acquaintance. He might even wind up married to Millicent. I couldn't bear it if he thought I was loose or immoral."

"You worry too much."

"You're from London, so you don't have any idea how these petty scandals play out in a small town. Everything matters, especially reputation, and I am quite sick with regret."

"I never deemed *regret* to be an emotion worth suffering."

"You wouldn't, but you're male and you're rich, so you can afford to act however you like. I can't."

She drew away and went to the window to stare out at the beautiful scenery. If he didn't speak up and tell her that he envisioned a future for them, she shouldn't ever come back to Oakley.

"Now that you own this property," she said without turning around, "will you change the name? Or will you keep it as Oakley?"

"I'll likely change it."

"To what?"

"To what it used to be."

"What was that?"

"Stone Crossing."

A shiver slithered down her spine. Was Mr. Melville's story about him being Raven Stone actually true? What else could it indicate?

"I have to get home," she said. "I'm positive people are frantically looking for me."

"You can visit me whenever you like. I figure you'll be curious about how the renovations are progressing."

"I can't visit again. It's too dangerous."

She glanced out a final time, then walked to the door, skirting by him so he couldn't touch her. If he did, she'd never escape.

"I was serious about Mrs. Carter," he said, "and I'll add your cousin, Clayton, to the list too. If they bother you over any issue, let me know. I'll put an end to it."

"I don't need any help with them. They're my *family*."

"Which isn't much in my book."

"I can't imagine what you're planning, Raven *Stone,* but please don't allow your rage to pummel me. I haven't ever hurt you, so I'd appreciate it if you wouldn't hurt me in return."

"I'll try not to."

As he voiced the remark, he appeared cold and bitter—and very, very alone.

"Are you still staying with us at Carter Crossing?" she asked. "Or have you packed your bags and snuck out without my realizing it?"

"Yes, I'm still there. Clayton's party is proceeding for the next fortnight. I intend to revel with him."

She didn't dare ponder what his *reveling* might involve. "I'll see you again then. Thank you for showing me the house. I've always loved it."

"I'm glad you stopped by."

He was so disconnected from her—as if they hadn't kissed a single time.

How did he switch his emotions on and off like that? She'd certainly never developed such an icy ability.

She hurried out without another word, being extremely relieved that Mr. Melville had arrived. If he hadn't burst in and yanked her to her senses, there was no predicting how she might have disgraced herself in order to make Mr. Shawcross happy. She definitely had a new understanding of how a girl got herself in trouble.

She practically ran down the stairs and outside, and she continued to run all the way home, not slowing until she was off the promontory and approaching the manor.

Hopefully, she hadn't been missed, but if she had been, she couldn't deduce what excuses she'd provide. What lie could she possibly tell that wouldn't land her in more of a jam than she probably already was?

# CHAPTER
## 9

"Will you come into Frinton with me?"

Clayton glared at his mother and scoffed. "No. I have a houseful of guests who are eager to be entertained. Why would I traipse off with you instead?"

"It's the day of the month when I stop by the shipping office to sign paperwork."

He waved toward the door. "So sign away. Why bother me over it?"

"It's been so long since you visited the company. When you're the owner, it's vital to occasionally display an interest."

"There's the problem for you, Mother. I have no interest whatsoever. Don't expect me to pretend about it."

"I wish you'd at least *try* to exhibit some authority." Beatrice's cheeks heated—as if she was about to confess a shameful secret. "I'm having trouble with the men you've put in charge. They don't listen to me."

"And you think *I* could make them?"

"Men like to deal with men. They don't heed women."

"With good reason," he muttered.

"It's been getting worse."

"Well, fire them and replace them with some idiots who are more malleable. Honestly, I don't understand why it seems so complicated to you."

They were in the dining room, which was the one spot you could be certain to find his mother. She was an absolute glutton, and it was humiliating to have his acquaintances discover what sort of parent he had, but he supposed everyone had relatives who were an embarrassment.

His sister was seated at the table too, and she chimed in with, "Don't be such an ass, Clayton. What could it hurt to escort her into Frinton? It will just be an hour or two. You'll be back in plenty of time to over-imbibe with your disgusting friends."

He glanced about, frantic to ensure no eavesdroppers were lurking.

"I caution you, dear sister, to shut your mouth. I've brought my favorite chums to the country with me. I won't have you denigrating them."

"I wouldn't dream of it," she sarcastically said.

He didn't really know Millicent. She was a decade younger than he was, so he'd grown up feeling like an only child. Her attitudes were like a gnat buzzing around his ear.

Girls were such a pricey annoyance, and smart families married them off quickly so some poor sap would assume their expenses. Four years earlier, Beatrice had ordered him to fund a lavish Season in London to snag a husband for Millicent, but he'd quashed that idea.

If money was to be spent, he would spend it on himself. *He* was the one who had an image to maintain. She simply dawdled at Carter Crossing, with naught to do and no future opening up.

He wouldn't waste a farthing on her, and he wasn't concerned that she was twenty and unwed. Whenever she became weary of waiting for Prince Charming, she could marry Preston Melville, and the match wouldn't cost Clayton a penny. Melville was so besotted he'd probably *pay* Clayton to have her.

"Why not oblige Mother for once?" Millicent badgered. "It's not as if you're busy this afternoon."

"I'm very busy," he insisted.

"Doing what?"

"I don't have to explain myself to you."

A sibling spat might have erupted, but Beatrice intervened. "Millicent, you're being a pest. What are *your* plans for the afternoon? Has Mr. Shawcross suggested another outing?"

"No, thank goodness."

Beatrice leaned nearer and said, "If you make one more disparaging remark about our guests—especially Mr. Shawcross—I will lock you in your room until they've all gone back to London."

Millicent was mulishly defiant, but she bit her tongue, and Clayton asked her, "What's this about you and Shawcross?"

"It was nothing. He simply took me on a carriage ride."

"He invited *you?*"

Clayton couldn't fathom it. His sister was pretty enough, but with Shawcross being so rich, he could have any female he wanted. Why would he notice Millicent?

Then again, he'd given her those blasted earrings. Clayton still couldn't figure out why, and he'd been pondering how he might convince Millicent to hand them over so he could sell them.

She never went anywhere fancy. Why did she need a pair of diamond earrings? But *he* always needed money, and suddenly, there were creditors around every corner. While usually he gamboled with a reckless abandon, he was being barraged with demand letters, and debt collectors were hounding him on the street.

Previously, he'd carried on like an aristocrat who never worried about his bills, but recently, his situation had altered drastically. He couldn't delve down to what it was, but he sensed peril swirling on his horizon. It was why he'd agreed to accept that silent investor. The extra fiscal cushion would be a blessing.

"Yes, Mr. Shawcross invited me," Millicent snottily said. "Don't look so surprised. You'd never admit it, but I'm beautiful and pleasant, and I would be a stellar matrimonial catch."

"Trust me, Millicent, Raven Shawcross could wed any woman in the kingdom. There's no reason he would set his sights on you."

"What a horrid comment," she complained. "Why don't you trot off and find some of your awful friends? I'm certain they'd be delighted to put up with you, but Mother and I shouldn't have to."

"I just meant that Shawcross is out of your league."

"Yes, I understood you, and I happen to concur. He's much grander than I am, and I like his brother better anyway." She flashed a caustic glower at Beatrice. "But Mother has already trampled that notion, so don't fret. I'm not gearing up to provide you with a wealthy, famous brother-in-law."

She was being so snide that he wondered why he ever came home. He tossed down his napkin and rose to his feet. "I'm weary of listening to the two of you whine."

"We're not too keen on listening to you either." Millicent gestured to the door. "Go drink yourself into a stupor. We're quite sick of having you in here with us."

His mother tried to smooth over Millicent's bitter words by saying, "I'll track you down later to tell you about my appointment at the shipping office."

"As if I care, Mother! Stop nagging about it!"

He stomped out, his temper sparking as he strolled through various downstairs parlors. He liked to gamble in the afternoon, before his head became too addled by alcohol. He didn't lose as much money that way, but no one was loafing.

He wandered out to the rear verandah, and Raven Shawcross was sitting by himself at a table and staring across the park toward the ocean.

He'd only known the man for a few months. Apparently, Shawcross had been dying for an introduction, and his brother—who was a regular at some of Clayton's favorite haunts—had made sure they met.

In reality, Shawcross had been the one who'd urged Clayton to host his birthday party at Carter Crossing. If it had been Clayton's choice, he'd have celebrated in town, but Shawcross had gushed over how he'd like to see Clayton's property, so Clayton had instantly offered the rural venue.

While Clayton had many lofty acquaintances, none of them tipped the scales with the sort of weight Shawcross exhibited. For him to have glommed onto Clayton, it was so fantastical as to be nearly unbelievable, but here they were.

"Shawcross!" He marched over and pulled up a chair. "I was just discussing you with my sister. She informs me you took her on a carriage ride."

"Yes, but you shouldn't read much into it. I had considered engaging in a flirtation with her, but I've changed my mind."

Clayton's spirits sank. "Why?"

"She's too young for me."

"I told her the very same," he hurried to say. "I told her you could never be intrigued by such a silly, frivolous girl."

"You're correct. I never could be."

Shawcross focused his gaze on Clayton, and he had such a potent manner of grinding a person down. Clayton squirmed in his seat, as if he was once again standing in front of the headmaster at school and about to be paddled for an infraction.

"Tell me about your cousin, Rebecca," Shawcross said.

"Rebecca? Why would you be curious about her?"

Shawcross's gaze sharpened. "What type of relationship do you have with her?"

"We're just . . . kin."

"You haven't ever tried to seduce her?"

Clayton suffered a fleeting vision—of a dark hall, a late night—when he'd been especially drunk. He had vague memories of attempting to drag her into a deserted parlor, but he wasn't positive it had occurred.

"I would never seduce her," he firmly stated, and he laughed. "If I was brave enough—which I'm definitely not—she'd steal of knife afterward and castrate me in my sleep. She has the tendencies of a harpy."

"Here's the problem I'm having. She has bruises on her arm. Would you like to explain to me how they got there?"

Clayton frowned. "I have no idea what you're talking about."

"Don't you?" Shawcross let the question hang between them, then he said, "Don't ever touch her again. If you dare, you'll have to answer to me."

"Now see here, Shawcross"—he huffed with genuine offense—"I won't be accused of nefarious conduct right on my own verandah. You're a guest in my home. Have a care for the insults you level."

"Leave her alone."

"I've never laid a finger on her, so I don't appreciate your insinuations."

He glanced away, certain he looked incredibly guilty. Had he accosted Rebecca? With how incensed Shawcross was, he must have.

Throughout his life, he'd viewed her as a kind of *lesser* sister, a second sibling who wasn't as annoying as Millicent. But she was very beautiful, and recently, he'd been noticing her in a whole new way. Clayton had supported her forever, so didn't she owe him some repayment? Why shouldn't he seize what he craved?

It wouldn't be the first time he forced himself on a woman, and it wouldn't be the last. If he proceeded, what could she do about it? Complain to Beatrice?

Any protest would be futile because his mother would never intervene.

Shawcross relaxed, evidently deeming the difficult conversation to be over. The man's gall was infuriating, and Clayton yearned to kick him out, to apprise him he was no longer welcome at Carter Crossing, but he couldn't guess how to accomplish it. What if he ordered Shawcross out, but he refused to go?

And Shawcross was much more popular with the other guests than Clayton was. If Shawcross left, they might all flee with him.

"You have another cousin," Shawcross said. "A boy of ten or so. Alex Carter?"

Clayton could barely swallow down a gasp. The boy was supposed to keep himself hidden for the duration of the party. Rebecca had promised he would.

"What about him?" he inquired. "I hope he didn't upset you."

"No. He was very polite. I ran into him by accident out in the stables. He asked about my adventuring."

"I'm sorry you were bothered. I'll deal with it. You won't have to fuss with him again."

"It was no bother. I liked him. He reminded me of myself at that age."

"Well . . . good. I'm glad he wasn't a nuisance."

"Who were his parents? I believe he's an orphan, but he seemed to be quite remarkable. Who sired him?"

Clayton was thrilled to have the little prick described in such glowing terms, and he was anxious to impress Shawcross. He puffed himself up and said, "We're both worldly men, so I don't imagine I'll shock you if I declare that he's one of my bastards."

"*One* of your bastards?"

"I met his mother years ago in London. She was a debutante, but you're aware of how they are."

"No, I'm not. How *are* they?"

"If a fellow pays them the slightest bit of attention, they start to hear wedding bells."

"Where is she now?" Shawcross asked. "What became of her? How did he end up living with you?"

Clayton wasn't about to admit that the stupid tart had died in childbirth. It wasn't the sort of news that would amuse Shawcross, so he said, "I didn't keep track of her, and her family didn't want him, so we took custody of him. My mother and I are magnanimous that way."

"Are you?"

"Look at Rebecca! We let her stay, and it's worked out swimmingly. She watches the boy for me."

"Alex," Shawcross said. "His name is Alex."

Clayton scowled. "I know that."

Suddenly, Shawcross leapt up, his chair toppling over, and he grabbed Clayton by the throat. His palm was massive, and he was strong as an ox. He squeezed with his fingers, cutting off Clayton's air.

Then he bent down and warned, "If you ever discuss a female in such a foul manner ever again, I'll kill you. Don't make me. I'd love to rid the world of you, but I'm trying to avoid that type of violence."

He tossed Clayton away—as if he were a ragdoll—and Clayton landed on the patio stones in a stunned heap.

He was struggling to breathe, was struggling to assert some aplomb, but was unable to find any. He wished he was tough enough to jump up and pummel Shawcross. At the very least, he should have given him a thorough dressing down. The man was a *guest*. How dare he act like such a barbarian!

"I . . . I . . . think you should head for London," Clayton wheezed.

"I'm not ready to head to London, and besides, at the moment, I have business in Frinton with your mother."

"What business could you possibly have with my mother?"

"I'll let her inform you, but I'd best be off so I'm not late for my appointment."

Shawcross sauntered off, and Clayton lay on the verandah, his throat swelling, his body throbbing. Finally, after a lengthy delay, he pushed himself up to a sitting position.

He peered around, praying there'd been no observers to the hideous incident, but he was very much alone. Praise be!

On wobbly legs, he pulled himself to his feet. He was swaying and off balance.

"I'd say this calls for a drink," he mumbled to no one in particular. "Actually, this calls for several drinks."

He smoothed a hand down his coat, then went inside. Vaguely, he wondered if he should locate his mother and notify her about Shawcross joining her in Frinton, but he decided Beatrice could fight her own battles with the deranged lunatic.

As to Clayton, he needed to calm down and figure out how to evict the sadistic madman. But Shawcross was powerful, vicious, and mentally unhinged, so how could Clayton ever force him to go?

⸻ ⊰•⊱ ⸻

BEATRICE APPROACHED THE ENTRANCE to Carter Imports. It was situated on the wharf in Frinton, tucked in among the taverns and boarding houses where sailors could rent cheap rooms when they were waiting for their ships to sail.

She would have liked to move to a different building on a better street, but Clayton refused to approve the expense, and their managers insisted they remain on the water so they could look out at vessels as cargo was being loaded and unloaded.

It was a bone of contention between her and them, and she kept losing the battle.

She was omnipotent at Carter Crossing, and it galled her that she had no authority at Carter Imports. It was all used up at home where women were allowed to rule the roost, and it was infuriating that she couldn't make her male employees tremble in the same way she terrorized footmen and maids.

Back when the company had been Stone Shipping, it had been a massive enterprise, and after Harrison Stone had been laid low by Charles's embezzlement, they'd had a fleeting growth spurt. Charles had been hailed in the newspapers for saving Lord Coxwold from Harrison's theft, so initially, people had rushed to become customers.

Yet Charles hadn't had the ability to administer such a large endeavor. Clients had gradually switched to other shippers, so the business was much smaller than it had been when Harrison owned it.

Charles had held on as best he could, but after he'd passed away, Beatrice had had naught but problems. If it hadn't been their sole source of income, she'd have chucked it all and walked away.

She'd told her driver to return in two hours. Their chief clerk, Mr. Wilson, would beg her to stay longer than that, but she wouldn't. For goodness sake! She visited once a month. What more could he expect from her?

She opened the door that led into a big room that was crammed full of desks. Clerks were usually huddled at them, adding numbers and reviewing contracts, but the place was empty. Where was everyone?

She headed for the stairs at the rear, as Mr. Wilson tromped down.

"Mrs. Carter!" he said. "I'm so glad you arrived."

He tried to steer her to a corner where, no doubt, he would browbeat her over some non-issue she couldn't abide.

"Let's proceed to your office, Mr. Wilson. Clayton is home to celebrate his birthday, and I have a house filled with guests. I have to get back."

She started up the stairs, and he flitted up behind her. He was always a nervous person, but on this occasion, he seemed overly anxious.

"I thought you and I should chat first," he said.

"We will chat. As I am signing all your infernal documents, you can chat until you're blue in the face."

"We have a dilemma to confront."

"You constantly have a *dilemma*," she complained. "I've never stopped by when you weren't in an absolute dither about some paltry crisis."

"Yes, but I hope you won't blame me. The fellow has ... has ... legal papers! He fired the staff before I realized what he was about!"

"What fellow? What papers? What are you jabbering about?"

Wilson yipped and yapped, as she reached the second floor and marched down the hall to the end. The more senior clerks normally toiled away in the side rooms, and their desks were empty too. Was it a holiday? Had Wilson given them the afternoon off? Was it a meal break?

If he'd been generous with the workers, there would have to be consequences.

She plodded into his tiny, cramped office, planning to round the desk and begin wading through the contracts he'd have laid out for her. But to her great astonishment, Raven Shawcross was seated there instead. His brother was positioned next to him, appearing to be some sort of guard.

They were tough and dangerous, and they studied her with steely expressions—as if she was in trouble.

"Hello, Beatrice," Raven Shawcross said. "May I call you Beatrice?"

"No, you may not, Mr. Shawcross. I have no idea why you're here, or why you're sitting at my desk, but I'm tired and in a hurry. I don't have the time or the patience for any nonsense. Move!"

She stepped toward him as if she'd assume her rightful spot, but his brother stepped too and blocked her way. The blasted boy stared her down, practically daring her to push on by, and she received the distinct impression that—should she try—he'd push her back.

Raven Shawcross hadn't stood to greet her, but was rudely relaxed in the chair and looking very smug, as if he knew something she didn't.

"What is the meaning of this?" she demanded. "And show me the respect I'm due. Stand when you address me!"

Mr. Shawcross didn't react, but his brother said, "Sit down, Beatrice."

"You will not boss me, sir."

The cretin grabbed her, dragged her over to an empty chair, and forced her down onto it. She'd never been treated so shabbily, and she could barely breathe from being so enraged.

"Mr. Wilson!" She glanced over her shoulder. "I can't imagine why you let these miscreants in here, but you will escort them out at once."

She paused, listening, but evidently, the disloyal toad had vanished. How had Shawcross scared him away? Well, Wilson was a glorified functionary. Beatrice was Mrs. Charles Carter, mother of Clayton Carter, who owned Carter Imports. She wouldn't be bullied.

"Speak your piece, Shawcross," she fumed, "and talk fast. When we're finished, I intend to have you arrested for trespassing."

He smirked. "That would be very hard to do because this business and property are mine now, so I can't possibly be trespassing."

She frowned. "What are you babbling about?"

"Clayton gambled it away," he bluntly announced.

Her heart literally skipped a beat. "You're lying. We just discussed the company yesterday. He's been in a bit of a financial slump, so he brought in an investor. Shortly, we'll have an infusion of cash."

"There was no investor," Mr. Shawcross said. "I had my lawyer tell Clayton that story so I could get my hands on your records. Are you aware that Clayton has a serious gambling problem?"

"Clayton is a gentleman and all gentlemen gamble."

"Yes, but some of them gamble too much. Some of them keep on and on until they squander all their possessions. I've always viewed it as an addiction some men can't shake. Take my brother here." He pointed to Lucas Shawcross. "He likes to wager occasionally, and he's grown very rich off it. Lucas, have you ever bet more than you could afford to lose?"

"Never," his brother replied. "Not even when I was eight and first held a deck of cards. I knew better."

"Your son *didn't* know better," Shawcross told her.

They were the most frightening words Beatrice had ever heard, and she cocked her head as if he'd spoken in a foreign language she didn't understand.

"How could that be?" she asked.

"It's simple really. Clayton is an irresponsible wastrel. To cover his losses at the gaming tables, he's mortgaged his assets over and over, and all of his notes were overdue. I purchased them at a bankruptcy sale."

"No, no, that can't be right." She felt off balance, as if the Earth had shifted and she might slide to the floor in a bewildered heap.

"I don't suppose he bothered to inform you."

"I'm certain he's confused as to the extent of the predicament," she said. "I'll confer with him, and he'll fix it immediately!"

Shawcross shrugged casually, as if they were conversing about the weather. "As I just mentioned, he's irresponsible, but I'm guessing you've learned that about him."

"You're spewing madness," she said. "This company is how we earn our income. How can you buy it at a sale? We didn't even offer it to you! I'll hire a lawyer and fight you!"

"With what money? I don't believe you have any anymore."

He displayed a folder full of papers, and he handed it to her, but she didn't reach for it.

"These documents explain it all," he said. "You can take them home and read them at your leisure."

"But . . . but . . . it's wrong that a family could lose all they have in the blink of an eye."

"Yes, I agree. It's very, very wrong that a *family* could lose everything, but then, I've always thought the world was a very unfair place."

"You have to give us a chance to buy it back!" she insisted.

He pretended to consider, then he grinned. "I could do that, but I don't want to." Then he shouted, "Mr. Wilson, attend me please."

The quivering idiot slithered in. "Yes, Mr. Shawcross?"

"Show Beatrice out, and lock the door behind her. She is to never be allowed inside again."

"I'll see to it." Mr. Wilson bowed as low as a serf. "Come, Mrs. Carter. I'll escort you down."

Beatrice was too stunned to move, so Lucas Shawcross lifted her to her feet. Before they could start out, Mr. Shawcross said, "There is another little issue I should probably raise."

She couldn't imagine what it might be. Any dire comment seemed likely. "What is it?"

"I've had accountants reviewing the ledgers, and there are huge irregularities with the numbers."

"What are you implying?"

"Someone with authority over the customer accounts has been embezzling for years. Mr. Wilson advises me that *you* are the only person who had complete access. Well, your son has it too, but we've already established that he's irrelevant. Who might have been stealing, Beatrice?"

Her knees were suddenly so weak she was surprised she didn't collapse.

Of course she had embezzled, but she didn't deem it to be theft. She'd merely utilized some of Charles's old tricks by pilfering from the larger clients. There was so much money flowing hither and yon. No one ever missed it, and it was so expensive to run Carter Crossing, so expensive to fund Clayton's fast living.

How could she survive on the paltry amounts the company generated? Especially when so many of their customers had fled. It wasn't possible to make ends meet without a bit of conniving.

"I can't fathom what you mean," she vehemently stated.

"Yes, I'm sure you can't, and jail is a very lonely spot. I've heard some people, after they're incarcerated, are so disgraced that they wind up hanging themselves."

The mention of *jail* had her utterly terrified.

Jail was for felons! Jail was for criminals! She wasn't a . . . a . . . criminal. She was a widow and mother who was simply trying to pay her bills. How could that be a crime?

"Let's go, Mrs. Carter," Mr. Wilson said.

Lucas Shawcross added, "Don't forget your documents, Beatrice. We want you to be very clear about what's happened to you."

He stuck the folder under her arm, then Mr. Wilson yanked her out and dragged her away. The sole benefit of the mortifying moment was that—when they passed through the main room—none of the clerks were present to watch her humiliation.

Wilson pushed her outside, tugged the door shut, and spun the key in the lock. She stood on the busy wharf, feeling as if a sharp ax had chopped her to pieces.

# CHAPTER

## 10

Nathan Blake, Lord Selby, grinned at his half-sister, Sarah Sinclair.

For most of his life, he hadn't remembered he had a half-sister. From the moment earlier in the summer when recollection had flooded in, he'd had teams of men searching for her, but he'd had no luck.

Then, with Fate guiding her steps, she waltzed in his front door and begged for his help. Their reunion had been accomplished that easily.

As opposed to him, she had always remembered she had a half-sibling, but she hadn't ever contacted him. She'd been too afraid he'd ignore any overture. The prospect would have crushed her, so she'd stayed away—until she'd been in dire straits and had had nowhere to turn but to him.

She'd run an orphanage in London, but the building had been sold, and she hadn't had the funds to restart it elsewhere. The facility had been her home for twenty-four years, and when she'd been tossed out of it, she'd ended up living with his best friend, Sebastian Sinclair.

Sebastian had promptly ruined her, then her problems had grown worse. When he'd been out of town, his mother had kicked her out, so she'd been imperiled for the second time in a matter of weeks. She still had custody of two orphans from her orphanage—Noah and Petunia Sinclair—and they'd been imperiled by Sebastian's mother too.

That string of catastrophes had brought her staggering to Selby, and he was delighted to be a person who fixed problems. He'd quickly fixed all of hers.

He'd gotten her married to Sebastian without delay, and Sebastian had rescued Noah and Petunia from the certain disaster his mother had arranged for them. So Sebastian—the consummate bachelor and libertine—suddenly found himself to be a husband with a pair of half-siblings he was about to adopt and raise.

Since Nathan had recently stumbled into his own happy marriage, he'd thought it only fair that Sebastian abandon his bachelor ways too.

Nathan and his wife, Nell, had hosted an immediate wedding for Sebastian and Sarah, and the newlyweds were loafing at Selby, with Noah and Petunia racing down the halls. It made everyone smile to hear the sound of children laughing and playing. It seemed as if the manor was being reborn, as if the ghosts were being driven out so that gentler, kinder people could take their places.

With Sarah's arrival, he'd been able to give her a special gift. While she'd recalled having a brother, she had completely forgotten that she also had a twin sister named Rebecca.

"I have a surprise for you," he told her.

"What is it?" she asked. "And in light of the calamities I've endured lately, will you forgive me if I apprise you that I'm not in the mood for any surprises?"

"Yes, I'll forgive you, but you'll like this one. I promise."

They were in his library, just the two of them chatting quietly. He was seated at the desk, and she was in the chair across. They were sipping a whiskey, with her husband having spilled the beans that she had all sorts of tendencies that weren't the least bit ladylike.

Nathan was thirty, and she was twenty-seven. They'd lived together for the first three years of her life. His mother had been an aristocrat's daughter who'd died birthing him, while hers had been the nanny their father had hired for Nathan after he'd been widowed.

Their parents had been very much in love, their home a cheery spot, but it had abruptly concluded when they'd been killed in a carriage accident. Nathan had become the Selby heir, and he'd been whisked off to Selby by his cruel, malicious grandfather.

Rebecca had been sent to her mother's relatives in an unrecalled town on *the coast,* and with England being an island, the possibilities of where that town might be located were infinite. Sarah—who'd been sick on the fateful day when they were separated—had been delivered to an orphanage. The cousin who'd shown up to retrieve the twins had refused to assume custody of her when she was so ill.

She might have suffered any dismal ending, but the orphanage owner had eventually adopted her, so she'd had a stable existence there. But what had Rebecca encountered? The question haunted him.

Shortly before his father had perished, when Nathan was six, his father had had a stern talk with him. He'd charged Nathan with the duty to watch over his sisters and to protect them if anything ever happened.

Considering how malevolent his grandfather, Godwin, had been, his father had been right to worry about the twins. Nathan's sisters had been gravely endangered by Godwin not letting them come to Selby with Nathan.

Nathan had taken his father's obligation to heart, but he'd been a little boy with no power or money. Gradually, his kin had convinced him he didn't have any sisters, and ultimately, he'd begun to believe them. Over the summer though, memories had rocked him, and he'd started his search.

He rummaged in his huge stack of correspondence to extract the letter he'd received. He tossed it to her and said, "Read that."

She gaped at it and frowned. "It's from your clerk—the one who's leading the hunt for Rebecca."

"He's positive he's picked up her trail. He doesn't provide much detail, but it's good news."

As she scanned the words, he could sense her frustration.

"He doesn't offer any significant facts!" she complained. "You've simply raised my impatience to a higher level."

"I asked him not to get my hopes up until he had firm information."

"You're torturing me," she said.

"If he finds Rebecca's relatives, he has a letter from me to present to them. In it, I request that it be given to *her*, so she can write to us—if she'd like to."

"Why wait for a response? Why don't we just go to her?"

"What if she doesn't remember us? Or what if circumstances would prevent her from leaving where she is? I decided *she* should initiate any contact."

"That's a deranged idea!" she huffed.

"I agree, so I've had second thoughts. I wrote him again and told him to introduce himself, then convey her to Selby. I advised him to act as if she has no choice in the matter."

Sarah grinned. "So . . . he could ride in any day, and she'll be with him?"

"Yes."

"Oh, my lord. Don't tell me things like that! You'll have me loitering in the driveway for the remainder of my life and praying for a carriage to roll down the lane."

"I figured as much, so I've had third thoughts."

"What are they?"

"If he meets with her, we should be there too."

"That's more like it, Brother. When will we depart for the coast?"

"I sent yet another letter to him. He's staying at a coaching inn in a town called Frinton. If he locates her, he's to notify me, and we'll join him before he proceeds."

"Do you really think we'll find her?"

"I have no doubt at all."

"What will it be like to come face to face with her?"

He smirked. "She'll probably ask what took us so long."

"And we'll bring her home?"

"Yes, we'll bring her to Selby—where Father would have wanted her to be—and we will never let her out of our sight again."

"You won't believe it."

"What won't I believe?"

Sarah Blake Robertson Sinclair gazed at her husband, Sebastian, and said, "Nathan heard from his investigator—the man who's looking for Rebecca?"

Sebastian froze. "He's found her?"

"No, but apparently, he's very close."

"That's wonderful news!" Sebastian said.

"It's the first genuine clue we've had."

They'd walked into the village and were headed back to Selby Manor. It was a cold, blustery autumn day, the wind lashing the trees, the clouds rushing by. Noah and Petunia were with them too. They were Sir Sidney's bastard children. Noah was twelve, and Petunia was six.

They'd visited the church cemetery so Sarah could show them where her Blake relatives were buried. Her father's grave was there, and she liked to stop by with a bouquet, feeling a desperate need to make up for lost time.

She couldn't guess where her mother had been buried. Since her parents hadn't been wed, the vicar would have refused to hold a funeral for her, and Sarah's horrid grandfather wouldn't have allowed her to be interred in the family plot.

She hoped, once she was reunited with Rebecca, that her sister would have information as to where her mother had been laid to rest. It seemed wrong to Sarah that she didn't know the site.

"What do you imagine your sister is like?" Noah asked. "Do you remember her?"

"I have limited memories of her, but we're identical twins. I'm betting, after we're together, you won't be able to tell us apart."

"I'll be able to," Petunia said.

"Why would you think so?" Sarah asked.

"No one could be as pretty as you."

Sarah smiled at her. "You're sweet to say so, but I swear she and I will be exactly the same."

Sebastian tsked with feigned offense. "How will I stand it? It's exhausting enough to deal with *you*. How will I bear up if there are two of you? Will she be as bossy and obstinate as you are?"

Sarah shut her eyes and reached out with her mind. With her having learned about her sister, it was getting easier to silently communicate as they had when they were tiny girls.

*Are you there?* she inquired.

*Yes, I'm here.*

*I'm searching for you. Where are you?*

*Come to me while I'm sleeping.*

Sarah never admitted that she could delve into her sister's mind. It would sound eerie and too much like witchcraft to be comfortable. But she *had* told them about her dreams where there was a girl who looked just like her.

Sarah had grown up assuming Rebecca was her guardian angel, and in a way, that's precisely what Rebecca had been. She'd watched over Sarah mentally— when she'd been sad or scared or forlorn. And Sarah had done the same for her.

Sarah had clear visions of her sister so, when she'd apprised Noah that they were just alike, she wasn't joking. At the moment, Rebecca was up on a cliff and staring out at the ocean.

*I'll be with you soon . . .*

She whipped her eyes open, and they were gaping at her, obviously worried about her drifting off, but she would never explain.

"I'm happy." She beamed with pleasure. "I was on my own for so long, and now, I have the three of you. I have my brother and Nell, and shortly, I'll have my sister with me too. Aren't I lucky?"

It was the sort of conclusion she'd always pictured for herself, but as the years had rolled by—especially during her recent tragedies—she'd begun to fear none of it would ever occur. Yet look where she'd ended up!

"I wish you wouldn't cry again," Noah said as tears threatened to overwhelm her. "I can't abide a weeping woman."

Sebastian nodded. "I agree. Don't be upset, Sarah. Everything is perfect."

He stepped in and hugged her, and he probably would have kissed her too, but they tried to behave themselves in front of the children.

"Are you going to kiss her?" Petunia asked, always the romantic.

"I was considering it," Sebastian said, "but I should wait until we're alone."

"You can proceed if you want," Petunia said. "We don't mind. Well, Noah minds, but he's a boy, so we don't have to care what he thinks."

"You're correct, little Petunia. As usual." Sebastian dipped in and kissed Sarah, adding, "No tears. There's no reason for you to ever despair."

"I'm not maudlin," Sarah insisted. "I'm merely feeling sentimental because I'm very, very glad."

She linked her fingers with his, and the four of them kept on toward Selby Manor.

---

"It's been quite a day."

"I thought the old harpy would drop dead from a massive heart seizure."

"We'd never have been that fortunate."

Rebecca was walking down the hall to Mr. Shawcross's room, and she could hear him chatting with his brother. It was late, supper long over, and she should have simply gone to bed, but she'd been too anxious to head there without talking to him first.

Odd events were happening, and she couldn't figure out what they indicated. Apparently, he and his brother had commenced the plot they were hatching.

Clayton had snuck off in the afternoon with some of his friends to revel with an acquaintance in Frinton. Before he'd left, he'd quarreled with Mr. Shawcross—a housemaid had witnessed it through a window—and he'd physically assaulted Clayton.

Then Beatrice had ridden into Frinton for her monthly visit to Carter Imports. She'd staggered back, looking stricken, and she'd locked herself in her bedchamber, declaring she wouldn't emerge until she could confer privately with Clayton.

The staff had prepared a huge meal, but there had only been a handful of people present to eat it. The entire affair had been awkward, and the few stragglers who hadn't traipsed into Frinton with Clayton had decided they weren't having any fun and would return to London in the morning.

Rebecca couldn't blame them.

The servants were rabidly gossiping about the Shawcross brothers. Rumor had it that they'd had a vitriolic encounter with Beatrice at the company office, but also that Mr. Shawcross was about to depart for good.

The news was terribly distressing. When she realized she might never see him again, she felt too despondent to carry on.

As she approached his door, she'd presumed she was being very furtive, but suddenly, he called, "Rebecca, is that you?"

She peeked around the frame, and they were over by the hearth. It was a chilly night, and they had a roaring fire burning. Mr. Shawcross was relaxed in a chair, his brother leaned against the wall. They were casually dressed, their coats off, their sleeves rolled back. They were drinking liquor, a decanter and two glasses on the table by Mr. Shawcross.

"Yes, it's me," she said.

"Why are you lurking? Did you need something?"

"Could I speak to you? Just for a minute?"

He sighed as if she was a heavy burden. "I suppose."

"Are we finished?" his brother asked him. "Don't we have to discuss our plans for tomorrow?"

"I'll find you in awhile," Mr. Shawcross said. "Where will you be?"

"I'll be in a parlor playing cards, but I've won from everyone. I'm sure they'll be rushing to town very soon—because I've emptied their purses."

Mr. Shawcross scoffed. "You don't amuse me."

His brother smirked, then asked Rebecca, "Dare I leave you alone with him, Miss Carter?"

"You needn't worry about me," she said. "I'll be fine."

"Raven is a renowned libertine. Were you aware of that? Don't be fooled. If you're silly about him, there can't be a good ending for you."

"Get out of here, Lucas!" Mr. Shawcross snapped.

"I'm simply telling her the truth. I like her, and I don't like you, and she has no business being in this bedchamber."

"Your concern is noted, now get! Or I'll toss you out bodily."

"All right, all right," Lucas Shawcross muttered. "When you're done—which I'm predicting won't be for hours—I'll be downstairs at a card table."

"Clayton and most of the men went into Frinton," Rebecca told him. "I doubt you'll stumble on anyone eager to gamble."

"I'll have to beg the footmen then."

"Lucas!" Mr. Shawcross said. "We've been through this. Don't steal from the footmen! They can't afford it, and you don't need the money."

"Yes, but they're so much more interesting than Clayton's tedious chums. They're real people, whereas his friends are idiots and whiners who are indescribably dull."

He headed out, and she was hovered in the threshold, so he had to walk by her to exit the room. He took a last glance at his brother, then murmured to her, "He bites, Miss Carter. Be careful."

He sauntered off, and she remained frozen in her spot as his strides faded. Mr. Shawcross refilled his glass and sipped the liquor. She didn't move, and he said, "Well? Are you coming in or not?"

"I'm coming in."

"Shut the door then."

"I shouldn't."

"I won't risk that a housemaid will sneak by and eavesdrop on our conversation. From your dour expression, it's clear you intend to raise a hideous topic, and I'd rather not have the servants tittering over it."

"If I was caught in here with the door closed, I'd be in so much trouble."

He scowled furiously. "Then go to your own bedchamber. I don't have the patience for your dithering. If you have something to say, say it. If you don't, then leave me be. I'm busy, and I'm exhausted."

She almost stomped out. Beatrice had addressed her in that same snide tone for most of her life, and she was heartily sick of it. But apparently, she had no pride at all.

She was sad and dejected, and she wanted to spend time with him. She wouldn't let him be horrid to her, wouldn't let him bark and complain and insult. If these were to be some of the final words they ever shared, then she insisted they be words she could mull with satisfaction after he left forever.

She shut the door. She didn't slam it, but secured it hard enough that he knew she was irked.

"Don't be rude to me," she said. "I don't like it, and I don't deserve harsh treatment from you."

He pondered, then nodded. "You're correct. I'm grouchy, so I'm behaving badly. I apologize."

He wasn't a man who apologized very often, and she accepted his comment for the olive branch it was.

"Why are you so upset?" she asked.

She thought he'd deny any distress, but he didn't. "I had a dreadful day. I'm getting the justice that is my due, but I don't feel any better."

"What justice are you due?"

He caustically assessed her, then he downed his liquor instead of explaining. "Why are you here? What do you need?"

"You fought with Clayton."

"What of it? If you're about to chastise me for it, you shouldn't."

"I won't chastise you. The staff is gossiping, and I figured I should learn what it was about."

"It was about you. What would you suppose?"

"Me!"

"I ordered him to never touch you again."

She sighed. "I wish you wouldn't have."

"I don't care."

"It will make things worse for me."

"No, it won't. Clayton has run out of opportunities to inflict himself on you."

"You keep spewing remarks like that, but you never clarify your plans. Stop speaking in riddles."

"This house doesn't belong to him anymore. I'll kick him out shortly, after I've toyed with him a bit more, but his days of being in residence—where he can terrorize you—are at an end."

She frowned. "What do you mean?"

"I *mean* this property is mine."

"How could that be? He hasn't put it up for sale."

"He mortgaged it over and over, to square his gambling debts, and he never tendered any payments. I bought it from his creditors—for pennies I might add."

"Give it back to him."

"No."

He poured himself another glass of liquor and pointed to the empty chair next to him. "If you dawdle over there, I'll strain my neck looking at you. Sit down."

She neared, but didn't sit as he'd demanded. She studied him, and there was an aura around him she hadn't noticed before. He seemed cold-blooded and dangerous, the kind of brigand you wouldn't want to meet in a dark alley.

Should she be afraid of him? She'd never worried about it in the past, not even the first afternoon when she'd been alone with him on the promontory. She'd never sensed any menace, but now, it practically rolled off him in waves.

"What did you do to Beatrice?" she asked. "The servants are gossiping about that too. She came home from Frinton and locked herself in her room."

"Is that where she went? I was wondering where the old bat was hiding."

"Tell me what you did!"

"I did what I've been dreaming about for two decades."

"Which is what?"

"I took my father's company from her, so she doesn't have anything left. She's about to discover what it's like."

"You *took* her company? Carter Imports?"

"Yes."

"Give it back," she said again.

'I can't. I've closed it down."

"But...but...how could that happen?"

"Ask your dear Cousin Clayton. He really shouldn't gamble."

"You've shuttered Carter Imports?"

He'd just admitted it, so her question made her sound like a dunce, but she couldn't wrap her mind around the disaster. She'd spent the day, seeing to her usual chores, carrying on as if everything was fine, but they'd lost Carter Crossing? They'd lost Carter Imports?

"Why would you do this to us?" she asked.

"I didn't do it to *you*. I did it to Clayton and Beatrice."

"It will impact me just as hard as it impacts them."

"Yes, tragedies have a terrible way of sweeping entire families to their doom. In my personal experience, I've found it can't be avoided."

"You hate us that much?"

"I don't hate *you* specifically. Or your cousin, Millicent. I'm ambivalent about her, but as to Clayton and Beatrice, my loathing for them knows no bounds."

He poured himself yet another drink, but before he could swallow any, she marched over and yanked it away. She set it out of his reach.

"Cease your barking," she said, "and explain what this is about."

"My father's name was Harrison Stone. Have you ever heard of him? Well, no, you wouldn't have. You were a child when he was sent to prison for a crime he didn't commit."

"What crime was that?"

"He was accused of embezzling from Lord Coxwold, and it was such a hefty sum that the pompous sot was almost bankrupted. The problem was that my father didn't steal a penny from him."

She'd already deduced the answer, but she posed her query anyway. "Who was the embezzler?"

"It was Charles Carter, but he blamed my father." He grabbed the decanter and downed a huge slug, then he toasted her with it. "He and Beatrice have lived high on the hog since then, haven't they? The root of their wealth was pilfered from my father, but that never seemed quite fair to me."

"No, it wouldn't."

"In case you were curious, my father hanged himself in prison."

She winced. "I'm sorry."

"Are you?" His gaze was brutal, as if she was responsible for the calamity.

"Yes, I'm sorry, you rude oaf. Why do you detest Clayton? Is it simply because he's Charles and Beatrice's son? Or are there other issues with him that you haven't revealed?"

"He ruined my sister."

"Oh."

"She wound up in the family way, and she and her baby died in childbirth."

Rebecca blanched with dismay. Evidently, this was a blood vendetta, so he'd never be satisfied, no matter how much retribution he obtained.

"It was years ago," he said, "and most people would probably insist I should be over it, that I should forgive and forget, but I'm not a forgiving man."

"I've figured that out about you."

"I was out of the country and far away in Africa, so I wasn't able to protect her. He destroyed her, then walked away. I've been waiting for my chance to get even."

"After you've extracted your vengeance, do you suppose you'll be happy?"

"Yes. A bit of revenge always makes me happy."

"So what will happen now?" she asked.

"What do you think will happen? I'm retrieving what belonged to my parents. Whatever is left—and Beatrice and Clayton have squandered nearly all of it—when I'm through, it will all be mine."

He stood suddenly and stepped in so they were toe to toe, and he towered over her in that thrilling manner she relished.

She wasn't sure what he intended—to strike her? to kiss her? to throw her out?—so she was unprepared for him to sweep her up and carry her into the bedroom.

"Raven Shawcross!" she scolded. "Put me down this instant."

"No."

He stomped over and flung her onto the bed, and he tumbled onto the mattress with her. In a trice, she was flat on her back, and he was stretched out atop her. Without a word being exchanged, he began kissing her as if they'd been separated forever and had finally been reunited.

Where he was concerned, she was a complete milksop, so of course she joined in with a great deal of enthusiasm, but why would she participate so eagerly? He'd just informed her that he'd ruined her cousins. Shouldn't she be incensed?

Beatrice had always behaved horrendously toward her, but despite her flaws, she'd fed, housed, and clothed Rebecca for twenty-four years. Shouldn't Rebecca exhibit some loyalty to her?

And what about her own situation? Was he planning to kick them out on the road? Where were they to go? How would they support themselves after they arrived?

Carter Imports had been the family's sole source of revenue. If it vanished, how would they survive? Would they move to London and become rag pickers and rat chasers?

She ought to be in her own bedchamber and analyzing her circumstances. If he was about to evict residents, she was positive he would include *every* Carter in that group, so she and Alex were at risk of losing their home. If Beatrice and Clayton found themselves in dire straits, Rebecca couldn't envision a scenario where they'd continue to extend charity to her and Alex.

Did Mr. Shawcross realize the wheels he'd set in motion with regard to her? Did he care that she might be imperiled? She was terribly afraid the answer was *no*, so she had no idea why she was loafing in his bed. She wasn't a prisoner. She could push him off and march out, but why would she? Each time she was with him in an intimate way, it might be the last time.

He was touching her all over, his hands stroking her arms, hips, and thighs. The caresses were like bolts of lightning, and she would never tell him to stop.

Because she was a spinster and hadn't expected to wed, she hadn't fully pondered the physical side of passion. How could it be that she'd never heard how exciting it was? How could she be twenty-seven and never been told how much she'd enjoy it?

He was in a peculiar mood, his temper raging, his emotions spiraling to a dangerous height, so the encounter swiftly burned out of control. He was unbuttoning her gown, untying laces and raising the hem of her skirt. His busy fingers slipped under the bodice of her dress, massaging her breast bare skin to bare skin.

The feel of it was so shocking, but also so wonderfully delicious, that she didn't order him to desist. He shoved fabric away, exposing a nipple and, stunning her, he dipped down and sucked it into his mouth. She hadn't ever imagined a man doing such a thing to a woman, and every portion of her anatomy, down to the smallest pore, was absolutely riveted.

An appalling notion occurred to her: Was she a wanton? Deep down, had she always harbored licentious tendencies?

All her life, Beatrice had warned her that her mother had been a slattern, that Rebecca had to fight the natural urges her mother's blood would foment. Rebecca had been aghast over the accusations and determined to prove Beatrice wrong.

But had Beatrice been correct?

Rebecca had only ever had her one brief amour when she was seventeen, so she'd never been enticed by immoral conduct, but she was definitely being enticed now. Her body had overwhelmed her common sense, her wits overruled by desire.

She yearned to do whatever he requested, so she couldn't guess what might have happened. *She* certainly wouldn't have called a halt, but abruptly, as if he'd been poked with a pin, he yanked away from her and rolled onto his back. He glared at the ceiling, his expression seeming a tad tormented.

"Why have we stopped?" she asked.

"You have to get out of here, Rebecca."

"Why?"

"I'm a lusty man, and I don't have many scruples. I have *some,* but not many. If you stay with me another second, I can't predict what I'll do to you."

"You would never hurt me."

"You can't guarantee that, and *I* am not willing to test the limits of my restraint." He shifted onto his side, so they were nose to nose, and he nodded to the door. "Go. Go now."

"I don't want to leave."

"Well, *I* don't really want you to either, but for reasons I can't deduce, you fascinate me. There's a powerful attraction between us, and I've been letting it flare, but I'm tamping it out. I know how to behave myself, and I have to start."

"You're departing for London soon. I'd hate to never see you again. These might be some of the final minutes we can be together like this. Would you rather we ignored each other?"

"I'm not Clayton," he said.

"Thank goodness."

"I loathe every Carter on the globe. That includes you, Rebecca. I won't lie to you about it."

"You don't mean that," she said. "You like me more than you care to admit."

"I don't." He didn't sound all that sure. Was he convincing himself or her? "You could never matter to me, so it's ridiculous for us to dally."

He'd stung her pride, and her temper ignited. "You're the one who carried me in here!"

"I shouldn't have. I have no honorable intentions toward you."

She scoffed with disgust. "You think I haven't figured that out?"

"Where would you like this to end? Shall I force myself on you, then abandon you to your fate? Is that the conclusion we should pursue? I told you I'm not Clayton, and I won't act like him."

From how much she'd relished the salacious episode, there would have been no *force* involved in whatever she'd tried at his behest. She was afraid he could coax her into any sinful antic. She didn't tell him that though.

He slid off the opposite side of the bed, and he sat up, facing the far wall, his back to her—as if he couldn't bear the sight of her.

She sat up too, her feet on the floor, as she straightened her dress and hair. It was an awkward, unpleasant moment. She was on the verge of tears, as if she'd lost a precious item and would never be able to retrieve it.

"You'd never force yourself on me," she murmured, needing to break the tension that filled the air like bile.

"I've paid some attention to you—when I shouldn't have—and I suppose, in that silly, feminine brain of yours, you've built up an entire fantasy where you believe I'll fall in love and marry you. You're a *Carter*, Rebecca. I would never proceed as you're hoping."

She *had* begun to dream about that very scenario, but she'd die before she'd confirm his assessment. While most people would describe her as humble and accommodating, in reality, she was bristling with vanity. It was likely her aristocratic father's blood that made her feel so superior.

Usually, she concealed it, but she wasn't always successful. Like now, for instance.

She wished she were a big, strong man, so she could march over and slap him for being so obnoxious. She'd visited him, being anxious to hear that he wasn't departing—or if he was, that he'd take her with him.

Was that prospect too outrageous to consider? Was she a ninny for assuming he fancied her? That he wanted her? Well, no one had ever wanted her. Why did she always conveniently forget that fact?

She stood and stomped out, and as she reached the door to the hall, he called, "I might have been a little harsh just then. I'm sorry if I upset you."

In light of how he'd insulted her, it was a paltry and completely useless remark.

"Jump off a cliff, Mr. Shawcross. There are plenty of them nearby, so I'm positive you can locate one easily enough. Please pick the highest one you can find."

She stormed out, telling herself that it was the last time—the very, very, very last time!—she would ever behave like such an idiot.

# CHAPTER

## 11

Lucas sat on a bench in the garden behind the manor. It was dark and cold, the wind blowing hard, so it seemed even colder. He was bundled in a coat, but it didn't provide the warmth he needed. London was chilly and damp, but *this* godforsaken spot, where the breeze rushed off the icy ocean water, was unbearable.

He wished he was back in town, snuggled at his favorite brothel. The lamps would be turned down low and the fires burning very hot. Why was he loafing at Carter Crossing?

Raven had asked him to come, and he always had trouble refusing his brother. He was such an imperious fellow, and it was difficult to ignore him.

And of course, they were the only two left in their small family, so they had a powerful connection. He was a great trial to Raven though. With his being reckless and negligent, he cheated people and constantly ran scams that brought him enormous satisfaction, but his conduct drove Raven to distraction.

Lucas never suffered regrets, and he hated that Raven fretted over his antics. He'd like to behave better, but he couldn't.

Raven had grown rich from his African explorations, and he'd given a ton of money to Lucas, but he'd been smart about it. Lucas's funds were stashed in a trust that was managed by his brother. Lucas received an allowance and had to request more when he overspent, but he rarely did.

He'd had too many lean years, and he'd learned to never count on money. It could vanish as easily as it arrived.

He'd agreed to help Raven roust Beatrice and Clayton Carter from their stable perches, and he was enjoying the chance to terrorize them. It was a bad habit, ingrained after he'd been sent to an orphanage, then had attended a charity school.

Both facilities had been foul and violent, and he'd been a gullible boy from a prosperous family who'd been completely unprepared for the experience. He'd developed the necessary skills quickly enough though, and he'd discovered that he had a real aptitude for brutality and vice.

He mostly felt dead on the inside. He was never merry or sad or angry. He simply coasted along, watching others, being cautious, and determining who could be counted as friend or foe.

Raven accused him of having no scruples or morals. He *had* them. He just didn't give them much exercise.

He didn't remember much about his parents or the life he'd had with them. He certainly didn't remember Oakley that Raven claimed had been their occasional summer home. Raven was remodeling it so it would once again be the fantastic mansion it had previously been, but Lucas had no idea if that was a good plan or not.

Since he recalled no link to the place, he possessed no nostalgia for it. But if it made Raven happy to live in it, Lucas wasn't about to tell him he shouldn't.

A brisk gust of wind whipped by, forcing him to wonder yet again why he was dawdling in the country. He'd accompanied Raven because his brother had wanted Lucas to guard his back, but also to present a united front to Beatrice and Clayton so they'd realize that Harrison Stone's sons had survived, and they were lethally enraged.

Raven had plenty of rage to display on his own, and he didn't need Lucas joining in to scare anyone.

Up on the verandah, Millicent exited the house, and he muttered to himself, "About damn time."

He wasn't the sort of idiot who trifled with innocents. There were hoards of trollops in the kingdom who were eager to revel in any disgusting fashion he proposed, so he couldn't figure out why he was bothering with her. He was a shrewd judge of character, and from the moment he'd first laid eyes on her, he'd recognized she was dying to expand her horizons. Why shouldn't he oblige her?

She was meeting him, but before she could dash down into the dark garden, her erstwhile beau, Preston Melville, exited the house too. He caught up to her, and they chatted, but Millicent's impatience was too obvious, and he slithered away so she could continue on.

But he lurked at a window, peering out and worried over where she was headed. The poor sap was madly in love with her, but she was too vivacious and spirited for him. If he ended up wed to her, she'd grind him to dust with how miserable she'd be as his wife. In Lucas's view, by flirting with her, he was saving Melville from making a hideous mistake.

She pranced up, looking pretty and sassy, and she grinned at him where he was relaxed on the bench like a lazy king.

"What took you so long?" he asked.

"My brother's guests kept stopping me to gossip about *your* brother. Is it true he pummeled Clayton this afternoon?"

"He didn't pummel him. He simply knocked him off a chair."

"Ooh, I'd like to have seen that! Why were they quarreling?"

"Why would you suppose? Clayton is an ass. He annoys Raven immensely, and Raven doesn't tolerate fools very well. I noticed Mr. Melville accosting you on the verandah. What did he want?"

"He just wanted to talk, and I can't stand to snub him. He's so nice, and he dotes on me."

"He should let you go or you'll eat him alive." He gestured to the spot next to him, indicating she should sit. "Did you bring a beverage?"

"Whiskey. Is that all right?"

"Whiskey is fine."

She handed him the bottle, then nestled down with him. Her bodily heat was very welcome, and he pondered whether it would be rude to suggest she shift to his other side so she blocked more of the wind. Her cloak was lined with fur, so she was better prepared for the frigid temperatures.

He downed several swallows of the liquor, liking how it warmed him. He offered it to her, and she enjoyed several hefty swallows too. He was turning her into a lush with hardly any effort.

"What about your brother and my mother?" she asked. "She's locked herself in her bedchamber, and she's refusing to come out."

"He merely put her in her place."

"How?"

"He took over your family's company today."

"What do you mean?"

"Clayton had mortgaged it over and over, and he never made any payments on the debt, so Raven purchased it."

"Why would he deliberately bind himself to this tedious estate at the edge of the world?"

Lucas smirked. "He has his reasons."

"I wish I'd seen him inflicting himself on Mother too. I've spent twenty years trying to put her in her place, but I've never managed it."

"Raven has a definite ability to frighten people to death."

"Was he always that way? Or have my mother and brother goaded him to new heights of indignation?"

"He's always been fierce. He had to be. So have I."

"What happened to you when you were a child? You constantly allude to tragic circumstances, but you never clarify what they were."

Should he persist with keeping their secret? Raven would spring the situation on the Carters all at once, then kick them out on the road. He wanted them to suffer as Raven and Lucas had suffered.

On the morning when the authorities had arrived to throw them out, their father had already died in prison, and their mother seemed to have lost her mind.

She'd grown so mentally befuddled that she hadn't understood their expulsion was imminent, or if she had, she hadn't moved to tamp down the consequences.

Lord Coxwold had obtained a judgment to sell their assets to recoup what had been stolen from him, and as they'd been shoved out the door, they hadn't even been allowed to pack their clothes. Poor Raven, who'd been just ten, had had to take charge so they didn't end up sleeping in a ditch. Their father's acquaintances had abandoned them—all except one—and the help he'd provided had been furtive and unenthusiastic.

Lucas had been four, so he had limited memories of that fateful period, but his life had been destroyed in an instant. With that dire scenario as his history, how could he have turned out to be stable and reliable? It simply wasn't possible.

Their mother had passed away shortly after their eviction, so he, Raven, and Lydia had been orphaned. They'd been delivered to an orphanage, then eventually shipped off to different schools.

He'd seen Lydia twice after that, Raven a few more times. Mostly, he'd been left alone in London, a terror at school and, later on, a terror in London who would commit any foul act.

It was a miracle, really, that he and Raven had survived. Not only had they survived, but they'd thrived in stunning ways. But it also wasn't that unexpected that Lydia had perished. She'd been an unprotected female, with no parent to warn her away from a scoundrel like Clayton Carter.

How could she have made it? Two of Harrison Stone's children had beaten the odds. The third one hadn't.

"You'll find out what happened to Raven and me very soon," he said.

"Why won't you tell me now?"

"Raven wants it to be a surprise."

"If he's taken over Carter Imports, what will become of my family? It was our sole source of income. How is he imagining we'll support ourselves?"

"I don't think he's concerned about it."

"Well," she huffed, "that's typical of him, isn't it? He's so surly and arrogant. Why would he worry about paltry old me? Is he figuring I'll wear rags and eat grass?"

"He hasn't considered *your* fate. He's too keen to ruin your mother and brother."

She tsked with offense. "You're being awfully blasé about it. If I begged you to stop him, would you?"

"I couldn't dissuade him even if I felt like intervening. He's quite determined."

"How about you?" she asked. "Are *you* determined?"

He was and he wasn't. He always liked to punish reprobates who deserved it, and he relished revenge as much as the next man, but Charles Carter's sins had occurred two decades earlier. Lucas wasn't burning with the fury that kept Raven up at night, but then, Lucas never burned with much emotion over any issue.

"I'm not determined," he said, "but I'll enjoy having your mother and brother laid low."

She grabbed his coat by the lapels and shook him. "What did they do?"

He sighed, as if she were an irksome burden. "Here's our story. I hope your frivolous feminine mind can bear it."

"Don't make fun of me. Just spit it out."

"Basically, your father was an embezzler, and when the theft was uncovered, he blamed it on *my* father. My father was arrested and prosecuted, and your father skated away with a huge reward. He used it to buy up everything that had previously been ours."

"Are you claiming Carter Imports was yours in the past?"

"Yes—but it had a different name. It was Stone Shipping."

She scowled. "That can't be right. My parents built it from the ground up."

"They lied to you, and in addition to that dubious conduct, Clayton seduced my sister."

"You have a sister?"

"I *had* a sister. She died in childbirth. It's difficult for a man like my brother to forget that sort of transgression. He's demanding his pound of flesh, and you're lucky he didn't get it from *you*."

"How?"

"He'd have liked to ruin you, then leave you in the lurch—as Clayton did to my sister—but he's too honorable. *I* wouldn't have hesitated, but he couldn't force himself to follow through."

"Is that why he was so attentive to me when he first arrived?"

"Yes, but he wasn't actually interested in you."

He thought she might be incensed, but she shuddered with relief. "I'm so glad to hear it was feigned. My mother ordered me to encourage him, but he scares the life out of me."

"He decided you were young and annoying." He shrugged. "I think you're annoying too, so I have no idea why I sneak off with you. Nothing much has transpired to entice me."

"As if I'd throw myself at your feet. If I ever succumb to passion, it will be after I have a ring on my finger."

He studied her, pondering how impudent she was, how spoiled. She was quickly growing to like whiskey very much, and he wondered what else she'd grow to like. He suspected she might engage in all kinds of mischief before she had a wedding ring, but he didn't tell her that. She wouldn't believe him anyway.

Instead, he asked, "After Raven makes his next move, have you envisioned a conclusion for yourself? You're not the type to have reflected much on the future."

"What are you saying? You constantly speak in riddles."

"Clayton has lost his shipping business. Raven shuttered it today, and you'll never guess what he has arranged for tomorrow."

"What?"

"Carter Crossing is his too, and you're about to be evicted."

She frowned. "How could it be his? Clayton would never have put it up for sale—at least I doubt he would have."

"Raven owns it the same way he owns your shipping company. Clayton has a serious gambling problem. You understand that, don't you?"

"Well, I know he *gambles*," the foolish ninny said, "but every gentleman does that."

"He's one of the worst, and he has no aptitude for it, so he has the worst luck."

"He wagered over Carter Crossing?"

"No, he just mortgaged it over and over—because he needed money. My brother bought it from his creditors."

She stared beseechingly, as if hoping he was jesting or merely trying to upset her. Ultimately, she said, "You're telling the truth."

"Of course it's the truth. Why would I lie about it?"

"What will happen to me?"

He noticed the exasperating girl didn't inquire about her mother or brother—or her cousin, Rebecca. He shouldn't have been surprised that someone so self-centered would only think of herself.

"I can't imagine what will happen to you," he said.

"Will you and your brother live at Carter Crossing?"

"No. Raven purchased that neighboring property that was abandoned. Oakley? He's renovating it, and he'll live there. As to Carter Crossing, I'm fairly sure he intends to demolish it."

"It's a perfectly good house!" she complained. "Why would he deliberately wreck it?"

"You're failing to comprehend how angry he is."

"If he stays at Oakley, and Carter Crossing is leveled, where will you be?"

"In London. I'm heading there shortly. Probably in the morning. I've had about all the excitement in the country that I can abide."

"But . . . but . . . I thought . . ."

When she didn't finish her sentence, he asked, "You thought what?"

"I thought you were sweet on me. I thought we were . . . well . . ."

"I've never been sweet on anyone," he bluntly admitted, "and I've certainly never been sweet on *you*. You're amusing though, and our trysts have been entertaining. It's been the only part of my sojourn here that was the least bit enjoyable."

Her shoulders slumped. "I assumed you'd save me from Carter Crossing. I assumed you'd save me from Preston Melville."

"I'm nobody's champion, and I'm definitely nobody's savior."

"So you've been toying with my affections?"

He scoffed. "You don't have any *affections*. Don't pretend to be hurt.

Female histrionics never work on me."

She peered at the manor, her mind whirring so fervidly that he could almost hear it churning away. Eventually, she said, "You're not married, are you?"

"Gad, no, and with the tarts who fill my world, I'd never shackle myself to one of them."

"Are you promised? Are you betrothed?"

"No! I've never seen a *good* marriage, and I would never risk the matrimonial noose. It holds no appeal to me whatsoever."

Suddenly, she flung herself against him, crashing into him so forcefully that, if he hadn't instinctively grabbed her, she'd have bounced off and tumbled to the ground.

He'd shared a few heated kisses with her that night out on the beach, but they hadn't gone any farther than that. She'd refused to meet him in a bedchamber, and *he* wouldn't deflower her on a park bench, so he hadn't gotten much of a benefit out of the flirtation he'd commenced.

She was pretty and shapely. With her wicked tendencies surging to the fore, she'd likely be a wildcat in a bed—once she learned the ropes—and he wondered if it would be worth it to teach her some tricks. He was sure not.

"Take me to London with you," she begged. "Please?"

"To be my what? I just told you I don't plan to ever wed."

"What other role is there? Mistress? Paramour? Friend? Confidante? I don't care what my position would be. Take me with you, and we'll figure it out later!"

He snorted with derision. "I'd have to be mad to bring you there."

"If you leave me behind, I'll just die!"

"Don't be so dramatic."

"You're aware of how tediously I live. According to you, I won't even have any of this much longer. You have to agree! You can't desert me!"

She searched his eyes, and he blandly stared back.

As Raven repeatedly scolded, he always did exactly the wrong thing. He had no scruples and no impulse control. In light of some of the trouble he'd caused over the years, he was fortunate he hadn't been hanged or transported to the penal colonies as an unrepentant nuisance.

When faced with bad choices, he glommed onto them. Why not? Life was hard, and most of what had been inflicted on him in the past hadn't been fair or just. Why not seize what he craved and damn the consequences?

It was so much fun to walk onto a moral cliff, to balance precariously, then topple over the edge. He'd never been the sort to plod forward like every other miserable oaf, and he was smarter than other men—men like Clayton Carter—whose dreadful habits overwhelmed their instincts.

*His* instincts were fine, and he noticed danger approaching, but he rarely jumped out of the way.

He grinned at her, recognizing that he was about to roll the dice and see where luck would land him.

"I might permit you to come," he said, "but what's in it for me?"

"What would you like to be *in it*?"

"I'll consider my answer and let you know."

"I have some money. You can have it."

"I'm filthy rich. I don't need money."

"Then what might I have that would interest you in the slightest?"

His torrid gaze wandered down her curvaceous torso. "I'm certain you'll think of something, and here's a hint: It will be shocking and salacious, but it will give us a chance to discover how desperately you yearn to escape. And if you don't realize what I want on your own, I'll be happy to show you what I mean."

"Will I like it?"

"Deep down, you have the heart of a harlot, so I'm positive you will."

# CHAPTER

## 12

"It's about time you staggered in."

"I'm here now, Mother, and you're lucky I am. Don't nag."

Clayton glared at Beatrice, his head pounding and stomach roiling from his hangover. It was two in the afternoon, and he might have stayed in bed and not risen at all, but his valet had roused him with the message that Beatrice demanded a conversation.

He'd gamboled in Frinton until dawn and had lurched to the estate as the eastern horizon was beginning to lighten.

With Shawcross manhandling him the prior afternoon, he'd been in no mood to return. The chums on his nocturnal bacchanal hadn't mentioned the incident, but he supposed those who'd remained behind were aware of the encounter. The servants probably were too.

When he'd still been sober enough to ponder his dilemma, he'd tried to figure out how to kick Shawcross out, but it didn't seem possible. Wasn't it better to leave for town himself? After significant reflection, he'd decided it was the perfect solution. He'd declare his party a dull bore and suggest they all go.

Once he announced his departure, his guests would accompany him. If Shawcross chose to dawdle after everyone left, who cared?

He had to sever ties with the mad African explorer, and after he was in the city, he'd spread quiet stories about Shawcross being deranged and that Clayton had dissolved their association because of it.

"Why are you hiding in your bedroom suite?" he asked his mother. "Why aren't you down in the dining room like a normal person?"

"I can't show my face down there."

"Why not?"

She was seated at a table by the window and stuffing herself with muffins. She waved to an empty chair, indicating he should join her, and he trudged over and eased down. He dished up some food and took small bites, wondering if he'd be able to keep any of it down.

"Will you tell me what's wrong?" he said when she didn't begin her tale of woe. "Or am I to guess?"

"I went into Frinton yesterday, for my visit to Carter Imports."

"Yes, yes, and if you intend to regale me with how horrid it was, this discussion will be finished before it's started."

"Mr. Shawcross was there—with his brother. He claims he's your silent investor."

Clayton froze, his fork suspended halfway to his mouth, as he frantically grappled with the information. Was this good news or bad?

*Definitely bad.* Considering how Shawcross had abused him, Clayton couldn't abide the notion of their being partners—silent or otherwise.

"Shawcross is?" he asked. "Are you sure?"

"He served me with some papers." She pointed to a folder on a nearby table. "We don't own the business any longer. *He* owns it now, and he's shutting it down."

Clayton scoffed. "Don't be ridiculous. How could Shawcross have purchased my company? I never offered it to him."

"He fired all the employees."

"We have ships coming and going. We have cargo and contracts to honor. We can't simply close our doors."

"*We* can't do anything. It's none of our affair."

He felt completely bewildered. "This is absurd. You have to be mistaken."

"Have you been borrowing money?"

"Maybe some here and there. It's hardly a crime."

"Have you arranged mortgages on Carter Imports?"

"A few."

She gasped with alarm. "Have you encumbered the manor too? Is the house imperiled?"

"I recall a loan or two on the house, but calm down. They're tiny. We'll pay them back like that!" He snapped his fingers, the sound echoing off the ceiling.

"How will we pay them?" she asked. "You don't seem to grasp that our sole source of income has vanished."

"What source has vanished?" he inquired like a dunce. In his hung-over state, he couldn't concentrate.

"Focus, Clayton! The business was how we earned our money. If it's not ours, how—precisely—will we generate any revenue?"

"You're making a mountain out of a molehill."

"I don't think so."

A niggle of dismay slid down his spine. From the time he'd first moved to town at age eighteen, he'd spent more than he had. There were simply so many intriguing activities to enjoy, and he had to keep up appearances. The minute it became known that a fellow couldn't afford to revel, his social status imploded, and he began to be ostracized.

It occurred to him that there were spurious forces at work he hadn't noticed. He sensed he'd been duped and hadn't realized it.

Why would Shawcross seek to ruin him? Why would Shawcross want his paltry shipping company? Due to Beatrice's inept management, it was a shell of what it had previously been. Why would Shawcross bother with it?

"I'm certain this is just a misunderstanding," he said.

"You need to find Shawcross and talk to him. I tried, but he wouldn't listen to me. It has to be you."

The words were frightening. It was Clayton's specific intent to *never* speak to the wealthy bully ever again. "That's not necessary, is it?"

"It's absolutely necessary. *You* have to approach him, for I'm afraid—whatever his scheme—he's not finished with us."

Clayton's lungs squeezed in his chest. "What can he have in mind?"

"I can't guess, but we have to learn what it is, then prepare to fight him. I threatened him with legal action, but he laughed and told me I don't have the funds to hire a lawyer."

She looked smaller all of a sudden, as if Shawcross had sucked out some of her spite and malice. Clayton had always viewed his mother as the toughest shrew in the kingdom. She ran roughshod over any idiot who stepped in her way, so how had Shawcross bested her?

Well, he wasn't like any of her prior adversaries. He'd traveled the Dark Continent with Sir Sidney, had seen sights and done deeds that would make ordinary men quail in fear. To him, Beatrice Carter would be like a buzzing gnat. He'd swat her away without breaking a sweat.

How could Clayton fare any better?

He was again mulling the prospect of heading for London. If he could just shift the party there, if he could just get Shawcross out of Carter Crossing, he was positive he could regroup and devise a plan to thwart him.

"How much have you borrowed, Clayton?" his mother asked.

He frowned. "I can't give you a solid number."

"Is it an amount sufficient to bankrupt us?"

"No. Don't be absurd."

"I've been pondering him. When I met with him in Frinton, he seemed to hate me, and I've been thinking . . ."

Her voice trailed off, and he said, "About what?"

"Rebecca told me a story about him. She claimed his surname isn't Shawcross, that it's Stone. Raven Stone."

"So? Why would I care if he's changed his name?"

"Your father had . . . ah . . . some issues with a man named Stone. It was long ago, but what if Shawcross is related to Mr. Stone somehow? What if he's plotting revenge over that old quarrel?"

Clayton wasn't interested in an ancient spat. "When did it happen?"

"Oh, it's been at least twenty years."

"Then I'm sure it's not that. Who would carry a grudge for twenty years?"

Even as he uttered the remark, dread swamped him.

Raven Shawcross was precisely the sort who would carry a grudge forever. Of all the men on Sir Sidney's expedition team, he was renowned as the harshest, shrewdest, and bravest. He was rumored to have killed dozens—perhaps hundreds—of enemies and malcontents, and he'd handled every dirty task that had vexed Sir Sidney, but that the great hero wouldn't stoop to handle himself.

Raven Shawcross wasn't the type to forget a single thing. Everyone said that about him.

"How should we proceed?" she asked.

"You expect me to have an answer?" He rubbed his throbbing head. "I think I'll declare the party to be over. I'll depart for town and take the guests with me."

"You can't leave me here with Shawcross! Don't you dare! The fiend terrifies me. His brother too."

"Well, I can't loaf in the country. Not with catastrophe festering. I'll return to London and hire a lawyer. I'll retain the most expensive one I can find too. I'll have *him* deal with Shawcross—so we don't have to."

"You're not paying attention, Clayton. Shawcross says we don't have the funds to hire a lawyer."

"Shawcross is an ass."

Clayton had had all the doom and gloom he could abide for one afternoon. He had to get downstairs and convince the guests that it was best to ride out in the morning.

After he was in the city, he'd track down new lenders and borrow a bit of money to tide them over. He'd use new money to square some of the older debts that were the farthest in arrears. It would stave off any argument with Shawcross.

Yes, that was the ticket! He'd borrow—and he'd gamble too! Maybe his luck would change, and he'd win some of what he required. He'd send a big, fat bank draft to Beatrice, and she could give it to Shawcross and repurchase the company.

He'd never have to talk to Shawcross, and everything would be fine.

He pushed back his chair and started out.

"Where are you going?" his mother asked.

"I have to prepare for my departure to London."

She sighed. "Your fleeing won't fix this."

"It won't make it any worse either, and for pity's sake! Stop moping and wringing your hands. You look like a defeated milksop. It's so unlike you."

He strolled out and hurried down to the front parlor, desperately in need of a few stiff drinks. Yes, the hair of the dog would definitely improve his mood.

———— ❦ ————

PRESTON MANEUVERED HIS GIG up the driveway at Oakley, although he wasn't positive it was still called Oakley. The sign over the gate had been torn down.

He always liked to welcome neighbors, but he wasn't keen to have the Shawcross brothers move in. In his view, they were scoundrels, and their continued presence boded ill for the young ladies in the Frinton area. For *two* young ladies in particular.

He'd been visiting Carter Crossing in the evenings, joining in Clayton's revelries. On each occasion, Millicent had been flirting with Lucas Shawcross. The prior night, she'd even snuck out into the garden to be with him.

He was worried about her, but worried about Rebecca too.

After stumbling on Shawcross kissing her in that secluded bedchamber, he was incredibly disturbed. It probably wasn't any of his business if she misbehaved, but then again, wasn't it exactly his business? He and Rebecca were friends, and she had no parent or relative to advise her in her choices.

He'd been endlessly debating his options. His initial idea had been to chat privately with Rebecca, but he'd quickly discarded the notion. He hadn't the slightest clue how to address such a difficult topic, and—if he warned her to be careful—she likely wouldn't listen anyway.

A conversation with Mrs. Carter was out of the question, so finally, he'd decided to confer with the obnoxious man himself. He'd remind Shawcross of the predicament he was creating for Rebecca. He'd point out the differences in their status and situation. He'd ask—no, he'd *beg*—Shawcross to leave her alone.

The door to the manor was wide open, and laborers were marching in and out, carrying in supplies, with renovation work already in progress.

He tied off his gig, climbed down, and went inside where it was organized chaos. Shawcross was standing in the middle of the foyer, holding what appeared to be restoration plans for the house.

Preston sidled over and waited quietly until Shawcross glanced up and noticed him hovering. Then he said, "Hello, Mr. Shawcross. May I speak with you?"

Shawcross could barely hide a grimace. "I'm busy, Mr. Melville, so no, I don't have time."

"Can you make time?"

Preston stared him down, ignoring his visible dislike. People thought Preston was an exhausting boor, and he never extended himself in a forceful manner. Generally, he was agreeable and courteous, but he could be extremely obstinate when stubbornness was necessary.

Shawcross was humored by Preston's display of bravado. Well, let him laugh! Let him tease and joke! Preston liked Miss Rebecca very much, and he wondered what Mr. Shawcross's opinion would be about her.

Somehow, he doubted Shawcross would have many kind remarks to share.

"Come with me," Shawcross said. "I'll give you ten minutes, then we'll be finished discussing it—forever."

He started down a deserted hall, guiding Preston away from the carpenters, hammers, and noise. Preston followed him into an empty parlor, and he shut the door, sealing them in.

Preston didn't dawdle, but seized the initiative. He had ten minutes, and he was sure, when the interval expired, he'd be escorted out—bodily.

"First off, I asked you about this once before, and you lied to me, so I'm asking you about it again. I'd appreciate it if you'd be truthful."

"Fine. What is it?"

"We briefly attended school together as boys, and your name is Raven Stone. You don't remember me, but my recollection of *you* is very clear. Please admit your identity."

Shawcross looked exasperated. "Yes, Mr. Melville, in another life, I used to be Raven Stone."

"Then you have no secrets from me, sir. I'm aware of the stories about your father, and you needn't clarify your early years. I'm certain it's painful for you to recall them."

"It's not painful. Those old memories make me really, really angry."

"Is your father's downfall the reason you've concealed who you are?"

"Wouldn't you have?"

"I can't imagine how I'd have reacted."

"My father had one acquaintance who stood by him, and he helped us stealthily, so the scandal wouldn't ever attach to him."

"I'm sorry to hear it," Preston said.

"He suggested we distance ourselves from my father as quickly as we could, so we adopted my mother's maiden name of Shawcross." He shrugged. "I shouldn't have, but I was only ten. What did I know?"

"Why haven't you told Clayton and Mrs. Carter who you are?"

Shawcross smiled a grim, frightening smile. "I'll let it be a surprise."

Preston tamped down a shudder. "You have plans with regard to them."

"Yes."

"What will be left of them when you're through?"

"Not much, I don't suppose." Shawcross announced it casually, nonchalantly, as if they were conversing about the weather.

"You're remodeling Oakley," Preston said. "Will you live here?"

"Probably."

"Should you tarry so near the Carters? Is that wise? It might be a burr under your saddle to be in such close proximity."

"They won't bother me for long."

Preston might have inquired as to what was coming, but the Carters' problems were their own. He had other fish to fry. "May I be frank, Mr. Shawcross?"

"Isn't that why we're in this deserted parlor?"

"Yes, I guess it is. It's about Millicent Carter."

"What about her?"

"I realize you went riding with her that one afternoon."

"I have no interest in her, so rest easy. She's too immature and silly for me."

"I'm glad of it, but what about your brother?"

"What about him?"

"He's been flirting with her quite outrageously, and I'm afraid he's leading her in a direction she shouldn't go."

"You've butted your nose into our business in a way that's irking me."

"I'm sweet on Miss Carter; I can't deny it. I hope to marry her someday, but your brother is handsome and exciting. As you mentioned, she's immature and silly. I'm sure he has no honorable motives toward her."

"I'm sure he doesn't," Mr. Shawcross bluntly concurred, "but here's the dilemma for us. My brother behaves however he likes. If he's decided to trifle with her, and I order him to stop—which I already have—he'll simply escalate his seduction merely to annoy me."

"What can we do then? Will you twiddle your thumbs until he ruins her? Is that where you'll allow this to end?"

Shawcross sighed with irritation. "My brother will tire of her very soon, and he's about to return to London. He's bored, and he hates the country. Once he's in town again, he'll never give her a second thought."

Preston nodded. "I'll take your word for it. Now then, I have to address the main reason for my visit."

"I know what it is, and I'm incredibly impressed that you'd dare. I wouldn't have deemed you to have the courage to confront me."

Preston huffed with offense. "It doesn't require much courage to remind you that Miss Rebecca is a very fine young lady. Out of the whole Carter family, she's probably the only one worth two farthings."

"You're correct," Shawcross said.

"But *you*, Mr. Shawcross, are a rich, sophisticated, famous man. You've journeyed around the globe and immersed yourself in wild adventures. Your acquaintances are rich and famous too, so you travel in the highest social circles."

"That's me in a nutshell."

"I didn't mean to stumble on you with her, and I had no idea she was here."

"She and I are very good friends."

"Is that what she is? A *friend?*"

"Yes."

"Will she ever become more than a friend?" Preston asked. "Might she become a fiancée?"

Shawcross glared at Preston, a myriad of emotions crossing his face. Finally, he said, "She's a Carter, so I would never envision her being my fiancée."

"Since you have no desire to marry her, you shouldn't be loafing in bedchambers with her. You shouldn't be kissing her in dark, isolated rooms, and you know it too. I'm asking you to leave her alone."

"You have no connection to her. Why would I listen to you?"

"I think she's extraordinary, and I think you agree. Will you deliberately hurt her? When you admire her so much, why would you treat her despicably? Will you destroy what little security she's managed to obtain for herself? If you continue on with her, and Mrs. Carter discovers your antics, have you considered what will happen to her?"

Shawcross studied him forever, then said, "I appreciate your concern for her, but I never let anyone order me about, so no, I won't leave her alone."

"Would it help if I beg you?"

"No."

He opened the door, and Preston's shoulders drooped with defeat. For a moment, he dawdled, struggling to formulate a different tactic he could pursue that might garner the guarantees he needed to protect her.

But Shawcross appeared resolute, and really, what authority had Preston in the situation? He wasn't her father or brother. He was a worried neighbor and that was it. He'd tried his best. What more could he do?

His other option was to approach Beatrice Carter, which he would never contemplate. She didn't have the temperament to handle the news in a sane way.

So . . . he would watch and fret—about both Rebecca and Millicent. He'd develop a plan of action, for he couldn't stand idly by while they were ruined by cads.

"Thank you for seeing me," Preston said. "I'd tell you it's been a pleasure, but it hasn't been, Mr. *Stone.*"

Then he stomped out without another word.

---

ALEX WALKED ACROSS THE garden, taking a circuitous route down the winding paths so he wouldn't be observed from the manor. It chafed at him to have to hide from their guests, but Rebecca had asked him to keep out of sight, and he would never deliberately upset her. Nor would he intentionally cause a conflict with Mrs. Carter or his father.

He should have been toiling away in the stables, which was his purported job, but he couldn't make himself care about his father's horses. The Carter family had never exhibited any interest in him, and he'd learned from their behavior. He didn't exhibit any interest in return.

He'd been on edge and restless, so he'd climbed the promontory to watch for ships, and he'd spotted two. They'd been big schooners operating with full sails, their bows cutting through the water like glass. He'd yearned to be on one of them so desperately that he could almost taste the freedom it would bring.

Though he'd skulked in the shadows for days, he hadn't seen Mr. Shawcross again, and he was anxious for a second conversation. He'd like to probe further into how a boy such as himself—with no sponsors or funds to get started—could join an expedition to a wild locale. Mr. Shawcross was the odd type of adult who would listen and offer sound advice.

Rebecca was up on the verandah, and he waved and went over to her—even though he should have continued on to the servant's door. She leaned on the balustrade and stared down to where he was loitering in the grass. If Carter Crossing had been a normal home and his relatives normal kin, he'd have marched up to her, but he was pushing his luck by being so close to the house.

If Mrs. Carter or Clayton stepped outside and saw him, there would be hell to pay. Not for himself—they ignored him—but Rebecca would be blamed and punished, and he couldn't bear for her to be in trouble.

"You scamp!" she said from up above him. "Why aren't you at work?"

He shrugged. "I was bored."

"Should I penalize you by dragging you upstairs and forcing you to do your school lessons?"

"On such a beautiful afternoon, that would amount to child torture."

She snorted at that. "Where have you been?"

"Up on the promontory."

"Were there any ships passing by?"

"A pair of three-masted schooners. And guess what else?"

"What?"

"People are moving into the old Oakley place. There are wagons of lumber parked in the driveway, and carpenters were carrying in their tools."

"Raven Shawcross purchased it."

The news was indescribably thrilling, and Alex beamed with delight. "Is he staying in the neighborhood?"

"It seems that he is." She leaned out a little farther and murmured, "We need to chat about an important issue. There's been some drama occurring among the grownups."

"With Mrs. Carter, wasn't it?" She was his grandmother, but he would never dare call her that. "Rumor has it that there was a situation at Carter Imports."

"Yes, and it involves Mr. Shawcross. The mess he's stirring might affect us. You and I should have a frank discussion about our options."

"Will we be swept up in it? Why would we be?"

"Let's not talk about it here. How about if you meet me in your room in a few minutes? We should probably make some contingency plans for ourselves—in case we're caught in the dilemma."

The comment was alarming, and he scowled. "What might happen?"

Suddenly, from behind her, his father bellowed, "Rebecca! Why are you dawdling? I told you to fetch me some whiskey! The decanters in the parlor are empty. Will I have to flog the servants to get them to do their jobs? What good are you as a supervisor if you can't accomplish such a minimal task?"

Rebecca sighed and furtively motioned for Alex to sneak off, but he was torn over how to proceed.

After the night he'd stumbled on Clayton harassing her in that dark hall, he'd been worried about her, and he hated to abandon her. He delayed a moment too long, debating the best choice, when his father loomed up next to her.

"Why are you loafing?" he inquired. "Who is distracting you from your duties?"

"I'm sorry you're irked," she claimed. "I'm coming in right now to assist you."

She turned away, and Alex was frozen in his spot, praying Clayton wouldn't glance down, but he'd learned at an early age that his prayers were never answered.

Clayton pointed a condemning finger at Alex. "Why is that boy standing at the foot of my verandah?"

"He's just leaving, Clayton. Calm down or your guests will hear you raging."

"I asked you a question!" When Clayton was angry, he couldn't moderate his volume, and it was definitely rising. "I have enough problems today without that boy traipsing around."

"No one will see him, and if they do, they won't wonder about him. It's not strange to find a child in the garden. It's silly to fret."

Rebecca was generally able to manipulate his father, but evidently, Clayton was in a worse mood than usual.

"He is your responsibility! If you can't manage him, I'll be happy to have someone else take charge. Perhaps—if I sent him to military school—he'd be taught to obey the rules."

"You're being a beast," she placidly said, "and you're aware that I will not let you shout at me. Locate me when your irritation has abated. We'll chat then."

She tried to walk off, but he grabbed her arm—as he had that night in the hall. Alex bristled with affront and leapt to rush up and pull him away, but before he could, Mr. Shawcross appeared like an avenging angel.

Clayton didn't notice the man's swift approach. Mr. Shawcross seized him by his coat, and with one hand, lifted him and flung him away from her. Clayton fell onto a table, the flimsy piece of furniture crumbling under his weight, and it crashed to the stone patio. He tumbled down with it and landed with a painful thump.

Mr. Shawcross wasn't even breathing hard, and Alex studied his posture and demeanor, deciding he would practice them in the mirror. He wanted to grow up to project that very same bearing.

"Are you deaf, Clayton?" Mr. Shawcross kicked Clayton in the ribs. "Or are you just stupid? I could have sworn I told you to never touch her."

"Bastard!" Clayton unwisely muttered.

"Don't insult my mother! I have it on very good authority that my parents were married." He kicked Clayton again, then he peered over at Rebecca and asked, "Are you all right?"

"Yes, I'm fine. He's drunk, which is his normal state anymore. You didn't have to over-react."

"Trust me," Mr. Shawcross retorted, "this is not me *over*-reacting. This is me controlling my temper. Go in the house."

"Don't boss me, Mr. Shawcross. You can't."

"Go in the house, *please*?" he snidely said. "Is that better?"

She frowned from him to Clayton, then back to him again. "What are you contemplating? If it's violence, I absolutely forbid it."

"I'm not contemplating violence. Clayton and I need to have a long conversation, and this is the perfect time."

"I demand to listen in!"

Rebecca was furious, and she looked amazing. Her feet were braced, her hands on her hips, as if she was ready to engage in fisticuffs with the much larger, imperious man.

"No, you can't listen," Mr. Shawcross said.

"I won't let you browbeat him," she insisted. "He's too inebriated to defend himself."

"Why was he scolding you? I could hear him yelling clear across the manor."

"He was livid about nothing. It's his regular condition when he's home."

She peeked into the garden, checking to discover whether Alex had tiptoed away. Mr. Shawcross followed her gaze and saw him. Since he was standing in plain sight, he would have been difficult to miss.

Mr. Shawcross smirked. "Hello, Alex."

"Hello, sir."

"It seems Clayton isn't overly fond of you."

"I'm sorry to have caused this upset," he replied, "and I should have crept off before he noticed me, but I couldn't leave her alone with him. Where she's concerned, he can be quite vicious."

"I know that about him," Mr. Shawcross responded, "and I appreciate your willingness to intervene. But why don't you run along? I'll take care of this, and she'll be safe from now on. I promise you that."

"Thank you."

Alex yearned to linger, to watch what would happen next, but he'd been dismissed, and he would never disobey such a dashing, heroic fellow.

He raced toward the servant's door, where he should have headed in the first place. It would have avoided so much trouble, but the damage was done, and it was too late to change the ending.

He glanced back for a final glimpse of the riveting scene. Rebecca stomped into the house, appearing annoyed at Mr. Shawcross for his ordering her about. His father was still hovered at Mr. Shawcross's feet.

Mr. Shawcross waited until Rebecca was inside, then he grabbed Clayton and raised him up. Clayton was swaying and off balance, and he uttered an idiotic remark that Alex couldn't hear, but whatever the comment, Mr. Shawcross punched him as hard as he could.

Clayton crashed into another table, and he plunged onto the stones and curled into a ball. He was gripping his nose, blood pouring from it as he wailed with dismay.

Mr. Shawcross lifted him yet again and dragged him off.

Alex dawdled for a few minutes, wondering if any of them would reemerge, but no one did. He smiled, being delighted with how his father had been bested. If he asked Mr. Shawcross, would the tough brawler teach him to fight? It seemed like an important skill for a boy to learn.

He whipped away and went into the manor to climb to his bedroom. Rebecca had mentioned there were problems brewing, and they had to discuss their options. He hoped she remembered that they needed to talk, for if she didn't, he couldn't go down to find her.

With the mischief he'd stirred by merely strolling in the park, he wasn't in any position to be out and about, and he definitely shouldn't be observed precisely where he shouldn't be.

———————— ❧❧ ————————

"You broke my nose!"

"Good."

They were in Clayton's library, and Shawcross tossed him into a chair, then sauntered around the desk and sat behind it as if it was his own. The man had the gall to fill ten castles.

After Clayton had been pummeled, Shawcross had hauled him through the front parlor and foyer, marching him past guests and servants alike. Although he'd been bruised and battered, none of them had been brave enough to intervene. They'd simply gaped at Clayton as if he was an ill-behaved mutt that had made a mess on the rug.

As they'd passed a footman in the hall, Clayton had wheezed, "Get my mother, would you? Have her attend me at once."

The footman had gawked as if he didn't comprehend English, and Shawcross had whacked Clayton on the head and spitefully reported, "Your mother can't save you from this quagmire. Don't expect her to ride to your rescue."

Gossip about the incident would travel far and wide. At that very moment, people would be packing their bags so they could hurry to London and spread the news of Clayton's disgrace. How would he show his face in town ever again?

"Your audacity is astounding, Shawcross," he spat. "How dare you attack me! How dare you embarrass me like this!"

"How dare I?"

Shawcross scoffed in a way that sent a shiver down Clayton's spine.

"Look at me!" Clayton waved a trembling hand over his person. "Look at my condition! You're a dangerous lunatic, and I categorically state that you must vacate the premises."

"I don't think I will."

"You've exceeded the bounds of what I should have to tolerate. You have inflicted yourself on my mother, and you have assaulted me. Not once, but twice!"

"I enjoyed it too."

"Go! Depart immediately!"

"One of us is going," Shawcross said, "but it's not me."

"Were you reared by wolves in the forest? What is wrong with you? I invited you here and this is how you act?"

Shawcross ignored Clayton's complaints and said, "Let's get down to business, shall we?"

"The only *business* that interests me is your announcement that you're leaving. Honestly, Shawcross! How can I force you out? Must I throw you out bodily?"

"As if you could." Shawcross chuckled crudely, then he picked up a stack of documents and flourished them at Clayton. "These will explain what's occurred."

"And what is that?"

"I've already clarified the situation about Carter Imports with your mother. Have you spoken to her?"

"Yes, and she spewed nonsense about your owning it now. I repeat, Shawcross: You are a lunatic, and you will never glom onto my property."

"Shut your mouth for a minute and listen to me. Listen carefully."

There were a thousand caustic remarks Clayton yearned to hurl, but he bit them down and asked, "What is it you feel so determined to tell me?"

"You're addicted to wagering, and you're really, really bad at it. You're in debt everywhere, and the payments on your numerous mortgages were overdue. I purchased them from your creditors."

Beatrice had told him much the same story, but he couldn't fathom it. He shook his head. "That can't be right. You can't simply butt into my life and seize what belongs to me."

"You ought to read your mail once in awhile. You were being sued constantly, and you never responded to any legal notices. Nor did you attend any court hearings. Weeks ago, you were adjudged a scofflaw, and it gave me the perfect opportunity to swoop in and ruin you."

"Meaning what?" he snidely inquired.

"Meaning Carter Imports is mine, and Carter Crossing is mine now too."

Clayton glared at him, certain he'd misunderstood. Beatrice had insisted Shawcross had stolen their company, but he'd stolen their home too? It was too improbable to be believed, so he wouldn't believe it.

"I'm sure you're jesting," he said, "but I have no idea why you would. It's cruel to spread these kinds of lies. You have my poor mother in an absolute dither."

"Your *poor* mother?" Shawcross snorted with disgust, then sarcastically added, "Yes, the prospect of her being upset is truly worrying me."

"How can I fix this?"

Shawcross scowled as if it was the strangest question ever posed. "You can't fix it. The business is mine, and with how revenue has fallen recently, there's no reason to continue it as a viable entity. I've closed it down."

"But it's how I earn my living! How am I to cover my expenses?"

"It doesn't matter to me how you cover them, but I suggest you check your bank account. I've obtained the appropriate writs and confiscated your remaining balances."

"You couldn't have."

"You're penniless, and I've learned from bitter experience that it's a very scary place to be. In the future, you'll have no ability to borrow again because you have no assets to encumber."

"You're trying to frighten me."

"No, I'm just stating the facts. It's the intriguing thing about England and its laws. The system is organized to punish debtors like you. When a rich man like me steps forward and agrees to square what is owed, any satisfying ending can transpire."

The door burst open, and Beatrice waddled in, and when she saw Clayton's bruised face, she demanded, "What happened to you?"

"Shawcross attacked me—with no provocation at all!"

"Didn't I tell you he was mad?" she asked as she approached and hovered over Clayton like a wicked witch on a broom.

"He previously informed you that he's gobbled up Carter Imports." Clayton gulped. "Apparently, he's gobbled up Carter Crossing too."

Her gaze narrowed. "He what?"

"The manor is his too."

For once, she'd been rendered speechless. She glared at Shawcross, flashing her usual glower, but he blandly stared back, his expression steely and terrifying to witness.

"Is this correct, Shawcross?" she asked. "You own our home?"

"Yes," he blithely said.

"You stole it from us!"

"There was no stealing involved. I got it the same way I got hold of your business. Clayton took out mortgages and didn't pay on them. So *I* paid them, and it means you've lost everything."

There was an empty chair next to Clayton, and she sank down into it. "Why? Why are you doing this to us?"

"I'm doing it because I can. I'm doing it because—when you squirm and grovel before me—I feel like a god!" Shawcross rose to his feet and declared, "My father was Harrison Stone."

Beatrice gasped with dismay. "That can't be true."

"Who is Harrison Stone?" Clayton asked her, but she didn't explain. Was that the man she'd mentioned earlier? Was it the dolt who'd had the ancient dispute with his father? Who cared about that?

"And my sister," Shawcross kept on, "was named Lydia. Might you recall a young lady named Lydia, Clayton?"

"Oh, no," Beatrice murmured, instantly deducing where the conversation was headed.

"I don't remember her," he hurriedly lied. There had been so many trysts, and Lydia was such a common name. Who could blame him if he'd forgotten her?

"You seduced her when she was sixteen," Shawcross said, "and she died in childbirth. Her baby died too. *You* did that to my sister—after what your parents did to my family. I was away in Africa when it occurred, which was lucky for you. If I'd been in England, I'd have snuck into your bedchamber and murdered you in your sleep."

At the threat, Clayton blanched, and it was on the tip of his tongue to blurt out that Lydia's baby hadn't died. Although Clayton had fervidly wished for its demise, the little bastard, Alex, was alive and well and prancing about at Carter Crossing. Why hadn't Shawcross been apprised?

Clayton's mind was awhirl as he wondered whether it was better or worse to admit it. Would Shawcross be glad to hear his illicit nephew had survived? Or would he be even angrier to discover how he'd been misled for years?

Before he could decide the best path, his mother reached over and patted his arm, warning him to be quiet. They needed to consider the situation. If he ever spoke up and revealed the boy's identity, he would definitely extract some concessions first.

Perhaps he could trade the boy for Carter Crossing. How badly did Shawcross want the bloody property? How desperate would he be to have the boy handed over? On the spur of the moment, there were too many variables to contemplate, and Clayton had to review them with his mother so they could wrangle a suitable conclusion.

"You have three days to move out," Shawcross suddenly stated.

"Three days?" Beatrice huffed. "Don't be ridiculous."

"It's the length of time my mother was given after final judgment was rendered on behalf of Lord Coxwold. You recollect Lord Coxwold, don't you, Beatrice? You shouldn't deny it. Not to my face."

"Yes, I recollect the old sot," she muttered.

"Lord Coxwold?" Clayton asked. "Who is he?"

They both ignored him, and Shawcross said, "My mother had three days to find somewhere to live with her young children—and so will you."

"We can't . . . move," Clayton complained, "and we're not going to. Carter Crossing has always been ours."

"No, it hasn't," Shawcross countered. "It's been *yours* for twenty years, and it was purchased with stolen money. I vowed that you would never keep it. It's the promise I made to my dead father at his grave. I've never faltered in that goal."

Clayton glanced at Beatrice, and she was pale as a ghost, as if she might faint.

"This is your mother's curse playing out, isn't it?" Beatrice asked.

"My mother cursed you?" Shawcross said. "Marvelous!"

"She swore I'd pay forever."

"She was correct."

"Mother!" Clayton cried. "Do something! Say something!"

"She can't do anything," Shawcross said. "She's tiptoed through life on a lie, and if I have my way, she'll be prosecuted for embezzling from my company."

"Mother!" Clayton almost squealed the word.

Beatrice simply tsked and said to Shawcross, "I can't believe you survived to pursue this."

"I survived—no thanks to you and your husband. But my parents didn't. My sister didn't, and I'm determined that your son repent that sin."

"Prove that you're Harrison's boy!" Beatrice said. "Prove that you have some connection to that pompous, loathsome family."

"I won't dignify your remark with a reply, but if you disparage my parents again, I can't predict how I'll react." He waved the stack of papers at Clayton again. "Three days, Clayton. You have three days to vacate."

"If we don't?" Clayton dared to inquire.

"I shall arrive with a team of men and put your possessions out on the road." He smirked. "That's what happened to my own mother. We'll see how *your* mother likes it."

He strolled out, and Clayton and Beatrice dawdled like a pair of marble statues as his footsteps faded down the hall.

After it was silent, he leaned toward her and said, "We can't let him get away with this! What can we do?"

"What can we *do*? I warned you this morning, but you wouldn't listen."

"He claims he's taken the last money out of our bank accounts."

"I'm not surprised."

He gaped at her, feeling annoyed, but alarmed too. *She* was the one who always had a plan. She couldn't be allowed to waffle in a crisis.

"You have to ride to London immediately," she told him. "You have to hire a lawyer and file an appeal. And it has to be someone with the power and authority to stop him."

In Clayton's opinion, Shawcross was omnipotent and untouchable. "How can I thwart him?"

"It doesn't matter how. Just do it!"

She pushed herself to her feet and, stunning him, she clocked him alongside the head. His wounds were still throbbing from Shawcross's assault, and he wailed with outrage.

"What was that for?" he asked.

"You are a failure, Clayton! As a man. As a son. As a human being. Now haul yourself to London and fix this!"

"What if I can't?"

"Then we're doomed, and shortly, we'll be living in a ditch."

She swept out, and he tarried in the quiet room, feeling miserable and alone and very, very tired.

The world was such an unfair place! A fellow such as himself, a fellow who simply tried to fit in and be friendly, never stood a chance.

He yearned to leap up and race to London as his mother had instructed, but he couldn't bear to show up there. Everyone in the house had observed how he'd been manhandled by Shawcross, and the gossip would be ugly.

Yet if he returned to London and resumed his regular habits, wouldn't the dilemma calm down? Surely Shawcross wouldn't evict his mother. Surely he wasn't serious. He wouldn't treat an older woman so despicably.

Clayton sat, and he continued to sit, and he couldn't make himself move.

The boy was key to any resolution. Yes, the boy had to be utilized. Clayton had chased him out of the garden, so where might he be hiding?

Rebecca would know. He had to find her and get control of the little bastard. Once he had custody, once Shawcross learned the identity of the boy's mother, then they'd see who held all the cards.

# CHAPTER
## 13

REBECCA STOOD IN FRONT of Oakley Manor, staring at the house. Most of the windows were still shuttered, but some boards on the ground floor had been removed. She could see inside, and it was dark and empty.

She walked around the building to where the master suite was located. It was a cold evening, so the windows were closed, but the drapes were pulled back, and a candle was burning. Someone was up there, and she had no doubt who it was.

The light called to her like a beacon.

She was struggling to understand her purpose. After her prior visit, where Mr. Melville had caught her kissing Raven Shawcross, she assumed she'd come to her senses about him.

She'd gone home, immersed herself in her chores, and ignored him completely. And she'd been so miserable!

When Clayton had accosted her earlier in the afternoon, Raven had blustered up to save her, and while she'd been thrilled to have Clayton pummeled, it would only make things worse in the end.

After the altercation, Raven had met privately in the library with Beatrice and Clayton. No one knew for sure what was discussed, but Beatrice was once again sequestered in her room, and Clayton was rampaging.

He'd bluntly announced to his guests that the party was over, and they would decamp for London in the morning. The staff had been tossed into a frenzy of preparation so people could depart on schedule. As to Rebecca, she'd been hiding because Clayton had been searching for her—and not with any cordial intent.

The maids had whispered warnings that he was drunker than ever, and he blamed Rebecca for the incident with Raven. She didn't dare cross paths with him. She'd hidden Alex from him too, having arranged for him to sleep in the hay loft in the stables, where he would remain concealed until Clayton rode away the next day.

When night had fallen, the manor had quieted. There was no nocturnal gambling in the downstairs parlors. No men chatted by the fire. Everyone was tucked away in their bedchambers, probably perceiving that an explosion was imminent.

Eventually, she hadn't been able to abide the tension or the isolation. She'd tiptoed to Raven's bedroom, but apparently, after he'd quarreled with Clayton and Beatrice in the library, he'd packed his bags and had left Carter Crossing.

His absence had been inexplicably depressing. How could he leave without a goodbye? How could she mean so little to him? Didn't he care about her at all?

The possibility was unacceptable, and before she could dissuade herself, she'd grabbed a cloak, lit a lamp, and climbed across the promontory to Oakley.

She went to the rear door and reached for the handle. If it was locked, she'd take it as a sign that she should go home. But if it wasn't, she would take that as a sign too.

As she gripped the knob, she whispered a prayer for strength—and for a wisdom she didn't seem to possess—then she entered into a porch. She didn't reflect on or question her mission. She simply wound her way through the deserted mansion to the grand staircase.

When she arrived at his suite, he was seated in a chair by the fire, drinking an alcoholic beverage. His coat was off, his sleeves rolled back. She couldn't see his face, but his posture was relaxed—like a man in his element, a man who'd finally ended up where he belonged.

"Hello, Rebecca." He spoke without turning around.

"How did you know it was me?" she asked as she blew out the lamp and set it on a table.

"I always know it's you. Where you're concerned, I have a second sense." He glanced over his shoulder. "Close the doors, would you? The room will stay warmer if we keep out the draft."

She obliged him, then walked over to where he was sitting. He clasped hold of her hand and linked their fingers.

"You left Carter Crossing without telling me," she said.

"Clayton and Beatrice will be departing shortly, and I had to give them a few days to make some plans. I didn't think I ought to be lurking."

"I missed you," she told him.

"I missed you too," he replied. "I was wishing you'd sneak over, but I wasn't expecting it. It's a nice surprise."

"I shouldn't be here."

"Of course you shouldn't be, but I'm glad you are. I was feeling . . . low, and you've cheered me."

It was quite an admission for him. He was such an imperious fellow; he'd never like to confess a bit of melancholia.

"Why are you feeling low?" she inquired.

"It's been a difficult year for me, and I've been pondering all that happened. Because of it, I'm incredibly morose."

He pulled her onto his lap, and he leaned in and nuzzled her neck as he untied her cloak and tugged it off.

"Are you all right?" he asked. "Clayton didn't bother you again, did he?"

"No, but he's been rampaging, so I've been hiding for hours. Alex too."

"Why does he detest both of you so much?"

"I have no idea. I've always been kind to him, but I suspect Alex reminds him of his failings. Were you aware that Alex is his bastard son? He was sired during one of Clayton's many peccadilloes."

"Clayton told me he was Alex's father, but I couldn't decide if he was being truthful or if he was just rudely boasting."

"It's the truth, and I'm a bastard too. My mother was Beatrice's cousin, and she was young and gullible and working for a nobleman who seduced her."

"That's a story as old as time. Who was the nobleman?"

She hesitated, debating candor, but she never discussed her dubious antecedents. "It doesn't matter who he was, and I don't like to talk about it."

Luckily, he didn't press. "I understand."

"Alex and I had nowhere to go when we were small, and Beatrice brought us to Carter Crossing, but she and Clayton have never been happy about it. They act as if they're better than me—because of my mother and how she misbehaved—and it saddens me. Beatrice insists I've inherited my mother's immoral tendencies, so I constantly try to prove her wrong."

"I predict that's been a futile pursuit. They're not the sort of people to change their views on any issue."

"You're correct. Every day of my life has been futile."

"And how about the hidden tendencies you've inherited from your mother? Is there a great wave of wickedness churning under the surface?"

"No. Yes. Maybe."

She groaned and nestled herself to his chest, and he stroked a soothing hand up and down her back. She snuggled with him while he sipped his liquor and gazed into the flames.

"You make me question everything about myself," she said.

"Why?"

"I like you more than I should. I hate it when you bark and snap and boss me, and I'm enraged that you're tormenting my cousins—yet here I am anyway."

He snorted at that. "I guess I like you more than I should too, and I've been struggling to figure out how I feel about that. My relationship with you is typical of how confused I've been the entire year. We're a pitiful pair, aren't we?"

"Yes, we are. What will become of us?"

"Nothing good, I'm sure."

"At least you're honest about it."

"Ever since Sir Sidney was murdered in Africa, I've been at loose ends."

"Were you terribly close to him?" she asked.

"Very close. He was like a father to me." He reflected for a moment, then smirked. "Well, perhaps if my father had been a wild, unrestrained roué."

"Sir Sidney was a roué?"

He wrinkled his nose. "Forget I mentioned it. I'm especially maudlin tonight, and I shouldn't denigrate him. I thought he was magnificent."

"Were you there when he was killed?"

"Yes, I was standing a few feet away. I saw my friend, Nathan, attacked too. Have you heard of him? Nathan Blake? He's Lord Selby."

"Yes, I've heard of him." She responded as casually as she could. "Wasn't he left for dead by all of you? You assumed he'd died, but somehow, he staggered home on his own."

He winced. "Don't remind me. I blame myself for our abandoning him."

It was another shocking admission. My goodness! If he would share such a stunning detail, he was definitely glum.

She scowled. "Was it your fault? Or are you suffering guilt that's not really yours?"

"It wasn't my fault, but it was absolutely my fault too."

"That makes no sense."

"A man from our team—a fiend named Judah—claimed he'd found Nathan passed away in the ferns, but the situation was too dangerous to retrieve his body. Later on, when matters had calmed, we went to locate his corpse, but it had vanished. I never wondered about Judah's story. I should have, but I didn't. If I hadn't been so distraught, it would have dawned on me that he was lying."

"Were you ever able to confront him about it?"

"I've confronted him," he coldly said, "but it doesn't wipe away my failing to protect Nathan."

She couldn't deduce what that might mean, and she didn't care about a stranger named Judah. But she cared very much about the other man: Nathan Blake. He was her half-brother, the one she remembered so vividly from the period before she'd been conveyed to Carter Crossing at age three.

"Have you spoken to Lord Selby since you returned to England?" she asked.

"Just once."

"How is he faring? Was he maimed during his ordeal? Has he recovered?"

"He's fine, thinner than he used to be, but fine. He's angry with us, which is completely understandable, but he got married recently. After he arrived home? I think it's helped to smooth over some of the trauma for him."

The news was unbelievably thrilling, but she was sad to realize how little she knew about him. It had her speculating again whether she shouldn't write to him and explain who she was. Would he reply?

"Have you met his wife?" she asked. "What's she like?"

"I haven't met her, and it's another mark of how awful this year has been. For over a decade, he was a best friend and constant companion, but he wed without informing me. He's so enraged about what occurred in Africa, and it haunts me."

"What's he like?" She prayed her query sounded blasé and nonchalant.

"He's smart and tough and brave. In any dicey debacle, he'd be the first to jump into the fray. You could count on him to guard your back."

"What a lovely compliment, and I'm sure—with your having had such a fond acquaintance in the past—you'll reconcile with him someday."

"I hope so. It's difficult to accept that he hates me now."

"I'm certain he doesn't. What was his childhood like?"

"He had a hard time as a boy. His father died when he was six, and afterward, he was forced to live with his grandfather—who was a monster."

"How was he a monster?"

"Nathan was incorrigible when he was small, and his grandfather finally threw up his hands and sent him away to school. He was never allowed to visit after that."

"He must have been so lonely. Had he any siblings?"

"No, no siblings."

*So . . . he wouldn't know about me.* The prospect crushed her like a heavy weight.

"How did he survive his rough upbringing?" she asked.

"He and Sir Sidney's son, Sebastian, were classmates, and Sir Sidney took him under his wing and shaped him into the man he's become."

Each tidbit was like a gold nugget that she would tuck away for later evaluation. He might have just confirmed her memories that she'd resided with her brother when she was tiny. Her father had perished when she was three, so Nathan would have been six.

She was disconcerted to learn that his childhood had been horrid. She'd imagined him wallowing in splendor at Selby, but it had been dreadful? Would his history make him more approachable? Might he be delighted to meet a half-sister he'd forgotten?

"I wish I could journey back in time and fix what happened in Africa," she said. "Or I wish I could wave a magic wand and erase all of it."

"Wouldn't that be something?"

"Will you ever travel there again?"

"I doubt it. It wouldn't be the same without Sir Sidney or Nathan. My other friend, Sebastian Sinclair? He'd have been the one to lead another expedition, but he shares my opinion. Our last trip was too harrowing, and it's the reason I'm at Carter Crossing. I decided I should move on with my life."

"What do you mean?"

"My work with Sir Sidney was carried out simply to earn enough money to execute my plans for Beatrice and Clayton."

"Can I convince you not to?"

He scoffed. "No. And don't stare at me with those pretty blue eyes of yours. You can't change my mind, so stop batting your lashes."

"I've never batted my lashes at a man, and I'm not about to start with you."

"What are you inclined to attempt? Why are you here?"

"I can't describe what's motivating me. I was at the manor—mostly hiding from Clayton—and I was suffocating. So I went to your room, but you'd packed and left."

"I'm no good for you. You shouldn't have sought me out."

"I know that."

"Whatever you're expecting to receive from me, I can't give it to you."

"I *don't* know that. I hate that we quarreled, and I hate that you're so angry. I hate that Clayton is so malicious. I hate that he's cruel to Alex. I hate that Beatrice has always been spiteful. I hate that I have no control over my fate."

"That's a lot of hating."

"Yes, and it's so unlike me to be disgruntled. I just want to feel better. I want *you* to feel better. I want us to both be happy. It seems wrong that we're not."

"You want me to be happy?" He pronounced the word *happy* as if it were an epithet. "There's one way you can improve my mood."

"Tell me what it is, and I'll try my best."

He paused, debating whether to apprise her or not. Ultimately, he said, "Let me show you."

He stood her on her feet, and he stood too and took a step toward the bedchamber. Through the open door, she could see the massive bed that was ostentatious enough for a king.

She hesitated, looking at the bed, looking at him. She was perched on a moral cliff. She could leap over the edge into sin and perdition . . . or not. She could stay where she was or she could cast caution to the wind.

A potent yearning swept over her. She longed to go with him. If she didn't accompany him, would she regret it forever?

She was positive she would.

By proceeding, wouldn't she bind herself to him? He liked her much more than he admitted. If she walked down this wicked road, wouldn't she snag him for her husband? If they behaved precisely as they shouldn't, he wouldn't be able to escape unshackled. He'd have to wed her. It was the required ending for dissolute conduct.

She had no parent or brother to speak for her. She was all alone, having to make her own choices, to forge her own path. She truly believed they shared a destiny and were being pushed in the same direction. When he tugged on her hand, she nodded and traipsed after him like a puppet on a string.

As Raven marched into his bedroom, he was keen to figure out his plan. He felt as if he was out of his body and gazing down on some other deranged idiot who was about to commit a grave error.

He never spent much time reflecting. He didn't lament over the past or fret about the future. He simply did what needed to be done, and he'd been driven by one goal: vengeance.

He was standing at the cusp of success, and he should have been celebrating, but he wasn't. He was thrilled to ruin Beatrice and Clayton, but their downfall couldn't alter history. His parents and sister were still deceased.

Once he was finished tormenting them, where would he be? He wondered if he might not become invisible and float off into the sky. What was there to tether him to Oakley or Carter Crossing?

Before Rebecca had strolled in, he'd been pondering her so furiously that—when she'd first appeared—he'd worried he was hallucinating. Since Mr. Melville had stumbled on them, she'd avoided him like the plague. On the verandah, when he'd intervened to stop Clayton from harassing her, she'd been snotty and ungrateful.

Yet she'd arrived and was offering herself up to his depraved intentions. He couldn't guess why she would, but he suspected—in her deluded feminine mind—she assumed it would encourage him to declare himself in love and wed her.

Unfortunately for her, he had few emotions—if he'd ever had any. From the day they'd met, he'd recognized that he needed something from her. Was this it? Would he use and abuse her in his grand bed? Then what?

He had no idea, but he was absolutely sure he would never regret what he was about to do.

He wouldn't give her a chance to reconsider, so he toppled them onto the mattress, rolling them so she was on her back and he was stretched out atop her. He kissed her as if he'd been drowning and she'd thrown him a rope, which wasn't very far removed from his pathetic situation. The losses of the prior year were piling up so high that he was feeling buried.

Might she ease some of his sorrow? If she surrendered what he should never have, would he be redeemed in some small fashion?

She joined in the embrace with an incredible amount of enthusiasm, and he was so relieved to cradle her in his arms, to have her body pressed to his.

His busy hands roamed over her torso, and her hair was driving him wild. It was tied with a ribbon, and with a nearly desperate yank, he jerked the ribbon away. Her beautiful locks fell free, and he riffled his fingers in the soft strands.

The more he caressed her, the more frantic he was. He started unbuttoning her gown, lowering the bodice so he could slip a palm under her corset to massage her breast. She was merrily willing to participate, even when he began to pinch and squeeze the nipple, even when he nibbled a trail down her bosom and sucked that nipple into his mouth.

She didn't draw away, but scowled and said, "This is so sinful."

He grinned. "Yes, it is."

"If it's a sin, it's wrong."

"The preachers claim it is, but I never listen to religious men."

"I'm not surprised."

"We came in here to dally. Will you talk me to death instead?"

"Maybe," she said.

"I don't think I can let you."

He dipped down and sucked on her nipple again, and she groaned with what sounded like resignation. He bit and teased as he tugged the hem of her skirt up her legs, past her knees, her thighs, so he could glide his hand into her drawers and touch her where he longed to touch her.

He slithered his fingers through her womanly hair and slid one into her sheath as his thumb flicked across the nub where all her pleasure was centered.

Just that fast, just that easily, she cried out and soared to the heavens. He laughed, delighted to discover she was as lusty as he'd imagined her to be. She flew up and up, the agitation never seeming to end, until finally, she reached her peak and tumbled down.

He captured her lips again, initiating a new round of torrid kisses that went on and on, and they were both so hot he figured they might burst into flames.

He was beyond the spot where he could practice any restraint, and while there was a very loud voice in his head ordering him to stop and send her home, there was another, much louder voice telling him to proceed and damn the consequences.

If he'd been more philosophical, he'd have paused to contemplate his motives. Though he appeared sinister and violent, when dealing with females, he was more or less a gentleman. He couldn't abide scoundrels, and he'd punished more than a few of them.

If he continued, was he any better or different from Clayton or any other cad? He held himself to a higher ethical standard than other men, so what was Rebecca's crime against him? Was there one? If there wasn't, why keep on?

He was simply feeling so adrift, and he thought—if he fornicated with her—he might find some pieces of himself he'd lost along the way. He wasn't about to hurt her so much as help himself during a rough patch.

If his masculine senses hadn't been ignited, if his cock hadn't been pushed to its limit, his reasoning might have been clearer, but he was so aroused that he couldn't fathom stepping away from the ledge where he was currently perched.

"I'd like you to do something for me," he said.

"I know what it is, and I'm not sure I should agree."

"Didn't you come to Oakley to give it to me?"

"I think so, but now that I'm in the middle of it, I'm waffling."

"You'll like it; I promise."

"Men always say that to women."

"And it will make *me* very happy."

She snorted. "I suppose it will. But what about me? Will it make me happy?"

"Yes, definitely—or I wouldn't consider it."

"We're not married," she pointed out.

"We don't have to be. It's just physical conduct."

"It's physical conduct that's expected to have a moral attachment."

He shrugged. "You're winding us back to the preachers, and I've already stated my view of them."

"What if I'd like it to have some meaning?" she asked. "What if *I* believe there should be a moral attachment?"

"Will you crawl out of this bed and sneak back to Carter Crossing? Is that the conclusion you'll accept?"

She pondered, then shook her head. "No, I'm not leaving."

He brushed a kiss across her lips. "I want to know you like this. It will be marvelous. I swear."

She moaned with dismay. "I have no willpower to resist you."

"This has been our path from the very start. Can't you feel it?"

"Yes, but where will I be when we're through?"

"You'll be right here with me—glad to have done it."

She gave the slightest nod, which he took as assent and permission.

He wasn't patient, wasn't the sort to dither and debate, and he'd engaged in all the discussion he could stand. If he didn't get on with it—and soon!—his body might explode. He was that anxious to finish it.

He began kissing her yet again, keeping her busy and distracted so she didn't have the opportunity to second guess.

Of course they shouldn't proceed. Of course she shouldn't participate, but it was too late to retreat and pick a different road.

As he teased and cajoled, as he tantalized and seduced, he was gradually stripping her of her clothes. There went her shoes and stockings. There went her gown and corset. When he had her down to chemise and drawers, he shifted away and removed his shirt.

She studied his torso and grinned. "I can't recollect ever seeing a man's chest before."

"What is your opinion of it?"

"May I touch you?"

"You'd better."

He clasped her hands and placed them on his skin, her palms like lightning to his phallus, and he was suddenly wishing he could make the event more special for her.

In many ways, it was her wedding night. After all, a woman only had her *first* time once in her life, but he was much too titillated to provide the amorous experience she deserved. He was too overwhelmed to slow down or talk about what was coming.

"Do you know what happens now?" he asked.

"I have a fairly good idea."

"It's very intimate."

"I've heard that."

"It's not like anything you've ever tried." A wave of guilt swamped him, but he shoved it away. "Promise me you won't ever regret this."

"Me? Regret being here with you? I never could." She scoffed and said, "You should promise *you* won't regret it. You not quite the scoundrel you pretend to be."

He smiled. "I won't ever regret it."

Swiftly, he divested her of her remaining clothes. All the while, he was caressing her, whispering encouragement about how beautiful she was, how much she pleased him. He'd have liked to strip off his own clothes, but he was in too much of a hurry. He unbuttoned his trousers and pulled them down to his flanks. Then he widened her thighs and centered himself, wedging his cock precisely where it was demanding to be.

She finally exhibited a hint of virginal alarm as she broke off their strident kiss and inquired, "Will it hurt? I've been told that it hurts."

"It won't hurt." He uttered the small lie with a straight face.

"And afterward, I'll be yours?"

"Yes, you'll be mine forever."

"Forever . . ." she murmured. "I like the sound of that."

He suspected she would interpret the comment in exactly the wrong way, that she'd assume he was offering marriage, but he couldn't predict what would occur the next hour, let alone the next day or week. He only knew that he had to be inside her or he'd melt with unquenched desire.

He kissed her and played with her nipples, as his naughty fingers stroked her down below. As her ardor escalated, as she cried out her passion, he gripped her hips, and he thrust into her, once, and again, and again, and he was fully impaled. He held himself very still, allowing her anatomy to acclimate to her new situation.

He gazed down at her, wondering what she'd thought of the monumental occasion, and she smirked and said, "I've got you now. I'm yours forever, but you're mine too. You'll never escape my dastardly clutches."

"Did it hurt?"

"A little, but I'm fine. Are we finished?"

"Just about. There's a bit more to it."

Tears flooded her eyes, and he couldn't decide if her deflowering had actually been painful, and she'd fibbed about it or if she was overcome by emotion. He was feeling quite overcome himself, which was strange. He was never barraged by sentiment, but he was being pelted by powerful male urges: to protect her, to cherish her, to keep her with him throughout eternity.

There were a thousand remarks on the tip of his tongue. He yearned to tell her how much he cared about her, how precious the interval was, but he never waxed poetic, and he wasn't about to start.

He tossed the peculiar sensations away so he could march down the carnal road to the end. He pushed in all the way and pulled out all the way, watching her expression as she adapted and joined in.

At first, it was awkward, but she rapidly figured out how the deed was accomplished. She wrapped her arms around him and hugged him as he proceeded toward the riveting conclusion. He delayed as long as he could, but much before he was ready, his seed surged from his loins. He shoved in and spilled himself against her womb.

He should have withdrawn to ensure they were safe from any consequences, but the pathetic fact was that she'd aroused him to the point where he couldn't restrain himself.

He took a few last thrusts, then collapsed onto her. He remained there, until he remembered he must be crushing her, so he rolled onto his side. She rolled too, so they were nose to nose.

Thankfully, she was smiling, looking none the worse for wear.

"How did you like it, Miss Carter?" he asked.

"I'm not a virgin anymore, am I?"

"No, you're not."

"I didn't need that old chastity anyway."

The tears that had threatened earlier overflowed and dripped down her cheeks. He was flabbergasted, but stricken too.

"You can't cry!" he said. "Don't you dare be sad!"

"I'm not sad, you dunce. I'm happy."

"You're crying because you're happy?"

"Yes."

He frowned. "I don't understand women."

"Men aren't supposed to."

He shifted onto his back and draped her over his chest. It was so quiet he could hear his heart beating. They dawdled, lost in thought, and he couldn't imagine what she was thinking. It was likely nothing close to what *he* was thinking.

He was aghast, but thrilled too. He shouldn't have forged ahead, but he never questioned his actions. He'd told her he wouldn't regret their conduct, and he didn't.

After a bit, she said, "Could I be with child?"

"It never happens from just one time."

He had no idea why he'd spew such an outrageous lie, and she was no fool.

"Are you sure about that?" she asked. "I presumed it could occur quite easily. There are certainly enough disgraced maidens in the neighborhood who've been rushed to the altar."

"I should have said it *rarely* happens from one time."

"If I'm unlucky, will you marry me?"

"Of course." It was another lie.

On the spur of the moment, he couldn't deduce how he'd respond, but he couldn't envision himself wed to a Carter. Despite how much he liked her, it was so far beyond the realm of possibilities that he couldn't begin to fathom it.

She sighed with what sounded like contentment, then she said, "What now?"

"Now we relax for awhile, then we'll try it again—if you're not too sore."

She grinned. "I'm not sore."

He settled her down so she was snuggled tight. The excitement was winding down, and lethargy swept over him. Without meaning too, his breathing slowed, and he fell into a deep, unusual slumber.

He never slept. Ever. From the minute his father had been imprisoned, his life had been in such a state of upheaval that he'd never been able to rest. Then, after he'd joined Sir Sidney, he'd been the lead scout and charged with noticing what others hadn't noticed. An added dose of insomnia had been stirred into the mix by his witnessing Sir Sidney's murder. How could a fellow sleep after all of that?

But with her in his arms, he dozed off, and he didn't move a muscle. When he opened his eyes, it was morning. She was gone, and he was alone.

She'd slid away in the night, dressed, and snuck to Carter Crossing—in the dark and by herself. He wondered how she viewed their antics and how they'd interact when they bumped into each other again.

Would it be uncomfortable or sweet? Probably a little of both, but he didn't reflect on it for long.

He'd ruined Rebecca Carter, and . . . ?

He wasn't sorry.

He shook his head—with amazement and disgust—and rose to face the day.

# CHAPTER

## 14

"It's about time you hauled your ass out of bed."

Lucas Shawcross glared at his brother who'd just staggered into the Oakley dining room. Lucas was seated at the table, dressed for traveling, and he'd been impatiently waiting for Raven to saunter in so he could say goodbye.

Raven had brought some servants from London, so the residence was more habitable. They'd gotten things squared away to the point where a breakfast buffet was laid out on the sideboard.

Lucas had initially thought it was fine if Raven restored the mansion, but after significant reflection, his opinion was that it shouldn't be restored. It was a decrepit, sorry building, and ghosts walked in the halls. He had no desire to linger and didn't comprehend or share Raven's fascination.

"What are you doing up at the crack of eleven?" Raven asked as he filled a plate and sat down.

Lucas countered with, "Why are you lurching *down* at the crack of eleven? Aren't you the kind of fellow who likes to leap up when the sun is rising?"

"I slept in for once. It's not a crime."

Lucas scoffed with disgust. As he'd sneaked in very late, having played cards at Carter Crossing, he'd been stunned to see Rebecca Carter sneaking out. She hadn't seen him though, and Lucas didn't have to be a genius to figure out why she'd been upstairs.

"I'm leaving for London," he announced.

"Why?"

"I've spent every minute here that I ever intend to spend. I hate the country, and I'm going home."

Raven shrugged. "So go. I'm not stopping you."

His brother voiced the remark casually, as if he couldn't care less what Lucas chose, but his expression was steely and irked, his exasperation impossible to ignore.

Raven had always been able to flash a glower and make Lucas realize he was a great trial. His brother's annoyance had Lucas eager to explain his decision. Not that it would do any good. There was no convincing Raven on any topic.

"You have the situation well in hand," he said. "The company is yours, and Beatrice is vanquished. You've tipped Clayton off his rocker."

"How?"

"Last night, he was shouting, throwing things, and bragging about how he would sue you into the next century. He was so drunk that he pissed himself, and the footmen had to carry him off."

"I wish I'd been there to observe it."

"He's declared the party over, and the guests agreed it was for the best. People can hardly abide him, and he put on such a deplorable show that they're all revolted by him. When he's in town again, he'll discover he has no friends remaining."

"He never had any in the first place."

"You don't need me to help you finish him off. You have a team of hired thugs coming to assist with the eviction. There's no reason for me to stay and watch."

"It would have been nice to have you guarding my back."

"From who? Beatrice? If you can't deal with her on your own, I don't know what to tell you."

Raven studied him, his fierce gaze digging deep, his ire so blatant that Lucas squirmed in his seat as if he were at school and about to be whipped by the headmaster.

"You're a mystery to me, little brother," Raven eventually said.

"No, I'm not. You understand me better than anyone."

"In most ways, I've figured you out, but in other ways, I'm completely clueless. Why, for example, would you be so blasé about how this ends?"

"I've never brimmed with your animosity. I was so young when Charles Carter bankrupted us. I don't really remember it, and I don't really remember Father. Or Mother for that matter. After we three children were separated, I saw Lydia precisely two times. If you asked me to describe her features, I couldn't."

"Can't you take my word for it that you should still be very, very angry? Think if we'd been raised like normal boys. Think of all we lost because of Charles Carter."

"What would that have been?" Lucas inquired. "Mother would probably have sent me to a seminary to become a minister. I'd have wound up as a preacher or maybe a bank clerk. Can you seriously picture me as an ordinary dolt? In some respects, Charles Carter did me a huge favor. He saved me from a life of tedium."

"No, he pushed you into a life of vice and criminality."

"I likely would have sought this path anyway. I doubt Mr. Carter had much of an effect on how I turned out."

"If you're not bothered by Father and Mother being destroyed, can you at least exhibit a smidgen of sorrow over Lydia? We weren't there to protect her from Clayton. Doesn't it make you want to lash out at somebody?"

"Lots of girls in my world are ruined."

The statement sounded terribly flippant, and it enraged his brother. Raven muttered, "Get the hell out of here. I don't need you hovering. You simply suck my attention away from where it should be."

"That comment came out wrong," Lucas claimed.

"No, it didn't. I heard you loud and clear. Lydia was just one more seduced maiden in a long line of them, and I'm just her brother. If she was killed by a roué, why should it concern me?"

"I only *meant* that her conclusion doesn't surprise me, and it shouldn't surprise you either. She was all alone. How could we have expected nothing horrid would occur?"

"Shut up, Lucas—before I pound you into the ground!"

Lucas's mind raced as he tried to deduce how to smooth over their paltry quarrel. He always hated to upset Raven, yet he always managed to upset him.

His brother blustered through life, and Lucas floated through it. His brother reached out and seized what he craved, and Lucas quietly stole it. His brother fought and won every battle, but Lucas furtively avenged himself when no one was looking.

He adored his brother. He worshipped his brother, but they never saw eye to eye and never would.

"What's your plan for the rest of the week?" he asked, anxious to depart on a calmer note.

"I'll mostly dawdle at Oakley to open up more of the house. In three days, I'll stroll into Carter Crossing with my thugs—as you call them—and I'll move Beatrice's possessions out onto the road. I'm sure she'll be in complete denial, and she won't have taken a single step to prepare."

"She'll be tossed out—as Mother was tossed out."

"Yes," Raven said, "but her experience won't be quite as dire. When it happened to Mother, she had three little children gripping her skirt. Beatrice's children are grown, so she doesn't have to fret over what will become of them. She won't have to die of a broken heart."

"I'm certain you won't believe me, but I'll be glad to picture the event—even though I'll be *picturing* it from my London bachelor's apartment."

"Heaven forbid that you stay and pitch in."

They'd already plowed this field, and he wouldn't plow it again. Instead, he asked, "What about Miss Rebecca?"

"What about her?" Raven was suddenly incredibly busy slathering jam on a muffin.

"What are your plans for her? Will you save her as you drive Beatrice to her doom?"

Raven scowled, as if it was the strangest question ever voiced. "She's a Carter. Why would I save her?"

"I saw her sneaking out last night."

Raven's knife halted in mid-air. "Really?"

"I don't suppose she was washing your dishes or doing your laundry."

"No, she definitely wasn't here for that."

"So you seduced her, and it was part of your scheme to destroy her cousins?"

"Pretty much."

Raven glanced away, giving Lucas the distinct impression that he had heightened feelings for the gorgeous, sweet-tempered blond woman.

"Isn't this precisely how Clayton treated Lydia?" Lucas asked. "If you ruin her and walk away, how does that make you any better than him? Doesn't that make you exactly the same?"

A muscle ticked in Raven's cheek. "Don't lecture me. You have no moral compass that would lead you to an honorable remark, and I suggest you butt the hell out."

"When your men begin evicting Beatrice Carter, Miss Rebecca will probably rush to you for assistance. If she begs you to help her, will you? Or will you simply lock the door, pull the drapes, and pretend she isn't knocking?"

Raven glowered at him forever, and he was so stoic and composed. It was always difficult to guess what he was thinking. Ultimately, he nodded to the door.

"Why don't you head out? It will be a hectic day, and as I finish this, I need to spend some quiet minutes, calculating how long it will take me to forgive you for running off like a coward."

Lucas bristled. "I'm not a coward."

"It seems like it to me. Or is it merely that our family's tragedy never truly mattered to you? You can be such a violent fellow, but it's usually over petty issues: women, money, dice. Yet in our past, the very worst thing happened that could ever happen to a pair of little boys, and all you can ponder is your next card game and how much you might win."

"Life *is* a game, Brother," Lucas facetiously said, "and if you would remember that, you'd be a lot happier."

"I've found happiness to be highly over-rated."

They stared, comments swirling, but Lucas had had all the bickering he could abide. He threw down his napkin and strolled out.

"Be careful," he cautioned as he went by his brother. "Watch your back."

"Yes, I'll be watching my back. It's not as if I'll have an ally present to do it for me."

"I'm not joking," Lucas fumed. "You deem Beatrice and Clayton to be fools, but you have them cornered and desperate, and they have nothing left to lose. That sort of person can be very dangerous."

"I'll keep that in mind."

Raven started eating again, ignoring Lucas, and Lucas frowned and continued on. His carriage was harnessed and waiting in the driveway. He'd only delayed because he'd thought he'd be courteous and tell Raven he was leaving. Why had he bothered?

He and Raven were two very different people. Raven never understood Lucas's choices, and Lucas constantly tried to explain himself—to no avail.

He climbed in and relaxed on the seat, and with the crack of the whip, the horses pulled the vehicle away. He told himself not to peer back at the aging, decrepit house, but he couldn't forget Raven's insistence that they'd come there as boys with their parents—before their lives had been wrecked.

Unable to resist, he peeked out, and he suffered a clear memory of his mother—he was very small—lifting him onto her hip and carrying him inside. She was young and beautiful and smiling. He sat very still, wondering if it was a genuine vision or if his imagination had conjured it.

Suddenly, a hint of her perfume filled the carriage, and he suffered another clear memory: that she'd smelled like the rosewater she'd bathed in.

He sighed with pleasure. Perhaps his mother's ghost had flitted in to say hello so he'd recollect that his brief history with her had been precious.

They reached the end of the lane and turned onto the main road. They hadn't journeyed very far and had just passed the entrance to Carter Crossing when his driver yanked on the reins and called to the horses to halt.

Lucas leaned out the window and asked, "What's wrong? Why have we stopped?"

"There's a girl blocking us, Mr. Shawcross."

"What are you talking about?"

Lucas opened the door and jumped down, and there was Millicent Carter standing in the way, her feet braced, a packed portmanteau at her feet.

She marched over to him, clutched the lapels of his coat, and shook him.

"You promised to take me with you," she said.

"I didn't specifically agree, and if you thought I had, I was lying."

"You can't abandon me! You absolutely can't! It's always been horrid here, but Clayton and my mother have gone totally insane—thanks to your brother. Can you picture what it will be like from now on?" She stamped her foot quite vehemently. "I'm sorry, but I can't allow you to leave me behind!"

He stared down at her, a myriad of bad choices arising, and it occurred to him that he could pitch in and give Raven some of the vengeance he craved. He could convey Millicent Carter to London and corrupt her in a very wicked fashion.

Why not?

Clayton had ruined Lydia, and Lucas was much more despicable than Clayton had ever dreamed of being. Tit for tat. It's what Raven kept clamoring about with regard to the Carter family. Tit for tat.

That conclusion certainly applied to Millicent too. Didn't it?

"I guess I can take you," he ultimately said, "but don't you dare whine about your fate after we arrive."

"Why would I whine about it? You're rescuing me, and I'll always be grateful."

"I doubt that," he muttered. "I doubt it very, very much."

He nodded to an outrider to grab her portmanteau, and as Lucas spun back to the carriage, she'd already dashed by him, climbed in, and settled herself on the seat.

PRESTON WAS MANEUVERING HIS gig toward Carter Crossing. A coach was approaching from the other direction, and he slowed down. It was fancy, with a driver and two liveried outriders hanging from the rear.

With Clayton Carter hosting his birthday party, Preston figured it might be a posh London guest heading home, and he prepared to wave in case it was a gentleman he'd met at the soirees.

The driver tipped his hat, and the horses rushed on by, so he only caught a quick glimpse of the passengers inside. He blanched with dismay.

It was Lucas Shawcross, and he was sure Millicent was snuggled next to him.

He warned himself not to read scandal into the discovery. She had accepted a ride with the older brother, and Beatrice had encouraged it. But Lucas Shawcross was on the road to London. Was there a reason Millicent would be traveling with him?

Preston couldn't think of one.

His mood glum, his spirits flagging, he continued on to Carter Crossing. It wasn't any of his business, was it? If her mother didn't keep track of her, was it Preston's place to mention the issue?

He was facing the same dilemma with Miss Rebecca. If he spoke up, he'd get her in a great deal of trouble, but if he remained silent, it was possible she'd land herself in plenty of trouble all on her own.

What was best? What was worst? How was a fellow supposed to know?

He decided to show up in his usual cordial condition. The party was still in progress, so men would be chatting in the parlors. He'd join in the socializing, and he would let circumstances push him to his next move.

---

BEATRICE TIPTOED DOWN THE stairs to the grand foyer. There was a general sense of abandonment in the air, as if the manor had been empty for months.

Clayton and his acquaintances had decamped for London shortly after breakfast. Her disloyal son had trotted off, so she'd have to tackle the pending calamity with Raven Shawcross by herself, and she viewed it as typical.

Men were worthless in a crisis, but the men of the Carter family were particularly useless. She'd ordered Clayton to hire a lawyer and commence legal proceedings against Shawcross, but she couldn't count on him to follow through.

She could only count on herself, and if their ship was about to sink, she would save herself. Clayton would have to hope he sobered up long enough to swim to shore before he was dragged under the waves.

The house was quiet, the servants tiptoeing too, as if everyone was bracing for catastrophe. They were wise to be alarmed.

How could she not have realized who Raven Shawcross was? Right from the start, she should have guessed. She'd been trying to recollect if she'd ever been told Lydia's surname. If she had been, she couldn't remember.

A decade earlier, when that sanctimonious vicar had arrived with Lydia's bastard in tow, Beatrice had been so stunned that she hadn't focused on the details. Now Lydia was wreaking havoc from the grave as her vengeful older brother ruined them all.

A footman was hovering by the door, and she asked, "Is that visitor gone?"

"Yes, Mrs. Carter, but he left a letter for you. He said it was very important and that you should read it immediately."

She'd been hiding in her room for several days, and during the interval, a stranger had stopped by on three different occasions and had begged to speak with her. He'd claimed they had to discuss a vital subject, but she'd refused to confer with him.

She'd presumed it would be more legal papers from Shawcross or perhaps a demand notice from the fired workers at Carter Imports, insisting she fork over their last wages. Well, they could parlay with their precious Raven Shawcross if they wished to be paid.

The footman handed over the missive, and she ripped it open, seeing that it was actually two letters folded together. The outside one was a note from her visitor, explaining his purpose. The inside one had gold trim on the edges and a fancy wax seal on the back. It was addressed to Rebecca, which was too odd to be believed.

*Mrs. Carter,* the stranger had written, *I have approached you on behalf of*

*Nathan Blake, Lord Selby. After significant investigation, he has learned that his sister, Rebecca Blake Carter, has been living in your home these past twenty-four years. He is interested in meeting her, and he intends to call on you at your earliest convenience . . .*

She quickly moved on to the second letter.

So! The exalted ass, Lord Selby, had finally deigned to worry about his dear sister. It had only taken him twenty-four years to get around to it! He wanted to travel to Carter Crossing to meet Rebecca! He wanted to introduce her to her twin, Sarah, the sickly child who'd been so ill that Beatrice had declined to bring her to Carter Crossing.

How had the feeble waif survived?

Lord Selby planned to waltz in like a magnanimous king and, if Rebecca was amenable, whisk her away to a life of splendor at Selby where she would be spoiled like a princess. The entire notion was so galling that Beatrice was surprised she didn't faint.

Her temper spiked. She hated rich people and always had. She'd come from meager circumstances herself, so when her husband, Charles, had begun to commit his embezzlement, she'd been delighted to help him steal as much as he could. Her loathing definitely extended to Rebecca's wealthy Blake relatives.

Beatrice had never forgotten how she'd been summoned to London by Rebecca's snooty, pretentious Blake aunt. The shrew had commanded Beatrice to assume custody of Rebecca, and Beatrice hadn't been able to stand up to her.

She'd corresponded with the witch numerous times to request financial support to defray the cost of raising Rebecca, but the annoying harpy wouldn't chip in. Ultimately, her lawyer had sent a cease-and-desist letter, warning Beatrice to quit nagging, so Beatrice had relented.

But suddenly, she was raging. If Mr. Shawcross had his way, she would lose everything. She didn't know if she'd be allowed to keep the clothes on her back, and she was certain her children would provide no assistance. They were lazy and foolish—Clayton especially—so Beatrice was gravely imperiled, and she had no allies.

The prospect that Rebecca might skate through it all, that her Blake kin might swoop in and rescue her just as Beatrice's world was collapsing, was too infuriating to abide.

She would have tossed the letter in the fire, but the front knocker was banged, and Preston Melville marched in. In her current mood, the irritating dolt was the last person she could tolerate.

"Mrs. Carter!" The cordial idiot smiled as if they were chums. "I'm glad to find you up and about. On my prior visit, I heard you were indisposed. I hope you're feeling better."

She wasn't about to engage in chitchat. "What can I do for you, Mr. Melville?"

He glanced into the receiving parlor, and it was empty. "The manor is awfully quiet. Where is everyone?"

"Clayton and his friends have returned to London."

"That's too bad. I was enjoying his guests. It's so rare that we have company. A new face is always welcome."

"What do you *want*, Mr. Melville?"

"Oh, yes. It's a brisk autumn afternoon, and I thought I'd ask Miss Millicent to go for a ride. Might she be available? Or if she can't, how about Miss Rebecca?"

Beatrice peered over at the footman. "Have you seen them recently?"

"No, ma'am. Not either of them. Not all day."

"Sorry, Mr. Melville, but I have no idea where they are, and I'm not about to search for them. As you've discovered"—she gestured to the deserted parlor—"we've finished entertaining, so you'll have to excuse me."

"Yes, yes, I understand." He frowned, dithered, straightened his coat, but didn't depart. "I realize you're busy, Mrs. Carter, but might we have a private conversation?"

"No." She nodded to the footman. "Show him out."

Melville was undeterred. "Please, ma'am? It's urgent."

She sighed with frustration. "I'll give you five minutes, and I suggest you use them wisely. Don't blather on and on. With how irked I am, I can't humor you."

She spun and stomped into the receiving parlor, and he followed her and closed the door.

"What is it?" she asked. "And for pity's sake, be brief."

"Before I start, I need to inform you that I'm speaking up out of affection for your family. I've been fretting over whether I should mention this issue, and I can't continue to be silent."

"Yes, yes, you're a veritable saint, aren't you?"

He dithered again, then wrung his hands. "I'm worried about your daughter and Miss Rebecca."

"Why?"

"They're spending too much time with the Shawcross brothers."

"Why would you think that? Millicent had a short carriage ride with the older one, and according to my son, he didn't like her enough to ever invite her again."

"She's been sneaking off with the younger one, with Lucas Shawcross."

Beatrice scoffed. "When would she have managed it that I wouldn't have observed her?"

"She's been waiting in the evenings until you went to bed, then she'd meet him in the garden."

"You're insane, Melville. I recognize that you're sweet on her, and I'm sure Lucas Shawcross has stirred your jealousy. But it's dreadful of you to spread gossip about Millicent merely because we've had a handsome rascal in the house."

Melville squared his shoulders. "I just saw Lucas Shawcross out on the road. He appeared to be headed to London, and I'm positive Millicent was with him."

"Well, *I* am positive she isn't. I am certain she's upstairs in her bedchamber. Will that be all?"

"No. I'm concerned about Miss Rebecca too. You're not inclined to believe me, but I'll spit it out anyway. If something terrible happens to her, and I don't warn you, I'll never forgive myself."

"What's she done—and I must confess that I can't picture any misconduct. She's such a timid mouse. She doesn't have the courage to misbehave."

"Are you aware that Raven Shawcross has purchased the Oakley estate?"

"No, I wasn't aware of that."

"It was a surprise to me too, but the other day, I was driving by in my gig. The door was open, and there were wagons filled with lumber in the yard, so I stopped and walked inside."

He paused and gulped with dismay, and she said, "And . . . ?"

"Miss Rebecca was there alone with him—in his bedroom suite."

Beatrice gasped. "In his bed?"

"No, no, they were just kissing—and it didn't look like their first embrace either."

"My, my." She studied him and said, "Swear to me that you really saw this."

"I swear, Mrs. Carter. I didn't approach you immediately because I wasn't clear on my role, but he's such a sophisticated fellow, and he can't have any honorable intentions toward her."

"No, he wouldn't."

"She's too trusting and wouldn't be able to ward off the charms of such a cad."

"You are a master of understatement, Mr. Melville."

"I hope you'll devise a good solution to this dilemma. She'll be dreaming of a future with him, but it won't be what he's thinking about at all. I'm convinced his motives are quite a bit more prurient than that."

"I heartily agree with you."

"I should also mention that his name isn't Raven Shawcross. I knew him as a boy, and his father was Harrison Stone. I won't say anymore about it, except that—with his arriving in such a furtive manner—he shouldn't be flirting with Miss Rebecca."

"I concur, Mr. Melville, and thank you for coming. I figured you would simply annoy me with ridiculous information. For once, I'm glad we talked."

"I'm sorry it's over such a depressing topic."

"I didn't find it *depressing* in the slightest. I found it to be extremely fascinating."

She went to the door and whipped it open, but he didn't budge.

"You won't punish her, will you?" he asked. "I apprised you with the expectation that you would handle this in a suitable fashion. I'll be so disappointed if I've created a huge problem for her."

"I'll deal with it in my own way, Melville. Don't you worry."

He sighed. "I realize you assume I'm fibbing about Millicent, but will you please check her bedchamber? I pray I'm wrong and that she is *not* headed to London with Lucas Shawcross—but I'm very afraid that she might be."

He tipped his hat, clicked his heels, and marched out.

She watched him until he'd exited the house, then her fury spiked to such a high level that she was amazed she didn't burst into flames.

Rebecca and Raven Shawcross? Seriously?

As the fiend was seizing their company and home, as he was preparing to take every item that had ever belonged to them, Rebecca was playing the whore for him!

Oh, Melville had claimed he'd only seen them kissing, but Beatrice had no doubt about Rebecca's true tendencies. Her mother had been a foolish slattern who'd succumbed to a nobleman's wily seduction, and Beatrice had warned Rebecca over and over that she likely possessed some of her mother's wicked proclivities.

Hadn't Beatrice been spot on in her assessment?

Rebecca had glommed onto the worst scoundrel she could have chosen, the one brute in the whole world who wanted to ruin every Carter, and Rebecca was a Carter! The girl was so stupid!

Beatrice was on her sinking ship, and as with Clayton, when she plummeted down, she'd be on her own. So would Rebecca. Rebecca probably believed Shawcross would rescue her as the calamity buried Beatrice, but the idiotic ninny was about to learn a hard lesson.

Rogues like Shawcross were dangerous, and when he boasted about how he would destroy the Carter family, he meant it. Rebecca was included in that group. Shawcross would never save her, and Beatrice wouldn't let anybody else save her either.

She was still clutching the letter from Lord Selby, and she stomped over to the hearth and tossed it in the fire. She observed until it dwindled to ash, then she whirled away and proceeded to her room where she would begin plotting her next move.

For days, she'd been frozen with astonishment and despair and confused over her options, but she'd finally been imbued with the energy she needed to fight back. She'd start with Rebecca, and when she was finished with her young cousin, the bloody tart would be very, very sorry.

# CHAPTER

## 15

"Psst!"

Rebecca had just stepped out of her bedchamber when Alex peeked out his door. He looked like a scamp who was contemplating mischief.

"I didn't think you'd ever wake up," he said.

"What time is it?"

"Almost noon."

"Noon!" She groaned with dismay. "I can't believe I overslept."

Of course that was the expected result when a female traipsed off and let herself be ruined by a scoundrel. She staggered home and fell into an exhausted stupor.

"Are you sick?" Alex's concern was evident.

"No, I'm fine. I worked hard yesterday, and with the stress I'm under, I was extra tired."

"I guess you were. I was about to come in and shake you to find out if you were still breathing."

"I am a bit off balance this morning," she said. "I'll perk up in a minute or two."

"You can't imagine everything that happened while you were loafing up here."

"What happened?"

"When you and I were hiding last night, Clayton rioted in the parlors, smashing vases and tearing down curtains. He was bellowing and shouting and generally making a fool of himself in front of his friends."

"My goodness."

"The servants are all gossiping about it. He was so drunk that he finally passed out, and the footmen carried him to bed."

"That's not the sort of sordid tale you should hear. The staff ought to be more careful about discussing it in your presence."

"They're all tittering. I couldn't *not* hear it."

"No, I suppose you couldn't."

"He called off the party, and he and his guests left for London."

"I knew they were planning to go, but apparently, I missed the chaos of their departure."

"The guests likely would have fled anyway—even if Clayton hadn't ended the celebration early. They were all disgusted." He grinned. "I'm betting he doesn't have any friends anymore."

She raised a brow. "If he's suffered a collapse of his personal situation, we shouldn't rejoice. If he loses his social standing, it might send him scurrying home where he'd be in residence constantly. Then where would we be?"

"True," he said. "I hadn't thought of that."

"I have to get downstairs, and I hope I'm not in trouble."

"Last I checked, Mrs. Carter was still locked in her bedchamber, so she probably isn't aware you slept in, and don't fret. If she's been inquiring, the servants will have invented a story to conceal your absence."

The news was so welcome that her knees were weak. She riffled his hair in an affectionate way that he hated. "You and I need to have our talk. There might be some awful consequences winging in our direction. We have to be prepared."

"What consequences?"

"Mr. Shawcross has taken over Carter Imports, and I've been informed that he owns Carter Crossing too."

Alex scowled. "It's the rumor that's swirling, but how could he own them?"

"Clayton gambled them away, and Mr. Shawcross bought them from Clayton's creditors."

"Well, that's a marvelous conclusion, isn't it?" Alex asked. "I like Mr. Shawcross very much, and he'll be much better at running the estate."

"Maybe, but I'm afraid he intends to kick the family out of the house this week."

She watched as he worked it out. "We're family too."

She shrugged. "Sometimes. Sometimes not. It depends on the moment."

"Will we have to leave with them?"

"I don't know. I've become friendly with him, so I doubt he'll treat us as he treats Beatrice." She whispered a silent prayer that her assessment would turn out to be correct. "In fact, I'm sure he won't treat us badly. I'm sure we're safe."

The prior night, she'd visited Raven because she'd been lonely and despairing and had been keen to share a private interval with him, but she'd had an ulterior motive too. She'd ruined herself for him, and for her efforts, he'd told her she would be his *forever.*

It wasn't exactly a nuptial proposal, but she considered it one. A man couldn't engage in the marital act with a young lady unless there was a marriage at the end. She declined to accept that he wouldn't wed her, yet she was terribly disoriented.

She wished she had a father or brother who could speak to him for her. That's how marriages were arranged. The two parties involved never made the decision themselves. Older, wiser people stepped in and organized it.

Since she had no one to assist her, she'd have to garner what she craved on her own. But how, precisely, did a female nudge a male into proceeding?

She had no idea.

"Should I walk to Oakley and talk to him?" Alex inquired. "He and I are friendly too, and I can ask his opinion about us straight out."

"No, I don't need you to talk to him. I'll see him later. I'll pester him until I receive some answers."

Actually, she was hoping she'd see him much sooner than that. She hoped he'd stop by, and she refused to think he wouldn't come.

Their conduct had been incredibly intimate, and she felt all jumbled on the inside. She was desperate to converse with him about what had transpired. She wanted to squeeze his hand and listen as he promised her that everything would be all right.

"If he kicks out Mrs. Carter," Alex said, "where would she go?"

"I suppose to town to stay with Clayton."

"Then what if Mr. Shawcross kicks us out too? Would Mrs. Carter invite us to go with her? Would my father allow us to stay with him?"

Rebecca had never lied to Alex, and she wasn't about to start. "I can't predict what's about to occur. This situation seems quite unreal to me. I can't imagine Beatrice departing or you and I having to make emergency plans for ourselves. Let's not panic."

"Not yet anyway."

"Not yet," she agreed. "Now I have to show my face downstairs. Would you try not to stir any mischief please?"

"I never stir mischief."

Rebecca scoffed. "If only that were true."

She left him and went down to the kitchen to grab a scone. The room was mostly deserted. Everyone appeared to be walking on eggshells, worried and murmuring in whispered tones about Clayton.

It would take days to get the manor in order, to repair the drapes and other items Clayton had damaged in his rampage. She was repeatedly asked about Raven and what might happen, but she kept her expression blank, not anxious to scare them.

As she'd mentioned to Alex, she felt she was dreaming. If the family was evicted, what would become of the servants? Would they be terminated? When Raven had seized Carter Imports, he'd fired the employees. Would the house servants suffer the same fate?

Rebecca couldn't guess how he'd behave, but she'd have a frank chat with him about the staff. Some of their relatives had worked on the property for generations. It would be cruel to send them packing.

She'd spent her life yearning for something exciting to transpire, for something to change, and she'd finally gotten her wish—merely to learn that she didn't care for *change* at all.

A maid came down to fetch her. Beatrice had emerged from her bedchamber, and she was in the library and commanding Rebecca attend her. At the news, people cast nervous glances. Beatrice's temper was always foul, and Rebecca bore the brunt of her low moods.

"I'll discuss Mr. Shawcross with her," she told them. "I'll share her comments with you as soon as I can."

"Find out if we'll be leaving," a footman said. "If that's Mr. Shawcross's scheme, where are we to go?"

Rebecca patted him on the arm. "Don't fret until we have solid information. For the moment, it's just gossip and innuendo."

She flashed a tepid smile and hurried up to the library. Even a short delay was an eternity to Beatrice, and it fueled her ire so sane discourse was impossible.

She was seated at the desk, and as Rebecca entered the room, she said, "Close the door."

Rebecca shut it and went over to sit in the chair across. "I'm glad you're up and about. We have to review several matters—especially Mr. Shawcross. The servants are pestering me with questions, but I don't know what to tell them."

Beatrice smirked derisively. "I'm not concerned about them. Nor am I concerned about Shawcross. He ambushed me at Carter Imports, so I was defeated there, but I'm ready for him now."

"Meaning what? How are you ready for him? And what about the servants? They're in a dither over whether or not they're about to lose their jobs."

"Shawcross believes he owns Clayton's business, and I've allowed him to think so, but he'll never take Carter Crossing from me. I'll kill him before I'll permit him to have it."

Rebecca could barely keep from rolling her eyes. "You'll *kill* Mr. Shawcross? Don't be melodramatic. Let's confer about real options that might help to resolve this dilemma."

Beatrice simply glared and asked, "Have you seen Millicent?"

"No."

"How about that impertinent scoundrel, Lucas Shawcross?"

"No."

"Over the past few days, have you noticed Millicent cozying up to him?"

"I've observed them chatting occasionally. Why?"

"Has she mentioned him to you? Has she been gushing about him?"

"Not to me, but then, I've been busy with our hosting such a large group of visitors. I've hardly spoken to Millicent."

"Yes, you've been very *busy*, haven't you?"

There was a caustic note in Beatrice's voice that set Rebecca's senses on alert. Clearly, she was about to be scolded for an infraction. What had she done?

"Well, I *have* been busy," she said.

"I'm not talking about your usual chores."

"What are you talking about then? It's obvious you're angry. Have I distressed you? If so, I apologize for whatever it is. You've been under a lot of pressure recently, and I would never deliberately make it worse."

"You're such a liar." Beatrice almost hissed the words. "You're not only a liar, you're a whore too."

Rebecca blanched. "What?"

"I've warned you for years," Beatrice said. "I've warned you about your mother and her immoral tendencies. You have her same blood flowing in your veins."

"Yes, and I'm weary of hearing you denigrate her. I wish you'd stop."

"Stop now? When you've proved yourself to be just like her?"

"What are you complaining about?"

"Whore!" Beatrice seethed again.

Rebecca's own temper flared. She'd frequently engaged in horrid discussions like this with her cousin. She'd sat through them, steaming with fury, then spending weeks afterward calming down. But the patience she had to muster to tolerate Beatrice's insults had vanished.

"As I just stated," she said, "you've been under a lot of pressure, so I will forgive you for hurling such a despicable falsehood, but I won't listen to it.

Summon me when you're feeling more yourself, and I'll return, but so long as you intend to chastise me for sins I haven't committed, I can't heed you. I don't have the composure to endure your diatribe."

She stood to march out, and Beatrice prevented any exit by demanding, "Tell me about your pathetic...*fling* with Raven Shawcross. How often have you spread your legs for him?"

Rebecca was stunned by the charge. Her affair had been discovered? Beatrice was aware of it? How could she be?

Rebecca's jaw dropped in astonishment. "Who told you that?"

"Did you think I wouldn't find out? This is a small household and a quiet neighborhood. Did you think you could revel like this and no one would know?" Beatrice scoffed. "I suppose that's what *he* claimed when he was seducing you. Is that how he coerced you into it? Did he insist no one would ever learn of your disgrace?"

Rebecca steadied her breathing. She didn't dare reveal—not by the slightest hint—that Beatrice possessed valid information.

"I have no idea why you're leveling such a spurious allegation against me," Rebecca said, "and I'm very hurt by it. I've tried to—"

"Be silent!" Beatrice shouted. "Have the decency to admit your shame to me. Don't pretend to be innocent, not when your guilt is so clear."

"I am innocent," Rebecca declared, even though her cheeks were heating.

"Raven Shawcross, Rebecca? The man is here to ruin me! It's his specific purpose! He'll seize everything I have and leave me with nothing."

"I realize that, and I'm sorry you've been forced into such a difficult predicament."

"He's determined to destroy me, yet you have blithely climbed into his bed. Are you his ally in this devastation?"

"No!"

"How can I believe you? Have you been feeding him details about me? As the two of you snuggle under the blankets, have you been whispering my secrets? How much worse will the damage be because *you* were on his side?"

"There are no *sides*. I want to help you. I want to smooth over this impasse with him. I don't want you to be evicted, and I don't want the servants to be terminated. He and I are friends! I can speak to him for you. Perhaps I can convince him to cease his torment."

"I took you in when you were three years old," Beatrice said. "I didn't have to. Your lofty Blake relatives were eager to be shed of you. I could have refused to assist you. I could have let them put you in an orphanage."

"Well, you didn't, and I've always been grateful."

"I have given you shelter and support for twenty-four years, and this—this!—is how you repay me!"

"Would you calm down? I hate it when you're in such a lather."

Beatrice snorted with contempt. "Still, you sit there and lie to me. Shall I send for Mr. Melville so he can describe what he witnessed?"

*So . . . Preston had tattled after all.*

Rebecca sighed. "You needn't summon Mr. Melville, but he merely saw me kissing Mr. Shawcross. That's it. We were only . . . kissing."

Even as Rebecca voiced the paltry defense, she understood how awful it sounded, and it certainly had no effect at dampening Beatrice's fit of pique.

"At least you've confessed that much. What about the rest? You decline to acknowledge the full scope of your transgressions. Shall we have the midwife in Frinton examine you? Is that what's required to drag the truth out of you?"

Rebecca flinched with alarm. She couldn't tamp it down. Could a midwife discern whether a maiden had been deflowered? The notion had never occurred to her, and she was terrified that Beatrice might demand it.

"Beatrice, honestly!" Rebecca scolded. "What a thing to say to me."

"You're exactly like your mother. Don't pretend you've simply been *kissing* Mr. Shawcross. With such a handsome rogue showing you a bit of attention, you couldn't have resisted him."

Rebecca's cheeks heated to an even hotter temperature. She held Beatrice's gaze, not glancing away, for she recognized that any retreat would be construed as an admission.

"Mr. Shawcross and I are friends," Rebecca repeated. "He's been cordial, and I've reciprocated his amiable gestures."

She would lie to the very end and had to hope Beatrice grew weary of the quarrel before it ascended to a cliff from which they couldn't step away.

"Friends . . ." Beatrice muttered. "You look me in the eye and brag that you're *friends* with my greatest enemy! The man who would crush me, the man who would wreck what my husband and I built! You kiss him behind my back. You ruin yourself behind my back."

"I didn't." Rebecca would deny any affair until she exhaled her last breath.

"What has he promised you?"

"Nothing!"

"Is it marriage? He must have claimed he'd wed you and install you as the mistress of Carter Crossing. Is that what you're expecting? You've always chafed over your lowly status in this house. Will you gleefully take my place?"

"No! You're being absurd."

"You've constantly thought you were better than me. You and your lofty Blake blood!" She pronounced the name *Blake* as if it were an epithet.

"Mr. Shawcross and I have never discussed marriage," Rebecca insisted, "and I don't want anything that's yours."

"Know this, Rebecca. Shawcross is a rogue and a scoundrel, a liar and a thief, a fraud and a criminal. Whatever he's promised you, whatever trick he used to entrap you, he'll never follow through."

Rebecca stared at Beatrice, wondering how they'd go forward after such a hideous conversation. They'd had many unpleasant chats over the years, and Rebecca always forgave the slights and snubs. She'd never had much choice but to pardon her cousin, but she didn't think it would happen this time.

Beatrice had persuaded herself that she'd been betrayed, and she was partially correct. Rebecca viewed herself as being allied with Raven. In any scheme he was pursuing with Beatrice, Rebecca would be on his side.

Her antics the prior night had left her feeling bonded to him in a manner she'd never been with anyone else. They were intimately connected, attached forever, so they could never be separated.

She belonged with him. His goals were her goals. While she was sorry for Beatrice and would guide her through the ordeal, Rebecca would assess it from Raven's vantage point.

As he carried out his plans, she would intervene quietly so he didn't wreak quite as much havoc. It was the maximum effort she could extend for

Beatrice. It was an important benefit for the servants who'd been kind to her.

"It pains me when you're so angry," Rebecca said, "and I'm sad that you've accused me of immoral conduct. I can't imagine how we'll interact in the future."

"You needn't worry about it."

"What do you mean?"

"Get out of my house."

"What? Don't be ridiculous. I'm not leaving—especially not when Mr. Shawcross is inflicting himself on you. I'll arbitrate for you to calm him down."

"Get out!" Beatrice rose from her chair, like a judge passing sentence. "Get out now. Pack your things and go."

"Go where? I don't have any money or acquaintances to offer shelter."

"Run to your precious Mr. Shawcross. I'm sure he'll welcome you."

"I doubt it," Rebecca felt compelled to state, even as she silently vowed to do exactly that. She would march across the promontory and stay with him at Oakley.

"You have one hour to be out."

"Beatrice Carter! This is my home. I'm not about to let you evict me on the spur of the moment simply because you're upset."

"When that hour is up, I will come upstairs to check your bedchamber. If your belongings are still in it, I will summon the law and declare you've been stealing from me. I'll have you arrested, and you can be removed from the premises that way—with the servants watching you dragged out in disgrace."

"Why would you treat me like that? Why?"

"Because I can. Because I want to," Beatrice coldly said.

Rebecca hovered, eager to continue the argument, to plead her case, or to defend herself. Why would she?

Beatrice was cruel and malicious. She'd worked Rebecca like a slave, had repeatedly abused her with taunts and insults, had exploited her gentle nature and sunny personality, but they'd arrived at the final junction in their relationship.

For her whole life, Beatrice had warned Rebecca that she'd turn out just like her mother, and isn't that precisely what had happened? It was embarrassing to admit how right Beatrice had been, but Rebecca—to her great astonishment—was very much in love with Raven Shawcross.

He might have seduced her, but she'd been a willing participant. She'd proceeded in order to make him happy, to encourage him to understand that they should be husband and wife.

They'd be wed at the earliest opportunity, so she needn't fret. And wasn't it time to depart Beatrice's home? Hadn't she been yearning to leave for ages? Here was her chance.

She would go to Raven, and he would take her in.

Unfortunately for Beatrice, when he rode to Carter Crossing to impose his penalties, Rebecca wouldn't be present to temper his wrath. But that was Beatrice's problem and not Rebecca's. Not anymore.

"Fine." Rebecca nodded, and she whipped away and headed out.

"One hour, Rebecca. Don't force me to send for the law."

Rebecca glared over her shoulder. "Trust me, Cousin. You'd receive too much enjoyment from having me arrested. I'd never give you the satisfaction."

She exited the room and slammed the door behind her.

# CHAPTER

## 16

"WHAT SHALL I TELL Mrs. Carter?"

"Why would it matter to me what you tell her?"

Raven glared at Preston Melville. They were in the front parlor at Oakley, and the carpenters were working in the kitchen, so he and Melville were alone. There was no one to overhear their conversation.

Melville was quite intrepid. He glared right back and said, "Miss Millicent was in your brother's carriage, and they appeared to be headed to London. Would you like to explain why that would be?"

"I'm not doubting you. I'm sure you couldn't lie if your life depended on it."

"Is it your opinion that he's absconded with her against her will?"

"No!" Raven scoffed. "Females trail after him like hens pecking at their feed. He doesn't have to kidnap one of them to obtain what he wants."

"She accompanied him of her own accord?"

"I don't bloody know! He left for London an hour ago. I assumed he was traveling by himself."

"She didn't stop by here? She didn't"—Melville gulped with dismay—"spend the night so they could get an early start?"

"I haven't seen that silly girl since the afternoon I took her on that carriage ride."

"Your brother has certainly *seen* her plenty. They've been sneaking into the garden every evening—after her mother went to bed."

The news lit a spark to Raven's temper. Shortly after they'd arrived at Carter Crossing, when they were still pretending to be horse traders, he'd caught Lucas flirting with Miss Carter, then Rebecca had mentioned a possible tryst between them. Raven had questioned him about it, and Lucas had insisted he'd been trifling with a housemaid. And Raven had shrugged it off.

It was the common tenet of their relationship: Lucas would dance out onto the edge of trouble, and Raven would nag at him about it. Lucas would lie through his teeth, and Raven would believe him. Why was that exactly?

Raven viewed himself as a shrewd, cunning judge of character and motive. He was never wrong. He never miscalculated. Why, when dealing with Lucas, was he so easily duped?

"What will he do to her?" Melville asked.

"What do you think he'll do?" Raven crudely retorted, and he muttered, "If he hasn't done it already."

Melville's shoulders slumped. "Aren't you the least bit concerned? She's a gullible maiden from a small village in the country, and he's a rich, worldly scoundrel. There's no predicting what might happen to her."

"Let your imagination run free. My brother is capable of any nefarious conduct."

"He'll ruin her."

"Yes."

"How long will he amuse himself?"

"A week? A month? His passing fancies never entice him for more than a month."

"Then what?"

Melville's expression was condemning. He was trying to make Raven feel guilty, but he never could. Lucas's foibles were his own, and Raven couldn't prevent or fix them.

"What are you demanding, Melville?" Raven inquired. "Should I gallop after them and force her home?"

"Yes, that's precisely how you should respond!"

"What would I be forcing her home *for* or *to?* In three days, I will march into Carter Crossing and evict the occupants."

"So the rumors are true?"

"I own their estate now." Raven admitted it without an ounce of shame.

"You're so eager to destroy them? You hate them that much?"

"Yes—for what they did to my father and for what Clayton did to my sister."

Melville scowled. "What did he do to your sister?"

"I'm betting you can figure it out without any clarification from me."

"Is that why you're content to have your brother ruin Millicent? Is it wrapped up in the revenge you seek?"

"I hadn't realized he'd seduced her, and I can't fathom what he's thinking."

"If he proceeds, how is he any better than Clayton?"

"Drop it, Melville. I'm not a philosopher, and I won't debate moral issues with you."

Melville switched to another topic. "You'll kick Mrs. Carter out on the road?"

"Yes."

"What about the servants?"

"They're not my problem."

"Some of their families have worked at that property for generations."

"Then this will be the *last* generation that works there."

"You don't care about Carter Crossing. Why take it? Why wreck the livelihood of so many people?"

"Because I can," Raven bluntly said.

"What are your plans for the manor? What about the fields and the gardens and the orchards?"

"I intend to raze the house, and I'll let the fields, gardens, and orchards go fallow. In a year or two, it will be as if the Carters never resided there a single minute."

Melville was a determined nuisance, and he looked aggrieved and heroic. "After you've carried out your horrible deeds, how can you remain in the Frinton area? You'll be a pariah who is shunned by all."

"Why would that bother me?"

"Everyone needs friends, Mr. Shawcross."

If Raven decided he needed a friend, he'd get himself a dog.

"Are we finished?" he asked. "I'm busy, and it appears you've fully shared your concerns."

Melville's lips were pursed in a tight line. "You won't go after them?"

"No, I won't."

"You are a famed member of Sir Sidney's exploration team, and Sir Sidney was practically a saint in this country. Is this how he'd like to see you acting?"

"Trust me: Sir Sidney wasn't a saint, and neither am I."

"Fine!" Melville fumed. "Evict Mrs. Carter. Fire the servants. Demolish the manor. When your vengeance is complete, will you finally be happy?"

"Yes. I expect I'll be very, very happy."

"What about Miss Rebecca?"

"What about her?"

"Will you kick her out too? I could have sworn you'd developed tender feelings for her."

"I haven't." As Raven uttered the huge falsehood, he hoped he wouldn't be struck by lightning.

"You were dallying with her merely for sport?"

"I guess."

"What are your plans for her?"

"I have no plans," Raven said.

"Just as I suspected." Melville scoffed derisively. "Your brother is a cad, and you are too."

"I wish you'd stop visiting me. Each time you stroll in, you annoy me a bit more."

"I shall save you from further aggravation, sir. It is my extreme desire that I never suffer the misfortune of chatting with you ever again. And I shall ride to London and confront your brother myself."

"You shouldn't. Miss Carter won't welcome your intervention, and she isn't worth the effort. You'll simply wind up embarrassing yourself."

"We'll see how she feels when I arrive. After spending a few days with your despicable sibling, she may have come to her senses. She may be delighted to be rescued."

"I doubt it, and if you irk Lucas overly much, he'll simply stab you in the heart and dump your body in the Thames. He's testy that way."

"If that is even remotely true, then I have to declare that the world would be a better place without either of you."

Melville doffed his hat and stomped out, and Raven stood in his decrepit parlor, listening as Melville climbed into his gig and drove away. The quiet settled, the only noise the hum of voices from the carpenters in the other section of the house.

From the moment Melville had slithered in, Raven's temper had been flaring, and with the oaf's snotty departure, his rage was burning even hotter.

He'd warned Lucas away from Millicent Carter, and Lucas had proceeded anyway. Raven could jump on a horse and race to London. He could beat Lucas to a pulp for being such an idiot, but what good would it do?

What had Miss Carter believed was occurring with Lucas? The foolish child likely thought handsome, dashing Lucas was madly in love and would wed her. Or perhaps she realized he wasn't ensnared *yet*, and she assumed she could convince him to fall in love.

But Lucas was broken on the inside. He didn't have the kind of feelings that a normal person experienced. He would trick, use, and abuse Miss Carter, then he'd discard her when a prettier, looser girl caught his roving eye. Where would she be then?

Well, her problems weren't Raven's problems, but he was devastated by Lucas's conduct. Even though he understood his brother's lack of emotion and his odd views, he was incensed that Lucas hadn't embraced his plot with regard to the Carters, that he'd fled to town and had left Raven to finish it on his own.

He'd desperately wanted Lucas to be by his side. Lydia was dead, so she couldn't be with him. There was only Lucas to mark the occasion, but Lucas didn't care about their parents or any of the rest of it, and Raven couldn't make him care.

There was a sledgehammer in the corner. A parlor wall was cracked beyond repair, and the plaster had to be chipped away, then a new layer applied. He grabbed it and began swinging it at the wall.

With the first strike, he slammed through the old plaster with thrilling force. He pounded at it over and over, his fury pouring into the blows. He would keep at it until his wrath waned or until his arms grew too fatigued to continue.

"Raven!" a woman snapped from behind him.

*Rebecca...*

He whipped around. "What?"

"What are you doing?"

"What does it look like? I'm remodeling."

"You're upset. What happened?"

"Nothing happened. Why are you here? What is it you need?"

"I have to talk to you."

"So... talk," he curtly said.

His rude attitude gave her pause. She studied him as if he was a stranger, and he supposed he was quite a sight: sweaty, breathing hard, covered in dust, his palms blistered from gripping the sledgehammer so tightly.

She squared her shoulders and forged ahead. "I've quarreled with Beatrice."

"I'm sorry, but I can't help you with that, and you shouldn't have bothered me about it." The words were out before he could bite them down. "You have to work it out with her."

She blanched as if he'd slapped her. "I can't work it out with her, and I didn't know where else to turn. She's evicted me, and I'm so distraught. Tell me what to do."

"I have no idea."

"Could I stay with you?" At her request, the horror must have shown on his face because she hurried to add, "Just for a few days? Until I can devise a plan for myself?"

"For pity's sake, I'm a bachelor, and this monstrosity of a house is barely livable. It's a totally inappropriate option."

Her expression darkened. She marched over until they were toe to toe, then she lowered her voice. "I spent the night with you."

"You shouldn't have."

She gasped. "That's your response?"

His cheeks heated. He was behaving like an ass, like a big, fat juvenile baby. He was angry with Lucas, so he was taking it out on her, but he couldn't seem to stop himself from acting like a complete bastard.

The weight of the prior year—which included Sir Sidney's death and Nathan's maiming—was crushing him with regret. His leaving the expedition team was crushing him.

Lucas was a wrecked human being who'd grown up alone and adrift. Raven hadn't been there to protect him. Lydia had been destroyed too, by Clayton Carter who'd never had to pay a penny of recompense.

As with Lucas, she'd been alone during her tribulations, and Raven had been far away in Africa, chasing the wealth required to save her. But he'd been too late to save her or Lucas.

Mr. Melville had asked—once he'd extracted his vengeance—would he be happy? He didn't think so.

He felt as if he was out of his body and staring down at Oakley and Rebecca. She was the only good thing he'd encountered in ages, but if he let her get close, he'd destroy her in the end too. He typically destroyed what he touched.

If he bound himself to her, he'd eventually ignore an important detail or he'd be absent when she needed him or he'd be too busy to focus on her, and she'd be imperiled. Why would he deliberately endanger her?

They shared a hot, searing attraction, and it had ignited on one torrid occasion. It had been incredibly grand, but he wouldn't claim it created a connection, and it didn't matter how fervidly she yearned for a different conclusion. He wouldn't oblige her.

He inhaled deeply, struggling to rein in his temper. "You shouldn't have come over here. I'm not having the greatest day."

"Mine hasn't been too keen either."

"You should be at home, planning where you and Beatrice will go after I've kicked her out. I'm shutting down Carter Crossing. I'm not jesting. You know I'm not, and people should begin preparing."

"I don't care how it unravels over there," she vehemently stated. "I just care about you, and I should be by your side as it unfolds. Actually, I should be by your side forever. You swore I would be, and I accepted your word about it."

He assessed her as if she were deranged. "You talk as if I'm in the market for a bride. Have I ever uttered a single comment to you that would make you think I was ready to be a husband?"

She flinched so violently he might have punched her. "I joined you in your bed! Or have you conveniently forgotten that fact?"

"I haven't forgotten. It was wonderful, and I'm glad we proceeded."

"You're *glad*?"

"What would you like me to say? Were you expecting me to propose?"

"Yes, Mr. Shawcross, I was expecting exactly that."

He blew out a heavy breath, then he said the worst thing he'd ever said, the one thing that couldn't be *un*said. "Rebecca, you're a Carter. Even if I was eager to wed, I would never marry a Carter. Surely you understand that, and if you don't, then it's clear you haven't been paying attention."

"I'm a *Carter*?" she spat. "Is that how you intend to avoid a commitment to me?"

He ran a hand through his hair. "Could we discuss this another time? As I mentioned, I'm having a terrible day, and my every remark sounds wrong."

"There's naught wrong with your remarks, Mr. Shawcross. I comprehend them perfectly."

"Don't call me Shawcross. Call me Raven."

"I can't, for it appears, *Mr. Shawcross*, that we are no longer on familiar terms."

If he'd had the energy to debate the issue, he would have, but he was too overwhelmed by events. He motioned to the door. "You should go for now. I'll try to stop by later, but you shouldn't come here again."

"Or what?" she snidely inquired. "Will you send me to bed without my supper? You are not my father or my husband. Don't boss me."

"I'm not bossing you. I'm simply asking you to depart so we can confer when I'm in a better mood."

She laughed a tad hysterically. "What is it that we would *confer* about when your mood has improved? Would we rehash the pesky problem that I'm a Carter and you hate all Carters?"

"I'm sorry."

"No, you're not." She shook her head with derision. "Were you fond of me in the slightest?"

"It's not a past tense sentiment. I am very fond of you."

She bristled with disgust. "Gad, I am such a fool. I . . . I . . . *love* you, and this is how you treat me?"

He scoffed. "You don't love me."

"I guess I was confused, but I thought maybe you were starting to love me too."

"I've never loved anyone. It's not possible for me. I've had too much happen in my life. I'm broken on the inside."

"We've all had awful experiences. Don't use your deplorable history as an excuse for being an ass."

"I won't." He pointed to the door again. "Would you please go?"

"Answer a question for me first."

"If I can."

"If we hadn't had this conversation, how many times would you have let me disgrace myself by climbing into your bed?"

"I don't know," he candidly said.

"You coaxed me into it because I'm a Carter, didn't you? You ruined me as part of your scheming on Beatrice and Clayton. There were no tender feelings involved. I was just easy bait."

"I can't explain my motives. I simply like you more than I should, and I've behaved badly because of it."

"Beatrice warned me about you. She swore you weren't sincere. She swore you'd never follow through on any promise."

"What promise did I make? I can't recall one. I'm not a man who makes promises because I don't like to be burdened by them."

"Truer words were never spoken, Mr. Shawcross."

Before he could brace himself, she raised a hand and slapped him as hard as she could. The blow landed square on his cheek, so ferociously that he staggered.

She whirled away and dashed out toward the trail that led over the promontory. He lurched out behind her and shouted, "Rebecca! Stop!" She didn't slow down, and he tried again. "Rebecca!"

Finally, she halted and glared at him over her shoulder. "I don't think any woman has ever cared about you, Mr. Shawcross. *I* would have. I would have loved you forever, and I hope you're happy with your vengeance and your decrepit, dreary mansion. I'm sure they'll keep you plenty warm on cold winter nights."

"I won't be happy. I'm certain of it."

"Well, *I* am certain that we all get precisely what we deserve in the end. Good luck to you!"

She continued on, and he yelled her name over and over, to no avail. He could have chased after her, but he wouldn't embarrass himself. They'd fornicated—once!—and it was widely acknowledged that virgins struggled with their emotions after they were initially deflowered.

No doubt she was distraught over their risqué tryst, and he should have been kinder, should have been more patient, but he'd been too grouchy to deal with her. He'd been a complete prick, and the slap he'd received had been totally warranted.

He'd go over that evening. He hadn't planned to visit Carter Crossing until he arrived with his team of men to throw Beatrice out. Now, with Rebecca in such a state, he'd have to visit much sooner than that.

It was another factor to aggravate him, to stir his temper and fuel his ire. She didn't . . . *love* him. She was being ridiculous, but he couldn't bear that he'd upset her.

He'd have to beg her pardon, and he'd spend the rest of the afternoon figuring out how to manage it because, clearly, he'd mucked up their meeting in the worst possible way. He'd talk to her later. He'd profusely apologize, and she'd forgive him. He just knew she would.

⁓⁓⁓

REBECCA RAN INTO THE manor and flew up the stairs to her bedchamber. As she reached it, several servants were there.

"What's wrong?" a footman asked. "Mrs. Carter sent me to check that you'd vacated the premises. She said if you hadn't left, I was to tell you your hour is up, and she would be summoning the authorities as she threatened."

"I've been fired and evicted." Tears streamed down her cheeks.

The group gasped with dismay, and there were mutters of outrage on her behalf, which were comforting to hear. After her hideous encounter with Mr. Shawcross, she was incredibly bereft. It was sweet to be reminded that there were people in the world who liked her.

"Shall I speak to Mrs. Carter for you?" the footman asked. "Or the butler might be willing to intervene. She can't treat you like this."

Even as he offered, she could see the dread in his gaze. It was never safe to confront Beatrice, so Rebecca calmed their fears. "I don't need any of you to intervene. You can't get yourselves in trouble over me."

"You can't leave as she's demanded!" a housemaid said. "Where does she expect you to live?"

"She's not concerned over my fate, and I'm reconciled to my departure."

They had an intense conversation, where they urged her not to obey, to wait for Beatrice to relent, but she was stoically resigned. And in light of Mr. Shawcross's cruel conduct over at Oakley, why would she remain?

She was a proud woman—Viscount Matthew Blake's daughter!—and she'd rather die than bump into Mr. Shawcross ever again. She'd rather die than let Beatrice discover how right she'd been about how he would behave.

She advised the footman to march down and inform Beatrice that she was packed and about to walk out the door. Then she passed around hugs. The maids were weeping, and their woe made Rebecca cry even harder. They were all so miserable, and she couldn't abide their commiseration.

She shooed them out, encouraging them to return to their chores. What with Mr. Shawcross about to kick them out, the manor was already in an uproar. They shouldn't ignite Beatrice's wrath as well.

Rebecca promised to write to the butler once she was settled somewhere—so they wouldn't worry. Finally, her room was empty and quiet, and she was able to focus. She had an old portmanteau Millicent had given her, and she pulled it out and laid it on the bed.

How was a female to cram twenty-four years into a single portmanteau? In her case, it wasn't difficult. She didn't have much: a few dresses and undergarments, a few pairs of shoes and stockings. For the most part, she was a poor person who'd never had many possessions.

Footsteps sounded in the hall, and Alex rushed in. She blanched. Her mental state was so disordered that she'd forgotten about him.

"I just heard the news," he said. "You're really going?"

"Yes, I'm going."

"Will you permit Mrs. Carter to chase you away? Why would you? Please put up a fight. Stay here and spit in her eye!"

"It's a delicious thought, but I'm not interested in further quarreling. It's pointless."

"Mr. Shawcross will arrive shortly to force her out. Why don't you tarry until he's dealt with her?"

"I don't care to see him ever again either." At her comment, he looked so surprised that she added, "I realize you think he's quite grand, but he's been awful to me. If I dawdled, hoping for his assistance, I'd only be in greater jeopardy."

Alex studied her, his fury growing. He could be such a fierce little champion. "What did he do to you?"

"It was . . . nothing," she claimed. "I assumed he and I were friends, but I'm a Carter, and that's how he views me. There's no reason for me to count on him. He'll evict me too—as if I was of no consequence—and I couldn't stand his disregard."

"He hurt you!"

"No, he didn't *hurt* me. I had entirely misconstrued his opinion about our relationship, and he was just brutally honest."

She'd ruined herself for him, believing it would make him happy, that it would make him love her, but wasn't that what every ruined maiden believed?

Well, she was done being gullible. She was done being a naive idiot. She was leaving Carter Crossing forever, and she would never wonder what happened between Mr. Shawcross and Beatrice later on. She was finished with both of them—and relieved to recognize it.

"I'm going with you," Alex suddenly said.

"You can't come. I can't imagine where I'll be living. For all I know, it will be in a ditch."

"As if I'd allow you to live in a ditch by yourself!" He scowled. "Would you like me to talk to Mr. Shawcross for you? Would you like him to apologize? I bet I could persuade him. Would that help?"

"I don't want him to apologize."

"Are you sure? He probably lashed out in anger. He's probably regretting his conduct."

"Trust me. He's not sorry."

Alex skipped over to his bedchamber, and in the blink of an eye, he was back. He had a packed satchel slung over his shoulder.

"I wish you'd reconsider," she told him.

"I won't, so don't argue about it. I would never remain here without you."

"All right, and I have to admit I'll be glad to have your company. You're a good boy, Alex."

"Of course I am, and don't fret. Maybe we'll find a ship in Frinton that's taking on passengers, and we can sail away together. Maybe we'll find a safe place, where people will like us for a change."

"Maybe."

She gave him a tight hug, and as she drew away, he said, "Can I tell you a secret."

"You'd better."

"You have to promise you won't be angry."

"I'm too sad to be angry."

He grinned. "It's the perfect moment to confess my crime then."

He reached into his shirt and pulled out a stuffed purse, and he opened it to show her it was full of money.

"Will this smooth over a rough beginning?" he asked.

"Where did you get that?"

"I've been stealing little bits from Mrs. Carter and my father."

Her jaw dropped in astonishment. "You've been stealing?"

"Yes. I always expected to be kicked out. Mrs. Carter constantly threatened it, and I thought I should be prepared in case she followed through."

"You're ten! Why would your mind work in such a convoluted way?"

"It seemed smart to plan ahead."

"You are in luck, Alex Carter. Any other time, I would have scolded you to Heaven and back. But not today. Today, I say: Let's hurry and depart before Beatrice comes up to check on me."

They marched out of her room and down the stairs, and as they stepped outside, he asked, "Where should we go?"

"We'll walk to Frinton for now and stay at a coaching inn. Then . . . ? I have an idea, but I'm not certain it's viable or wise. I have to think about it."

"Will I like it?"

"I can't decide."

"Mr. Shawcross will be upset when he learns that you left."

She stopped and stared at the promontory, picturing him across the hill, all alone in his deserted mansion.

"Mr. Shawcross won't be upset. He barely knows I'm alive."

They rounded the house and strolled down the lane, her portmanteau banging into her leg. Servants had tiptoed out to watch them leave. They stood at attention, and the stable hands removed their caps as if it was a funeral procession. Lest Beatrice hear them voicing fond farewells, no one uttered a word.

They continued on until they were in the trees, then she turned and waved. The crowd waved back, and she tarried for a minute soaking it in, but it was unbearably depressing. She whipped away and kept on until she vanished in the shadows.

In an instant, it was as if she and Alex had never resided there at all.

# CHAPTER

## 17

"What was Mrs. Carter's response?"

"She claimed my clerk was misinformed, and we have the wrong Carters. Apparently, they have no cousin named Rebecca."

Sarah stared at Nathan and asked, "Did your man believe her?"

"He wasn't certain what was happening. He had no opportunity to speak directly to Mrs. Carter. On each visit, the butler insisted she was indisposed, but the stable hands were gossiping that there was some sort of massive drama occurring."

"What sort of drama?" Sarah inquired.

They were in the front parlor at Selby Manor. The afternoon was waning, evening on the horizon. It was her favorite time of day. The house was quiet, the servants down in the kitchen having tea before they began the busy push to get supper on the table.

The children, Noah and Petunia, were upstairs in the nursery, and Nathan's wife, Nell—who was in the family way—had been feeling under the weather, so she was taking a nap.

Sarah had Nathan all to herself, although her husband, Sebastian, was with them too. She could hardly demand he leave them alone. He and Nathan had been best friends since they'd met at school at age seven. Their relationship had nearly been destroyed during their final trip to Africa, and they were bonding again. They couldn't stand to be parted for a single second.

Nathan had almost died in Africa, having barely survived the maiming he'd received during the melee that had resulted in Sir Sidney being murdered by natives. Then he'd been declared deceased by Sebastian and left for dead on the Dark Continent. He'd staggered home on his own, and he still hadn't explained how he'd managed the amazing feat.

After that hideous incident, it had seemed he and Sebastian would never reconcile, but they had. Their connection was too vital for them to carry on without it. Nathan regarded Sebastian as his brother so, when Sarah and Nathan enjoyed a whiskey, Sebastian blustered in, and neither of them would tell him he shouldn't.

"I guess Mrs. Carter's son is addicted to wagering," Nathan said, "and he's gambled away their property. Some fellow from London bought it from his creditors, so they're about to be evicted. It means she has bigger issues on her mind than my clerk and a long-lost sibling."

Sebastian jumped into the conversation. "Did you say that woman's surname is Carter?"

"Yes," Nathan replied. "Mrs. Beatrice Carter."

"They live out on the coast?"

"Yes."

"I could swear Shawcross once told me he had his sights set on a Carter family and that he was intending to implement some mischief against them."

"Why would he?" Nathan asked.

"It's wrapped up in the trouble his parents had when he was a boy. His father was swept into a quagmire he didn't deserve, and they were ruined. I was never sure on the particulars. He didn't like to discuss it, so I didn't press."

"He was the same with me. He never mentioned any details."

"When I last talked to him," Sebastian said, "he was headed to the coast, to execute the scheme he envisioned."

Sarah asked, "You think it might be the same people?"

Sebastian pondered, then scowled. "It would be too much of a coincidence, wouldn't it? I probably have the names confused, and he's probably in a completely different area of the country."

"I hope you're correct," Sarah said. "You're fond of him, but I loathe him. I wouldn't want him within a hundred miles of my sister."

Nathan chuckled. "You don't like Shawcross? I didn't realize you'd met him."

"Oh, I met him all right." Just from remembering the pompous ass, her blood boiled.

"Your dislike is understandable, I suppose," her brother said. "His normal demeanor is severe and daunting, but what did he do to you specifically?"

Sebastian answered for her. "He was simply his usual overbearing self."

"Before I was married"—Sarah cast a glower at her husband—"when I was staying at Hero's Haven, Shawcross was an obnoxious prig who constantly lectured and manhandled me."

Nathan smirked. "I'm surprised he was brave enough."

"I almost punched him in the nose a few times." She shook off thoughts of the despicable oaf and focused on her sister instead. "What about Rebecca? What if Mrs. Carter was lying about her? If they're pushed into an eviction, Rebecca would be imperiled too."

Sebastian said, "And if they're scattered to the four winds when they're kicked out of their home, it will become even more difficult to find her."

"If any of that is a possibility," Sarah said, "we can't ignore the situation."

"Why would Mrs. Carter lie about Rebecca being her cousin?" Nathan asked.

Sarah shrugged. "Why does a person commit any crazed act?"

"A valid question," Nathan retorted.

She rose and went to the window to gaze outside. For several days, she'd been anxious and apprehensive. She'd always been able to mentally communicate with Rebecca, but for some reason, the ability had abruptly stopped.

She couldn't figure out why she was sensing it, but she was certain Rebecca was in danger. She would never explain her heightened perception to her brother or husband though. They weren't twins, so they wouldn't comprehend the bond she and Rebecca shared.

"I'm so restless," she murmured more to herself than them.

"I agree," Sebastian said. "You're either pacing or fidgeting. Why don't you have another glass of whiskey? Perhaps it will calm you."

She frowned. "I just feel that something's about to happen."

"Something bad or something good?"

"Just . . . something. I can't describe it. It seems as if my skin is itching or maybe that I've been electrified." She glanced over her shoulder. "If I pointed a finger at you, sparks might fly from the tip."

"Please don't shoot any at me," Sebastian said.

"Or me," Nathan added. "I've been wounded enough. I don't need more scars."

She stared outside again, wondering if she shouldn't walk into the village. It was cold and blustery, the seasons changing. The fresh air would be invigorating. Even though it was growing late, she could visit her father's grave in the cemetery behind the church, which was soothing.

She'd decided to announce that very plan when she noticed two people approaching the manor. They were down the lane, and she studied them, seeing that it was a woman and a boy about Noah's age. The woman was carrying a heavy portmanteau, and the boy had a satchel slung over his back—as if guests were about to arrive.

As far as she was aware, Nathan wasn't expecting any company.

She continued to watch them, and her anxiety spiraled out of control. There was a ringing in her ears, and suddenly, her heart was pounding so hard that she feared it might simply burst out of her chest.

"Oh, my lord," she muttered. "I think it's her. But it can't be, can it?"

"What are you talking about?" Sebastian asked.

"It is!" she whispered, agog with amazement. Without peeking over at the men, she mumbled, "Would you excuse me?"

She dashed out of the room, and as she fled, they leapt to their feet, and Sebastian called, "Sarah! What's wrong?"

Not slowing to reply, she ran down the hall, through the foyer, and out the front doors, blind to the shocked expressions of the servants she passed. She raced down the grand stairs to the driveway, and she flitted across the grass.

"Rebecca!" she shouted. "Rebecca! Is it you? Tell me it's you!"

She was crying so vehemently she couldn't hear a word so—if her sister answered—she had no idea.

---

"WHAT IF WE'RE TURNED away?"

"You know the old adage," Rebecca said to Alex. "Nothing lost, nothing gained. If Lord Selby refuses to meet with us, we'll keep on to London."

It was probably what they should have done anyway, but when the mail coach on which they'd purchased seats had stopped in a village near Selby, it had felt as if invisible ropes were dragging her to visit her half-brother.

She had fleeting memories of him as a brave, fierce boy, but she couldn't judge whether they were accurate or not. She might have simply conjured a picture of him in her mind to counter Beatrice's horrible stories.

According to her, he was a typical aristocrat—lazy, imperious, cruel—and he was especially harsh with his servants, that he flogged them and had them jailed for petty infractions, that he never paid their wages and retaliated against any who complained.

Rebecca couldn't guess what was true and what wasn't. He'd joined Sir Sidney Sinclair's expeditions, and his close friend was Sir Sidney's son, Sebastian. Sebastian had penned travelogues about their adventures, and Nathan Blake had been at the center of their escapades, with his exploits and daring-do constantly praised.

Mr. Shawcross had praised him too, had claimed he was tough, courageous, and loyal, but in light of Rebecca's current predicament, she didn't put much stock in Shawcross's opinion about any issue.

Despite the conflicting tales, she was an optimist, and she wouldn't accept that her brother would be awful to her. Her biggest worry was that he wouldn't remember her, but why would he?

When their parents had died, he'd been six and she'd been three. He'd been whisked off to Selby, and she'd been sent to Carter Crossing. Why would he have looked back for a single second? Why would he have fretted over her?

It was merely a fact that illicit children were born into noble families, and she was a disgraceful little secret wedged onto a branch of the family tree.

She would politely request an audience with Lord Selby. If he was away from home or if he declined to see her, she would try not to be too disappointed. If he agreed to speak with her, she would brace for any sort of reception.

If her brother was dreadful, she had Alex by her side, and they had a purse full of money. They would head to London and build a new life there. She wasn't concerned about the future. At least that's what she was telling herself.

"Does Lord Selby know Mr. Shawcross?" Alex asked.

"Yes. We discussed him once."

"I wonder what Lord Selby would think of how Mr. Shawcross treated you."

"I can't imagine."

She gnashed her teeth, determined to avoid talking about Raven Shawcross. Alex had developed a serious case of hero worship, and he was eager to confer about him. Her heart was absolutely broken though, so whenever Alex mentioned him, she'd slyly steer the conversation to a different subject.

"What do you suppose Lord Selby will be like?" she asked. "Cousin Beatrice told me he was rich, lazy, and obnoxious."

"Well, we should ignore her view on every topic. Sebastian Sinclair described him as a great fellow."

Boys around the kingdom had read stories about the notorious pair, and it had left them yearning to have the same adventures. Alex was no different.

"Yes," she said, "Mr. Sinclair was extremely complimentary of Lord Selby."

Alex grinned. "I hope we're about to encounter Mr. Sinclair's version—and not Mrs. Carter's."

Rebecca nodded. "I shall hope for the very same."

They'd walked to the estate from the village, having gotten directions from a blacksmith. They'd found the entrance easily enough, the name *SELBY* carved into the wood over the gate. Then they'd continued down the lane toward the manor, winding through orchards and finally being spit out of the trees.

They staggered to a halt and gazed up at the enormous building. It was much more imposing than she'd been expecting. As a girl from the country, who'd only ever lived at Carter Crossing, she'd thought Carter Crossing was large and ostentatious. Clearly, she'd had no clue as to the type of residence real wealth could bestow.

Selby Manor was magnificent, constructed from a light-colored brick, with turrets on one end, as if the older section had once been a castle. There were hundreds of windows gleaming in the afternoon sun, and a circular driveway that, in the summer, would have been lined with flowers. An impressive set of stairs rose to ornate double doors.

There were meadows with horses frolicking. She could see the park behind the house, the paths groomed, the grass swathed. It was so beautiful, so peaceful and bucolic, like a scene in a painting.

For a minute, they tarried, taking it in. She tried to envision her father being raised in the splendid spot, but she couldn't picture it. Her opinions about him had been tainted by Beatrice's constant sniping about his being an unrepentant philanderer.

She pondered Nathan though and how two children, sired by the same man, could be reared in such diverse circumstances. Mr. Shawcross had claimed Nathan's childhood was unhappy, but was that true? Or had Nathan been content at Selby? Had his life been one of tutors and expensive clothes? Had he studied fencing and languages?

She was cognizant of his years of exploring with Sir Sidney Sinclair, but what other experiences had he enjoyed?

What had she to offer him by way of acquaintance? She'd never gone anywhere or done anything, and with her being confronted by the majesty of Selby, she felt dowdy, ordinary, and completely out of her element.

Suddenly, the strangest surge of energy was coursing through her body. All day, she'd been restless and out of sorts. Initially, she'd assumed it was nerves from her traipsing off on such a wild journey. Previously, she'd never traveled more than a few miles from Frinton or Carter Crossing. Now she was off to London—where she'd never been.

She kept telling herself it would work out. They'd rent a room, and she'd find a job. She was smart and educated, and she presented herself well. She refused to think she would face adversity.

With so many changes occurring, who wouldn't be nervous? Who wouldn't be on edge?

Still though, she was practically electrified—as if she could point her finger and sparks would shoot from the tip. There was the oddest ringing in her ears. It was growing louder and louder, and she was incredibly dizzy, as if the world had tilted off its axis and she couldn't maintain her balance.

"Are you all right?" Alex asked his question as if from a far distance.

She frowned, but was paralyzed and unable to respond.

"Rebecca!" He physically shook her. "You can't suffer a fit of the vapors in Lord Selby's driveway. It would be a very bad introduction."

"I'm ... I'm fine," she stammered. Her head was pounding, and she rubbed her temple. "I'm just tired. The past few weeks have been so stressful."

"They certainly have been. Let's get you to the manor. Hopefully, they'll provide us with some refreshments. If we can put some tea and biscuits in your stomach, you'll feel better."

"I'm sure you're correct."

She forced a smile and had spun to the house when a woman burst out the elaborate front doors. The moment was startling and disorienting, and Rebecca's vertigo was worse by the second.

It seemed as if *she* had burst out of the mansion. The woman racing toward her was her exact double—white-blond hair, slender figure, same height and shape—but she, Rebecca, was standing with Alex. Her mind couldn't process what she was witnessing, and she wondered if she wasn't extremely ill.

The woman was laughing, crying, and shouting, "Rebecca! Rebecca! Is it you? Tell me it's you!"

"Who is that?" Alex's anxious gaze shifted from the woman, to Rebecca, then to the woman again.

"I don't know," Rebecca mumbled.

"Are there two of you? Is it possible?"

"You see her too?" Rebecca asked. "I'm not going mad?"

"I definitely see her."

The woman uttered the most peculiar comment. "Bec-Bec, it's me! It's Sissy! You have to remember me. You can't have forgotten!"

"Sissy?" Rebecca's voice sounded young and breathless and nothing like her own.

"Who is Sissy?" Alex inquired. "Who is Bec-Bec?"

Rebecca couldn't answer. Her dizziness spiked to a frightening level. She tipped one way, then the other, and she fainted dead away.

RAVEN MARCHED INTO CARTER Crossing. He'd promised Beatrice and Clayton that he'd be back in three days, but here it was—*two* days later—and he was staggering in like a whipped dog.

But then, Rebecca had that effect on him.

When she'd trotted over to Oakley, when she'd thrown herself at him and begged him to catch her, he'd behaved dreadfully. Needing to apologize, he'd nearly ridden over a dozen times, but he'd tamped down any embarrassing overtures.

He'd spent a torturous night, where he'd convinced himself that he didn't care about her, that she was a Carter, and he had to let her leave with the rest of them, but he had an unusual connection with her, so he could never act as he ought.

He was tormented over how forlorn she'd been, and after she'd fled, he'd meticulously reviewed their conversation. She'd mentioned that Beatrice had kicked her out. What had she meant by that? He'd been so furious over Lucas that he'd barely heeded her woeful remarks.

Mostly, he'd been shocked over her request to tarry at Oakley. As if unwed adults could cohabitate! What lunacy had afflicted the deranged female?

She had him so flustered he couldn't think straight, and eventually, he'd decided he had to visit her. He'd use the occasion to remind everyone they'd be departing. He doubted Beatrice would have informed the staff, and they had to be apprised.

He'd confer with Beatrice too, to insist he wasn't joking, that he intended to evict her the following morning. She'd have persuaded herself it wouldn't really happen, that Clayton would save her, but they couldn't change their circumstances.

Raven would arrive with a team of men, unemployed veterans who were happy to have the temporary jobs. He'd been planning to have them tear down the house, then have the fields grow to weeds, but when he was calmer and debating more rationally, he accepted that he shouldn't be so immature about it.

The property was large, the manor in good condition, and he could sell it for a tidy profit. Why shouldn't he?

He'd be rid of Beatrice and Clayton and make money off them at the same time.

The butler entered the foyer just as Raven entered it too, and the man blanched and shot a derisive glower. He couldn't hide his disdain.

"If you're here for Mr. Carter"—his tone was quite snotty—"he and his guests have returned to London, so there's no one with whom to socialize."

"I couldn't abide any of them anyway. Fetch Miss Rebecca for me."

"Miss Rebecca has left too."

Raven scowled. "Left for where?"

"I don't believe her whereabouts are any of your business, and if you'll excuse me, I'm busy." He gave a stiff bow. "I'm sure you can find your way out."

Raven ignored him. "Fetch Mrs. Carter for me then."

"She remains indisposed to callers."

Raven stepped in so they were toe to toe. "Fetch her," he commanded, "and be quick about it. If you won't, I'll tromp about and locate her myself. You'll have difficulty explaining how I walked into her bedchamber without you stopping me."

A muscle ticked in the man's cheek. "I'll search for her, but I can't guarantee she'll attend you."

"Tell her—if she doesn't—I'll drag her down to speak with me." He whirled away and started down the hall, saying, "I'll be waiting for her in *my* library."

The man trudged up the stairs, and as he reached the landing, he leaned over the railing. "Is it true we're all leaving tomorrow?"

"Yes, it's true."

"Will *all* the servants be fired? Will you permit anyone to stay?"

Raven glared up at him, and he looked old and a bit haggard. Raven wondered how long he'd toiled away for grouchy Beatrice. It couldn't have been easy. It was on the tip of his tongue to declare, *Bloody hell, yes! You'll all be fired!*

But an irksome wave of pity washed through him. These people had worked with Rebecca. They'd been her friends, and she would hate him if he was awful to them. And what was his quarrel with them?

There wasn't one, so he said, "I'm not certain what will occur. Mrs. Carter is departing and that's all I know. After she's gone, I'll decide on the rest of you."

"Very good, sir. The staff has been in the dark, so I appreciate the information."

He kept on up the stairs, and Raven continued to the library. He poured himself a whiskey, then seated himself behind the desk. It took forever for Beatrice to appear, but ultimately, she did.

She stomped over, and for a moment, it was clear she'd considered circling around to try and push him out of the chair. She realized she never could though, and she plopped down in the chair across.

"You have an enormous amount of gall to have blustered in," she complained.

"Yes, I've always had plenty of gall."

"Where is my daughter?"

"She's not here?"

"No."

"Then she's likely in London with my brother."

"And . . . ?"

"She's likely in a lot of trouble."

"Is that all you have to say about it?"

"Yes, except that she's a fool to have accompanied him."

"I agree, and I demand you rescue her."

"I can't."

"Why can't you? You inflicted him on us, and he's kidnapped her. You must exert some energy to fix what he's done."

"If she's with him, he didn't *take* her. She went willingly, and trust me, after she's adopted a few of his habits, you won't really want her back."

"You and your brother are immoral fiends. If your precious father, Harrison, was still alive, how would he view the two of you?"

"Let's not wander down that road, Beatrice. I'm not in the mood to hear my father's name spring from your lips."

"It's Mrs. Carter to you, and you're not welcome in my home. I insist you leave. If you won't, I'll summon the footmen to have them haul you out."

Raven rolled his eyes. "It would be humorous to have them try."

"You think you're so smart," she fumed. "You think you're so tough, but you'll get yours soon enough."

"How?"

"Even as we speak, Clayton is in town hiring a lawyer. We'll have this repaired shortly, and once it's reversed, we'll sue you for harassment."

"You can't reverse it. The court proceedings have been over for weeks. Clayton was served with subpoenas over and over, but he never showed up for any of them. Eventually, he was held in contempt and adjudged a delinquent without his ever mounting a defense."

For an instant, her wall of condescension fell, and she looked quite alarmed, but she swiftly shoved that wall back into place. "My son is completely competent. He would never have allowed that to happen."

"Lie to yourself if you wish, but I've simply come to repeat that you have to vacate the premises tomorrow."

"And *I* told you Clayton will return with legal papers to stop you."

"If you truly believe that, you're living a fantasy. There will be no last-minute reprieve, so I advise you to make plans for yourself."

"I won't."

"Then I shall personally carry you out to the carriage that will whisk you away. It's up to you whether you have a destination in mind or not."

"You're doing this as revenge over your father's troubles."

"Of course I am."

"It was twenty years ago!"

"Yes, it was, and I've suffered through each one of them, imagining this conclusion."

"How could the courts permit such an injustice? It's not fair!"

"I guess that depends on whose vantage point you're using."

"We'll see who goes and who remains," she furiously retorted, "but for now, this house is still mine. Get out!"

She stood and huffed to the door, apparently assuming she could shoo him out, and he said, "The butler informs me that Miss Rebecca has left the property."

"Yes, she has."

"I need to speak to her. Where is she?"

"How would I know?"

"Why would she depart?"

"I found out she'd ruined herself with you, and I don't tolerate salacious behavior under my own roof. I tossed her out."

He gaped at her as if she'd babbled in a foreign language he didn't understand. "What did you say?"

"I discovered she was spreading her legs for you. For you! My sworn enemy! How could you think to keep it a secret from me? I kicked her out—with just the clothes on her back."

He thought of how distraught Rebecca had been when she'd arrived at Oakley. Evidently, Mrs. Carter had accused her of being a harlot and had evicted her on the spot! Because of *him* and their carnal antics! She'd rushed to him for help—and he'd refused to supply it! What was wrong with him?

He rose to his feet, so angry that he worried he might march over, wrap his fingers around her throat, and choke her to death.

"Where is she?" he seethed.

"I have no idea. I ordered her to go—and to take that little bastard Alex with her. In light of your conduct toward me, I shouldn't have to continue providing shelter to your nephew."

"My . . . nephew? What are you talking about?"

She smirked. "I hadn't realized until a few days ago that his mother—stupid, gullible, deceased Lydia—was your sister. Once I figured it out, I didn't suppose I should have to waste another penny on him. They slunk off together and good riddance!"

She started out, and he said, "Wait! You're claiming Lydia's baby didn't die with her?"

"Who told you that? No, the boy didn't die. He's been here all these years, and *I* have had to support him. My well of mercy has run dry!"

She stormed out and slammed the door as hard as she could.

He was frozen in place, listening as her strides faded down the hall, then he sank into his chair, feeling more confused than he'd ever been.

# CHAPTER
## 18

"I'm going to Africa someday."

"How will you manage it?"

"I haven't figured out that part yet. I simply know it's my destiny."

Noah Sinclair grinned at Alex Carter. Noah was twelve, and Alex was ten. From the moment he'd arrived with Miss Rebecca, Noah had realized they'd be fast friends.

The house was awhirl with activity, the adults in a frenzy, so Noah had decided it was best to get out of their way. He and Alex were out in the park, throwing rocks in the lake.

"Sir Sidney is my father," Noah explained, "and Sebastian is my half-brother. Sebastian initially journeyed to the Dark Continent when he was ten, so I'm already two years behind."

"I feel as if I'm falling behind too."

"I have to finish my schooling," Noah said, "then when I'm sixteen,

Sebastian has promised to buy me a commission in the army. I'm hoping I can earn a fortune there so, in the future, I can fund my own expeditions."

"You're so lucky. I wish I had someone who would buy me a commission. I'd love to be a soldier."

"We should devise a plan to make it happen. Perhaps we can figure out how to join the army together."

Noah was a great judge of character, and Alex would be worth having by his side. He saw many of his own traits in the other boy, traits such as loyalty and bravery. He believed in Fate too. Lord Selby and Sarah had been searching for Miss Rebecca, and she'd suddenly strolled up the lane—as if magnets were drawing her to them.

Alex had been with her, and Noah didn't suppose it was an accident that he'd appeared. Fate had brought Alex to Noah so their paths would cross.

"I want to go to Africa with you!" Alex vehemently said. "I could be your second in command. Or I could be your scout like Mr. Shawcross."

Noah scowled. "How do you know about Mr. Shawcross? Have you met him? Or have you simply read Sebastian's travelogues?"

"I know him—all too well," Alex admitted.

"I found him to be a very dodgy fellow."

"At first, I thought he was amazing, but now, I'm wondering about him."

"How are you acquainted with him?"

"My father's estate, Carter Crossing? He's seized it."

"Seized it how?"

"My father is a gambler, and he owed money everywhere. Mr. Shawcross purchased his debts and foreclosed. He showed up a few weeks ago, and he's been causing problems ever since."

"The news doesn't surprise me. I was staying at Sebastian's home of Hero's Haven, and Shawcross was there too. He was awful to me. He bossed me and ordered me about, but I never listened to him on any topic. He was even more horrid to Sarah."

"He was horrid to Rebecca too. I'm not sure what occurred between them, but it was the reason we had to leave. I assumed they were friends, but we had to depart because of him."

To Noah's ears, the story was incredibly similar to Sarah's story with Sebastian, and he asked, "Was Miss Rebecca sweet on Mr. Shawcross?"

"How would I know that?"

"Did you ever notice them sneaking off or whispering in the corner when no one was looking?"

"Maybe."

"My grandfather often warned me about young ladies and scoundrels. From how pompous Mr. Shawcross could be, he's probably a cad. A female like Miss Rebecca is never just *friends* with a man like him. They always wind up in trouble."

"What sort of trouble?"

"It's the kind that requires adults to marry quickly so they're not sinners."

"Oh. I'd like it if Mr. Shawcross married Rebecca. In most ways, he was remarkable. It was just there at the end that I had my doubts about him."

"We should return to the manor," Noah said. "I need to tell Sebastian that you met Mr. Shawcross. He's been worried about him, and Sarah should hear about his relationship with Miss Rebecca. She'll be able to learn if he hurt her, and if so, she'll find him and punch him in the nose."

"I'd like to see that."

Noah threw a last rock into the water, then they went back to the house.

---

"Everything will be fine. It will be fine forever."

"I didn't remember you. I remembered Nathan, but not you."

Sarah grinned at Rebecca and said, "I didn't remember you either."

"Our cousin, Beatrice Carter? She's the woman I lived with. For several years, I pestered her about you, but she constantly declared that I didn't have a sister. I was certain you were real, but she insisted you weren't. She claimed I imagined you."

"I always felt you rummaging around in my mind."

"I felt you too. I thought you were my guardian angel."

"You're joking! I thought the same about you! Do you recall what happened to us?" Sarah asked. "Do you recall the day we were separated? Do you ever dream about it?"

"Yes, I frequently dream about it. You and I are sitting nose to nose and holding hands. The people with us are shouting and weeping. Then a wicked witch swoops in and carries you away."

Sarah's jaw dropped. "That's my dream exactly! I bet I've had it a thousand times."

They were in an upstairs bedchamber that had been opened for Rebecca. When she'd fainted in the driveway, Nathan and Sebastian had chased Sarah outside, and when they'd realized who Rebecca was, they nearly fainted themselves.

Nathan had picked her up and rushed to the manor, with Sarah bellowing instructions to the servants. Rebecca had roused without too much of a delay, but it had taken an eternity to calm her down, to get the room situated, to shoo everyone out.

Finally, it was just the two of them: Sissy and Bec-Bec, reunited once and for all. Rebecca was stretched out on the bed, propped against the pillows, and Sarah was seated in a chair next to her, their fingers tightly linked.

"Did that event with the witch actually occur?" Rebecca asked.

"Yes. The *witch* was our Aunt Edwina. She's Father's sister-in-law, and when he and Mother died, Edwina came to shut down our house and deal with the three of us."

Rebecca frowned. "We were split up?"

"Yes. Edwina dragged Nathan to Selby, but our grandfather wouldn't let her bring us too. We were the family's dirty little secret."

"I went with Cousin Beatrice. Where did you go?"

"The day Mrs. Carter arrived to fetch us? I was sick, so she refused to keep me with you. Aunt Edwina sent me to an orphanage."

At the terrible news, Rebecca started to cry, and Sarah leaned in and swiped her tears away.

"Please don't fret over it," Sarah said. "My comment sounded much worse than it was. The facility was a private home for the natural children of the wealthy and notorious, and the owners liked me so much that they adopted me. I grew up poor, but cherished."

"When I was small, Cousin Beatrice repeatedly stated that Father and Mother gave me away because I was too expensive to raise and they didn't want me."

Sarah sighed with dismay. "Mother and Father were killed in an accident. Were you aware of that?"

"Yes. Beatrice was truthful about that at least."

"They loved us very much. The villain in this sad saga was our grandfather, Godwin. Aunt Edwina wasn't the kindest person either. She made some bad choices on the spur of the moment with regard to us."

"Do you remember our mother?" Rebecca asked.

"I have glimpses of her in my sleep, but I'm not sure if they're accurate."

"Was she a trollop?"

Sarah gasped. "Gad, no! Who told you that? Beatrice again?"

"Yes. She described Mother as a doxy who deliberately seduced Father. Supposedly, she believed she'd get rich if she wound up with child. Beatrice insisted she was stupid and greedy."

"It appears that Aunt Edwina isn't the only witch in this story," Sarah said. "Mrs. Carter is quite horrid too."

"She was very cruel to me."

"I'm so sorry to hear it. I've been jealous of you because you were given shelter by our Carter relatives, while I was cast aside by them. I assumed you had the better ending."

"It was awful there," Rebecca admitted, "and she spewed such dreadful nonsense about the Blake family—and especially about Nathan."

"Nathan is a remarkable man—which you'll discover as you become acquainted with him. As to our parents, I don't recollect much about them, but Nathan does. I'll have him tell you about them."

"So Mother wasn't a slattern?"

"No! She was a nanny. Nathan's mother died after he was born, so Father was a widower with a young baby. He hired Mother to work for him, and their affair commenced. They were very happy, so you have to ignore Beatrice Carter's false narrative."

"I'm so glad I stopped at Selby. I wasn't going to. We were headed to London."

"The boy with you? Alex?" Sarah hadn't had two seconds to speak to him and, carefully, she asked, "He's not your son, is he?"

"No. Beatrice has a son who's thirty. Our cousin, Clayton? He had a fling when he was a student at university, and Alex was the result. After his mother passed away, a vicar visited Carter Crossing and practically dropped him on our stoop. Beatrice couldn't abide him, so he's been my responsibility."

"I guess immorality runs in our Carter blood." Sarah smirked. "Why were you on your way to London?"

"Clayton is a gambler, and he wagered away their property."

"There are more and more tales of woe like that. Men can be so reckless."

"Beatrice is about to be evicted, so there was no place for Alex and me anymore. She's lost everything, so she wasn't about to continue supporting us."

"In light of how she treated you, I'm thrilled you were forced to leave. If she hadn't kicked you out, you'd never have staggered in here."

The door opened behind her, and she glanced over to see Nathan peek in. She waved him over. He came to the bed and rested a hip on the mattress.

"How are you feeling?" he asked Rebecca. "Any better?"

Rebecca studied his features, and she said, "I dream about Father occasionally, and he looks just like you."

"I have an old portrait of him that was painted when he was about my age. I'll show it to you tomorrow."

Sarah said to him, "Our Carter cousin, Beatrice? The woman who whisked Rebecca off to the coast that day? What a shrew she turned out to be! You won't believe how she lied to Rebecca over the years."

"What were her lies?" Nathan asked.

"She claimed Mother and Father dumped Rebecca on Beatrice because they were sick of her. She grew up thinking they gave her away!"

"Oh, my goodness," Nathan murmured.

"I recalled that I had a brother," Rebecca said, "but I constantly nagged her about Sarah, and Beatrice told me she didn't exist, that I imagined her."

"I didn't recall that I had sisters either," Nathan said. "Our grandfather and aunt convinced me I was an only child, and I gradually forgot you. It flooded in over the prior summer though, and I've been searching for you ever since."

Sarah was still holding Rebecca's hand, and Nathan reached out and clasped the other one.

"When I was six," Nathan said, "Father had a very stern talk with me about the two of you and how you would have a very hard life. If anything ever happened, I had to protect you for him. Back then, I didn't comprehend why he was telling me that, but I've decided he must have been afraid of Grandfather and how he might behave toward you. I had a difficult childhood because I recollected there was a task I should carry out for Father, but I couldn't remember what it was. It left me angry and frustrated."

"His burden from Father was *us*, Bec-Bec," Sarah said. "He was supposed to take care of us."

"Now I'll have the chance," he said.

"Why do you call me Bec-Bec?" Rebecca asked Sarah.

"I couldn't pronounce Rebecca when I was little."

Nathan added, "And Sarah was *Sissy* to both of us."

"I'm so relieved that I came here," Rebecca said.

"We were about to head to Carter Crossing to meet you," Nathan said. "We'd planned to introduce ourselves and invite you to Selby. Didn't you get my letter?"

"What letter?"

"I wrote you a few weeks ago, and my clerk delivered it to Mrs. Carter. She didn't share it with you?"

"No. She never mentioned it."

Nathan bristled. "She and I probably need to have a long chat about that, and I predict she won't enjoy it very much."

"She has plenty of her own problems," Sarah said. "Her son gambled away their property, and they're being evicted."

"Good." Nathan snorted. "I love it when horrid people suffer horrid consequences."

Sarah smiled at her brother and sister. "We're together—the three children of Viscount Matthew Blake."

"About time," Nathan muttered.

"Is Grandfather Godwin rolling in his grave?" Sarah asked.

Nathan chuckled. "I'm sure of it."

"Is Father finally resting easy in his?"

"I'm sure of that too."

---

RAVEN MARCHED UP TO the front doors of Carter Crossing. He tried the knob, but it was locked, and no footman peeked out. The servants couldn't have missed his entourage. He'd come with a dozen men and several empty wagons.

Beatrice wouldn't have made any preparations to depart, and he was happy to let her have a bit of furniture and the personal belongings that were special to her. He'd paid for lodging for her for a week at a coaching inn in Frinton. Or if she'd rather, he'd convey her to London, so she could move in with Clayton.

Fleetingly, he wondered if Clayton had slunk to the country to stand by his mother in her hour of need. This very same scenario had been inflicted on Raven's mother when he was ten. He'd recognized the unfairness of the episode and how wrong it was to have powerful fiends swoop in and steal what was theirs.

He'd yearned to stop it, but he'd been a child, so he hadn't known how to battle such dominant forces. Clayton was an adult though, so he could have clashed with Raven over what was occurring, but he hadn't bothered. He was losing everything, but he was such a lazy fool that he wasn't willing to fight for what was his.

Raven had spread word at Clayton's clubs about his bankruptcy, but he was late with his dues everywhere, so no one was surprised. He was months behind on his rent, and his landlord was about to throw him out. He was out of options and wouldn't be able to borrow from the moneylenders.

They'd incurred too much of a loss when Raven had bought up his debt, so Raven figured he'd hear from Clayton after he visited his bank and learned his account had been closed. The drunken dunce would likely ride to Oakley then. They'd hash it out to the bitter end, and Raven couldn't wait for him to show up.

He had an interesting conclusion arranged for Clayton, with punishment being the ultimate goal.

With Beatrice having shared the shocking news that Lydia's son was alive and well, his fury was raging at an even hotter temperature. How could such a lie have reached him in far-off Africa? Why had it been disseminated and by whom? Though the mistake wouldn't have been Clayton's fault, Raven blamed him anyway, and his penalty would be even grimmer than Raven had originally envisioned.

He knocked loudly, but there was no answer, so he raised his boot and kicked the door as hard as he could. The wood splintered, and he glanced over his shoulder at his men and said, "Let's go in, shall we?"

He entered the foyer, and he was humored to find Beatrice positioned at the foot of the stairs, a footman on either side. They looked ill, as if they wished they were anywhere else on the globe.

She was holding an old musket, and it was so heavy and unwieldy that she could barely lift it.

"Stay right where you are, Shawcross," she warned. "This is my home, and it's been my home for twenty years. You can't have it."

"Don't be ridiculous."

"I'll shoot! I mean it!"

He had no idea if the gun was loaded or not, but before she could swing the barrel in his direction, he stomped over, grabbed it, and yanked it away.

He gave it to one of his men, even as he realized he was slightly impressed. Clayton hadn't felt the need to protect what was his, but *she* had made an attempt. It was a futile and paltry attempt, but at least she'd tried.

Two of his men circled around Raven and seized her, quickly binding her wrists so she couldn't attack.

"You dog! You cur!" she spat. "I'll kill you for this! I will!"

"Not from where you'll be."

"We'll see about that!"

Another man, the sheriff's man, stepped forward, and he said, "Beatrice Carter? I arrest you in the name of the Crown."

"On what charge?" she huffed.

"Embezzlement, theft, and double-dealing at the business previously known as Carter Imports."

She blanched with astonishment. "That company was my son's! The money was ours. There can be no embezzlement from our own accounts!"

"Yes, but it was client funds," he said. "Your fingers were very busy, pilfering from them."

"You're mad! I only took what was mine! I took what I deserved to have!"

"The law will sort it out," the man told her, "but I'm predicting—since you stole from your customers—you won't have much of a defense."

Raven grinned at her. "You should have covered your tracks better, Beatrice. Didn't your husband, Charles, teach you how to do it? When he tricked my father, he had fake books and fake numbers to display. Where are yours?"

Suddenly, she was a bit green around the gills. Then she puffed herself up and announced, "This brute—Raven Shawcross—is duping you. I've never stolen a penny in my life!"

"Must we continue to listen to her?" one of Raven's men asked.

Raven shook his head. "No, we don't have to listen."

The sheriff's man addressed her. "If you'll come with me please?"

He clasped her arm to escort her out, and she planted her feet and tried not to oblige him, but he pulled her away against her will.

"I'm innocent!" she shrieked. "I'm completely innocent!"

"Tell it to the judge, ma'am," someone muttered.

As she passed Raven, he said to her, "Jail is a very lonely place. I'd send my father to explain what it will be like, but he didn't fare very well when he was incarcerated. I wonder how you'll manage."

She was yanked out of the house, and Raven was frozen in his spot as she squawked, fussed, and protested. Finally, she was in the jailor's carriage and whisked away. It grew very quiet, as if the building was holding its breath.

His first, very juvenile impulse was to have his men bring in sledgehammers and start smashing down the walls, but he refrained from giving that order.

Instead, he turned to a footman and said, "Assemble the servants for me. I have to figure out where we go from here."

———————◈———————

"Where were you last night?"

"I went to a brothel. Why? Did you miss me?"

Millicent glared at Lucas, and her temper flared. How dare he flit off to a brothel! How dare he voice such a despicable word in her presence!

"You left me at the theater by myself," she complained. "I had to find my own way home."

"Are you upset? Why would you be? It appears you made it safe and sound, and I didn't sign on to be your nanny."

"It was scary!"

He chuckled. "I constantly forget that you're a country mouse. Yes, I suppose it was horrid of me to abandon you like that, but you have to learn how to take care of yourself. If you can't, this city will eat you alive."

They were in his bachelor apartment, which was a small suite of rooms in the theater district. It was a neighborhood of actors, musicians, and other artistic types who didn't have the most stellar morals. He had exactly two servants: a valet and a footman.

She'd suggested he hire a maid to tend her, and he'd gaped as if she were a lunatic, so she'd been forced to struggle with her clothes and hair by herself. It was embarrassing to realize how unprepared she was for real life.

His lodging was very modest and not what she'd been expecting. He and his brother were obscenely rich, so she'd presumed he'd have an ostentatious mansion in a posh area. She'd been planning to rub elbows with the cream of London's High Society.

When she'd politely expressed her disappointment over his meager residence, he'd claimed he didn't need a monstrosity of a house where the marble floors echoed when he walked across them.

Well, he might be happier in humble surroundings, but *she* wasn't, and she had no idea how to persuade him that he ought to improve his situation.

He never dawdled at home, and when they'd initially journeyed to the city, she'd begun traipsing off to various entertainments with him. He drank, gambled, and gamboled, and he had a thousand friends, but they weren't the sort of acquaintances she'd yearned to acquire.

As she'd slowly suffocated at Carter Crossing, she'd fantasized about how grand things would be if she could just move to town, yet it was nothing like she'd imagined.

While she liked imbibing of hard spirits until she grew silly and out of control, she didn't like any of the rest of it. His male chums talked about risqué, salacious topics, and they were quite lecherous. They viewed her as loose and available to misbehave.

In the sheltered, rural world where she'd been raised, she'd been unaware that adults carried on in such a foul manner. Clayton had wallowed in London for over a decade. How could he stand the dissipation and vice? She was already exhausted, and she'd only been reveling for a week.

Her biggest disillusionment came from what she'd been doing at night. With her begging him to take her to London, she'd assumed he had a mansion, with plenty of servants and bedchambers, so there would be minimal impropriety over her staying with him.

But he had only one bedchamber, and she'd drunk too much liquor and had wound up in his bed. After that carnal encounter, he'd explained that subsequent encounters were to be allowed and enjoyed, so she'd continued to participate without argument.

The physical deeds he'd shown her were shocking and thrilling, but she was sinning egregiously, and her conduct went against all she'd ever been taught about right and wrong. Marriage was the sole remedy that would make her whole, but it was obvious the notion hadn't occurred to him.

It was the middle of the afternoon, and he'd just risen to face the day, while she'd been up for hours, pacing and fretting. So far, the boons she'd envisioned hadn't transpired, and she was fairly sure none of them would.

He was at the dining table, eating breakfast, but sipping whiskey too—as if the approaching evening of parties had commenced. He was handsome as ever, suave and urbane, attired in expensive garments, but his cold, steely reserve was firmly in place.

During their first assignations, she'd convinced herself that his demeanor indicated a deep and fascinating personality. Now though, he was staring at her as if he wasn't certain who she was or how she'd gotten into his apartment, and she had to accept that she might have completely misjudged his character.

It was very possible that he was simply an odd, detached fellow who might engage in any reprehensible act, but who never regretted any transgression. She hadn't understood that such peculiar people existed.

"You were at a brothel?" she asked, a tad dizzy from mentioning the subject.

"Yes, I'm a member of a very elite one."

"You lie down with women who are paid for their intimate services?"

"Actually, I pay dues to belong. It's a private club."

"But . . . but . . . what about me?"

"What about you?"

"I thought we were a . . . a . . ."

She had no term to describe what they were. A couple? A betrothed pair? Bound lovers? None of those conditions applied in the slightest.

"I'm ruined!" she pointed out as if he might not recollect.

"Yes, and it's been very fun, hasn't it?"

She wouldn't deny it, but in her world—which he'd definitely never inhabited—there was a consequence for their antics. That consequence was matrimony.

"Will we wed or what?"

"Wed!" He pronounced the word as if it were an epithet, then he laughed. "You are so naïve. No, Millicent, we won't ever wed."

"What will happen to me then?"

"You'll figure it out. London can be very lucrative for a girl as pretty as you."

"What do you mean?"

"You should put yourself out for bids."

"What kind of bids? What are you talking about?"

"You should be a mistress. I know several females who are making a bloody fortune at it. We can spend a bit more time in the bedchamber, and I'll teach you some tricks so you have lots to offer the men who are interested. It will drive up your price."

"A mistress?" She shuddered. "I'd be paid for doing what you and I have been doing?"

"Yes, but it's not tawdry. You'd be in an exclusive relationship, and if you play your cards right, you'd walk away with a pile of money and jewelry. You'd be set for life."

"I don't want to be *set*. I want to be settled."

"They seem the same to me."

"I assumed—when I came here with you—that I was coming *with* you. I assumed we'd be together."

"We are together, aren't we? I'm happy to have you tarry until you can devise a plan for yourself, but you can't remain with me forever. The Madam who owns my club can help you find a protector, and she can write the contracts. She frequently assists girls like you."

She was aghast. "There are contracts?"

"You have to guarantee that the fellow follows through on his promises. You'd be mad not to."

"I would never sell myself."

"What will become of you then?"

He studied her over the rim of his glass. He looked cocky and magnificent, but totally removed from her too. Clearly, he didn't care what path she picked, and she felt like a big ninny.

"I thought this would be different," she murmured.

"Of course you did." He reached out and patted her hand. "As I mentioned, you'll figure it out. You have quite a few immoral tendencies, and in town, you can let them flow free and have the exciting life you always dreamed of having."

Suddenly, she burst into tears. "I want to go home!"

He was horrified. "To Carter Crossing? I'm a Shawcross, and you ran away with me. Why would your mother take you back? Besides, I doubt she's there."

"Where else would she be?"

"The property is my brother's now, remember? He'll have evicted her. Or she may have been arrested."

"Arrested! For what?"

"She was embezzling from the client accounts at Carter Imports, so he intended to summon the sheriff. If she's left, he might have already burned the place to the ground."

At the news, she was enormously stricken. "Why would he wreck it?"

"Because he hates your family. He and I both do. I explained it to you when we were still in the country. You can't have forgotten."

"You seduced me as part of his scheme, didn't you? You didn't really like me. You proceeded so I'd be shamed and disgraced."

He pondered the accusation, then he nodded. "I guess my ploy was two-fold. I brought you to town so you could escape Carter Crossing, but I brought you for my brother too. He might have seduced you himself, but he's too honorable, so I did it for him." He shrugged. "I'll admit to having mixed motives, but don't be so glum! All of London is open to you. You should embrace this chance."

"I'm so stupid," she muttered.

"Everyone is out of their element when they first arrive, but you grow up fast." He stood and tossed down his napkin. "Now then, I must be off. I have an important card game tonight for very high stakes. I have to prepare."

"May I come with you?"

"No."

"How should I amuse myself for the rest of the evening?"

"You're welcome to do whatever you like, but you should make an appointment to confer with the Madam at my club. She can tutor you on how to keep from winding up with a babe in your belly. If you wallow in iniquity, you have to be cautious."

Millicent blanched with dismay. She was such a dunce that the prospect of a baby hadn't occurred to her. "I could be with child?"

"Probably not yet. I've been careful, but other lovers might not be, so you have to take the appropriate action. A man never will. It's up to the woman."

He started for the door, and she said, "When will I see you again?"

"Tomorrow morning? I'm not sure how many hours the game will last, but I'll be winning, so I won't quit until the other players' purses are empty."

"How can you be certain you'll win?"

He grinned his devil's grin. "Because I cheat."

Then he sauntered out, and she loafed at the table, listening to the silence. His servants were running errands, so she was by herself. Lucas had given her some pin money, so she wasn't exactly broke. She could have gone shopping or visited a museum, but she didn't like to bustle around the busy streets on her own.

She wondered how much it would cost to buy a ticket on the mail coach to Frinton. What if she traveled to Carter Crossing, but Beatrice wouldn't let her inside? Or what if she staggered in, but Raven Shawcross had foreclosed? What then?

Perhaps she should write to Rebecca to ask what was happening. Rebecca would know, and she'd respond too. Of all the people at home, Rebecca was the only one who'd fret about Millicent's disappearance.

Yes, she would write immediately, then, depending on Rebecca's answer, she'd decide her next step. It was obvious she couldn't continue on as she was.

She couldn't imagine how long she dawdled, but with autumn ending and winter approaching, the afternoon waned quickly. She stared out as the colors faded from the sky.

A knock sounded on the door, but she was too morose to react. It sounded again, and she figured a servant was back and had forgotten his key.

She rose and trudged over, feeling more wretched than she'd ever been, and when she glanced out, she was incredibly confused.

"Mr. Melville?" she said. "What are you doing here?"

"Hello, Miss Carter." An awkward interval festered, then he asked, "May I come in?"

"Yes, yes, of course."

He blustered in, and as he studied the room, his expression was furious.

She gestured to the sofa. "Won't you sit?"

"No, thank you."

There was another awkward pause, where neither of them could begin. Finally, she couldn't bear it, and she asked, "How did you find me?"

"It wasn't easy; I'll tell you that."

"What do you want?"

"I want you to return to Carter Crossing with me. I want you to accompany me right now."

"Really?" She was swamped by such a wave of relief that she nearly hugged him.

He clasped her hands very firmly. "I realize you have a low opinion of me. I'm stuffy and stodgy and boring. I could never compare to a dashing rogue like Lucas Shawcross, but Miss Carter—Millicent—I can't permit you to remain with him."

"It's so sweet of you to worry about me."

"I have worried. From the moment I discovered you'd left with him, I've been in an absolute dither, and I have to admit that *I* am the only one. Raven Shawcross isn't concerned that his brother absconded with you. Your mother isn't concerned. There's only me, Miss Carter. I intend to wrench you from Lucas Shawcross's dastardly clutches. Will you let me?"

The tears she'd shed earlier had dried up, but on hearing his poignant entreaty, they started in again. "You're being very kind, Mr. Melville, much kinder than I deserve, but I can't show my face back there. I fear I am . . . am . . . ruined."

"I had no doubt you would be. Lucas Shawcross is a fiend, and I guessed at once that you would be imperiled."

"He didn't abscond with me. I begged him to bring me to London."

"Are you wishing he hadn't? You look positively glum, so it can't have turned out as you were hoping."

"No, it hasn't turned out as I was hoping at all."

"You're young, Miss Carter, and you've never encountered a scoundrel like him. I comprehend how and why he tempted you, but when you recognize you've made a bad decision, you're allowed to change course. We can go home, and you can put this incident behind you. I'll never tell a soul what I observed. It will be our little secret, but please assist me as I keep you from making it any worse."

"I might be with child!"

He gulped at the news, then pulled himself up to his full height and valiantly announced, "If you are in the family way, I shall wed you and save you from disgrace."

"Why would you?"

"I've been inordinately fond of you, Miss Carter. In the past, you discounted my affection, but perhaps this escapade will have smoothed over your ambivalent feelings. It's amusing to think about having wild adventures, but there is great solace in the normal, common parts of life. I'm sure—in your traipsing off with Mr. Shawcross—you didn't completely consider the ramifications."

"No, I didn't."

"So . . . I forgive you for your transgressions, and I ask that I have a chance to prove my devotion to you."

It was a pretty speech, and he was flummoxed by it. His cheeks flushed bright red, and she supposed they were a pathetic pair. He was embarrassed and discomposed, and she was crying like a baby.

"If you can forgive me, Mr. Melville, I have to categorically state that you might be the dearest man who ever lived."

"I might be boring and tedious, Millicent, but I'm steadfast and true as well." He nodded to the bedchamber. "Will you pack your bags? Will you leave with me? You must understand that this is the sole time I'll stop by. If you refuse to depart, I won't try again—and you'll be on your own. Don't permit pride or foolishness to push you into the wrong choice."

"What would I be returning to?" she asked. "I'm afraid my mother has been evicted—or maybe even arrested."

"We'll worry about all of that later. For now, we'll simply remove you from where you are."

She peered around the small parlor that so clearly indicated how Lucas had failed to deliver the future she'd dreamed of having. She'd tossed the dice, had cast caution to the wind. In her naïve condition, she'd glommed onto a wastrel and a gambler, and if she tarried, who could predict how it would wash out in the end?

That very instant, she could have a babe growing in her belly, but if she was in trouble, Lucas would never rescue her. His remedy was for her to visit the proprietor of his brothel and be instructed in the methods of harlots.

It was the existence she'd risked all to have, and it had been a hideous mistake.

And here was Mr. Melville. Kind, dull, clumsy Mr. Melville. In running off with Lucas, she'd sinned dreadfully, yet he'd fretted over her. He'd searched for her. He'd found her, and he forgave her.

What woman could ignore that sort of marvelous fidelity?

"Yes, I will go with you," she said. "Let me grab my portmanteau. I just need a minute to pack."

# CHAPTER
## 19

"Do you know where Mother is buried?"

Rebecca pulled up short and gaped at her sister. "I just realized I have no idea."

"She wasn't brought to Carter Crossing?"

"No. There's a family plot at the cemetery behind the church in Frinton. She's not buried there."

"She was a sinner—due to her affair with Father—so the vicar wouldn't have let her be laid to rest in hallowed ground."

"Gad, I hope she wasn't dumped in a pauper's grave."

"I'll have Nathan ask Aunt Edwina. She might have details about what happened—if she'll share them with him. She can be awful."

"I'd consider writing to Cousin Beatrice, but when I left Carter Crossing, I swore I'd never contact her again."

"We can have Nathan speak to her. I believe he has some comments for her about that letter we sent you."

"I wish I could claim I'm surprised she didn't give it to me, but I'm *not* surprised. She was horrid."

"Why would she care that we wrote to you?" Sarah inquired. "Why would it bother her if your relatives reached out?"

"She never had a positive remark about the Blakes, and she hated that they were aristocrats. She was probably afraid I'd flit off to live with you, and my life would be wine and roses from that point on. The notion would have driven her mad."

Sarah smirked. "Were you aware you have a dowry?"

"I don't have a dowry."

"Nathan dug into it. He'd been wondering whether Father had a Will when he died. When we were born, he put some money aside for us. At the beginning, it wasn't much, but it's been sitting in an account for a quarter of a century, so it's quite a lot now."

"Are you telling me I'm an heiress?" Rebecca was very skeptical.

Sarah chuckled. "I hadn't thought of it that way, but I guess you are."

Rebecca was a tad astonished. "What a bizarre discovery."

"You could wed if you wanted."

"I don't want to wed. Not ever."

"I used to feel the same, but then, I met Sebastian. He changed my mind."

"Not right away. According to him, you were incredibly stubborn."

"He deserved for me to be stubborn. His family behaved atrociously toward me, and I refused to be connected to such hideous villains."

"You're lucky though. From what I've observed so far, he's a fine man."

"Rich and famous too," Sarah added. "How often does a girl get to marry a national icon?"

"Not often."

They were strolling arm in arm, bundled in cloaks and hats, their noses red from the cold wind. They'd walked to the village outside Selby so Sarah could show her the Blake section at the cemetery. She'd seen her father's grave for the first time, and it was a precious gift she would always cherish.

They were headed home, enjoying the brisk air and solitude. Everyone at the manor was glad they'd been reunited, glad Rebecca had arrived, so it was difficult to chat privately.

"Noah told me a secret about you," Sarah said.

Rebecca frowned. "I'm barely acquainted with him. How could he have learned any of them?"

"Alex spilled the beans."

"Those two are thick as thieves."

"They're planning to join the army together in a few years," Sarah said. "Then, after they have stellar careers as soldiers, they're starting an exploration company like the one Sir Sidney had. Noah will be the leader, and Alex will be his second in command."

"That's not a bad idea, although I can't imagine how they'll afford it."

"Did I mention that Sebastian is disgustingly rich?"

"I believe you did."

"He'll take care of it. And if he won't, I'll nag at Nathan so he pitches in."

Rebecca sighed with contentment. "People here are so kind. I should have staggered in a decade ago."

"Back then, you wouldn't have received much of a welcome. From Nathan especially. He wouldn't have remembered you."

"What was the secret Noah told you?" Rebecca asked. "My past has been so boring. It can't have been too shocking."

"He tells me you know Raven Shawcross."

Rebecca missed a step, and Sarah leapt to steady her.

"Yes, I've met Mr. Shawcross." Her tone was very bland.

"Alex revealed to Noah that you were very close friends."

"We might have been."

Sarah halted and pulled Rebecca around to face her. "How close is *close*?"

"Ah . . . cordial?"

"You expect me to accept you were *cordial* with that handsome rogue?"

Rebecca's cheeks flushed with shame. She'd only just arrived at Selby, had only just bonded with her siblings. She couldn't bear to confess how she'd disgraced herself with Mr. Shawcross. To her sister in particular.

She doubted Sarah would judge her, but when she was working so hard to fit in, it would kill her to dampen the esteem that was building. How could she admit she'd allowed herself to be seduced by a scoundrel? Yet at the same time, she was terrified about how the future might unfold.

She'd engaged in marital relations with Mr. Shawcross precisely once, and she'd always been unlucky. What if she was increasing? What if she had to inform her new-found brother that she was in the family way? If that humiliating moment ever occurred, she'd throw herself off a cliff.

"Mr. Shawcross was a member of the Sinclair expedition team," Sarah said.

"I'm aware of that."

"He, Sebastian, and Nathan are great chums."

"Yes, I suppose they would be."

"Before I married Sebastian, I stayed at his home of Hero's Haven for a bit, so *I* know Mr. Shawcross too. So does Noah. It's why he apprised me of your connection."

"What was your opinion of him?" Rebecca asked.

"He was a conceited, pompous, ridiculous ass. He constantly shouted at me and ordered me about, and I couldn't abide him. But that's just me. What is *your* opinion?"

"It's pretty much the same as yours. Initially, I thought he was fascinating, but after I learned more about him, I decided he was a fiend and a liar."

"A fiend *and* a liar? That's quite a description."

Rebecca was inconsolable over the loss of him, which was patently absurd. The last day at Carter Crossing, when she'd desperately needed his help, he wouldn't provide it. Why then would she feel any regret or remorse about their parting? She ought to be ecstatic that she'd escaped his clutches! She ought to be celebrating!

"Could we not talk about him?"

"I think we have to."

"I can't stand it."

"I'm going to ask you a question, and you have to answer truthfully: Are you ruined?"

Rebecca was so mortified that she couldn't reply. When she didn't respond, Sarah's query landed in her mind:

*You can't hide what happened from me. Are you ruined?*

*Yes, but I practically begged him to proceed.*

"Oh, you poor girl," Sarah murmured.

She wrapped her arms around Rebecca, and they hugged each other tightly, dawdling until they realized they were freezing and had to keep moving.

"He broke your heart," Sarah said.

"Yes."

"Then I'll hate him forever!"

"I hate him too."

"Might you be increasing?"

Rebecca blanched with dismay. "It's too soon to be sure."

"Would you like to have him as a husband?"

"Are you joking? Who would want such a stubborn, horrid man as a spouse?"

"Who indeed?" Sarah mused. "Occasionally, Fate intervenes though, and we women don't have a choice about how this sort of situation ends."

"We always have choices," Rebecca vehemently insisted. "You won't tell Nathan, will you? Or Sebastian? I'd die if they discovered how I've disgraced myself."

"Don't worry. I won't tattle. If they found out about this, they'd probably ride to Carter Crossing and murder him."

Rebecca chuckled miserably. "Considering how he treated me, that conclusion might please me very much."

---

"IT'S ABOUT TIME YOU arrived." Nathan grinned at Sarah and toasted her with his whiskey glass. "We got tired of waiting and started without you."

Sebastian toasted her too. They were in Nathan's library, seated on comfortable chairs in front of a warm fire. It was chilly outside, and they were glad to be snuggled inside.

"What took you so long?" Nathan asked her.

Sarah poured her own glass of whiskey, then came over and sat down across from him. "Rebecca and I tarried at the church, then we chatted on the way home."

"Where is she now?"

"She was exhausted by our visit to the cemetery. It was emotional for her to see father's grave. She went upstairs to have a nap."

"While you and Rebecca were walking, we heard some curious gossip from Noah."

Sarah didn't react to his remark, making him suspect that she already knew what he intended to discuss.

"That's odd," she said. "What gossip could Noah possibly share that would interest you whatsoever?"

Sebastian answered her question. "It seems your old nemesis, Raven Shawcross, is closely acquainted with your Carter relatives."

"Yes, I recall Rebecca mentioning it."

"Evidently, he's implementing all kinds of mischief with regard to them."

"Yes, he has a vendetta against my cousin, Beatrice, and her deceased husband."

"Raven's parents lost everything when he was a boy," Nathan said. "He never explained exactly what occurred, but I received the distinct impression that it was incredibly traumatic."

Sebastian said to Nathan, "When Sarah was still Miss Robertson and staying in my cottage at Hero's Haven, she and Raven had a few altercations."

"A few!" Sarah huffed. "He is an arrogant bully, and I can't abide him."

"Which brings us to Noah," Nathan said. "He claims Raven and Rebecca were very friendly."

"Maybe," Sarah blithely stated.

"In fact, according to Alex, they might have been romantically involved."

Sarah stared right at him and said, "I have no information about it."

"Liar. You should never play cards for money. Your face is an open book."

Sebastian scowled at her. "Did you promise Rebecca you wouldn't talk about it?"

"I don't have any comment."

Sebastian smirked. "I'll take that as a *yes*. And I concur with Nathan. You should never gamble."

"Is she ruined?" Nathan asked. "Will I have to insist on another fast wedding?"

"I swore to Rebecca I would never betray her confidence," she said, "so I will merely reveal that Noah and Alex might have divulged a pertinent problem that concerns me very much."

Nathan's rage ignited. He was renowned for his wicked temper, and despite his wife's best efforts, he couldn't always tamp it down. But then, he deemed anger to be a very valid emotion, and some circumstances simply called out for a strident response. Why pretend otherwise?

Sebastian asked, "Have either of you hard-headed Blakes thought about how strange all of this is?"

"What do you mean?" Nathan said.

"Well, you, Raven, and I traveled together for years. You found out you had two sisters—whom you didn't remember having—and I ended up married to one of them. Now we've discovered that your other sister has wandered down the same path with Raven. What are the odds of that happening?"

"I couldn't calculate a number that high," Nathan said.

"Would Rebecca like to have him as her husband?" Sebastian asked Sarah.

Nathan cut off Sarah's reply. "Rebecca doesn't get to decide. If he's behaved badly toward her, he has to pay the appropriate price, and that price is matrimony."

"He can be so obstinate," Sebastian said. "If he was opposed to the notion, who could make him proceed?"

Nathan tsked. "Are you expecting you and I couldn't persuade him?"

"We might have to *persuade* him with our fists," Sebastian pointed out.

"I'm happy to pound on him," Nathan said. "How about you?"

Sarah scoffed with disgust. "You're not going to beat him into submission and force him. I refuse to allow it. First, you have to discuss it with him and learn his opinion about her."

"And if he won't willingly consent?"

Her eyes flared with her own bit of temper. "Then you can thrash him until he agrees."

———※———

"SHAWCROSS!"

Lucas heard his name bellowed, and he glanced over to the door of his club. Clayton Carter was waving, anxious to get his attention.

"Shawcross!" Clayton tried again.

It was early in the evening, so the establishment wasn't busy yet, but there were customers scattered about. They turned to look at who was creating the disturbance. Men mumbled and snickered.

Poor Clayton! He struggled so valiantly to be liked and accepted, but the dissolute crowd where Lucas socialized had never embraced him. His antics at his birthday party had only made it worse. They existed in a world where dubious conduct was encouraged, but it was considered bad form to have others witness your foibles.

It left your acquaintances with the sense that you were weak and couldn't control yourself, which described Clayton exactly. The dolt had no allies. Well, he hadn't actually had any to begin with.

Lucas nodded to the ruffian guarding the door, so he let Clayton through. As he marched over, Lucas assessed him, thinking he was a tad frayed around the edges.

He hadn't shaved, and his coat was wrinkled and missing a button. The garment should have been given to his valet, but Lucas suspected Clayton didn't have a valet anymore. How could he afford it?

Servants weren't stupid. No doubt his London footmen had abandoned ship.

"May I help you, Mr. Carter?" Lucas didn't stand to greet Clayton, but remained rudely slouched in his chair.

"I was wondering if you could vouch for me."

"Vouch for you where?"

"There's been a mistake. I've been a member of this club for years, but they're claiming I've been revoked."

"How embarrassing for you!"

Lucas hadn't invited him to sit, but Clayton grabbed a chair and sat anyway.

"You have to assist me," Clayton absurdly stated.

"Why would I?"

"Your brother caused this trouble. It's only fair that you rectify my situation."

Lucas pretended to ponder, then shook his head. "Sorry. I'm not interested in aiding you."

"Shawcross! You have to!"

"You're looking a little desperate, Mr. Carter."

"Creditors are hounding me. My landlord has put a chain on the door to my lodging so I can't even retrieve my clothes. My banker advises me that my accounts have been emptied. I can't latch onto a single penny, no matter where I turn."

"Yes, I suppose the walls are closing in, aren't they? Raven warned you about these dire consequences. You should have listened to him."

"If I could play cards, I'm sure I could win a few pounds—just to tide me over."

Clayton peered nervously at the guard. The man was watching his every move and would drag Clayton out if Lucas indicated he should.

Most times, Lucas thought he hadn't been swept up in Raven's enjoyment of Clayton's downfall, but apparently, there was a lot to enjoy after all.

"Have you seen your sister, Mr. Carter?"

"My sister?" Clayton asked the question as if he didn't have a sibling.

"Yes, Millicent? I'm certain you remember her."

"Why would I have seen her?"

"She came to London with me. She's been staying in my apartment, but she vanished. I figured she got sick of me and slithered over to stay with you instead."

"Don't be ridiculous. Millicent wasn't living with you."

"Yes, she was." Lucas grinned. "I ruined her too."

"Liar."

"I often lie, but not about this. She was a pretty piece of work, and I relished her carnal company. I hope she's all right. London is a dangerous place for a young lady on her own." Lucas shrugged. "Maybe she headed home, although I can't imagine how she expects to be safe there."

"Why wouldn't she be safe at home with my mother?"

"Your mother has been evicted, Mr. Carter. Have you forgotten?"

"She couldn't have been. I'm dealing with the problem. I'm hiring a lawyer, but legal proceedings are slow as molasses."

"Your mother's been arrested."

"Arrested! What are you talking about?"

"You should keep better track of the women in your life. Aren't you the *man* of the family?"

Clayton waved away Lucas's remarks as if he'd been babbling nonsense. "Let's play cards. Tell the oaf at the door that you'll permit me to join you for a game."

"I'd rather not."

"I need funds, Shawcross! Your brother has destroyed me!"

"When I was four," Lucas told him, "my father was imprisoned. I didn't understand why, but several weeks later, the sheriff came. He forced us out of our house, and we weren't allowed back in. I had a little toy soldier I carried in my pocket, but I didn't have it on me that day, and I never saw it again. The loss haunted me for years."

"You poor bugger!" Clayton snidely said. "I don't care about the stupid toy you lost when you were four."

"No, you wouldn't, would you? Your father's crimes caused that to happen to me."

"What are you blathering on about? If you're angry over that incident between our fathers from two decades ago, I can't help you. I was a boy myself, and you ought to stop obsessing."

"Have you any clue of what sort of adult a child like that grows up to be?"

"I can't be held responsible for the sins of my father."

"What was your excuse for being a prick when you were nineteen?"

Clayton frowned. "What do you mean?"

"Weren't you nineteen when you seduced my sister, Lydia? You weren't a boy then."

"Is that what this is about? You're incensed about your sister spreading her legs for me?"

"I wasn't at first, but Raven convinced me I should be furious, and I'm livid. I persuaded *your* sister to spread her legs for *me*. Shall we call it even?"

"Don't lie about Millicent!"

"Get out of here, Mr. Carter. You've exhausted my patience, and since you're no longer a member, I don't have to put up with your boorish presence."

"You Shawcross brothers think you own the whole bloody world."

"We own your tiny portion of it anyway, and you'll never retrieve it from us."

"Yes, I will," Clayton sneered. "I have a trump card up my sleeve that will make your brother return everything to me."

"Let me guess: My nephew is alive and well. He didn't die with his mother, and he's been residing at Carter Crossing."

Clayton was dumbfounded. "How did you know that?"

"We're not dunces, you dunce. Were you hoping to trade him? Might you have presumed—quite wrongly—that Raven would give you money in exchange for custody?"

Clayton gulped, proving that, *yes,* that was precisely what he'd assumed.

"I've supported that bastard for nearly ten years," Clayton said, "so you owe me plenty. I shall be suing for full reimbursement."

"Mr. Carter, you just might be the most unpleasant person in the kingdom."

Lucas rose suddenly, shoving back his chair so forcefully that it wobbled the table. His glass and liquor bottle went flying.

"Stand up, Clayton," Lucas said.

"I don't take orders from you. Sod off."

"My brother is in the alley. He'd like to speak to you."

"Your brother can choke on a crow."

Clayton pushed himself up, his balance unsteady, and Lucas supposed he was inebriated, which was his usual state.

"When Raven declared himself ready to implement his revenge," Lucas said, "I figured it wouldn't be very much fun, but it's been very entertaining."

Lucas's temper ignited for once. Evidently, it required an idiot like Clayton

Carter to set a spark to it. He stepped around the table and hit Clayton as hard as he could. He tottered, then collapsed in a stunned heap. Blood spurted from his nose, and he curled into a ball and wailed with dismay.

The other customers glared at him and tsked with disgust.

"What was that for?" he asked after he caught his breath.

"That was for my sister—for you seducing her."

"It was worth it," he unwisely taunted.

Lucas kicked him in the ribs, viciously enough that he likely broke several. "That was for *your* sister because I ruined her and you don't even care."

Lucas gestured to the guard, and the man stomped over, grabbed Clayton, and dragged him to the rear door. The other patrons jeered as Clayton passed by, and Clayton didn't put up a fight. He was disoriented from being battered, so it was easy to haul him out. Lucas didn't even have to pitch in.

After they were outside, the guard dropped him in the muck, then vanished. No spectator would have witnessed a thing, but then, Lucas didn't need to worry. Who would ever wonder what had become of Clayton Carter?

Raven was loafing next to a carriage, waiting for Lucas to arrive.

"I told you he'd show up," Lucas said.

"I'm impressed by your shrewd assessment."

"It wasn't that shrewd. He's been slinking in every night, whining at the members to help him."

"I was certain he'd stagger to Oakley, and I'd get to kill him in the country."

"You still can if you want. It would be fine by me."

Clayton was finally able to focus on their conversation. "You're a pair of fiends. I will not accompany you anywhere."

Lucas hit him again, knocking him unconsciousness.

"Little brother," Raven said, "I typically assume you're never angry, but occasionally, you surprise me."

"I trifled with his sister, and he wasn't concerned in the least. It almost seems like it was a waste to have bothered with her."

"I warned you to leave her alone."

"I never listen to you, so why continue to harangue at me?"

"Has there been any news about her?"

"No, and Clayton hadn't seen her either. I'm betting she went home."

"I hope so. If she met with a bad end, it will be your fault."

"I'm never at fault," Lucas said. "I make sure of it."

Raven leaned down and tied Clayton hand and foot, stuffing a kerchief in his mouth so he was trussed and gagged. Then he and Lucas lifted the oaf and threw him into the carriage where he landed with a painful thump.

"Would you like to ride to the docks with me?" Raven asked.

"Do you need me to?"

"I'd *like* you to, but it's not necessary."

"I won't come, but I will visit you at Oakley very soon. I enjoyed it there much more than I expected I would."

"I'd be delighted if you'd visit."

"Have you found our nephew?"

"No. He and Rebecca stayed at an inn in Frinton for two days, then they took the mail coach to London. They didn't mention their destination to anyone."

"If they're in London, we'll likely never locate them."

"I refuse to think we won't," Raven said.

"I will attempt to muster some of your optimism."

"I'll see you at Oakley."

"I'm actually looking forward to it."

"If we don't watch out, we'll begin to seem like a real family."

"Heaven forbid. We could never be that ordinary."

Raven jumped into the vehicle, and Lucas waved him off, observing until he rounded the corner, then he walked inside to finish his whiskey. It had been a night worth living for a change, and all in all, he felt quite grand.

———※※———

CLAYTON ROUSED SUFFICIENTLY TO recall being assaulted by Lucas Shawcross, then being dragged to the alley and tossed at Raven Shawcross's feet. The brothers were deranged, and he was positive he was simply one man in a lengthy line of unfortunates who'd been destroyed by them.

It was dark and difficult to get his bearings, but it appeared he was lying on the floor in a moving carriage. He tried to sit up and was alarmed to
discover that his hands and legs were fettered. He would have cried out, but
he was gagged too, so he couldn't summon assistance. If he'd been prone to
emotional displays, he might have burst into tears and bawled like a baby.

He shifted about, seeking a more comfortable position, and for his efforts, a man's boot was firmly wedged on his stomach to hold him in place.
Raven Shawcross bent down and muttered, "You've been out so long that I
was afraid Lucas had killed you. I guess not."

"Mm! Mm!" Clayton complained.

"What was that?" Shawcross asked. "I couldn't understand you."

He yanked the gag away, and Clayton swallowed and spat to clear his
throat.

"Where are you taking me?" he demanded.

"You'll find out in a few minutes."

"If you don't tell me, I start shouting, and I won't stop until someone
comes to my aid."

"If you annoy me, I'll put the kerchief back in your mouth. Or I can
knock you unconscious again. From the earlier blow Lucas administered, it's
obvious you have a very soft head. It would be easy to silence you. You can
shut up on your own or I can shut you up. Your choice."

"Dog! Cur!"

"Your mother hurled those same epithets when she was being arrested.
You two ought to devise more cutting insults."

"What has happened to my mother?"

"I conducted an audit at Carter Imports, and she'd been embezzling."

"The old bat was stealing from me?"

"Not from you, but from the clients. I learned from experience that they
get really irked by that sort of behavior."

"I can't believe she'd be smart enough to engage in a scheme like that."

"Your father was a thief too, and he taught her all his tricks—except how
to conceal her crimes."

"She was always too stupid for words."

"She didn't feel you were particularly bright either."

Clayton was quiet for a bit, wincing and moaning as they bounced over ruts and bumps. His mind whirred furiously, anxious to formulate a plan that would thwart Shawcross, but he seemed omnipotent. How could a normal fellow like Clayton fight him and win?

An idea floated to the surface. He'd used it with Lucas Shawcross, to no avail. Perhaps he'd have better luck with his evil brother.

"I'd like to make a trade."

"What type of trade?"

"I'll give you an item you want very much, and you'll let me go. We'll forget this little . . . *incident,* and we'll call it even."

"What is the item you'd like to trade?"

"I have your bastard nephew."

Raven snorted. "You don't have my nephew."

"I do have him! I've hidden him from you, and if you won't release me, you'll never see him again."

"He's with your cousin, Rebecca."

"He's not with her!"

Shawcross kicked him. "The more you talk, the more I wonder if I shouldn't just murder you. The world would breathe a sigh of relief if you weren't in it."

"Why not proceed then?" Clayton rashly taunted.

"I murdered a man a few weeks ago, so for the moment, I've had my fill of violence. But if you keep pushing me, I'll be happy to oblige you."

Clayton pondered whether Shawcross was being truthful. Might he have slain someone? Or was he trying to frighten Clayton? If so, his boast had definitely succeeded!

In Clayton's view, Shawcross was capable of any nefarious deed. Hadn't he traveled in Africa for over a decade? Rumors swirled that Sir Sidney's team of explorers had shed their British ways, becoming like savages in their attitudes and habits. He might do anything to Clayton—and he'd likely get away with it too.

"You won't harm me," Clayton insisted. "This is England! There are laws against homicide."

"Laws have never prevented me before," Shawcross brashly stated, "but a hasty demise would be too easy for you. I have a more suitable ending arranged."

Clayton shivered. "What ending?"

"You seduced my sister, Lydia, when I was in Africa. She was alone, without me here to protect her. I fret over how she must have suffered."

"I was kind to her!" Clayton lied. "She was pretty and sweet. I would have married her, but ... ah ... my mother wouldn't agree to the match. Can't we admit that Lydia's difficulties were Beatrice's fault?"

"No, we can't admit that." Shawcross seized Clayton by the throat, cutting off his air. "I often think of Lydia. I think of her being tossed out of her boarding school and sent to that unwed mother's home in disgrace. I think of her slowly bleeding to death and, while it was transpiring, being informed her child had died. Those visions haunt me, Clayton."

"I can imagine!" he heartily concurred as Shawcross pitched him onto the floor with a hard thud.

"So ... while I would have loved to kill you, I don't want you to have a quick conclusion. I want your misery to persist until you feel as if you'll go mad if it doesn't stop."

Clayton scoffed with disgust. "It wasn't enough that you ruined my life?"

"No, it wasn't the beginning of enough."

The carriage rattled to a halt, the cessation of movement incredibly ominous.

"Where are we?" he asked.

"At the docks."

Before Clayton could blink, Shawcross stuck the kerchief back in his mouth. He tugged a flour sack over Clayton's head too, concealing Clayton's features in case there were any bystanders to observe them. Then he climbed out. Clayton writhed and jerked and attempted to free his wrists, but they were tied too tightly.

Shawcross was outside, talking to another man in low tones.

"Don't bring him back to England for at least five years."

"That should be simple," the man replied. "We're bound for China, with visits to India and Africa. We'll be at sea for a very long time."

There was a clinking sound that could only be money changing hands. Then Clayton was dragged out and onto his feet. He was dizzy, swaying to and fro, and with the flour sack over his head, he was so disoriented he couldn't tell up from down. He started moaning, but it merely bought him a whack on the belly and a fierce order to be silent.

Shawcross stepped in and whispered, "I've sold you to a merchant ship."

Clayton blanched. A ship required dozens of sailors, and unsavory captains had trouble finding able-bodied men for their crews. Occasionally, convicts were released from prison to join up, but gullible men were conscripted too—very much against their will.

They were drugged or beaten unconscious, then hauled aboard without their realizing what was occurring. They woke up in the middle of the ocean, with gut-wrenching nausea and no means of escape.

There were always stories about such terrible events, but Clayton hadn't believed them. They were true? What?

*No! No! No!*

"This is a prison sentence for what you did to my sister," Shawcross said.

*I didn't hurt her! She liked it! She wanted it!*

Shawcross continued, "You never paid a price for your sins toward her, so you'll pay it now. It will be a tough voyage, and I expect you'll be in agony each and every day of it."

*You fiend! You deranged animal!*

"Try not to get yourself killed." Shawcross chuckled. "I take that back. I don't care if you survive or not."

Suddenly, a cloth was pressed to Clayton's face. He was so surprised by the abrupt feeling of being smothered that he inhaled deeply, and it caused him to ingest a potent chemical that burned through his nose and into his lungs.

He tipped one way, then the other, and as he collapsed, strong arms caught him and carried him away.

His last cognizant thought was hearing Shawcross say, "Good luck, Clayton. You're definitely going to need it."

# CHAPTER

## 20

RAVEN SAT IN THE front parlor at Oakley, his back to the fire, so he could look out the open door. It was Sunday, so his carpenters were off with their families. He'd hired a few servants too, and they were off as well. His cook had left him a plate of food in the kitchen, but he hadn't had the energy to eat it.

The residence was quickly becoming habitable, so he should have been ecstatic, but with every improvement, he wondered what he'd been thinking when he'd decided to buy it and move in. He wasn't a farmer or country gentleman, and while he owned many businesses, he didn't run them himself. He hired clerks to administer them.

A man was supposed to belong somewhere though, but he'd never been tied down by property. From the time he was ten and his father had been arrested, his life had been one of change and flux. Once he'd joined the expedition team, he'd sailed and trekked with Sir Sidney, having rarely lingered in one spot.

With his Africa days behind him, he'd convinced himself that he should have a genuine home, and it would be wise to purchase Oakley. He possessed a poignant attachment to it due to a handful of summer holidays spent in it as a young boy. And, of course, its proximity to Carter Crossing had provided easy access from which to torment the Carters.

His scheme had worked out precisely as he'd dreamed. He'd ruined Beatrice and Clayton. He'd retrieved what remained of their assets. He'd punished Clayton for seducing Lydia.

He often pondered his sister. How and when had she met Clayton? Had she loved him? Had she believed—to the bitter end—that he'd relent and wed her?

The facility where she'd died had been closed for years, so Raven had never been able to ask the attendants about her final hours. Who had been with her? Had there been anyone? Or had she staggered through it alone?

There were probably some people in the world who would declare he'd been too hard on Beatrice and Clayton, but he disagreed. Not when Lydia's fate was recalled.

He should have been celebrating. He should have been congratulating himself. But he was so miserable!

He'd shuttered Carter Imports, but it had brought him no satisfaction. He'd already had several visits from civic officials in Frinton who'd demanded he reconsider and let the employees return to their jobs.

To his great disgust, he was contemplating it. If he yielded, why had he expended so much effort to wreck the stupid company? If he simply planned to revive it, why had he bothered?

He was vexed over Carter Crossing too. He'd intended to evict the occupants and level the bloody house, but he hadn't. As he'd faced down the dozens of servants, he'd found he couldn't. He'd put the butler in charge and had slithered away, being extremely conflicted over what he'd like to have happen.

Why demolish a perfectly good house? Why tear down barns and stables? Why uproot fields and crops? Beatrice and Clayton were vanquished, their ownership revoked. Wasn't that enough?

He recognized that his wanderlust was fueling his discontentment. He'd meander like a ghost down the quiet Oakley halls, until he couldn't stand it. Then he'd climb the promontory to stare at passing ships. Why wasn't he on one of them?

Winter was about to arrive, and a smart man would have been headed south to warmer climes. For once, he wasn't headed south, and he was wretched because of it.

The worst part was how desperately he was missing Rebecca. He couldn't stop reviewing their last conversation where she'd raced over the hill to seek his help, but he'd been too annoyed to give it. Every time there was a noise in the old mansion—a board would creak or a window would rattle—he'd whip around, certain it would be her, but it never was.

He simply couldn't accept that she'd vanished. According to the servants at Carter Crossing, she hadn't had any money, friends, or kin other than Beatrice. Where would she have gone? And how could she have afforded to get there?

She had his nephew, Alex, with her too, and he would be an added burden. How would she manage?

After he'd discovered in Frinton that she was bound for London on the mail coach, he'd nearly suffered an apoplexy. Women from all over the kingdom traveled to town to start over in the teaming, chaotic city, but he'd never heard of a single one of them having a decent ending.

He wanted to tell her he was sorry. He wanted to apologize and atone. He wanted to officially meet his nephew, to support him, to assist him so he'd have the path he deserved to have.

If he ever saw Rebecca again, he'd kiss and hug her, then he'd shake her until her teeth rattled for being so irresponsible, for causing him to worry so much.

It was chilly and drizzly outside, and he had a warm fire burning in the hearth, but he felt as if he was suffocating, so he'd left the front door wide open. He was gazing out, watching a light rain fall and enjoying the smell of the fresh air. It tantalized his senses, increasing his perception that he was in the wrong place, doing the wrong thing, after having made all the wrong choices.

Suddenly, a rider trotted up the lane. Because the weather was inclement, he was bundled in a canvas slicker, a hat pulled low, so Raven couldn't discern his identity. Nor could he imagine who it would be.

Not his brother. Lucas was too lazy to come on a horse, and he liked to lounge in a plush carriage where he could drink, smoke, and relax while on a trip. He wouldn't traipse about in dicey conditions either.

With Lucas off the list, he couldn't settle on who else it might be. He loafed in his chair, curious as the man dismounted and tied off his reins. When he marched in and removed his hat, Raven blinked with surprise.

"Mr. Melville? You're the last person I was expecting."

"I'm sure I am, Mr. Shawcross. Why is the door open? It's cold as the devil. May I close it?"

"Be my guest."

He observed as Melville shut it, then shed his hat and slicker.

"Where's your gig?" Raven asked.

"I sold it."

"That's too bad. You were very sporty when you dashed around the neighborhood. You enlivened this dreary spot."

"I'm not the sort to own such a flashy vehicle. I forced myself to admit it, and I reverted to less exciting transportation."

The poor fellow looked positively glum over the decision, and Raven said, "I have some servants now, so I might have had someone tend you, but I gave them the day off so they could spend Sunday with their families."

"It sounds like a completely normal idea. If you're not careful, people will begin to assume you're absolutely ordinary."

"There's no chance of that," Raven muttered. "Why are you here? I could have sworn—after your prior visit—I told you to stay away."

"Yes, well, we have a few matters to discuss." He motioned to an empty chair. "May I sit?"

"I suppose, so long as you promise you won't aggravate me."

Melville smirked. "I'll try not to."

He walked over and plopped down, which meant Raven had to turn toward the hearth too so he wasn't facing in the opposite direction.

"It's wet and miserable out there," Melville said. "This fire is wonderful."

"We're not chatting. What is it you want? Get on with it please."

"Fine, fine. You needn't snap and bark at me. I've brought Millicent home to Carter Crossing."

"Oh. Good. After you explained her situation, I went to London to pry her away from my brother, but she'd departed on her own—smart girl that she apparently is."

"I realize you're fond of your brother, so I will not call him any of the names I'd like to use when referring to him."

"You can call him whatever you like. He is not a mystery to me, and you won't be telling me anything I haven't already figured out."

"I have offered to marry her."

"Really? You'll save her from disgrace?"

Melville's cheeks flushed. "Yes."

"That's gallant of you. I guess Lucas's antics were totally to your benefit then. I doubt she'd have wed you without his mischief."

"It appears to be the case, so I will not argue the point."

"Praise be."

"I have to ask you about Carter Crossing."

"What about it?"

"I've spoken with the butler, and he has notified me that the staff is in a state of limbo. They had expected to be terminated and that you would tear down the house, but you haven't done any of that."

Raven shrugged. "I'm still debating."

"May I beg for mercy on their behalf?"

"You don't have to convince me. I've listened to plenty of nagging to calm down and let them remain. I probably will."

"Millicent and I plan to marry next week."

"It's awfully fast. Can you accomplish it that quickly?"

"I've applied for a Special License. I didn't think we should delay, although she's advised me we needn't hurry. Evidently, there's no babe on the way, so your brother is off the hook." Melville scowled. "I can't fathom how she would know she's not increasing, but better safe than sorry."

"Melville! We're not discussing female bodily functions."

"Yes, yes, I agree. And . . ." Melville gulped and forced himself to continue. "I'd like to invite you to our wedding."

"Is that wise? Your betrothed's mother has been arrested, and it was due to facts I furnished to the authorities. She might not be keen to gaze out into the pews during the ceremony and find me there."

"I don't believe Millicent is surprised by her mother's crimes."

"So she won't mind if I attend?"

"No. We'd both like you there."

"Are we to be friends, Melville? Is that what you're hoping?"

"Not friends precisely. You're such a surly, unlikable brute. It's not possible—not with what I've learned about you—but perhaps neighbors? Cordial neighbors?"

"If we're to be neighbors, it indicates that you presume you'll be living over the hill at Carter Crossing."

"Yes . . . ah . . . about that. When I arrived back from my trip to town to rescue Millicent, I'd received correspondence apprising me that I won't be granted a church posting after all."

"I'm truly devastated to hear it," Raven said. "You possess the necessary qualities to have been especially proficient at that line of work."

"I appreciate the sentiment, but it means I won't have the funds to support a wife or the rectory to give her a home."

"I get it now," Raven mused. "You want to stay at Carter Crossing with her."

"I'm determined to provide for her, Shawcross, but I have the worst luck. Nothing ever goes right for me. I'm quite despondent over it."

"You're wrong on your assessment of the situation. You yanked her away from Lucas, and it proves you have all kinds of spunk and character. Those attributes will take you a great distance in life."

"I'll pray you're correct, but so far, I haven't had much fortune shine on me. I'd like it to, but it never does."

"Is your loss of the church job the reason you sold your gig?"

"Yes. I needed the money, but it dawned on me too that I should stop pretending to be someone I'm not."

Raven studied him, and an interesting idea popped into his head. He never made hasty decisions, and he always considered the angles of any choice, but his sudden spurt of inspiration ignited a spark he couldn't ignore.

If he did a good deed, a deed that was a relief to many, would he cease feeling so wretched?

"I have a proposition for you, Melville."

"What is it? Before you explain, I must inform you that I view you as a very dodgy fellow. I might not ever be a vicar, but my morals are still firmly in place. Please don't suggest any project that would have me blushing."

"I wouldn't dream of it."

He stared at the fire, the seconds ticking by as he poked at the notion once more, then he resolved to simply bluster forward. Why not? If it turned out to be a disaster, he'd pick up the pieces and try something else.

"I had planned to raze Carter Crossing," he said, "then let the fields grow to weeds."

"I realize it, and I understand what Charles Carter did to your father, so I won't judge you. If I'd lived through your predicament, I don't know how I'd have reacted. I'd like to assume I'd have avenged my parents too."

"With your comment, I find myself liking you more than I should. I will admit to you that I've changed my mind about the property. It's a fine residence, and it would be asinine to ruin it."

"I'm delighted by this news. Millicent and the servants have been distressed. You've calmed many fears."

"I've shuttered Carter Imports too. The ledgers were a mess, and Beatrice had embezzled from the clients so often that I figured it was best to close it. But I've had numerous people beg me to reopen it."

"Will you listen to any of them?"

"I think I will."

"You're becoming an accidental philanthropist."

"Or maybe I'm the biggest fool ever."

"Maybe."

Melville grinned, and in an abrupt flash, Raven remembered him from their months together at school. He'd been a quiet, funny boy, with an absurd sense of humor, and his quirks had made him a pariah. Other students had bullied him relentlessly, and on one particularly awful occasion, Raven had chased them off.

Preston had been embarrassed at having to be rescued, so he'd never spoken to Raven again. Then Raven's father had been arrested, and he'd been sent to a different school. If his life had gone in a better direction, might they have been friends? Could they be friends in the future?

"I need a manager to run Carter Imports for me. It has to be a person I can trust, a person who will rebuild it—and not rob me blind. What is your opinion? Would you like to take charge of it for me?"

"Me!" Melville blanched, then sat up straighter. "Well, *yes,* I believe I would like to do that."

"We'll settle on a salary later."

"I'm amenable to receiving whatever you deem to be fair."

"You're a pathetic negotiator." Raven rolled his eyes, wondering again if this was a sane idea. "If I'm not razing the manor, I have to have someone live in it and manage things there for me too."

"Are you offering the position to Millicent and me?"

Raven nodded. "I guess I am."

"We enthusiastically accept!"

Raven chuckled. "Good decision. I'm glad to note you won't be stupid about it. Now get out of here, and let me enjoy a whiskey by myself. I've been as cordial as I can be for one afternoon."

Melville jumped up and grabbed Raven's hand, and he shook it vigorously, his fervor overblown and awkward. "Thank you, thank you!"

"You're welcome."

Raven pulled away, and Melville smiled and went over to don his damp hat and slicker. As he prepared to depart, he was almost skipping with excitement. In contrast, Raven supposed he was a pitiful sight: alone in his cold, drafty mansion, with no family, friends, or servants to keep him company.

Melville seemed to sense his dejected state, and he hovered, obviously anxious to share a pertinent thought, but Raven had meant it when he'd said he was exhausted by so much cordiality.

He'd likely spend the next week, scolding himself over his generosity and speculating over what peculiar urge had possessed him, but he suspected he'd done it because it would make Rebecca happy. If she learned that he was being kind to Millicent, that he was saving their childhood home, might she return?

Just as Melville opened the door to leave, Raven peered over his shoulder and asked, "Melville? While you were in town, Rebecca left Carter Crossing. She took the boy, Alex, with her. They had a fight with Beatrice, and she kicked them out."

"I heard about that, and actually, I was hoping she might be staying with you."

Raven wasn't about to confess that she'd begged for shelter, but he'd been too much of an ass to provide it. "They rode the mail coach to London. Might she have had kin or acquaintances there? Could you ask Millicent for me? I'm not positive Rebecca had a destination in mind for when she arrived, and a young lady can land herself in a lot of trouble when that's her plan."

"I'm not aware of any London acquaintances, but you might check with her Blake relatives. It's quite a lofty family, and I can't imagine she's had contact with them lately, but it might be worth inquiring."

"Her Blake relatives?"

"On her father's side? You don't appear to have been informed about her lineage. Her mother was a Carter, but her father was Viscount Blake of the Selby Blakes. Apparently, he was a philanderer, and her mother was seduced by him."

Raven almost fell out of his chair. "Are you joking?"

"Ah . . . no? Her half-brother is Nathan Blake, the current Lord Selby? He's the famous explorer."

"I know who Nathan Blake is," Raven snapped in a surly tone.

Melville pondered the remark, then perked up. "Oh! Yes, I expect you would. He's one of Sir Sidney's men."

"He and I have been close for over a decade, so I'm cognizant of the relevant details about his past. He doesn't have any siblings."

"I can't guess what he was ever told about it, but Rebecca *is* his half-sister. Her mother was Nathan's nanny when he was a baby." Melville wrinkled his nose. "I shouldn't be spreading gossip about her. If Rebecca never confided in you—"

"She never did."

"—it's clear she didn't think it was any of your business. She never talks about it either. Her Cousin Beatrice always taunted her over her connection to them, so she tried to pretend it didn't exist."

"Nathan Blake! He's her brother? You're certain? You're not confused or mistaken?"

"No. Millicent could stop by to tell you about it if you'd like."

Raven shook his head with amazement, but a bit of shock too. "I believe you, Melville. I don't need your fiancée to verify it."

"You ought to write to Lord Selby. He might have some news, but other than him, I really can't picture where she might be."

"When is your wedding?" Raven asked.

"Friday."

"I'll be away for a few days, but I'll be sure to be back for it."

"Where are you going?"

"I'm traveling to Selby to discuss Rebecca with Nathan Blake."

"If he doesn't know about her being his sister, should you apprise him? In my humble opinion, aristocrats are odd ducks. He probably wouldn't like to discover that his father was a libertine. He might shoot the messenger."

"I'll brace myself for a rude reception," Raven said, "and I'll return in plenty of time for your ceremony. I'll buy you an expensive gift."

"You're growing nicer by the minute."

"Don't get used to it."

"If you find Miss Rebecca at her brother's home, bring her to the wedding too. Millicent would love to have her sitting in the front pew at the church."

"I will do that, Melville. If I find her, I definitely will."

RAVEN WAS NERVOUSLY PERCHED on a sofa in a small parlor at Selby Manor. He'd arrived without warning, introduced himself to the footman at the door, and asked to speak with Nathan.

A servant had been dispatched to track him down, but it was a large estate, and he'd been apprised it would take awhile to locate him. Nathan had important guests in residence, and he was busy entertaining them.

What would Nathan think of Raven blustering in? Would he be irked? Or would some of his temper have waned so he'd be happy to have an old friend stop by?

Raven was hoping it was the latter.

He'd never previously visited Selby, and he was stunned by the opulence. Yes, Nathan was an earl, but during their expeditions, he'd simply been a member of the Sinclair team, so his disparate wealth and status hadn't mattered.

Raven wasn't exactly a stranger to affluence. He was very rich too, as were several members of their group, particularly Sebastian Sinclair who'd inherited Sir Sidney's fortune after he'd been murdered.

Raven and his companions had existed in two worlds. In one, they'd camped and cooked over fires and lived like vagabonds. They'd rarely bathed or shaved or laundered their clothes. In the other, the one they inhabited whenever they returned to England, they wallowed in conditions that were grandiose and pretentious.

But Selby Manor put all their other mansions and properties to shame. It was exquisite, Nathan's position and prosperity visible in every direction. How far would he have reverted into his aristocratic life? Had Raven any part in it now?

Since they'd been home, Raven had bumped into Nathan on precisely one occasion: the public inquest held to review the circumstances leading up to Sir Sidney's death. When they'd chatted, Nathan had been cool and dismissive, his attitude demonstrating that he considered himself to be separated from his prior acquaintances.

Months had passed since then. Might some of his hostility have abated? Nathan was tough and brave, possessed of many of Raven's same traits. Because they were so similar, he'd always been one of Raven's favorite people. He couldn't bear for them to be at odds.

The door opened behind him, and he braced for anything. If he'd been a religious man, he'd have murmured a prayer for strength, that Nathan would have forgiven him for the mistakes he'd made in Africa. At the very least, he'd have prayed for a display of cordiality.

He'd have prayed too for news about Rebecca and Alex, but because he wasn't religious, he simply inhaled a deep breath, rose to his feet, and spun to discover who had entered.

"Rebecca!"

Her name burst from his lips, and he felt a tad dizzy at finding her hale and present. He hadn't been optimistic that Nathan would have information about her, so this was such an unexpected surprise. He was so relieved he could barely maintain his balance.

"I'm so glad to see you!" he said.

She marched over, and he dipped in to kiss her. He probably didn't have the right anymore, but he was so overjoyed that he couldn't resist. She lurched away though, so he grazed her cheek.

"Hello, Mr. Shawcross."

Her mode of address was so formal, and his spirits sank. Clearly, she was angry, and he supposed it would be difficult to alter that opinion, but then, he deserved her scorn.

"Don't call me Shawcross. Call me Raven. We're still friends, aren't we?"

"Friends? Really? Your gall knows no bounds. Imagine my astonishment when I learned you'd slithered in without an invitation."

"I've been searching everywhere for you."

"A likely story," she scoffed.

"Mr. Melville told me you were a Blake, so I came immediately to ask Nathan if you'd contacted him."

"Oh, he's heard plenty from me, but I won't repeat any of it. I'm not sure you'd like it."

His spirits flagged even further. Nathan had been left for dead in Africa, and Raven blamed himself for their abandoning him. He'd been mourning Nathan's demise, then—when Nathan had turned up alive and at Selby—Raven had been too much of a coward to visit and check on him.

He'd tried to apologize that afternoon at the inquest, but his overture had been rebuffed. If Rebecca had been filling his ear with tales of how Raven had mistreated her—tales that were true—any chance for them to mend their bond had been destroyed.

"Is Alex with you?"

"Yes, he's with me."

"Good. I have the greatest secret to share about him."

"What is it?"

"He's my nephew! My sister, Lydia, was his mother. Can you believe it?"

"You can't have him. I won't let you steal him from me."

"It hadn't occurred to me that I would."

"Well, *don't* think about it."

She was acting so strangely. He'd figured she'd be curious about his announcement, that she'd be eager to discuss it, but she looked bored and ready to move onto a different topic.

He regrouped. "When you rushed to Oakley that day and begged to stay with me, you were in such an agitated state."

"I certainly was."

"I was in quite a state too. I'd just had a fight with my brother, so I was distracted, and I didn't listen to you."

"That seems to be a problem of yours. You never listen!"

"I admit it. You pleaded for my help, and I refused to provide it. I've been kicking myself ever since."

"You poor, poor man."

Her tone was so snotty, and he was taken aback by it. Rebecca was never snotty. Even if she was furious, which she had every right to be, she would never deliberately offend someone.

What had happened to her? Had his terrible conduct changed her into a harsh and unforgiving person? It wasn't possible.

"I have interesting news from Carter Crossing," he said.

"Why would I care about that? I never had a positive minute at that stupid place. My cousins were horrid to me. Why would I be dying for news?"

It was another odd comment that he didn't understand, but he forged ahead, anxious to calm her sparking temper.

"I realize Beatrice and Clayton were awful to you, but I doubt Millicent was. She's marrying Mr. Melville on Friday! They want me to bring you home for the wedding." She stared blankly as if she'd never heard of Melville or Millicent, but other than that, she evinced no reaction. "I thought you liked Mr. Melville. I thought this would make you happy."

She didn't respond, but inquired instead, "Why are you here, Shawcross? You haven't given me a single reason to suppose we should be glad you strolled in."

"First off, I'm stunned to stumble on you. You've caught me off guard."

"Why would you be stunned? Nathan is my brother. Why would it be peculiar for me to stop by?"

"I wasn't aware he had a sister."

"Not that it's any of your business, but he has two sisters."

"Oh. I had no idea."

"You'd be amazed by the details I could supply about him and me."

"You never mentioned your connection to him. Nathan has always been my friend, and I would have been thrilled to learn you were related."

"Why is that precisely?" she snidely asked. "Would you have treated me better? Would you have been more polite? If you'd known I had lofty kin, would you have ceased being such an unrepentant ass? Would you have behaved like a human being?"

He scowled at her, and his confusion escalated. He was looking at Rebecca, the woman he apparently couldn't live without, but it seemed as if some other, more callous woman had swooped in and assumed control of her.

Yes, he'd been dreadful to her at Carter Crossing. Yes, he'd ignored her plea for help, but it was so unlike her to be dreadful in return. Even though she'd been constantly abused and maligned by Beatrice, she'd remained kind and unflappable, and everyone at Carter Crossing cherished her for it.

He sighed with regret. "I'm sorry you're so angry. I'm sorry I hurt you. I'm sorry for everything."

"Are you?"

She stepped in so they were toe to toe, and he was desperate to reach out and snuggle her to his chest, but he didn't dare touch her. From how she was glowering, she reminded him of a rabid dog that might bite.

She studied him, and he was so disoriented. She had Rebecca's eyes, but they weren't her eyes too. He felt totally overwhelmed, as if he was gazing at Rebecca, but not gazing at her. They'd been apart for such a short interval. How could she have altered so completely?

"Tell me what I mean to you," she said.

"What you *mean* to me?" he repeated like a dunce.

"You've chased after me, so obviously, you must possess some heightened affection. Describe your level of sentiment."

When she'd still been at Carter Crossing, he'd told himself she was just another female in a long line of them who'd tickled his fancy. But after she'd left, it had dawned on him he had genuine feelings for her that couldn't be tamped down.

He suspected he might . . . might . . . *love* her, yet he was the consummate bachelor who didn't believe in love. He was so utterly besotted though. If it wasn't love, what was it?

With her glaring as if he was a stranger, as if they'd never shared an intimate moment, he couldn't imagine declaring himself. It would sound fake and forced, and she'd laugh him out of the room.

Suddenly, the door opened again, and he glanced over, yearning for it to be Nathan so he could save Raven from the wretched encounter. But the sight that greeted him was so bizarre that the Earth must have tipped off its axis.

Rebecca was standing directly in front of him, but a second Rebecca was standing over by the door. There were two of her, and he couldn't process what he was witnessing.

Then the Rebecca by the door said, "Raven Shawcross! What are you doing at Selby? And Sarah Robertson Sinclair, leave him alone before you give him a heart seizure!"

Raven whipped his focus to the woman in front of him, and it was then that he noted the minutiae that should have revealed something very unusual was occurring.

"Sarah *Robertson*?" he asked, and he staggered back, his calves banging into the sofa. He plopped down, astonishment rendering him speechless.

"Yes, Shawcross, it is I, your nemesis, Sarah Robertson. I am staying with my brother, Nathan Blake. My sister, Rebecca, is staying with him too."

Miss Robertson had been a thorn in his side for several weeks after she'd lost her home and Sebastian had permitted her to tarry in a cottage at his estate of Hero's Haven. She was an obstinate harpy who barged through life as confidently as any man. She presumed it was perfectly appropriate for a female to exhibit male traits.

After Raven had quit the expedition team and headed to the coast to fuss with Beatrice and Clayton, one of the benefits had been that he wouldn't have to spar with the annoying shrew ever again.

"You're Rebecca's sister? You're twins?"

"Yes."

"She called you Sarah Robertson *Sinclair*. Please tell me I'm wrong. Please tell me it doesn't indicate what I think it indicates."

"It you *think* it indicates I married Sebastian, then your worst fears have been confirmed."

"Oh, no," he breathed.

"Noah is with me too, and Sebastian is adopting him. We're having a grand Blake family reunion, and I'm still hoping to discover why we should allow you to dawdle and be part of it."

"Sarah!" Rebecca said again. "Stop tormenting him."

"He deserves it," Miss Robertson—no, Mrs. Sinclair—replied to her sister.

"Yes, he probably does," Rebecca agreed, 'but *I* will handle this."

"You? Handle it? You are completely incapable of standing up to such a bully."

"I'll try my best."

Miss Robertson/Mrs. Sinclair whirled away and sauntered over to Rebecca. "Don't tolerate any nonsense," she murmured, "and don't listen to any of his drivel."

"I won't. Will you go?"

Miss Robertson shot a final, nasty glower at Raven where he remained collapsed on the sofa like an enfeebled halfwit, then she said to Rebecca, "I'll be right outside. If he upsets you, just summon me. I'd be delighted to punch him in the nose for you."

"He won't upset me."

The two siblings stared fondly, and it was very odd, but he received the distinct impression that they were talking about him in their minds. Then Miss Robertson stomped out. Rebecca shut the door and spun to face him. They gaped forever, neither of them able to start.

"I thought she was you," he eventually said. "She walked in, and I thought it was you, but at the same time, it *wasn't* you. She was so angry, and you never are, so I couldn't figure out what had happened to you."

"She and I are the same, but we're very different too."

"I know her. Remember when I first met you on the promontory? I accused you of being her."

"Until I arrived at Selby, I didn't recall I had a sister. I used to ask Beatrice about her when I was little, but Beatrice constantly insisted I was imagining her."

"I'm sorry to hear it."

"She was here waiting for me—as if she realized I was coming. The shock of it nearly killed me."

"She doesn't like me," he said.

"Who does?"

The question hung in the air between them, and there were a thousand ways he could have answered. He'd always been a lonely, solitary man. It was difficult for him to make friends, and he didn't trust people.

But he was changing, wasn't he? He was improving. He was being kinder. He was assisting others—servants, employees, and those such as Melville—who needed his assistance. If he mentioned any of it though, would she scoff at his positive actions?

He pushed himself to his feet and went over to her. She was still hovered across the room, as if she was afraid of him.

"Mr. Melville told me you were Nathan's sister," he said. "I wish you'd told me yourself."

"I never discuss my parents."

"I appreciate that, but Nathan and I have been close for ages, and he's remarkable. I'm glad he's your brother. I'm happy for you."

"Beatrice filled my head with terrible lies about him, so I was scared to come to Selby, but I tossed the dice and knocked on his door. He welcomed me with open arms."

Raven was anxious to begin fixing their problems. "The day Beatrice kicked you out, I treated you so badly. I'd been fighting with my brother, and I—"

"I can't talk about it."

"I think we should. I think we have to."

"You're wrong, Mr. Shawcross. We don't have to talk about any topic."

"The minute you left, I regretted it. I visited Carter Crossing later on to apologize, but you'd already departed."

"I didn't *depart*. I was thrown out, and if not for Nathan, I'd have been gravely imperiled."

He nodded. "I understand that, and I was an ass to you. I didn't listen, and I didn't help you."

"No, you didn't, but then, that's been the story of my life. Those I should have been able to count on were never on my side."

"I'm on your side, Rebecca. I want to always be there."

"We're past that point."

He clasped her hand and tried to link their fingers, but she yanked away and said, "I can't have this conversation with you."

His shoulders drooped with defeat. "It's always been easy for us to communicate. It's one of the best things about us."

"There is no *us*. There never was. Would you go? And please don't return. It's extremely distressing for me to have you here, and I really can't bear it."

She pulled the door open, and he was incredibly irked. He hadn't said what he'd intended, and he grabbed for the knob to shut it, but she glared at him with such disdain that he relented.

"Just like that?" he asked. "You're through with me?"

"There's no comment you could utter that would appeal to me in the slightest." She gestured into the hall. "Go! Don't make me beg."

He stared at her, his mind working furiously to deduce how he could smooth over their impasse. He'd never been particularly verbose, and he'd certainly never suffered such a painful moment with a female.

He had absolutely no idea how to calm her down, how to coax her into caring about him again. They'd been separated for such a short period, and she'd previously been so fond of him. How could all that affection have vanished?

Obviously, he needed to devise a better plan of action. He'd assumed he could bluster in and, with his usual steely determination, force her to forgive him. Why had he thought it would be that simple?

He wasn't typically so perplexed, and he blamed his befuddlement on his initial discussion with her twin—whom he couldn't abide.

"Fine, I'll leave you be," he said, "but we're not finished."

"Yes, we are."

"We'll see about that."

He stomped out, and she closed the door behind him with a firm click. He was so aggravated that he nearly pushed back inside to resume their quarrel, but he managed to refrain.

He was at Selby. He'd tell the footman to find Nathan, and he'd confer with her brother about the situation. He wouldn't depart until he'd cleared up several subjects with the sane, rational man of the house. He had to locate Alex too and inform the boy of their connection.

He marched toward the foyer, and as he approached it, two very large, very irate men stepped in to block his way. It was Nathan and Sebastian, and they were dearer to him than anyone in the world—except for his wastrel brother. He was delighted to observe them, but wary too.

"Hello, Shawcross," Nathan said. "Fancy meeting you here."

Sebastian added, "Would it surprise you to learn that we were about to ride out to the coast to have a chat with you?"

"Yes, it would surprise me," Raven replied.

"It shouldn't," Nathan said. "I've recently been apprised that my sister, Rebecca, has been seduced by a scoundrel, and it appears that scoundrel is *you*. I don't take kindly to that sort of behavior."

Raven's cheeks flushed with chagrin. "No, I don't suppose you would."

Sebastian chimed in with, "Rebecca is my sister-in-law these days, so I don't take kindly to it either."

"I just saw Miss Robertson," Raven said, "ah . . . I mean . . . Mrs. Sinclair. You married her?"

"Yes."

"I imagine there's a long and convoluted story behind your decision."

"There is, but at the moment, we have other issues to address."

Before Raven could stop himself, he mumbled, "You and Miss Robertson?"

"Careful, Raven," Sebastian warned. "I let you complain about her in the past—when I admit she was driving me quite mad—but from now on, you can't denigrate her."

"You're correct of course," Raven hastily concurred. "I'm simply a tad astonished to discover that you're married." It was the understatement of the year! He was so stunned he could barely function. "I'm sorry I missed your wedding. I wish I'd known about it so I could have attended."

"It happened quickly," Sebastian said. "There wasn't time to send invitations."

Nathan asked, "Are you leaving?"

"I intended to track you down first," Raven said.

"Have you spoken to Rebecca?" Nathan inquired. "Sarah left you alone with her, and it's only been a few minutes, so it must have been the briefest conversation in history."

"Yes, I've spoken to her," Raven muttered with disgust.

"And . . . ?"

"She told me to go away and never come back."

"So you'll just obey her? You'll scurry away like a whipped dog merely because she insisted?"

"Well . . . ah . . . she's so angry. I thought I should wait for her to calm down, and I'll return later—like maybe in the next century."

"Rebecca is ruined, and she isn't permitted to have an opinion about how this resolves."

"It's what Nathan and I want that matters," Sebastian said.

"What is it you want?" Raven asked.

"We want a swift wedding," Nathan answered, "and the instant I heard you'd arrived, I dispatched a rider to London to fetch a Special License. We'll be holding the ceremony right away."

"Oh."

Sebastian smirked with what looked like glee. "Your bachelor days are at an end, Shawcross."

"Head down the hall to Rebecca," Nathan commanded. "Talk fast and talk plenty, and don't show your face until she's agreed to marry you."

Raven sighed. "If she won't?"

"That's not an option. Get in there and convince her you're worth having."

Nathan and Sebastian stood like a pair of livid sentinels. Their feet were braced, their arms folded over their broad chests. Raven studied them, the two friends in his life who'd helped to carry him into adulthood, who'd helped him to become a man.

If he could persuade Rebecca to be his bride, they wouldn't just be his friends. They'd be family too.

"I'll definitely talk to her," he told them, "but you might have the butler deliver food and drink. This could take weeks."

"We're not going anywhere," Nathan said.

The three of them smiled a conspiratorial smile, and Raven spun and marched back to the parlor.

# CHAPTER
## 21

REBECCA STOOD, FROZEN IN place, as Raven hovered on the other side of the door. She could practically feel his temper wafting through the wood.

He never let himself be bossed, and he behaved precisely as he liked, without regard to anyone else, so she'd assumed he would ignore her request that he depart.

She'd insisted it was too painful to confer with him, and he'd simply left without argument. Didn't he care that she was inconsolable and forlorn? Didn't he recognize how effortlessly he could have changed her mind and made her his own?

He was such a rude, domineering idiot! Why had she wasted a single second pining away over him?

Her sister and brother had been debating about him for days. Nathan and Sebastian had intended to ride to Carter Crossing to ascertain his opinion about having her as his bride. If he'd declared that he had no interest in matrimony, they'd planned to pummel him, then haul him to Selby and force him into it.

She'd been vehemently opposed to the scheme. If he'd brazenly claimed he wouldn't proceed—which was a definite possibility—she'd have been mortified. Why would she agree to wed a man who had to be dragged to the altar?

For several minutes, she tarried, expecting him to storm back in and tell her they were marrying and that was that. But the hall was dreadfully silent, and she had to accept that he didn't believe she was worth fighting for.

She staggered over to the sofa and fell onto it; her regret was that profound. What now? What next?

From the moment she'd fled Carter Crossing, she'd lurched forward, feigning confidence and acting as if she was fine, but she'd constantly glanced over her shoulder, being certain he'd follow her. At the coaching inn in Frinton, on the mail coach to London, she'd watched for him, being positive he'd trot up to stop her, but he'd never arrived.

Once she'd been safe at Selby, she'd sent a letter to the butler at Carter Crossing, so the servants wouldn't worry. The whole time, she'd told herself Raven might see it too, that he might come, but he hadn't.

Finally—finally!—he'd strutted in, and after the shortest conversation imaginable, he'd strutted out again.

Well, she'd realized from the outset of their relationship that she'd had no business glomming onto him, no business thinking he'd reciprocate her affection. She had to cast off her foolish dreams and look ahead to the future. She deserved better, and she would forget about cold-hearted, selfish Raven Shawcross.

Suddenly, the door banged open, and it was shoved with such strength that it flew all the way in on its hinges and crashed into the wall. She jumped to her feet and whipped about to discover what had caused such an explosion.

There, looming in the threshold like an evil specter, was Raven Shawcross. He was dressed in his typical black clothes, and with how his eyes were shooting daggers, he appeared frighteningly sinister. As he marched in and slammed the door, she yelped with alarm and rushed behind the sofa, using it as a barrier to keep him at bay.

"I could have sworn I asked you to leave," she said, "so why have you slithered in? Do you simply love to torment me?"

"No. I decided I had neglected to mention a very important point."

"What was that?"

"I never listen to women, and I'm not about to start with you."

He studied her as if he were a wolf and she his unlucky prey, and they engaged in an odd sort of dance, circling the sofa as they bickered. His temper hadn't abated, and as she remained out of his reach, he grew visibly annoyed.

"Hold still, Rebecca!" he demanded, fury in his tone. "I won't chase you around this stupid piece of furniture."

"Tell me what you want."

"I want you to cease behaving like such a shrew."

"Me! A shrew? I've never behaved like a shrew in my life."

"Really? What would you call your current conduct then?"

"I'd call it survival. You're an imperious lunatic who likes to boss and command me. You manipulate me as if I'm your puppet. You yank on my strings and expect me to obey."

"I haven't begun to yank on your strings," he muttered. "Now hold still!"

"Your days of ordering me about are finished."

She braced her feet and rammed her fists onto her hips, which she'd recently learned was precisely how Sarah stood when she was angry. As he observed her posture, he smirked with disgust.

"Gad, I should have figured out you were Miss Robertson's sibling. You're an exact copy of her."

"If I cared about your opinion, I'd ask what you mean by that, but I don't care."

"Your sister is a harpy who flaunts herself as if she were a man."

"So? Maybe if a few more females pushed against you idiotic males, the world would be a better place."

"Since you're living with her and being subjected to her haughty influence, I'm not surprised by that remark."

His denigration of Sarah lit a spark to her own temper. "Be silent, Mr. Shawcross! I won't let you disparage her."

"It's Raven, remember? I suppose she's filled your ears with despicable stories about me."

"She didn't have to. I have plenty of stories generated from my own experiences with you. She didn't have to share a single one."

"Yes, I've been a complete ass, haven't I?"

His admission startled her. "Yes, and I'm sick of you and how you've treated me."

"Why didn't you tell me Nathan was your brother? Why keep it a secret?"

"Why would I have told you? First off, I previously explained that I never talk about my parents. And second, are you implying—if you'd known I was a Blake—you might have been nicer to me? Pardon me if I sneer at the notion. I'm certain you'd have been horrid no matter what."

"I confess that I was predisposed to loathe you."

"We're finally delving to the truth of our situation."

"You are a Carter after all, and I've spent twenty years plotting revenge."

"Yes, yes, you've been very clear about it, and I've heard your insults. Are you about to repeat them? You needn't bother. I recollect each and every one."

"I've had such a lengthy vendetta, and it's definitely causing me to wonder about my fascination with you."

"Give yourself a bit of time. I'm sure it will wane. You're such an intriguing fellow, what with your schemes and plans and retribution. You're likely too busy to focus on me."

"That's what I assumed, but guess what?"

"What?"

"I rather like my obsession."

"Am I to believe that you've suddenly developed a strident affection for me and you can't put it aside?"

"Yes, that's exactly what you should believe."

Her pulse raced. During their short fling, she'd convinced herself that he was fond. Had she been correct? Was he fond? If so, where did it leave her? Where did it leave them?

The prospect of his having a heightened attachment was thrilling, but she shoved it away. If she allowed herself to think he was besotted, she'd turn into a gullible dunce who would swallow any lie he spewed.

Looking very sly, he asked, "Would you like me to tell you what's been happening at Carter Crossing since you left?"

"No. I resided there for twenty-four years, but it was never my home. I'm not concerned about what's happening."

"Your Cousin Beatrice has been arrested."

She gasped. "On what charge?"

"Embezzlement at Carter Imports. She constantly pilfered from the client accounts."

Rebecca couldn't decide if she was astonished or not. In her view, Beatrice seemed capable of any foul conduct. "She's a thief? You're not joking?"

"No, I'm not. As opposed to her dead husband, Charles—who stole from my father—she didn't cover her tracks very well. She's in jail, awaiting trial."

"What will become of her?"

"She'll either end up behind bars for an eternity or she'll be transported to the penal colonies. So far, she hasn't demonstrated the slightest remorse, and judges tend to frown on that sort of attitude. When she's brought to court, she'll face a harsher sentence because she refuses to evince any regret."

Rebecca's mind frantically whirred as she tried to deduce her feelings about Beatrice's plight.

Beatrice had been cruel and had enjoyed torturing Rebecca, but she'd given Rebecca shelter for over two decades. Yet when Rebecca and Sarah were tiny girls, she'd been complicit in Sarah being sent to an orphanage. Then she'd hidden the contemptible deed by pretending Rebecca had had no sister.

What was Rebecca's opinion about that? She and Sarah had been separated in the most painful, destructive way, and they were lucky that the orphanage had been managed by a sympathetic couple who'd been kind to Sarah. What if it hadn't been? What if Sarah had been mistreated or abused?

She hadn't been mistreated though, so was Beatrice resolved of guilt or blame? On the spur of the moment, Rebecca couldn't determine the answer to that question.

He yanked her from her conflicted reverie. "She's gone from Carter Crossing, and she'll never return."

"Has Clayton been informed? Has he visited her? Has he hired a lawyer to defend her?"

For a fleeting instant, there was a disturbing amount of mischief in his gaze, but it was swiftly masked. "Clayton has disappeared from London."

"What do you mean by *disappeared*?"

"No one can find him. Gossip has it that he was being hounded by creditors and facing prison himself as a debtor, so he fled the country."

"Where might he be?"

"I have no idea."

He had such a virtuous expression, as if he was an innocent choirboy, and she tsked with disgust. "*You* have no idea?"

"He could be anywhere about now."

She studied him keenly, overcome by the strongest sense that he was responsible for Clayton vanishing. He'd never admit it though, and she'd never be shrewd enough to pry the truth out of him.

"I don't believe you," she told him, "but I'm not in the mood to dicker over my relatives. If you're finished dispensing your news from Carter Crossing, you can leave."

"I've hardly begun."

"Must I reiterate that I don't care about what's occurring there?"

Of course he ignored her. "The estate is mine and Carter Imports is mine too. I closed it, and I intended to tear down the house, but I've reconsidered. I'm reopening the company, and I won't wreck the manor. The employees at the business have been rehired, and the servants at the manor have been retained."

"What stirred this burst of generosity?"

He shrugged. "When it was time to take the final steps, I wasn't nearly as happy as I had assumed I'd be. I was just hurting blameless people who didn't deserve it."

"I'm glad there's a warm heart beating in your chest. Perhaps you'll become a decent person after all."

"Maybe. Maybe not." He grinned. "I'd ask you to supervise the house for me, but I already found someone else."

His remark had dueling effects. Initially, it created a flutter of excitement. She'd have loved to run Carter Crossing, without Beatrice there to snipe and chastise her every move, but she wouldn't have liked to run it for *him*. Then again, she was irked to hear he'd given the position away so she couldn't arrogantly decline it.

"I wouldn't have accepted it because I wouldn't work for you if you were the last man on Earth."

"I figured as much, and I wouldn't have wanted you there. I have plans in mind for you, and they don't include you working for me."

He pronounced the word *working* in an odd fashion. No doubt he envisioned an illicit affair where he would coax her into further immoral antics, and why wouldn't he presume he could coerce her?

In their brief acquaintance, she'd repeatedly proved she was no better than she had to be. If he viewed her as loose and wicked, it was her own fault.

She was about to scold him, but before she could, he inquired, "Aren't you curious as to who will be in charge of the two ventures?"

She was dying of curiosity, but he looked so annoyingly smug. "No."

He ignored her yet again. "Mr. Melville and Millicent will take the reins for me. By the way, they're marrying on Friday. They asked me to invite you to the wedding and bring you to Carter Crossing so you could attend."

Her jaw dropped. "Millicent is marrying Mr. Melville?"

"Yes."

"When did that happen? How did that happen?"

"I should keep your cousin's secrets, but they're too scandalous, so I can't. She flitted off to town with my brother, Lucas."

"Oh, no."

"Oh, yes, so she landed herself in quite a jam. Dear, faithful Mr. Melville rescued her, and as his reward, he gets to have her as his bride."

"They're marrying!" Rebecca said more to herself than to him. "Mr. Melville will be miserable forever."

"Probably," he agreed, "but for the moment, he's happy as a lark, and *I* have supplied them with a home and an income to live on. Won't you tell me how wonderful I've been?"

She scoffed. "If you extended any kind gestures, I'm sure you had an ulterior motive."

"I confess it. I'll make plenty of money with Carter Imports, and Melville is disgustingly honest. He won't steal from me. At least he promised he won't, and I've decided to trust him. What do you think? Will you attend the wedding with me?"

As they'd chatted, they'd stopped circling the sofa, but suddenly, he was sidling around it again as if he might catch her off guard. She held out a hand. "Stay right where you are, you bounder!"

Of course he didn't listen. He kept coming, so she started walking again too.

She couldn't let him touch her or she'd melt like a blob of hot wax. She'd never been able to resist him, and whenever he was near, her brain ceased to function. She'd behave like a ninny and believe any foolish comment, no matter how bizarre.

"I must share one other pesky detail," he said. "The boy, Alex? Is he officially your ward? I'm not certain of your authority over him."

She braced for any horrid news. "What about him? If you utter a hideous insult, I can't predict how I'll react."

"His mother was a girl named Lydia."

"I know that."

"Lydia was my sister," he declared.

"What?"

"Lydia was my little sister. It's why I hate Clayton so much. I was in Africa when she passed away. I didn't learn of her death until over a year later."

"You mentioned the calamity before, but I didn't realize she was *your* Lydia."

"The tragedy—if there could be *more* of a tragedy than her dying—is that Lucas and I were apprised her baby had perished too. This entire decade, I had no idea that I had a nephew out there in the world."

She was a bit slow in unraveling the situation. Like a dunce, she said, "Alex is your nephew?"

"Yes, and I intend to adopt him and rear him as my own son, but a boy needs a mother, so I should have a wife to help me."

At the announcement, she felt as if he'd poked her with a stick. Alex was *hers,* and Raven Shawcross couldn't have him!

"You want to adopt him?" she scornfully asked. "I'd be quite strongly opposed to that scheme."

"Yes, I thought you might be."

He preened as if he was toying with her, as if it was all a big joke, but at the prospect of losing Alex, she was particularly bereft. Alex would love to attach himself to rich, famous Raven Shawcross, but where would that leave her?

"You look upset, Rebecca," he said.

"I am upset. You're the most irritating brute I've ever met. You ruined me and broke my heart. I was evicted from Carter Crossing, and you didn't even care. Then you track me to my brother's home, and you torment me with threats of taking Alex. I can't abide it. I really can't!"

"I broke your heart? You admit it?"

"Yes, you broke it, you dolt!"

"That must mean you were fond of me."

"If I was, you drummed it out of me that day at Oakley. You made your opinion very clear, and I'm over you."

He raised a brow. "Are you?"

"Yes," she lied.

He'd started walking faster, so she sped up too. They were racing around the sofa again, but at a frantic pace. He thwarted her by stepping onto the cushion and hefting himself over it so he landed in front of her.

She tried to scoot away, but before she could escape, he pinned her to the back of the sofa, his large, male body pressed to hers all the way down.

"Let me go!" she fumed.

"No. I like having you this close to me. I loathed talking to you when I couldn't touch you."

"You surrendered the right to touch me."

"Tell me again how forlorn you are," he said. "Tell me how miserable you've been without me."

"No."

"Then at least tell me you missed me."

"I haven't."

As she voiced the falsehood, she couldn't hold his gaze, and he chuckled. "You always were the worst liar."

"Why would I miss you?" she asked. "What was there about our short acquaintance that furnished any benefit to me at all? Name one thing."

He pretended to ponder, then he shrugged. "I can't think of any benefit."

"You're correct! There was no benefit to me. I came to you that one time and begged for assistance. I never doubted that you'd take me in; I was that certain of your affection."

"I can be so horrid, can't I?"

"Yes, so what woman would want a man like you in her life? Not me, that's for sure."

She couldn't believe she'd uttered the terrible comment. She'd love to have him for her very own—if he ever acted like a sane human being. He flaunted his wealth and used it to destroy people. He'd seduced her with wicked intent, having no inclination to wed her afterward. How could he look at himself in the mirror in the morning?

"Can I share another secret?" he asked.

"No. If your conscience is bothering you, you should find a preacher."

He snorted. "Your brother and brother-in-law are lurking out in the hall."

She scowled. "Why?"

"They ordered me to propose." He huffed with offense. "They didn't give me any choice about it either."

She bristled. "Is that what this is about? My brother ordered you to come in here, so you did?"

"Yes. After you were so rude to me, I was about to slink off to Oakley with my tail between my legs, but he wouldn't let me leave."

"Has he threatened to pummel you if you can't persuade me?"

"Not specifically, but I understood the warning beneath his words."

In case Nathan and Sebastian were listening, she called toward the door, "I won't wed you simply because Nathan is insisting!"

"I told him you were much too angry to consider it, but are you really?

Didn't I mention that you're an awful liar? We should discover if you're being truthful or not."

He stepped away, then he clasped her hand and dropped to one knee. There was only one reason a man knelt in that position, and she was startled.

"What are you doing?" she asked.

"What do you think I'm doing?"

"If I had to guess, I'd say you're about to propose, but I could swear I just advised you that I won't consent merely because Nathan is demanding it."

He scoffed with what sounded like disgust. "You haven't known me very long, but have I ever seemed like the sort of person who would proceed if I didn't absolutely wish to?"

"No. You're dreadfully stubborn, and I hate that about you."

"You don't hate anything about me."

"I might!" she furiously stated. It disturbed her to have him prostrate before her, and she grabbed his arm and attempted to lift him to his feet. "Get up. You're embarrassing me."

"I won't stand until I receive the answer I seek."

"I haven't heard a question," she said.

"I realize that, so here it is: Rebecca Carter Blake, will you marry me?"

"No." The rebuff slipped out; she couldn't swallow it down.

He sighed with exasperation—as if it was the idiotic reply he'd expected. "I'll ignore that response and try again."

"It won't do you any good."

"Are you sure about that?"

She gazed into his delicious blue eyes, the eyes that had always riveted her, and muttered, "No, I'm not sure."

"You figure I'm simply eager to please your brother."

"Aren't you?"

"Yes and no. Nathan has been my friend for over a decade, and I would never deliberately distress him, but even though we're close, he could never force me into it."

"Are you claiming you *want* to marry me? Are you claiming this is your idea?"

"Strange as it must seem, yes, this is my idea. I came to Selby because— when you fled Carter Crossing—you gave me the fright of my life."

"I couldn't possibly have."

"You did! I've been pestering the servants and the hotel staff at the inn in Frinton, searching for someone who could provide the slightest clue as to where you went. Preston Melville suggested I talk to Nathan, and I rushed here immediately."

"You were planning to marry me all along? Is that what you're hoping I'll believe?"

"Well, I wasn't positive I'd stumble on you, but now that I have, it's made my task incredibly easy. I don't have to chase all over England, hunting for you. I can just get to the point."

"Which is?"

"You have to wed me, Rebecca. You have to." She opened her mouth to offer another ridiculous complaint, and he cut her off. "I understand you have reservations about me. I'm bossy and domineering, and I have to have my own way."

"Yes, and it drives me mad."

"But let's disregard my failings for a minute."

"You don't have that many," she grumbled.

"I'm glad you admit it."

"What I meant was that you don't have *many* faults, but the few you do have are big, egregious, and annoying."

"Yes, they are, but I'm rich, and you're poor, and that fact should place me in the running as the perfect spouse for you."

"I recently learned that I have a dowry." She stuck her nose up in the air, feeling extremely pompous at being able to mention it. "I don't necessarily have to settle for you."

He frowned. "How could you have a dowry?"

"My father put money aside when I was a baby, and it's been sitting in a trust. I'm not insisting I'd ever like to wed, but if I decide to bite the bullet, I could use it to lure a husband."

He appeared a tad jealous. "You are not dangling a dowry in front of any candidates. I won't permit you to behave so foolishly."

"Why shouldn't I proceed? I'm not such a bad catch these days. I'm no longer a poverty-stricken cousin living on a small estate at the end of the earth. I'm half-sister to the Earl of Selby, so I could have suitors lined up at the door—if I was interested."

He scowled ferociously, gripped her waist, and shook her. "Listen to me! You are not encouraging any suitors!"

She rolled her eyes. "See? We can't converse on any topic without you bossing me."

"Well, when you spit out a deranged notion like that, what can you expect?"

She stared down at him, and a huge wave of emotion coursed through her. She was overwhelmed—by him, by events—and she couldn't bear to have him begging her to be his wife. She'd once craved it more than anything, and she probably still craved it, but she was terrified of what such an arrangement would be like.

He was brash and magnificent, and she was ordinary and reserved. He was like a comet streaking across the sky, lighting up her world. She was satisfied simply to have watched him fly by. Where would she fit in any scenario that included him?

"You don't want to wed me, Raven," she said.

"You don't think so?" He scowled even more fiercely. "Now you're just being silly."

He rose to his feet, and he towered over her in the manner she relished. He dipped down and kissed her, and she couldn't resist joining in. She pulled him even nearer and hugged him as tightly as she could. The embrace went on and on until she began to worry they might simply burst into flames.

He drew away and rested his forehead on hers as he murmured, "I love you, Rebecca."

Her initial instinct was to deny his statement, but it ignited such a thrilling surge of pleasure that she couldn't. She responded with, "I love you too."

"If you don't tell me you'll have me, if you won't allow me to stay by your side forever, how will I survive without you?"

He gazed down at her, seeming—for the only time since she'd met him—a bit lost and adrift. What would he do without her? He was so solitary and alone. Might it be possible that he desperately needed her? At the prospect, her rage melted away.

"I have to take pity on you," she said. "If I reject you, you'll spend your life as a grouchy, unlikable bachelor—and it will be my fault for spurning you."

"I don't want to be grouchy and unlikable. I want to be the man I am when I'm with you. You look at me and assume I could be better than I really am. I want to be that *better* man for you. Won't you let me try?"

"Oh, Raven ..."

Her defensive walls were quickly crumbling, but then again, they hadn't ever been very sturdy. The whole reason she'd danced around the sofa for so long was because she grew befuddled when he was too close. She knew it, and he knew it too.

"My sister can't abide you," she said, the main problem rearing its ugly head.

"I'm betting I can charm her—if I work at it. She'll start to like me. I guarantee it."

Rebecca chuckled miserably. "On the other hand, my brother and brother-in-law think you walk on water."

He smirked. "I've tried. I can't."

"If I refuse you, I'm afraid they'd beat you bloody just for sport."

"They're not tough enough."

They stared silently, a thousand comments swirling. She yearned to offer a profound remark, but couldn't imagine what it should be.

She finally settled on, "What now?"

"Now you answer my question, then we wed and live happily ever after."

"You say that as if it will be easy."

"It will be *so* easy. Every minute with me will be filled with contentment and joy. I swear it!"

"You couldn't gallivant off to Africa. I won't have a husband who's never home."

"I'm done with all of it. I will be so firmly glued to your side that you'll be sick of me."

"You can study the horizon, but you can't ever ride off to see what's over the next hill."

"If my wanderlust ever flares, I'll climb the promontory above Oakley—with you—and we'll count the passing ships. We'll entertain ourselves by inventing stories about their destinations and that will calm me. *You* will calm me."

He dropped to one knee again and clasped her hand. "My dearest, Rebecca, will you do me the honor of becoming my bride?"

She hesitated for an eternity, savoring the opportunity to have him wait, to have him squirming, then she smiled and said, "Yes, Raven Shawcross. I will marry you and become your bride. I will make you happy each and every day that we're together. I promise."

"I never had any doubt."

She pulled him to his feet, and he kissed her again, then asked, "Shall we inform everyone?"

"I should find Sarah first and get her accustomed to the idea. This news just might kill her."

"I'm planning to charm her, remember? Once she realizes how hideously I'm spoiling you, she'll wind up glad you snagged me when you had the chance."

"Here's hoping."

"It will be perfect now," he said. "You'll always be mine."

"And *you* will always be mine."

He grinned. "Perfect from this point on."

# CHAPTER

## 22

A FOOTMAN HAD ESCORTED Raven to a bedchamber, and he was alone in the ostentatious room and staring out the window at the park. He was frozen in his spot and feeling a tad stunned. Events of the past two hours had left him completely drained.

He'd found Rebecca with no problem at all. His proposal had been accepted, and they would proceed the next day with a Special License. Rebecca was searching for her sister, to apprise her of their decision, while he had enjoyed a celebratory drink in the library with Nathan and Sebastian.

Since both men had recently donned a leg shackle, they'd displayed no sympathy whatsoever over Raven's change of circumstance. In fact, they'd appeared gleeful to have had him ensnared by the matrimonial noose.

He was thrilled to find Nathan and Sebastian reconciled, thrilled to find their friendship once again firmly in place. It seemed as if the prior terrible year hadn't transpired. With their forgiving each other, some of Raven's own guilt and remorse had floated off his shoulders.

He'd yearned to ask Nathan if he was forgiven too for his mistakes in Africa, but he hadn't inquired. Obviously, if he hadn't been pardoned, Nathan wouldn't have permitted Raven to wed his sibling.

In Raven's view, the ending was perfect. Nathan and Sebastian would be his brothers-in-law, and he couldn't have engineered a better conclusion if he'd worked it out with his usual meticulous plotting.

His head was spinning, and he couldn't relax, couldn't calm down. He'd pleaded fatigue and had trudged out. As he'd staggered away, Nathan and Sebastian had snickered, insisting his mood would gradually improve—after his new condition settled in and he realized it wouldn't kill him to be a husband.

Footsteps echoed in the hall, and he peered over as Noah Sinclair strutted in. Alex was with him. In all the chaos, Raven had forgotten that he had to speak with Alex right away.

"Mr. Shawcross!" Noah said. "We heard you had arrived, but we wanted to check for ourselves."

"Yes, I'm here, you little fiend."

Noah was twelve, but acted like he was forty. He was the spitting image of his father, Sir Sidney, and he possessed the exalted man's same confidence and bravado. Raven suspected he'd lead nations as his life unfolded over the decades.

"Is it true you're marrying Miss Rebecca?" Noah asked. "All the servants are gossiping."

"Yes, it's true."

"What is Sarah's opinion of the idea?"

"None of your business." He smiled at Alex. "Hello, Alex. It's nice to see you again."

"Hello, sir."

Noah was determined to monopolize the conversation. "Alex and I have become fast friends, and we've planned a grand future for ourselves."

"What have you envisioned?"

"We'll be joining the army," Noah explained, "then, after we've gained some experience, we'll mount an expedition to Africa."

"I'll be his second in command," Alex added.

"That's a fine notion."

Raven could already picture the two of them slashing their way down a jungle path. With Noah directing their route, any destiny could await them. Raven had the fortune to assist them in making it happen, so Alex would never have to gamble, cheat, or steal in order to buy a stake in the ventures he chose.

"Alex will be my Shawcross," Noah said, "like you and Sebastian during your journeys."

Raven smirked. "He'll be good at that."

He studied Alex keenly, reflecting again—as he had when they'd first met at Carter Crossing—that he looked just like Lucas had as a boy. But of course he was incredibly similar. Lucas was his uncle.

"Could I talk to Alex?" Raven asked. "Alone?"

Noah frowned. "Is it your intent to browbeat him over some issue? If so, I can't allow it."

"I won't browbeat him, you obnoxious oaf. Now get."

Noah and Alex exchanged a glance that indicated how powerfully their relationship had blossomed.

"I'll be out in the hall," Noah told Alex. "Call if you need me."

"I won't need you," Alex replied. "Mr. Shawcross and I are fast friends too."

Raven chuckled, liking the sound of that.

Noah cast a glower at Raven, warning him to behave, then he marched out and closed the door. Raven sighed, thinking he'd have to figure out how to handle the brash miscreant. It appeared they were about to be family.

"Is Rebecca all right?" Alex inquired once it was quiet.

"She's terrific," Raven said.

"You're marrying her? You weren't fibbing?"

"No, I wasn't fibbing." He'd never been particularly verbose, and he wasn't sure how to commence their discussion. There was a small table in front of the hearth, a chair on either side. He gestured to it. "Will you sit with me for a minute?"

Alex scowled. "I'm not in trouble, am I?"

"No. I merely have to tell you some important news."

They went over and plopped down, but Raven was tongue-tied and couldn't begin. He was gaping in a manner that had Alex squirming in his seat.

He was stunned by their strong bloodlines. Alex had dark hair and blue eyes, so he was definitely a Stone/Shawcross. As far as Raven could surmise, there wasn't a hint of the Carters in his features. He couldn't locate Clayton anywhere.

"You claimed I'm not in trouble," Alex said, "but it certainly feels as if I am."

"I'm sorry. I can't stop looking at you."

"Why is that?"

"When I was still at Carter Crossing, I learned a huge secret about you."

Alex's shoulders slumped. "Is it about the money I stole? If it is, I won't apologize."

"You stole some money?"

"Oh. You didn't know about it? Then I guess I didn't pinch anything from anybody."

At the comment, Raven was startled. It was precisely the sort of remark Lucas would utter when his mischief was exposed. Not only did Alex physically resemble Raven's younger brother, but apparently, he possessed some of Lucas's shady tendencies too.

"Whose money was it?" Raven asked.

Alex dithered, then admitted, "My father Clayton's and Mrs. Carter's too. She's my grandmother, but I'm not supposed to mention it. I took little bits—in case they ever kicked me out. They always threatened they might, and I thought I ought to be prepared."

"That was shrewd planning."

"I'm glad I had it too. Mrs. Carter evicted Rebecca without any notice, and I used it to pay our expenses so she wasn't imperiled."

"You departed with her—even though you didn't have to. Why?"

"I couldn't let her blunder about on her own. She's awful at taking care of herself."

"I agree," Raven said, "so you and I will have to take care of her from now on. Is it a deal?"

"Yes, it's a deal."

Raven reached out, and they shook hands.

"What was the secret?" Alex asked. "If it wasn't the money, what was it?"

"I realize Clayton was your father, but were you ever provided any facts about your mother?"

"Just that she was a doxy who tried to trick him into marriage, and he got lucky when she died birthing me—because he didn't have to wed her."

Raven's temper flared. "Who told you that?"

Alex pondered, then shrugged. "It's what everyone at the estate said about her."

"Well, Alex, here is a piece of information that I'm betting will shock you and—I hope—delight you."

Raven had to swallow several times before he could impart the details. The moment was so emotional, much more than he'd understood it would be. If he'd burst into tears, he wouldn't have been surprised.

"What is it?" Alex asked. "Is it horrid? Please spit it out."

"It's not horrid, Alex. Your mother's name was Lydia."

"I know that."

"She was my sister."

"Why *didn't* I know that?"

"We had no idea you existed. We were wrongly apprised that you perished along with her when you were a baby."

Alex was ten, but he was smart as a whip. He stared at Raven, his mind working it out. Without too much mulling, he deduced what Raven had been too befuddled to clarify.

"If she was your sister, then that would mean you're my uncle."

"Yes, I'm your uncle, and my brother, Lucas, is your uncle too. For ages, we assumed there were only two of us left out of all our kin. Now that we've found out about you, there are three of us. We're very excited."

"We'll be a family? You'll wed Rebecca, and we'll be together?"

"Yes, we'll live at Oakley—together."

"I don't have to go back to Carter Crossing?"

"Never."

"Do I have to still be a Carter?"

"Not if you don't want to be."

"I don't want to be. I want to be a Shawcross like you."

"I'll be ecstatic to make that a reality."

The interval grew awkward, and it was difficult to fully capture the significance with words. Finally, Alex seemed like the adult in the room. "This is the best ending I could have had."

"For me too," Raven said.

Alex assessed Raven in a calculated way that was so much like Lucas it was uncanny.

"Will you be able to help me in the future?" Alex asked. "How about with my schooling or my buying a commission in the army? How about my traveling to Africa?"

"Yes, I can assist you with all of that."

"Noah has such big goals, and I like to listen to him talk about them, but I never thought it would actually be possible for me to join him."

"It's all possible."

"May I tell Noah? We've been discussing our enlisting in the army, but we had no idea how I would manage it."

"You'll manage it now. Your dreams can all come true."

Alex grinned a grin—Lucas's grin—that nearly knocked Raven off his chair.

"I don't have to filch pennies from my relatives ever again?"

"Never again," Raven said.

"Is there anything else I should hear?"

"That's plenty for the moment. We'll chat more, once matters have calmed."

Alex jumped up and dashed to the door. He raced out and ran down the hall, shouting, "Noah! Noah! Where are you? You won't believe what happened!"

Raven smiled, feeling as if all the luck in the world had fallen into his lap.

———❦———

SARAH WAS WALKING UP the stairs to her bedchamber. She'd spoken with Rebecca and had been informed that her sister was about to be a bride. Changes were occurring too rapidly, and she was almost dizzy with trying to keep track. She'd just been reunited with Rebecca, and already, she was gearing up to plan her wedding.

She'd stopped in the library to have a drink with Nathan and Sebastian, but she hadn't stayed. They'd been obnoxiously preening, amused to have Shawcross leg-shackled, amused to have his bachelor days end as theirs had ended. As to herself, she couldn't decide her opinion about any of it. She could learn to like any sort of person, she supposed. Even Shawcross.

She reached the landing as someone was traipsing down. She glanced up, and there was the would-be groom himself, descending toward her. They couldn't avoid each other.

"Well, Shawcross," she said, "here we are."

"You're about to be my sister-in-law. You should probably call me Raven."

"You'll always be *Shawcross* to me."

They stared, temporarily rendered speechless, then he said, "This is a strange turn of events."

"You are a master of understatement."

"You and I have to negotiate a truce."

"We haven't been in a war, Shawcross. I just never liked you. I can't abide stubborn, insufferable men."

"So you picked Sebastian Sinclair to be your spouse?"

She chuckled. "Point taken."

"We should cease our bickering."

"Yes, we should."

"And we can't snipe and bark. Rebecca would be upset by it."

"I agree."

"If we don't need a truce, how about if we claim it's a lull in the fighting?"

"We're not fighting."

"Good." He nodded. "I've been hiding in my room, struggling to figure out how Fate meddled in all our lives and led us to this conclusion. What has it been about?"

"I wouldn't try to guess."

"I love Rebecca," he suddenly declared.

"You'd better."

"I'll always love her."

"Will you watch over her? Will you protect her? Will you cherish her and be her unwavering ally until your dying day?"

He scoffed. "I can't believe you'd question my intentions."

"It's what worries me the most about you. I'm so afraid you don't deserve her."

"Ask Sebastian about me. He'll tell you I'm fiercely loyal."

"Yes, he's waxed on exhaustively."

"Maybe you should pay attention to him."

"I'm persuading myself to accept that he's correct." She studied him meticulously, wishing she could open up his head and rummage around inside it. "Rebecca is precious to me."

"To me too," he said.

"I'll take you at your word—that you love her."

"I'm completely bowled over."

She snorted. "I like the sound of that. It makes you seem more human."

"I told Rebecca that I will work hard to be the person she thinks I am. I won't ever let her down. I won't ever let *you* down. You'll be glad she wed me. I swear."

"We'll see about that, and if you ever supply me with a reason to doubt you, I have a tough, strapping spouse who will keep you in line."

"I know."

"So behave yourself."

"I will."

"I left Rebecca in the library with Nathan and Sebastian. Why don't you find her? You look a tad lost."

"That's putting it mildly."

"Marriage won't kill you, Shawcross."

"I'll have to hope not."

"But if you ever hurt my sister, *I* might murder you."

"After a remark like that, it's difficult to imagine we're not at war."

"I'm not easily swayed," she said. "You'll have to convince me you're worth the bother, but then, Rebecca loves you. As do my husband and brother. They can't all be wrong, so I might—might!—learn to love you too."

She flashed a warning glower, and they continued on in their opposite directions.

※

It wasn't a grand wedding or a large one. Rebecca and Raven weren't acquainted with anyone at Selby but for a few family members. With their using a Special License, they'd had to hurry, so there'd been no time to invite guests who would have been required to travel.

Rebecca's social world was at Carter Crossing, and Raven had promised her a second ceremony after they returned to Oakley. They would have it later, so they didn't interfere with Millicent and Mr. Melville's big day.

They were thinking of having it in the spring, which would give Raven months to refurbish Oakley so the mansion would be ready for their company.

Rebecca had been alone forever, living with cousins, but not welcomed or embraced by them. The greatest gift she'd received by coming to Selby was the realization that she had a sister, in-laws, a niece, and nephews. Nathan's wife, Nell, was having a baby, so their numbers were swiftly growing.

Originally, Nathan had urged her to have the service at Selby Manor. He'd been elated over the notion of how it would have annoyed their grandfather who'd been instrumental in separating them. But Rebecca had refused to proceed in a spot where the underlying motive would have been so petty.

So she was in the vestibule of the village church near Selby. Their father was buried in the cemetery behind the building, and it made her feel closer to him.

And her mother? No one remembered where she'd been buried, and it was the saddest information ever. But on such a glorious morning, Rebecca wouldn't ponder that depressing situation. She would simply assume her mother was with their father in Heaven and smiling down on them.

Nathan was with her and about to walk her down the aisle. Sarah was there too, as were Alex and Noah who'd served as ushers. Noah had just escorted Nell down to the front pew. Noah's sister, Petunia, was sitting with her. Lucas was on the other side, so Raven had a relative in attendance.

It was a small gesture, but Rebecca was happy that the corrupt scoundrel had deigned to show up. Raven would never admit it, but it pleased him very much too.

The servants at Selby had generously filled the altar with hothouse flowers and had decorated the pews and entrance with ribbons, so the place was festive. Outside, it was clear and crisp, and with how the sun shone in the stained glass, it painted everything in shades of pink and orange that soothed her nerves.

Except for the cooks who were preparing their nuptial breakfast, the whole staff had come, so even though she was a stranger at Selby, dozens of people would cheer her on as she spoke her vows.

"Do you have the ring?" Nathan asked Alex.

"Yes, sir. I have it."

Noah said, "I checked, Lord Selby. I'll ensure he gets it to Mr. Shawcross with no problem."

"Let me see it anyway," Nathan said.

Alex was Raven's nephew and would carry it to him. He held out a pillow, the ring prominently displayed in the center. There hadn't been time to buy an expensive one in London, so they'd pilfered one from an old jewelry box in the attic. It was a simple gold band that was very pretty and that matched the kind of woman she deemed herself to be.

Raven was irked to use such a paltry piece, so he'd insisted—at the earliest opportunity—they would ride to town and purchase a gaudier trinket. She'd merely nodded and agreed, but she didn't need one that was bigger or costlier.

The gold band was lovely, and once he slipped it on her finger, she would never remove it.

"Are we ready?" Nathan asked the group in general.

"We're ready," the boys said together, their bond so firmly established that they finished each other's sentences.

"How about you, Sarah?" Nathan inquired.

Sarah was pacing and fidgeting, and her unease was humorous to witness. "I'm so anxious! I wasn't this flustered at my own wedding."

"Raven will take good care of her," Nathan said. "Would you stop worrying?"

"I'm not worried. I've seen how he looks at her when he believes no one is watching. Besides, he swore to me he'd be the husband she deserves. If he ever fails her, you and Sebastian will push him in line very fast." She smirked. "You'd probably enjoy it too."

They were waiting for the vicar to step out to the altar with Raven and Sebastian. Sebastian would stand with Raven, and Sarah would stand with Rebecca.

"Are they ever coming out?" Alex asked.

"Maybe Mr. Shawcross snuck out the back," Noah said. "Occasionally, bachelors get cold feet and panic."

Nathan scowled severely. "Raven didn't scoot out the back. Don't be so irritating."

The organist began to play a hymn, and the vicar emerged. Raven and Sebastian followed him out. Rebecca studied them, thinking how handsome they were, how dashing.

Sebastian was wearing the suit he'd donned when he'd wed Sarah, and Raven had borrowed some clothes from Nathan. As usual, he'd picked black, but the garments were more formal than his typical attire. He appeared stylish and elegant and nothing like the horse trader he'd pretended to be when she'd first met him.

A wave of gladness swept through her. She was so lucky! When Fate had been cruel for so many years, why had it suddenly pointed its fickle finger in her direction and fixed what was wrong?

Nathan motioned to Alex and Noah. "You two head down the aisle. Don't trip and behave yourselves."

"We always behave," Noah said.

They took off, marching to the music. Rebecca observed them, and she pondered Fate again, wondering what would be in store for the pair as they grew up. They might have so many wild adventures and become so famous in their own right that Sir Sidney's legacy would pale in comparison.

Noah slid into the pew next to Lucas, and Alex continued to the altar. He offered the ring to his uncle, and Raven leaned down and whispered a comment in his ear that made him beam with pride, then he went to sit with Noah and Lucas.

The three Blake siblings were left alone in the vestibule. Nathan extended a hand to her and Sarah, and they clasped hold, the three of them huddled in a tight circle.

"I've told you this story before," he said, "but I'd like to tell it again. My most powerful memory of Father occurred when I was six. It was just prior to his death. I imagine Grandfather was harassing him, so he was fretting about us. He snuggled me on his lap, and we had a very stern discussion. He ordered me—in case something ever happened to him—to look after the two of you."

"You feel so guilty about your inability to keep us safe during that terrible ordeal," Sarah said, "but you were just a boy. You have to forgive yourself."

"I know, and I eventually found both of you."

Sarah chuckled. "It's more correct to state that *we* found you."

"You're with me at Selby," Nathan said. "It's what Father would have wanted, and I'm so relieved that we can have this day together."

Tears flooded Rebecca's eyes, then Sarah's, and Sarah said, "Don't you dare get all sentimental on me, Nathan. You'll have me weeping."

"Sebastian and Raven are the best men I've ever met," he said. "With them as your husbands, I'll never have to worry about either of you."

Rebecca asked, "Do you suppose Father and Mother are gazing down on us from Heaven?"

"I'm sure they are," Nathan said, "and I'm not even religious. I just sense that they're present."

"So do I," Rebecca said.

"Oh, you two!" Sarah complained. "I'm going down the aisle. If I remain here another second, I'll be bawling like a baby, and I refuse to stagger past everyone with my face all blotchy."

She spun to Rebecca, and they fell into each other's arms. They hugged, as they had a quick conversation in their minds:

*Can you learn to like Raven?* Rebecca asked.

*Are you joking? He loves you, so I will always love him.*

"Are you about finished?" their brother inquired. "If you delay much longer, people will strain their necks peering back at us."

Sarah pulled away, and she patted Rebecca's hair and kissed her on the cheek.

"You're the most beautiful bride I ever saw," Sarah murmured, and the tears that had threatened overflowed. "Ah! I *am* weeping. I'm going down!"

She headed off, as Rebecca and Nathan watched her. When she arrived at the altar, Sebastian noted her distress. He drew her close, then they turned toward the vestibule. The organ music swelled, and it was time for Rebecca to head down too.

"You'll never regret marrying him," Nathan said.

"I already figured that out on my own."

"He's a bit rough around the edges, but he's fierce and loyal. He'll always cherish and protect you."

"I know that too." She smiled. "You don't have to convince me. I think I loved him the first minute I laid eyes on him."

"I guess he simply needed a few weeks to deduce that he loved you too."

"Men can be so obtuse," she said.

"Truer words were never spoken, little sister."

"Little sister . . ." she repeated. "I like the sound of that."

"Now then, Raven is glaring impatiently. I better get you down to him before he storms over and drags you down."

"I want to walk as slowly as we can. I want to relish every step."

"I'm not in any rush," he said.

They started off, and the guests stood as they passed. Joy wafted from the crowd, and it all seemed to be happening in a vivid dream.

She'd hoped she might eventually have the chance to marry, but she'd never believed it would actually occur. She'd told herself to be content with what she had. She'd told herself not to pine away for what could never be, then, without warning, Raven Shawcross had swept into her life, and naught had been the same since.

Finally, they reached the altar. Nathan put her hand in Raven's and said, "I swore to her that you'd be her staunchest champion. Don't ever make me a liar."

Raven grinned at his old friend. "I will love her forever."

"I expect nothing less," Nathan replied.

Raven studied her emotional expression, and he asked, "Are you all right? You're not about to swoon on me, are you?"

"I won't swoon."

"I'm relieved to hear it."

They turned to the vicar, and the man asked the assembly, "Who gives this woman in holy matrimony?"

"Her sister and I do," Nathan responded.

Then he sat in the front pew with Nell and Petunia.

Rebecca glanced at the throng of guests, at Lucas, Noah, and Alex smiling their encouragement from one side, Nell, Nathan, and Petunia from the other. Rebecca couldn't bear it, and Sarah realized it.

She leapt over and hugged Rebecca again, whispering, "I wish Mother was here so she could see how happy you are."

Her words caused a deluge of tears to gush for both of them. Sebastian whipped out a kerchief for Sarah, and Raven produced one for Rebecca, which had the audience indulgently chuckling and tearful too.

Rebecca was trembling, and Raven squeezed her hand. "You're beautiful, and we're being buoyed by so much affection. There's no need to be distraught."

"I'm so overwhelmed that I just might faint after all."

"I'll never allow you to fall," he vowed. "Hold onto me and don't ever let go."

"I won't."

"Remember what I promised when I proposed? You'll always be mine."

"And *I* will always be yours," she said.

"It means everything is perfect."

The vicar asked, "Shall we begin?"

They nodded, and her dearest Raven answered, "Yes, we can begin—and I feel as if I've been waiting for this moment my whole life. Please hurry."

## *THE END*

# ABOUT THE AUTHOR

**CHERYL HOLT** IS A *New York Times*, *USA Today*, and Amazon "Top 100" bestselling author who has published over fifty novels.

She's also a lawyer and mom, and at age forty, with two babies at home, she started a new career as a commercial fiction writer. She'd hoped to be a suspense novelist, but couldn't sell any of her manuscripts, so she ended up taking a detour into romance where she was stunned to discover that she has a knack for writing some of the world's greatest love stories.

Her books have been released to wide acclaim, and she has won or been nominated for many national awards. She is considered to be one of the masters of the romance genre. For many years, she was hailed as "The Queen of Erotic Romance," and she's also revered as "The International Queen of Villains." She is particularly proud to have been named "Best Storyteller of the Year" by the trade magazine Romantic Times BOOK Reviews.

She lives and writes in Hollywood, California, and she loves to hear from fans. Visit her website at www.cherylholt.com.